Together at last—two magnificent novels from the New York
Times *bestselling author who has captivated millions with*
thrilling tales of love and betrayal, loyalty and passion . . .

FERN MICHAELS

THE
Delta Ladies

Wild Honey

FERN MICHAELS

THE
Delta Ladies

Wild Honey

POCKET BOOKS
New York   London   Toronto   Sydney   Singapore

This book is a work of fiction. Names, characters, places and incidents are products of the author's imagination or are used fictitiously. Any resemblance to actual events or locales or persons living or dead is entirely coincidental.

An *Original* Publication of POCKET BOOKS

 POCKET BOOKS, a division of Simon & Schuster, Inc.
1230 Avenue of the Americas, New York, NY 10020

ISBN: 0-7434-3999-6

First Pocket Books trade paperback printing January 2002

10 9 8 7 6 5 4 3 2 1

POCKET and colophon are registered trademarks of Simon & Schuster, Inc.

For information regarding special discounts for bulk purchases, please contact Simon & Schuster Special Sales at 1-800-456-6798 or business@simonandschuster.com

Printed in the U.S.A.

These titles were originally published individually by Pocket Books.

CONTENTS

THE
Delta Ladies

CHAPTER ONE

———— ❦ ————

*A*t an altitude of five hundred feet, a pilot could expect to experience occasional patches of scudding clouds misting against the windshield and ruffling like hazy feathers as they were chewed in voracious bites by the twin-engine Beechcraft. But the day was cloudless, the sky a vibrant blue. The early morning sun had scorched away the sporadic tufts of cloud and blazed through the cockpit, giving off a steady, baking heat that even the direct flow from the air vents could not dispel. It was a glorious day, the kind of day Cader Harris associated with dropping a baited hook from the fertile banks along the river and snagging a pike, or, with extraordinary luck, a meal-sized catfish. It was a good day for returning to his hometown of Hayden, Louisiana.

By squinting his eyes and looking off to the west, Cader could see the long stretch of hard-packed clay leading to the black-topped strip of the local small-plane airport. A glance at his fuel gauge assured him he had another fifteen minutes of flight time before the spiky needle pointed to empty. On a sudden whim, he banked to the left twenty degrees, heading east now, away from the airstrip. He hadn't called in to the flight tower for permission to land as yet, and he allowed his impulses to take him on a long, slow circle of the town. From his increased altitude of seven hundred feet, he imagined he would experience a new perspective on the place of his beginnings.

There, on the Louisiana Delta, on a lazy spur of the Mississippi flowing into the greater waters of the Gulf of Mexico, rested the town of Hayden. The white-spired steeple of the Baptist Church, circled by an expanse of new, lushly green lawn and dotted at its rear by neatly tended tombstones, was easily discernible. A peaceful town, populated by some fifteen thousand upright, law-abiding citizens, it was named for Jatha Hayden, its founding father, and had carried his name proudly for nearly one hundred seventy-five years.

Cader smiled to himself. Seen from up here it could be any small town in the country. The myriad styles of architecture from the Greek Revival to the New England saltbox represented a kaleidoscope of life styles. Even seen from the ground Hayden could have been anywhere in the continental United States, with its street names like Magnolia Drive and Chinaberry Circle, and Sunday dinners of fried chicken and pecan pie. But Cader knew it was the people, their values and prejudices, the highs and lows of their humanity that made Hayden what it was—just another town.

Cader's sharp eye caught sight of the narrow strip of railroad tracks that divided the town. Deliberately, he veered his Beechcraft again, preferring to remain on the north side of Hayden, away from the overgrown tracts and rows of ramshackle hovels where he had been born. Instead, he concentrated his attentions on the more favored side of Hayden, the scrupulously tended lawns and neat rows of houses.

Cader remembered the markers the Junior Women's League had erected amid the tree-lined streets that denoted the supposed, rather than the exact, location of such historic and memorable events as Jatha Hayden House, first established homesite, or the Jatha Hayden Library, founded by Jatha and Cloris Hayden, nestled in among other interesting and necessary tidbits of the town's history. Cader's back teeth clenched and he grimaced in a way that passed for a smile. In newfound, mature understanding he realized the only thing "historically accurate" about these markers was that the ladies agreed on where they should be placed.

The blacktopped roof of the Jatha Hayden High School tipped into view. Cader had attended the school for four of the most important years of his life: four years of fame and glory on the football field that eventually led him to college and ultimately into the flamboyant world of pro ball.

While a young student at Hayden High, Cader's ability for football had come into prominence. In spite of his poor beginnings, coming from the wrong side of the tracks as he did, he drew the notice of Foster Doyle Hayden, the last living descendant of the founding father to carry on the Hayden name. Football had always been Hayden's obsession, and when Cader had come into the lime-light during his high-school career, Foster Doyle noticed him, tak-ing vicarious pleasure in the young man's success. Rumor had it that Cader had been offered a scholarship to Tulane University and had accepted it.

Cader's mouth tightened to a grim line. Some might call what he'd done "selling out." Cader preferred to call it cutting his losses. And when Cader cut his losses, he cut everything, including Irene Hayden, Foster Doyle's white-skinned, golden-haired daughter. Irene, the original golden girl, with the autocratic temperament of a thoroughbred racehorse and the lusty appetites of a high-class whore. When Foster Doyle told Cader that Irene was pregnant with his child, Cader saw all his ambitions going down the drain.

Expecting Hayden to ride his back and demand he marry Irene, Cader visualized a future with himself under Foster Doyle's impe-rious thumb, running the bases at the man's whim. Instead, Hayden floored Cader by offering him an escape—leave town . . . never see Irene again . . . and Cader would be rewarded with enrollment at Tulane University, tuition and all expenses paid, not to mention a very healthy allowance paid to a bank once a month.

Escape . . . a way out . . . a path with which Cader Harris was very familiar. More than an escape . . . a dream . . . something he'd wanted all his life and always believed was beyond his reach.

Tulane . . . the gem of the Southern universities . . . money for clothes, a car, enough left over to see to his drunken father's sup-port. All he had to do was agree to Hayden's bargain.

Still, there was Irene to consider. Hayden had sneered at Cader's hesitation. Irene had a position to maintain and the family name to consider. Irene's problem could be solved.

Cader hadn't been able to reach an immediate decision. He loved Irene, but the lure of escaping his humble beginnings to the upper echelons of Tulane, paid for and supported by Hayden, was impossible to resist. He would have everything going for him. He already had the magazine looks, the physique to wear the maga-zine clothes and the athletic and sexual prowess to bring it all together. He would be a star! A football hero! Pursued by the girls, envied by the guys.

To Cader's own amazement, breaking ties with the hometown

had proved to be difficult. While in attendance at prep school to gain the necessary credits to enter the university in the fall, he had subscribed to the town paper. It was there he learned of the surprising marriage of Irene Hayden and Arthur Thomas. The news depressed him. Despite the enthusiastic female attention surrounding him, his thoughts still clung to Irene. He admitted a sense of loss, a heartfelt regret, yet upon reflection he was relieved to have made his escape with so few scars.

One evening, after football practice with the Tulane team, he happened to read the Hayden paper. In the social column was the announcement that Irene Hayden Thomas had given birth to a son, Kevin Hayden Thomas. A quick count on his fingers gave him his answer. A son. His son.

When Foster Doyle had proclaimed he would "take care of everything," Cader had assumed he meant an abortion for Irene.

Looking out of the cockpit down on the town of Hayden, Cader brought himself back to the present. Somewhere, down in that green patchwork, was his son. A boy known as Kevin Thomas. And Cader would see him, find him.

He had merely cut his losses, Cader justified; he hadn't really traded Irene and his son for a chance to cross the tracks into acceptable society. And he'd kept his bargain, until now. Not even when his father had died had Cader returned to Hayden. Not that he would have been so inclined anyway. But he had kept his bargain, and if in a weak moment his conscience pricked him, he knew with supreme arrogance and utter confidence that with a snap of his fingers he could cancel it all out and Irene would come running. So far, he hadn't had to draw on his one last reserve; he'd never snapped his fingers.

Having flown beyond the limits of town, the landscape below had become low, flat plains; he was over the truck farms that skirted Hayden. Six or seven miles to the south the tall stacks of the catcrackers belonging to the Delta Oil Company were visible and the eternal flame of the flare-tower smoked hotly into the noonday sun like an angry, fire-breathing sentry. In a natural progression of thought, Cader smiled, squinting against the glare bouncing off his windshield as he accelerated his Beechcraft toward the offensive sight of gray steel and blackened machinery and sterile girders that were the Delta Oil Company. One thought just naturally seemed to follow the other these days; old man Hayden, the granddaddy of us all, and good ol' Delta oil.

Long before he approached the blackened Erector-Set construction of the oil refinery, Cader glanced down and was able to pick out the wide three-mile strip of beach and the hundreds of acres of pampas grass behind it that were the bone of contention between the magnates of Delta Oil and the citizens of Hayden. It was there, on what had always been referred to as Jatha Beach, that Delta wanted to erect those ominous-looking and lethal-sounding liquid natural gas holding tanks.

Although the title and deed for the innocent playground of the young people of Hayden rested in the town's hands, Foster Doyle Hayden, last living descendant of the original founding father to carry on the name, was bitterly opposed to the plan. His opinion weighed heavily in the small, sleepy town.

Foster Doyle Hayden was pleased when he heard himself referred to as the genteel, soft-spoken, white-haired town father. He was a paternal figure, upheld for his civic responsibility and generous endowments to *his* town. He was a paragon, a model of virtue. Secretly, he likened himself to Teddy Roosevelt, speaking softly and carrying a big stick.

On more than one occasion the members of the town council, on which he served as president, had seen Foster Doyle's big stick. And on the matter of Delta Oil's infiltration into the town, they had felt it.

Foster Doyle was a reactionary of the first order. All argument proclaiming the economic advantages Delta Oil would bring was lost on him. He liked the town as it was, sleeping and submerged, untouched by progress. Delta Oil's intrusion would mean a change. Any commercial growth would involve an influx of trade and people into *his* town. If Delta Oil meant growth, and growth meant change, Foster Doyle would have none of it. He didn't want to lose control of Hayden to a pack of upstarts with revolutionary ideas and possibly more money than he had to see those ideas to fruition.

Foster Doyle was confident of his control as it now stood. The council understood his thinly veiled threats, just as they were meant to. They comprehended his stated concern that the new medical center could be delayed indefinitely; that financial contributions for the library's new wing and various and sundry other pet projects of the council would never see the light of day without his financial support.

The town of Hayden rested in Foster Doyle's gnarled hand, a hand that could close like a vise if and when he chose. Delta Oil needed someone to combat Foster Doyle's influence. Who was better for the job of turning opinion in favor of the LNG (Liquid Natural Gas) than Cader Harris? A native-born son of Hayden, retired from a football career in which he became a national hero and pride of his hometown, Cader filled Delta Oil's bill. He was a handsome, vital man of thirty-six, irresistibly attractive to women, while at the same time considered a "man's man." Delta considered their problem practically solved.

The title of Public Relations Advisor was dreamed up by Cader himself. It was meant to salve his conscience, while in truth Harris needed no second urging, trumped-up title or no. He had too much to gain to be concerned with scruples, even if the least of these advantages was the easing of the lifelong grudge he'd carried around with him against the town of Hayden and its democracy-loving citizens. Cader saw his position with Delta as an ideal opportunity to retaliate for the hurts and slights he had suffered at their hands while he was growing up among them. He'd make them accept those natural gas tanks, accept them and love them even. And then he'd take the money and run and never look backward to see if those great gray giants ever blew up in their faces.

Revenge wasn't the only reason Cader jumped at this chance. The success or failure he brought about for Delta was tied in with his own personal success or failure. He knew what it meant to be a "has-been." The popularity Delta Oil insisted Cader enjoyed in Hayden was not indicative of the status he experienced beyond the town's limits. The high salary and financial rewards he'd earned as an athlete had been lost to extravagance and poor management. All that remained was several thousand in the bank, this twin-engined Beechcraft given to him by the enamored daughter of a manufacturing scion who expected love in return for her generosity, and a rapidly crumbling identity. Cader knew there was no middle of the road. You were either a "somebody" or you were a "nobody." Money went a long way in ensuring you the former status.

A quarter-of-a-million-dollar commission and a contract for commercials and advertising endorsing Delta Oil would have been inducement enough for Harris to set fire to the whole damn town, let alone *persuade* them that the LNGs would be *good* for them.

Just thinking about it caused a fine beading of perspiration to moisten his upper lip. Taking his powerful, sun-gilded hand from the stick, he wiped it away. He knew this was do or die. The end of the road. He knew he couldn't make that uphill swing from nobody to somebody again, no matter what. This was his last chance and he had to make the best of it. A sinking, gut-churning feeling, like a steel rod stirring his insides around, hit him full force. The way things had been running these last few years he'd need everything Lady Luck could blow his way. It was almost as though he had grease on his sneakers and he was on a downhill slide. This was it, everything, and he *had* to make a good job of it. Delta Oil was his salvation; indeed, it had become his redeemer.

The faint cough from the right engine caught Cader's attention. Immediately, his eyes flew to the fuel gauge. Empty. Just enough reserve to land. Christ! Just when he almost had it all, it would be just his luck to daydream his way into a tailspin and finish his life where he started it—in the rubble outside the limits of Hayden. He reached for the headset and adjusted it, tuning for the air control, requesting permission to land.

Sunday Waters brushed her long, honey-blond hair out of her eyes and concentrated on guiding her blue Mustang down the quiet, tree-lined street. She gently pressed the clutch with her neat, white-sandaled foot as she glided to a stop at the corner light at Jatha Hayden Boulevard and Leland Avenue. A quick look at the gold circle on her wrist and she sighed with relief. She was early for her appointment with Marc Baldwin, the gynecologist.

With her slender hand on the gearshift as she waited for the line of traffic to move on Hayden Boulevard, she caught sight of a low-flying plane circling over the high school. Narrowing her light blue eyes against the glare of the sun, Sunday leaned forward and peered up at the craft. She supposed it was one of the crop dusters who earned extra pocket money by taking on aspiring students who were bent on earning their pilot's license. However, on closer examination, the plane didn't appear to be one of the patched and repatched disasters the pilots around Hayden used to spread their insecticides on the crops.

A pinch of memory nearly caused her to stall out the '72 Mustang. A memory of Cader Harris and herself stretched out in the tall grass skirting the airport, watching the planes take off and land on the steaming, sticky blacktop in the midday heat of summer. Cader had always been crazy for anything connected with flying, and he had dragged her out to that landing strip more times than she could count to watch the fragile machines soar into the air and to listen to their engines sputter and finally roar to life as they wound up for takeoff.

The tall, scratchy grass would whisper all around them, concealing them from passers-by. The millions of insects hiding there with them would often sting them in buzzing protest at this invasion. But Sunday would have cheerfully walked into a snake pit with Cader Harris if she could lie there beside him and watch the excitement mount in his dancing dark eyes and know that soon, when he had had his fill of watching the aluminum birds sweep the sky, he would turn to her, take her in his arms and teach her to fly even though her bare little ass never left the dry, sunbaked ground.

Sunday was lifted from her reverie by the sight of a young boy and two girls approaching the boulevard. How young they were, as young as Cader and herself all those many summers ago. God, was she ever that young? Of course she was, but she had never looked like the youngsters approaching the crosswalk. They were Ivy League, spit and polish, Ivory soap and Crest toothpaste. She had spent her teen-aged years wearing made-over dresses from her aunt who lived in New Orleans. New clothes and even decent meals took second place to Bud Waters's daily consumption of liquor.

She recognized the young people as they neared the curb. Kevin and Bethany Thomas, Arthur's children, and Judy Evans. Sunday blinked when she saw Kevin throw back his head and laugh at something his sister had said. A knot of nostalgia tightened in her chest. She remembered being carefree and smart and having someone look at her that way. Cader Harris had when Sunday had been his girl—his blond and bouncy and wonderfully happy girl. Until he tried to make that leap across the tracks into

Hayden's inner circle via Irene Hayden, who could open those doors for him. Sunday sighed; one way or another, even without Irene, Cader had opened those doors. And the result was the same; Sunday had been left behind.

The Mustang bucked slightly with the pressure of her foot, and as the children passed the car, Sunday noticed the proprietary look in Judy Evans's eyes. Young romance, she mused to herself, as she eased the car onto Jatha Hayden Boulevard. And what was that glimmer of hostility on Bethany's face? Sunday frowned. If she hadn't known they were brother and sister, she would have marked it down to jealousy. Now what the hell did that mean? Whatever, it was none of her business. Sooner or later their father, Arthur Thomas, would tell her every niggling little problem riddling his family. It was impossible to have an affair with a man and not be aware of his problems. *If* they were problems. And somehow, in her gut, she knew the Thomas kids were a problem. With Irene Thomas for their mother, how could it be otherwise?

Stopping for yet another traffic light, Sunday let her eyes travel the length of the boulevard with its patriarchal sycamore trees. Everything looked normal and tranquil. Yet she fully expected that at any moment the world would turn upside down. Cader Harris was coming back to Hayden. To open a sporting goods store, rumor had it. She had been serving the usual Scotch and water to Gene McDermott in the Lemon Drop Inn, where she worked as a cocktail waitress when Neil Hollister broke the news. It was a miracle her hand remained steady when she placed Gene's double Scotch in front of him. Neil had said he was writing up a feature story on Cader, and he knew the wire services would pick it up. Then he had winked at her and grinned. "Stud Harris," he had laughed. "Every woman in town will either run for cover or else they'll become overnight sports buffs." Sunday had remained silent, smiling vaguely, trying to hide the fact that her heart was leaping up her windpipe.

Why was he coming back to Hayden now? After all this time? Oh, she'd heard that tale about the sporting goods shop, but Cader wasn't a merchant type. Unless he had changed drastically over the years, he'd never make a go of it. A business took time, effort, and money. Money was something Cader had always been short of, saying it was something to be spent and enjoyed; let someone else take care of the rainy days. Still, after a career like his, money should be the least of his worries. Maybe he had changed now that he was older and settled. But somehow she didn't believe Cader Harris had changed one bit.

Behind her a horn sounded, and she pushed the clutch to the floor and moved with the traffic. She still had ten minutes to make it to Dr. Baldwin's office for her monthly Pap test. Now, there was a man, she thought. Marc Baldwin. Attractive and virile, and no doubt a master of a woman's psyche. She shook her head to clear her thoughts and pulled into his parking lot, obeying the sign that said to park "head on." *A Freudian slip, doctor?* She laughed to herself. It was funny, but she had never thought of Marc as making known his sexual preferences. She had always thought of him in the context of complying with a woman's preferences. Lucky Julia, Marc's wife.

Sunday stepped from the car and smoothed her cornflower-blue dress over her hips. She knew it matched her eyes perfectly and did wonderful things for her complexion and honey-colored hair. Squaring her shoulders, she headed for the Medical Building, which housed an ophthalmologist, two dentists, an optician, and, of course, Marc Baldwin's ob-gyn offices.

When Sunday stepped into the cool of the air conditioning, she frowned slightly when she noted Marsha Evans sitting at the reception desk. She chastised herself for making her appointment on Marion's day off. Sunday didn't care much for Marsha. She couldn't say why, exactly; Marsha had always been very pleasant and never looked down her patrician nose at Sunday for being a mere cocktail waitress. Still, it was hard to read Marsha. All the signals got crossed somehow.

"Hi, Sunday. Marc will be ready for you in a bit." Marsha smiled, her voice soft and friendly. "Have a seat. It must be getting really hot out there."

Sunday forced herself to answer politely. She found herself actually clenching her back teeth to keep from spitting out the replies. Why did Marsha Evans have this effect on her? Going one step further to hide her hostility, Sunday volunteered, "I just saw Judy crossing the boulevard with the Thomas kids. She looked so pretty, all smiles and giggles."

"I'd guess she had a lot to giggle about," Marsha answered,

looking at Sunday levelly, her dark green eyes holding a soft, maternal humor. "The last day of school. Remember how that felt, Sunday? Three long months out of jail to play and swim and have a good time?"

"Yeah, I remember," Sunday answered, reaching impatiently for a dog-eared magazine and pretending to see something of profound interest in its pages. She supposed Marsha hadn't meant anything in her remark about fun and swimming and good times. Maybe that's what *her* summers were like, but there was nothing in what Marsha said that even faintly resembled Sunday's summers. Hers had been an endless chore of taking in ironing with her mother and slaving away in the tobacco fields while the sun burned half her brain to a crisp, and forgetting what it felt like to stand up straight until someone came along and cracked her back so she could hobble over to the truck that would take her back to town.

Sunday was suddenly nervous. Even the quiet beige tones of the waiting room couldn't quell the jittery feeling creeping over her. Cader was coming back to town.

A buzzer sounded on Marsha's desk, and she closed her appointment book. She fixed a crisp, professional smile on her face and walked into the examining room, her hips swaying seductively in the white uniform.

Sunday sighed as she looked around the office. Besides her, the only other patient was an older woman whose name eluded her at the moment. Discarding her hastily chosen magazine, she reached for one with a new-looking glossy cover, relieved to note it bore the latest date. Leafing through the silky pages, something caught her eye. The caption read, "Is it possible—the multiple orgasm?" She suppressed a smile. You betcha! Her smile widened to a grin. Once, when she was in high school, she had had a triple with Cader who almost went out of his mind as he matched her, O. for O. So much for novices who claimed it was merely a myth, she thought smugly, closing the magazine and tossing it onto the glass-topped table.

Was it warm in here or was it her? She noticed the soft hum of the air conditioner. No, it was her. Gently, she brought her fingers to her cheek, careful not to smudge the rosy blush on her high cheekbones. She felt flushed. Even as she thought of the word, she had an instant vision of herself disappearing down the botttom of a filthy toilet and Cader Harris pushing the handle again and again as he laughed down at her. *Flushed, all right, right down the old john.* Well, that's what he had done, wasn't it? When he'd gotten that "too good to turn down" offer to attend Tulane. She wondered vaguely if she were running a temperature. God, she couldn't get sick now, not with Cader coming back to town. *And,* she reminded herself, *I have to stop by Arthur's funeral home.* "Damn!" she muttered, why had she promised she would stop by today? For the hundred dollars, she admitted with rare honesty. Pap tests every month were expensive, not to mention the douches when you used them as often as she did. Besides, the extra money would come in handy just about now. There was a stunner of a dress in the Monde Boutique that would knock Cader's eyes right out of his head.

She shrugged. As fly-blown as she felt today, she would keep her promise to Arthur. He needed her and in some small way she was able to make him happy, temporarily, until he went home to face his wife, Irene Hayden Thomas. Well, there was nothing she could do about his home life. Everyone had problems. It seemed enough for Arthur that Sunday offered him her friendship and a quick piece of ass in the casket display room. Funny thing about that though, Arthur had become a special friend to her. It had nothing to do with the money he pressed on her and she readily took, it was much more. He had become someone who was really interested in her, in what she was feeling. Sunday had shared some of her most personal secrets and fears with stodgy old Arthur Thomas and, most important of all, he seemed to care. At least he never laughed at her, not to her face anyway. She was bursting to tell him that Cader was coming back to town, but somehow she knew she wouldn't. How could she admit, even to herself, that even after nearly twenty years she could still get herself into a flap at just the mention of his name. Eighteen long, frustrating years since she last saw the tail end of Cader Harris. What would Hayden's wonder boy think when he saw her now that she lived on the right side of the tracks and wore the right clothes and makeup?

"Sunday, Dr. Baldwin will see you now," Marsha Evans said in her most professional tone as she stepped aside to allow Sunday to pass into the examining room. "You know the procedure; you can hang your clothes there on the rack. There's a fresh gown on the shelf. The doctor will be with you shortly."

Sunday's eyes narrowed and she shot Marsha a quizzical glance. Was that some kind of crack, that bit about, "you know the procedure"? You could never tell with Marsha. Sometimes butter would melt in her mouth, and other times she could be as caustic as the lye vat Granny used for making soap. Stepping into the cool, almost cold, examining room with its austere stainless steel fittings, Sunday reached behind her and shut the door with emphasis. As she struggled with the long zipper on the back of her dress, she wondered why Marsha's remark should rub her the wrong way. So what if she was a fanatic about these Pap smears? Wasn't it a known fact that her own mother had died of pelvic cancer that was discovered long after there could be any help for her?

And Ma had been a good woman, she thought as she wrestled with her panty hose, not like . . . me! She finished her thought with determination. Admit it. Ma always said only women who lived sordid lives got diseases in their female organs. Ma's shame about the cancer had almost been greater than her pain and fear of death.

Marsha Evans stepped back into the confining cubicle just as Sunday was folding her panties and placing them neatly on the little swivel stool. She handed her the pale blue paper gown and tied it at the neck after Sunday pushed her arms through the armholes.

"It'll be a few minutes yet before Marc is ready to see you," Marsha explained. "Have a seat. Would you like a magazine while you're waiting?"

Sunday shook her head. "I'll be fine."

Marsha heard the phone on her desk buzz and made a quick, smooth exit.

Sunday lowered herself onto the stool and crossed her elegantly long legs. She wanted a cigarette but knew Marc wouldn't approve.

Being naked under the tissue gown made her vaguely uneasy. Being here in this sterile atmosphere was different from being naked in her apartment or being naked with a man. Here, she felt exposed.

She could hear Marsha's voice speaking to a patient on the phone. Her voice was softly modulated, quite unlike the harsh scream Sunday knew she was capable of. During their high school years Marsha was a member of the cheerleading squad. Sunday laughed to herself. This was the fourth time in a single hour that she had paused to reflect on those long ago days. She supposed hearing about Cader's return to town had everything to do with her turn of thoughts.

As she listened to Marsha's voice, her thoughts spun back again to when she was a freshman in Jatha Hayden High School.

The day had been warm for the end of September, even by Louisiana standards. Notice had been posted on the bulletin board that tryouts for the cheerleading squad would be held on the athletic field immediately after school. In honor of the occasion Sunday had changed to her least faded pair of shorts and had carefully whitened her broken-down sneakers with shoe polish the night before. More than anything, she wanted to make the squad. She knew she was good. Her slim, graceful body was agile and when she made her jumps and splits her thick, honey-blond hair would bounce appealingly.

Sunday knew looks counted and was optimistic about making it, but she had certain apprehensions concerning Irene Hayden, the stuck-up captain of the cheerleading team, and her covey of cohorts, which included Marsha Taylor and Julia Wilson. But they had always been nice to her, even if there was a distinct flavor of condescension in their attitudes. Sunday wasn't in their league and she knew it. More important, they knew it too. Girls from the wrong side of the tracks just didn't find a welcome in the ranks of Hayden's leading families' darling daughters.

At the far end of the football field the Jatha Hayden High School Band marched through its paces, the sound of the snare drums setting the beat, the blare of the trumpets reverberating through the air. On the bare clay patch near the bleachers the contenders gathered, observed and measured by Mrs. Hurley, the girls' gym teacher, and the existing cheerleading squad. Sunday saw Irene Hayden watch her arrival on the field. Sunday lifted her chin and smiled a greeting that was ignored by the modishly dressed Miss Hayden. Marsha Taylor and Julia Wilson sat on either side of the squad's captain, and both of them gestured a greeting. But Irene's eyes were hard and cold and appraising.

A commotion of masculine voices startled Sunday and, turning to her right, she could see several members of the football team gathering to feast their eyes on the bare legs and sweatered bosoms of the contenders for the two open positions on the squad. A bright golden head caught her attention, and she knew without looking that it belonged to Cader Harris, Jatha Hayden's star player. She heard Rudy Barnett's jeering comments as the first girl went through her routine of cheers. Sunday flushed pink. Why did Rudy Barnett have to be here now? Rudy, with his leering eyes and coarse comments and groping hands. He played fullback for the team, and his influence over the guys was second only to Cader's. Sunday hated Rudy. He was a pig. Only last week he had followed her home, trailing behind her in spite of her determination to ignore him. Long ago, Sunday had learned that boys like Rudy Barnett thought she was an easy lay. And what infuriated her more than anything was that their opinion was derived more from where she lived than from what kind of girl she was. Girls born and bred in the row of shacks lining the tobacco fields always had a rough time of it, and Sunday was no exception.

When Sunday was next in line to go up, she glanced into the bleachers and saw Irene Hayden whispering to Marsha and Julia. Their giggles and stares told her that she was the subject of their laughter. Sunday wanted to run off the field, but then her eyes fell on Cader. He smiled at her encouragingly, his eyes squinting against the sun, his strong teeth flashing. In spite of her self-consciousness, Sunday smiled back. Cader Harris had always been one of her favorite people. Even though she came from the row of shacks on the other side of town, he ignored her reputation. The few times he had even spoken to her she had gotten the feeling that he liked her.

Mrs. Hurley was calling her name. She was up. After a quick glance into the bleachers and seeing the expression on Irene's face, Sunday knew she wasn't going to be picked. She had seen Irene's curious glance move to Cader and then back to Sunday. It was as simple as that. Sunday Waters was a loser again.

She went through the cheers mechanically. Her voice cracked as she yelled the familiar cheer, and she shrank from the puzzled frown on Mrs. Hurley's face, a frown that said Mrs. Hurley knew Sunday was capable of a much better performance.

A titter of excitement trilled through the other contenders as they waited for the results to be called. Sunday sat alone, her heart sinking lower and lower. She hadn't made it. Of that she was certain. She hadn't done her best. She had been put off by Irene's glaring looks and Rudy's lewd comments.

The two girls were picked and called amid a clapping of hands and hoots from the boys. As she had predicted, she was not named. Not even as a substitute. Sunday slunk off the field, heading for the locker room and the showers.

The locker room was empty, as she had anticipated. She kicked off her sneakers, now smudged with dirt and clay from the field and, with a true aim, they landed with a rumble in the bottom of her locker. Impatient fingers tore at the button at the waist of her shorts and pulled them down over her slim, curving hips. As she sat on the long bench to tear off her socks, her emotions welled. *It isn't fair! It isn't fair!* The injustice of it all overwhelmed her. *If* she had been born a Hayden, not a single boy in town would have had a word to say about her, even if she were the biggest put-out in the school. *If* she had nice clothes and lived in a nice house like the rest of the girls, she would have been accepted. *If* Irene Hayden wasn't such a snot, she would have had a better chance of making the squad. *If* Cader Harris hadn't looked at her and if Irene hadn't seen him, she wouldn't have been the object of ridicule, and she could have done her best. *If If If!*

Furious with herself, she slipped the light sweater over her head and fumbled with the clasp of her bra. Impatiently, she slipped her arms through the straps and twisted the garment around so the hooks were at the front. She stepped out of her panties and grabbed the thin, frayed towel she kept in her locker.

The showers were empty and would most likely remain so. All the other girls had nice houses with nice bathrooms and indoor plumbing. The best thing about school was being able to take a shower, even in the winter, when the water from the pump at home would freeze to a thin layer of ice in the dishpan unless it was left heating on the stove.

The needle-sharp spray stung her shoulders and the steam rose near her feet. She wouldn't think about the cheerleading squad. She'd been dumb to think she could have made it anyway. Besides, if you were a cheerleader, you were expected to look nice all the time. Her two outgrown dresses and three skirts and four blouses didn't exactly compose a wardrobe. And then there were the homecoming dances and the Varsity Hops. . . .

A sound echoed through the hiss of water. Turning to the doorway, she almost fainted when she saw Rudy Barnett and his cronies leering at her.

"Get out of here, Rudy Barnett," she screamed, "and take your trash with you!" She turned to face the wall, conscious of her bare behind exposed to their gaping stares.

"We didn't know you were in here, Sunday. Honest! Right guys?" His voice betrayed him as a liar. "We just heard the water runnin' and we came in to shut it off. Right guys?"

"I don't care what you're here for. . . . Get out!" She was crying, humiliated.

They knew she was alone in here. They had come after her. Silently, she prayed.

"Now, Sunday," Rudy mocked, "why don't you shut that water off and bring your lil ol' ass over here? We only want to see if that's all you. We got a little bet ridin' on it. Some of the guys don't believe that's all you under those tight sweaters. . . ."

"Get out!" There was hysteria in her voice.

"I told them that was all Sunny Waters in those sweaters. I told 'em how I ought to know, only they don't believe me." Rudy spoke smoothly, sneeringly, threateningly.

"You don't know anything, you pig. Now get out of here!"

"Come on, Sunny, don't make a fool out of me in front of my friends. All we want is a little fun, right guys?" She heard his step on the tile floor and pressed herself closer against the wall. "All we want is a little of what you're givin' to everybody else. It's for the good of the team, ain't it, guys?" There was a low rumble of voices and jeers and taunts.

"Let's see it, Sunday, c'mon. Just let us see it, we won't touch you, right guys?"

"Please, leave me alone," Sunday pleaded through her tears and the rushing water. "Please, leave me be. . . ."

"You heard the little lady," a voice strong with purpose, in contrast with Rudy's wheedling, echoed in the shower room and contracted the muscles in Sunday's back. "Now get your asses out of here and make sure I don't hear of you pulling another stunt like this. Leave her alone and that goes for now as well as later."

"Christ, Cade, we didn't mean nothin'; we was only havin' a little fun," Rudy whined.

"I don't give a shit what you thought you were doing. Now get out of here!" His voice rang with authority.

Vaguely, through her terror, Sunday recognized the shuffle of feet leaving the shower room. She crumpled to the floor, her face hidden in her hands. Her whole body was in flames of humiliation.

She heard Cader moving through the shower room and realized he had turned off the water. Her towel fell over her. "Sunny, Sunny, I'm sorry this happened to you." His voice was soft with compassion and closer than she would have imagined. She took her shaking hand away from her eyes and looked up into his. He had dropped to one knee beside her. "I'd give anything if those animals hadn't done this. If I'd known what they were up to, I would have stopped it long before this. Better not come into the locker room alone for a while. Okay?"

Her head nodded automatically.

"Now get yourself dressed. I'll be waiting for you outside the door. I'll walk you home so those guys don't get any funny ideas. You gonna be all right? Should I get Mrs. Hurley in here to help you? I wouldn't want to get the guys in any trouble, but you could say you were feeling sick. . . ."

Sunday shook her head. Her voice became unstuck and sounded feeble. "I'll . . . I'll be all right."

"You sure?" His hands closed over her shoulders, helping her up. When she looked up into his eyes again, she saw that he held her gaze, being certain not to allow his eyes to wander.

When she heard him close the door behind him she set about dressing. She wanted to get out of the shower room, out of the lonely locker room. She wanted to be out of the school. Out of Hayden itself. If she let herself think about what had happened, she knew she would die. *Not here, get home. Just get home.* The thought of the dark little shack on the other side of town became her target. *Just get home.* Never before had she realized how comforting that word could be. Home.

Cader held true to his word. When she stepped out into the hallway, he was waiting for her. "You don't have to walk me home; I'll be all right." Her voice was shaky.

"I'm going that way; it's no problem." His tone was still soft, compassionate.

She fell into step beside him, her eyes fixed on her old loafers with the now-dull pennies in the slots over the instep.

If the sun was still warm, she didn't feel it. She only felt the warmth of the friendship Cader was offering her. And if there were sounds in the street, she didn't hear them. She was only conscious of the sound of his voice.

"Feeling better?" Cader asked when they were almost to the lane that turned down toward her house.

"No," she answered flatly, candidly. "I'll never feel better again."

"That's no way to be, Sunny. Those jerks can't get you down; you're made of better stuff than that."

"But they *saw* me! They *saw* me!" Her tone rose to a pitch, just below hysteria; her face flushed scarlet. "They think I'm a whore and that I'd put out for anybody. And the truth is I never . . . never . . ." She broke off into sobs.

"Hey, don't you think I know that?" Cader placed his arms around her and soothed, "I know what kind of a girl you are, Sunny. Look, I can't let you go home like this, c'mon." He took her hand and led her onto the dirt road through the tobacco crop. Still crying, Sunday followed, unmindful of the crusty black dirt beneath her feet and the breezes bending the yellow-green tobacco plants that stood sentinel as they awaited a late harvest.

Cader led her to a grassy oasis on the far side of the field over which one lone oak provided shade. Leaning against the trunk of the gnarled tree, he took her in his arms. "Cry, Sunny. Cry it all out."

"I can't cry like that, Cader. It won't come out like that. I'm too mad. Too humiliated."

"Aw, why are you humiliated? You've got nothing to be ashamed about. Don't you know that? You're beautiful, Sunny. The most beautiful girl I've ever seen. You're too good for those jerks and they know it. You watch, they won't be able to look you in the eye, not the other way 'round. You just hold up your head 'cause you know you're too good, too beautiful for the likes of them."

Sunny lifted her head, blue-gray eyes swimming with tears, a look of wonder on her face. She could hardly believe this was Cader Harris, *the* Cader Harris, talking to her this way. She had always liked him because, while he was brash with the other boys, he had always been nice to her. But she hadn't known how kind he could be, how sweet and gentle. Cader Harris was the only boy in school who never frightened her, who had never looked at her as though she were a piece of meat. She had always supposed he had never noticed her, but now, here he was telling her that she was beautiful.

Softly, his lips brushed her cheek. Lighter than the wings of a butterfly, softer than the touch of the sun and gentler than the caress of her mother's hand. Cader kissed her.

He told her she was good, that she was beautiful, and she knew he was sincere. As she leaned her head against his chest, she could hear the thumping of his heart. In that instant she knew that she wanted to belong to Cader Harris. For ever and ever. And with a knowledge beyond her experience, she knew she would give herself to Cader Harris. Soon. Soon. And that would be the happiest day of her life.

Sunday Waters smiled to herself when she remembered that hot afternoon in a tobacco field. Cader had been warm and understanding and caring. He had shown her the person inside the football hero, the gentleness behind the rough exterior, the generosity beneath the selfish facade. Sunday knew intuitively that whatever else Cader Harris displayed to the world, she had seen the real man that day in the tobacco field. Beneath the hot Louisiana sun, shaded by the outspread arms of a lone oak, Sunday Waters had given her heart to Cader Harris.

Marc Baldwin knocked perfunctorily before admitting himself into the examination room. Sunday had seen him only two nights ago at the Lemon Drop Inn; now, somehow, he seemed different, taller, leaner in his white coat with his stethoscope hanging casually from his neck. His dark hair was trimmed to exactly the correct length and his face was still smooth from his morning shave. She could even pick up the faint aroma of his Aramis cologne.

"How are you today, Miss Waters? Any problem or just the Pap smear?" Marc always referred to her as Sunday whenever she met him socially, but in the office it was always "Miss Waters." And it was nice the way he always said, "How are *you* today," rather than using that cutesy medical lingo of "How are *we* today?" He knew how to treat people, especially women, as individuals. He was never patronizing.

"The Pap smear . . ." Sunday said softly, grateful for the fact that he didn't lecture her about the ridiculousness of these frequent tests. He had long ago explained to her that if these checkups gave Sunday peace of mind then she was entitled to his time and patience. She adored Marc Baldwin, just as all the other women who comprised his practice loved him. He was the answer to a woman's prayers. A progressive thinker with a true appreciation for the female species. Women's Lib had invaded Hayden, and Marc's office was littered with appropriate reading material, such as *Ms.* magazine and *Viva.* Even *Playgirl* made its appearance among the copies of *Cosmopolitan.* Not for Marc Baldwin's office were the ragged copies of *Good Housekeeping* or *House Beautiful.* His approach to his patients was friendly and capable and he made them feel comfortable discussing their most intimate problems as he lent an interested ear. And consideration! Marc Baldwin was the leader in his profession as far as consideration was concerned. Didn't he actually warm his instruments under hot water before inserting them into the tensed vaginas of his patients? This alone, the ladies of Hayden agreed, proved that Marc Baldwin was an understanding friend and physician.

Attaching the blood-pressure cuff around Sunday's arm, Marc instructed Marsha to prepare the slide for the Pap test. While the scratchy sleeve swelled on her arm, Sunday watched through narrowed eyes as Marsha took her place behind the stool where the doctor would sit.

"Blood pressure's normal. Now, for your heart." A moment later, "Everything sounds just fine." Stepping closer, the fragrance of his Aramis wafting across the small space between them, his long, gentle fingers probed the neck of the paper gown, exposing her breasts. He lifted her left arm. Tension. Quickly and expertly, his slender fingers probed and prodded. A silent sigh. "Fine, Miss Waters. Now for the Pap test and then you can take advantage of what's left of this beautiful day. It's really getting a head start on summer, wouldn't you say?" he asked, smiling warmly, waiting for her answer, giving every impression that he was interested in her opinion. In truth, Marc Baldwin was prolonging the moment before he began the examination.

"I would say," Sunday answered, her voice tight as she slid down on the paper-covered table and hooked her bare feet into the icy stirrups.

Dr. Baldwin motioned for Marsha to hand him the speculum that had been warming in the pan of warm water in the sink. He lowered himself onto the stool at the foot of the table, his eyes level with the tender pink between Sunday's spread legs. Another examination to get through. Whenever he conducted pelvic examinations on any except pregnant women, he dreaded the ordeal. It was like looking into a bird's vacated nest. Damp and dark, void of all life. During pregnancy, it was suffused with color, a nesting place, a nurturing place, a place of miracles.

Half listening, he heard Sunday say something. "Hmmm," he murmured. *Goddamn it!* Why did all women think they were duty bound to keep up a running conversation while he probed their vaginas.

Marc let his breath out slowly as he inserted the instrument. Deftly, his hand steady, he scraped her cervix and wiped the swab across the glass Marsha held out for him.

Sunday felt the machinations connected with her examination, aware of the slightest touch, even of Marc's breath feathering against the inside of her thigh. There was no shame here, no feeling of being immodest or clinically explored beneath the indecent light which cast its warmth between her spread legs. When Marc Baldwin was at the helm, even the awkward position necessitated by the examination was like a sensuous pose for a girlie magazine. Marc wasn't the kind of doctor who hurried through the exam, tittering nervously and barely touching his patient with his sterile rubber gloves. When Marc touched you, you knew it. His grip was firm and personal. His attitude confident and unembarrassed. God! Lucky Julia. Here was a man with a true appreciation for the female body, inside as well as out.

"Everything looks fine, really fine," Marc assured her in a deep voice. Inside the dark depths of her own vagina was the one place a woman could never look. It wasn't as if it were her liver or kidneys. No one else could look there either without the help of machines. This was a private place, her own place, where others could look only with compliance on her part and a good strong light. It was the place where she gave and received pleasure during the sex act, the place from which she bore her children. And yet, lovers, husbands, strangers even, could look into the depths of a woman's vagina and see what she herself could never see.

"No sign of irritation," Marc continued. "Good color, a healthy pink. No sign of blood or swelling. Everything looks better than normal."

That was another of the phrases Dr. Baldwin used to make

Sunday, as well as his other patients, feel special. "Better than normal." Somehow those words put a woman above all others.

Unceremoniously, he removed the speculum. Sunday Waters, Marc thought to himself, was the only one of his patients who didn't flinch when the clamp was inserted and who didn't squeal "Oh, what a relief!" when it was removed. Marc could feel the tension leaving his jaw as he saw out of the corner of his eye Sunday unhooking her feet from the stirrups and sliding backward on the high table to a more dignified position. Jesus, he thought for the millionth time since he began his career in gynecology, why, when he peered into the dim, rosy depths of a woman's vagina, did he always expect to see teeth? Christ! What was it that Sunday was saying about multiple orgasms? He nodded to show her he had heard and made a pretense of studying her words. "Anything is possible, Miss Waters. So many women, unfortunately so, consider discussion about orgasms . . . embarrassing," he managed to choke out before returning to his chart.

Sunday rearranged her paper gown. "On the contrary. I find it very interesting," she bubbled delightedly. "I once had a friend who had a triple orgasm." A sigh from Marsha. "It must be one hell of an experience, don't you think, Doctor?"

Marc Baldwin swallowed hard, his head bent over the chart. Jesus, sweet Jesus. He looked up from the chart, a smile warming his lips, his expression conveying little else besides a physician's concern. "An unforgettable experience, in my opinion." Then, changing the subject, "There's no need for you to come into my consultation office. Everything looks fine. That is, unless you have something you'd like to discuss with me."

Sunday returned his smile. "No, everything is fine in every other department too."

"In that case, have a nice day, Miss Waters."

Back in his office Marc Baldwin sat down on his swivel chair behind his massive desk and turned till he faced the blank wall behind him. *Jumping Jesus!* He got them all. Multiple orgasms, triple orgasms! He wondered if Sunday herself was the one with the triple. No doubt. He swallowed again as he rubbed his temples. This time her vagina had smelled like tangerines. Last month it had been Listerine and the month before that, lilacs. He turned on his chair and wished fervently that the hospital would call, telling him that Sara Stone had gone into labor. Anything to avoid Mrs. Gallagher's pelvic examination. He hated to see the wrinkly, leathery skin of her thighs and the sparse, white hair between her legs. And she always smelled of dry urine. Not to mention that she was the worst squealer of the lot. "Oooh, Doctor! That hurts!" she would cackle and he knew damn well she loved every minute of it. He also knew the day some woman had an orgasm on the examination table was the day he would end his practice.

Marsha Evans opened the door and spoke quietly. "Mrs. Gallagher is ready in room three and your wife called. She said for you to call her back when you have a free moment. I made an appointment for Sunday Waters for next month, and she paid by check."

"Thanks, Marsha. Tell Mrs. Gallagher I'll be right in. Did her report come back from the lab?"

"I enclosed it in her file. It's on your door shelf."

"Marsha, if you'd like to leave a little early today, Mrs. Gallagher is our last patient, and there's no need for you to straighten up. The cleaning woman comes in at five. By the way, Marsha, I really appreciate your filling in for Marion."

"Love doing it, Marc. But I will take you up on your offer to leave early. Today was Judy's last day of school, and I promised we'd go out for dinner."

Sunday exited the doctor's office, her mood lightened now that the examination was over. She knew she was paranoid about uterine cancer, but she couldn't help it.

She backed her Mustang out of the parking space, narrowly missing Mrs. Gallagher's Mercedes. That's what her name was. Gallagher. God, she was old. Imagine having to examine a pussy like hers. Poor Marc Baldwin. She wondered if Mrs. Gallagher would be as uncomfortable in Marsha Evans's presence as she had been. She shivered in the warm closeness of her car and flipped on the air conditioning and headed for Arthur Thomas's funeral home.

First, she would park in the lot and walk toward the drugstore, and, if no one was about, she would go in the back door of the mortuary. She looked at her watch. Four forty-five. A quick one, home for a shower and then on duty at the Lemon Drop at five-thirty. It would be cutting it close, but she had promised Arthur, and she wouldn't go back on her word. Just as she climbed from her car she noticed Kevin and Beth round the corner and enter the mortuary. *Damn! How long would they stay? At least fifteen minutes,* she told herself. She looked around again and climbed back behind the wheel. She would call Arthur from home and make other arrangements. Later in the week, Friday or possibly Saturday afternoon. This way, when she went to the bank on Monday, she could deposit her pay and Arthur's contribution at the same time.

Once again, she backed her Mustang from its parking place and this time headed for home. She would try to make it Friday.

That way she could feel secure with his hundred dollars in her purse.

CHAPTER TWO

*T*he well-oiled hinges of the mortuary door opened and closed silently. Arthur Thomas looked up from the magazine he was reading and was surprised to see his children standing there. Furtively, he glanced at his watch and prayed Sunday would be late. Of all days for the kids to stop by, why today? "What brings you down here?" he asked heartily.

"It was the last day of school. Did you forget, Daddy?" Beth asked, bouncing over to plant a kiss on her father's fleshy cheek.

"Yes, I guess I did. Still, what are you doing down here? You know your mother . . . I know, you need an advance on your allowances, right?"

Beth laughed, her long, strawberry blond braids bouncing. "No, Daddy, we still have our allowances. Kevin wants to talk to you about something. Tell him, Kev," she said, digging her elbow into her brother's side.

"Dad," the young man said respectfully, his dark eyes grave and glowing beneath his shock of sun-streaked blond hair, "would you mind if I applied for a job at the new sporting goods store that's going to open on Leland Avenue? I saw a sign on the window this morning on the way to school. I asked the real estate agent who rented the store, and she said she had put the sign in the window at Cader Harris's request. It's going to be his store, Dad."

Arthur felt an unreasonable jealousy rise in his chest. It was the way Kevin's eyes sparkled and the way his voice became so animated that caused the cold stab in his chest. The whole town was talking about the returning hero. A sports hero. Just the kind of man a boy like Kevin could look up to, unlike himself who was fighting the battle of the bulge and losing and who didn't know one end of a golf club from another.

When Kevin didn't receive an immediate reply from Arthur, his strong, indomitable chin rose in the air, just like Irene's, Arthur thought. "Southern aristocratic supremacy," Irene would chide whenever he pointed it out to her.

"Look, Dad, I can do the job; I know I can. I've helped out here with the bookkeeping and running errands. And I know I can handle sports equipment."

"Say yes, Daddy, please say yes," Beth pleaded.

Kevin put his arm protectively around his sister's shoulders. "What d'you say, Dad?"

Arthur Thomas knew from the moment Kevin mentioned working in Harris's store that he would have to put a stop to the idea. Irene wouldn't like it one bit. *Her* children working like common folk? She would find the idea appalling. But when Kevin put his arm around Beth, Arthur knew that, for the children's sake, he must answer yes. They needed to get out of the house, away from Irene's smothering. Since they had been born, she had coddled them, kept them apart from other children, saying they would catch unholy childhood diseases. Finally, after the threat of chickenpox and scarlet fever was over, Irene admitted the true nature of her obsession concerning the children. According to Irene, Kevin and Beth were not *ordinary*. They were descendants of a long line of Haydens; they were a part of her own late, great family of southern aristocracy and should only socialize with children from similar backgrounds. Arthur's protests were feeble. He had been so involved in making a success of the funeral home he had left the child-rearing to Irene. His children had grown up with only their mother for company, having outside friends only in carefully controlled doses and an overbearing, autocratic grandfather, Foster Doyle Hayden himself. Naturally, Beth and Kevin were close, he told himself, closer than most brothers and sisters. They needed each other. But soon Kevin would be going off to college, and it was time to break him from this mutual dependency. Likewise for Beth. There had been times when the two of them complemented each other so completely that one seemed to know what the other was thinking. It was incidents like these that planted a distinct uneasiness in Arthur. Sometimes, it even gave him the creeps.

"Please say yes, Daddy," Beth pleaded, her green eyes sparkling, and the lamp from the foyer making a red-gold nimbus of her long, silky hair.

Looking around the waiting room as he tried to decide upon his answer, Arthur thought of how he hated the hushed quiet and the odor of embalming fluid which always surrounded him. The wire flower stands and the thickly padded carpet all seemed to stand in silent rebuke. The courtesies and gentle ministrations to the bereaved families were painfully dull. This business, this funeral home, had been chosen *for* him, not *by* him. His dreams had been to become a first-rate medical examiner in a bustling city. Noise, confusion, drama: those were the elements missing from his staid, well-ordered life. He had been intent on embarking upon that exciting career when Irene telephoned him at medical school and told him she was pregnant. Pressure and conscience pointed Arthur's short, fat feet in the honorable direction. Gone was the dreamed-of career as medical examiner; in its stead was the humdrum life of the undertaker.

Looking up at Kevin, seeing the excitement and anticipation in his dark eyes, Arthur decided he would give the boy the answer he most wanted to hear. He would do all he could, even confront Irene head on, to save his son from discarding his dreams and missing opportunities. Arthur's fate would never be Kevin's. "I think it's a fine idea, son. It would be good for you. A good way to spend your summer," he added, keeping his eyes away from Beth, thinking that what he really meant was that it was a good way to get Kevin away from Beth and Irene.

"That means I can apply for a job there too, right, Daddy?" Beth chirped, her eyes meeting her father's levelly. "I can work in the ladies' sportswear," she added confidently.

"Now, wait a minute, little girl, there was nothing in this deal concerning your working for Mr. Harris."

Beth's eyes turned to chips of ice. "If Kevin can, so can I," she argued unreasonably. "Why don't we ask Destry what he thinks."

Arthur Thomas turned to see his black associate, Destry Davidson, standing in the doorway.

A wide grin appeared on Destry's face. "Little miss, I never mess in other people's business, especially white folks' business. Your Papa will give you sound advice. There's only two things in this life that I could offer advice on—dead bodies and . . ."

And Aunt Cledie's house of ill repute, Arthur added silently. "Can I help you, Destry?"

"Mrs. Marlowe passed on; the family just called."

"Is she one of yours or one . . ."

Destry's grin tightened and then vanished, leaving his almond-colored face devoid of all expression. "Mrs. Marlowe was the cook and housekeeper at Aunt Cledie's," he said softly.

Arthur couldn't help it; the words were out even before he stopped to think. "That should slow down business for about thirty minutes."

Destry's face remained impassive, but his eyes were mocking when he spoke. "Give or take a few minutes either way."

Arthur cringed. Life did go on. Aunt Cledie wouldn't let a little thing like death interfere with her thriving brothel—service with a smile, twenty-four hours a day. Jesus, would she close up shop for the viewing and funeral? He knew he should say something, any-thing. Destry was waiting. "Take care of it, Destry. If you need my help . . ."

"I'll call you," Destry replied coolly as he walked from the room. Why in the Goddamn hell did white people always think a black color would rub off? His gut rumbled as he remembered the first time Arthur Thomas had seen him drain the blood from what he called "one of his own." He had looked shocked when he saw that the blood ran as red as his own! That was a long time ago, and Arthur Thomas had come a long way with regard to the black pop-ulace of Hayden. Now, he merely considered them second-class citizens deserving of Destry Davidson.

Arthur blinked, knowing he had somehow offended Destry

without meaning to. He was uptight, he told himself. He would apologize later.

"Daddeeee," Beth said through clenched teeth. "Are you listening to me?"

"Of course, I'm listening. Now what were you saying?"

"If Kevin can work, so can I."

"What would your mother think, Beth? You know how she is; she would never agree to your working in a shop this summer." Something had gone wrong here, Arthur thought; he was being conned and he couldn't give one goddamned good reason for telling Beth he didn't want her hanging around Kevin's neck.

"Mama has no choice. I've decided I'm going to work for Mr. Harris right along with Kevin. Just let her try to stop me!" The girl's lower lip jutted out and her chin rose in defiance.

"Dad's right, Beth," Kevin tried to soothe. "Besides, you've already signed up for tennis and water skiing. You can't back out now."

"Kevin!" Beth whined. "I don't want to spend my summer with a bunch of kids. I want to have fun like you! Please, Daddy," she turned back to Arthur, "don't say no!"

"Beth, honey, there's no assurance either one of you will get the job. Perhaps Mr. Harris wants more mature sales help. And you wouldn't want to narrow your brother's odds of landing the job, would you?" he appealed.

"Kevin won't take the job if I'm not hired too, will you, Kev?" she said with stubborn certainty. Kevin looked at her blankly, and Arthur read the boy's thoughts. Poor kid, he was being torn in two between his sister and wanting the job.

"Now look, Beth," Arthur said sternly, "that's an unfair position to place Kevin in. And it doesn't show much maturity on your part." This wasn't going the way he had intended. The only reason he had decided to confront Irene head on was to get Kevin away from his mutual dependency with Beth. Now she was going to get herself a job working right alongside him!

"I don't care how mature it seems to you, Daddy. I'm going to apply right along with Kevin. And if I'm hired, neither you nor Mama can stop me!" she said hotly. Beth had Irene's angry determination in getting her own way. Arthur knew argument was useless. Sighing, he nodded his head.

"Provided you don't make it a stipulation that both of you are hired. Understand? Beth," he said again, "do you understand? The whole matter rests with Cader Harris." Arthur frowned at the change in his daughter. Her sparkling green eyes were murky, and there was a strong set to her jaw.

"Well then, go to it and good luck. Both of you," he added reluctantly. "I'll see you at dinner, okay? Don't be late. Your mother's going to resist this idea, and we don't want to add more fuel to her fire." He clapped Kevin heartily on the back and lowered his cheek for Beth's kiss, but not before he looked into her bright eyes. He was stunned by the calculating, manipulating look that met his gaze. A chill washed over him as she backed off, her eyes unwavering, almost defying him to say something.

Beth had always been manipulative. From the time she was able to talk she had managed her mother and thought she managed him. It amused him at first to give in to petty little demands. Why was it only he who saw through her shallowness and not Irene or Kevin and, least of all, her grandfather? Another chill washed over him as he stared at his daughter. It was one thing when only he had been aware of her deviousness, but now that Beth was aware of his knowledge, he felt frightened. Frightened somehow for Kevin and for himself. God, didn't he have enough problems? He would deal with it later. Later when he could force himself to take a good long look at what Beth was becoming.

When the door closed behind their excited chatter, Arthur Thomas's shoulders slumped. It was ten minutes after five and Sunday wouldn't show up today. Not if she had to be on duty at the Lemon Drop at five-thirty as was her custom. He would stop by the Inn on his way home and set up another date. He needed to tell someone about these uneasy feelings he got about Kevin and Bethany, and Sunday was always a good listener.

Pastor Damion Conway shifted his long, lean body behind the desk in the rectory of the First Baptist Church. His cobalt-blue eyes focused on the blank sheet of paper before him. He had to concentrate and come up with a soul-stirring sermon for next Sunday's services.

Don't desert me now, he pleaded silently as he raised his eyes heavenward. Lately, it was becoming more and more difficult for him to gather his thoughts together and put them on paper.

He cleared his throat several times, forcing himself to cough. Then he brought his long, slender, artistic hands together, making a steeple of his fingers. *Get on with it*, he scolded himself. *Pick up the pencil and make notes. Anything. Just get your mind rolling.* Viciously, he tossed the yellow pencil across the quiet, masculinely paneled study and rose to his feet. Perhaps a walk to clear his thoughts.

Hands jammed into the pockets of his faded jeans, he straightened his stiff back and gazed out the mullioned window toward Jatha Hayden Boulevard. Damion saw Keli McDermott before she raised her eyes to the rectory window. He frowned as he watched her hand go to her throat. She paused a moment, indecisive, her blue-black hair glinting in the bright sunlight. She closed her door quietly and hitched her arm through the strap of her handbag. She didn't walk, Damion observed as he watched her cross the parking lot, she floated.

When she had left his line of vision, he walked back to his desk and scribbled a few words. "Testing the emotional winds," he wrote. Next Sunday's sermon. Now, all he needed was another nine hundred ninety-six words and he had his sermon.

Unlike the other times Keli McDermott came to his office to deliver the prepared sermons she had volunteered to type for him, he was anticipating her soft knock on his study door. Everything Keli did was soft. She looked soft; she moved softly. Delicate and soft, like a moonbeam on the water. Soft hair, skin silky and the color of a summer peach.

Damion Conway had long since come to terms with the emotional response Keli McDermott evoked in him. A minister was also a man, and a man couldn't help but be moved in some way by the sight of Keli. She was the incarnation of all that was feminine. Even the western clothes she had adopted in place of her native Oriental costumes looked soft and crushable.

She entered his study, an expression of childlike bewilderment on her features. The look was a part of her; she wore it the way other women wore makeup. Damion made no move toward her. He smiled and motioned for her to sit down. Her features became the epitome of Oriental inscrutability as she sank down into the leather chair opposite his desk.

He waited. At times she just sat, saying nothing. When some indeterminate span of time elapsed, she would rise and leave, never uttering a word. At other times she would talk about every-thing and nothing. Keli had been coming to the rectory off and on for the past six months, and Damion still didn't know what her problem was. Or even if she had a problem. Yet, she presented a picture of pain, willing him with her dark, oblique gaze to make it go away. For the past three months, since she had volunteered to do his typing, she had been coming regularly twice a week. Each time it was the same; yet each visit was different.

He spoke quietly, gently, so as not to frighten her. Gradually, she relaxed and leaned back in the chair, her hands folded primly in her lap and her small, narrow feet planted firmly on the floor.

"You wonder why I come here like this," she said quietly. "It would be simple to leave the typing downstairs with your house-keeper." Her voice was husky, femininely throaty, with just a touch of accent to enhance her sometimes awkward choice of words and phrases. "I don't know why, Damion. It is so peaceful here. Sometimes, when I rise from sleep in the morning, I know I must come and sit. Perhaps talk."

When she spoke his name, she made it sound like two words, enunciating each syllable with gravity. Dami-on, she called him, giving his name an Oriental flavor, making him one of her own. Although her English was nearly perfect, her speech had a cadence that was undeniably foreign, almost exotic. He waited for her to say more. Suddenly, without any outward sign of movement, she withdrew from his presence. Her long sloe eyes closed; her hands gripped each other a bit more tightly. There would be no further words between them, and the silence would become a special kind of communication. Like an oasis in the desert the silence was a balm giving peace and respite from a world where words could become meaningless sounds masking the emotions and abrading the senses. These silences were uplifting; a type of intimacy with-out touching.

When Damion's eyes went to Keli again, she was staring at him. She had beautiful eyes and the thickest, longest lashes he had ever seen on a woman. He smiled at her. He was here, ready to talk, ready to listen. He said nothing. He knew by some finely honed instinct that Keli was afraid of words.

She stood, moving away from his desk, away from him and, for the first time since entering his office that day, Keli smiled. Her dark sloe eyes became lit from within and a feeling of sunshine filled the room. Because of him Keli had smiled.

There had been rumblings of racial discrimination against Keli in the beginning, but the "power of the pulpit" had quickly squelched it in one fire-and-brimstone sermon from Damion. When she was gone, he tried to remember what she had been wearing. Something soft. Even the colors eluded him. All he could see was the utter bewilderment and the picture of pain that was Keli McDermott here in the inner sanctum of the rectory office. Someday, he would sit down and write that book, and he knew that his hero would love a girl just like Keli.

The sermon. He must get it done. His mind wandered again. Was Gene McDermott Keli's problem? Perhaps Keli was homesick for her family in Thailand, Damion speculated. No, she would share those feelings. He decided, as he had in the past, that it was retired Colonel Gene McDermott, USAF, who was Keli's problem.

Hastily picking up the yellow pad and opening the desk drawer where he intended to stow it, hiding the visible proof that he couldn't concentrate today, he saw the daily paper he had put there earlier that morning. He had shoved the news out of his sight, irritated that Cader Harris was coming back to Hayden. Why not admit it to himself? Cader Harris's return threatened him in some way. Cader Harris meant trouble. As if there wasn't dissension enough already with the town's opinion divided because of those liquid natural gas holding tanks Delta Oil wanted to install on the beach strip. It was growing into a heated problem fraught with all the furies of another civil war. Brother against brother, only this time all the brothers lived right here in Hayden. As their pastor, Damion felt his congregation looked to him for unity and guidance. A fantasy of self-importance, he chided himself, yet in every fantasy was a grain of truth. So far, he had managed to remain neutral on the subject, but that state of cowardice wouldn't continue for long. The Junior Women's League and the Masons were already clamoring for him to speak at their meetings, and it had been hinted at that his opinion would be asked concerning Delta Oil.

What this town doesn't need right now, if ever, is good old jock Cader Harris. He was a wiseass even when they had been in college together. The "punting parson," Cader would tease in the locker room after the games. The nickname had caught on and even the media sportscasters had picked it up and used it over the air.

Use and abuse, that's Cade's policy, Damion thought uncharitably. As long as Cader Harris was *número uno,* all was right with the world. Always *número uno.*

There was no putting it off; Damion gritted his teeth. He supposed he could find Cader at the sporting goods shop. Cader would show those square white teeth and clap him on the back and make him feel like some local yokel while he pinned up photos of all the celebrities he had hobnobbed with during his fantastic career on the gridiron.

The ride to the new sporting goods store belonging to Cader Harris was a short one. The air conditioner really hadn't had a chance to change the temperature inside the black, somber-looking Dodge. All it had done was blast him with the odor of stale cigarette air. Beneath the shade of the striped awning Damion found the door locked and the storefront dark. But deep in the dim recesses he had seen a burgeoning of daylight and decided to walk around the block to the store's loading dock. He stepped over cartons and skirted a stack of baseball bats that were wired together. As he inched his way around a crate of tennis rackets, his eye caught movement in the corner of the back room. "Cade, is that you?"

"Yo! Over here," came the jocular reply. "Damion, you son of a gun, what brings you down here?" Cader Harris said, stretching out his hand in greeting.

"Would you believe to welcome you to the flock?" Damn, now why had he said that? He wanted to steer things away from his ministry; he didn't want to give Cade an easy opening for his jokes. "Don't believe it, huh? How about downright curiosity on my part?"

"You got it," Cader grinned, his square white teeth gleaming in the dark tan of his face.

Damion flinched at the show of teeth. Nobody had that many teeth! It was hot in here despite the dimness. The aroma of leather and new wood, along with excelsior packing, stung his nostrils. Cader muttered something about fresh air, but he made no effort to move toward the door and outside. Damion felt as though he were once again in the locker room; all that was missing was the sweet-sour smell of manly sweat. It was obvious that Cader Harris was once again in his own element. "What say we go outside?" he offered, moving toward the door. He'd get Harris outside beneath God's blue sky, Damion Conway's element.

"You son of a gun!" Cader slapped him on the back. "It's good to see you. Ever get yourself hitched? I didn't think so," he said at Damion's negative nod. "Listen, Damion, Catholic priests are supposed to remain celibate, but not Baptist ministers. Whatever happened to the old 'punting parson'? Nobody around here in Hayden got your blood moving?"

"Don't you ever think about anything besides sex?" Damion snapped, knowing that Cader was thinking his own thoughts. The sportscasters had picked up the polite form of Cader's nickname for Damion. The original version was "cunting parson" after word got out about a particular drunken orgy where Damion was discovered in a back bedroom with two girls from a nearby sorority house.

"How do you handle the celibacy, Damion? Or do you go into New Orleans every once in a while?"

"How do you handle your thing, Cade?"

"Gently, very gently. But I do think about other things. Money and football. What else is left?"

"Believe it or not, there are a few other things."

"For Christ's sake, Damion, you aren't going to give me a lecture like back in the old days. Don't you think we're a little old for that crap? You live your life and I'll live mine. You know you rode pretty hard on me when we were in college. I guess we rode pretty hard on each other."

"Yeah, only your mouth was bigger than mine. What I considered private, you considered public. I still haven't forgotten that little handle you pinned on me."

"We were boys then, Damion; we're men now. Forget it, will you? Don't start preaching fire and brimstone to me like your old man did. You go about your business and I'll go about mine."

"Which is?"

"Hell, man, did all that religion go to your head? My sporting goods store!" Cader Harris smiled winningly, the same smile he used on women when he was cajoling to get his own way.

Conway's guts were churning and his instincts were fully aroused. "There's something else, Cade. I know it in here," he said bitterly, pushing his fist against his chest. "There's something you're not telling. This isn't the right town to open a sporting goods store in, or any other kind of store, for that matter. The town's dying. It's all the established merchants can do to keep Hayden's business from floating down the highway to New Orleans. It's fine for incidental stuff, a drugstore and that kind of business. But sporting goods? That's expensive equipment you've got stashed there," he said, kicking at one of the cartons with the Adidas trademark stamped on its face. Damion noted the grim set to Cader's jaw and his tightly clenched fists. Everything concerning Cader Harris was physical. Super jock, macho hero.

"I don't know what you're talking about, Conway. What you see is what you get."

"Yeah!" Damion scowled. "But this has got to be the quickest operation I've ever seen. Word only leaked about you coming back last week, but from the looks of all this," he gestured toward the merchandise, "it's been in the planning for months."

Harris shrugged. "All it takes is a connection, a phone call and a show of credit cards, and it's delivery the next day."

Damion's scowl deepened as he watched Cader with a speculative eye. "How many football jerseys can you sell? How many tennis rackets? Once the school athletic teams pass through, what's left? Why did you come back here, Cade?"

Cader Harris's dark eyes looked straight into Damion's. "To open a sporting goods store," he said slowly and distinctly. Damion turned away in disgust.

"Of all the things I know you to be, Cade, I know you're no shopkeeper. Two months and this little enterprise will go down the drain."

"Why did you come here, Conway? To tell me I'm not your usual merchant type?"

"I don't really know. Or at least I didn't until I walked in and saw that you'd actually come back to Hayden. Now, I realize it was to tell you that I know in my gut you're here for another reason entirely and to tell you that I'll be watching you. These are my people here in Hayden, and I'll stand between you and them."

Harris threw back his head and laughed. "Now you sound just like your old man, Damion. I guess his preaching got to you more than I thought. He used to lecture me too, whenever he lowered himself for the good of the souls on the wrong side of the tracks. Funny thing is, I never thought you liked your father well enough to follow in his footsteps. I was always of the opinion you agreed to enter the ministry more out of fear of him than anything else."

Damion Conway blanched. Cader had hit closer to the truth than he cared to admit even to himself. How many times had he asked himself what he was doing wearing a clerical collar? Recovering quickly, he said gravely, "You know where the church is. If you ever want to talk to someone, that's where you'll find me. Just call," he said, swinging his leg over the low iron rail on the side of the steps.

"Hold it, Damion. Listen," Cade said, leaping the railing, landing next to Damion. "What's this I hear about Delta Oil? If they set up shop, why, man, this town will boom. And," he said whacking Damion on the back, "you told me this was a dying town." He eyed the minister, watching for reaction. Was his alliance with Delta Oil still secret? Damion would know.

"It is, dying, that is," Damion said seriously. "Delta will never make it. The people are up in arms." He shook his head, watching Cader carefully. "Don't count on Delta to make your business boom. It's too dangerous," he repeated ominously.

"Why?" Cader asked, seeing nothing in Conway's demeanor that revealed any knowledge of his undercover assignment for Delta.

"I know you don't give a damn, but I'll tell you anyway. Pollution, the possibility of an explosion. Human life, Cade. Any environmentalist will tell you liquefied natural gas is a hazard. Even though Delta will store it in tanks, they have to get it here; it has to be transferred from ship to terminal. Cade, stored liquefied natural gas or LNG, as it's called, has the energy potential of several atomic bombs if it's ignited. Now, do you understand? I care; the people of this town care. Delta will never get into Hayden."

"Pity," Cader said airily.

"Yeah, a real pity," Damion repeated coolly. "If you need me, call."

Cader laughed again. "And you'll give aid and comfort as is your calling, right? I'll try to remember that. Thanks for stopping by and wishing me luck. Hey, Damion," he called out, "d'you play racquetball?"

"No!" Damion yelled, not bothering to turn around.

As always, when he was distressed, Damion tugged at his earlobe, mashing the plump flesh between his thumb and finger. He climbed behind the wheel of his car and turned the key in the ignition.

Damion pulled into the flow of moving traffic, his mind occupied with thoughts of the effort it would take to monitor Cader Harris's activities. As he pulled to a halt at the red light on the corner, Damion's thoughts indexed over his relationship with Cader Harris like a two-million-dollar computer. "Harris" was a synonym for "humiliation" as far as Damion was concerned, and one little file from out of the past stood out from the rest and demanded review.

Methodical and orderly, his thoughts brought him back to senior year at Jatha Hayden High School and the debating team, the one area where the talents of Damion Conway could shine. He had been surprised to discover that Cader Harris, already the school favorite because of his prowess on the gridiron, was a fellow member of the debating team. This had puzzled Damion and, upon questioning, Cade had answered, "Look, man, I've got to get myself into a good college if I'm going to make anything of myself. You've got your old man and your Honor Society to get you where you're going. I've got to get there by the hair on my balls and scholastic achievement. What better way than the debating team? I know that college admissions boards are interested in things like that." He grinned at Damion, an ingenuous, dazzling grin that suggested a more serious attitude than Cade admitted.

"As captain of the team," Damion said, extending his hand, "we're glad to have you. It takes a lot of work, Cader, let me warn you." Damion tried to keep his voice easy, which was the opposite of the way he was feeling. He felt intruded upon. This was *his* territory, something he excelled in, and he didn't like Cader Harris interloping on his domain. Why couldn't Harris stay in athletics, where the limelight was certainly brighter?

As the weeks rolled by and Cader continued making extraordinary plays on the field, Damion was watchful and wary. A captain was responsible for the performance of his debating team, and he was ever mindful of the fact that Cader seemed to lead a very busy life. Training for football, other studies, and the arrival on the scene of Sunday Waters, Cader's new girl. Yet, each week, when the debating team met, Cader's material was prepared and his theories held water. They had already participated in two or three debates when they were informed that admissions officers from four separate colleges were to be present at the next competition. Damion's team had achieved a "no loss" status. This debate was an important one.

The subject was social security and the pros and cons had been meticulously explored. On either side, each member of the four-man team knew his arguments, and Damion himself was to be the last speaker, sending their arguments home with a punch. Cader was to speak just before him, and his theories were presented in such a manner as to establish Damion's arguments. They had it in the bag; they couldn't lose.

In Jatha Hayden auditorium, the debating team waited in the wings. Cader was peering out from behind the curtain when he turned to Damion. "Which ones do you think they are? Those college admissions officers."

Damion shrugged. "We only know they're out there, Cade." He had warmed to Cader over the weeks, seeing he had a real zeal for winning, the same zeal he displayed on the gridiron each Saturday. Cader knew where to stress a point, where to emphasize a phrase.

Cader glanced hastily at his notes, and Damion noticed his apprehension. "Not scared, are you? Don't freeze up on me now. We're a team, Cader, and none of us can win this on our own. It's not like out on the football field."

"Yeah, yeah," Cader answered impatiently. "I know."

Damion walked away feeling confident. His team was going to win. More important, he would send the winning argument home. Pro or con, whichever the toss of the coin said was the side they would take, they were going to win. He imagined this was the adrenaline flow Cader got when he ran out onto the field every Saturday. Sure, the football team won, but everybody knew they won only because of Cader Harris. Same thing here, the debating team would win, and everyone would know it was because of Damion Conway. He prided himself on his quickness of thought and his agile maneuverings during debate. He knew his voice had a clear, masculine ring over the loudspeakers, and he was confident of the tone of sincerity he could bring out in his delivery and the haunting look of zealousness which shone in his indigo eyes. Damion Conway was impressive; everyone said so, and he would stand second to none on the pulpit when he became a minister.

Halfway through the debate, the time clock buzzed before the second man on the opposing team could finish his argument. More points for Damion's team. Cader would speak next. Damion sat at attention, listening to every word the moderator spoke. The palms of his hands tingled. Soon, he would have his chance, and he would bring the victory home. He, Damion Conway, would be a hero.

Cader began his argument. Damion was so familiar with the material as they had programmed it that he allowed his mind to wander, dwelling on the impression he would make on the college admissions officers. Suddenly, something Cader said caught his attention, and he realized that Harris had skipped over some very important points of argument and was plunging into the end of his speech. Damion's thoughts clamored. This was terrible. Cader would be left with time on the clock and nothing to say. Their team would lose its point advantage!

Cader drew to the end of his argument. His eyes flew to the clock. Only for an instant, for a syllable, did his voice falter. Cader continued.

Damion's mouth opened in shock. Instead of backtracking to the section of the argument he eliminated, as Damion had expected, Cader Harris bounded on, presenting the argument that should have been Damion's. Unbelieving, Damion listened. He wouldn't! He couldn't! He had. Cader Harris had stolen Damion's argument! He brought the final statements home to a rousing finale, his voice clear and vibrant, emotion rising, just as he had seen Damion practice it.

The clock buzzed for time. The audience applauded, something unheard of in the middle of a debate. Applause was saved for the end.

Aghast, Damion realized the last man on the opposing team was struggling with his point of view. Cader's argument, no, *Damion's* argument, had unnerved him. Damion watched the clock with terror. There was nothing to say. Cader had said it all, using Damion's words! Anything at this point would be anticlimactic. Open-mouthed and staring, Damion willed the clock to stop. He couldn't think! He had had it all wrapped up, and Cader had made a fool of him. It was his turn. The moderator's eyes were on him; the audience's eyes were on him. He groped for theory, for argument, for his voice. Nothing came. Dumbstruck, Damion stood up abruptly, knocking over his chair, and ran from the stage, humiliation burning the backs of his ears, hatred for Cader Harris choking off all reason.

The night was black, protective, covering his shame, hiding his hatred. Footsteps.

"Damion? That you?" Cader Harris asked.

Damion stood tall, willing the night to conceal him, furious that Cader had followed him and found him.

"Christ, Damion! I don't know what made me do it! I forgot the whole middle of my argument. Must have tightened up knowing those officers were in the audience. Christ, I'm sorry, Damion. I couldn't think of a thing to say. Only those closing statements of yours came to my mind. I guess I was pretty impressed with them to remember them. . . . Hey, Damion, you believe me, don't you?"

"Get away from me, Cade." His voice was flat, belying the roiling emotions he was experiencing. Cader Harris had stolen his thunder. There he was, everything any guy in school would give his back teeth to be, and he had to go and steal from a nonentity, Damion Conway.

"You've gotta believe me, Damion. I didn't realize what I was doing until the words were out of my mouth. . . ."

"Shit, you didn't know! Don't give me that crap! You took from me, Cade. Just as if you'd put your hand in my pocket, you stole from me!"

"I deserve that, I know it. But I didn't mean to. It just happened, believe me; it wasn't as though I'd planned it."

"I might believe anyone else, Cader, but never you! Now, get away from me before I kill you." Damion's hands closed into fists.

Now, honking horns broke through Damion's thoughts. The light had changed, God knew how many times, and he was holding up traffic. His foot tromped the gas pedal, and the car burned rubber as it sped across the intersection. Damion's hands were clenched on the steering wheel, and with mental effort he loosened his grasp. He could feel the backs of his ears burning as though he had suffered the humiliation only yesterday.

His reverie had reinforced his position. Cader Harris would

bear watching. Cader Harris was a man without virtues. He was arrogant and self-serving. Cader Harris could turn his back on honor and obligation. Cader Harris was without conscience.

Cader was busy storing cartons when he heard a sharp knocking at the locked front door of the shop. He reached for a football and tucked it into the crook of his arm. Now, he felt dressed. *Never meet your public without feeling dressed,* he grinned to himself. He decided he would saunter to the front of the store. *Showmanship. Always give the public what they want.* Stepping into the dimness of the shop, he saw two young girls and a tall, well-built young man staring in through the glass at him. He immediately surmised they had come to apply for jobs. Hayden, being what it was, offered limited employment for young people. He expected to be swamped with applications.

Cader fixed a lopsided grin on his face, the grin he was known for, and sprinted to the door and undid the latch. The football was held loosely in his suntanned, brawny fist. His nut-brown eyes quickly took in the youngster, and he tossed the ball to the tall blond young man. "Great catch! You handle the pigskin like you know what to do with it," he praised, clapping the boy on the back. He held out his hand. "Cader Harris."

"Kevin Thomas." He handed back the football and waited a moment. "I played first-string quarterback for the school team."

Cader felt the wind knocked out of him. His hand gripped the boy's involuntarily. His son. Recovering, he purposefully released Kevin's hand and forced his voice to work. Even as he spoke, he eyed the boy's handsome features and measured his physique. His son. His son. The thought reverberated in his head.

"Yo! That's what I played when I went to that school. Hey, gang," he addressed himself to the others in the small group that had followed the Thomas boy and the two girls into the store, "is he any good?"

"The best. And he's my brother," Beth Thomas said quietly. "The coaches compared him to you all season. They said his arm was every bit as good as yours, and he could run faster than you."

"Did they, now? Is that what they said, Kevin?" he asked, a speculative look in his eye, squelching an earthquake of paternal pride.

Embarrassed, Kevin said, "More or less."

"If business gets slow, we can take a run out to the field and toss a few. Been awhile since I had a workout. Okay, let's get down to business," he said, remembering the crowd of job applicants. There would be time for these alien emotions later. "The applications and pencils are on that packing case. Just fill them out, and I'll give you a call so a schedule can be set up. I only need part-time clerks and one full-time," he said, eyeing Judy Evans, who, much to Beth's rancor, had found her way to Harris's store at the same time as Kevin.

Casually, Cader draped his arm around Judy's shoulder and grinned down at her. Christ, no kid this age had a right to have that kind of expression in her eyes. "What's your name, honey?"

"Judy Evans. My mother's name used to be Marsha Taylor. She says you went to school together." Judy's shoulder pressed tighter against Cader's arm. All the while her eyes were on Kevin to see if he noticed or cared that Cader Harris had chosen her over his fairy princess sister.

Cader laughed and tweaked her cheek. "I thought you reminded me of someone." His dark eyes watched her as she strained to see the others filling out their application forms. A smile formed on her full lips when she saw Kevin Thomas straighten and glance around. Beth hastily scribbled her name on the bottom line of the application and inched her way toward her brother. Both of them walked toward Cader. Simultaneously, they handed him their applications and waited while he scanned them quickly.

Cader was most interested in Kevin's application; there was no question that the job was his. Beth was something else. If there was one thing he didn't need, it was a brother-sister act. "Beth, is it? I'm sorry, honey, but I don't think you're what I'm looking for. I need someone more aggressive, someone who knows how to sell, like this little chicken." He waved the application toward Judy. "You've got the job. Kevin, that is, if you want it, and I assume you do. Every day from one to six P.M., and ten to six on Saturday. You can start tomorrow. I want everything in shape for Saturday's opening. We have a lot of stocking to do, and there's more merchandise coming in every day."

Judy narrowed her eyes at Kevin and waited expectantly.

Would he take the job without Beth? Poor, poor Bethie, look at the tears. Kevin saw them too and inched a little closer to his sister. "Mr. Harris, I know my sister hasn't had any experience, but she can learn. Couldn't you give her a chance?"

" 'Fraid not, son. Once I start with a kid I like to keep in step with him. What would be the point in hiring her for just a few days and letting her go? Are you telling me, by some chance, you don't want the job unless I take on your sister?" Cader asked harshly, dreading the answer. He wanted to get to know his son but not under the overly possessive eye of his half-sister, Beth.

"No, sir, Mr. Harris. I'll be here tomorrow at one." He moved another step until he was directly behind Beth. Lightly, he placed a hand on her shoulder. The fierce protectiveness and the alliance between the two was disconcerting.

The moment Kevin's hand touched Beth's shoulder, Cader felt Judy stiffen beside him, and he could see the tight set to her full lips. *What have we here,* he wondered. He wasn't surprised to see tears gather in Beth's light green eyes. Just like her mother. Irene had also resorted to tears when something didn't go her way. "You're Irene Hayden's kids, aren't you? I'd heard she married Arthur Thomas while I was away at college. Tell me, are you off to college in the fall?" he asked pointedly, wanting to know every- thing there was to know about Kevin. When Cader knew he was returning to Hayden, he had supposed that sooner or later he would run into Irene's son. He had never imagined the tidal wave of emotion that would engulf him when he came face to face with his own flesh and blood.

"Yes, sir, it's right there on the application, Mr. Harris. Tulane. I leave on the twenty-second of August."

Jesus! His own alma mater. It was almost like coming full circle. Soaring emotions plummeted when he realized that Kevin would never know he was walking in his father's footsteps.

Cader was aware of the hostility that surrounded the three young people. Judy was suddenly relaxed, and young Beth was strung as tight as a clothesline. There was more here than met the eye. "Good school. I'll keep my eye open for a replacement at the end of the summer. Who knows? You may find your way back to Hayden next summer to rest up from all the attention you'll get from the girls at school. If everything works out, you can depend on a job for next year." He smiled enthusiastically, catching the slight narrowing of Beth Thomas's eyes when he had mentioned girls at school. "The job's yours, Kevin. I'm sorry, little lady," he said to Beth, "try me next year when you're a little older." Beth ignored him, her hazel-green eyes full of disdain. It had to be disdain, Cader thought. Denying her the job wasn't cause for murder, and that was the only other word that came to mind when he felt her eyes finally turn to look at him.

Cader watched the Thomas kids hold open the door for a woman to enter as they left the shop.

"Hi, Mom," Judy called.

"Hi, honey. Cade, it's good to see you. Remember me? Marsha Taylor. How are you?" she said, stretching out her hand to meet his.

"How could I forget the prettiest girl in Hayden? How are you, Marsha? Heard your husband died. Sorry about that. He was a real talented guy." He saw Marsha's eyes go to Judy, then back to him. "What have you been doing with yourself, Marsha? It's been a long time. I met your girl here. You should be proud. She's as pretty as her mother at the same age."

"Prettier." Marsha laughed. "As for what I've been doing, it's just a little of this and a little of that, I'm afraid. Actually, it's a whole lot of nothing. Today was my day to help out in Marc Baldwin's office."

Cader looked at the white Qiana uniform with the mandarin collar and long sleeves. It was all under there; everything in its tidy, sexy little place. "How about this bachelor and this bachelorette having dinner? How's Tuesday of next week? We'll go out to the Lemon Drop."

Marsha smiled. "Why not? Pick me up around seven. Listen, honey," she addressed Judy, "do you think you could walk home? Keli McDermott is having car trouble, and I said I would pick her up and drive her home. She's at the garage."

"Okay, Mom. Mr. Harris, I didn't fill out an application and I really want the job. You weren't kidding when you told Beth you were going to hire me, were you?"

"Me? Kid a nice little girl like you? You've got the job, Judy. Same hours as Kevin." Now, why the hell had he said that? He didn't need two full-time clerks. He shrugged. It wasn't his money, so what difference did it make? Besides, it might give the boys at Delta Oil something else to squawk about, something other than when and how he was going to start putting pressure in the right places to get those tanks into Hayden.

CHAPTER THREE

*K*evin's stomach churned as he walked beside Beth down tree-lined Mimosa Lane. He should say something, anything, to wipe away the hurt look in her eyes. It wasn't his fault that Mr. Harris didn't want to hire her. He had intervened on her behalf, hadn't he? Damn, why did she have to make him feel this way?

His dark eyes lightened as he laid a hand on her arm and stopped at the crosswalk. "I'm sorry, Beth." Damn! There he went apologizing to her again. He held his breath, waiting to hear what her answer would be. *Say anything,* he pleaded silently, *just don't keep looking at me that way!*

Beth imperceptibly shook off his hand and raised her eyes. Stunned by what he saw there, Kevin could only stare at her. Where was the hurt, the wounded look he had expected to see? Instead, a pair of glazed hazel eyes glared through him as she spoke in a carefully controlled voice: "If only one of us could have the job, I'm glad it was you. Mama said she was giving you a limited allowance this summer, so the money will come in handy for you."

Say it, Beth, his mind shouted. *Say I want the money for college in the fall. Say it! Don't pretend I'm not going and that I want this money to blow on good times this summer. Say it!* He walked along beside her as they crossed Mimosa Lane toward their house. Taking a deep breath, he blurted, "The money will come in handy when I leave for Tulane at the end of August. I can manage for the summer with

what Mother gives me; it's September that'll put me in a bind."
Kevin swallowed hard and looked down at Beth. She raised tear-
filled eyes and sprinted ahead of him down the street to the white
neo-Grecian house that was home.

Kevin remained on the curb, his eyes narrowed against the late
afternoon sun. Should he race after her? Should he apologize to her?
It wasn't his fault he got the job and he was going off to college.

Leaning back against a gnarled sycamore trunk, he scuffed at
the moss near the base of the old tree with the toe of his sneaker.
The older you got, the more complicated life became, he told himself sagely. He knew in his gut that as of today his life was going to
change. Meeting Cader Harris, graduating from high school
tomorrow night, working at a bona fide job were only the first of
many changes. He could feel the presence of change in the air.

Telling his mother that he'd taken a job would bring about
another change. Getting Beth to come around and cheering her out
of her sulk would be another. Judy. Beth hated Judy for her good
looks and free, easy spirit. Tacky was the word Beth used for Judy.
He grinned. There was a lot to be said for tacky. He blinked and his
ears felt warm when he imagined what Judy's round, full breasts
would feel like cupped in his hands. Guilt and disloyalty erased
the fantasy. Beth hated Judy, had hated her since grammar school.
The same animosity still raged between the two girls, even after all
this time. Beth was just entering her senior year, and Judy was
graduating in his class.

Kevin lowered his eyes to the destruction he had created at his
feet. Emerald-green moss lay in clumps, and specks of rich, brown
earth dotted his white sneakers. He hunkered down and carefully
fitted the clods back into place. Satisfied that no outward sign of
damage showed, he rose to his feet, dusting off his hands. He
squared his shoulders and jogged home. To home and Beth.

Keli McDermott watched Kevin jog down the street and smiled
to herself. She turned slightly in the car seat and spoke to Marsha.
"Kevin Thomas is such a nice boy. Irene must be very proud of him.
Gene . . . Gene told me the boy was going to Tulane in the autumn. It
must be wonderful to have children. Children to make one proud."

Marsha turned slightly and looked at Keli. She frowned when
she spoke. "What you say is true, Keli, but sometimes a mother
and a father, too, take children for granted. We want so much for

them, and when they fall short of the measure, we feel cheated. Somehow, I can't imagine Kevin Thomas ever falling short. Irene wouldn't stand for it."

Keli said softly, "I would like to know how it feels to be a mother."

Again, a quick, light glance and then back to the road. "One day soon, you'll know. Then you won't wonder any longer."

"Marsha, are you wondering why I asked you to drive me home?"

"Glad to do it. Is Gene out of town that he couldn't pick you up at the garage?"

Warily, "I . . . I called him and there was no answer."

"But doesn't Gene always work on his book from nine in the morning till five? He made a point of saying that, boasting about it, at Julia's dinner party last week. He said it was all a matter of discipline," Marsha said, risking another quick glance at Keli. How beautiful and defenseless she was. Like a butterfly perched on the edge of a blossom, tentative, with a kind of trembling sense of her own beauty. God would only know how, with the protective cocoon Gene wrapped around his wife, this beautiful little butterfly managed to emerge, she thought sourly.

Shyly, Keli said, "He may have been walking in the garden; he does that to clear his head when things don't go right for him at the typewriter."

"I'm sure that's what it is. I don't mind giving you a lift. Keli, will you pick us up tomorrow as planned? Remember, we all have to be at the school at noon."

"I would be most happy," Keli breathed softly. Keli's natural graciousness always made Marsha feel as though she had the tact of a buzz saw. "If Gene will permit me to use his car, I will pick you up first and then Irene and Julia. Thank you for the ride, Marsha," Keli said, opening the door almost the moment Marsha braked in front of her house. "See, Gene is home and waiting for me." She pointed a slender finger at a burly man walking down the flagstone path toward the car.

Marsha's jaw tightened as she saw Gene McDermott peer intently into the car, trying to recognize the driver. She slipped the car into gear, but not before she saw the colonel's arm go around Keli.

Marsha drove furiously, her mind whirling. She could have a hand in teaching Keli to speak English and to dress stylishly, but she couldn't protect her from her own husband, retired USAF Colonel Gene McDermott. *Christ!* Any woman living under his roof, let alone soft, uncomplaining Keli, would have a tough time keeping her spirit from being buried under his bush. Gene McDermott was reducing Keli's identity to a thin shadow. She had never met such an overbearing, self-righteous man in her entire life. He was a bull. He was just the type to marry an Oriental girl, thinking that they, above all other women, would be acquiescent and obliging to his demands. Hating Gene McDermott, she jammed her foot to the floor and rounded the corner onto Mimosa Lane on two wheels.

Arthur Thomas climbed from his car and stood watching Marsha as she careened around the corner, her tires screeching. If she didn't watch it, she would soon be availing herself of his services at the funeral home.

He was tired. God, he was tired, he thought as he wiped at his wide brow. If he had his way, he would slip out to the garden and lie down in the hammock and sleep for a week. Oh, no, he had to shower and change for dinner so Irene wouldn't be able to complain that he smelled of embalming fluid. And he would have to shave. "I hate shaving at six in the evening," he muttered to himself as he let himself in the front door.

"Irene," he called without enthusiasm, "I'm home."

"You have ten minutes until dinner is ready. You're late, Arthur," she said, walking into the dining room to place a silver bowl of yellow tea roses precisely in the center of the lace cloth. She walked over to her husband in a cloud of White Shoulders and dutifully presented her cheek for his light peck. "Oooh, you positively reek, Arthur! You are one man who always brings his work home with him." She frowned.

Arthur ignored her. "What's for dinner?" He wrinkled his nose to see if he could get a clue to her culinary masterpiece of the day.

"Great-Aunt Matilda Hayden's famous meat loaf," she answered quietly, her eyes daring him to reproach her.

Again, Arthur ignored her. "Must we go through this Cecil B. DeMille production for meat loaf?" he asked, waving his hands toward the lace cloth, the bone china, and the sterling silver cutlery. "Why can't we have dinner on the patio?"

Irene sucked in her cheeks and issued her favorite retort to Arthur's comments on her elaborate dinners. "Daddy always said you can't make a silk purse out of a sow's ear. If you want dinner on the patio, I'll have Dulcie serve you out there—alone. The children and I will dine in the manner to which we are accustomed, the manner in which all civilized people dine."

"One of these days, Irene, I will do just that, and," he said ominously, "I will wear the suit I wore at the funeral home, my *work clothes,* as you call them, and I will enjoy eating on the patio." Turning on his heel, he left her standing, her mouth agape at his sharp tone. "And spare me another of your daddy's homespun philosophies."

Dressed in what Irene called his "at home dinner suit" of light blue seersucker, he paused and looked at his reflection in the cathedral mirror. "I am sick to death of the Haydens. I am sick of Daddy Hayden, and I am even sicker of Great Granddaddy Hayden. As a matter of fact, Irene, I'm getting pretty sick of you!" Enraged by the close-fitting tie that was an essential part of his dinner outfit, Arthur struggled with the knot and ripped it from beneath his collar. He stared at himself in the mirror and didn't like what he saw there. There, in his place, was a middle-aged, running-to-fat man with a receding hairline, who had somehow managed to snag the heiress to the Hayden money.

Arthur never understood why *the* Irene Hayden noticed him in the first place. She was from the finest family in town and had never given him any indication she was, or could ever be, interested in a simple country boy from a middle-income family. It had been when he had come home from college on spring vacation that she had all but thrown herself at him. To this day, when he thought of that night in his old '53 Chevy, he couldn't believe that the girl who had wrapped herself around him and welcomed him to her with soft moans of delight was the same Irene he had married. A hasty, whispered phone call placed to his fraternity house announced she was pregnant and he had to marry her.

When Kevin was born, eighteen years ago, Arthur imagined himself to be the luckiest man in the world, and all thoughts of abandoned ambition and becoming a medical examiner were banished from his mind. A year later, when Bethany came along, Arthur knew he had the world on a string. It was then his relationship with Irene changed. From an eager young girl who sought his arms and his lovemaking whenever possible, she had become a nag, fighting off his advances, at last resigning herself to her "wifely duty." There was no joy left, no anticipation, no anything. Screwing Irene was like screwing one of the corpses in his preparation room.

Resignedly, Arthur once again wrapped the tie around his neck and began knotting it. In spite of it all, in spite of everything, he still loved Irene. Regardless of his thwarted career, regardless of hearing over and over again how he owed his prospering business to his father-in-law, in spite of her unresponsiveness in the bedroom, Arthur Thomas loved his wife, and he knew he always would. He was in awe of her, and although she dressed in staid, matronly clothes and allowed her hair to darken to its present mousy color, Irene was the most beautiful woman who had ever come into his life. Even Sunday Waters, lovely as she was, could not compare with Irene's inborn class and charm.

A sound from above reminded Arthur that the kids had applied for work at Cader Harris's. Dinner was going to be unpleasant at best, he thought morbidly. Once Irene was told about their applying for work, that was. His face brightened momentarily when he thought that for once Irene was going to get her tail feathers singed a little and ol' Daddy Hayden and Great Granddaddy Hayden, deceased, couldn't do anything about it. He was still smiling when he entered the dining room in time to see Irene seat herself and pick up the small silver bell which rested near her place. "Try for a dirge tonight, Irene. Great-Aunt Matilda's meat loaf could use a little mood music."

"It must be your obnoxious profession, Arthur, which makes you behave in such an uncivilized manner. I wouldn't be surprised if rigor mortis hadn't settled in your brain." The silver bell tinkled and she announced in a musical tone, "Dinner is served."

Beth and Kevin came into the dining room and seated themselves at their mother's graciously appointed table. Beth's eyes were downcast. She toyed with her fork and the thin slice of meat loaf on her plate. Kevin helped himself generously and then, looking at his sulky sister, resisted the impulse to begin eating.

Arthur's eyes scanned the members of his family, concentrating on the faces of his children. He sighed and spoke. "Irene, Kevin applied for a job this afternoon. How did it go, son?"

Before the meaning of her husband's words settled in her consciousness, Irene heard her son say, "I was hired, Dad. I start work tomorrow."

"Fine, son, I'm proud of you." Turning to Irene, he said, "Kevin will be working for Cader Harris in his new sporting goods store."

"A job! Kevin, what in the world are you thinking of?" Irene hissed, her fork poised in midair. "Haydens never seek employment until after college. A job! Never! You just call . . ." Her words were cut off in midstream. It had suddenly dawned on her that Arthur said Kevin would be working for Cader Harris. Her heart began a mad thumping in her breast. Irene knew Cader had returned to Hayden. How could she help knowing when the whole town was buzzing with the news? She had even been formulating a plan which would throw her into contact with him again. But to have Kevin working for him! Never! She didn't want Kevin anywhere near Cader Harris. She leaned against the high-backed chair, her gaze challenging Kevin, a war of emotions erupting within her.

"Look, Mother, you know as well as I do that I could use the money." Kevin chanced a sidelong glance at his sister and saw her chewing through her salad, a smug expression on her face.

"You have your inheritance from Granddaddy Hayden, Kevin," Irene protested. "And Haydens never . . ."

"Kevin is a Thomas, Irene," Arthur said curtly, jumping to the defense, "and we Thomases have been known to work for a living. The money isn't the only consideration here; it's a question of independence. Finding a job like this is commendable. Commendable!" he emphasized as he cut into the dirt-colored meat loaf.

"Mama, I happen to agree with you," Beth said pertly, her eyes sparkling. "Kev doesn't need the money, and why should he take the job from some poor person who really needs it?"

His daughter's statement caught Arthur's attention. Apparently, Beth had applied for the job and was turned down. Arthur loved his daughter, but, as a man, he sympathized with his son. So, Kevin would be free of his sister around his neck, and Beth didn't like that idea at all. Now, more than ever, he supported the idea of Kevin working for Cader Harris. "Kevin needs the experience of responsibility. This will be a good way for him to gain a knowledge of the working world, and it will prove profitable."

Irene swallowed hard and forced her hands to be still in her lap. "Kevin can learn responsibility by looking after Beth this summer."

A flurry of rage rose in Arthur. "That's what he's been doing since Beth was born, Irene, and it's time things changed. Beth will have to learn to get along without him. Kevin's graduation will mark the beginning of his adult life. He can't stay with Beth for the rest of his life, and Beth might as well begin knowing that now!" He pounded his fist on the table.

"Be reasonable, Arthur." Irene gulped. It had been years since she had seen Arthur work himself up over the children this way. Usually, he acquiesced to her wishes. Not since Kevin came home telling them he had tried out for the football team and was accepted had Arthur interfered this way. She was going to lose this battle, she knew it, and there wouldn't be a thing she could do about it. "I still say the answer is no!" she said with all the imperiousness of generations of Haydens.

"No one was asking you, Irene," Arthur said quietly. "Therefore, your answer is not required. Kevin has landed the job at the sporting goods store, and I'm proud of him."

"Mama is right, Daddy. You always take Kevin's side," Beth accused.

"It's not a question of taking sides, Bethany. Find friends of your own and leave Kevin to do as he wants. The two of you spend too much time together as it is." He glanced at Irene accusingly.

"Arthur!" Irene shrilled. "The answer is no! For one thing, think of what it will do to our dinners together. You know as well as I what a task it was to convince Dulcie to come back in the afternoons to serve dinner," she whispered, looking toward the kitchen door for signs of the black housekeeper. "I do declare, she's getting more and more independent. This civil rights thing has destroyed genteel Southern living. . . ."

"Irene! We are not talking about your house-help," Arthur said forcefully, familiar with Irene's ploys to change the subject. "We are talking about Kevin's job. What time do you quit every day, son? Six, did you say? Good. See there, Irene, surely you won't be too inconvenienced by holding dinner another fifteen minutes. If not, I'd be happy to eat out on the patio with Kevin."

"Arthur . . ."

"Mother, I'm taking the job. I gave my word, and I told Mr. Harris I'd report for work tomorrow. I'm going to," Kevin said in a hard, cold voice. He purposely avoided Beth's eyes when he made his declaration.

Irene sputtered, "How . . . how will it look? Think of how it will look! I forbid it!" Her hands were trembling; tears formed in the corners of her eyes. *Cader. Cader.*

"I've got the job, Mother, and I'm going to take it. Excuse me, Dad, I'm not hungry," he said, rising from the table and making a hasty exit.

Beth jumped to her feet, tipping her water glass onto the lace cloth in the process. Tears glistened in her eyes as she ran up the stairs behind Kevin.

"Now, what am I going to do with this meat loaf?" Irene asked nervously. Cader Harris was back in town. *Cader Harris,* her mind repeated over and over.

"Do what you always do with your great-aunt Matilda's meat loaf. Give it to the cat," Arthur said callously.

Irene sat at the table long after the others had left, her mind churning at what Arthur had said. Kevin was going to work for Cader Harris. Kevin was going to work for his father. Wearily, she massaged her throbbing temples. What had Cade thought when Kevin appeared in his store? More important, what did he feel when he looked at the boy? Surely, he recognized his own features in Kevin. She had to be careful and not say too much in front of either Kevin or Arthur. She couldn't give it away, not now after all these years. Kevin was Arthur's son, that's what the child's birth certificate read, Kevin Hayden Thomas. Panic coursed through her for a split second. Cade wouldn't claim parentage now, would he? Oh, God, what had the boy thought when he saw Cader Harris? Was he impressed with him? Did he like him? Did he notice any resemblance to his own clean-cut good looks? She had to do something, make some kind of plan. Plead, beg with Cade not to divulge their secret. Daddy! Oh, no, not this tine. Cade, she would go to Cade and straighten out everything.

Irene stared at the lace tablecloth and then down at the severe dress she wore. The sensible walking shoes and less-than-sheer hose. Dowdy. How had she allowed herself to become dowdy?

Arthur, that was how. Arthur was dowdy—a balding, pudgy old man at forty-two. If she sprinkled embalming fluid over herself and fluffed up her hair, he would be in seventh heaven. And for what? His hands were always so cold. All those customers of his made his hands cold. Cade's hands had always been warm, hot and searching and then conquering.

Defiantly, Irene reached behind her to the sideboard and pulled a package of crumpled cigarettes from the drawer. She puffed steadily, drawing the smoke deep into her lungs.

Nineteen years since she last saw Cader Harris. Almost an eternity by some people's standards. Where had the years gone; what had she done with them? *Existed*, she told herself, crushing out the cigarette and immediately lighting another. Just existed, knowing that Cade would come back and they would live happily ever after. In her fantasies she had imagined Cade looking at Kevin and then rushing to her and taking her in his arms. First, he would thank her for giving him such a wonderful son and then he would tell her he loved her, had always loved her and that was why he had come back, because he knew now he couldn't live another day without her and his son. Arthur. Arthur would always manage to weave his way into her fantasies at this point and spoil everything. Arthur always spoiled everything. Still, she could really hurt him by telling him Kevin was Cade's son. Arthur genuinely loved Kevin and the boy returned that love. Arthur was Kevin's father and that was all there was to it. When you really stopped to think about it, Arthur had everything. He had the love of his son, a sweet daughter, a perfect wife, and all those bodies to while away his days. And what did she have? She had a respectful son, a whiny daughter, a less-than-perfect husband who smelled, and meetings. It wasn't enough. "I want more. I deserve more." She grimaced as she let ashes drop into her coffee cup. "Tsk, tsk," she muttered, "ashes in the old Hayden china. Who in the goddamn hell gives a good roaring fuck," she said viciously. She lit another cigarette and blew a perfect smoke ring and then she laughed. That was what she needed, a good fuck, frontwards, backwards, sideways, and hanging upside down, dangling from the window, on the beach, in a pile of leaves. Anywhere, anytime, anyplace. It had been a long time since she had had a big O. and here she was just thinking of Cader Harris and getting it off.

Nineteen years ago she had felt like this, but then she didn't have to depend on fantasies or memories. Cade was real and always ready. A smile tugged at the corner of her mouth. How well she remembered the first time she had been physically aware of Cader Harris. It was in her senior year in the lunchroom at school. Sunny Waters had walked in and sat down at a table, and Cader Harris, who was carrying his tray, noticed Sunny just as he passed Irene. Because she was sitting down and at eye level with his crotch, she had seen the immediate swell in his pants as soon as he set eyes on Sunny. She had made up her mind right then that she wanted to cause the same response in him.

Irene Hayden leaned back in the cane-backed chair, the cigarette dangling from her fingers, as she became the eighteen-year-old cheerleader who had cheered Cader Harris to victory on the emerald field.

"You're edgy today, Irene," Marsha Taylor said irritably, "your cheers are off beat. Can't you stay in tune with the rest of us?"

"Five minutes to halftime," Irene said, twirling her pompom under Marsha's nose. Her eyes sparkled with what she intended to do. Before the night was over she would have superstar Harris eating out of her hand.

"I don't like that look in your eye, Irene. What are you up to?" Marsha demanded, her eyes glued to the battling figures on the grassy carpet.

"I've decided that I want Cader Harris, and I'm going to get him, tonight after the game," Irene said loftily.

"Ha! You and every other girl in this school. Besides, Cader Harris already has a steady girl, Sunday Waters, or hadn't you noticed?" Marsha snapped.

"Of course, I noticed. Everyone has noticed. He's only taking her out for one thing and you know it. I know it and so does everybody in school. Why, I could get him just like that!" Irene said, snapping her fingers.

Marsha Taylor stared at Irene Hayden and knew she meant every word she said. Poor Sunny, she wouldn't have a chance with the likes of Irene Hayden. "And when you get him, what are you going to do with him?" Marsha demanded.

"Do with him?"

"Yes, do with him. Cade Harris is physical. By that, Irene, I mean he is going to want to do more than hold that lily-white hand of yours."

"Well," Irene sniffed delicately, "he is almost acceptable now that he's been nominated for All State. I don't see any harm in kissing him."

Marsha laughed at the vague look on Irene's face. She wanted to shock her, drive her out of that gilt and ivory tower she lived in. "Are we talking about kissing your mouth or your pussy? Somehow, Irene, I can't picture you opening your legs, and it's always been a mystery to me how you put your bloomers on."

"Marsha Taylor, for shame!" God, was that what Cader Harris would expect? Did that tacky Sunny Waters let him do . . . Oh, God!

"Well, which is it?" Marsha demanded in a laughing voice. "Boys like pussy, face it. You shower with the rest of us after gym and you've heard the girls talk just as I have. Cade Harris only wants one thing from you or any other girl."

"Oh pooh, Marsha. He'll respect me just the way all the boys do. If he doesn't, then I'll tell Daddy and have him booted off the team. I'm no slut like Sunny Waters."

"You don't know Sunny Waters is a slut, so just watch it, Irene. I happen to like her and so does Julia. The only reason you don't like her is because she has Cade wrapped around her finger."

"She puts out," Irene said huffily.

"So will you if you go out with Cade," Marsha giggled, "and then what is Daddy going to say?"

"You hush, Marsha. I'd never go all the way. Have you?" she asked curiously. Marsha and Julia Wilson locked stares and then scampered away to Irene's acute discomfort. She couldn't . . . she wouldn't . . . !

The opportunity to speak with Cade came during halftime when she tossed her pompom into the air and purposely shot wide, knowing exactly where it would fall. Giggling, her cheeks flushed, she raced to the fallen pompom and scooped it up, but not before she winked at Cade and whispered. "You're playing a great game. If you make another touchdown, I'll let you take me to the Shrimp Boat after the game."

Cader Harris blinked and did a double take. Old man Hayden's kid asking him for a date. There certainly was a lot to be said for football. Here was his chance to see how the other half lived. Irene

Hayden asking him, Cader Harris, for a date! Why in the hell was she licking her lips like that, he wondered uncomfortably. He couldn't be too eager and he didn't really have enough money to take her to the Shrimp Boat, and, besides, he had promised to take Sunny to a late movie. He raised his head and narrowed his eyes. "It depends on how tired I am."

"Tired! Somehow, I never thought of you ever getting tired," Irene cooed. If she didn't pull this off and make him promise now, Marsha would have it all over school that Cade Harris turned Irene Hayden down in favor of that slut, Sunny Waters. "Sorry, football man," Irene said coolly, "you have to let me know now, because there are other guys who asked me out and I thought I would give you first choice since you are the star and all."

"Okay," he grinned. "Did you say one touchdown?"

"I'd like two, but one will do." Irene preened.

"You got it and I'll meet you at the gate after I shower."

Irene danced her way to the other cheerleaders and smirked. "Cader Harris is taking me to the Shrimp Boat after the game. I told you I could get him to ditch that slut. From this point on Cader Harris belongs to me. Pass the word along so that all the girls stay out of his way. He's mine!"

"Now that you got him, what are you going to do with him? I know I asked you that before, but at the time it was just in the talking stage, but now that he's definitely yours, I'd like to know what you're going to do with a big, virile he-man like Cade Harris. You're just an itsy-bitsy lil ol' Southern gal with a starched petticoat, and you're a Hayden to boot."

Irene stared at Marsha, hating her for what she was saying. "I'm going to play with him until I get tired, that's what I'm going to do, and when I'm tired of him, I'll still be a virgin, not like you and all those others. Haydens don't mess around, so there, Marsha Taylor."

"That's only because they never met up with a Cader Harris, and don't be so damned pompous. My mother told me your father is Cledie's best customer, so don't get snotty with me."

"I'm talking about Hayden women. Cader promised to get me two touchdowns, what do you think of that?" Irene said, trying to change the subject.

"I think he's just as crazy as you are." Marsha grimaced.

Cade was as good as his word; he scored a touchdown in the first ten minutes of the third quarter and a second one in the final five minutes. Each time he tossed the pigskin onto the turf, he looked toward the row of squealing, bouncing cheerleaders and grinned.

Irene was beside herself with the second touchdown, preening and giggling for the other cheerleaders, knowing they envied her and would have given their own virginity, if still intact, for the evening ahead of her.

Marsha had to literally restrain Julia from strangling Irene when she pranced her way to the bleachers and looked straight at Sunny while she spoke to a friend sitting two seats away. "I'm going to the Shrimp Boat with Cader Harris after the game, so don't wait for me." Marsha watched Sunny's knuckles go white and her face drain of all color. It was to Sunny's credit that she sat out the remaining minutes of the game before she left, her slim shoulders in their faded sweater slumped for all to see. "I hope you get a good dose of the clap, Irene Hayden," Marsha hissed.

Irene ignored Marsha, her eyes on the field and Number Fourteen, who was standing staring at her. Cader Harris was hers. She won him just like he was winning the game for Jatha Hayden High. He was hers. As far as she could tell, her only problem at this point was her father, and when she tried, she could wrap him around her finger. Still, she would have to sneak around, but that would only add to the excitement. A date with Cader Harris and two touchdowns, what more could any girl ask for? By tomorrow every girl in town would know she had staked out Cader Harris and Sunny Waters had gone down the drain. Irene giggled as she waved her pompoms.

Irene waited in her brief cheerleading costume near the gate for Cader, knowing she should have changed her clothes, but she wanted Cade to see how her legs looked up close. Boys always admired girls' legs and she had good legs, might as well put them to good use. "Oweeee, Cader, over here," Irene squealed. She watched his loose-limbed stride as he approached her. He didn't look as though he was in any hurry to make his way to the gate, stopping to talk to first one boy and then a girl and then a parent. He wore a wide grin, accepting the admiration of his fellow students with ease.

Irene liked the way he stood before her and stared at the short red skirt and her tan legs. His voice was low and husky, sending shivers up her arm. "I kept my promise, now what are you going to promise me?"

"Why, Cade, to go to the Shrimp Boat with you. That's what I promised, all that I promised," Irene said nervously.

Cader Harris leaned against the fence post, his muscular arms folded across his chest. "Maybe," he drawled, "we better get something straight before we take off for the Shrimp Boat and I go blowing my money on you. The coach has all the players on a ten o'clock curfew. Tonight, because of the game the ban is lifted till eleven-thirty." He looked at his watch pointedly. "It's nine-twenty and I sure as hell hope you eat fast because I have other things in mind. Make up your mind now before we leave because I don't spend money on any girl unless I get some kind of a return."

Irene pretended not to understand. If she backed off now, she'd be the laughingstock of Jatha Hayden High in the morning. She stared at Cader and suddenly didn't care what she had to do. She wanted to walk into the Shrimp Boat with Cader Harris and have all the girls sigh in envy, especially Julia and Marsha. So what if he stuck his hand down her sweater and felt her breasts, and so what if he stuck his tongue in her mouth? Who would know? Her heart thumped wildly when she remembered all the stories she heard about Sunny Waters. Sunny certainly didn't spread them so it must have been Cader. He must have bragged to the other boys and . . . oh, God, would he say those things about her? She would make him promise with the threat of Daddy booting him off the team. "Cader Harris," she said arrogantly, "I didn't ask you to pay for me at the Shrimp Boat. All I did was say I would let you take me. I intended to pay my own way. Heaven's sake, what kind of girl do you think I am?" She had a quarter tucked into her saddle shoe and would order a cherry phosphate and that would be it. She would pretend she had an upset stomach from all the excitement.

Cader was silent for a minute. "I know exactly what kind of girl you are, and you know exactly what kind of guy I am. You want to be seen with me so you can brag to your friends, and it won't hurt my image to be seen with you. You want something from me and I want something from you. Simple. Now, are you going to put out or not?" he grinned, moving closer to her and touching her cheek with his thumb.

Irene swallowed the lump in her throat and knew in that second that she would do whatever Cader Harris asked of her. He knew it too. "All right, Irene Hayden, you're my girl. I'll give you my football sweater and you give me your class ring." Irene had the ring off her finger before he stopped speaking and could barely wait for him to slip off the bright red sweater. He really was hers. The sweater said so. Now, she could order the shrimp platter and forget about the cherry phosphate. When you were going steady, the guy paid, and all she had done was sell herself to the number-one guy in Hayden.

Irene's entrance into the Shrimp Boat was everything she hoped it would be. The girls all stared at her with envy and the boys looked at her differently, and it wasn't just her imagination.

Irene watched Cader as he wolfed down his shrimp while she toyed with hers, pushing the succulent morsels from one side of her plate to the other. God, it looked like he wasn't chewing the shrimp but swallowing it whole. The sooner he finished, the sooner he would want to leave. "Eat mine, Cader, I don't think I can finish it," Irene said hastily.

"I have a better idea," Cader grinned, "let's take it with us and I'll eat it in the car. We are taking your convertible, aren't we?" Cader asked, a hint of envy in his voice as he eyed the gleaming, customized Ford Fairlane with the rolled and pleated interior.

"If you want. Do you want to drive it? Daddy gave it to me for my birthday and it only has fifteen hundred miles on it," Irene babbled.

"Sure, get in," Cader replied, taking the offered keys. Irene was left to open the door herself.

"Where are we going, Cade?" Irene asked, watching the wild and reckless set of his features as he tooled the convertible onto the open highway.

"How about Jatha Beach? We can watch the submarine races," Cade shouted to be heard above an eighteen-wheeler whizzing by.

"Why don't you take me some place you haven't taken another girl. Some place that will be just ours, yours and mine," Irene said, a tinge of hysteria creeping into her voice.

Cader slowed the convertible and glanced at her. "On your side of the tracks or mine?"

"I think we should stay on this side of town because my car

might be noticed. . . . What I mean is . . . over there you people don't . . . I don't care," she said suddenly, "you're driving, let's just drive till we find some place you like."

Cader laughed and pressed his foot to the floor, the yellow car shot forward and sailed down the highway as though on wings. Irene's hair whipped about her head, and she felt exhilarated beyond belief. She couldn't wait for the car to slow down and come to a stop. She wanted Cader Harris. She realized she no longer felt frightened or apprehensive.

When Cader maneuvered the car into a rutted road that was dark as ebony, she let her breath out in a long sigh. Before he turned off the lights, Cader looked at his watch and said, "We have exactly sixty-two minutes." The moment the engine died he had her in his arms and was crushing her mouth to his while his busy hands searched and probed her soft flesh.

In the darkness Irene felt herself being crushed against Cader's chest. There was a faint aroma of deodorant and aftershave, and, although his grip was tight and rough, his lips were soft, caressing her mouth, teasing it and persuading it to open to his.

His hands were in her hair, on the back of her neck, on her throat. This wasn't like the fumbling of some of the other boys who had tried to seduce her. This was the expert handling of a man, the man of the hour, Cader Harris.

She had been determined to charm him into obedience, flirt with his ego and eventually have her way with him by leaving him panting with desire yet respecting her virginity. But the touch of his mouth on hers, the caress of his tongue searching for hers, the unhurried exploration of his hands on her breasts seemed to beat the will out of her.

She had never felt this way before. She had sometimes allowed a boy to kiss her and even to slip his tongue into her mouth. And if he were very nice, she might let him go so far as to touch her breasts, but never, ever, had she wanted a boy to open her blouse, undo her bra, and run his tongue over her nipples. Now, here with Cader Harris, she wanted this more than she wanted breath.

Her own fingers fumbled with the buttons on her blouse. Unashamed, she impatiently worked the hooks on her bra and tore it free from her body.

He acceded to her demands, allowing her to lead the pace and set the limits. She heard her own gasp when his hand touched her flesh, heard his moan of passion as he bent his head to touch his lips to the rosy crests, felt a curling heat build within her and ignite between her thighs.

With the same impatience she had displayed with blouse and bra, Irene removed her skirt and panties. She didn't dare to stop to think what she was doing. She only knew she wanted to be naked with Cader Harris. She wanted him to touch her all over in that same teasing and feathery way that he touched her breasts.

There, on the front seat of her Ford Fairlane, Irene Hayden gave herself to Cader Harris. And when she felt him tremble as he entered her, she was unaware of the sharp momentary pain. She was only aware that Cader was saying her name over and over.

They stayed out long past Cader's curfew. Loving and kissing and exploring one another. They were both naked now, the chill of the early October air making their bodies smooth and silky against each other. Irene forgot all about her decision to save herself for marriage; she forgot entirely about the fact that she was a Hayden, one of the privileged, and that Cader was from the wrong side of town; she even forgot that she had met his challenge and lost. The only thing she could think of was Cader, his mouth, his hands, the way he whispered her name. Irene Hayden, for the first time in her life, loved someone else more than she loved herself.

Her inexperience was no deterrent to her inventiveness. When the passions flared between them again, she moved him into a sitting position and straddled his lap. His hands played with the firm flesh of her bottom as she lowered herself onto him, greedily taking him inside her. Her long, tapered thighs were strong and her body agile as she moved her hips in slow, undulating circles. And when she pushed herself against him and his mouth found her breast, she cried out his name and the wind carried it above the treetops. Irene Hayden had found passion and fulfillment and love. Irene Hayden had found Cader Harris.

Dulcie entered the dining room and had to repeat her question before Irene could break herself from the memory of that night. Even as she responded to Dulcie's question of "Will that be all for the day? Can I go home now?" she was aware of the wetness between her legs.

Cader Harris was back in town. Had he come back for her? Did he still love her? Or had he come back for Kevin? A dull heaviness weighed on her chest as she looked at Kevin's place at the table. She swallowed hard, choking back her dread. Irene Hayden knew from experience that Cader Harris always got what he wanted.

Hours after Dulcie had cleared away the half-eaten meal, Bethany paced the ruffled confines of her room. She wrung her hands together to keep them from trembling with anger. How could Kevin do this to her? How could he take a job with that awful Cader Harris? *How could he work with Judy Evans every day?*

Judy Evans. She'd had her eye on Kevin since kindergarten. She wanted Kevin for herself! Well, she couldn't have him. Kevin belonged to her, Beth, his sister, and nobody, nobody in this whole world could take him from her. Not Judy, not Cader Harris, not Tulane, not anyone or anything!

She paused before the pier glass and studied her reflection. Slowly, as though afraid to look, she pulled her robe apart and saw her nakedness reflected in the mirror. She scrutinized her slimness, curling her lip in distaste at the whiteness of her skin and the smattering of freckles left over from last summer's sunburn. Why couldn't she tan like the other girls, like Judy Evans? She was always as white as a fish's belly except for the patch of bright red hair at the V of her thighs. Even that looked pale and washed out to her eyes. She had seen Judy many times showering after gym, and her pubic hair was thick and glossy and black against her skin.

Her hands cupped her small, symmetrical breasts and she bemoaned the fact that they weren't full and ripe like Judy's. With a jerk she pulled the flaps of her robe tightly around her nakedness, blocking it from her view in the pier glass. Well, she was herself and not like Judy at all. Judy was a different type altogether. There were lots of beautiful women in the world whose breasts were small and whose skin was white, she reasoned. *Just think of all those women Kevin and I used to look at in Daddy's girlie magazines.* The ones he had kept hidden in the bottom drawer of his bureau. Lots of the girls in there had been milk-skinned and slim. Once Kevin had even pointed one out, saying that Beth would grow up to look just like her. She remembered studying the glossy page, noting with satisfaction the way the girl's legs had a long, sensuous curve to the slim hips and the way her breasts were high and firm, not like some of the others whose breasts hung halfway to their waists.

Beth had asked Kevin if he thought the girl in the picture was beautiful.

"Gee, yeah, Beth! If she weren't beautiful, do you think she'd have her picture in the book?"

That had been years ago, Beth thought, pulling herself back to the present. A lot of magazines and rainy afternoons when they had been left alone had gone by since that day, and each time they had experimented and explored each other's bodies with the offhanded innocence of children.

One day, shortly after Kevin's thirteenth birthday, Beth had suggested they take a peek in Daddy's bottom bureau drawer. It had been months since the two of them had gone into Mama's room together. Kevin had glanced at Beth uneasily and then quickly looked back to the book he was reading. "Aw, c'mon, Beth. That stuff's for kids. It's better to forget all about it." He was embarrassed; Beth could sense it and it puzzled her.

"Have you forgotten about it, Kevin?" she sulked.

"Yeah, Sis, all about it." He closed off any further discussion by immersing himself in his book, but Beth knew he was aware of her standing there, looking down at him with tears smarting her eyes. Kevin could tell her he'd forgotten about those times in Mama's room till the cows came home and she'd never believe him. She sensed she would make him angry if she continued to push in that direction, and she decided she would never make an issue of it again. But she'd never forget. Never. How could she forget her very own brother? Her own, very own, beautiful brother, Kevin.

Beth heard a sound from the room next to hers. Before she realized what she was doing, she was out in the hall and quietly knocking on Kevin's door. He murmured something and came to open the door. She heard the snick of the lock. When had Kevin started locking his door? Was he locking himself in or locking her out?

He stood there facing her, a book in his hand. He was forever studying and restudying, trying to get a jump on the courses at Tulane. "Beth, if you've come to argue with me again or to pull another of your sulks, forget it. I'm taking the job with Mr. Harris and that's final."

"That's not why I'm here," Beth began, her mind racing to find another reason. She didn't want him to expel her from his room and to widen the breach that existed between them. "I just wanted you to know that Luther Guthrie asked me out. Do you think Mama will let me go?"

The shocked expression on Kevin's face amused her. "Boomer? Boomer Guthrie wants to take you out? You've got to be kidding!"

"And what if I'm not, Mr. Bigshot? What's wrong with me anyway that you don't think a boy would ask me out?" she shot back in annoyance.

"Don't get me wrong, Sis. It's not that I don't think Boomer wouldn't want to take you out. That's easy enough to believe, you're so pretty and all. What gets me is you'd actually consider dating him. Boomer?"

Hotly, "Darn right I would, Kevin Thomas! Luther is one of the best looking boys in the graduating class!"

"Yeah, and one of the horniest! You're not going out with him, Beth. That guy's a menace to the flower of Southern womanhood."

"Luther is not! He's a perfectly nice boy and there's not a thing you could do to stop me from seeing him!" Beth enjoyed seeing Kevin react this way. Groping for a reason for coming to his room, even though it was a lie, she had hit on just the right mark.

"Beth, listen to me, I've heard girls complain that Boomer has more hands than an octopus and he's got a very nasty temper when he's turned down. Be serious now, find some okay guy to date."

"I don't know what you're talking about, Kevin Thomas. Luther is nice and he wants to take me out!" she lied again.

"Look, Beth, they don't call him Boomer for nothing. And that's not a name he got on the football team either. He's been called Boomer ever since sixth grade when some of the guys caught him playing with himself in the boys' room going, 'Boom! Boom! Boom!' at the top of his voice. That's all he could think about then and that's all he still thinks about, and no sister of mine is going out with him!" Kevin's rage flushed his face and his ears were burning.

"I won't be dictated to, Kevin. Why should I listen to you? You don't care what I think! You're going to work for Mr. Harris and be with that tacky Judy Evans every day."

"Just where did Boomer ask you to go with him?" Kevin asked, trying to get the subject away from Cader Harris and Judy Evans.

Beth's mind raced for a reply. "Just to that movie over in Dunstan that I wanted to see. The one with Barbra Streisand," she pouted.

"Tell you what, Beth. I'll take you. Would you like that?" Kevin asked, his eyes pleading with her.

Suddenly, "Oh, Kev, you're the best brother ever! Would you really take me? When?" She threw herself at him, hugging him tightly around the neck, waiting for his arms to go around her.

"How about this Friday? I'll get the car from Dad. Okay?"

"You betcha!" she exclaimed, giving him a final squeeze, pressing close to him, very aware of her own nudity beneath the thin robe.

"Okay, get yourself out of here for now," he pushed her toward the door, "I've still got some studying to do and then I want to hit the hay early."

CHAPTER FOUR

Cader Harris sat quietly atop a packing crate and made no effort to answer the shrilling phone. When a phone rang at the ungodly hour of 7:30 in the morning, it could only mean one thing; anyone who wanted to reach him didn't have one damned good thing to say to him. He stretched his thick, muscular neck and wiped at the perspiration on his brow. He had just arrived at the store a few minutes ago and the air conditioning hadn't had time to cool off the stale air hanging like a shroud in the topsy-turvy shop.

The thin madras shirt he wore was open to his waist, revealing a wide expanse of chest dewy with sweat. He flexed his shoulders and felt the moisture trickle down his sides. Christ! Was this the way he was going to start every day here in Hayden? Fear and uneasiness gnawed at him. Sooner or later he would have to answer the fucking phone, and he damn well better do it before his new sales help came in for the first day on the job. But not now. Now he just wanted to drink the coffee he'd picked up at the carry-out sandwich shop and savor the wet, cardboard taste.

The shrilling phone cut off in mid-ring, causing Cader to flinch as though he'd been struck a blow. It would ring again, and soon. It would ring and ring until he picked it up and said what he was supposed to say. What he was getting paid to say. *They're really going to bust my balls till they hear for the hundredth time what I've already agreed to do. What the hell happened to a man's word and a hand-shake?* Everything had to be done yesterday and the day before that. "When you stick a poker up someone's ass, make sure it's red hot!" he said aloud. "Sixty lousy days to whip this town into shape," he muttered. It was just like the gridiron, you could either run with the ball or stick around with your finger up your ass and wait to get clobbered. Just stick with the game plan and then take the money and run.

The phone shrilled again; this time he picked it up. "Cader Harris," he bellowed into the receiver.

"Mornin'. How's our man?"

"Mornin', Mr. Fairfax, how's things at Delta Oil?"

"Now remember, Cade, we agreed no names, right?"

"Right."

"How's things going?"

"It's too soon to tell."

"We know we can depend on you, boy. You'll have it all sewed up in a week's time."

"I wouldn't be too sure of that, Mr. . . . ." He stopped himself just in time.

"No names," he was reminded. "What do you mean, 'don't be too sure'?"

"It's just that it will take a while. This town isn't going to be easy to convince that they want, even need, those storage tanks."

"We've all got a lot riding on you, Cade. You know that. There's even something in it for you, or did you forget?"

Forget a quarter of a million dollars? he thought to himself. He said, "No, sir, I haven't forgotten." Harris knew Delta Oil had sixty days to bid on a huge shipment from Algeria. It was imperative to have a firm decision on Hayden accepting the erection of the holding tanks. Failure to have the okay for the tanks could cost Delta millions of dollars.

"Good, then. As we arranged, we'll be in contact daily. If there's anything I can do . . ."

"Yes, sir."

"Good. One of us will talk to you tomorrow. Till then." The receiver on the other end of the line clicked quietly, leaving Cader's half-said goodbye to fall on a dead line.

Christ, he thought to himself. It was going to be hard enough to convince the right people that the storage tanks should come into Hayden, let alone have a time limit on it. That sixty days bit had been something they had thrown in at the last minute. The bastards. He could see it now. He'd do all the ground work and then his time would be up. Then some sharpshooter would come into town or they'd put a few healthy bribes in the right places and he, Cader, would be out in the cold. When he had suggested a payoff to them in the first place, he was met with strong opposition. Delta Oil wouldn't risk the possibility of a scandal. It would be better, much better, if the town opted for the LNGs on their own. No, it would be better, much better, if Cader would go back to Hayden as a merchant. That way it would appear that he'd have a natural interest in seeing the industry come into town.

"Sure, sure," he kicked out at a carton of tennis balls, "you'll come in when everything else is done and grease a few palms and I'll be out in the cold. Well, I won't let it happen. I've got too much riding on this deal. My whole future. I'll squeeze the quarter mil out of Delta Oil before the ink even has a chance to dry!"

In his mind Cader began reviewing the tactic he would take to inveigle himself into the town's confidence. Sure, he was already their returning hero, but that didn't count for much when there was so much at stake. He had, at one time, thought of befriending the men on the town council. That was until he began studying the town newspaper and noticing that the Junior Women's League of Hayden had among its rolls all the wives of the men on the council. Marvin Guthrie, Hayden's own mayor, was married to the

Women's League president, Alma. That's where he would begin, he smiled to himself confidently, aware of his past successes with women. Hell, if he could get them to pull down their pants, it would be easy to get them to endorse the LNGs. A good-looking jock tells a woman the marvelous things Blass and Halston could do for her and bingo . . . she wants her husband to provide them. And this jerkwater town would need a healthy boost in commerce that only Delta Oil could provide.

He went down the list of members in his mind, finding the names familiar and recalling the way most of them had looked in high school. Some ladies' names he didn't recognize, but he recognized their husbands' names, remembering jocks he'd played ball with and which ones had sat in the bleachers wishing they were Cader Harris. One name that didn't make any connection at all was Keli McDermott. Must be new in town. Her old man too. His dinner date with Marsha Evans would help break him into the right circles. Marsha, he knew from studying the back issues of the paper, was secretary of the Junior Women's League as well as being a real fine-looking piece of ass. He thought of Marsha and how she looked in that clingy white uniform, but his mind kept turning to the name of Keli McDermott, and he wondered if she was a blonde or a brunette.

Colonel Gene McDermott (ret.) added the coffee to the percolator and plugged it in. At the sound of the first plop of the bubbling water, he cracked eggs into a bowl and stirred them carefully. Just as he was about to add them to the hot butter, the phone rang. "McDermott here," he said briskly.

"Dr. Baldwin's office calling. May I speak to Mrs. Dermott?"

"Mrs. McDermott can't come to the phone right now, would you care to leave a message?" A worm of concern began biting into Gene's flat, drum-tight stomach, making him sound raspy and unsure of himself.

"Well, tell Mrs. McDermott Doctor Baldwin will see her tomorrow at one o'clock. I've had a cancellation and this is the earliest I can fit her in," the clinical voice at the other end of the receiver explained.

"Is this her regular checkup?" the Colonel asked, licking dry lips.

"Goodness, no. Checkups are made a month in advance. This

visit is for a consultation concerning the lump in her breast. The doctor knows and understands how worried you both must be, that's why I scheduled her as soon as possible. We'll see her tomorrow at one."

"Yes, yes, I'll give her the message. Matter of fact, I'll bring her myself."

Gene McDermott listened to the last plop-plop-plop of the coffeepot and looked at the eggs in the bowl. Suddenly, he felt sick. Sick and beaten. The one beautiful thing in his entire life and they were going to mutilate her. Never. Gene knew all about lumps and breasts and doctors. Hadn't he seen his own mother undergo a mastectomy and hadn't she died an excruciating death?

He'd never let them get their hands on Keli, mutilate her and scar her body. He'd seen what a woman looked like after her breast was removed, and nobody was going to hack away at his beautiful wife and mar her perfection. When something was perfect, you didn't tamper with it. He wouldn't let them touch her. Asshole doctors, what did they know? Put an M.D. after their names and you might as well smear the word "God" across their foreheads. And that Baldwin was the asshole of the lot. "Like hell you'll take a knife to my Keli!" he shouted hoarsely.

A towel wrapped around her body, Keli walked into the kitchen and was shocked at the hateful look on her husband's face. Her doe eyes fearfully raked the room for some sign, some clue to his apparent outrage. "What is it, Gene, did you burn yourself? What is making you angry?"

At the sight of the slim woman standing before him, his outrage cooled immediately. "Honey, why didn't you tell me you had an appointment with Dr. Baldwin?"

Keli sucked in her breath and reached out an arm in entreaty only to remember she needed both hands to hold the towel around her nakedness. "I didn't tell you because I didn't have an appointment. The office said they would call me when there was an opening. I don't want to upset and worry you, Gene."

"Honey, honey," he said gruffly, "what do you think I'm here for? I'll always take care of you. As long as I'm alive, you have nothing to worry about. I'll never let anything happen to you. I love you, don't you know that?" Tenderly, he cupped her face in his hands and looked into the velvety depths of his wife's eyes.

"You should have told me," he chided gently. "There's no need for concern. I'll take you to see Doc Baldwin and I'll set him straight. No one is going to touch you. I give you my word."

"But, Gene, I am not a child. I am a woman. I know that sometimes surgery is needed. Ever since I discovered the little lump I have done some reading. At times they take a little piece of it and make the necessary, what they call biopsy."

"It's only necessary if I say it is necessary." He spoke distinctly as though she were a backward child. "You're my wife and I swore to take care of you and that's what I'm going to do. Scoot now and get dressed. I'll make eggs Benedict as a special treat. You just put this whole thing out of your mind, and we won't mention it again. Go on, now, get dressed," he prodded sternly.

Tears glistened in her velvety eyes as Keli turned to leave the copper and brick kitchen. What was the use? No matter what she did, no matter what she said, Gene would have his way. If he said she wouldn't have an operation, then she wouldn't have an operation. She would have to endure the pain and try to ignore it. A fatalist by nature, she fully and completely believed that her life was predestined. She knew the lump was cancerous, and she knew she would eventually have her breast removed or she would die. She had learned to live with other things and she would live with this. Gene would take care of her. Gene would always take care of her.

While she dressed, she let her mind wander to Julia and Marsha and how they would have reacted to her situation. Would they, with their Western ways, be better able to handle what she was going through? Julia would, of course, she was married to Doctor Baldwin; Marsha would bite her lower lip and see it through to the end. And then there was Irene. Irene had a philosophy and a solution for everything. Besides, no cancerous lump would have the audacity to inflict itself on Irene's body. A small smile tugged at the corners of Keli's mouth. After all, some time or another, Irene's Daddy Hayden must have come across the same problem and would have handed down to his daughter some sage advice.

Her bra secure, Keli flinched when she tugged it into place and felt it dig into the soft flesh under her arm. Now it was swollen, she noticed and once more tried to adjust the soft silk cupping her breasts. Perhaps she could go without the bra today if she wore a dark blouse. Quickly, she removed the offending garment and let her breath out in relief. Gently, she worked her arm up and down and shrugged her slim shoulders. It was definitely easier to bear the nagging soreness once the bra was removed.

Her eyes fell to the neatly typed pages resting on her dressing table. Damion's sermon for next week. It had taken all her concentration to overcome the pain in her breast and under her arm last evening when she had drummed out the sermon on the typewriter. She didn't think she'd be able to type for him again. At least not until something was done to alleviate this almost constant discomfort. How was she going to tell him? She frowned. She liked to think he depended on her. That someone depended on her and thought of her as a capable adult. It was terribly confining to be the kind of individual who aroused the protective instinct in everyone around her.

Colonel McDermott downed the bitter liquid at the bottom of his coffee cup and slammed it down into its saucer. The phone call from Dr. Baldwin's office had unnerved him, and he was aware of a creeping fear swelling in the pit of his stomach. He could hear Keli's movements from down the hall as she dressed and was aware of the faint scent of her perfume. His beautiful Keli.

Gene rubbed his heavy-knuckled hand over his short-cropped hair, feeling the hard bones of his skull beneath his fingers. Though his hair was mostly silver now, his physique and unlined features were those of a man considerably younger than his fifty-eight years. Out of those fifty-eight years thirty had been spent crawling up the ranks of the Air Corps until he reached the rank of colonel. It had been a tough struggle at times, but he had known that a life amid a world of men suited him perfectly.

It had been during his last campaign, while he was serving in Vietnam, that he had discovered Keli. While on assignment with Thailand's forces, he had been attracted by a local religious ceremony being conducted in a public square. Kneeling before a shrine, dressed in traditional costume, was the most beautiful creature he had ever seen. Her black hair was wound atop her head and fresh exotic blossoms were arranged between the strands. Her face had been a study of innocence and virtue as she knelt with her offering to the strange god. She represented something that Gene had always suspected was absent from life: goodness and purity.

Gene McDermott's experience with women had always been

of the basest nature. Women were available for men's use; they were the providers of necessary sexual release. The Air Corps provided everything else in the realm of comfort. Meals were prepared and laundry done with none of the hysterics or messy emotional reparations he had noticed his married colleagues being forced to endure. Everything in the Corps was done cleanly, efficiently, unemotionally. A man could take his meals in the mess and not feel obliged to make small talk with the cook. He felt no indebtedness to the person who washed his Jockey shorts and who pressed the creases in his uniform slacks. Life was clean, without involvement.

It was when a man became involved with a woman that his values were upset, and the orderly life that was natural to the male species became emotional and peppered with havoc. Fights erupted in the bars among friends who had their eye on the same prostitute; married men were obliged to leave the officers' club early, even during a winning streak in an endless poker game, muttering some vagary about the "little woman." Even on a battlefield women impaired a man's judgment, even if that instant appraisal of a situation was necessary to self-preservation. He'd seen it over and over again. That instant of hesitation, that error of judgment, that irrevocable choice. "Come back to me, darling," they would write in their voluminous letters to husband or lover, imposing on a man the determination to survive the war not for the sake of his own life but for some higher, more noble reason which surpassed even the will to live: that of returning to the woman who had assured him she could not live without him. That was until he received his "Dear John" letter and then was so demoralized, so confused about his own value, that he would walk into the line of fire, leaving his chances of survival to a much higher authority.

Some lived and some died, and according to Gene's observations, it was always because of some woman.

Being an astute individual, Gene had decided never to be entrapped by a woman. He would take what they had to offer, use it or turn away from it, as was a man's inalienable right. It didn't seem strange to him that he equated all women with the prostitutes with whom he traded money for sexual release and irrevocable proof that he wasn't a queer. He didn't hold with the theory he had heard expounded at great length that prostitutes were products of their circumstances, that their entire economy was simply a matter of supply and demand, a demand created by men, an economy created by society. There was only one theory which seemed plausible to Gene McDermott: there were "good" women and there were "bad," and the worst of the lot were the prostitutes who frequented the watering holes of the United States Air Corps.

Being a man committed to his conviction, many times after paying a prostitute for her services, Gene would give her a sound beating in the bargain. Bad women had to be punished. Bad women spread diseases. They passed their corruption and infections onto men, smiling as they did so, distracting the unwary male with sighs of passion and hungry lips. In his rage and hostility directed at women in general, Gene never stopped to wonder where the women became infected in the first place. To him, disease and corruption were synonymous with the name "woman," and it was bred and festered within their bodies, in the dark regions between their thighs.

When Gene McDermott saw Keli, he recognized the difference between her and other women immediately. Keli was pure where other women were sullied. She was guileless and beyond reproach.

Having made subtle inquiries, he discovered she was from a fine, if impoverished, family, and she was, in fact, as pure and unworldly as his every instinct told him she was. He made arrangements with her family to marry her, see to her family's safety and make financial arrangements to provide for Keli. His tour of duty separated him from her for nearly four years, and the only contact he had with her was through stiffly interpreted letters.

Throughout their separation, Keli studied English and learned to read and write until she finally produced her first letter to Gene in his own language. It was formal and held her own quality of innocence. Gene treasured it.

Finally, political upheaval and red tape cleared, he retired from the Air Corps and brought his beautiful wife home to the States, settling with his young bride of twenty-two in the town of Hayden.

With a successful military career behind him, financial independence, a nice home in a nice town, friends at the country club and a beautiful wife, Gene McDermott should have had the world by the tail. Yet, somehow, it was all disconnected and he knew himself to be unfulfilled. It never occurred to him that his discontent stemmed from his unfortunate and twisted view of what his wife should be. Somehow, the shrine where he first saw Keli had become an altar for her purity. In the two and half years of living with her and sleeping in the same bed with her, he had never been able to achieve a sexual relationship with his lovely, sloe-eyed bride. Each attempt ended in failure, leaving Keli with quiet tears shining in her dark eyes, and leaving Gene with a profound feeling of inadequacy.

Since the first time he had seen Keli praying in the pageant and making contact with her family, Gene had abstained from sexual encounters, telling himself that a girl as chaste as Keli deserved a man of moral fortitude. He would make himself as worthy of her purity as possible.

Somehow, it had all backfired. Gene had become totally incapable of having a sexual relationship. He glossed over this fact by telling himself that it was because he couldn't bear to take from Keli that one quality which set her apart from and above all other women: her virginity.

He had seen Keli's eyes following the children in the playground. He had heard her sweet bubble of laughter when a particularly precocious child appeared in a television commercial. He knew she wanted a child. But a pregnancy would be a violation of her body, robbing her of her innocence, submitting her to a life growing within her, a life that would share an experience with her that he could never share. He wanted to protect her from that violation, from the indignity of childbirth, from the acknowledgment that she was like all other women.

This is what he told himself. He was informed about the practices of contraception and could have put any number of them to use. He never bothered. He knew, even without admitting to himself that he knew, that everything else was a lie. His adoration of his wife, of her purity, of her beauty was all a lie. They were excuses and he knew it. What Gene McDermott couldn't and wouldn't admit to himself was that he was impotent.

CHAPTER FIVE

*J*udy! I'll be leaving in a few minutes!" Marsha Evans
called, her voice carrying up the stairwell to the second
floor bedroom where her daughter primped with pimple cream
before her bedroom mirror. Determined, she tried to soften the strident tone which habitually crept into her voice when she dealt
with Judy. If there was anything she didn't want this morning, it
was an emotional scene with a petulant sixteen-year-old whose
face was dotted with chalky, flesh-colored acne ointment for a skin
disorder that didn't exist.

Ever since Rod and Marsha had been divorced three years ago,
Judy had become more and more difficult to handle and the situation had worsened since his death in an automobile accident the
summer before.

It didn't take a fancy, high-priced psychiatrist to conclude that
Judy accused Marsha of Rod's death and found her guilty. With the
inimitable logic of a teenager Judy had reasoned: "*You* were the
reason my father left us. *You* were inadequate and he went away
and divorced *you* and me too! If *you* were the kind of wife he
needed, he never would have left *me!* He never would have been
in that car when it crashed!"

"Judy, did you hear me? I said I'll be leaving in a few minutes!"

No answer.

Taking a deep breath to steel her nerves, Marsha waited for a
response. Receiving none, she called again, hearing that dreaded,
strident tone rise upward to her daughter. "I said I'll soon be leaving! I would like to talk to you before I go. Now, please come
down here!"

Still no answer. Instead the sound of footsteps scuffing along
the upstairs hall. Judy appeared at the top of the stairs enveloped
in a pink wrapper, her face predictably disguised with pimple
cream and her hair wrapped around lethal-looking electric curlers.

"I can't talk to you while you're up there and I'm down here. If
you would, please."

Judy stomped down the stairs. "I didn't hear you, Mom."

Near exasperation, Marsha took another breath and purposely softened her tone. "Judy, I'm going out this morning. Mrs. McDermott will be picking me up any minute now. But I'll be back later this afternoon. Before you leave for the day, I expect you to pick up your room and straighten the bathroom. It's beyond me how you manage to create such a mess. . . . A new client will be coming by this afternoon to discuss my redecorating her home. You know I like to take prospective clients through our house to show them some of my ideas. It would help a lot if your room and the bathroom were in order. Okay?"

Judy lifted her eyes heavenward in a display of boredom. "I've heard it all before, Mother. Yes, I'll pick up my room. And the bathroom. But I think you should consider that I'm working now too, and I don't have all that much time."

"You've still more time than I do, young lady, and your working for Mr. Harris doesn't excuse your responsibilities around the house."

"Mr. Harris, Mother? I thought you called him Cader. The two of you seemed awfully chummy when he hired me for his new store." Judy grinned.

"What are you getting at? Cader and I went to school together, we're old friends." Marsha laughed, relieved to hear the light note in her daughter's voice. Their relationship had improved in the past few weeks and Marsha suspected that reason for improvement was Kevin Thomas. The accusations concerning Rod's death had ceased, and Judy seemed content with judging her mother merely inadequate.

"I'm not getting at anything. I was just wondering how you got to be 'Johnny on the spot' and managed to connive a dinner date with him, that's all," Judy teased.

"You were right there. You know how it came about!"

"Yeah, you're right, Mom. I saw that little maneuver and I don't blame you. I believe in going after what you want."

"Is that how you feel about Kevin?" Marsha asked conversationally.

"That's right. I want him. I went after him and I've almost got him. And I'm not going to let him get away."

The answer was curt and truthful and Marsha knew Judy compared herself to her.

◆ ◆ ◆

Keli settled herself behind the wheel of Gene's Camaro, a look of dismay marking her exquisite features. Stick shift. She didn't know if her arm could hold out, and she didn't want the others to know she was in pain. Mentally she counted how many stops she would have to make and how many corners there would be before she arrived at the high school. Weakly, she leaned back in the bucket seat and toyed with the idea of staying home or calling one of the others and asking them to drive.

Rejecting the idea, her foot eased the clutch down as she slipped the car into first gear and then into second. A fine beading of perspiration glistened on her smooth brow, and alabaster teeth dug sharply into her lower lip. Third and fourth, cruising speed. When she stopped for Marsha, she would slip it into neutral, as she glided to a stop, and then into first. That way, she told herself, there would be less of a jolt on her arm.

Keli rounded the corner and Marsha recognized Gene's Camaro. Marsha smoothed her pearl-gray silk shirtwaist over her hips and wished she'd waited inside in the air conditioning. The day was humid and the sun baked the dew off the lawn into sticky vaporous waves. The cream-colored sports car came to a jolting halt at the curb and Marsha strode down the path, the strap of her bag slapping against her leg. Tucking her knees below the dashboard and fastening her seatbelt, she turned to Keli. "Hi," she said huskily.

"Good morning, Marsha. I'm sorry I'm late but sometimes I am not used to this car and my hands and feet don't work at the same time," Keli apologized softly.

"You're here and that's all that matters." Marsha smiled. "Are you picking up Irene or Julia first?"

Keli let her mind wander to the various stops along the way and finally decided Julia would be her first stop. "Julia, I think."

Out of the corner of her eye, Marsha watched Keli's trembling hand close over the gearshift and was momentarily alarmed by the tense grip the slim girl applied to it. Keli's whole body was ramrod stiff and her jaw clenched tightly. Something was wrong. "Would you like me to drive? You look like you're upset about something. Do you want to talk about it?" Thoughts of her problems with Judy flew out of her mind as she waited for Keli's response. She had never seen her this way, so tense, so frightened.

Tears gathered in Keli's eyes. The kind offer had disarmed her and she suddenly felt very much as though she wanted to tell her best friend. "Marsha, there is something I wish to ask you. No. That is wrong. There is something I want to tell you; something I want you to keep in confidence."

Alarmed by Keli's soft, urgent words, Marsha could only nod.

"I . . . I have a lump here," Keli began, touching her long, slim fingers to her breast. "Tomorrow, I am to see Doctor Baldwin. Gene . . . he insists on taking me himself. He answered the phone this morning about my appointment." Her voice broke and Marsha cursed Marc's bumbling, busybody nurse for not asking to speak to Keli instead of blurting everything out to Gene.

"Gene has already decided he will never allow me to have an operation if it is called for."

"Oh, my God!" Marsha breathed, thoughts whirling around in her head.

Keli heard Marsha's intake of breath and continued. "Once, when Gene was telling me about his family, he told me how his mother died. It began with a lump in her breast. . . ." She fought to gain composure. "He said he would never let anyone scar my body. . . ." It was impossible to continue. Impossible to talk about it without condemning Gene for his attitude.

"I understand, Keli. You don't have to talk about it if you don't want. Poor baby." She reached for Keli and gathered her into her arms in an embrace. Gently, she stroked the silken head and crooned soft words of comfort. "Poor baby, I'll stand by you. I'll speak to Marc. He's the most understanding man I know. I'll explain about Gene. Don't worry, Keli, I'll make it right for you." Squeezing her eyes shut against the torrent of tears gathering there, Marsha silently prayed for the wisdom to say the right words to comfort Keli.

Finally finding her voice, Marsha crooned, "Keli, honey, it may not be what you're thinking." Somehow she could not utter the word "cancer," yet it stood between them like the shadow of a carrion bird circling for the kill. It carried with it every fear common to all women. Disfigurement and death. "Lots of women get lumps and bumps and most of them turn out to be nothing. Don't go thinking the worst, honey," she murmured, still cradling Keli's head against her shoulder.

Swallowing hard, Keli moved away from Marsha and spoke hesitantly. "If you would not mind, Marsha, take me to the parsonage and go on to the high school with Irene and Julia. I think today is not a good time for me to be with other people. I promised Damion I would deliver his sermon today, and if I do it now, perhaps I can help him with something before . . . tomorrow." In spite of her determination, she couldn't help the slight hesitation. "Tomorrow," a word meaning "the future," yet it sounded like the end of the present.

"The hell with the rest of them, Keli, you shouldn't be alone. I'll just run in and call the girls. . . ."

"No, please. I would like a little time to myself. Gene . . . he doesn't understand that I sometimes need time to be alone. . . ."

"I understand, honey. I'll pick you up when we finish the uniforms," Marsha said, climbing from the car.

"I have thought again; I will walk to the parsonage. I'll find my own way home. Thank you anyway. Drop the car off at the house and Gene will give you a ride home. Today I feel the need to walk and be alone."

Bewildered, Marsha could only agree. Sadly, she climbed behind the wheel and looked up into Keli's face. "Keli—," she began, then cut off her words. What could she say? What could she possibly say to lessen the fear, the pain? "If you need me, you know where I'll be. I'd rather not go and listen to those gossipy . . ."

"No! You must go, Marsha!" A note of hysteria tinged Keli's voice. "I won't need you, Marsha."

Keli turned in the direction of the parsonage, her head bowed, her jet hair falling over her face and forming a curtain between herself and the world. Instinctively, she knew she had hurt Marsha by telling her she wasn't needed. Just as she knew she had hurt Gene by not telling him of the lump in her breast, by having him find out about it through a casual phone call. Marsha and Gene had little use for one another, yet in some ways they were remarkably alike. She pushed the thought from her mind. *She* was the one who needed help. She needed someone, and she knew she could find that help, that strength, in Damion Conway.

Her thoughts still centered on Keli, Marsha pulled the car over to the curb in front of Julia Baldwin's sprawling ranch-style home.

Looking as though she stepped out of the pages of *Vogue*, Julia smoothed her gleaming cap of auburn hair and adjusted the collar of her pink silk blouse.

"Marsha! Isn't this Gene McDermott's car? Where's Keli?"

"Something came up and I dropped her off to see Damion Conway. Maybe she'll join us later, although we can manage without her for the day. Irene told me there were only nine band uniforms that still needed new braid and one that needs repairs on a sewing machine. Christ! The way she goes on about sending the band to Disney World you'd think it was for a command performance at Buckingham Palace!"

Julia laughed. "Irene takes on about everything. It's her style. I only asked about Keli because she doesn't seem to have her normal vitality lately. She's withdrawn. Have you noticed? I'm concerned about her."

Marsha swallowed and tried to keep her voice from quaking. What was she doing here prattling about this and that with Julia when Keli, her best friend, was sick and troubled and needed someone? "I'm sure it's nothing," Marsha answered. "I know she wanted to get a job and Gene won't stand for it. It has something to do with not feeling useful," Marsha lied.

"I can understand it. We all need something to get us through the days. There was supposed to be a meeting at the school auditorium last night about Delta Oil. Marc had a delivery so he didn't go. I was wondering how it all came out."

"Want me to turn on the radio? We might catch the news."

"No. I've got a miserable headache this morning. I hope Irene doesn't keep us waiting. I'm not in the mood for sewing today. And to tell you the truth, I'm absolutely not in the mood to listen to any more tales of Great-Granddaddy Hayden and how Arthur always smells like embalming fluid, however that smells. I'm sorry, Marsha, I didn't mean to bite. It's this ghastly headache, and, for God's sake, don't mention headache to Irene or she'll be expounding all day about how only really intelligent people get migraines and the rest of us have to suffer with plain old aches in the head!"

Marsha laughed and felt some of the tension leave her shoulders. "I'm kind of in a funk myself today. Let's just get the job over with as soon as possible. Relax," she said, guiding the Camaro to the curb. "Irene is ready and waiting. That is Irene, isn't it?" she asked, pointing through the windshield.

Julia narrowed her eyes behind the polished glasses. "She's gone and got herself a new hairdo and she's lightened it! Christ! She must have dragged her hairdresser out of bed at the crack of dawn!"

"I like it," Marsha added. "It makes her look more feminine. Younger. She was getting awfully dowdy there."

Julia smiled, "I wonder what Daddy Hayden thinks of his little magnolia now. The word 'chic' almost comes to mind."

"Girls," Irene greeted them as she climbed into the back seat. "Hot, isn't it?" Her hand patted her new hairstyle which hung loose to her shoulders in place of the tight, heavy, drab knot she'd worn at the back of her head for longer than anyone could remember.

Almost by tacit, mutual consent, Marsha and Julia murmured something about the heat and said nothing about Irene's coiffure.

"Where's Keli?" Irene added, almost as an afterthought, chagrined that neither Marsha nor Julia mentioned her hair. She'd choke before she brought it to their attention and fished for a compliment. Her mirror told her all she had to know. Now, if she could only lose those eleven pounds before meeting up with Cader Harris.

"Keli couldn't make it today, but she was good enough to lend me Gene's car. That should make you happy, Irene. We all know how you just 'love' Keli," Marsha said nastily.

"Marsha, I refuse to allow you to bait me today. You know I just adore Keli."

"My ass you adore Keli," Marsha all but sputtered. "You were the one who said, 'Oh, dear, those slanted eyes will never go over in this town,' and if you had had your way, you would have run her out of town on a rail. Admit it, Irene!"

"I'll admit to no such thing. You're a terrible person, Marsha, to even . . . to even think I didn't like that child."

"Keli is not a child!" Marsha shouted. "And I don't want to hear any more from you about her."

Always a gracious loser, Irene said, "Well, what's wrong with your car, Marsha? Why did you have to borrow Gene's?"

Changing the subject, Marsha said snidely, "I like your new hairdo. Don't tell me the morticians' union is having a dinner dance!"

Irene ignored her caustic words and plunged ahead. "I'm tired.

I thought a change would do me good. As a matter of fact, I'm off to New Orleans tomorrow to do some shopping. I've been thinking of going to Elizabeth Arden and getting the works."

"That's a wonderful idea," Julia said, leaning over the back of the seat to look at Irene. "I've been thinking about going to New York for a week or so. It never hurts to improve the outer shell a little."

"New York is frightfully expensive," Irene offered.

"Irene, dear, the Haydens aren't the only people in the world who have money. Marc's income is more than substantial and I can afford to go to New York if I please," Julia said testily.

"For heaven's sake, Julia, you are touchy this morning. I didn't mean to infer he didn't make enough money. Gracious, his practice is certainly successful. It's possible he has almost as much money as Daddy."

Julia gagged and turned around in the seat. If Irene said another word, she would leap over the seat and strangle her, new hairdo or not.

"I'm just so tired this morning. Arthur had a late viewing and was called for a removal before he got home. My daddy always says you should never lock up before the man of the house is snug in his bed."

"Was that with or without his wife?" Julia snapped.

"Did someone singe your tail feathers last night, Julia?" Irene asked, her claws showing in the tone of her voice.

Marsha jumped into the verbal exchange and blurted, "Cader Harris invited me to dinner on Tuesday. Have either of you seen him since he came back to town?"

At the mention of Cader Harris, Irene stiffened. Her eyes pierced the back of Marsha's head as she pushed down her jealousy and felt herself almost choke on it.

"Really? You're not joking, are you?" Julia asked.

"Would I joke about something like that? Of course he asked me, and I'm going shopping for a new outfit tomorrow."

"Marsha, did you say Tuesday? Listen, how would it be if I gave a dinner party and invited all of Cader's old friends? We'll give him a rousing welcome." Julia's face brightened and for the first time she removed her sunglasses.

"Julia!" Irene complained. "That's really not fair. After all, it is Marsha's date!"

"Not at all, Irene," Marsha said, "I think Julia has a wonderful idea."

"In that case, we can have the party at my house," Irene insisted. "Let's do it up right."

"Meaning I don't?" Julia challenged.

"No . . ." Irene hastened to amend her words. "It's just that I have all the Hayden china and silver, not to mention the stemware. It can be a formal affair. . . ."

"Not on your life, Irene," Julia interrupted. "I refuse to eat another of your old Aunt Matilda's meat loaves. Shrimp Creole, my grandmother's recipe from the bayous. What do you think, Marsha?"

"Fantastic."

Irene pouted. This had nothing to do with jealousy over Cader Harris. This was something nearer the point of honor. *She* had always been the one elected to have important dinners. Like the time the Governor visited the Delta Oil refinery and had stayed in Hayden. The dinner had been a marvelous success and from that time on she had more or less become Hayden's official hostess. There had been a little write-up in the town's paper. . . .

"Shrimp Creole, a crisp green salad, what kind of wine do you think?" Julia asked Marsha.

"Hrmmph! And on what do you intend to serve this provincial masterpiece, Julia? Paper plates?" Irene grumbled nastily.

"How about my Wedgewood? Would that suit you?"

"Nobody, absolutely *nobody* eats on Wedgewood!" Irene stormed, oblivious to Julia's sarcasm.

"Then bring your own plate," Julia said callously. "I can't wait. As soon as I get home, I'll make all the calls. Ten people should round it out quite nicely."

"Why not just eight. Eight is so much more intimate," Irene pleaded.

"Irene Hayden Thomas . . . shut up. This is my dinner party and not yours. This town isn't ready for another of your Cecil B. DeMille productions. But I won't embarrass myself, I promise you. I'll even use a tablecloth!"

"Are you going to invite Keli and Gene McDermott?" Irene demanded. "I don't like Gene. He's a foreigner."

Marsha smiled. It was just like Irene to refer to Gene as the "foreigner" and pretend to accept his Oriental wife as one of her own.

"Irene," Julia said, exasperated, "just because Gene came from Connecticut doesn't mean he's a foreigner."

Irene defended herself. "Well, I wouldn't be surprised if he starts dinner off by singing the 'Battle Hymn of the Republic.' Great-Granddaddy Hayden was in the military, and he never behaved like Gene McDermott."

"Do I have to remind you the South *lost*, Irene?"

Irene was about to retort when she saw that Marsha was pulling into the parking lot behind the school and she clamped her mouth shut.

CHAPTER SIX

*D*amion Conway closed the Bible with a loud snap and impatiently raked his hands through his hair. The Bible wasn't going to help him cope with Cader Harris. In order to cope with Cade, you always had to be one step ahead of the arrogant bastard. He could just hear Cade call him the "punting parson" in front of the town's leading citizens. He sighed. Everyone had his cross to bear, and Cade Harris and the title he had bestowed on Damion in college was his. He knew in his gut that sooner or later old Cade would spill the beans and then he would be in for it. Discretion was not one of Cade's virtues. Come to think of it, Cade had no virtues.

Damion pushed back the old-fashioned, wooden swivel chair and started to pace the floor. Cade meant trouble. He knew it as surely as he knew he had to take a next breath. He wasn't opening a store for the reasons he said. Cade never did anything without a reason and whatever that reason was Cade always came out *número uno*. What could he possibly be up to and why? For days he had been torturing himself with these questions and what he could do if he found out.

"Damn!" Damion exclaimed just as Keli walked in the door, his sermon clasped in her hand. Something was wrong. It was in the set of the slim shoulders, in the trembling hands. Why was there a look of pain in her eyes?

Shyly, arm extended and hand trembling, she handed him the folder with Sunday's sermon. "Damion, I must talk with you. I will not be able to type your sermons anymore."

Damion waited. When he realized there was to be no further explanation, he smiled and motioned for her to sit down. "I understand, Keli, and it's all right. I'm surprised that you put up with my chicken scratching as long as you have. I'll throw myself on the mercy of one of the good ladies of the town. I wish I could have paid you more, Keli, but that's all that was allowed in the clerical budget."

Her dark eyes were filled with tears. "No, Damion, that is not the reason. I . . . I have a small problem and until it is . . . resolved, I cannot help you. It is not that your writing is bad or that the money is not sufficient. It is a personal matter," she said, lowering her eyes to stare at her folded hands.

"Keli, do you want to talk to me about it? If I can, I want to help you. Sometimes, not all the time, but sometimes it helps to talk out a problem. If I'm not the one you want to talk to, then perhaps you should talk it over with a relative or someone close to you. You did say you had a cousin in Los Angeles, didn't you?"

Her face showed overwhelming relief. "I feel very disloyal," Keli said, letting her breath out in a whisper. "It is not easy for me to talk of this . . . this problem with you or with anyone."

"Sit down, Keli, and let me get you a cup of coffee. Tell me," he said, his voice purposely light, "what did you think of this week's sermon? Will I reach the good people of Hayden and will they understand what I'm trying to tell them?"

Keli's sapling spine straightened imperceptibly. She felt rather than saw Damion leave the room. She would take a deep breath and say what she had to say and then it would be over. Damion would understand why she had come to him.

She saw the tray.

It wasn't just a tray, Damion was holding it. The silver winked and glittered in the sunlit room, making her blink.

And Damion. Quiet. Still. His presence reassured her. Offered her strength . . . an escape from the fear. He watched her, his eyes riveted to hers. Still. Quiet. Only her own people were that quiet. That still. She knew an overwhelming relief. A sense of coming home.

Unhurried, Damion set the tray on the corner of his desk and then took his place in the swivel chair. He wasn't too close, that was good, Keli told herself. He had a quiet, almost serene, face. A serenity that added to his handsome features and gave him a quality of maturity beyond his years. There was nothing to cause fear in Damion Conway's face. There was a certainty about him, a touch of infallibility. Then his expression changed. The lines around his mouth tightened and she read there concern. Concern for her, she knew. He made no sign. No overture. Yet, when their eyes met, she felt free to speak.

Confident now, she spoke slowly and distinctly, her almond eyes staring straight into Damion's. "My marriage to Gene has never been consummated." She waited, her gaze unwavering.

Damion's thoughts lingered on the way she had pronounced "consummated." As though she had never heard the word before but had read it in a book and wasn't quite certain of where the inflection should be placed.

When Damion said nothing and his expression remained unchanged, she continued. "Why is not important. But it will never be what other people . . . it will never be a marriage."

Strangely, he felt relief at Keli's words. Relief because, although he had refused to face it until now, he had always turned away from the thought of Keli belonging to Gene. "The 'why' is important, Keli," he said softly. "Is it because of his age?"

Keli lowered her eyes, refusing to answer.

"Look at me, Keli. I can't help you unless you tell me."

She looked at him, her eyes liquid and shining, willing him to understand, reluctant to answer his direct question. "Gene is . . . is impotent," she whispered, "and it's my fault. He tries . . . so hard . . . but he can never . . . never . . ."

"I understand," Damion said, seeing the relief in her face. "But why? Is it physical?"

"No," Keli blurted. "There is no physical reason. Gene doesn't want a wife; he wants an idol, a goddess, not a flesh and blood woman."

The heaviness in Damion's chest lightened. He understood. Gene was reluctant to mar Keli's perfection, her purity. He wanted her always to be a virginal maiden. Damion remained motionless. He hadn't known what to expect, but this wasn't it. Saliva swirled in his mouth, and he found it difficult to swallow. If he swallowed, Keli would see his throat working and know that she had shocked him. He could feel Keli was about to say more. He felt it in the way she braced herself in the chair. Swallow, damn you, he cursed himself. Swallow and wait.

Momentarily, Keli's dark eyes shifted and Damion swallowed, his stomach muscles relaxing. He felt cold, chiseled, like the figure on the cross hanging from wires in the center of the church.

"I will never know what it is to give birth and feel the warmth of a child against my breast." It was a statement. Her oblique, dark eyes widened and filled with tears. "How true," she whispered, "I never realized . . ."

Her spine stiffened and Keli rose to her feet. She advanced a step and then another. When she was a foot from Damion, she dropped to her knees and held out her hand. He reached for her slim fingers and clasped them in his two hands. Again, he waited. Instinctively, he knew he could not speak, could not move or frighten her in any way.

"I have a . . . there is . . . I know . . ." She gulped. "Damion, I have a lump in my breast. I know it is cancerous. I need strength. Gene will not . . . Gene will not permit me to have it removed. I know I am going to die, and I have come to you for strength." Her eyes brimmed with unshed tears and she lowered her lids.

His voice, when he spoke, was almost a gurgle. "How do you know it's cancerous? Have you seen your doctor?" First things first . . . get to Gene later . . . the marriage was something else. No child to her breast. . . . Help me, God, he prayed silently.

"I know," she said simply. He believed her implicitly.

Damion's eyes narrowed slightly as he watched her tears well and remain in her eyes. How could that be, he thought incongruously. Tears always had to fall. He was suddenly aware that her hands were not trembling. Where were the words he should say? Why weren't they bubbling from his mouth? Why wasn't he being the good minister he was? There were words. He only had to search for them. Words. Gentle words of comfort, of strength. Soft words. Soft like Keli. Slow words, safe words. They wouldn't come. Keli didn't want words. There were none. Keli knew it and Damion knew it.

Softly, she said, "I have upset you and for that I am sorry."

"Keli," he whispered, finding his voice. "You say Gene will not permit you to have it removed. I can't pretend to understand why, not now, at least. I only question your sense of responsibility to yourself. It is your body, your life." He tried to keep the tone of urgency out of his voice.

Keli sank back against her heels, shoulders slumped; head bowed, long, jet hair shielding her face from his view. She spoke so softly he strained to hear her. His gaze was centered on her hands which had fallen to her knees, palms up, fingers curved. Slowly, she began to tell him of the circumstances under which Gene had first seen her. She told him of the political danger her whole family had been in and how Gene's contracting to marry her had saved them. Because of Gene they had been able to relocate and place themselves under the protection of the American forces in Thailand. Gene was a powerful man. He was a generous man. He deserved her total respect and obedience.

As she spoke, Damion began to understand. Gene had been placed in the position of an honored ancestor. To Keli and her family and because of their culture, he was venerated, nearly deified. Respected without reservation. Revered. "I cannot, I will not, disobey Gene. I am grateful I see no questions in your eyes. I could not bear that, Damion."

She was wrong. His mind was filled with questions. Yet, he made no comment. Then at last he murmured, "Your answers will come from within you, Keli." He spoke gently, with great difficulty, aware of the pain his words could inflict. "I can listen to you, Keli; I can at least do that. You have a choice; you haven't denied that. I only ask that you not make it quickly. Consider, Keli."

"Gene . . ."

"Not Gene, Keli. Choice. Gene's an intelligent man; he'll reconsider his decision." He saw in her eyes that she knew Gene would not. Damion winced when Keli reached out to grasp the corner of his desk to pull herself to her feet. He saw the pain reflected in her eyes. Where had the tears gone? He wanted to know, he needed to know. He wanted to know everything about Keli McDermott, where she drew her strength, her serenity, where her tears went instead of falling on her cheeks.

"Thank you, Damion," she whispered. "I will try to remember what you have told me."

She was gone and Damion was left standing in the center of his study, the saliva gathering in his mouth again. He reached for the white linen handkerchief he always carried in his pocket and never used. She had thanked him. For what? What had he said to her? He couldn't even remember. Words, meaningless words. What good had he done her? What comfort had he brought her? Instead of doing the human thing, taking her in his arms and letting her cry it out, he had done what his father had always done. Lecture. Only he wasn't as proficient with gracious phrases and calling down the Lord's blessing as his father had been.

Damion's white clerical collar felt tight around his neck; his skin felt chafed. The Reverend Ephram Conway, Damion's father, had been Hayden's evangelist for nearly thirty years while Damion was growing up. He, Damion, had suffered all the pains of being the minister's son, and Ephram had fulfilled all the clichés of the tyrannical father with a calling for the Lord's work. Because of a stroke, retirement was forced on Ephram by the bishopric. As a last favor, Damion had been granted a position in his father's former congregation. The people seemed to accept him as an extension of old Ephram and to all outward appearances everyone was happy. Everyone except Damion.

All his life Damion had done exactly what was expected of him. It was expected, as the minister's son, that he be exemplary in his behavior. It was expected that his grades be the highest, that his morals be beyond reproach. It was expected that he follow in his father's footsteps. It seemed to Damion that everyone knew what to expect from him except himself. Countless times he had asked himself why he had allowed himself to be pushed into the ministry. The closest he could come to an answer was that, perhaps, he would at last have something in common with his father. A common ground that would open communication between them. But it hadn't. If anything, the sparring and conflicts now ran deeper than ever. Each week at least, he could expect a phone call from old Ephram, asking about how the congregation was getting along. Never how are *you*, Damion. Always how are *things*. As though he had no identity apart from that of the spiritual leader of the people of Hayden.

And mother Rachael Conway. A whirlwind of activity. Visiting the sick, leading the choir, teaching Bible school. On and on, her list of Christian duty read. She was a veritable knight pitted against the forces of evil. A perfect mate for Ephram and together they shared and enjoyed their lives and interests. Mother's light never hid behind the proverbial bush. She was right up there, up front. She had father, and father had his church, and together they were happy. Damion grew to manhood feeling like the little urchin with his nose pressed to the bakery window, always feeling outside of things, yet never wanting for anything. Rachael's family was well founded in land and transportation. That alone eased their lives, providing them with a generous living, never reducing them to the generosity and the stipend that the congregation bestowed.

Damion sighed. This was old hash. He had come to terms with this ages ago. Keli was his main concern right now. He could almost hear his father chastise, "A good minister never involves himself *personally* in the lives of his congregation. You are called upon to give spiritual counsel. You mustn't become emotionally involved, Damion. That can be a minister's downfall."

Goddamn it! He was involved. Keli had involved him. Everyone who came to him for guidance or advice involved him. Involved him and drained him. Perhaps he hadn't inherited his father's glibness of speech, but he had developed it, been cursed with it sometimes it seemed, out of a responsibility to his congregation. And practically the whole town was his congregation. The only other church was nearly fifteen miles away, aside from the small church attended by the blacks on the other side of town.

Damion reached for the manila envelope Keli had left on his desk: He saw how his hand trembled and knew why. He knew why his body was shaking, and he also knew there wasn't a thing in this world he could do about it. Keli. Dear God, not Keli. One of the truly beautiful people he had ever known. Brave, tranquil, with an inner beauty which just happened to coincide with her outer appearance. Tender, gentle, good. Honorable and loving. Keli. His fist slammed down on the desk, the pain shooting into his wrist and forearm a companion to the weary dread he was experiencing. Keli.

He rose from his desk. He had to do something and do it now. He had to get out of this office and away from his thoughts. Thoughts and feelings he couldn't afford if he was to be any help at all to Keli. Walk. He'd walk. Go to the library and get something heavy to read. Something to force his concentration. Don't think about anything, he warned himself. Don't admit anything to yourself, he cautioned. Slow and easy. Walk. Don't think.

As always, the library represented comfortable, happy times. Hours spent among books researching one project after another. He loved the sight of the spines in muted colors stacked on the shelves. The smell of books, slightly moldy with the dry, almost antiseptic odor of paste.

Suddenly, a laugh bubbled from his throat and he stopped in midstride—seeking solace and comfort in the library when he had his own church. He was a minister, a preacher, and he was seeking peace in a small, ivy-cloaked library. The tension eased and he took the steps two at a time and thrust open the screen door that squeaked on rusty, protesting hinges. He made his way through the anteroom to the laden, tiered shelves.

As his eyes explored titles and authors, he decided he wanted something not quite as heavy as he originally intended.

Dodsworth, Dostoevsky, Dumas. He wasn't in the mood for Dostoevsky and the way he explored the souls of his characters. He knew Dumas and *The Three Musketeers* the way he knew his Bible, and there was no way he was going to get into Dodsworth and his Nobel Prize literature, not today. He finally settled on Hemingway's *A Farewell to Arms*. As an afterthought, he picked up Oscar Wilde's *Lady Windermere's Fan*. Perhaps his witty, funny dialogue would lift his spirits, and, in his opinion, Wilde was better than Shaw any day of the week, although he knew he would get strong arguments from some of Shaw's fans. "Why not?" he muttered to himself as he laid the books down on the scarred oak table and settled himself comfortably.

Before he opened his book, he looked around and was surprised to see Beth Thomas seated down the table and across from him. He drew his brow into what his mother always called the "numeral eleven" and stared at her. Engrossed in her book, she did not notice his close scrutiny. School was out, so what was she doing in the library?

From time to time Damion lifted his eyes, but the young girl made no move except to turn the pages of her book. What could she possibly be reading that was so engrossing on such a beautiful summer day? He had to know.

Quietly, he laid the book on the table and stood up. He breathed a sigh of relief when the chair made no sound on the slick floor. He felt like a sneak when he walked up behind her and leaned over. Jesus! Eustace Chessar's *Love Without Fear.*

Beth Thomas lifted her head and stared at Damion while making no move to close or hide the book she was reading. He was shocked at her clear, level-eyed look that almost dared him to make a comment.

Damion forced a smile and spoke lightly. "I could say something like 'What's a nice girl like you doing in a place like this on such a beautiful day?' but I won't."

Beth smiled with her mouth, but the clear, sharp eyes were piercing and still level. "And I could say something like 'I don't like people peering over my shoulder!' but I won't."

"Touché," Damion said softly.

Damion backed away from her chair and was not surprised when she lowered her eyes and was again totally engrossed in the book. He picked up the two books he had selected and took there to the librarian to be checked out. While he waited for the card to be stamped, his eyes traveled again to Beth. She had treated him almost with defiance. It bothered him. Everything was bothering him lately, he realized. Everything and everybody.

Beth Thomas closed the book the moment she heard the screen door close. A smile tugged at the corners of her mouth. *And that, Reverend, should give you something to think about all day.* She glanced at the watch on her wrist. A few minutes before closing should be a good time to stop in the sporting goods store to see what was going on. The tennis racket at her feet needed restringing and what better place to take it than the shop where Kevin worked. By now, he was probably bored to tears and would welcome a chance to take a break and talk to her. And if he were busy, although she doubted it, she would wait out on the loading platform till he was free.

Covertly, she looked around the library and deftly slid the book into her tote. When she got home, she would put a book cover on it and no one would be the wiser.

CHAPTER SEVEN

―――――――――◆―――――――――

oster Doyle Hayden looked around his musty office and felt as dry and dusty as the contents of the room. This was his private domain, an office he had kept long after retiring from his professional life—a place to come and think and to smoke the forbidden cigar which he allowed himself along with a double shot of Wild Kentucky Bourbon. He liked the aroma of the cracked leather and the stale cigar smoke; it reminded him of his middle years when he abandoned his law practice for a seat on the bench in the county courthouse.

Gently, he touched the peeling leather on the humidor that rested in a prominent position on his desk—the last gift from his wife before she died. Now, why was he thinking about her at a time like this? Because, he answered himself, Irene was coming to the office. If there was ever a time that he longed for the company of his wife, this was it. He was going to tell Irene that he would not tolerate any shenanigans with Cader Harris now that the bastard was back in town.

Why had Cader come back? It couldn't be because of Kevin! Even if Cader recognized Kevin, there wasn't a damn thing he could do, was there? Cader had been gone so long no one ever gave Kevin's resemblance to him another thought. But with Cader back, the resemblance was going to be there for all the world to see.

In a way it was good that Cader had fathered a Hayden child. The old blood had been in need of a little rejuvenation, and Kevin was the proof that it worked. Hayden blood was good for girls like Bethany, but no matter how Foster Doyle tried to fool himself, he had to admit that Harris's bloodline was what made Kevin what he was. Christ! He loved that boy and nothing was ever going to change that.

Foster Doyle was becoming agitated with such thoughts; he could feel it in the wild flutterings of his heart. Or was it the forbidden cigar he was chomping? Cader Harris could spoil everything. Irene, if she wasn't controlled, could spoil everything. Even Arthur, milquetoast Arthur, could spoil things if he ever got down-wind of the fact that Kevin was Cader Harris's son. Kevin and Cader had to be kept apart. That was all there was to it. It could be easily done. Kevin was leaving for Tulane at the end of August, and if Foster Doyle knew anything at all about Cader Harris, it was that he wouldn't last in this town. Irene was the only stumbling block, and surely, she wasn't so stupid that she couldn't see what would happen if she so much as glanced in Harris's direction.

A tight ache that was closer to a pain ripped across his chest, and he sat down, forcing himself to a calmness he didn't feel. He stubbed out the cigar with regret, knowing full well that the tobacco wasn't what was giving him the pain. It was fear. Fear of Cader Harris. Fear of what Irene would do. She wasn't a giggling teenager any longer. She was a grown woman with a grown woman's pas-sions. Cader Harris would be like the forbidden fruit. And Irene would reach for that fruit like a drowning man clutches at straws. Foster Doyle rubbed his hand over his eyes. If Irene should ever discover that Cader Harris had been bought off, she would never, never forgive Foster. She would accuse him of meddling, and he would be the object of her tearful outrage. She would never once stop to judge the man who had left her alone with a child in her belly for a paid college tuition. He could never allow Irene to find out that her own father had paid Harris off; Irene was all Foster Doyle had left. Irene and Kevin, Cader Harris's son. And, of course, Bethany, he reminded himself as an afterthought. For some reason he always forgot about Bethany, possibly because she was so much like Irene, spoiled and whiny and always demanding.

Why did Harris have to come back to Hayden now, when Delta Oil was threatening intrusion into his beloved town of Hayden, named for his own great-grandfather?

Irene Hayden Thomas stood in the doorway, observing her father. Her emotions were mixed. She loved him, and yet there were times when she almost hated him, such as now. He had sum-moned her to his office, demanded she be here to discuss Cader Harris's return. She had ignored the first summons, pleading one thing and then another, but she knew she couldn't avoid a second demand. Foster Doyle looked so vulnerable sitting there behind his desk with his eyes closed. Vulnerable and yet formidable. She continued to stare at him, hardly believing he was approaching seventy years of age. The steel gray hair and the piercing blue of his eyes belied those years. His flesh was firm and more than one person had commented on the square cut of his jaw and his masculine form. Momentarily, she was proud of him until she remembered why she was here. Apprehensively, she said, "Daddy, are you sleeping?" as she walked into the room.

"Good heavens, no. Sit down, Irene, I want to talk to you. It's apparent to me that you've been avoiding me, and I know it's because of Cader Harris's return. There's no reason for you to fear discussing this with me. After all, I am your father and the grandfather of your children. . . ." Foster Doyle's words drifted off into space. He was looking at his daughter, actually looking at her. She had done something with her hair; it was lighter, younger looking. Makeup, jewelry. . . . Foster Doyle almost moaned aloud. It was too late, Irene had already determined that she would throw herself into Cader Harris's company. Why else this overhaul that had turned a dowdy matron into a smartly dressed, attractive woman?

"I'm not afraid of you, Daddy, I just haven't been able to get over here before now. I've just been over at the school working on the band uniforms. Honestly, you can't imagine the wear and tear those uniforms . . ." Foster Doyle displayed his contempt for the turn in her conversation, and Irene halted abruptly. "What is it you want to talk about?" she asked testily.

"Cader Harris," Foster Doyle boomed, angered by his observations of the change in Irene. "I want your solemn word you will do everything in your power to keep Kevin away from him. Everything in your power, Irene," he repeated forcefully. "I won't settle for anything less than your word."

Irene blanched. "It's too late, Daddy. Kevin applied for a job in Cader's sporting goods shop and was hired. Arthur insisted he keep the job. There was nothing I could do."

"Nothing you could do!" Foster Doyle Hayden shouted. "You're a Hayden and you sit there and tell me there was nothing you could do. Are you telling me that . . . that . . . keeper of dead bodies tells you, a Hayden, what to do? May all the Haydens that walk the heavens have mercy on you."

"Daddy, you don't understand. Kevin already had the job. Arthur is the boy's father and he insisted. For me to nag and nag would have made him suspicious. There was nothing I could do! I tried! You have to believe me. Daddy, say you believe me."

"I'll give the boy whatever sum he's earning in the shop if you can keep him home. The Haydens don't work, Irene. I can't believe you allowed this to happen," Foster continued to shout, thumping the shiny surface of his desk with his clenched hand. "And I want to know why Cader Harris is back in town. Have you been in touch with him over the years? Don't lie to me, girl," Foster said, leaning over the desk, his blue eyes staring into Irene's. "That business was settled eighteen years ago, and it's over and done with," he said, not waiting for her denial.

Irene flushed and lowered her eyes. "No, I haven't been in touch with him, and I have no idea why he's here in town. Oh, Daddy, do you think he wants to take Kevin from me?"

"That's the kind of thinking that got you into this mess in the first place. I don't know why he's here, but I intend to find out. I want you to send Kevin to me tomorrow. If necessary, I'll force the boy to quit the job. I'll carry it one step further. I'll tell the boy I'll cut him *and* you out of my will. Bethany too. He'll come around when he realizes I mean what I say. If you have a mind to, Irene, you can reinforce my . . . request . . . with cutting off his funds for Tulane. You did tell me that you were paying for his education because business was bad and Arthur had to . . . what is it those keepers of the dead have to do?"

Irene was stunned. "Daddy, you wouldn't! You can't do that to Kevin! He would hate you."

"Better he should hate me than come to like that . . . that football jock."

"Oh, God," Irene mewed. "We have to discuss this calmly, Daddy, and not do anything any of us will regret later. Daddeee, are you listening to me?"

"Irene, you will do as I say or I will indeed remove your and your children's names from my will. I will leave everything to the Jatha Hayden Foundation for the elderly," Foster Doyle said slowly and distinctly to be sure his daughter understood.

Irene's eyes took on a dangerous glitter as she matched her father's cold stare. Her shoulders squared imperceptibly and the gesture of defiance was not lost on Foster Doyle Hayden. "Your days of threatening me are over, Father. You almost ruined my life once, but you won't do it a second time. It's time you and I had a father-daughter talk. I'll do the talking and you do the listening. I know that you had something to do with Cader leaving here, but I can't prove it. You've maneuvered and manipulated all your life, and sometimes you're so smug I almost believe you put the squeeze on Cader because you thought it would get you what you wanted. Eighteen years ago I was a gullible, frightened young girl. I'm not that girl any longer. The biggest mistake of my life was in telling you I was pregnant with Cader's child."

"Irene, there's no need to go through all this," Foster Doyle said testily, not liking the determined took on his daughter's face.

"Well, I think there is every reason. I'm just a little too old to be threatened. I won't tolerate it. Now is as good a time as any for me to tell you that I only *seemed* to go along with your plans to send me away to have the baby and then bring him back as a distant relative who was conveniently orphaned. I never had any intention of following through. I knew that once you got your hands on my child, mine and Cader's, that you would raise him your way. And if you think for one minute that this town would have bought that story of some long-lost relative suddenly bestowing a baby on you for safekeeping, you're wrong. I just want you to know that I saw through all that. I might not have said anything at the time because I feared your wrath, but this is today. I had made up my mind to have Cader's baby one way or another."

"Irene," Foster Doyle interjected, "you're overwrought and you're upsetting me. I don't want to hear any more of this nonsense."

"Well, I'm not finished yet, and you're going to hear it whether you like it or not. I loved Cader Harris. I loved the idea of bearing his child. When he left here so suddenly, I wanted to die. He left not knowing I was going to have a baby. How in the name of God do you think that made me feel? Part of me died then and now that part of me is alive again. Cader's back."

"Yes, Harris is back," Foster Doyle said coldly. "Have you given any thought at all to what will happen to you if he decides he wants Kevin? If you haven't, I suggest you think about it."

"Kevin is not a football to be tossed back and forth. He's my son. Mine and mine alone. For the public, Arthur is his father, but he's mine, all mine, and I intend, for the time being, to keep it that way. And speaking of Arthur, it's time for you to know that I maneuvered and manipulated him just the way I've watched you do over the years. When Cader left town, I moved in on Arthur so fast, he didn't know what hit him. I opened my legs and prostituted myself so that I could keep my baby. To this day, Arthur thinks Kevin is his son. What do you have to say to all this, Daddy? Defend yourself," Irene said bitterly.

Foster Doyle felt himself shrink beneath his daughter's penetrating stare. He never in his life had to defend himself, and the feeling was so alien, he felt the need to gag. "It wasn't the child I objected to, Irene, it was Harris himself. He wasn't the man for you; he still isn't. He may be Kevin's biological father, but that's all he is. And I knew all along what you were doing. After all, you are my daughter. It's not doing either one of us any good to rehash all this and open old wounds. You can't do anything foolish now that will jeopardize Kevin's well-being and future."

"I told you to stop telling me what to do. If I want to see Cader, I will. If I, and I said *if I*, decide to tell him about Kevin, it will be my decision and mine alone. And last, but not least, your threats about the children's and my inheritance don't scare me at all. I have Mother's money and I control the children's trusts," Irene said stonily.

Foster Doyle snorted. "Only on paper, Irene. I'm the one who drew up the papers, and I know exactly what they say. I control everything. If I wanted, by noon tomorrow, you would be penniless. Am I making myself clear?"

"You're threatening me again, Father, and I told you not to do it. You do what you have to do, and I'll do what I have to do. Do you understand that?"

Foster Doyle winced. She was his daughter all right. "Yes, I understand that you're turning against me, your own father."

"If that's the way you see it, there's nothing I can do about it. I will do what I think is best, and I'll do it without any interference from you or anyone else. Kevin is my first concern. Arthur can take care of himself just as you can take care of yourself. Neither of you needs me, but my son does. I will be the one to handle matters from now on."

Foster Doyle's heart started its mad fluttering as he stared at his daughter. Did he dare to pull his fainting trick on her or was it better to sigh and leave it all in the hands of God. God and Cader Harris? The moment he sighed, Irene knew she had won. She too sighed. It was so nice to have a father to depend on. A father who always saw things the way she saw them . . . in the end.

As Cader Harris sat in the comfortable leather chair behind the impressive-looking desk, his eye wandered to the main part of the shop. Kevin was a good worker; he had been hustling his butt for the past three hours without a break. And that was saying something, with that sexy kitten hot on his tail. He grinned. Another hour and either Judy would have him cornered in the back room or he was a backwoods country boy who didn't know where to put his peter. You could bang a girl leaning against a wall just as easily as you could in bed. He had lost count of the number of times he had banged Sunday Waters in the janitor's basement of the school, and it had been good, damn good. Maybe he should offer the kid some advice; he looked like he needed it. Just a little good old Harris philosophy.

His grin widened and he hoped Judy's old lady was as good as the kid was. Marsha had class while her daughter had . . . an "earthy" approach to getting what she wanted. The word surprised him and he laughed aloud. If he could get Marsha to mix a little earth with her class, would be doing just fine.

Kevin Thomas hefted a case of Spalding gloves onto a work table and prepared to slit open the top. He turned to get his knife and bumped into Judy. She was so close he could feel her warm breath on his neck. His heart pounding, he stared at her. He had to say something. "If you would do a little more work and less following, we might get home by six. I don't wanna stay here past closing."

"I wouldn't mind if you were here with me . . . and we were alone," Judy said, moving still closer. "Perhaps I can arrange it . . . we could do all sorts of things." Her voice became husky, her eyes searching.

"Like what?" Kevin challenged, reading the answer in her flashing eyes, feeling the curl of heat in his loins.

"Like unpacking the rest of this junk. Or we could neck," she cooed, leaning closer till he felt the round fullness of her breasts against his chest. "You name it, Kevin. I'm game."

"You're crazy for talking like that, Judy. Some guy might take you up on it."

"I wouldn't mind, Kevin, as long as you're that guy." She pressed closer, her voice a murmur, her gaze direct, defiant.

"If Mr. Harris heard you, he could take it into his mind to fire both of us. I don't know about you, but I need this job, so knock it off."

"Kevin, are you afraid of me?" Judy persisted. "I bet you never made it with a girl, did you? Of course not, how could you with your fairy princess sister hanging around your neck every minute of the day," she snorted.

"Drop it, will you, Judy? What are you doing back here anyway?" Kevin said gruffly.

"I came back to use the dressing room. Mr. Harris wanted to know what I thought of these new tennis outfits. I thought I'd try a few on." Judy looked up at him from beneath lowered lids. She smiled, sweetly, but Kevin saw the challenge glittering in her smoky gaze.

Beth pressed her face against the plate glass window and peered into the depths of the sporting goods store. Kevin was nowhere in evidence. Her heart skipped a beat as she pondered her next move. Fifteen minutes till the store closed. Kev must be either on the loading dock or in the back storeroom. If he were in the storeroom, then Judy was with him. The tennis racket in its plastic mitten banged against the brick wall as she swiveled and raced for the side driveway that led to the loading dock.

Quiet was the name of the game, she thought viciously. She would creep up the stairs and watch and see what dear old Judy was doing. After all, she had a perfect right to be here; her tennis racket needed restringing. She took the concrete steps two at a time and once again squinted into the dimness of the storeroom. No one. Voices. Carefully, she inched her way into the vast storeroom with its leather smells and wide assortment of athletic equipment. Laughter.

"How do you like it, Kevin? These Chrissie Evert outfits should go over big," Judy said, laughing as she twirled and preened for his benefit. She had deliberately left off her bra, knowing the taut pink crests of her breasts would strain against the thin nylon outfit. Kevin too, she could see, was aware of the straining fabric. "Let's play mixed doubles next weekend, and I'll talk my mother into buying this outfit for me."

Kevin felt his face flush and grinned, enjoying Judy's modeling. "If you wear that outfit, you'll win hands down. No thanks. I have to keep my mind on the game."

"Oh, Kevin, I knew if you were away from that snotty little sister of yours, you would open up and be human. Why do you let her tag around after you like that? All the kids in school call her your albatross."

Kevin's mood changed abruptly. "Leave Beth out of this. She's no concern of yours and I don't care what anyone says about the way she 'hangs around me,' as you put it. She's my sister."

Judy swung her arms out and then thrust them behind her, clasping her hands, making her full breasts jut out even further. "So okay, she's your sister. Are you taking her to Jackie's party on Saturday?"

"I didn't know Jackie was having a party and, no, I'm not taking her," Kevin said, hefting a carton of footballs onto a shelf.

"Will you go with me?"

"What makes you think I'll be invited?" Kevin hedged.

"Because Jackie came into the store today and told me she was sending out the invitations this afternoon. Her parents are going out and won't be home till after eleven." She giggled.

Kevin stared at Judy, his mind racing. Why not? Judy was a tease, a flirt, but he liked the way she played up to him. It had been awhile since he went anywhere without Beth and really enjoyed himself. Did the gang really think of Beth as an albatross around his neck?

"Well?"

Kevin ginned. "Okay, you got yourself a date."

Judy squealed in delight, throwing herself into Kevin's arms.

"We'll have such a good time, you'll see. Boomer said he was going to sneak some beer into the party, and he promised there would be enough for everyone. Did you ever drink beer before, Kevin?"

Kevin reached up to loosen Judy's grip around his neck and felt his breathing quicken. She smelled warm and sweet, like a wildflower in the meadow. Even her hair smelled nice. Suddenly, he felt reckless and daring. "Sure," he lied.

Judy moved and let her hands drop to her sides. "Great! Then I know I'll be in safe hands," she said softly, never taking her eyes from him.

"You'd better get out of that outfit and put it back before Mr. Harris sees you." He felt hot, feverish. "Hurry up, Judy. All we have to do is stack these T-shirts and we can leave."

"Will you walk me home, Kevin?" Judy called from behind the dressing room door.

"Sure, if you get a move on."

"Kev? Are you back here?" Beth called as she moved into sight from behind a loaded dolly.

Kevin felt like a kid with his hand in the cookie jar as he swung around to see his sister advance further into the storeroom. How long had she been standing there? How much did she hear? What was she doing here in the first place? Irritated, his eyes swept over her. She carried her tennis racket, the one that needed restringing. One look into her bright, accusing eyes and he knew, without a doubt, she had heard and seen enough. She had heard him agree to take Judy to Jackie's party and to walk her home. She had seen Judy in the skimpy tennis outfit and she was angry. He wondered what Cader Harris would do in a similar situation. In his gut he knew Cader Harris would never allow himself to be placed in a situation like this.

"Here I am," Kevin called out in a tightly controlled voice.

Beth's eyes were furious when she stared at her brother, but her voice was calm and sweet when she spoke. "I brought my racket to be restrung. Take care of it for me, will you? I hope you don't mind stopping by the drugstore. I need some shampoo. Then Daddy can give us a ride home."

Her accusing glance dared Kevin to defy her. "Sure, if that's what you want," he heard himself answer.

Judy emerged from behind the cartons and laughed openly. "Thanks for the offer, Beth. Your father won't mind dropping me off too, will he? And I have to get some toothpaste at the drugstore myself. You're a sweet . . . kid, for reminding me of that. I'll just tell Mr. Harris we're going and, Kevin, don't worry, I'll tell him I'll come in a half hour early tomorrow to fix the shelves. As a matter of fact," she smiled brightly, "I'll ask Mom for the car and pick you up." With a lofty wave of her hand she sauntered into Cader Harris's office and closed the door behind her.

Beth watched Judy weave her way among the boxes and cartons and felt bile rise in her throat. Her mind sought a word for Judy and the only thing she was able to come up with was one of Irene's favorites—Jezebel.

While Kevin tidied up his work area, her mind raced. She had to find a way to get to the party—with or without Kevin. Boomer. Boomer would take her. Boomer would love to take her. He'd been puffing and panting after her all year. If Kevin could take that . . . that Jezebel, then she could take Boomer. Only she would pretend that it was Boomer who invited her. Why not? Why not anything? Kevin was changing right before her eyes. Any other time he would have been glad she dropped by to go home with him, but now, today, he actually seemed to resent her.

Tears gathered in her eyes as she watched him place her racket in a box marked for restringing and come back to her, a wary look in his eye.

"I'm ready when you are," she said lightly, a forgiving note in her voice. Her heavily fringed eyes were still furious and now openly calculating as she linked her arm through Kevin's.

Judy and Cader Harris emerged from Cader's office and approached the pair. Harris smiled a welcome to Beth and boldly removed her arm from Kevin's. He turned and began leading her toward the front door. "Little lady, where I come from, actions like that are suspect." His grip was tight and unrelenting as he led her from the store, Judy and Kevin trailing behind.

Cader Harris didn't like her, Beth knew. She had seen it that first day when she and Kevin had applied for the jobs. She didn't care; she hated him. It was all because of *him* that Judy was getting her claws into Kevin.

"Didn't anyone ever tell you, little missy, that big brothers aren't supposed to be sissies? What are you trying to do to Kevin? Don't you think you're a little old to be hanging on to his shirt-tails?" Not bothering to wait for a reply, undaunted by the venomous look she was giving him, he continued in a conspiratorial tone, "Can't you see that little temptress next to him is trying to make out and you're standing in their way? You know what I'm talkin' about, don't you? Right?"

"Wrong, Mr. Harris. Kevin has a mind of his own and can do whatever he pleases." With a quick, almost violent gesture Beth was free of his grip. Her voice was choked when she turned to Kevin and said, "I just remembered that Mother bought shampoo this morning, and I promised Boomer I'd stop by his house late this afternoon. Why don't you walk Judy home?" Without another word she sprinted down the street.

Cader narrowed his eyes at the stricken look on Kevin's face and then at the grateful expression on Judy's. He winked, as if to say, "All in a day's work."

Kevin's mouth tightened as he looked from Cader Harris to Judy. He knew he'd just been manipulated. "You can pick me up in the morning, Judy. I'll see you, Mr. Harris." Before either of them could say another word, he was loping after Beth, his young face set into lines of anger and frustration. Frustration for himself for running after Beth and anger with Cader Harris for involving himself in what was none of his affair.

When something went wrong, it really went wrong, Judy thought angrily as she walked home alone. She'd been after Kevin ever since junior high and now, just when she almost had him, Beth screwed it up. She brightened momentarily when she realized that Beth wouldn't be in the way come fall. So far, it was her secret, hers and her mother's, that she had only last week been accepted to Tulane. If she played her cards right, she could arrive at the same time as Kevin. Wouldn't he be surprised! A whole year without drippy Beth to contend with. Kevin liked her, she knew he did. She could see it in the way his eyes followed her when he thought she wasn't looking. Mom liked Kevin; she'd be happy that he was taking her to Jackie's party.

Judy wondered why she was sometimes so rude to the only person she had left in this whole, entire world. She loved her mom, but sometimes. . . . If Dad were still alive, she wouldn't be having these troubles. Dad had always been so easy to talk to. He would have listened to her when she wanted to talk about Kevin, and he wouldn't ever have ruffled her hair and smiled indulgently as though it were just kid stuff the way Mom did. She would have been able to tell him about Beth and how she was always trying to keep Kevin to herself. If only he hadn't been in that car when he had that heart attack. Even the doctors said it was the crash that killed him, not his heart.

It was all Mom's fault. Stress and strain killed people, everyone knew that. It was the stress of fighting with Marsha, the bitter quarrels they didn't know Judy was aware of that killed him. Especially that last night when they had argued over custody of Judy. Dad wanted her with him and Mom said absolutely not.

It had all been Mom's fault. Dad had had the heart attack almost immediately after that last bitter quarrel. It had happened as he was driving from Hayden. Mom had driven him away because she was somehow inadequate. Daddy had died because he loved his daughter, and Mom wouldn't let them be together.

Judy opened her change purse and counted her money. Three dollars in change and a wilted one-dollar bill. She sprinted down the street and around the corner, skidding to a stop outside the florist shop. With any luck Mr. Carpenter would have some kind of arrangement for four dollars.

Breathing heavily, she swung open the door, apologizing to the stoop-shouldered old florist. "I'm so glad I got here before you closed, Mr. Carpenter. Do you have something already made up for four dollars? I want to take a run out to the cemetery and put them on Dad's grave."

Adam Carpenter looked at the young, breathless girl and saw the grief in her eyes. She was the only kid he ever knew who saved her pennies and bought a single Shasta daisy to take to the cemetery. So many times he wanted to add extra flowers or a sprig of fern but she would decline his generous offer. She paid for whatever she bought, even if it was just a single flower. "Nothing made up, Judy, but it will take only a minute to wire a bouquet of Shastas for you. Would you like colors or white?"

"Make them all different colors. Dad always liked colors. If I have enough money, would you add a little fern? Wait, I have an extra quarter in my jeans that I forgot about."

"Judy, how many times do I have to tell you there's no charge for the fern?"

"You're just being nice, Mr. Carpenter. You have to pay for the fern. I want to pay for it, really I do."

Adam Carpenter's pale gray eyes lightened and he smiled crookedly. "You always were too smart for me, Judy. A quarter it is," he said, twisting the wire around the stems of the daisies, careful not to damage the leaves. "That will be four twenty-five." Judy handed over the money and accepted the flowers. Judy sure was different from her mother, he thought sourly. Not once in all the time Judy's father had been laid to rest did Marsha ever come into the store to order flowers. Come to think of it, she hadn't even sent a spray to the mortuary, and he knew that for a fact because Arthur Thomas had made a point of mentioning it. It was the least she could have done. After all, she was married to him for a long time and he was Judy's father. There's just no accounting for some people's actions, he told himself as he locked up for the night. Just no accounting at all, he continued to mutter as he walked out to his car.

Beth looked over her shoulder, and when she saw no sign of Kevin, her eyes burned furiously.

Deftly, she skirted the corner and headed for the driveway that led to the mortuary. She'd show him and Judy too. She'd go into Daddy's office and call Boomer. "I'll show them," she muttered as she brushed impatiently at the tears burning her eyes.

Kevin sprinted along, his mind whirling. Lately, it seemed all he did was run after Beth. Girls! Mother! Beth! Judy! Why couldn't they just leave him alone? Everything was a problem lately. Damn!

He slowed at the corner of Jatha Hayden Boulevard and Mimosa Avenue and looked both ways. Beth was nowhere in sight. A grin tugged at the corners of his mouth when he realized he had stopped and when he also realized that even though he'd been doing a lot of running after Beth, for some reason he never caught up to her. Was he doing it unconsciously or . . . no point in wasting his energy now. He could take his time and walk home and appreciate the warm day and the thought of taking Judy to the party. Guys were supposed to think about girls on days like this, so why shouldn't he? Judy was okay. A little different but still okay. Too bad Beth didn't like her. Beth didn't like anyone. Maybe Dad was right and they had been spending too much time together. Now was as good a time as any to wean Beth away. The end of August would arrive all too soon and then what would Beth do? The question bothered him and the muscles in his shoulders constricted. He was worried about Beth and he didn't know why.

Kevin brightened momentarily when he thought of the active life at college and all the new friends he would make. He would be alone and on his own for the first time in his life. The end of August couldn't come soon enough for him.

As Kevin's mood brightened, Beth dialed Boomer's number. She wasn't surprised when she heard his voice on the other end of the line. "Boomer? This is Beth. Beth Thomas. Are you surprised?" she asked in what she hoped was a coy voice.

"Oh, yeah, sure, Beth."

His voice sounded distracted and she babbled on anxiously. "I just thought I'd see what you were doing with yourself. Being summer an' all, I haven't seen you around." Beth bit into her lower lip to keep it from trembling. Boomer Guthrie had always terrified her, ever since grade school, when he would find every opportunity to corner her alone and say dirty words. Once, he'd even pushed her down in the playground and she could still feel his eyes on her when her dress flew up, exposing her panties. Even this last year he seemed to take delight in eyeing her hotly and making lewd gestures until she blushed in embarrassment.

"Yeah. Well, that's how it is. I've been busy," he answered indifferently.

"Yeah, I know how it is," she plunged on, trying to seem casual. "I was just wondering if you were going to Jackie's party." She held her breath.

"Who? Oh, yeah, I am. What of it?" Suddenly, there was a ring of interest in his question.

"Oh, nothing, I was just wondering if you'd asked anyone to go with you." Beth heard her heart thumping madly. He couldn't have, he just couldn't have asked anyone.

"Yeah. Well, as a matter of fact, I didn't get a chance yet. I thought I just might go stag to this one," he lied. He'd been trying Judy Evans's number all day and there'd been no answer.

As though reading his thoughts, Beth said breathlessly, "Judy is going with Kevin. If you're going stag, maybe you'd like to come along with us instead."

"Yeah?" She could almost see his face pinch up the way it did when he became thoughtful. "You asking me to take you to the party, Beth?"

"Well, I thought, I mean, if you weren't going to take anyone, you could go with us and not have to go alone."

"Alone? Me? You know better than that, li'l Bethy."

"Yeah," she said tonelessly. This wasn't going the way she had intended. What was wrong with him? He'd been after her all year and now he was acting as though he didn't know what she wanted. He couldn't be that dumb, could he? She held her breath, listening to the silence on the other end of the line.

"You wanna go with me, Beth?"

"How nice of you to ask me, Boomer!" She hoped her voice sounded convincing.

"I said, you wanna go with me? You asking me to take you?"

Beth recognized that tone of voice. That sly, baiting tone he used when he whispered dirty words to her. She wanted to hang up on him before it went any further. But she couldn't. This was so important. She couldn't let Judy get her hooks into Kevin.

"Yeah, Boomer, I'm asking you to take me," she managed to choke out.

"Yeah? No kiddin'? Sure, I'll take ya, li'l Bethy, but first you gotta tell me what you're gonna gimme if'n I do."

God, she hated him; he was a slime. "Wh-what do you want, Boomer?" She squeezed her eyes shut, dreading to hear his answer.

"Me? What could a guy like me want?" She could hear the sneer in his voice.

"Oh, I don't know." She tried to keep her voice level as she glanced quickly around to be certain she was alone. "Look, Boomer, I'll give you anything you want. I've just gotta go to that party," she blurted, covering her mouth with her hand, not believing what she had just said.

"Yeah. Well, what d'you know? Li'l Bethy's finally come around. You plannin' on wearin' a bra?"

Beth felt scared. "What difference does that make?"

"Well, it makes a difference. I always had a yen for your nice little titties." He lowered his voice but Beth heard him loud and clear. Again, she glanced over her shoulder.

"Boomer, I don't wear a bra," she gulped.

"That's nice, Beth, real nice."

"Well?"

"Well what?"

"Do we have a . . . a date or not?"

"Yeah. Sure, why not?"

"We . . . we'll double with Kevin and Judy. Okay?"

"Does good ol' Kev know about this?"

"Of course. He's one of your best friends, isn't he?" She held her breath, daring him to deny it. She had to get off the phone with him before she lost her nerve. "Pick me up around eight, okay?"

"Yeah. Maybe I'll call you tonight, around nine. Be home. You and me can talk some more. I like to hear you talk, Bethy."

Perspiration broke out on Beth's brow and she felt damp under her arms. She knew the kind of talk Boomer wanted to have and she felt sick thinking about it. She should hang up on him right now. She should tell him it was all a joke, a dare. She should make a fool out of him. Instead, she steadied her voice and answered, "That would be nice, Boomer. I always like to hear from you." To her own amazement, she actually had pulled it off. Her voice dripped syrup.

"So there, Kevin," she muttered as she replaced the receiver in its cradle with a trembling hand. "So there!"

CHAPTER EIGHT

*K*evin knew something was amiss when he woke to find his grandfather having breakfast in the kitchen with his mother. Kevin eyed the two of them carefully as he withdrew a container of orange juice from the refrigerator. "Good morning, Grandfather," he said respectfully as he bent down to peck his mother on the cheek.

Foster Doyle rose from the chair and clapped the boy on the back. "Fine morning, so I decided to go for a walk and decided at the last minute to stop by. I understand Dulcie left some of her famous cinnamon buns, and you know I can't resist those."

They were conspiring against him, he could sense it, almost smell it. Where was Dad? For that matter, where was Beth? He knew he needed an ally—desperately.

"Your mother tells me you have a job for the summer at the new sporting goods store," Foster Doyle said affably.

Kevin grimaced. Well, he might as well get it over with now. Dad was on his side and that was all he needed. "Yes, Mr. Harris hired me on the spot. He gave me good hours and is depending on me. I shook hands with him and gave him my word that I would do a good job," Kevin said tightly. "And, Grandfather, I mean to do just that."

"Commendable idea, boy, commendable, but the Hayden young never work till they're through college. What are the towns-people going to think of you? You surely don't need the money, and by accepting the job you're taking it from some poor, deserving youth. Tell me what Harris is paying you and I'll ante up the same and you'll have your summer free to do what you want."

Kevin's eyes narrowed. "I appreciate what you're saying, Grandfather, but I want to work; I think I'm going to like working in the store and I like Mr. Harris. He's an okay guy. I've already taken the job; Dad gave his approval."

"I agree with your grandfather, Kevin, let some other deserving boy have the job and you can spend your summer with Beth. After all, you're going to be going away at the end of August and she's going to miss you terribly. A little consideration is all we're asking, Kevin," Irene pleaded.

Kevin stared at his mother and then at his grandfather. They were doing it to him again. They took sides against him and against his father. He'd always given in to his mother's pleas, but not this time. This time he was going to do what he wanted. Dad was on his side.

"If you're such an independent fellow, then how would you like to work your way through Tulane?" Foster Doyle snapped irritably.

"I've given that some thought too," Kevin replied, watching Foster Doyle carefully. "I applied for a job in the cafeteria for the dinner hour. My meals would be free."

"Kevin," Irene screeched. "What's happened to you? Where are you getting these ideas?"

"I've always had them, you just never bothered to listen. Dad thinks it's a good idea. Look, I have to go now or I'll be late. It was nice seeing you, Grandfather. Mother, I'll be home at dinnertime. If I'm late, don't hold it for me. I'll eat with Dad."

Foster Doyle unclenched his hands when the screen door closed and stared at Irene. "Is that what you call taking care of things?" he said harshly.

"I told you his mind was made up. Arthur is on his side, and now that I've had time to think more on the subject, I don't think it's such a bad idea at all. If Cader suspects anything, I'm sure he won't say anything. After all, Kevin is his flesh and blood and he wouldn't deliberately hurt the boy, and Kevin would be hurt. Cader is no fool, Daddy."

"We've lost this battle, but the rest of the war is still not finished," Foster Doyle said thoughtfully. At that moment he made up his mind to see Cader Harris and set things straight. And the sooner the better.

Irene was dabbing at her eyes and wishing she had a cigarette. "I'll take care of matters, daughter. Wipe your eyes and go out shopping. Buy yourself a new hat, one with lots of feathers, the kind I like. I'll take care of Kevin, that asinine husband of yours, and Cader Harris."

Irene's stomach churned. Why couldn't he let her handle her own affairs? Kevin was her son, and Cader's. She and Cader should be the ones to settle things. At that moment Irene Hayden Thomas hated her father with an all-consuming passion. The intensity of her feeling frightened her, so she left her father standing with his mouth hanging open. She ran to her room and searched wildly for one of her menthol cigarettes. She fumbled with the crumpled package and succeeded in mutilating four of the slender cylinders before she finally managed to bring the cigarette to her mouth and light it. A sob caught in her throat.

Arthur Thomas tugged at the vest of his somber, blue-striped three-piece suit before walking into the viewing room near the back of the mortuary. The room was reserved for the black wakes and was appointed in dark turkey reds and bright gilt which catered to their taste for the flamboyant. Arthur always flinched slightly whenever he came into this room. He had long ago reasoned that it was because it was the scene of unbridled grief. Unlike the formal, carefully controlled funerals and wakes common to whites, blacks were far less repressed, more prone to outbursts and wailings. He supposed that after all these years he would have become used to the wailings and public weepings, but he had not. It still embarrassed him. He much preferred the quiet, solemn ceremonies of his own people. With his own people it was only necessary to be considerate of their grief, to be polite and carry out his duties in the most efficient way possible. Grief among the blacks was a more personal emotion and weighed heavily upon anyone who came in contact with it. Their prayers, their hallelujahs, their gospel songs required an emotional response, something that was too easily aroused in Arthur Thomas.

It was because of his discomfort in dealing with black funerals that he had hired Destry Davidson, his black associate. Arthur's eyes sought out Destry and signaled him to come out into the foyer.

Destry Davidson was tall and immaculately groomed. He carried his height with dignity and he never seemed to hurry, although Arthur knew him to be a man with economy of motion. The word "conservative" always came to Arthur's mind when he looked at Destry. Even his woolly hair was tailored, cut and shaped to his head so that no stray hair was visible. His shirt was niveous white against his almond-colored neck. Irene said Destry was spit-and-polish but more spit than polish if Arthur knew what she meant.

"Will you be coming back this evening, Mistah Thomas?" Destry asked in his serious, somber tone.

"Not tonight, Destry. You've been here alone . . . with your people before tonight; you don't need me. As a matter of fact, I've been meaning to talk to you about me being here when one of your own is laid out. Somehow, I think it would be better if you managed alone."

Destry folded his long arms over his muscular chest and stared at Arthur Thomas, the man he had called "Mistah Thomas" for the past ten years. "Does that mean you don't want me in attendance when one of . . . your own is laid out?"

"No, that's not what it means, Destry. You know I couldn't run this place without your help. All I'm saying is I think your people feel more comfortable when I'm not around."

Destry's licorice eyes were inscrutable as he stared at Arthur. "How did the council meeting go today? Did anyone make any firm decisions?"

"A lot of bickering and fighting but that was what I expected. You're in favor of the tanks, aren't you, Destry?"

"Yes, Mistah Thomas, I am, as we have discussed many times. This town needs a black mortuary and one day I hope to open it. If the tanks come to Hayden, then black people will come too. Personally, I don't think the pollution and danger is what the people of this town say it is. This town is going to stagnate soon enough, so why not get ahead on some kind of industry? If not the tanks, then something else. We need new blood and new ideas. I speak for my people and myself, of course."

"I think it's too early to tell what's going to happen. The Town Council meeting is just a few days away and then we'll see which way the wind is blowing. I haven't made up my mind either way. My wife now, she has very definite opinions about this whole thing, but I have no intention of letting her influence me one way or the other. I want what's best for this town and everyone in it."

Destry looked pointedly at his watch and then at Arthur Thomas. "Miss Bethany is waiting for you in your office, Mistah Thomas, and if you don't leave now, you'll miss your dinner."

"What time is your viewing?"

"In fifteen minutes. I made a special concession this evening for the immediate family. It's going to be . . . er . . . emotional," Destry explained, aware of Arthur's abhorrence of unbridled grief. "When a black child dies, it's not something that's easy to handle."

"Good night, Destry," Arthur said, heading for his office.

"G'night, Mistah Thomas. Enjoy your dinner," Destry said softly.

When Arthur sat down at the carefully appointed dinner table, he fully expected to enjoy his meal. He had noticed Irene's new hair style and that she had had it lightened almost to the color it was when they were first married. He had been generous with his compliments and for the first time in years Irene had blushed beneath his appreciative gaze.

Only a few minutes after Dulcie served the ham, Arthur knew that Irene's new hairdo wasn't going to defuse the charged atmosphere. Beth picked at her food and Kevin jabbed at his ham with his fork, never bringing the succulent meat to his mouth. Arthur looked from his children to his wife and back to Kevin. Pretending to eat, he watched Beth's covert glances toward Irene, and he knew something was in the wind, and whatever it was, it wouldn't do Kevin any good. Sooner or later, Irene would get around to whatever it was Beth wanted from her. He was proved right when Dulcie served the pecan pie and whipped cream.

"Kevin, Beth tells me you're going to Jacklyn's party with Judy Evans. Beth has been invited to the same party by Luther Guthrie and I think, as it's her first more or less grown-up party, that you should double date and keep an eye on her. I'll feel more comfortable if you're together."

"Irene!" Arthur almost shouted. "Why do you insist on pairing these children off together? In the first place Luther is too old for Beth to date, and in the second place Kevin doesn't need to look after his sister. Stop arranging their affairs for them. How do you know Kevin isn't doubling with another couple? The least you could do is give him the courtesy of asking before you make these arrangements."

"Arthur, children are a mother's responsibility, and I think Beth has every right to go to the party, and Luther is such a nice boy. Don't you remember how adorable he looked when he was the ring-bearer at Anna Delphine's wedding?"

"Irene, that was ten years ago. If you're so worried about Beth needing someone to look after her, then she's too young to go. Kevin will not double with Beth and that's final!" Arthur said, standing up from the table, his eyes fierce and cold.

"It's okay, Dad, really it is. I don't mind," Kevin mumbled.

"There, you see, Arthur, even Kevin says it is all right."

"The boy knows that's what you want. I mean it, Irene, Kevin will not take Beth to the party. It's time she did things on her own!"

Beth jumped up from the table, her eyes tear-filled. "You hate me, Daddy! You always side with Kevin. My very first party and you spoil it for me. Now I don't want to go; you ruined everything!" she wailed.

Arthur stood his ground, puzzled by the strange look in his daughter's eyes. She really expected him to back down, he could see it. When she saw that he had no intention of rescinding his order, Beth flounced from the room and raced up the stairs to her room.

"Now see what you've done," Irene cried.

"I've done nothing and you know it, Irene. Kevin has a right to a life of his own, and it's time he started living it. He's done everything you asked of him for the past seventeen and a half years.

Enough is enough!" Arthur roared, banging his fist so hard on the lace-topped table that Irene almost fell from her chair.

"Very well," Irene said coldly, "but if anything happens to Beth, it will be your fault. You just remember that, Arthur Thomas. And you, young man," Irene said, poking a finger under Kevin's nose, "you remember that you, by your very actions, if not words, made it clear that you don't want your sister to go with you to this party."

"Mother . . ." Kevin entreated.

"I'm not interested in hearing any more excuses from you, and you're excused from the table, Kevin. Leave my sight. I never thought I would live to see the day when my very own husband and my very own son would turn against their sister and daughter like this. Haydens," she said imperiously, "do not do things like this. Why, I can almost see Granddaddy Hayden turn over in his grave over such goings on."

"Irene, Granddaddy Hayden was the biggest rake going, so stop pretending he was some sort of saint. I hardly think he would turn over in his grave because his grandson wanted to go to a party without his sister. As a matter of fact, he would probably cheer Kevin on. This is the end of the matter, Irene, and I don't want to hear another word about it again, do you understand me?"

Irene ignored him as she rose from the table. She would ignore Arthur the way she always did. When she really concentrated, she could pretend he didn't exist.

Cader finished his solitary cardboard sandwich and tossed the remnants into the trashcan next to him. He leaned back, his feet propped on the scarred desk. His eyes were glued to the parking lot and the long, sleek Lincoln Continental that was maneuvering its way between the white lines. *A whole damn parking lot, and he has to worry about the white lines.* Cader grimaced. He waited.

Foster Doyle Hayden came in through the storage room and then through the shop before he noticed Cader sitting in what passed for his office. Cader let his eyes lock with those of the old man and deliberately remained seated. Since there was no other chair, the old man was at a distinct disadvantage and Cader wanted it that way. He was in control and Foster Doyle Hayden knew it.

"Why are you here? Is it the boy?" he asked bluntly. Cader said nothing. Strategy. Let the old geezer talk and, hopefully, he would get so rattled something worthwhile would come of the confrontation. "Surely, it can't be Irene; she's married. This town doesn't need a sporting goods store any more than it needs you. This town never needed the likes of you. What do you want? How much, Harris, to pack up and get out?"

Cader lit a cigarette and tossed the match on the floor. What a wonderful thing power was. Now he knew why the old man thrived the way he did. *Jump, you old bastard,* he thought bitterly.

"Well? How much?"

Cader eased the chair down softly and leaned across the desk. "You bought me once and you owned me for four years. We played by your rules, crooked rules. But I played because that was the bargain we made. You told me Irene was getting an abortion, and I halfway believed you. Right now, you son of a bitch, we're playing by my rules and those rules say I don't have to tell you anything. My debt has been paid."

"I'll have you thrown out of town," Hayden blustered.

Cader laughed. "And all the while you're having me escorted through the main street, I'll be playing pied piper. Irene and Kevin will be right behind me. In case you don't understand, you wise-assed bastard, I'm holding all the cards."

"Surely, you wouldn't hurt Kevin, your own son. If you tell him now, it could do only harm. The boy is happy, content, with Arthur Thomas as his father. I'll pay you whatever you want, give you whatever you want, if you'll just give me your word," Hayden pleaded.

"Right now, my word is just about as good as yours was eighteen years ago. And. Mist-tah Hayden, there isn't enough money in the world to buy me off a second time. I'm not for sale. I rarely give advice, but this time is an exception. Get your skinny ass in that hearse you're driving and get the hell off my property. And don't come back. I've developed a deep sensitivity over the years, and you're offending me. What that means, Mist-tah Foster Doyle Hayden, is you're being dismissed by one football jock named Cader Harris."

Foster Doyle's face reddened and then turned a deep shade of blue. He gasped and placed his hand over his heart and then groped in his pocket for a small vial. With shaking hands, he popped the pill into his mouth and waited, his white-knuckled hands clutched on the rim of the desk. Cader's eyes narrowed but he made no move to help or hinder the old man. Blind hatred surged through him.

"You would have let me die, wouldn't you?" Foster Doyle asked in stunned shock as his breathing and color returned to normal.

"I don't know," Cader said honestly.

The old man's slumped shoulders straightened. Cader Harris would never know what that effort cost him.

Cader Harris locked the store and stood a moment looking up and down the quiet street. All the merchants were gone for the day and the storefronts stood sentinel.

Deftly, he backed the rental car from the parking area and at the last minute decided to go to the Lemon Drop for dinner. Food was the least of his interests right now, so it made no difference if he ate his dinner or if he drank it. A couple of short ones and a trip to the other side of the tracks to Aunt Cledie's and a little poontang was what he needed. A little dark meat went a long way and was always better after a long abstinence. He grinned to himself at the thought and then sobered. He bit into his lower lip as he wondered how the council meeting went. Perhaps someone at the Lemon Drop would know.

While he drove, Cader let his eyes pick out sites he had long ago forgotten. Damn town never changed. He grimaced. Christ, if he had to live forever in this jerk-water burg, he would go out of his mind. Bright lights and firm flesh were what he wanted. And, by God, he was going to make damn sure he got it . . . one way or another. Hayden was the end of the rainbow for him, and his pot of gold was going to be filled to overflowing. He would invest a little and spend a lot. Let the twilight years take care of themselves.

Sunday Waters, a tray in her hand with a double Scotch on it, spotted him immediately when he entered the room. It was all she could do not to drop the tray and run over to him and throw her arms around his neck. Damn it to hell, no man should be able to do this to a woman after eighteen long years. In a split second the years were erased and he was the Cader of high-school days. He couldn't see her as yet, she thought, since coming from the outside into the dimness of the supper club would momentarily blind him. Give the customer his drink and then walk nonchalantly over to the bar where he would be sitting and say something cool and mocking. Something with class.

Her hand shook slightly when she placed the drink in front of the waiting customer. "Would you care for some nuts or pretzels?" she asked softly. "Enjoy your drink, sir."

Thank God she had taken pains with her makeup and dress tonight. She'd had her hair done this afternoon. She looked good. She knew she looked good; the man with the double Scotch had looked at her with more than approval, and if she had cared to make a small overture, she could have had him eating out of her hand in a minute.

Deep breath. No subterfuge for Sunday. Straight from the hip. Why bother with small talk? What was wrong with showing Cade she was glad to see him and just winging it from there? "Hello, Cade," she said, smiling as she perched on the stool next to his.

Cade's eyes widened as he let his eyes drink in the sight of the attractive woman sitting next to him. "Yo, what have we here?" He grinned. "Don't tell me; it can't be, but it is . . . Sunny!" The bar stool swiveled and he had her wrapped in his arms in a hard embrace. "Damn if you aren't a sight for these eyes. Jesus, you're all grown up."

"How do you like it?" Sunday grinned. "You don't look so bad to these eyes either," she said softly. So what if her lips trembled; so what if he saw. He could stop them; he knew how. "I've thought of you often, Cade. More often than is decent. Tell me a lie, Cade, tell me you thought of me too."

"Baby, it wouldn't be a lie. I thought about you more than I thought about any woman. Before . . . that was a long time ago. I had things to do and places to go. What we had . . . well, it was fine, but we both knew it couldn't last . . . we both knew that, Sunny."

"You're wrong, Cade. I never knew that. I wanted it to last. I loved you, don't you remember? Tell me another lie and say you remember."

"Eighteen years is a long time," Cade said, his throat constricting at the open, hungry look on her face. Who said people change? Whoever said change affected Sunday Waters? She might be wearing her hair differently and she might smell different, but she was still the same. There was that ever-present vulnerability in her glance and the sexy pout of her full, shapely mouth that just bordered on trembling. She was still that young girl who had clung to him out of shame and fear. People who were born on the wrong side of the tracks like Sunday Waters and Cader Harris never changed. Times changed, circumstances changed, but never the people.

Cader leaned his elbows on the polished bar, his drink sitting in front of him. The Lemon Drop Inn was new in town. At least it had been established during his absence. It was nice, in a New York style, polished and plush with a separate dining area. He had seen better and he'd seen worse. For a town like Hayden, this was definitely better.

In the wide frosted mirror behind the bartender, Cader's eyes followed Sunday as she went about her duties. He could hear her soft, husky laugh. Her figure was better than ever—fuller, more womanly, although it hadn't lost the girlish firmness and smooth curves. Men looked admiringly at Sunday, openly appraising her.

Cader realized he was frowning because of something someone said that made her laugh. He recognized the expression in the man's eyes as he looked at Sunday and it annoyed him. No, things hadn't changed that much. The boys had become men, and now, instead of leering at Sunday Waters, they lusted.

Taking a swallow of his drink, Cader suppressed the old, dredged-up feelings of possessiveness and protectiveness. Sunday didn't need him anymore. She had learned to handle herself. Regret made his drink taste bitter. Then he caught a glimpse of Sunday's face as she turned away from the table to take the order to the kitchen. There, buried behind the glossy facade of sophistication, was still that scared little-girl expression. Somehow, his drink tasted sweeter.

When Sunny Water left the Lemon Drop Inn, she was only slightly surprised to find Cader Harris parked beside her in the lot. She walked over to him as he leaned out the window, the lamppost light falling on his blond hair and making it silver. His dark eyes bordered by those incredibly long lashes looked up at her and she felt her knees go weak. "Shall I follow you home or do you want me to drive you?" It was a statement more than a question. Just like Cader, bypassing all the amenities and getting right to the heart.

"Follow me," she heard herself say. As she was driving down Main Street to her apartment over the boutique, she went over all the games she might have played with him. She might have played hard to get, but that wasn't her style and no one knew that better than Cader. It had been so long, so damn long, and yet here she was getting wet between her legs. *Pavlov's dogs!* She grimaced. *One look at Cader and a bell goes off in my head and my pussy starts to lather.*

Sunny fumbled with the key in the lock, distracted by Cader's presence pressed against her back. Finally, the door opened and her hand reached for the light switch. He gripped her wrist, pulling her hand to his mouth and pressing his lips to her palm. "Don't touch the lights, Sunny, we don't need them, do we? Don't we remember each other as though it were only yesterday?" His voice was husky, sweet. His mouth had come so close to her ear that she could feel his breath against her neck.

Somehow, the door closed behind them. Without ceremony he pulled her against him. She could feel the length of him, the hardness of his body, the quivering jump of the muscles in his back through his light sport jacket. Her mouth met his hungrily, washing away the years they had been apart, kindling all the excitement just being near him could bring.

He followed her into her bedroom and inhaled the fragrance of her perfume that had permeated the draperies and bedspread and mingled with the spicy aroma of hair spray and talcum powder. "I wanted you to see my apartment," she said softly. "I wanted you to see how far I've come since we lived on the wrong side of the tracks."

"Shh," he murmured, "I'll see it all later. Right now, I just want to look at you." He reached down to the bedside table and flicked on the night lamp; it glowed dimly, illuminating the room in a pale pinkish glow. "Let me see you, Sunny."

Sunny gasped, was it possible he remembered the first time they were together like this, in the run-down shack he lived in with his father? They had been alone that night too. His father had been out at Aunt Cledie's on a binge, and Cade had assured her they wouldn't be disturbed. That night too, after he had kissed her and petted her and told her that he wanted her, loved her, he had whispered, "Let me see you, Sunny," as he reached down to undo the zipper on her skirt.

It was like being in a whirlpool, in water that was blood warm. The past and present were becoming confused in her mind. She was sixteen again and she loved Cader Harris, and she was on the brink of her first sexual experience. There was no right or wrong; there was only Cader and the fulfillment that he promised by the touch of his fingers caressing her breasts and touching her tenderly between her legs. He made her feel beautiful; he made her feel desirable. He made her want to give to him. Give, give, give, wholeheartedly, without reservation.

Slowly he undressed her, tenderly he touched her, pressing his mouth lovingly against her soft flesh. She heard herself moaning with pleasure. His lips ignited tiny flames of fire that she had thought were long dead. At the very last he unpinned her hair, running his fingers through it and pulling it down around her shoulders.

"You're so beautiful, Sunny. So beautiful," he whispered before he sat down on the edge of the bed and pressed his head against her flat stomach.

She wanted to be beautiful for him. She wanted to make him happy, bring him pleasure. In Cader's pleasure she would find her own, just as he had taught her to do when she was fourteen. He laid her down on the bed, leaning over her, caressing her mouth with his own, licking at her lips, probing deeper with his tongue. She offered her mouth to him, answering his kisses, touching his lips with the tip of her tongue in the way she knew he liked.

His mouth left hers and pressed against the fragrant column of her neck while his hands explored her gently, tentatively, softly. Over her breasts and down the flat of her stomach to her haunches. Silkily gliding over her flesh, arousing in her a fever that came down to her from the past to make the present sweeter. No longer was she that shy tittle girl, afraid of her own responses, needing to be gentled like a wild colt. She opened herself to him willingly, expectantly, waiting for his remembered caress, feeling his mouth travel the length of her until he found her center. A shudder went through her as her thighs yielded to him and the bed sank beneath his weight. He fell to his knees and stroked and explored her with his lips.

She watched him as he undressed and carelessly dropped his clothes into a heap on the floor. He was beautiful. The promise of his slenderness as a boy had come to fruition in the hard-muscled flesh of the man. His chest was broad, his arms powerful, his hips narrow. The golden hair on his chest threaded over his taut stomach to bloom again in a darker grove between his thighs. His legs were long and well-muscled, but it was to the darkness between his legs that her eyes returned.

She reached out her hand to touch him, her fingers lovingly grazing his maleness and falling between his thighs. She propped herself on her elbow, drawing him closer with her hand, her mouth finding him and taking pleasure from the sound of his indrawn breath.

"God, Sunny. Your mouth, your beautiful mouth . . ." he whispered so quietly she thought she was imagining it. His hands touched her head, her neck, her shoulders. ". . . Oh, Sunny, your mouth." She brought him closer still, holding him, her palms on the smooth roundness of his haunches. "Love me, Sunny. I need you to love me. . . ."

He pulled away from her, slipping himself from between her lips and pushing her back against the bed, following her, pressing against the length of her. When he kissed her, she could taste herself on his mouth, knew he could taste himself on hers and the thought excited her.

His mouth tasted her, relished her, devoured her as it covered her breasts, her midriff, her haunches. His hands stroked her, loved her, took possession of her as he moved between her thighs.

Sunny's eyes closed, her lips parted, her body undulated against his exploring, tantalizing fingers. She reached down and grasped him in her palm and held his throbbing virility in her hand and began to rub it against her wet, yearning body, murmuring over and over, "Love me, Cade . . . love me."

She felt him rise and envelop her in his powerful arms, kissing her, his tongue coming into her open mouth. She opened herself to him so that he might come into her and fill the pulsating emptiness and yearning inside her. He entered her, the velvet tip entering slowly, ever so slowly and gently, pausing, waiting, demanding that she reach out for him and take him into her warm moistness.

He watched her, his eyes studying her face. Eyes heavy with desire, he saw the same emotion reflected in her smoky, glazed depths. She was beautiful, so beautiful, and never more beautiful than now. Time had not changed her; there was still that sweet innocence about her full mouth and the same honesty in her eyes. Even now, on the brink of orgasm, her eyes widened in surprise, as though this were a totally new experience, as though this were her first time. A smile broke on her lips, she gazed up at him, eyes shining, as though he had given her a wonderful gift.

Cader began to move within her, thrusting gently, becoming more insistent. Thrusting and withdrawing, taking his pleasure from her, immersing himself in the soft, honeyed flesh she offered. She offered and he took, pushing against her, burying himself within her, filling her with a savage, insatiable hunger that demanded more . . . more!

She welcomed him, met each thrust with one of her own. Taking him, holding him, wanting him deeper, deeper and deeper. Undulating her hips in a slow, swaying circle to his insistent rhythm.

Together they reached remembered heights. Ecstasy became heaving, curling waves of indescribable rapture.

Sunny lay with her head on Cader's shoulder. His arm around her offered comfort, and tears threatened to spill from her eyes. How long she had wanted this, prayed he'd come back for her. And now he was here. "Cader, why did you come back to Hayden?" she asked softly, wanting to hear him say he'd come back to be with her.

"Hmmmn?"

"I asked you why you'd come back to Hayden. You've always hated this town. What made you come back?"

"You know, Sunny. Why do I have to tell you?" His voice was sleepy, but he couldn't fool her. Cader Harris never went to sleep on a woman, not even in his callous youth.

She propped herself on her elbow and looked down at him. "I don't know, Cade. I want you to tell me."

He looked up at her in a pretense of nonchalance. "I came back to open the sporting goods store." He could see in her frank appraisal that she didn't believe him. Suddenly, it wasn't necessary to lie. Sunny knew the score and he'd always been able to be honest with her. No matter what he did, no matter how he had betrayed her with other girls, she had always taken him back.

Sunny never played games. She had come from the same side of the tracks as he had and she knew what a hard climb it was to get to the other side. If there was one person in this whole fucking world who would understand what he was doing in Hayden and why, that person was Sunday Waters.

"I'm here doing a job for Delta Oil," he told her, expecting to see surprise in her frank gaze. Instead, she nestled back against his shoulder.

"I thought it must be something like that. I knew you couldn't have changed that much. Being a merchant just isn't your style. Tell me about it. Maybe I can help."

Cader told her. "So, if I can change the town's opinion by a little careful persuasion, there's quite a bit in it for me, Sunny. I don't have much to show for my career on the gridiron. My plane, a little in the bank and some big plans. This time I won't be so foolish."

"How much is in it for you, Cade?" she asked, nuzzling her lips against his neck.

"A quarter of a mil and a contract as public relations spokesman. It'll mean commercials and advertising. There's a lot of money in that, babe, and I mean to cash in. And the contract is open; I'd be free to endorse other products. Once it gets around that a big outfit like Delta is using me in advertising, the offers will come rolling in." She heard the satisfaction in his tone.

"And then what, Cader? After you cash in, I mean."

"Then I'm going to have to blow this town. There's no way I can stay here, not after people realize that I was just feathering my own nest with *their* feathers."

"And then what?" she asked hopefully, waiting to hear him say that he meant to take her with him.

Cader was silent as his hand moved possessively over her face, bringing her mouth to his once again. In the urgency of her renewed need for him she forgot that he'd never answered her question.

CHAPTER NINE

❧eli McDermott transferred the contents of her shoulder bag to a flat clutch. Now the heavier bag wouldn't be weighing her down. Sometimes, she would almost forget the dull ache in the left side and hang the shoulder bag there, wincing with pain every time the leather swung against her body.

A last, cautious look around the room and she knew she couldn't postpone the inevitable a moment longer. If she dallied now, she would be late and Gene would be annoyed with her. It was time to go, time to put all thoughts from her mind, time to think of nothing else save the visit to Marc Baldwin's office.

The beige sheath blended with her tawny skin, and her rope sandals and clutch bag made her seem all of a piece, she noted as she walked toward the door with its long, narrow mirror. Was that beige person her? Where was her life and color? Would she slowly fade away to nothingness, this slim, beige person who was closing the door now and walking into the kitchen?

Gene rinsed and placed his coffee cup in the dishwasher, his eyes on Keli, making his movements awkward and clumsy. How beautiful she was. He would make certain nothing happened to her even if it meant making a punching bag out of Marc Baldwin. No one was going to hurt her or mar her.

"I'm ready, Gene. Do you have the checkbook?" she asked quietly.

"No problem, honey. Now there's nothing for you to worry about. Nothing is going to happen to you; no one is going to hurt you. Trust me, honey," he said, putting his arm around her shoulder comfortingly. "You don't even have to go there if you don't want to," he coaxed, hoping she would take his suggestion. "It's a simple matter of a phone call."

"Gene, please, I must know what is wrong with me. . . ."

"All right, honey," he sighed.

Tears gathered in Keli's dark chocolate eyes as Gene led her toward the waiting car that would take her to Marc Baldwin's office.

The waiting room was empty, the air conditioner whirring softly as bright afternoon sunshine spilled through the separation in the drapes. Keli walked over to the receptionist's desk, glad that Marsha wasn't working here today. She didn't want Marsha to take her under her wing the way Gene was doing. They were so alike in so many ways, she thought wearily. Her husband and her best friend imposed themselves on her. This was *her* business, *her* body. She should be allowed to do this for herself.

The middle-aged woman at the desk looked up, her skin ruddy against the stark white of her uniform. "Your name, please?"

"Mrs. Keli McDermott."

"If there's one thing I appreciate, it's a patient who arrives on time." The receptionist smiled, striving to put this lovely woman before her at ease. A quick look at her notes beside each name on the appointment book told her why Keli had come to see the doctor. A shame, a tragedy, her eyes said.

Keli's oblique glance narrowed slightly as she correctly interpreted the look the receptionist was bestowing on her. "Mrs. McDermott," she heard the receptionist say, "is this your first visit with Dr. Baldwin?"

Keli nodded.

"In that case you wouldn't mind filling out this information sheet, would you?" She slipped a long, yellow sheet of paper out of the desk drawer and handed it to Keli.

"Do you have a pen? Never mind, here, use this one." The woman smiled, suddenly made uneasy by Keli's quiet manner. "You can sit over there with your husband."

Keli took her place beside Gene on the soft, apple-green bench that rested against a matching wall. She was glad Gene hadn't picked the beige chairs next to the beige wall covered in heavy burlap. She couldn't bear to be part of the office even if it was only for a few moments. She needed color . . . she needed life. She needed . . . God, how she needed.

Gene helped her fill out the information sheet. She was surprised that she was able to hold the pen—her insides were quaking. Yet her hand was steady, her handwriting smooth. When she had finished, Gene took it back to the receptionist.

"Thank you," she murmured, giving the paper a cursory glance. "Mrs. McDermott, if you'll please come with me. You can get ready while the doctor is on the phone."

Keli stood, her knees feeling as though they would buckle beneath her. She followed the white uniform into an examining room, Gene close behind.

It wasn't until the receptionist turned to close the door behind Keli that she noticed Gene. Her expression showed her surprise. "Er . . . Mr. McDermott, why don't you wait outside? Mrs. McDermott is in good hands, I assure you. . . ."

Gene pushed his way into the small cubicle. "I'm staying with my wife," he said gruffly, daring the woman to contradict him. "She needs me."

"This is quite unusual. . . ."

"I don't give a damn, I'm staying!" His voice rose in anger, his tone commanding.

The receptionist glanced at Keli, who was slowly unbuttoning the front of her dress. "If Mrs. McDermott has no objections . . ."

"Why the hell should she? I'm her husband."

The woman hastily handed Keli a paper gown and quickly retreated from the room. The doctor wasn't going to like this, not at all. She closed the door behind her, leaving Gene and Keli alone.

"Here, let me help you with that," Gene murmured solicitously as he helped Keli out of her dress. He was about to unfold the paper gown and slip it over her when he saw Keli lifting the hem of her slip.

"What are you doing?"

"I can't be examined with my clothes on, Gene," she said softly.

"Here, let me help you, then," he offered, deciding not to argue. His hands gently grazed her skin as he pulled the lace-edged garment over her head and dropped it onto the circular stool. He unhooked her bra and removed it, his eyes traveling to her breasts, searching for a change in their symmetry. Keli stepped out of her panties and took the paper gown from the examining table and poked her arms through the slits. She climbed up onto the table, her feet hanging over the sides. Gene bent to undo the buckles of her sandals. She almost told him it wouldn't be necessary, then decided it didn't make any difference. Besides, it gave him something to do. His hands touched her slim ankles as he removed her shoes. Tentatively, she felt him caress her leg, sliding his fingers over her smooth, honey-colored skin. Keli squeezed her eyes shut. It had been so long since Gene had touched her this way. She didn't want him to touch her, to caress her, to explore her. It was too indicative of what their whole marriage had been based on. Gene, touching her, caressing her, as he would a fine piece of art. Then he would hold her against him and lie down beside her, his arms wrapped possessively around her. And then, nothing. How ashamed she had been those times when his gentle hands had elicited a response in her, when her body cried out to be loved, loved as a woman wanted to be loved. Poor Gene, she thought, a tear forming in the corner of her eye. He knew, he had felt her need for her husband to love her, to make love to her, to give her children. Sometimes he would cry, great heaving sobs, and she would hold him and comfort him. They never spoke of it; words were meaningless and wouldn't change anything.

Marc Baldwin knocked on the door before entering. Keli could see he wasn't surprised to find Gene with her. The receptionist had warned him. "Hello, Keli. Gene."

They both nodded perfunctorily.

"Gene, why don't you wait outside? This can't be very pleasant for you, and sometimes a husband can make things more difficult for the patient. . . ."

"I'm staying. I'm Keli's husband and I'm staying." Gene glared at him defiantly.

Marc's eyes flew to Keli. "It means so much to him, doctor," she said resignedly.

"All right, then. Look, Gene, sit over there and try to keep out of my way."

Gene picked Keli's clothes off the stool and held them on his lap, obediently following Marc's directions.

Marc unhurriedly began his examination procedure. Blood pressure. Temperature. Reflexes. "All right, Keli, now if you'll just lie back."

Gene watched as Keli lay back on the table, the crisp paper beneath her slim body rustling. He watched as Marc Baldwin lowered the paper gown to Keli's waist and placed his hands on her right breast.

"Lift your arm over your head, Keli. That's right." His fingers probed, touched, massaging her breast, squeezing the coral nipple gently. "Now the left," he murmured tonelessly.

Gene's eyes followed Marc's fingers as he began the examination of Keli's left breast. Then back to the right, back to the left. There was something wrong. Keli flinched each time Marc touched the soft flesh on the outer side of her left breast. Time and again Marc's fingers returned to that spot.

"Okay, Keli. Now just slide down on the table and I'll help you put your feet in the stirrups. . . ."

"The hell you will!" Gene burst out, standing suddenly, Keli's clothes dropping to the floor. "Get away from her!"

"What the hell's the matter with you, man?" Marc challenged.

"You're not going to touch her down there! She came in because of something in her breast."

"Now, look! This is routine." Marc was beginning to perspire. The grape-sized nodule in Keli's left breast was highly suspect and filled him with the same sense of dread he experienced whenever the possibility of cancer reared its ugly head.

"Routine or not, get away from her!"

"Gene . . . please . . ." Keli's voice was almost a whimper.

"No! He's not going to touch you!"

Keli turned her face to the wall.

"I thought you came here for help," Marc persisted. Keli was in trouble and he needed to complete the examination. Often abnormalities in the breasts were reflected in the reproductive organs. "Don't make this any harder on Keli than it already is," Marc said authoritatively.

Gene seemed to acquiesce. Marc persisted. "Now, sit down over there and be quiet!" To his amazement, Gene obeyed, his squarish head lowered in resignation.

Marc quickly positioned Keli and began the examination. He was relieved not to find any swelling or growth. Skillfully, he took a smear from her cervix and dropped the prepared slide into an envelope with her name on it. He couldn't find any signs of abnormality but what he did find was just as puzzling. Keli's hymen was still intact! Keli was still a virgin. Marc's eyes fell on Gene, who was still sitting there with his head hanging. Now he understood his reluctance to have Keli examined. Marc shook his head. Christ, you just never knew! Here was Gene McDermott, all man, all Air Corps, and he probably couldn't get it up. Marc helped Keli up to a sitting position, determined not to add to her discomfort by showing any sign that he had discovered their secret.

"You can get dressed now, Keli," Marc said as he turned quickly to avoid looking into her frightened eyes. "We'll talk in my office. Why don't you wait for Keli in the waiting room, Gene . . . ?"

"I'll wait right here," the colonel interrupted fiercely, his face reddening with fury. His arms crossed threateningly over his massive chest.

"Have it your way," Marc answered shortly as he closed the door behind him.

"Get dressed, honey," Gene said softly as he wrapped the crisp white sheet around her shoulders to cover her nakedness. "Remember what I told you. No one is going to hurt you or do anything to you."

"Yes, Gene, I remember," Kell sighed as she slipped from the cold table and picked up her clothing. Before she turned her back on her husband to begin dressing, she gave Gene a last little-girl-lost look.

The colonel sensed Keli's terror and his heart sank. He knew Marc Baldwin had found something, otherwise he would have set their fears to rest immediately.

In his quiet, booklined office Marc Baldwin sat solemnly in his swivel chair, his gaze fixed on the partially open door. He licked at dry lips and breathed deeply when he saw Gene McDermott hold the door open for Keli and usher her solicitously to a deep leather chair.

Marc cleared his throat and began talking. His eyes were warm and compassionate as he addressed Keli. "It is suspect, the lump. I want to arrange a mammography for you, at once. But I'm certain of the results. It will have to come out, the sooner the better. I'll make an appointment for you with Doctor Adam Clayton in New Orleans. He'll want to examine you, and, of course, run the mammography test. For now, I can give you some literature to look over. I don't want you to be frightened, Keli. Clayton is a good man, some say he's the best."

"No operations, Baldwin!" Gene McDermott snapped, jumping to his feet. "No one is cutting into Keli ! And there won't be any other appointments either! Did you hear me? No one is cutting into Keli!"

Astounded, Marc Baldwin stared at the man who was daring to take responsibility for his wife's life. Her very life! He turned away from Gene, ignoring him. His gaze was directed at Keli, who was huddled down in the deep chair, fear distorting her lovely features. "This is not your husband's decision, Keli," he said softly, hoping his words were getting through to her. "You must decide for yourself. From a medical point of view, you have no other choice."

There it was again. That word. *Choice.* Decision. Choice. "I understand, Marc," she whispered, not daring to raise her eyes to meet Gene's.

"I'm waiting, Keli." Marc pierced her with a questioning look. "I'm waiting for you to tell me to go ahead and make the appointment for you with Dr. Clayton in New Orleans. No, no, don't look to Gene, this is *your life, your* decision." Behind him he could feel the colonel was about to explode. He imagined it was the feeling a matador gets when the bull was charging for his back.

Keli's head bowed, her long silky hair forming a curtain between herself and the rest of the world. Gene sniffed loudly and Marc anticipated another outburst. But Keli raised her head, her eyes tearless, her mouth set in a grim line and a look of hopelessness on her face that quelled her husband's outburst.

Softly, she said, "You do not understand, Marc. You have no idea of the kindness my husband has shown me . . . me and my family. Without him, his love for me, we would have all perished in the war." She said this without an excess of emotion, but her eyes fell on Gene and delivered a message of gratitude and respect. She looked back at Marc Baldwin, her gaze level and direct. "I will not disobey my husband."

Marc understood. But she was so young, so lovely to be bound by such loyalty and with so much at stake. "Keli, I understand, believe me, I do." He leaned forward, over his desk, his hands clasped in front of him. "I am your doctor."

Keli knew he was referring to the examination just a few minutes before. He was aware she was still a virgin. He knew that Gene had never claimed her as his wife.

Suddenly, Marc slammed his fist down on the desk, papers ruffling. "Damn it, Keli! It's your life we're talking about here, not some cultural belief! Gene is your husband. He's only a man! Don't, I beg you, don't allow his fears, his terrors to stop you from preserving your own life!"

Gene had had more than enough of this. He stood abruptly, his bulk seeming to fill the room, his rage seeming to suck all the air. "C'mon, honey, we're getting out of here." Roughly, he pulled her up from the chair, causing her to wince with pain.

Keli stood, pulled to her feet by Gene's force. She leveled him a calm, unblinking stare and extricated her arm from his fingers. She turned and left the office without another glance at the doctor or her husband.

Out in the parking lot she raised her eyes to see a swoop of starlings circling in the sky. Even birds made decisions. To fly or not to fly. She had to decide between life or death. Even then there would be no guarantees. If she disobeyed Gene, she could die anyway and she would have disgraced her family, her husband. If she disobeyed Gene and lived, she would be in disgrace.

Keli stumbled once on her way to the car. She threw her hands out in front of her and balanced herself. She smiled. Of course she wanted to live. Just the way she had caught herself from falling and doing herself possible harm. She wanted to live. Life was her choice. Somehow, she had to make Gene understand.

Marc Baldwin felt his insides churn. He'd handled Gene and Keli all wrong. He should have disregarded the fact that they were personal acquaintances; he should have been more professional. He shouldn't have allowed the colonel to get under his skin; he shouldn't have involved himself at all, he finally decided. *That's right*, he thought, disgusted with himself, *always take the coward's way out.*

"Nothing personal, Keli, but if you have cancer, I don't want to know it. You may be calm and serene and believe in destiny and all that stuff, but, you see, I have trouble holding on to my breakfast when I'm confronted with a life-and-death situation." The sound of his own voice brought a taste of bitter gall into his mouth. What the hell was wrong with him? What kind of doctor was he? "I should have been a dermatologist. No house calls, no worries, no life-and-death decisions. If a rash doesn't clear up in two weeks, it will in a month. No need to get involved."

Suddenly, before he could change his mind, he picked up the

phone near his left arm and told his receptionist-secretary to get hold of Adam Clayton in New Orleans. He'd at least inform Adam of Keli's case and ask, as a personal favor, for him to see her without delay when and if she decided to seek consultation.

While he was waiting for Dr. Clayton's return phone call, Marc busied himself with two pregnant patients and happily announced that everything was progressing normally with each of them. Later, while going over his case files, the phone on his desk rang.

"Doctor Clayton returning your call, Doctor Baldwin," Marion announced in her most professional tone.

"Put him through."

"Marc? How are ya? How's your golf game?" Adam Clayton, surgeon, asked in his congenial, Southern accent.

"Just up to par," Marc answered tonelessly. "Look, I'm not calling you to wrangle an invitation to play on that fancy golf course you've got down there in N'Orleans. I'm after another favor."

"What's up, Doc?" Clayton joked.

"Cut the shit, will ya? I'm not in the mood."

"Sorry, Marc. What can I do for you?" Clayton leveled his tone and asked somberly. His physician's antennae snapped to attention and signaled an alert. It would be about a patient, he knew. How often had he heard that same note in his own voice when a situation was critical?

"I've got this patient, name's Keli McDermott," Marc began without ceremony as he went on to describe Keli's condition.

"How's she handling the pain?" Adam Clayton asked while penciling notes as Marc spoke.

"So far, so good."

"It can get worse, a lot worse," Clayton said flatly.

"Yeah, I know."

"Sounds to me as though you've made an accurate diagnosis from what you tell me. Of course, you'll need tests to back you up."

"Yes, and that's where the problem arises." Succinctly, he told his colleague of the problem between Gene and Keli, omitting his findings when he had examined Keli internally, telling him only that there didn't seem to be any involvement of the reproductive organs.

"Tell me what I can do for you, Marc. You know there's nothing you can do unless this woman seeks medical attention. You sound as though you're pretty much involved with her. It's hard, I know it is, but . . ." Marc could envision Adam shrugging his burly shoulders when he didn't complete his statement.

"I want you to see her. That is, *if* she decides to . . . Shit, Adam! When the pain gets bad enough, they'll come to me for the answers. What I want is for you to handle it when they're ready. I only hope it's soon enough to save her. Take down her name and have your secretary keep on the alert. If she calls, give her an immediate appointment. Okay?"

"You've got it! Listen, is there anything I can do in the meantime? You say you and Julia see the McDermotts socially. Perhaps you can talk to the man, try to make him understand."

"Adam, that bastard doesn't want to understand. He's afraid his beautiful wife will be mutilated and he can't handle that."

"Look, that's what I'm getting at. Hold out some hope for the guy. You say this girl is an Oriental, right? Small breasts, right? Did you say anything about breast reconstruction? It can be done within a year after surgery."

"I'm not up on these new techniques, Adam. I've heard about it, read about it, but I didn't know it was in widespread use."

"It's not. At least it wasn't until women discovered there was such a thing and began demanding it. There was a gal up in New York who brought her plastic surgeon into the operating room during her mastectomy. We've had several cases right here in N' Orleans. The results are spectacular! Some of the old relics in the surgery service are against it but not me. Hell! If a little bag of silicone can give a woman back her self-confidence, I'm all for it!"

"No kidding! What about the nipple?"

"The surgeon takes it off and grafts it onto the woman's thigh or groin area. When she's ready for reconstruction, he grafts it back into place. In the cases where the mastectomy was performed without preparation for reconstruction, a small circle of vaginal tissue substitutes. The results are fantastic. Tell you what, I'll send you some literature and the best of the photos. You can show them to this McDermott guy and let him see for himself. If it is cancer, it may just give his wife something to live for. Christ, can you imagine being married to someone who's only interested in your physical attributes and doesn't give a shit whether the person you are lives or dies? Christ! Someone should do a frontal lobotomy on that guy."

CHAPTER TEN

———— ❦ ————

*J*ulia Baldwin cast a critical eye over her dinner table and was satisfied that even Irene would not be able to find fault. A quick glance at the sunburst clock on the wall of the dining room told her she had a little over an hour till the first guests started to arrive. Where was Marc? Surely, he wouldn't be late, not tonight, when he knew she was having a dinner party. Her mind raced—was anyone due to deliver? No, only Sara Dunlap and she still had a month to go. Where was he?

Halfway up the polished stairway, she heard his key in the lock. Finally. Not bothering to turn around, she called over her shoulder for him to hurry. She would lay out his clothes while he showered, since he didn't like it when she steamed up the bathroom.

Marc tossed his medical bag onto the foyer table and didn't bother to answer Julia. What good would it do if he told her he needed a drink—a drink to wash out the taste and thoughts of Gene McDermott. Ever since the consultation in his office he couldn't think about anything but Keli and Gene. "Damn!" he muttered to himself as he climbed the stairs. Tonight he would have to keep his mind on dinner table conversation. Dinner table conversation that would all be about Delta Oil. Everyone would voice an opinion and then they would all talk it to death. Irene Thomas could talk the hide off a buffalo if she got the chance. Christ, how was he going to keep his mind on what was going on if Keli and Gene sat within eye range of him? How would the obnoxious colonel behave? He knew how Keli would act, quiet and serene like she always was. "Damn it to hell," he mumbled as he stripped down and entered the shower.

Marsha Evans removed her ruffled apron and stood looking at her sullen daughter. "You barely touched your dinner, Judy. Is something wrong? Is something bothering you?"

Marsha felt her brows knit into a frown as she watched Judy

toy with the food on her plate. "Why don't you have a few of your friends over for a little television or to play some records? Are you just going to mope around all night?"

"I'm in the mood to mope tonight; is that all right with you? You mope when you feel like it; why can't I? Is that dress new? You never bought new dresses when Daddy took you out to dinner," she accused.

"Judy, that was a long time ago. When are you going to understand that the divorce was not *all* my fault? It takes two people to make a marriage or a divorce. You can't go on blaming me the rest of your life. You're old enough to understand that being miserable is no way to live."

"And now Daddy's dead," Judy said, jumping up from the table and running from the room.

Marsha sat down at the wrought-iron table and nestled her face in her cupped hands. Patience, she warned herself. Judy would come around. She had already taken long strides since the accident. This was no time to cry, she told herself. If she cried, she would have to redo her eye makeup, and she wouldn't be ready when Cader Harris arrived. She could always cry later, when she was in bed with the lights out and no one was around.

Cader Harris stretched his neck and straightened his tie before he rang Marsha's doorbell. He wished he'd worn his white sport jacket and slacks, with his copper silk shirt which he always left unbuttoned halfway down his chest. Women liked skin and masculine gold chains. Instead, he had worn his dark blue suit with shirt and tie. Hell, if you wanted to do business with people it was always a good idea to at least try and look like them. His lip curled in distaste. He *never* wanted to look like the local yokels in Hayden.

The door opened, revealing Marsha standing there in some kind of green thing that hugged her curves. "Hello, Cader. What's so funny? You look like the cat that swallowed the canary."

"I was just thinking about a cat," he answered, widening his grin.

From the way his eyes flicked approvingly over her, Marsha figured *she* was the cat. "How about a drink before we go," she said warmly.

"Why not?" Cade grinned. "Double Scotch will be fine. Nice place you've got here," he added, roaming through the living room and pretending interest. When she handed him the squat glass containing the amber liquor, he took a long pull from his drink and sized up the woman before him. She was beautiful in a sultry kind of way. The dark of her hair whitened her skin, lending it a luminescent glow. He liked the way her brows winged upward toward her temples and the way her full mouth lent itself easily to a smile. And her figure was excellent, long limbed and full breasted. It always had been, ever since he could remember.

But even in school Marsha had been a "hands off, eyes only" kind of girl. And there was no reason to assume her attitudes had changed.

Uncomfortable because of Cader's scrutiny, Marsha stammered, "We'd better be going; we don't want to be late."

"Who's going to be at Julia's tonight?" he asked as he led her out the door and to his car.

"Same old crowd. Julia and Marc, of course. And there's a new couple in town, Gene and Keli McDermott. I suppose the Guthries will be there, they always are somehow. Oh, you wouldn't know, but Marvin Guthrie is Hayden's mayor now. Do you remember him?"

"Little fat guy, isn't he?" Cader climbed behind the wheel and inserted the key into the ignition.

"That's him," Marsha laughed. "And I think Damion Conway will be there. And of course, Arthur and Irene Thomas." She eyed him covertly to see how the mention of Irene's name would affect him. Seeing no response, Marsha settled down in her seat.

"Somehow, I never figured you for a vulture, Marsha." His statement was offered matter-of-factly but it had the required results.

"Cader?"

"Don't pretend ignorance. You know perfectly well what I mean. You wanted to see if you could get a rise out of me by mentioning Irene. Well, even if it didn't show, you did. I've been wondering when I would run into her. Tonight's as good a time as any."

"Cader, I'm sorry, I didn't mean . . . Yes, I guess I did mean," Marsha sighed. "No one ever understood why you left for college the way you did and why Irene married Arthur Thomas when she'd never shown the slightest interest in him. Guess I was just feeding my curiosity."

"That's okay," he excused her, patting her hand. "Friends, right?"

"Friends."

"Okay, old buddy, I'll tell you. Sure, I want to see Irene, I don't suppose I've ever really gotten over her. We really had something going for a while. But, you know, it was the old bit about the right boy from the wrong side of the tracks and the little princess. I just wasn't good enough for her; old man Hayden made that pretty clear."

"This is where we turn," Marsha instructed, sorry that Julia's house wasn't farther away. She had the distinct impression that Cader would have gone on talking, telling her, after all these years, what exactly had come between himself and Princess Irene Hayden Thomas.

Irene sat beside her father as he wove the long Lincoln through the narrow streets. Her nerves were taut and she kept glancing at Foster Doyle. Nothing in life seemed fair somehow. When she had learned earlier that evening that Arthur had unexpected commitments at the funeral home, which would prevent him from accompanying her to Julia's party, she had bubbled with secret delight. If only Foster Doyle hadn't been there when Arthur called and insisted that he would take Arthur's place as her escort. Foster Doyle might be a crafty old fox, but he wasn't going to outfox his own daughter. He knew as well as Irene that Cader Harris would be at Julia's tonight, and he intended to make sure Irene's emotions didn't lead her astray.

Foster Doyle maneuvered the car toward the curb and threw the gear shift into park. Irene waited for him to come around to the passenger side and open the door for her. She would have been quite willing to open it for herself and was annoyed that she forced herself to sit there, as her father expected, while he played the gentleman.

Irene drew in her breath and felt her heart pounding in her chest as Foster Doyle held the door open and she saw Cader Harris in the flesh for the first time in more than eighteen years. He was the same. Tall and brawny, blond and handsome, with still a hint of the boy about him. Were her eyes playing tricks on her? Time was the ancient ravager, why should Cader have escaped it? Suddenly, she was nervous and unsure of herself. She wished she had had more notice that he was coming back to town. She could have prepared better. Started on that diet sooner, taken more time for facials. What would he see when he looked at her? What would she read in his eyes? She had had opportunities to see Cader before this, Kevin working for him being the most plausible one. But she hadn't availed herself of the right to visit her son at the sporting goods store. She had been too frightened, more so of what she wouldn't see in Cader's eyes than of what response she would find there. And now she drank in the sight of him and reveled in the sensuous pull of his magnetism.

Irene was simultaneously aware of her father's controlled astonishment when he fastened his eyes on the tall bulk of Cader Harris, Cader's wry smile and the static shock waves charging through her. It was Irene who spoke to Cader and Marsha as they advanced toward the house. She held out her hand and Cader took it in his. "Welcome back to Hayden, Cader."

Harris's eyes widened as he held Irene's hand. Jesus. Was this Irene Hayden? This regal, soft-spoken woman who had enough class and good looks to depose Princess Grace? He grinned, showing perfect white teeth. "It's good to be back," he answered, a surge of long-remembered tenderness softening his voice.

Irene was surprised her hand was steady. How could she be so outwardly calm and be in such a turmoil on the inside? "It's nice to see you again, Cade."

"It really is true what they say on the commercials, isn't it?" Harris continued to grin, looking down into Irene's upturned face.

"What's that?" she asked coyly, almost knowing what he was going to answer.

"That you don't get older, just better."

"How nice of you," Irene rejoined demurely, to Marsha's astonishment. This wasn't the same simpering, flighty Irene. This was an attractive woman, no, a beautiful woman, looking up into the eyes of a man whom she found irresistibly attractive. There was no pose of the spoiled Southern belle in Irene's demeanor. Her gaze was frank and open and perhaps speculative, but certainly not simpering or self-indulgent. This was an Irene Marsha had never seen.

"I think we should be getting inside; we don't want to be late for Julia's 'happy hour.' After all, Cade, you are the guest of honor," Marsha said, taking him by the arm and tearing him away from Irene. She was the only woman in Hayden who could clutch with her eyes, Marsha thought nastily. Irene Hayden Thomas clutched with her eyes because she didn't have the guts to clutch with her hands.

Julia opened the door and smiled warmly at Cader Harris as she ushered the guests into the long, formal living room with a light, airy, "You know everyone, so why don't we just have our drinks and settle down to some cocktail chatter?"

Foster Doyle crossed the room, his back tall and straight, his distinguished gray hair smoothed close to his head, and seated himself in a high-backed Queen Anne chair near the fireplace. He lowered himself onto the chair and sat stiffly, hands placed firmly on knees, and seemed to preside over the room. By his posture and appearance he commanded attention and respect, like a Supreme Court judge deliberating his verdict.

As always, people were drawn to him. Marc Baldwin, Mayor and Mrs. Guthrie, Marsha Evans hovered near him, seeming to hang on his every word and basking in the attention the old man paid them.

Cader watched, sneering inwardly, half expecting to see them all kowtow in obeisance. Turning his scrutiny away from the silver-haired gentleman, he accepted his drink and smiled at Julia's guests, making each feel special under his gaze.

Julia settled herself in a low, comfortable chair—her eyes never leaving the muscular figure of Cader Harris. Her mind whirled and refused to focus on the conversation floating around her. God . . . he was good looking. Virile and . . . God . . . he was virile! Every woman in the room was looking at him. Was this the way it happened? Was this the way women decided to have affairs? Did they lock eyes with a man and know instinctively that sooner or later, preferably sooner, they would end up in bed together? She felt the beginnings of a flush on her cheeks. She let her eyes travel to her husband, Marc, who was saying something about the weather. He looked bored to death and mechanical. There was certainly no animal magnetism there. She turned her head to look at Cader Harris who was leaning against the mantel in the relaxed pose of a man about town. It never occurred to her that the pose was studied, and, if he had a pipe in his hand, he could have come right out of the pages of *Town and Country*. He was talking to Marvin Guthrie about the cost of freight, but his eyes were talking to every woman in the room.

Irene rose from her chair and moved across the room. She could feel Cader's eyes follow her as she moved past him. The silky fabric of her white jersey sheath hugged her hips and restrained the movement of her legs. Now, instead of feeling confining and restricting, it felt good against her limbs, brushing against her skin, sending a flush of pleasure through her. The back was draped in a long cowl, baring her superbly tanned skin to the waist and outlining the high swell of her buttocks. She knew it set her figure off to an advantage. An advantage, she knew from experience, Cader Harris would notice and appreciate.

Cader Harris took Irene's hand in his and smiled down at her. "I want you to sit here and tell me everything you've been doing since we last saw each other."

Irene felt deliciously wicked in this crowded room, aware of Foster Doyle's disapproval. For the first time in her life Irene didn't care what Daddy thought. She was all grown up now and she didn't need Daddy's blessing. She knew she was a full-grown woman; the proof was there in Cader's enveloping gaze.

She smiled up at him, her heart beating a rapid tempo. She should hate him. She should want to scratch his eyes out. He didn't even remember when they'd seen each other last, when they'd last spoken to each other. What they had meant to each other. But *she* couldn't forget. Did not want to. She only wanted to have him smile down at her the way he was doing and to listen to his voice, which still held a soft edge of a Southern accent. He liked her. She could see it in the way he looked at her. The years hadn't changed her that much. Out of the corner of her eye she saw Foster Doyle give her a forbidding look. It was a good thing he couldn't read her mind.

Irene listened to Cader as he spoke of inconsequential things, reminiscing on the past. Her thoughts were blown from her like leaves before a wind. She watched his hands, felt them as they reached for hers. They were gentle, warm . . . just as she had remembered, just as she had dreamed all those nights. All those years. Where did they go? How could you suddenly see someone you hadn't seen in so many years and have that time wiped away? You just couldn't erase eighteen years. Or could you, she asked herself. From the look in Cader's eyes, *he* thought you could.

While Cader and Irene were reminiscing, the doorbell rang and Colonel and Mrs. McDermott arrived. Keli McDermott accepted a drink from Gene, her face soft and serene as she gazed about Julia's graciously appointed living room.

Keli glanced over the rim of her glass to see Marsha staring at her. Quickly, Keli glanced away, swallowing hard, feeling the cold liquid burning her throat. She didn't want to talk to Marsha, didn't want to answer her questions and defend herself against a barrage of demands for explanations of why she wasn't taking Marc Baldwin's advice. Marsha would never understand, not the way Damion understood. She would harass Keli, saying things such as "It's your *life!* You've got to get another opinion. Why? Why? Why?"

Keli centered her attention on Cader Harris, the guest of honor. He was a forceful man, she decided. Even from here she could feel his presence, and he hadn't even spoken to her as yet. He reminded her of an animal prowling the confines of his cage, stopping every so often to peer between the bars, gauging his chances of luring some unsuspecting soul close enough to devour. She decided it was his eyes—sleepy eyes, strange eyes. Calculating eyes.

"Keli, Gene! How nice to see you," Damion Conway said, smiling down into Keli's lovely face.

"Reverend," Gene said curtly, acknowledging the minister.

"You look lovely tonight, Keli," Damion complimented. The slim-fitting slacks topped by a narrowly cut dress that came only to her knees and was slashed from the hem to the hip line on each side was reminiscent of the garments worn in her native Thailand. Even though the high neckline was opened to the top of her breasts, and the simple white dress was sleeveless in a compromise to Western apparel, the association was unmistakable. She was wearing her long silky hair twisted into a coronet on the top of her head, giving her unexpected height and revealing the graceful length of her slim neck. She was lovely, Damion thought, but it was in her eyes that her real beauty was to be found.

"Have you met our 'guest of honor'? No, stay here and I'll

bring him over and introduce you. Cade Harris and I go back a long time. Kids through school and then fraternity brothers at the university," Damion explained to Gene.

As Damion crossed the room to where Cader was talking to Irene, Keli's eyes followed him. If it weren't for the clerical collar, one would have thought Damion was a musician or an artist, or even a dancer. He was tall and lithe and his dark hair that always seemed to be a week past needing a haircut tumbled over his forehead in a casual, unruly manner, softening his slightly craggy, yet unmistakably handsome features. But it was his hands that revealed his sensitive, creative nature to Keli. Long and agile, fingers with slightly splayed tips, gentle hands, soothing hands.

Damion clapped Cade on the back, a smile pasted on his face. "Come over here; there's someone I want you to meet. You are the guest of honor at this shindig, aren't you?"

"Well, if it isn't the 'pun—' the local minister." Cader grinned, noticing the warning in Damion's eyes. He spread his arms loftily and grinned again, white teeth flashing. "You got it, old buddy, the guest of honor. Be happy to meet your friends. You should have gone into public relations, Damion. I never did think this preaching business was for you. What the hell do you get out of it? And don't give me any of that shit about inner satisfaction," Cade murmured as he walked beside Damion to the bar.

"Then I won't give you any. Actually, I'm going to devote my life to saving your soul: You *do* have one, don't you?"

"Hell, no! But I do have a cock which I use regularly. Can you say the same?"

"It might surprise you to know I have one too, but it wouldn't get the workout yours gets if I lived to be a hundred," Damion rejoined coldly.

"You shot your load back in college, is that it?"

"One of these days someone is going to put the screws to you, Harris, and I hope I'm around to see it. You have the balls of a Saint Bernard."

"At least I got 'em."

"You're up to something, Cade. I don't believe you'd ever come back to Hayden unless there's something in it for you. I'm going to watch you carefully, Cade. I mean it. These are my people and you're not going to do anything to hurt them."

"Fuck it, Damion. Watch me all you want. Just remember that the hand is quicker than the eye."

"Smile pretty, Cade, and try not to act like the animal you are." Coming up to Keli and Gene, Damion made the introductions. Damion's eyes were cloudy as he watched the handshakes and Cader turn on his charm.

"Well, if you aren't the prettiest thing these old eyes have ever seen," Cader said, grinning down at Keli, "and Colonel, I've heard about that book you're writing. I always wanted to be in the military, but I didn't have the guts. You guys are rough and tough; I knew I could never hack it."

Gene McDermott fastened his eyes on the athlete. "With a little training and discipline you would have made a good soldier. I have an eye for a good man when I see one. Shame, damn shame, you didn't join the service."

"I'm sorry myself," Cader lied. "Hell, man, you got it all. Retirement as a colonel, a beautiful wife, and you're still young enough to enjoy life. Yes, sir, you've got it all. Makes a man sit back and wonder where he went wrong. Sure would like to read that book you're working on."

"Stop by the house and I'll let you take a squint at the outline. Any time this week would be fine. I'm just researching for the next few days, so you won't be interrupting any writing."

"I'll just do that." Cader grinned.

Damion grimaced. The only thing Cade Harris read was *Hustler* and *Screw*, and then he only looked at the pictures. *Bastard*, he seethed. His eyes went to Keli who was sipping at her drink, her eyes traveling around the room. "How are you, Keli?"

"Just fine, Damion. It's a lovely party, isn't it? Julia and Irene always have such . . . exquisite parties."

Damion smiled. "A party is a party. It's the people who make it a success." His voice was gentle, almost paternal.

Her soft doe eyes questioned his tone, not the words. "Yes, I agree." Short, clipped words that merely agreed with something he said. Well, what the hell did he expect her to say?

"Doesn't Irene took lovely this evening?"

Damion turned and stared at Irene Hayden Thomas. "I really hadn't noticed till you mentioned it, but, yes, she does look nice. I don't think I've seen Irene that dressed up since Marsha's clambake last year."

Keli giggled and Damion was shocked. He had never seen her do anything but smile. She looked so young and . . . vulnerable. Keli giggled. *Amazing,* he told himself. *Absolutely amazing!* Did Cade Harris have anything to do with it, he wondered. Perhaps it was some kind of inside joke that only women understood. He shrugged.

When Cade turned to include Keli in the conversation, Damion backed away on the pretense of getting another drink.

Marsha Evans's voice was low as she conversed with Julia about her dinner and how stunning everyone looked, including Irene.

"I think your dinner parties bring out the best in everyone, Julia. Of course, I'm the first to admit that Cader Harris just might have something to do with it. I've never seen Irene look so animated, not since her father's appointment to the bench. And, Julia," she said, lowering her voice to a whisper, "when have you ever seen any of the men in this room so . . . so spruced up or standing so straight? Look at Mayor Guthrie; he looks like he's in mortal agony holding in his stomach."

"Cader certainly is a virile-looking man," Julia agreed. "You must feel pretty flattered that you're the one he brought tonight."

Marsha's eyes darkened momentarily. "I'm not interested in Cader Harris or any man right now. I've had enough of men to last me the rest of my life. A dinner here, a movie or a concert, that's something else as long as there are no ties and no strings. I'm not looking for a relationship, Julia."

"And why not? Relationships are what makes the world go 'round," Damion Conway said, coming up to the two women.

"Damion, I do wish you had brought a date for the evening," Julia chided the reverend. "You threw off my seating arrangement, I want you to know."

"I'm sorry, but there just wasn't anyone I wanted to bring this evening. I know you'll forgive me. I've read somewhere that hostesses adore single men at parties."

"Only if there are single ladies and you have one strike against you by being a minister." Julia smiled.

Damion slouched against the mantel. "It looks like your party is a success. Cade is having the time of his life."

"That's what it's all about," Julia retorted. "The party is for Cader, to welcome him back to town. Do you think he'll make a success of the sporting goods store, Damion?"

"It's too early to tell. If charm was the only thing he needed, then yes, it would be a roaring success. He seems to have an adequate supply of money, so, off the top of my head, I'd say he has an excellent chance of succeeding. I just heard him tell Gene he was thinking of hiring a tennis pro and expanding his tennis line. It's a good idea if I do say so myself."

"Yes, tennis is the *in* game," Marsha agreed. "I've been thinking of taking it a little more seriously myself. I could use a little help with perfecting my backhand."

"I hope he can get Marc interested in some kind of sport," Julia said through tight lips.

"Leave it to Cade, Julia. Before you know it Marc will be out there with a racket or running or something. I have a feeling that every man in town will be taking up some kind of sport, and soon," Damion said coolly.

"You don't like Cader, do you?" Marsha asked bluntly.

"Does it show that much?" Damion retorted just as bluntly.

"Yes."

"Let's just say he's not one of my favorite people and let it go at that."

"We're going to have to; dinner is now being served," Julia said as she acknowledged the cook's silent signal that all was in readiness.

As Julia's guests milled around the dining room looking for their place cards, Marc encountered Keli and Gene McDermott just as they were placing their half-finished drinks on the bar. Gene stiffened his spine and purposely avoided Marc's glance. Realizing that a strain would be placed upon dinner, Marc attempted to bridge the gap. "Gene, you came to me for medical advice and I gave it to you. My opinion hasn't changed and I'm trying to understand your feelings on this matter. Let's not have it affect our friendship."

Gene puffed up, his squarish head thrust forward on his bullish neck. "Look here, Baldwin, I only came to your wife's dinner because it seemed to matter so much to Keli. I can well imagine what you think of me and I don't give a damn. Just stay out of our lives!" His voice was guttural and he seemed to hiss between clenched teeth.

Keli placed her hand on Gene's arm, her cheeks reddening

with embarrassment. "Gene . . . please . . . Marc didn't mean any-thing. . . ."

"Don't you go defending him, Keli. I didn't want to come here in the first place. . . ." He turned to Marc. "Now just stay out of it, Baldwin, and leave us alone! I'm warning you. One more word and I'll drag Keli out of here."

Marc's eyes narrowed and his gaze centered on the throbbing pulse evident just above Gene's too-tight collar. "Don't get your pressure up; I only wanted to say I will stay out of it, for tonight, at least. Come on, Keli, everyone's being seated." He placed her arm through his. "Coming, Gene?" He glanced backward to see the colonel pouring himself another finger of Scotch and downing it. The man is scared, Marc thought in surprise. It's not just stupidity or stubbornness, it's fear. He sighed heavily. It would seem that before Keli found help Gene would have to overcome his fear and ignorance. He only hoped the intractable Gene McDermott came to his senses while there was still time for Keli.

Keli found herself seated beside Damion Conway, and throughout the dinner she was aware of his silent understanding. She was conscious of Marsha's eyes constantly searching hers and of the close attention of Marc and Gene. Why couldn't they leave her alone? Why did they have to keep watching her as though she were suddenly going to explode all over the dinner table? Only Damion understood. He was the only one who saw beyond the body to the woman she was. He offered her a quiet consolation. Unlike Gene who denied her the right to make decisions concern-ing herself, her own body. Unlike Marsha, who watched her with puzzled eyes, wanting to help in some way, yet wanting to take control in much the same way as Gene. Only Damion understood, not forcing his will upon her, telling her she had a choice, even if that choice was not to his liking. Damion saw the woman, the per-son within.

Her thoughts were interrupted by Marvin Guthrie's loud guffaw. "Now, Cade," he was saying, "we like our town just the way it is, don't we, honey?" He turned to his rotund wife, Alma, who auto-matically nodded while pushing another shrimp into her mouth. Actually, his words were for Foster Doyle's benefit. Next year was an election year and old man Hayden's support was important.

"And I like the town just the way it is too, Mayor," Cader

answered jocularly. "It's refreshing. I've lived in cities where you couldn't turn your back and you needed three locks on the door. No, Hayden may be just the way I left it, but I like it that way."

"We're glad you do, Cader," the Mayor said in his gravelly voice between bits of crisp lettuce. "Hayden is a fine place to live and rear children. Some say we haven't progressed beyond the year 1945, but that's all right with us, isn't it, honey?" Again he looked to his wife for confirmation, and again she nodded automatically just as the perfect politician's wife should do.

"I know just what you mean," Harris bantered. "Some may say it's a dying town, but we know better, don't we?" His words had the required, calculated effect. Mayor Guthrie nearly choked.

"Dying! Who says Hayden is a dying town?" He challenged with all the furor of a town politician.

"For one thing, the merchants of Hayden are having a rough go of it. I know. I had to look into it before I opened my sporting goods store here."

"Why did you open it here if, as you say, the merchants are having a rough go?" Foster Doyle interjected, his cold gray eyes piercing Harris suspiciously.

Harris shot him a glaring look. "Because I felt a loyalty to my hometown. Because it was time to settle down a bit, and I'd rather be here in Hayden than anywhere. This may not be a boom town but there's enough here to warrant my investment."

"That's admirable of you, boy. Your loyalty, I mean." Foster Doyle smiled to himself. Keep talking, Harris, I'll find out why you're here and then I'll blow it for you.

Cader Harris seemed to read Foster's intent and fell suddenly silent. But the mayor had uncovered a political bone and would not leave it alone.

"See here, Harris, you wouldn't be referring to Delta Oil, would you?"

"Actually, I don't know enough about it to come to a decision. It certainly would appear to be just the boost Hayden is looking for."

"Well, I can tell you about it!" Marc offered seriously. "Of course everyone understands I'm speaking strictly from a medical point of view, but I believe installing those holding tanks would be the worst thing possible to come into our town." Marc saw he had the attention of everyone at the table, and he unconsciously squared his shoulders and lowered his voice. "My concern is with the health and safety of Hayden's citizens. It is well agreed that the Mississippi area is already saturated with nearly thirty percent of the entire United States petrochemical industry. It is second only to the New York–New Jersey metropolitan area, which boasts over forty percent. I'm concerned with the children who attend schools here, not only in Hayden but also in surrounding towns. The pollution. The hazard of explosion. The possible adverse effects on our air and our water supply. My concern is with human life. Once Delta Oil gets a foothold here there's no telling how far it will go. Other towns will follow our example and allow similar installations to be built. I'm totally against it."

"I can understand that, Marc," Cader said, "and I certainly sympathize with your reasons. Only your livelihood doesn't depend upon commerce. You're a doctor. You can relocate. I'm thinking of the small businessman. If there's no work, people can't help the economy of Hayden. How long before they sell out . . . leave town? What of the teachers? Struggling towns can't afford top salaries. Our children will suffer educationally. Only second-rate teachers will be attracted to Hayden. That's where I'm at and a lot of other people here in town are thinking the same thing. Otherwise, why this split, this division? If you ask me, this town is on the brink of another Civil War."

"Nobody's asking you, Harris," Gene said quietly, "or haven't you noticed? However, I'm for progress and I've made the unpopular decision that Delta Oil should come into Hayden. What's the sense of trying to save the environment when no one will be living here anyway?"

The mayor coughed and cleared his throat in preparation for his speech. "I've looked into this matter, and I must admit I've every guarantee from the state environmental agencies that if Hayden decided to allow Delta Oil's holding tanks in here, they would be on top of the issue every step of the way. That's not to say that I'm in favor of the tanks, understand." Marvin Guthrie looked around the table making certain everyone did understand, especially the president of the town council, Foster Doyle Hayden.

Cader Harris smiled to himself. The pompous jackass. He knew for a fact that the mayor straddled the fence where Delta Oil was concerned. In no way, shape, matter or form did he want to offend potential political supporters. Reelection was coming up next year and Cader knew that Mayor Guthrie's stand was quite different when he was talking to the Chamber of Commerce and the Rotary. Nothing that could be quoted, of course, nothing that would offend the opposing faction, but it was obvious that if Mayor Guthrie could be convinced he wouldn't be drummed out of office because of this issue, he'd push for the installation of the tanks.

"As far as danger of explosion, Baldwin," Gene McDermott was saying, "the odds are strictly against it."

"Then you admit it's a gamble," Marc retorted.

"Life is a gamble. However, I've been studying this situation, and I even have letters from the federal environmental agencies. The problem in Hayden is that so many people are uninformed."

"Then inform us, please," Cader interjected. He could tell by the vibes that Colonel McDermott wasn't a popular man in the community, and he probably skimmed along on the strength of his wife's charm. But he was pro-Delta and what he had to say could be important.

"For one thing, the liquefied natural gas, or LNG, is proposed to be stored in two huge tanks. Environmentalists contend that the gas in its liquefied state presents a serious safety hazard if not handled correctly. In this I bow to Dr. Baldwin. Handled irresponsibly, it would be a serious hazard to area residents. LNG is actually frozen to two hundred sixty degrees below zero and is thus condensed six hundred times to a liquid state."

"We all know that, Gene," Marc said impatiently. "And we also know that stored LNG, as proposed by Delta Oil, has the energy potential, if ignited all at once, of several atomic bombs."

"True," Gene continued. "However, the real risks involve not so much the storage of LNG but its transfer from ship to terminal."

"Yes," Marc leaned forward, his face drawn into grim lines, "and a spill, according to many experts, could result in a vaporized plume that if ignited could result in a flash fire engulfing several miles, depending on wind direction."

"The state of Louisiana has approved the installation as proposed by Delta Oil," Cader interjected. "Certainly it meets all safety standards."

"That's only because a terminal here would ensure the state's energy supply for years to come," Marc said hotly.

"Gentlemen, if the real danger is in the transfer of the liquefied gas, surely Delta's proposal should be considered. A pipeline, extending miles out from Hayden into the Gulf . . ."

Foster Doyle, who had sat quietly throughout the discussion, suddenly cleared his throat. The effect was instantaneous and predictable. The room was immediately silent. All eyes focused on the gray-haired gentleman, waiting for him to speak. It was almost as if he had slammed his fist on the table. "Delta Oil will *never* come into Hayden," he said, looking pointedly at the mayor, knowing how Guthrie straddled the fence. "I will never allow it. This discussion is pointless. There will be no threat to health or environment because there will be no tanks. There will be no increase in business for the same reason. Hayden will remain as it is."

Cader focused on Foster Doyle, his expression a combination of humor and grudging respect. "*Never* is a long time, Foster." He purposely used the old gentleman's first name, reminding him that he was no longer the boy from the wrong side of the tracks; now he was an equal. "I remember when you said 'never' to me. As you can see, it's only a word and doesn't mean a thing."

Foster Doyle nearly choked. How dare Harris say that in front of all these people who now were scrutinizing both men curiously. Fleetingly, his gaze fell on Irene whose startled expression showed perplexity rather than curiosity.

Foster Doyle stood up abruptly, the muted scrape of his chair against the carpet a nerve-grating shriek in the hushed room. He tossed his napkin onto the table. "I will be leaving now," he stated in a barely controlled voice. Always the gentleman, showing his fine breeding, he expressed his thanks to his flabbergasted hostess.

Irene ignored her father's penetrating, silent command. She was staying!

Several moments after Foster Doyle's dramatic departure, the conversation buzzed with inconsequential subjects. Cader Harris looked speculatively at each of his dinner partners, mentally assessing their stand on the possibility of Delta Oil coming into Hayden. Only Gene McDermott was pro-LNG and he was not well liked. It may have looked like a Mexican standoff to anyone other than Cader Harris. He had now made a foothold in society and had been included in the discussion of Delta Oil. Now it wouldn't seem strange or unusual if he should discuss it with any of the merchants or be seen in the company of anyone who approved the proposal. It wasn't going to be easy; he had known that before returning to Hayden. But a quarter of a million dollars was a lot of money, and it was imperative that he wrap things up here before Delta Oil became impatient and sent in a few of their own men with nice fat bribes to put in the right places. Damn! He wished he had more working capital. He'd have gone that route himself in spite of Delta Oil's objections that bribery was only a last resort. And it would be done by their own people, men who weren't working for them for a promise of an enormous sum of money or a contract as their public relations advisor.

CHAPTER ELEVEN

*I*rene Thomas stood on the patio, gazing up at the clear blue sky. God, it was hot and humid! Or was it she who was hot and humid? She felt drained, empty.

She sat down on a colorful webbed chair and continued to stare at the scrubbed blue sky. She looked at her Bloody Mary and winced slightly. This was new, this drinking in the afternoon. She admitted that the afternoons were the worst time of day to get through. Was this her second or third? Who gave a good rat's ass, anyway? What if it were five or six? Who cared what she did, how much she drank? No one, she answered bitterly as she drained her glass and poured another.

Glancing at her watch, she grimaced. She had expected Cader to call before now. Why hadn't he called? Last night at Julia's house hadn't his eyes told her she would be hearing from him? Soon? Very soon? It was now twelve hours since the party broke up; she should have heard from him by now.

Idly, she dipped her index finger into the drink and stirred. At first the movements were slow, then, as she watched, her finger moved faster and faster, till the tomatoey drink slopped over the sides of the glass and down onto her white tennis outfit. She stared at the blood-red stain on the stark whiteness and flinched slightly.

It suddenly occurred to her that before Cader had returned to town she would sit and secretly browse through *Viva* and *Playgirl* magazines and make endless checks in the boxes of the self-revelation tests in *Family Circle* and *Woman's Day,* all the while wallowing in self-pity. But she didn't need a slick magazine article to tell her that the multiple orgasm was not a myth. It was Cader Harris who had taught her that and who now filled her thoughts while she filled her afternoon with Bloody Marys.

Cader's failure to call her was linked in her mind to the way he skipped out on her eighteen years ago. She wasn't fooling herself; he had done just that—skipped out, leaving her with a full belly that turned out to be Kevin. Bitter that Cader had failed to call, Irene smiled smugly. She wondered what Cader would say if he knew that Kevin was his own son, his own flesh and blood. Perhaps if he knew, it would strengthen the ties between them. Irene gulped, shoving back the thought that was very close to being a temptation. Cader must never know. What if he took it into his mind to take Kevin away from her? It was unthinkable. Kevin was Arthur's son. No! Kevin was *her* son! Her very own son, he belonged to her and her alone! No one, nothing, would ever take him away from her.

Her basic fear and distrust of men overtook her. She was aware of her own ineffectiveness in the face of masculine dominance. First, there was Foster Doyle, powerful, self-assured, almost revered, even by other men. He had always held a strong, if indulgent, hand over her. And Cader, he'd always gotten what he wanted, hadn't he? Even Arthur, in his own milquetoast manner, held the high cards over her. She only had to think of Kevin's love for Arthur to know this. She drained her glass. If keeping Kevin to herself meant she must never let Cader know he was the boy's father, then so be it. It would be the only trump card she could hold against him. And Irene needed something to hold on to. God help her, in spite of everything, she still wanted Cader Harris. Wanted him more than she'd ever wanted anything. And by Jesus, she'd have him. She'd gone after him before and she would do it again. And this time, it would be on her own terms.

Squaring her shoulders and slamming her glass down on the table, Irene bristled. She chortled quietly, remembering that time-worn axiom, "Hell hath no fury . . ."

Tears welled in her eyes at the horrible injustice of it all. She had nothing without Cader and now that she had seen him again, this realization shook her foundations. A single tear slid down her cheek and she felt the taste of salt on her lip. There was an answer. She just had to find it. She had to think of something! Do something!

Irene's eyes lowered to the crimson stain on the short white skirt. The outfit was ruined, and it was her favorite. Even if she didn't play tennis, she felt good wearing it. It was a pretend thing. Like her life. *Let's all pretend everything is all right and it will go away.* Pretend. There was nothing left to do but go out and buy another tennis outfit. She needed a tennis outfit to pretend while she drank her Bloody Marys.

She got up from the deck chair and reeled slightly. Yep, guess it was five instead of three. Laughing, she trotted into the house and up the stairs to her bedroom. Let's see, she mused, what did you wear when you went to buy a tennis outfit? A golfing outfit, of course. She giggled as she pulled up the zipper. This was another of her pretend outfits. It had been years since she'd been on the golf course.

The moment she pulled her car into the empty lot of Cader Harris's new store, she realized her mistake. Today was Wednesday and all the stores were closed after one o'clock. Maybe Cader was still in the shop and would open it for her. She really needed that outfit. She opened her bag and popped a Chiclet into her mouth, and it wasn't till she started chewing that she realized it was a Feenamint. *Shit!* A fit of laughing overtook her as she pounded on the frosty glass of the shop. "Cader, are you in there? It's Irene."

"Yo, I sure am. I was just getting ready to leave," Cader said, opening the door for her to enter. "Come in, pretty lady. What can I do for you?" He caught the glitter in Irene's eyes at the same moment he got a whiff of her breath. He could feel his adrenaline begin to surge as feelings of revenge, danger and scorn bounced around within him. Was Irene a secret drinker or had she been drinking because she needed the courage to finally confront him for leaving her the way he had eighteen years before? *Play it cool,*

Cade, he warned himself. He put his brain into gear and pasted his number-six smile across his lips, the one he had used for the new toothpaste he had endorsed.

"I need a tennis outfit and I need it right away. You can't play tennis if you don't have an outfit." Irene giggled.

A tennis buff and from the looks of the outfit she was wearing she must be into golf too. Strong legs. "Good thinking, Harris," he muttered to himself. Jesus! He had never seen such hot eyes. "They're hanging up over there; take your pick," he said, pointing to a rack at the far end of the store. He continued to wear the number-six smile as he contemplated her next move.

"I'll take six, just wrap them up. Size nine. Why is it so hot in here?" Irene asked, looking around.

"Beats the hell out of me." Cader grinned, shifting into smile number-seven that held a trace of a leer and showed off his porcelain to the best advantage.

Irene frowned. "I don't remember you having all those teeth. I like them," she said, throwing back her head and laughing with delight. "Makes you look like a super jock. Are you a super jock, Cade?" she teased lightly.

"Depends on who's doing the asking." She wanted to play games from the sound of things. He liked games as long as he won. Irene would be a good loser.

"Ma-cho stud. Super jock. It fits you, Cade. God, I can't get over all those teeth. I bet you made some dentist real happy."

Cader laughed, enjoying the conversation. "I heard he took off for Aruba for a month's vacation after I paid the bill."

Irene purposely widened her eyes, drinking in the sight of him. She wanted him, needed him. Eighteen years was too long a time to wait for anything, and she had no intention of waiting another minute. She wasn't Irene Hayden Thomas, she was an eighteen-year-old again, bent on getting the one thing she wanted most. Her eyes narrowed slightly. No, if she was going to be honest, she wasn't just an eighteen-year-old again; she was a bitch in heat. "That figures. Pull the blinds and take off your clothes," she commanded.

"I thought you came in here for a tennis outfit." Cader laughed as he closed the Venetian blind on the front door.

"I did."

"It would appear to me you have something else on your mind.

It goes without saying that I've been wrong on occasion. . . . Christ, you have hot eyes. Exactly what do you have in mind?" Cader demanded, knowing full well what Irene wanted and experiencing a response that displayed itself in his nether regions.

"Whatever goes after you take off your clothes. I thought you would have figured it out by now. Sit on that chair. I'll do the rest."

"Will you, now?" By God, she was something. He'd had women come on to him before, but this time there was something different. He stared at her and suddenly understood her need. What was so astounding was that he never, ever thought Irene would reach out and take it. He shrugged inwardly. Hell, he'd always been a giver. "I was never one to drag my feet," he said, taking off his shoes. By the time he had his socks off Irene was down to the buff, her feet slightly parted, her face serious, her eyes smoldering. And he thought Sunday Waters had it down for speed. This was faster than the Indy 500.

A smile played around the corner of Irene's mouth. "Sit. I'll get on top." Cader Harris sat. He knew how to obey orders. Irene straddled him, her long, muscular legs hanging over the sides of the chair. It was over almost before it started. Twice more she repeated her frantic gyrations. Finished, she slid off him and stood looking down at him, a dreamy, faraway look on her face.

"If you want an explanation, you aren't getting one," Irene said, picking up her clothes.

"Hey, Irene, this is me, Cade. If that's your style, you don't owe me an explanation. But," he said, wagging a finger, "why do I have this feeling that I've been used?"

Irene laughed. "Let's just say I wanted you to see what you've been missing for the past eighteen years." She tilted her head to one side. "As fucks go, you were all right." The sound of the zipper being pulled up on the golf shorts seemed unusually loud to Cader.

"Jesus H. Christ, is that what you call it? I was all right?" He grimaced in pretended outrage. "You fucked me, lady. I just came along for the ride. Don't stand there and tell me *I* was all right. If you want to get fucked, I'll fuck you, but we'll do it *my* way. Then you can tell me if it's all right. And I am well aware of what I've been missing."

She was Irene Hayden Thomas again. "Are you saying I hurt your manly pride? You got it off. What more do you want?" she asked, stuffing her bra into her handbag. She buttoned her shirt and continued to stare at the naked man sitting in the chair. Suddenly, she felt very powerful, like that time at the football game when she snared him away from Sunny Waters. Cade Harris was hers; he always had been.

"You used me!" Cade said in a miffed tone. "Goddamn, you came into my store to buy a tennis outfit and you used my cock for your revenge." When the full enormity of the situation hit him, he doubled over laughing. "You used my cock to . . ." Unable to continue, he lunged for Irene.

Irene stepped neatly to the side, her eyes laughing merrily. "Come off it, Cade. How many times have you used a woman? We both know you're a taker. You know that old saying; there are givers and takers. Are you going to hold it against me because I took a little?" She smiled. "See you around, Cade. You better get dressed; it's awfully cold in here."

"The next time, we do it my way, agreed?" Cader called to her retreating figure.

Irene stopped in midstride. Her tone was serious and all the merriment was gone from her eyes. "I'd like that. I'd like that very much."

"Son of a bitch!" Cader cursed as he watched the door close behind her. He had one leg in his pants when the door opened and Irene stuck her head in and grinned.

"Thanks, Cade."

One leg in his pants, the chair wiggling beneath his grasp, Cade teetered and went down. He was just too tired to get up. Jesus, how could he have forgotten how much of a woman she was? She had drained him and she was still as perky as a frisky pup.

Irene stepped from the shower and wrapped a bright lemon bath sheet around her just as the phone rang.

Suddenly, the day was different, the phone was a rare pearl in her hand, Cader's voice was a symphony in her ear, and the bright sun shining through the window making dappled patterns on the carpet, the rarest of fine laces. It was a moment before she could trust herself to speak. "Hello, Cader," she whispered. It was going to be a perfect day, she could feel it, sense it, almost taste it.

"I'm calling to ask you to have lunch with me. Can you make it?"

Could she make it? Could she breathe? Of course, she could

make it. She'd die before she declined. "I think so," she breathed heavily. "Where shall I meet you?"

"I was thinking about the Cottage Inn on Westover Drive. It's far enough off the beaten track that I think you'll be safe meeting me there. I should be able to clear things away here at the shop and be there by one. Is that convenient for you?"

Of course it was convenient for her. She'd have dropped the bath sheet and started this minute if he said so. "One will be fine, Cade. I'm looking forward to it," Irene said softly.

"Irene, do you remember the time . . ."

"That you took me there after the Thanksgiving game? Of course I remember. I'm a little surprised that you remember, though."

"I could never forget that day. I'll see you at one, then."

"Goodbye, Cade," Irene said, replacing the receiver in its cradle.

A pot and a half of coffee and a pack of cigarettes later, Irene was ready to leave. God, she hoped she wouldn't have an accident on the way.

A heavyset hostess led Irene to the back of the inn and settled her in a black leather and knotty pine booth. Irene ordered a vodka gimlet and settled back to wait for Cader.

As she sipped at the tart drink, she looked around. She hadn't been here since that day she had come with Cader after the Thanksgiving game eighteen years ago. It looked the same, with its rustic atmosphere. The heavy ferns in their copper baskets gleamed brightly from the dimly lit wall sconces. The worn red brick and the rough-hewn beams made her think of times of old. It was pleasant; quiet and pleasant. She knew that she and Cader could sit here in the booth the entire afternoon, and no one would bother them or even notice them in the semidarkness.

"I'm glad you chose this place," she said to Cader as he slid into the booth and immediately reached for her hand.

"I'm glad that you're glad." Cader grinned. "Yesterday we didn't have much of a chance to talk." He was still grinning, and Irene flushed but said nothing. There was no way she was going to apologize to him for her actions yesterday. "How are you?"

"I've never been better."

Irene Hayden Thomas squirmed on her seat and wished there was something she could do about the wetness between her legs.

Sitting across from Cader Harris in the dimly lit cocktail lounge at high noon was something that didn't occur every day of the week. She had to try to concentrate on what Cader was saying.

"Hmmmn," she murmured as she sipped at her vodka gimlet. "Hmmmmn," she repeated. God, what had he said? Whatever it was, her murmured response must have been right.

"And so you see, Irene, if Delta Oil doesn't get into Hayden, I'll have to pack it in," Cader confided. "You just don't know how hard that would be for me to do."

"Hard, yes, very hard," Irene choked as she squeezed her thighs together.

"You of all people understand what it means to belong." His voice was lowered to a whisper. "What Hayden needs is a place on the map. You know, some new life, the shot in the arm, economically, that Delta Oil could give it." His voice dropped another octave. "Can I tell you a secret? Actually, it isn't a secret, but I want to confide in you."

Irene's heart pounded in her chest so loudly she was certain he could hear it from across the table. She couldn't speak. She was dumbfounded. Just being here with Cader, looking at him, listening to him, watching his hands play with the cocktail stirrer and trying not to think about the wetness between her legs required almost more control than she could muster. She nodded, her eyes glazed and filmy as she sipped again at her third gimlet.

"I'm almost broke, Irene," Cader whispered. His breath fell with gentle caresses on her cheek as he leaned closer to her. "I need your help, Irene." He leaned closer, taking her hand in his. "Look, I'm not going to con you into anything. I'm leveling. I've had women, Irene, lots of women. But, Irene, none of them were half the woman you are. I can't count the times I've thought about you and being here with you this way. You're the best," he said huskily.

When Irene raised her eyes from the table where their hands were touching, she stared at him in open-eyed wonder. Cader swallowed hard. He grasped her hands and looked into her tear-bright eyes. "You've got to use your influence to get Delta Oil into Hayden. You've got to make it clear that you want Delta Oil, that it would be good for the town." His voice was gruff, but it was sensually husky to Irene's ears.

"Is that all? It won't be easy," she warned. "I'll have to go against Daddy and I don't know if I want to do that. I'd . . . have to think about it. I know if I went against Daddy it would kill him."

"Foster Doyle is from a past generation, Irene. This is today, the here and now. Think of the present generation; they're all leaving Hayden. Face it, it's a dying town. Aside from my own interests in the project, you have to admit Delta Oil would be good for this town. Besides," he whispered closer to her ear, "if things work in my favor financially, it would be that much sooner that I could leave Hayden and take you with me."

Irene looked up into his eyes, hoping he wouldn't notice how she ignored his statement about leaving Hayden. "Someday, Cade, I'm going to tell you a secret. A secret that will make you forget all about leaving Hayden and me."

A sinking feeling descended in Cader's gut. He knew he had asked for too much too soon. Irene would never willingly leave Hayden. She liked being a big fish in a little pond. He would have to convince her; he must.

Cader reached for Irene's hands and with his elbow slid her drink away. "I like my women to have their wits about them," he murmured.

"I do, I do!" Irene whispered in return. "Oh, I do, Cade."

"Come on, baby, I'm taking you to the best damn motel I know. We have a lot of lost time to make up for."

Cader looked down at Irene. Her blond hair was strewn across the pillow and tangled around her white throat. He kissed the hollow beneath her ear and blazed a trail to the fullness of her breasts. She sighed, turning beneath him, offering herself up to his loving.

She was still magnificent, a little fuller, a little older, but still magnificent. With her, here like this, Cade was only eighteen years old again. Her passions were more sophisticated now, as were her practiced touch and her responses. If anything, she was better than she had been when they were younger. Tenderly, he pressed his lips to hers, the touch lingering, becoming more ardent, more urgent.

The afternoon sun filtered through the draperies into the room, lighting his hair to gold. Irene raised her hand, running her fingers into the wealth at the nape of his neck, feeling the strength of him, the muscular length of him, as he covered her body with his. His lovemaking was slow, languorous, titillating her senses, filling her with an unquenchable need for him.

He teased her, taunted her with his light touches, grazing her skin with his fingertips, awakening her responses. Every nerve in her body cried out for him, ached for him, damned him for playing with her this way, loving him for it. He watched her, his eyes burning where they touched her flesh. A smile played about his mouth, his beautiful mouth, his mouth that was doing such indescribably lovely things to her. He loved seeing her this way, she knew. Watching her tense, arch herself toward him, begging for more, always more.

She reveled under his gaze, knowing the picture she created: lips parted with passion, hair tumbled, skin flushed. She watched as his eyes followed the path of his hand, watched his fingers play against her flesh. The lowering sun ignited the downy hair on her belly to gilt, and farther down, where it became darker and delineated her firm thighs, his fingers strayed.

The first touch sent a quiver of pulsating throbs through her. Then, as the novelty became familiar, her body moved of its own accord beneath his hand. She raised her eyes, locking them with his, and saw that his pleasure was in pleasuring her.

Wanting him, needing him, she clasped him to her, driving herself beneath the weight of his body, her hips stating her demands, her cries voicing them.

He drove into her with fury, locking her legs over his shoulders, taking his pleasure in her, giving pleasure. Together they spiraled the heights of carnality, each enhancing the other's sensuality, each feeding the other's lusts.

Breathless, shaken, Irene lay in Cader's arms, her head on his chest, making it wet with her tears. When she was calm enough to speak, she said softly, "I don't know if I'll ever be able to forgive you for robbing me of this for all these years."

Beth Thomas tied the right sash of her sun dress into a neat bow as she squirmed and struggled before her mother's pier glass. "How do I look, Mama?" she asked, her eyes unnaturally bright.

Irene frowned slightly at her child's intensity as she watched her yank at the side of the mirror to get a better view of the bow at the back of her dress. "You look sweet and lovely, Beth," she answered honestly. "You just look like my sweet little girl."

"What's that supposed to mean, Mama?" Beth said, whipping around and challenging Irene with her eyes.

"Why, darlin', it just means that you look nice and pretty. Just like my little girl. . . . Whatever are you takin' on about?"

"How old do I look?" Beth demanded irritably.

"Old? I never thought about it, but now that you mention it, you look right this minute like a little girl going to her first party. Remember? You were twelve years old and you wore a sun dress almost like that one?"

"Twelve years old! Sweet!" Beth cried in outrage. "Oh, Mama, how could you say such a thing? I hate this dress!" She shouted as she pulled and tugged at the bow. "Why do you buy me such ridiculous clothes? If I had worn this to the party, my first real party, they would have laughed at me. How could you, Mama?"

"Beth, honey, calm down. You look like a little lady, like a Hayden should," Irene said defensively.

"A lady!" Beth screamed at the top of her lungs. "Mama! Well, I'm not wearing thi-this . . . baby dress," she snapped as she pulled it over her head and tossed it onto Irene's bed.

"Beth Thomas, where is your brassiere? I don't believe I'm seeing what I'm seeing," Irene exclaimed.

"It's in the drawer. Nobody wears a bra. I have to find something to wear!"

"You're not 'nobody'! Now, you put it on this minute. Don't you dare walk down the hall to your room in just your bloomers. I forbid it!" Irene ranted. "What if your brother should see you, or, God forbid, your father? Young lady, I don't know what's got into you. Maybe your father was right and you're too young to go to this party. You're not leaving this house without a brassiere, Beth Thomas, and that is my final word!" Irene scolded, following her daughter at a near run down the long hallway.

Once inside the girl's room, she sank into a bright scarlet beanbag chair. She watched in horror as Beth pulled a tube top from her drawer and pulled it over her head. More frantic searching in the closet and she had a short denim skirt in her hands.

"You look like a trollop," Irene gasped in a hushed voice as though afraid someone would hear. "I only agreed to buy you that ridiculous outfit so you could wear it over your bathing suit. You look scandalous! Now, take it off!"

"Mama, do you want the other kids to mock me out? I'm wearing this. All the girls dress like this. I can't imagine how I let you talk me into wearing that babyish sun dress. Ask Kevin; he'll tell you all the kids wear these outfits."

Irene threw up her hands in despair. "It's just that you've grown up before my very own eyes."

"Oh, thank you, Mama." Beth smiled, her eyes narrow and keen. "I knew you would see it my way. Don't worry about me; I'll stay with Kevin every single minute."

"Darlin', I know that Luther is such a nice boy. You'll probably be the most envied girl at the party with Kevin and Luther to watch over you. Why, I can well believe that the boys will be standin' in line to fill your card," Irene doted.

Beth sighed. "Mama, when you boogie, you don't use cards, and this is not a formal dance. It's just a get-together." Beth squinted at her image in the mirror and fluffed her long, red-gold hair. "Can I use some of your perfume?"

"Just use a little. Perfume can drive men to dangerous lengths," Irene said knowledgeably.

"Just a dab," Beth said brightly as she skipped alongside her mother. "Come on, Kev," Beth squealed, "it's time to go. You did say we were picking up Boomer and Judy, so let's hurry. I told Boomer we would be on time."

Kevin frowned but said nothing when he noted Beth's skimpy outfit. If Mother thought it was all right, who was he to stick his nose in and get it bitten off? Besides, he didn't like the look in Beth's eyes. They were almost feverishly bright and there was a noticeably tight line around her mouth. He didn't say anything when she hopped into the front seat of the car and sat down next to him. Instead, he clenched his teeth and jabbed the key into the ignition.

"Are you picking up Boomer or Judy first?"

"Boomer, and then you can move in back with him," Kevin answered curtly.

"In the back! Only niggers ride in the back, Kev. I'll sit up here with you, and Judy and Boomer can have the back seat," she said slyly, watching him out of the corner of her eye.

"It doesn't work that way. If you think you're old enough to date Boomer, then you're old enough to follow the rules. *You* and Boomer go in the back seat, and I'm telling you now, watch him, he's got seventeen hands."

"You just want to be with Judy by yourself. You don't want me around anymore; all you want is Judy. She's no good, Kev; everyone talks about her. She has a bad reputation," Beth cried wretchedly.

"Well, I happen to like her, so lay off, Beth. You're going to have all you can do to handle Boomer."

"Are you going to kiss her?" Beth asked in a childish voice.

Kevin's face flamed. "I might and I might not. Don't you go making out with that stupid Boomer, hear?"

"If you kiss Judy, I can kiss Boomer," she continued in her childish vein.

Kevin seethed. He knew every trick she was pulling on him. What should have been a fun evening was going to be a nightmare, he could feel it in his bones. So what if he kissed Judy? And, maybe, he grinned to himself, a little something else if things went all right. He would have to keep his eye on that stupid Boomer every minute or Beth would be going home without her skimpy little tube top, and without a few other things too. Damn it, how did he allow himself to get trapped into this? He was tired of playing mother hen. He wanted to be a rooster for a while, cock of the walk, like Cader Harris.

Kevin steered Arthur's Lincoln into the driveway and gave a light tap on the horn. Boomer came racing through the garage and sprinted to a stop, his eyes taking in Beth and her outfit. "Oh, man," he said, his eyes lighting up as he climbed in the back seat. With a firm shove from Kevin Beth opened the door and slid in next to Boomer. Boomer leered. "I like that thing you're wearing."

"This old thing! Why, Boomer, I didn't even think you'd notice."

"Are you kidding? I love it when girls don't wear bras," he whispered in Beth's ear, ogling her small, nubile breasts through the clinging, skimpy jersey top. "Kev, are you a leg or tit man?"

Kevin almost choked as he backed the Lincoln from the driveway. He knew he had to give some kind of answer or by tomorrow it would be all over town that he was a fag. "A little of both," he said nonchalantly.

"Yeah. You ever been over to Aunt Cledie's, Kev?"

"Not lately," Kevin lied, pretending firsthand knowledge of Hayden's infamous cat house. Beth was certainly getting an education. Well, she asked for it.

Boomer, not used to sitting with his hands idle, made a grab for Beth and pulled her against him and whispered in her ear. "Remember, Bethy, you said you would do *anything*. Those were your exact words, *anything!*" His whisper became softer, huskier. "I want your panties for a souvenir," he groaned as Kevin pulled the car to a stop outside Judy's door.

"Be right back," Kevin said warningly as he climbed out of the car. "Watch it, Boomer, that's my sister. Any funny stuff and I put you through a wall."

"She's as safe with me as she is with you," Boomer grimaced, waiting for Kevin to approach Judy's door. "Come on, Beth," he said urgently, making a wild lunge for her, his hands groping with her tube top.

"Stop it! Get your hands off me! Stop it, Luther, or I'll scream!"

Luther retreated sulkily. "Is it so goddamned much to ask from a girl who said she would do 'anything' if I took her to this party? I didn't bring you for your looks, you know."

"Just leave me alone!" Beth pouted, her eyes intent on Kevin's back as he waited for someone to answer the door.

"You're nothing but a cock teaser," Boomer shouted. "You said you'd do anything, and this is anything. Go to the party yourself. I'm leaving," he said, opening the door.

Beth paled. If Boomer walked out on her, Kevin would take her home and go to the party alone with Judy. She couldn't let him take Judy, not without her. "Wait a minute, Boomer. What I meant was here comes Kevin and Judy. Later, after . . . when it gets dark, we'll go outside and . . . I'll do what you want!" she almost shouted hysterically.

"You mean it, Bethy? You'll do it?"

Beth gagged but managed a sickly smile. "Come on, Boomer, get back in the car; here they are. Don't say anything to Kevin . . . he's a . . . a turkey."

"Yeah, I know," Boomer said, getting back into the car. "He's never been to Aunt Cledie's, I know. I asked."

Judy settled herself beside Kevin and turned around to smile at

Boomer and spoke to Beth. "This is your first party, isn't it . . . honey?"

Ill at ease and out of her depth with Boomer breathing heavily next to her, she answered coolly, "Yes, and I plan to have a really good time. Don't you worry about me; Boomer is going to take care of me and make sure I enjoy myself." Her defiant eyes met Kevin's in the rearview mirror.

"You and Boomer are staying with me and Judy," Kevin said quietly.

"That's so . . . big brotherly of you, Kev. If that's what you want, then I'll do what you say, won't we, Boomer? By the way," she babbled, "don't you think Boomer looks just like Nick Nolte? He's so handsome, Nick I mean. Don't you just adore him?"

"Yeah, just adore him," Boomer grumbled. "Just remember what you promised, little cock teaser," he hissed to Beth beneath the sound of the car stereo blaring the latest rock tune.

Beth giggled nervously. With Kevin in close range Boomer could make all the threats he wanted, but Kev would take care of her. And Judy could have Boomer. They were two of a kind as far as she was concerned.

"Guess what I heard at the tennis court today," Boomer said excitedly. "Sally Davis and Jack Matthews have the clap. Sally gave it to him, Jack said, and to Sam and Will. Jack gave it to Andrea and her old lady found out and now everyone in town is having a fit."

No one said anything and Beth sat back against the seat warily. Why should everyone be having a fit? What was the clap? She made a mental note to ask Kevin later.

"I'm surprised you don't have a dose of it yourself. I heard you've been hanging around Aunt Cledie's. All of her girls have it. Mom said they're always in the office for treatment." Judy watched in malicious satisfaction as Boomer's face paled and then flushed.

"You putting me on, Judy? Whores are supposed to be the cleanest women going; they take care of themselves. That's what it says in *Hustler* magazine."

Judy smirked. "Listen, if you don't believe me, ask Janice Harper. She works in the drugstore and she sees how many prescriptions they get, and my mother will tell you the same thing. I bet you got it, Boomer." She laughed.

"Just shut the hell up, Judy."

"What are you going to do, Boomer?" Judy taunted.

"I'm not going to do anything because I don't have to do anything. Do you think I'm so green I wouldn't have used protection?" he said glibly.

Judy wouldn't let up. "You just walk in that place and you got it, turkey; those germs are all over." She laughed. "Maybe you better put him out of the car and take Beth home, Kevin. She might get contaminated."

"I'm warning you, Judy, shut your mouth. I don't have anything. Guys like me watch out for themselves. You can just knock it off or I'll give you a sample right now."

"Kevin wouldn't let you hurt me, would you, Kevin?"

Before he could answer Beth spoke up, not wanting to hear her brother commit himself to Judy over anything. "Why don't you drop us off right here, Kev, and park the car. The driveway looks full. We can wait out by the pool with the kids. I think you passed a parking space back there near Hibiscus Drive."

"Sure thing." Kevin nodded.

"I'll stay with you," Judy said, smiling, "and you won't have to walk by yourself." It was too late for Beth to change her mind; Boomer was yanking her by the arm and dragging her out of the car.

As twilight descended, Beth found herself hard pressed to find excuses to keep herself out of Boomer's clutches. Kevin was always within close range, Judy hanging all over him. Beth's lips tightened and a muscle twitched in her cheek as she watched one of the boys place a new record on the turntable.

"This is great, isn't it, Bethy?" Boomer whispered in her ear. "Come on, let's dance, I want to feel you against me. Pretty soon it will be dark and then, yeah, man. I found a good place down at the end of the garden. I staked it out in our name," he said, leering down at her.

Beth's stomach lurched and she was almost nauseated. Or was it Boomer who was making her feel like this? No, it was Judy draped all over Kevin by the pool. Just wait till she told Mama he was so busy with Judy that stupid Boomer could have dragged her into the bushes and he'd never have known the difference.

A low, throaty laugh from Judy wafted toward her. Kevin must have said something funny to her, or something. . . . Her hand went to her mouth and she swallowed hard.

"Boomer," she said, turning and placing her hand on his arm, "let's make it the next dance. I want to go to the powder room and comb my hair," she muttered distractedly.

"Yeah? You better not be teasing me, Bethy. I hurt," he said lecherously, "and you, Bethy, are the only thing that will make the hurt go away."

Beth skirted around Boomer, pretending to head for the house. Glancing over her shoulder and seeing Luther dancing with Sue Ellen, she backtracked and took off on a dead run for the pool. Her small face puckered into a look of hate as Kevin moved closer to Judy on the chaise longue. They were whispering and, oh, God, he was going to kiss her. Kevin was going to kiss Judy. He couldn't kiss Judy; he just couldn't. If he kissed Judy that meant. . . . It was dark out. People kissed in the dark and it meant . . . it meant other things. . . . He couldn't kiss Judy. She, Beth, wouldn't let him.

"Kevin, Kevin, where are you?" she shouted. "Kevin, I don't feel well and I want to go home. Kevin, can you hear me? I feel sick; I want to go home."

Kevin was off the chaise and on his feet when Beth skidded to a stop at the edge of the pool. "What's wrong? Is Boomer putting the arm on you? You were fine when we got here." Ignoring Judy, he walked over to Beth and put his arm around her shoulder. "I tried to warn you; you aren't ready for the likes of Boomer. You have a lot of growing up to do yet, Beth, before you can handle something like this."

"And I suppose you're grown up!" Beth challenged. "I saw you!" she hissed. "I saw you, Kevin. You were going to kiss Judy."

Anger shot up Kevin's spine. He was humiliated that Judy was witnessing Beth's tantrum and chagrined that Beth caught him in what Irene would have called a compromising situation. "Why don't you ask Sue Ellen for some aspirin, and then if you don't feel better, I'll call Dad to come and get you."

"Sure! Take two aspirin! And while I'm doing that you'll be making out with Judy, right Kevin? You brought me and you're going to take me home. Now!" she shouted.

"Oh, grow up, Beth." Judy laughed. "Why must you spoil everything? Kevin's right. You're not ready for this kind of party.

Why don't you just go call your father to come and get you. Don't spoil Kevin's good time."

Beth sneered, her face drawn into an ugly mask. "And I suppose you're going to show Kev that good time. Right? There's a name for girls like you. . . ."

"Shut up, Beth," Kevin threatened, seizing her by the elbow and shaking her violently.

"Let her go, Kevin," Judy soothed. "Boomer is putting on the squeeze and she can't handle it, right Beth?"

"Make her stop talking to me like that, Kevin!" Beth wailed. "Slap her! Hit her, Kevin! Make her stop!"

Kevin threw his hands up in disgust. "Fight it out between yourselves," he said coldly as he headed for the area where couples were dancing. "Okay, Boomer, I get the next dance with Sue Ellen," he called.

"You stupid, whiny, bawlbaby." Judy turned furiously on Beth. "Now look what you've done! Grow up or drop dead."

Tears streaming down her cheeks, sobs tearing at her throat, Beth clenched and unclenched her fists. She wanted to smash Judy's face till it was no more than a bleeding pulp. Judy was taking Kevin away from her! And Kevin was letting her do it! Judy was going to kiss Kevin and make him forget all about everything except making out with her.

"Beth! Beth!" she heard Boomer call. Mindlessly, she turned and ran, darting through the bushes, careful to stay in the shadows until she made her way into the house and stumbled to the powder room. Once inside, she locked the door and sat down on the toilet, a thick terry towel pressed to her mouth to stifle her sobs of self-pity.

After what seemed like hours, she stood and went to the sink to splash cold water on her face. She looked terrible and she felt terrible. A rapping on the door and a muffled "How long you gonna be in there?" broke her attention away from her reflection.

"Just . . . I'll be awhile yet. Can't you use the powder room upstairs?" she managed to reply, fresh tears threatening to choke off her voice.

"No problem. Just didn't want to hike upstairs," the voice answered. Beth waited expectantly for another sound from behind the door. She relaxed when she realized whoever it was had gone away. She wanted to be left alone. She didn't want anyone to see her this way. She couldn't face herself in the mirror, so how could she face Judy or Boomer? Worst of all, she didn't want to face Kevin and see his indifference.

Damn that Judy! God, how she hated her! Why couldn't Kevin see Judy for what she was? A conniving bitch! Beth lowered her head onto her arms, pressing against the cool ceramic sink. What was happening between Kevin and herself? Why was she behaving this way? She couldn't blame Kevin for hating her, not after the way she'd been treating him. But she couldn't help herself somehow. It was just that she was so scared of losing him. Without Kevin she wouldn't have anyone. Bad enough he was going away to college in a few weeks; now Judy was stealing whatever precious time they had left together.

And just now, when she'd asked Kevin to take her home, he had acted as though he didn't care what happened to her as long as it didn't interfere with his making out with Judy. Judy, Judy! Always Judy! What would it take for Kevin to see how much his own sister needed him?

Everything had changed since Mr. Harris came back to town and hired Kevin to work in his store. Kevin was away from home so much of the time now, she didn't have anybody to talk to, no one to rely on. It wasn't even as if they had parents like other kids. It didn't take a genius to see that there was something wrong between Mama and Daddy. It had always been just the two of them, Kevin and Beth. Hadn't they always been close? Closer than any other brother and sister because they only had each other? Now, Cader Harris and Judy were wrecking everything, taking Kevin away from her. Well, she wouldn't let them. No matter what she had to do, Kevin was hers; he would always belong to her.

"Come on, Bethy, you've monopolized the bathroom long enough." Judy's voice held a note of contempt. "You're hiding out, aren't you? Come on, I have to use the bathroom and I'm not going upstairs."

Beth riveted her attention on the closed door, the only barrier between Judy's contempt and her own inadequacy. She wished she could strike Judy Evans dead, right through the wooden panel. Hatred grew in her, matching her panic. Kevin. She couldn't lose Kevin. She had to make him see that she needed him. Her panic became almost tangible and drums sounded in her head. Home. She wanted to go home. Home with Kevin. She had to get him away from Judy, whatever the cost!

Judy's voice called again, her words indistinguishable through Beth's desperation. The eyes that looked back at Beth in the vanity mirror were wide and frightened, glaring out of her whitened features, staring back at her until all perspective was lost and she could perceive only the hollow, empty eyes of the skull on a bottle of iodine. Only one of them could have Kevin, she realized that now. Only one of them—either Beth or Judy.

Her throat was dry, parched, closed against a choking knot of despair. Her hand trembled as she reached for the bathroom glass and turned the cold water faucet as far as it would go. She held the glass beneath the full rush of water, watching it fill and overflow.

"Did you hear me, Beth? When are you coming out of there?" Judy insisted.

"Never," Beth muttered beneath the sound of rushing water. "I'm never going to come out of here. I'm going to die in here and then Kevin will be sorry."

"Beth Thomas!" Judy called again, her tone barely concealing her contempt. "Answer me! I know you're in there, Bethy." Suddenly her tone changed. "Beth, are you all right?" she questioned, concern edging her words now. "Answer me, won't you? Bethy?" After a breath or two, her concern changed to impatience. "Bethy Thomas, open this door. Do I have to pry the lock? I can do it, you know. I only have to turn this little thingamajig with my fingernail. Beth!"

Beth's attention was centered on the doorknob. Hysteria mingled with resentment as she watched the circular insert in the knob slowly turn. Every nerve in her body tightened. Her fingers closed over the slippery glass, crushing it into lethal shards. Blood mixed with running water, turning it pink before it churned and whirlpooled down the drain. Shocked by what she had done, Beth happened to catch sight of her reflection in the mirror. A reflection of a sly creature peering out from behind her own eyes.

The bathroom door swung open. "Bethy?" Judy's harsh intake of breath. "Bethy! What have you done to yourself?"

Beth fixed her eyes on her upraised hand which still clutched the fragments of glass, the crimson of her blood running down her arm. Her fingers opened. The shards of glass fell into the sink.

"Oh, my God! Are you crazy? What'd you do that for?" Judy cried, reaching for the towel and rushing toward Beth.

"Don't touch me!" Beth screamed. "Don't you dare touch me!"

"The bleeding . . ."

"Don't touch me!"

Judy proceeded toward her with the towel; the blood was now running freely, dripping onto the white tiled floor. The shock of seeing what Beth had done was evident in her whitened features and her look of horror. She was barely keeping herself under control in the face of so much blood.

Just as Judy was about to wrap her hand in the towel, Beth screamed at the top of her voice, "No! Don't touch me! Don't ever touch me!"

"You're covered with blood. . . ." The words were cut off in Judy's throat. Beth's eyes had become pinpoints of madness and her movements were frantic as she rubbed her bloodied hand over her left arm and across her neck. Splinters of glass scratched her skin and pricked painfully and then went unnoticed.

"Kevin! Kevin!" Beth screamed, only slightly aware that the hum of conversation and celebration in the next room had suddenly ceased. She pushed her way past a dumbstruck Judy and stumbled through the doorway. "Kevin!" Her face contorted into a mask of frenzy as she ran from the room screaming. "Kevin! Kevin!" The sound burst from her lungs and echoed shrilly above the blare of the stereo. She moved toward the doors leading to the swimming pool, her bloodied arms extended like a sleepwalker's, her eyes glazed with panic and madness. "Kevin, help me!" she wailed pitifully between sobs rising from her throat.

Beth hardly noticed the horror and confusion in the faces of the others as they made a path for her between their ranks. The only sound was the melodic rhythm of "Hotel California" and the sound of her own pleadings. "Kevin! Help me! I'm bleeding!"

Suddenly, she saw him, standing alone and she began to run to him, frantically waving her arms. "Kevin! Kevin!"

Kevin's face was wild with horror. Boomer leaned against the wall muttering over and over, "Oh shit, oh shit!"

"What happened?" Kevin demanded, trying to force her arms from around his neck to quiet her down.

"I'm bleeding! I didn't mean to do it! I'm bleeding! Take me home, Kev, please take me out of here!" Her words ended in a chattering shudder that frightened him.

"We have to stop that bleeding. . . . Judy . . . where's Judy?" His eyes frantically scanned the crowd gathering around them. "For Crissakes, get me a towel or something. . . ."

Beth pulled herself away from him, leaving a trail of crimson across his shoulders. Judy . . . always Judy! Here she was, bleeding to death, and all he could think about was Judy! "I want to go home, Kev," she wailed weakly. "I want Mama!"

Kevin grasped her by the shoulders. "We gotta stop that bleeding! We gotta make sure you didn't cut an artery or something. . . ."

"No!" Beth shrilled. "I want Mama! Mama! Take me home to Mama!" But Kevin wasn't even hearing her. He was looking at Judy, who had brought him the towel from the bathroom.

Beth broke away from Kevin and pushed her way through the gathering crowd. "Mama!" she continued to scream as she raced across the patio and around the front of the house.

As Kevin raced after her, the last thing he heard as he rounded the side of the house was Boomer shouting at the top of his lungs, "Oh shit! Oh shit! She tried to kill herself!"

CHAPTER TWELVE

Irene Thomas powdered her slim body and felt satisfied. Tonight was going to be Arthur's night. She was no fool; she could read him like he read his undertaking manuals. Carefully, she pressed the thin material of the prim-looking nightgown over her hips and smiled at her reflection.

"I've been a good wife, Arthur," she mouthed silently. "It's just that sometimes I . . . sometimes I remember another time and another place. I'm thirty-six years old and women . . . *I* start thinking about that other time and that other place. I *have* been a good wife and mother. I'm not a selfish person. Didn't I give you Beth? Didn't I give you a daughter who looks like you? I did that for you, Arthur. If I wasn't a good person, I would never have wanted to have a child with you. You'll never know that Kevin isn't your son. I atoned for that by giving you Beth. I don't feel guilty." *If you don't feel guilty, then why are you defending yourself?* a small, niggling voice asked the reflection in the mirror. Irene straightened and moved back from the square mirror. "Because . . . because I know that I still love Cader Harris. I gave you Beth as your own. My obligation to you has been paid and now I can do what I want. You have a beautiful home, lovely children, your rightful place in the community and a devoted wife. I am devoted . . . in my own way," she said grimly. "All these years, all the unsatisfied, sleepless nights. It's my inalienable right. You never knew about Kevin, and there's no reason for you to know anything about this. I'll protect you, Arthur," she whispered to the mirror.

A dab of perfume on each ear lobe and a quick splash between her breasts, and she was ready. She opened the door a crack and stood for a moment watching Arthur turn the pages of one of his pathology textbooks. She opened the door wider and leaned languidly against the frame, her eyes moist and warm as she stared at her husband. "Artie," she called softly.

Arthur's head jerked up and his eyes widened. She hadn't called him Artie since the first time she let him seduce her. Sweet Jesus! Before he could say another word she was on top of him, her breathing out of control, her hands caressing his naked chest as her lips clung to his. He'd been reading too many of his own magazines. He must be dead and on his way to heaven. Was this Irene Hayden doing all these delicious things to him? "Sweet Jesus," he moaned as he felt her tongue begin to work its special magic. He knew, he just knew, that this was going to be one of those once-in-a-lifetime fucks. "Oh, Jesus," he moaned over and over as he straddled his panting, heaving wife. "Oooooh, oooooh . . ."

What seemed like hours later, Arthur spoke. "God, Irene, it took you eighteen years, but you finally did it. I'll never forget this night, ever," he said as he patted his limp penis.

Irene was still gasping like a fish out of water as she listened to Arthur's words. She wanted it again and she knew she was capable, right this minute, right this second. It was Cader Harris. All she had to do was substitute Cader's face and cock for Arthur's and she could get it off. If it worked once, it would work again.

She rolled over, her eyes closed tightly as she slid beneath the covers, her hands and mouth searching desperately for Arthur's penis that he clasped protectively in both hands. "I want it," she moaned hoarsely. "Now. I want it now!"

"Oh, God. Oh, God. Oooooh. Oh, God. Oh, God. Ooooooooh."

Arthur's last thought as he drifted off to sleep was that he hoped no one would die during the night. If they did, they were on their own, and he couldn't give a good roaring fuck.

Cader Harris gave the Venetian blind on the front door of the shop a vicious tug and was stunned to see Beth Thomas racing down the street screaming, "Mama! Help me! Do something; I'm bleeding!" Her brother was in hot pursuit. Now what in hell was that all about? He walked outside, hands on hips, staring after the running twosome. *Everybody was screwed up, why should those two be any different,* he thought philosophically. He had other things on his mind, important things. Things that wouldn't go away by thinking about something else. The phone would ring shortly. "What the hell," he muttered as he walked back into the shop and slammed the door. Another hour to piss away before the phone call. An hour that could be spent making time at Aunt Cledie's.

Irene Thomas woke, fear clutching her throat. "What . . . what is it?" she called in a shaking voice. "Beth, stop the screaming and answer me! What's wrong?" Quickly, she scrambled into her robe before Beth could burst into the room and catch her nude from the lovemaking.

"Arthur, wake up!" She poked the sleeping form beside her. "Arthur!"

"Oooooh," he groaned, rolling over and burying his head under the pillow, trying to drive Irene's screams of passion from his ears. Why was she bleeding to death and what did Kevin have to do with it? . . . Kevin!

"Mama! Make it stop! Make it go away!" Beth cried hysterically. "I'm going to die," she bellowed, "and Kevin didn't do anything to help me! I ran all the way home by myself! Mama!"

Irene's mouth dropped open as she was confronted with the sight of her daughter smeared with dried blood.

Kevin burst through the front door and bounded up the stairs. He was breathless and his face was white with shock. "Bethy!"

Beth extended her hand for Irene to examine. The bleeding had slowed considerably, and it was difficult for Irene to imagine how Beth had managed to cover herself with blood. One glance at Kevin and his bloodied shirt and Irene felt dizzy. "Oh, my God, you've had an accident with the car!"

"No, we didn't . . ." Kevin rushed to explain before Irene interrupted.

"Arthur! Arthur! Get yourself up and come out here! Hurry! Kevin's had an accident with the car and Beth is bleeding to death!" she called as she put her arm around Beth and half dragged, half carried her to the bathroom.

"We didn't have an accident with the car! Beth cut herself somehow! Christ! The kids are saying she tried to kill herself!" Kevin ran his hand through his hair, a deep, vertical crease forming between his brows.

Irene paused for a moment before she grabbed Beth's right hand and brought it up for examination. "Arthur! For God's sake, get yourself out here and call Marc Baldwin. Tell him we need him right away! Now, Arthur!"

Arthur Thomas staggered out of the bedroom. His pajama bottoms kept slipping around his waist, and he had to keep hitching them up so he wouldn't trip on them. In his haste to put something on he had screwed up the string ties. His robe flapped open and his hands kept groping for the elusive belt.

"Look, Dad, I don't know what happened to Beth. She came running out of the bathroom, screaming she was bleeding to death. She was covered with blood. When I tried to do something to stop the bleeding and see what was wrong with her, she ran away from me. I ran after her, but she had a good head start on me, and I still don't know what's wrong with her. I left your car at the party. I'm sorry, Dad. All I could think of was to run after her. God only knows what she's gone and done to herself. Now the kids are saying she tried to kill herself."

"Take it easy, Kevin. I know that whatever it is, it's not your fault. Beth's always been high-strung. It must be the Hayden blood in her. Go and change your shirt. Beth's got you covered with her blood."

As Kevin changed, he could hear Arthur talking quietly to Dr. Baldwin. He heard Arthur lower his voice as he said, "Irene wanted you to come over here. Look, Marc, if Beth did try to do something to herself . . . well, things get around this town as it is. If we took her to the hospital, there would be no stopping the rumors and people would just make it out to be worse than it is. It can't be serious. The only blood I saw on her was already dry. . . ." Kevin listened as Arthur said his thanks to Marc Baldwin.

Low tones, then Irene's voice penetrated the silence in the house. "But, Beth, I don't understand. If you cut yourself on the bathroom glass, how did all this blood get all over you?" Irene pried Beth's hand open and looked at the wounds. "That's pretty nasty; there's imbedded glass. Not to worry, Marc will get it all out," Irene soothed.

"Where's Kevin?" Beth asked, wincing slightly.

"He's out in the hall, dear. You gave him quite a scare." Irene looked at Beth and for an instant she got the impression of some sly creature peering out of her daughter's eyes.

"I just don't want him to be angry with me, that's all," Beth explained. "I just ruined his night, I know I did. But I couldn't help it, Mama! I got so scared! And Kevin was no help at all! He just wanted to wrap a towel around it! And I wouldn't let him." *Just like I wouldn't let him stay and mess around with Judy*, Beth thought exultantly.

"I just can't understand all this blood!" Irene complained as she worked feverishly with a soapy washcloth and towel while Beth stood quietly, only wincing occasionally when her mother plucked a sliver of glass out of her palm. "What could you have been thinking of to be so careless with a glass, of all things? And did you hear what Kevin said? They . . . they think you tried to commit . . . Oh, God! It's too horrible! Think of the rumors! I won't be able to hold my head up in this town! And neither will you, Beth Thomas. What in the world did you do to yourself?"

Arthur knocked on the closed bathroom door. "Beth? How are you? Irene, what's going on in there?"

"It's open, Arthur. Beth just cut her hand on a bathroom glass. Isn't that right, honey?" Irene said with false brightness. "All it needs is some cleaning up. Did you call Marc?"

"I got that poor man out of bed to come and clean a few cuts?

We could have taken her over to the emergency clinic!" Arthur complained.

"No, we couldn't. Imagine, this town would be rife with rumor of terrible things about Beth and . . . and her mental condition." She eyed Arthur frantically so that he would shut up and let her handle it.

"Where's Kevin?"

Arthur ignored Beth. "What do you mean, 'her mental condition'?"

"Daddy! Where's Kevin?" Beth whined.

"You know as well as I do," Irene said hotly. "You heard what Kevin said. Some of the children are saying that Beth tried to . . . Oh, never mind!"

"Daddy! Where's Kevin?" Beth demanded.

"Out! I told him to go and get the car," Arthur answered impatiently.

"Now, Arthur, go downstairs and wait for Marc. I'll help Beth get into bed. Laws! Did you ever see . . ."

"Daddy! Are you saying Kevin went back to the party?" Beth directed her gaze on her father.

"No, I didn't say that. I said he went to get the car. But I wouldn't blame him if he did go back to the party. If only to make up for all the unpleasantness you've caused tonight."

"Arthur, this isn't the time for that." Irene shook her head warningly. "Kevin must be very upset. Are you certain he'll be all right to drive?"

"Mama," Beth whined, "here I am, bleeding like a stuck pig, and all you could think about is Kevin! It's always Kevin. Kevin this and Kevin that. You've always loved him more than me!"

Disgusted, Arthur turned and left the room.

Insensitive as always to her husband's feelings, Irene complained to Beth, "Honestly, now what's gotten into him? Here, now let me wrap this towel around your hand. We'll get you all nice and cozy in your bed. Now, how does that sound . . . ?"

"Shut up, Mama," Beth said flatly. Beth's eyes were glaring, her mouth was set in a tight thin line as she thought of Kevin returning to the party. And to Judy.

Cader Harris hunched over his desk, his face cast in shadows by the downward tilt of the gooseneck lamp near his left hand. The phone receiver was pressed to his ear. His expression betrayed his misery while his voice strained to exude confidence. "Well, what if it is taking longer than we planned?" He braved a chuckle. "The results will be the same. Look, I've been meeting with the town's merchants and they're on our side. Even the Board of Education sees the advantages to having Delta Oil come into town. They know the value of a buck."

Cader listened, his face grim, while the voice grumbled discontentedly on the other end of the line.

"I've made a friend here in town, a very influential friend. She's promised me her support, and she's making good on her word. Who do you think got me in to see the Board of Ed?" He listened again to the voice at the other end of the line.

"You've got to make certain, Cader, that you keep to the deadline. We at Delta Oil are getting edgy, I don't have to tell you that. The only reason we haven't stepped in before now is because we don't want any reverberations a year or two from now. That's why we sent you as our emissary. We don't want some loudmouth blabbing about a payoff. But I'm warning you, Harris, at the price we're paying we can't afford to make mistakes. If we have to bypass you and handle things ourselves, we will. Then you'll be out in the cold, and you won't get your percentage."

"You're not telling me something I don't already know," Cader said bitterly. "I don't mind telling you I don't trust you bastards as far as I can throw one of your oil tankers." A fine beading of perspiration stood out starkly on his brow. "Just keep your cool; things are working out fine. Just leave it up to me; I'll handle it."

Kevin walked the deserted street, putting one foot in front of the other. He'd wait until later to get the car. Much later. After the scene Beth had made he didn't want to face anyone. He raised his head from between hunched shoulders and noticed he was rounding the corner near the sporting goods store. A dim light glowed from within. He tested the door and found it open. Curious, he moved inside. The light was coming from Mr. Harris's office, and Kevin could hear the faint murmur of conversation coming from behind the closed door.

Cader had just hung up the phone when he noticed the doorknob on his office door turn. *What the hell?* He stood and rocked back on his heel, a paperweight gripped tightly in his hand as he stared at the door in fascination.

"Yo! What have we here?" He grinned as Kevin entered the room.

"Mr. Harris, I found the front door open and thought I'd take a look around. I didn't realize you were in here," Kevin mumbled, shuffling his feet.

"Damn white of you, boy. But what are you doing around town at one in the morning?" Cader reconsidered his last statement. "Listen, kid, you don't owe me any explanations. Your business is your business and my business is mine. If you want to talk about it, that's something else." The boy looked as though something was bugging the hell out of him. He could spare a few minutes for wise and sincere counsel, Cader told himself. Aunt Cledie's girls never slept. There sure as hell was a lot to say for twenty-four-hour service. Kevin's problem must have something to do with his whacked-out little sister.

"It's not important, Mr. Harris. Just a little family hooray. I was just out walking."

"I can think of better things to do to work it off. Listen, Kevin, you ever been to Aunt Cledie's?" At Kevin's negative nod, Cade continued. "How would you like to come with me? I'll fix you up with some poontang and a little white lightning, the likes of which you'll never get anywhere else."

Cader waited for Kevin's response and smiled to himself. Arthur Thomas may have raised Kevin at his own knee and influenced the boy's upbringing, but he, Cader Harris, would see to his own son's sex education. Let Arthur Thomas handle the insignificant matters; Cader would handle the important ones.

Shit, out of the frying pan and into the fire, Kevin thought wildly. If Judy was right about what she told Boomer, the last thing he needed right now was a dose of the clap. Or was Judy just putting Boomer on? "No, I've never been there. The guys say all the girls have the clap." His face flushed; Kevin backed off a step and watched Cader Harris to see his reaction.

"Yo, is that what they're saying? Cledie spreads those rumors herself so she doesn't get all those unseasoned high-school kids. Cledie's girls are so clean they squeak. Do you think I'd risk a dose of the clap? Come on, kid, take my word for it. You haven't lived till you've had poontang. What do you say?"

Kevin's misery weighed against him, pressing down on his shoulders. He'd sell his soul to be like Cader Harris, who seemed to have no problems in hanging it all together. If a little poontang could straighten out Mr. Harris's head, maybe it would do the same for him.

"You got it, Mr. Harris. You're right, that's exactly what I need."

"If we're going to get poontang together, you can stop calling me Mr. Harris. Make it Cader. And as a special favor to you, I'm going to personally handpick your girl. You want one or two?" he asked as an afterthought.

Kevin blinked. *Why the hell not?* "Two sounds good to me."

"Not that it's any of my business, but have you ever . . ." Cade grinned at the wretched look on Kevin's face.

"Oh, kid, is Aunt Cledie gonna love you. When she gets a virgin, she rolls out the red carpet. Cledie keeps a sort of track record of her 'virgins.' Reads like *Who's Who*. You get a plaque after ten years. See what you got to look forward to? Any time you're ready, kid. The sooner we get there, the sooner we get what we want. Look at it this way, in one month you got two diplomas, one for school and one for life. Yo, I would have made one hell of a good teacher!"

Cader drove his rental car down the deep rutted road with its low-hanging trees. "Jesus, this is the only thing I hate about this place. One of these days Cledie has got to get some kind of light around here. A man could kill himself on this fucking road. Kid, it's worth it." He grinned in the darkness. "To your left, see those lights. That's going to be your home away from home from now on. Night or day, you'll always find a welcome here."

Kevin laughed nervously as he watched Cader maneuver the car between a dilapidated pickup and a long, pearl-gray Lincoln that looked like Destry's status symbol.

"Take a good look, kid. Once you go through those hallowed doors, you ain't never gonna be the same."

Kevin risked a quick glance around the junk-filled yard and at a stray chicken scratching near the rickety steps that led to a sagging front porch. "I thought chickens slept at night," he said inanely.

"Boy, there ain't anyone that sleeps at Cledie's! Okay, this is it, kid; smile. Always smile, makes the girls think they're getting something special. It's when *they* smile and show too many teeth that you have to worry."

Kevin fixed a smile on his face and followed Cader into the room which seemed to be overflowing with overstuffed burgundy furniture and people. He squinted into the dimness and wished that Aunt Cledie used something brighter than a fifteen-watt bulb. Inside, the air was stifling; not a breeze blew in through the windows where light, lacy curtains were knotted to allow any stray breath of air free passage. As his eyes became adjusted to the yellowish light, he could see several women, some of them young, some not so young, lounging around on sofas and chairs, their bare legs exposed by scanty, bright satin robes. Kevin got the impression of glistening brown skin and white teeth.

Several black men were sitting near a makeshift bar constructed of wooden planks and a barrel. One of them was Destry, his father's associate. When Destry's dark glance flicked over Kevin, the boy felt like running, afraid to be seen here, afraid Arthur would find out. But the way Destry turned his back on him, Kevin knew that his secret would be safe.

Several women smiled at him. There seemed to be more teeth in this one room than all of the Osmonds' put together. His stomach lurched slightly as he noticed a buxom, dark-skinned woman bearing down on Cader. She was dressed in a ruby-red wrapper and her bare feet were pushed into silver sandals. Her breasts were huge and swayed with each step she took, and her plump hand brushed at her frizzy hair, wiping the perspiration which trickled down her face.

"Lordy, lordy, twice in one week! Ah jus' don' believe it! Mah gals are shoah ta go up in smoke! What's this youah bringin' me, honey?" She grinned at Cader, showing bright gold caps for front teeth.

"Jus' what you like best, Aunt Cledie. An eighteen-year-old virgin. Treat him just the way you would me, you hear?" Cader said piously.

Cledie's eyes swallowed Kevin whole and spit him back for the other girls in the room to devour. "Honey, we've all been jus' sittin' here pinin' for somethin' lak this. Pretty baby," she crooned, patting Kevin's head, "Auntie Cledie is jus' gonna make a man outa you. If'n you live to be a hundred, you ain' never gonna get an edjucayshun lak you're gonna get t'night." She laughed, a deep, husky laugh that made Kevin want to shrink into the farthest corner.

"Stop lookin' like you're ready to crawl up your own asshole!" Cader whispered fiercely. He then turned to Aunt Cledie, who was already speculating which of her girls would have the treat of breaking this youngster in. "Don't rush with him, Cledie. We don't have to leave until around sunup."

"Honey, edjucaytin' a man's not somethin' we do in a hurry. This pretty baby is gonna learn and he's gonna learn Aunt Cledie's way. Y' can settle up when you leave. I jus' might throw this one in for free. Too soon to promise, though. You take it easy on my gals, you heah, Cader Harris? I got a whole passel of young studs comin' up from N'awleans, but theah ain' a virgin in the bunch," she said disgustedly. "Ah specialize in virgins, in case you haven't heard," she said as she fixed Kevin with a scorching look.

"Don't just talk about it, Cledie. Show him before he wets his pants. I'll just take Charlene upstairs with me. She's just a little too frisky for our young man here. See ya 'round, kid." Cader grinned. "Don't thank me, just enjoy yourself."

Aunt Cledie snapped her fingers. "Viola, chile, c'mon over heah. There's somebody ah wants you ta meet."

The girl Aunt Cledie called Viola stood up from an oversized chair in the corner. Kevin gasped when he saw her. He remembered her from school, only Viola had dropped out in ninth grade. Kevin gulped. How was he going to get it on with somebody he knew? He thought everybody here would be a stranger, not some girl he'd gone to kindergarten with! Kevin's eyes were fastened on Viola as she picked her way across the room. She was tall, almost as tall as he was, and the scanty slip she was wearing clung to her full, round breasts and almost boyishly slim hips. He could see that she wore nothing beneath the slip, and the slight protuberance of her belly was sharply indented near the center where her navel was, almost as though someone had punched his thumb into soft dough.

Kevin suddenly felt wet under the arms, and he became aware of a buzzing in his ears as he gulped and swallowed. Viola looked at him with shining dark eyes, her finely defined lips parting over strong white teeth. "C'mon, honey," she said huskily, a knowing smile on her face, "we ain't got all night." She moved closer to him and he could smell the slightly musky femaleness of her, he could almost feel the warmth of her body radiating across the space between them.

"G'wan, chile." Aunt Cledie laughed throatily. "An' when y'all come down them stairs, yo ain' gonna be a chile no moah." This seemed to strike the other occupants of the room as funny, and a titter of laughter danced through the room. A tremor ran down Kevin's legs and sparked between his toes, feet ready to run. Viola reached out her slim arm and touched him lightly, calming his apprehensions.

"Y'all jus' follow me, honey. Viola's gonna take real good care of you." She led him toward the stairs. As she mounted the steps, Kevin in her wake, he focused on the exaggerated swing of her narrow hips and the remarkable length of her legs, shown off to perfection in her run-down high-heeled slippers.

Just when he thought he couldn't take another step, when he felt the irrepressible urge to turn around and slink down the stairs out into the safety of the dark night, something happened. Viola turned and looked down at him, a radiant smile lighting her pretty face, and in her shining eyes was a look that said, "I like you, Kevin Thomas; I've always liked you, and thank you for letting me be your first."

Kevin returned her smile and jogged up two steps to catch up with her. They mounted the remaining stairs together, arms around each other, and when she pressed her warm body close against his, Kevin laughed out loud. If he had anything to do with it, Viola was going to come away learning a few lessons herself!

CHAPTER THIRTEEN

*D*estry suppressed a grin as he watched Arthur Thomas make an ineffectual swipe at the stainless steel table. His chocolate eyes noted the almost silly expression on his associate's face and the haphazard way he had been doing things all morning. The suppressed grin blossomed when Destry remembered that it had been Kevin at Aunt Cledie's the night before, and not Arthur. There wasn't another thing in the entire world that could make a man look like Arthur Thomas looked except a trip to Cledie's and a good roll in the sack. This just might be the right time to talk to Arthur, when he was in this expansive mood and agreeable to what looked like almost anything. Son of a bitch, hadn't he offered to let him, Destry, embalm a white man? That alone set some sort of precedent. After lunch, he told himself as he watched the last of the embalming fluid drain through the tube. Done. And another white man has bit the dust.

Arthur matched his silly grin and said, "You just finish up in here, Destry. I'm going into my office and . . . and finish that Anaïs Nin book. Carry on, Destry," Arthur said airily as he flounced from the room.

"I'll be a ring-tailed son of a bitch." Destry laughed aloud as he watched Arthur's retreating back. It just might pay to find out where the white man had spent his night.

In his office with the door closed and locked, Arthur Thomas sat back in his comfortable swivel chair and propped his legs on the corner of the sleek mahogany desk. The hell with Anaïs Nin. Nothing could top last night. It had been so long since Irene got it off, he'd been thinking her twat was as dry as good ol' Aunt Matilda's meat loaf. Was Irene experiencing her second awakening? Jesus! Even though he wasn't a Catholic, he crossed himself reverently and prayed that last night was a preview of things to come. Jesus! The phone shrilled on his desk.

"It's Sunny, Arthur. I was wondering if it would be all right to stop by around four-thirty."

"Sunny, good to hear from you. Why don't you stop by now? If you're not busy, that is. Destry is . . . Destry is busy and we'll . . . Look, why don't you come over now? I'd like it if you could stop by," he said firmly as his hand found its way to his crotch.

Arthur smiled to himself and continued to talk in what he thought was his sexiest voice, "I'm just going to close my eyes and keep them closed until you get here. I'm going to sit here and think of all the beautiful things you're going to do to me when you do get here."

Sunny bit into her lower lip as she hung up the receiver. Arthur had it all wrong, and she was too much of a dummy to tell him over the phone. He thought she was coming over for a little nooky and her hundred-dollar tip. Nothing could be farther from the truth. What she wanted to see Arthur about was his wife, Irene.

Late yesterday afternoon Cader had come to her apartment. She was delighted to see him, but there was something strange about him. To quote the poets, one could say he almost had "stars in his eyes." After an unabashed drilling, he admitted to her that he had renewed his relationship with Irene Thomas.

Cader's revelation had stunned her. She feigned a lightheartedness she couldn't feel. It was happening again, after all these years; she was losing Cader Harris to Irene Hayden all over again.

After Cader left, Sunday Waters agonized for the remainder of the day and long into the early morning hours. She came to the conclusion that she wouldn't lose Cader to Irene twice, not without a fight. She would nip this little romance in the bud, doing anything she must. Sunday figured she had nothing to lose. If she did nothing, Irene would win, just as she had the last time when Sunday waited for Cader to come back to her. She knew she risked losing Cader if he ever discovered she went to Arthur with the information, but she had to take her chances.

During the short ride to the funeral home, Sunny rehearsed what she would say to Arthur. She hated doing this to him; he was one of Irene's victims, just as she was. She didn't place any blame on Cader, he was an innocent who had never grown up and was still trying to cross the tracks by making love to Princess Irene.

Arthur was waiting for her just as he had promised. His face was wreathed in a smile of genuine affection. Arthur was always happy to see her, and not only on these quiet afternoons. Arthur was a friend, and whatever else existed between them was for their mutual benefit.

With a sinking feeling, as if someone was churning her insides with a red-hot poker, Sunday realized she could no more break this man's heart by squealing on Irene and Cader than she could whip a sick puppy. Arthur Thomas was probably the only real down-to-earth, hundred-percent human being in this whole eff'n town. Sunny told herself she might be a lot of things, but a fink wasn't one of them.

It wasn't so much the expectant look on Arthur's face, it was the more than noticeable bulge in his trousers that prompted

Sunny to whisper, "Just sit there, Arthur." She opened the buttons of her blouse and clicked the lock on the door behind her. "I'll do all the rest."

Later that night, sitting alone in the living room, Arthur reflected on the rebirth of Irene's sex life. Ever since he'd returned from the funeral home that evening she'd been casting him sidelong glances that promised him "everything." Arthur shifted in his chair, pulling the center seam of his pajama bottom away from his crotch. The head of his penis was sore and red. But it was happy! One good ol' happy cock expertly serviced by Irene and Sunny!

Arthur Thomas closed his magazine and walked into the hallway when he heard Kevin's key in the lock. The boy looked happy, happier than he had seen him in a long while. "Have a good time, son?" Arthur asked as he slipped his arm around the boy's shoulder.

"Yes, sir, I did. The movie was great and then we walked on the beach for a while. Judy had to be home at ten-thirty or we'd still be there. We just talked, Dad."

"I know that son. But where'd you go after that? It's nearly one A.M." Arthur pierced Kevin with a curious glance. He had picked up the slightly sour odor of beer and whiskey almost the moment Kevin had walked in the door.

Kevin hung his head and couldn't meet Arthur's eyes. "Well, some of the guys got together and we had a couple of six-packs. I met them on my way back from Judy's house," Kevin lied. He couldn't tell Arthur that he'd run into Cader Harris and had spent the last few hours talking man-talk and drinking boilermakers.

Arthur sighed. "Well, I suppose boys'll be boys. You didn't have too much, I hope." He bent his head to look up into Kevin's guilty expression. Hell, he shouldn't make it hard on the boy. After all, he would be going off to college in a few weeks. From his own experience Arthur knew about the "beer brawls" that were a part of campus life. It was better that Kevin had his first taste here, close to home, rather than among strangers miles away, where he could really get into trouble. Let the kid learn to handle the stuff while he had some kind of supervision. He could see Kevin was very uncomfortable under his scrutiny and he tried to calm him. "Look, son, you don't have to explain anything to me. I'm glad you feel you can be open with me."

"I don't mind telling you about what I do, Dad. All I had was a few beers. As for Judy, I like her a lot. I'm taking her to the clam-bake."

"That's good, son. Listen, are you hungry? Beer can do that to a guy. D'you want a sandwich? A glass of milk, maybe?"

"No thanks, Dad. We had a hamburger and a Coke at the stand in town. I'll sit with you if you want something, though."

"I don't need it, Kev." Arthur patted his belly. "It's late and we both have a busy day tomorrow. Get a good night's sleep. I'll see you in the morning."

In his room Kevin peeled his clothes off. *A cold shower should do it,* he thought as he stripped down. Cader Harris said it was the best thing for what ailed you when things got temporarily postponed.

As he shucked out of his jeans, a dull thunk caught his attention. Christ! The flask Cader had given him. He must have had more to drink than he thought to forget that and leave it where Mom might find it. He fished through the pocket and extracted a slim, shiny flask. He shook it and realized it was still half full. He considered dumping it down the sink and then rinsing it out, but instead put the flask to his lips and downed it. He choked as the liquid rushed down his throat and began to warm his insides. Still coughing, he went into his bathroom and rinsed the flask under the cold water tap. Before he left to tuck the cylinder into his drawer, he turned on his shower.

He suddenly felt the need for the bracing water for more than a general feeling of horniness. That last drink had packed a wal-lop all its own. The moment the needle-sharp spray touched his body he felt better. Cader was right again. He was always right. Tonight, after his early date with Judy, Kevin had gone to see Cader hoping he would suggest a trip out to Aunt Cledie's. Instead, they had gotten into a heavy discussion about sex and drinking. Cader sure knew what it was all about, Kevin nodded to himself. Just like he told him about cold showers. He'd also told him not to jerk off, that only kids did that. He said there was enough free ass around so that a guy didn't ever have to waste himself on his own hands. Kevin supposed Cader was right, but it sure would be a welcome relief along about now. At least he had the clambake to look forward to. Judy wouldn't have her period then and she had all but promised they would "get together," if he knew what she meant. He believed her. He liked her and was glad she would be going to Tulane with him. He was suddenly glad his life was changing and he owed it all to Cader Harris. Without him he would still be dragging his little sister around behind him. Not that he didn't like Beth, he told himself, but a guy had a right to do his own thing. Kevin crawled beneath the thin sheet, not bothering with his pajamas. Men like Cader Harris and Kevin slept in the raw.

Beth lay for a long time after the sound of the shower in Kevin's room stopped. She knew why Kevin was showering so long. To wash off the smell and feel of Judy Evans. He would have to shower for hours, she told herself, to get rid of Judy Evans. He must be in bed now. What was he thinking about? Was he thinking about Judy?

Beth's eyes circled the dimness in her room and came to rest on a bevy of stuffed animals Kevin had won for her at various state fairs. She loved each and every one of them because Kevin had given them to her. She loved them almost as much as she hated Judy Evans. Hate, hate, hate!

She couldn't sleep. Was Kevin sleeping? Crawling from her bed, she walked over to the open window and looked out into the still, quiet night. *Starlight, star bright, first star I see tonight. Wish I may, wish I might, have the wish I wish tonight. I wish Judy Evans would drop dead. Dead, dead, dead!*

Her stomach churned and she fought back the tears that burned her eyes. It was so hot, so hot she couldn't breathe. Quickly, she pulled off her thin nightgown and stood before the window. She shivered. It wasn't hot, it was cold. Reaching down, she grabbed at the terry robe and gratefully snuggled into its warmth. Something was wrong with her. Her head felt fuzzy and her mouth was dry. Her breasts felt funny. Funny and good at the same time. It must have something to do with periods, she thought as she sat down on the edge of the bed. Now she was hot again. Maybe she should wake Mama and see if she had a fever. Kevin. Kevin would know what to do. Kevin always knew what to do. She would wake him and ask him.

Quietly, she tiptoed down the hall to Kevin's room and carefully opened the door. He was asleep. She could hear his regular breathing above the hum of his air conditioner. Dropping her robe to the floor, she turned back the sheet and slipped in beside him. Immediately, she detected the sour smell of stale whiskey on his breath. As her hand slid over his chest, he mumbled something. It sounded like a name . . . Viola.

CHAPTER FOURTEEN

*D*amion Conway checked off each name on the clipboard as the band members climbed aboard the bus that would take them to Disney World. He wished he felt like they did, carefree and happy. No worries except to have a good time. He glanced around. Looked like the whole town was out to see the kids off.

He knew she was there before he turned his head. He could feel her presence. His eyes narrowed slightly beneath the polarized lens. She was so still, so quiet, as she stared at the laughing, chattering youngsters. Her eyes met his and locked. Time stood still. The desire to reach out, to run through the crowd of milling people, was almost unbearable. He wanted to touch her, say something to her. Words, any kind of words, just to speak to her. Just to say her name. Keli. Keli.

"And what do we have here?" Cader Harris mocked as he slapped Damion on the back. "Surely, we don't have a case of unrequited love, or do we? Doesn't one of the Commandments say, 'Thou shall not covet another man's wife'? For shame, Damion."

"You bastard!" Damion hissed through clenched teeth. "What the hell do you know about the Commandments? Watch it, Cade, or I'll knock every one of those pearly whites right down your lying throat."

"Here? Before the pillars of the community?" Cade taunted. "You have a look in your eye and a bulge in your pants that says you lie. Now, just what the hell kind of parson does that make you? Makes me downright sick to think these people come to you for spiritual guidance. I bet you have a thing going, like that dentist back in New York who got his jollies with his patients when they were gassed up. Makes me downright sick. And profanity . . . I'm appalled!" Cade clicked his tongue to show his disapproval and moved slightly so that he was out of Damion's reach, just in case he decided to throw a wild punch. There was no way he wanted all of his porcelain scattered around the town of Hayden. "As to those Commandments," Cader continued in a mocking tone, "I made up the eleventh one. It's called 'Harris Eleven.' Want to hear it, Parson?"

"I don't want to hear anything from you. You're disgusting, Cader. Now why the hell don't you buzz off and leave me alone?"

"Now is that any way for you to talk to an old friend?" Cader goaded, knowing Damion's temper was at the boiling point. He didn't like himself for the way he always needled Damion, but he was beyond helping himself. Grudges died hard and he supposed he never forgot the way Conway refused to let bygones be bygones over that stupid debate in senior year. "From those moonstruck looks I saw you giving Keli, I think you got a good thing going. But," he wagged a playful finger, "she don't want to play, right? Hell, I'd give that situation a wide berth myself. That crazy colonel she's married to would just about cut off your balls if he caught you with his wife. Either way you could lose. I read somewhere that those Orientals are some kind of nuts. An eye for an eye, that kind of thing. What is she? A Filipino? A Sap? Yeah, I read it in *East Wind Rain.* They just cut a man's cock right off if he gets caught messing with someone's wife. The colonel probably learned it from her. Watch it, Damion."

"You son of a bitch, I'll kill you yet," Damion grated, his fists clenched and knuckles itching to pound Harris's face to a bloody pulp. Glancing around at the children, he forced himself to regain control.

"There's nothing worse than a cockless man unless it's a man with *no* balls and *no* cock." Cader grinned as he feinted to the left out of Damion's arm's reach. "See you around, ol' buddy. Hey,

Damion!" he added as an afterthought. "I've had a few Chinks in my time, and take my word for it, they ain't what they're cracked up to be. They're nonmovers. Shit, man! You could masturbate and get the same effect. But," he grinned, "they do say 'Thank you' when it's over." Cader laughed all the way back to his car.

Cader felt a deep anger gnawing away at his insides. Words kept surfacing in his brain. No matter how he tried to put them out of his way, they refused to budge. It was true he had old scores to settle and he was going to do it before he left Hayden. It was a piss-ass world and he didn't like it one bit. Who the hell did these people think they were? His hand was on the doorknob of the shop when he saw the reflection of the long black Lincoln going by. Foster Doyle Hayden. Now, there was an old score and one he had every intention of settling. And soon.

The sporting goods store was cool and dim after the direct glare of the sunlight. For some reason that angered Cader. He likened it to the time the old man had come to the shack he called home. It had been cool and dim that day too, beneath the tarpaper roof of the shanty.

Cader's hands toyed with the empty coffee cup on his desk as he let his mind swirl back in time to that hateful day when he had sold his soul to the devil: Foster Doyle Hayden.

"Mr. Hayden, what brings you way over here?" Cade had asked nervously, debating whether he should invite the impeccably dressed man into the shabby two-room shack. The decision was made for him when Hayden shouldered him aside and marched into the room. His eyes took in the peeling paint, the sagging furniture and the linoleum-covered floor in one swift, appraising glance. Cader's back stiffened as he moved three days' worth of newspapers from the one good chair so the older man could sit down. Hayden peered at the chair and remained standing.

"I'll get right to the point, Harris. I'm here to do you the biggest favor of your life. But first, I want you to understand something. I am aware that you've been seeing my daughter, and, as of this minute, it must cease! Don't deny that you've both been sneaking behind my back. If there's one thing I won't tolerate it's a lie at this stage of the game."

Cader bristled at the old man's tone. Just who the hell did he think he was, coming to his house and looking down his nose at him? "Did you tell Irene you were coming here?" Cader asked brazenly, all the while quaking in his shoes.

Foster Doyle Hayden ignored Cader's question and continued. "I said I was here to do you the biggest favor of your life and I mean it. How would you like to go to Tulane University, all expenses paid?"

Cader was dumbfounded. "What do I have to do? Are you talking about a football scholarship?"

"I'm talking about me paying for your education, four years of it along with off-campus housing, a car and a five-hundred-dollar-a-month allowance."

"Just like that?" Cader asked quietly, his nimble brain running over the numbers. "Why? Why me?"

Foster Doyle Hayden pulled a cigar from his breast pocket and bit off the end. He didn't bother to look around to see if anyone was watching; he just spit the tip of the cigar on the floor. "I feel like being generous. You have great athletic potential and I feel that it can be developed at Tulane. I personally guarantee that you'll be All-American the first year out. This is your chance, Harris, to get away from here," he said, a sneer in his voice as he looked around the shabby room. "Here," he said, handing Cader a slim, white folder. "A one-way ticket to a prep school where you'll obtain the credits you need to enter Tulane in the fall."

There was more to this than a generous man offering to help a kid from the wrong side of the tracks and Cader knew it. "I don't know. I'll have to think about it, talk it over with my father."

"There's nothing to talk over. I'm giving you the opportunity of your life to shake this . . . squalor and move among decent people. Take it or leave it. Now!"

Cader stood up. "No. I said I'd think about it. I might be a dumb kid from the wrong side of the tracks, but I know you want me out of here for a reason. If you tell me what the real reason is, maybe I might give you the answer you're looking for now."

The old man's face was mottled and his hand, holding the unlit cigar, held a slight tremor. "Very well, there are strings, certain promises I want you to make. The minute those promises are broken, all aid ceases. Do we understand each other?"

"Spell it out, Mr. Hayden," he said curtly.

"As I said, you are not to see Irene anymore. Nor are you to get in touch with her, ever again. I want you to leave tomorrow. A friend of mine will meet you and take you to your apartment, where your new car will be waiting along with your first month's check in the amount of five hundred dollars. You'll receive your monthly stipend on the first of each month. I don't much care what you do with it."

"As long as I keep my mouth shut and do what you say?" Cader said arrogantly.

"Exactly."

"You're sending me away just so I won't see Irene anymore?"

"More or less," the old man hedged.

Cader was suddenly aware of the older man's acute discomfort each time he brought up Irene's name. His eyes narrowed. At that moment he became a gambler. "I don't think so, Mr. Hayden. I like it here, and if I work summers and weekends, I can make it through junior college. If I'm lucky, I might get a scholarship. Thanks for the offer, though. It was nice of you to think of me. Tell Irene I said hello when you see her."

"You stupid fool!"

Cader's gambling instincts rose to the fore. "Tell me why? Tell me why you're buying me. Tell me why I'm selling myself. I want to hear it. If I'm selling out, I want to know why."

Foster Doyle Hayden lowered himself into the lopsided armchair and lit his cigar. "Very well. You leave me no other choice. You've impregnated Irene, and there's no way I plan to welcome you into the family. The matter will be taken care of."

"Is that the same as Irene being pregnant?" Cader asked stupidly, knowing full well what the old man meant. He had to stall for time while he digested the words. Irene was pregnant. Jesus. No wonder the old geezer was upset. He was going to take care of it, he said. The word "abortion" rattled around in Cader's brain. He was too young to be a father. A baby! Jesus. Cool, he had to be cool, pretend he knew all about it. Just like Irene to let him be the last to know. The old man was right, if he cut and ran now, he was selling out. Selling out for the chance to shake this place and move among all the straight arrows out there. Tulane! An apartment of his own! A car of his own! Five hundred bucks a month! Jesus. All he had to do was walk away and never see Irene again, and let Foster Doyle Hayden "take care of things."

"What kind of car?" Cader asked craftily, already knowing he was going to accept the offer.

"The best."

"You want me to leave tomorrow?"

"Yes."

"And you'll pay me five hundred dollars a month for four years along with all my expenses?"

"Yes."

"In turn, all I have to do is walk away from Hayden and keep my nose clean?"

"Yes."

"One last question. How are you going to explain all of this to Irene?"

"I don't have to explain anything to anyone," Foster Doyle said huffily.

"That's what you said when you came in here and look at you now." Cader laughed, enjoying the old man's annoyance.

"I'll handle matters. For now, I want your word that you're accepting the terms I've offered, and from this moment on, my daughter is off-limits. That means you don't see her, speak to her, or write to her. Is it a deal?"

"It's a deal, but if it's all the same to you, Mr. Hayden, I'd rather not shake hands with you."

Hayden was surprised at the remark. "And why not?" he asked harshly.

"Because it goes against my grain to see a father sell his daughter for fifteen thousand bucks plus expenses."

Foster Doyle Hayden's face turned ashen at Cader's words. "I don't ever want to see you back in Hayden again. Be sure you understand that, Harris. I'll keep my part of the bargain as long as you keep yours. The moment you back water, I'll squash you like this," he said, and tossed the smoldering cigar onto the worn linoleum and ground it beneath his heel.

The screen door slapped against the frame and was still. Cader bent down to pick up the warm cigar. He stared at the frayed tobacco leaves and grimaced. He bunched the leaves in his fist and tossed them across the room. Wiseass old bastard buying and selling people like they were cattle.

The remains of the coffee in the cardboard container dribbled down Cader's arm as he realized he was crushing the cup like he had crushed those tobacco leaves so long ago. "Well, you wiseass old bastard, your days of buying and selling people are over," Cader snarled to the quiet office. "You may not know it, but they're over, old man."

Judy Evans settled herself some little distance from Kevin and slowly unwrapped her sandwich. She wriggled experimentally to get herself more comfortable and stretched out her legs. "Ah, that's better," she sighed. "I wish Mr. Harris would get some chairs in here. I don't mind sitting on the floor to watch TV, but I hate to eat my lunch in the storeroom while I'm on the floor. Yuk," she grimaced, "I hate egg salad."

"Trade you," Kevin said quietly. "I've had ham and cheese every day this week." He leaned over and changed his position slightly so that he was nearer the packing crate Judy was leaning against. He liked the look of her long suntanned legs. They looked so silky and shiny, almost like the girls at Aunt Cledie's, and she didn't have half as many teeth when she smiled.

A light flush crept up his neck as his hand touched hers. "I like egg salad." He grinned. Cader said you always had to grin. Anyway, he told himself, he felt like grinning. Every time he saw Judy Evans, he felt like grinning.

As they ate in silence, Judy repeatedly glanced over at Kevin, who was quietly munching at his sandwich instead of wolfing it down the way he usually did. He had seemed unusually quiet all day, now that she thought about it. "What's the matter, Kevin? You got something on your mind?"

"Huh? Oh, no." He grinned again to show her everything was fine. Only the smile didn't quite reach his eyes.

"I just thought there might be something wrong. You're pretty quiet today. You're not mad, are you? That I had to be home by ten-thirty last night? Did you go right home after you dropped me off?"

"Nope. I'm not mad, that is. Nothing like that. I just guess I'm tired today. On my way home last night I ran into Mr. Harris and we killed a couple of six-packs between us." He didn't confide in Judy about the boilermakers they were drinking or the slim flask that Cader had given him as a gift. There was no sense in arousing Judy's curiosity about the relationship that he'd developed between himself and Cader Harris.

"Well, it doesn't look as though beer agrees with you, Kevin. You've been so out of it all day." Judy went back to nibbling at her sandwich. She didn't want Kevin to see that she was annoyed that he hadn't gone directly home after leaving her. She absolutely didn't want to start nagging at him the way Beth did.

Kevin swallowed the last of his container of milk. His stomach still felt queasy from the drinks he had consumed the night before, and his head still throbbed, but he'd die before he'd admit it to Judy. He didn't want her to think he was such a hick he couldn't handle his booze. But that was the last time he'd ever drink like that, he swore to himself. Kripes! He didn't even remember getting out of the shower last night or how he got to bed. The last he really remembered was taking the last hit out of the flask and the bracing feel of the needle-sharp spray of icy water. And dream! He'd had wet dreams before, but never like that! He'd dreamed he was screwing Viola, then Judy, then Charlie's Angels, all three of them. Actually, he hadn't even remembered his dream. Not even when Dad had had to come into his room and shake him awake so he wouldn't be late for work. It wasn't until he'd gotten down to the breakfast table and saw Beth that he'd remembered. It was something about the way she looked at him, almost as though she knew what he dreamed in his sleep.

"Did Mr. Harris say where he was going or what time he would be back?" Judy asked, biting into the ham and cheese sandwich.

"Just that he wouldn't be back till after three and to tell you to work the register. He also said you should set up a display of the Spalding balls."

"That's so boring. I would rather stay out here with you; at least we can talk. If there aren't any customers, I just doodle on a pad. It's boring," she repeated.

"I'll yell at you from time to time so you won't get lonely," Kevin grinned. "You *are* going to the clambake with me, aren't you?"

"If that's an invitation, sure," Judy said, flexing her long legs. "Ah, Kevin, is . . . what I mean is . . . you aren't . . ."

"No, I'm not bringing Beth if that's what you're trying to say."

"That's what I was trying to say. It's not that I don't like her, it's just that . . . well, what she does is . . . she clutches at you. I don't like to hear the kids mock you out over your sister. It's not right. She should have her own friends, Kevin."

Kevin swallowed hard. He should say something in defense of Beth but the words wouldn't come. All he could think of was Cader Harris's words, "Grin, kid! Makes 'em think you know something they don't. You have to set women up. They expect it. Hell, they want it, and I've known a few that begged for it. But," he had warned, "it goes two ways. Women, if you don't watch them, can set you up and *bam*! They get you right in the balls, which was their intention all the time. I knew this one broad that I swear to Christ had the balls of a Saint Bernard. When I tell you she set me up, she set me up. I fixed her ass, though. I knocked her up and took off like greased lightning. And for Crissakes, kid, remember to grin. You got good teeth; show them."

Kevin grinned.

"What's wrong with you, Kev, you look like you have a toothache. You know, you have nice teeth. Not as nice as Donny Osmond, but nice. I go for nice teeth."

Kevin grinned again. "You want to go to a movie tonight?"

"I'd love to go to a movie with you, Kevin. First show or second?"

"Let's make the first show and then we can take a walk along the beach."

Judy thought about it for a moment. She leaned forward slightly and rubbed her hands over her thighs. "I like to sit on the beach. Will you bring the blanket or should I?"

"I'll bring it. I think there's one in the trunk of Dad's car. I like to sit on the beach too." He grinned again. Maybe, just maybe . . .

"Ooops, there's a customer. Thanks for the trade, Kev. I'll look forward to tonight," Judy said, getting up and smoothing her short skirt.

"I'll pick you up at quarter to seven." He grinned again.

"Kevin, are you sure you don't have a toothache?" Judy asked, concern in her voice. How could he neck with someone on the beach if he had a toothache?

Kevin continued to grin, only this time it wasn't a practiced grin. "I have an ache, but it isn't in my tooth."

Judy laughed. "I'll just bet you do. If you get bored out here, come into the store and we'll set up the balls together."

"You got it," Kevin called after her as he hefted a carton of football helmets onto his broad shoulder. *Boy, I hope you know what to do with it when I give it to you.* He shrugged philosophically. Now that he was experienced, he could teach her if she didn't know. He laughed to himself. Cader Harris called it higher education of the first order. And just think, if it weren't for Cader Harris coming back to Hayden, this might have been just another dull summer.

Keli McDermott busied herself at the stove, stirring the spaghetti sauce Gene had taught her to make. From time to time she glanced out the window into the backyard where her garden grew. The tomato plants were nearly as tall as she was and the bright, gleaming purple of the eggplants peeked through the luscious green leaves which protected them from the sun. If the weather kept up this way, the children would have a good time at their clambake. They would be returning from Disney World, Florida, in triumph as they did every year, looking forward to the annual clambake with anticipation and a little sadness. Summer was almost over.

Everything looked so bright and clean outside. The light rain during the night had made everything smell fresh and clean and somehow honest. Almost like a new beginning. If Keli wanted, today could be the first day of the rest of her life. She had read that somewhere and liked it. Today is the first day of the rest of your life.

She heard a light step on the back porch and raised her eyes. The screen door squeaked as Marsha opened it and stepped into Keli's colorful brick and copper kitchen. "I have to talk to you, Keli, she said in a strangled voice. "You haven't been answering your phone or returning my calls."

Keli nodded, her eyes wary and watchful. "May I offer you a cup of coffee, Marsha?"

"Yes. Yes, I'd like that. Thank you." She watched her friend Keli go about her kitchen duties as though there were nothing more pressing on her mind than measuring the correct amount of coffee.

Softly, the words almost a whisper, Keli said, "It will have to be instant."

"That will be fine." Marsha's eyes followed Keli as she busied herself with cups and boiling water. The gleaming copper pots against the dull old brick with its vivid hanging baskets of ferns made no impression on her. Her mind boiled with the words she had come to say. "Keli, I have to talk to you. I have to know what you're going to do." Impulsively, she reached her hand across the table to grasp Keli's and winced as though she had been struck when Keli pointedly withdrew her hand and placed it on her lap. "I read your file, Keli. I know I had no right to do that, but I had to know. Do you understand?"

This could be the first day of the rest of her life. If she wanted. Sorrowfully, she said, "I wish you had not done that, Marsha."

"Keli. For God's sake! They have excellent surgeons in New Orleans. I've heard about the doctor Marc wants you to see. He's magnificent. If . . . if it's serious, they say he's the best for reconstructive surgery. Keli, you can't wait! Oh, my God! Why can't I make you understand? You hear me but you aren't listening. Damn you, Keli," Marsha shrilled, "you could die! You're the best friend I ever had; I won't let you do this to yourself."

Before Keli could frame a response to Marsha's statement, a shadow fell across the table.

"Gene!"

"What are you trying to do to Keli, Marsha?" Gene demanded as he braced his hands on the tabletop, his heavy body threatening.

"Trying to talk some sense into her, since you don't seem to want to do anything," Marsha shot back, not in the least intimidated by his menacing manner.

"Keli's no concern of yours and never will be. I'm going to pretend I didn't hear what you just said, and Keli is going to pretend she never heard it. I want you to leave this house, and I don't want you to ever come back. Do you understand? You're an interfering busybody, a crepe hanger; you're sick!" he spat vehemently. "Now, get your tail out of here before I throw you out like the garbage you are."

"Sick!" Marsha hissed. "How would you know? If anyone is sick, it's you! What kind of maniac are you that you won't allow Keli to have a lifesaving operation? You'd let her die, wouldn't you? And you call me sick? I want her to live. I read the file in Marc's office. I saw her chart. If you don't allow her to have that operation, I'll tell everyone in town that you wouldn't 'permit' it. They'll run you out on a rail, Gene McDermott!"

"It's Keli's decision, not mine. You ever spread a rumor like that and I'll kill you!"

Frantically, Marsha turned to Keli, who was sitting at the table, eyes lowered, head hung low. "Is that the truth, Keli? Is he allowing you to decide for yourself? Or are you going to let him have his way. Don't you see what he's doing? He'd rather have you dead than alive. If you're dead, he would have had you all to himself. He'd never have to worry that someone else would love you. He's a madman, Keli. Don't, I beg you, don't sacrifice yourself to his insanity!"

Keli stood up from the table and looked first at Gene and then at Marsha with utter calm. "I will be the one to make the decision. I have already called the surgeon in New Orleans and made an appointment. It is my body, my life. I made the decision for myself, not for you, Gene, nor for you, Marsha. For myself. I want to live and I want to love," she said softly, looking into Gene's eyes.

"Now see what you've gone and made her do?" Gene turned viciously on Marsha.

Keli was almost to the doorway when she turned and said quietly, "Today is the first day of the rest of my life. I made my decision today, and, whatever happens, I'll live with it. It is my life."

Cader Harris mounted the stairs behind the Monde Boutique two at a time. This news was too good to keep to himself, and he only had Sunny to share it with. *Hurry up!* he thought. *Christ! This is too good to keep to myself I've got to tell somebody about it!* He glanced down to the alley where she parked her car. It was there. She had to be home. "Sunny! For Crissakes, open up! I wanna talk to you!"

A fumbling sound, and the door swung open. "Cader? What time is it? I was sound asleep."

"Yeah, I know," he muttered as he shoved past her into the dimness of her apartment. "Listen, I had to talk to you. I've got the greatest news! I did it! I did it!" he crowed. "Get a couple of glasses; this deserves a toast!"

"Sure, sure." She smiled, catching his excitement, shuffling out to the kitchen on bare feet and groping in the cabinets for two clean glasses. "Okay, shoot!" she said as she presented the glasses and watched Cader struggle with the wire on a bottle of sparkling Burgundy.

"I did it, baby! Ole Cader Harris pulled it off!" To her questioning look, he explained. "Delta Oil! I did it! There's a town council meeting right now, and the vote is expected to come in a definite 'yes.' I have it on the best source."

Sunny's blue eyes lit and the smile touched her lips. She loved to see him this way. Victorious. And her joy was complete with the knowledge that he'd come to share his victory with her and not Irene Thomas. "I knew you could do it, Cader, I just knew it."

"Yeah! Well, here's to me and Delta Oil!" He clinked his glass against hers and downed the burnished liquid. He refilled his glass and offered another toast. "And here's to me getting out of this stinking town. The Peyton Place of the South. Screw it!" He drained his glass again.

A frown developed between Sunny's brows. She didn't like to hear Cader talk that way about Hayden. After all, she was a part of the town too, and she always took it personally. She forced herself to be honest and admit that if Cader had said "we" were going to get out of this stinking town, it wouldn't have bothered her a bit. She always waited for him to say something about taking her away with him when he left, but he never did. Leaving her half-finished drink on the counter, she moved toward the stove to put on a pot of coffee. "Tell me about it!" she coaxed above the sound of rushing water from the sink. "How do you know this thing with Delta Oil is going to go through?"

"Friends, baby," Cader chortled. "The right friends in the right places."

"So tell me who your friends are. Don't leave me out in the cold." She struggled with the manual can opener on an unopened can of Maxwell House. "Shit!" She dropped the can opener and studied the thumb of her right hand. "I broke another nail."

"Yeah. I told you to get yourself one of those electric openers," Cader said disinterestedly.

Sunny glanced up at him quickly: "I don't like to be dragged down by owning too many things. I like to travel light. Know what I mean?"

She begged him to understand her, to know that she was talking about him and that she'd be ready to leave with him anytime he said the word.

"I know what you mean, baby. Sure do. Anyway, about my friend in a high place, you'll never guess who it is."

Sunny slammed the coffeepot onto the stove. There were times

Cader Harris's skull was as thick as a hog's. What did she have to do? Spell it out for him? "Who's your friend, Cade?" she asked in a monotone, hoping he'd see her annoyance and ask her about it.

"*The* Irene Hayden Thomas! Would you believe it? Right now, she's down at the Town Hall fighting her little heart out for Delta Oil and me."

Sunny raised her eyebrows. "Does Irene know your stake in it?"

"Yes and no. All little Irene wants is for me to stay here in Hayden, and I told her in order for that to happen this town's gotta boom. Hence, Delta Oil. We've already got Mayor Guthrie on our side, the greedy little man. And you know about the town's merchants and the Board of Education. It's gonna go, Sunny! It's gonna go! With Irene Thomas at the helm, it's gonna go! And then I'm gonna go! And this time when I leave this town it'll be for good. And in my pocket will be a nice fat check!"

"I hope so, Cader, for your sake."

"What d'you mean, you 'hope so'? It's a sure thing, honey, a winner," he cackled as he poured another glass of the sparkling Burgundy. "What could go wrong now?"

Sunny hesitated. The sound of assurance and confidence in his voice reverberated through her head. He wasn't going to like what she had to tell him, and she only wished it didn't have to come from her. "If you'd come by last night the way you'd promised, I could have told you then."

"Told me what?"

"Two men came into the Lemon Drop last night. Strangers. They were staying at the motel in the back. I know because they asked me to reserve a room for them. When they finished their dinner and drinks, they paid their check and left. I cleaned off their table and I found this." Sunday fished in her handbag and withdrew a slim, silver, executive ballpoint pen. She pushed it across the Formica counter top toward Cader, who stared at it in disbelief. He picked it up as though he were touching cat shit or something equally disagreeable. On the side of the pen was engraved DELTA OIL.

Suddenly, the fizz of the sparkling Burgundy became flat on his tongue.

CHAPTER FIFTEEN

*I*rene Thomas busied herself in the kitchen, hoping that activity would calm her nerves. It wouldn't be long now before Foster Doyle discovered how she had gone before the Board of Education with her plea to admit Delta Oil into Hayden. She had gone well armed, with the support of the Junior Women's League and the League of Women Voters. And, because she was Foster Doyle's daughter, he would have to forgive her campaigning against him. Hence, everyone else who opposed Hayden must be forgiven right along with her.

"It's a perfect evening for the clambake, Beth, don't you think?" Irene asked Beth, a look of concern on her face. "Is something wrong, dear? You haven't been yourself lately. Beth, if you're dwelling on what happened to you at Jackie's party . . . well, you just can't. I'm certain everyone's forgotten about it by now, and you're just going to have a grand time at your first clambake. Is Luther picking you up or are you going with Kevin?" As she spoke, Irene began whipping egg whites with a wire whisk in the gleaming stainless and white confines of her practical kitchen.

"I'm not even sure I want to go!" Beth retorted hotly. "Luther is taking Sue Ellen and Kevin is going with Judy."

"Not go to your first clambake? Whatever are you thinking of, Beth Thomas? If you don't go, then for certain everyone in town will start talking *again!* You've looked forward to this all year. It's your special time, and I can't imagine why you would even contemplate not going. You're not the only one without a date. And to think that this minute your father and Destry are working on the barbecue pit so everything will be nice for you young people." Irene adjusted the gay scarf she wore on her head to protect her hair. It always struck Beth as funny that her mother wore the scarf like the tignons that old nigger women wore.

Beth listened to her mother's ramblings and knew she had intended to go to the clambake all along. In fact, there wasn't anything in this whole world that could keep her away from the beach tonight. Not anything. She had to talk to Kevin; she had to get him alone, some place where he couldn't turn his back on her. Everything was wrong. How could Kevin treat her this way? As if she didn't even exist. He should be treating Judy Evans the way he was treating her. A deep flush stained her cheeks and clashed with her red-gold hair. Irene droned on and on about how she was only young once. Ever since that night when she had been feeling sick and she had gone in to Kevin for help and he had done that to her, just the thought of the special secret she had to share with him could make her feel all jumpy inside. It was a secret, her secret. But soon, tonight, it would be their secret. Beth's and Kevin's. She hugged the thought to her. Kevin would be so happy to know that she really loved him. Then he could stop pretending to like Judy and things would be the same again, just like when they were little kids. When there were just the two of them. Only now they were grown up and it would be better than it ever was. Kevin was going to be so happy when she told him what he had done to her in bed that night.

"You can wear your new halter sun dress, the one I bought you last week. I know how you young people love to show off your suntans. You're going to look just perfect, and Luther will be sorry he invited Sue Ellen. Why, Sue Ellen's mother told me herself that Sue Ellen was going to wear those tacky blue jeans she's glued to. And the child needs a wave to her hair. I can't believe her mother allows her to go out in public dressed that way. Now you, Beth, are a perfect lady. You have to admit that no one would ever say you look tacky." Irene played with the meringue she was heaping on top of the lemon custard pie. "It's a shame the river has changed so much since your daddy and I were your age. Then, it was our only place to swim. I suppose it was dangerous then too, but we just didn't realize. I have cautioned that no one should go swimming at the clambake. It's one thing during the daytime, but at night . . ." Irene shuddered. She continued to chatter. "Thank God, there haven't been any drownings there this year, but wasn't it only just last summer that nice nigra boy, Johnson was his name, I think, drowned."

Beth nibbled on a piece of pie crust and listened patiently. "Ummm."

"I suppose it's because most people have swimming pools, and the children don't use the river for swimming as much as they did in my day. But, Beth, that river is treacherous! I was the one who brought that up at the town council meeting yesterday. You know, the one concerning Delta Oil taking over the beachfront for those tanks. People have very short memories, but not we Haydens. *I* reminded them of the lives that river has claimed. Yes, indeed. As for boating, well, most everybody who's into that sort of thing uses the marina further downriver anyway." Irene patted her apron and adjusted the scarf on her head. "It's the foolish mother who allows her child to swim in that river!"

"Have you seen Kevin, Mama?"

"Not since lunch. Today was only half a day at the sporting goods shop. Did you forget?" Irene hummed tunelessly as she placed the pie in the oven. Suddenly, she turned and looked inquisitively at her daughter. "Beth, do you know what's bothering your brother? He's acting so strangely. So withdrawn and remote. Why, he's barely civil to me, and I'm his very own lovin' mother."

Beth shrugged, her mind questioning Kevin's whereabouts. Irene continued to babble as she covertly watched Beth out of the corner of her eye. Beth noticed her mother's glance and began toying with the sticky utensils on the countertop. "He's probably out somewhere with that Judy Evans." She watched her mother's reaction. It came right on cue.

"I spoke to Daddy about Kevin, but, as usual, your father's no help at all. He refuses to listen to me and says Kevin is old enough for a girlfriend and old enough to choose his own friends. What troubles me the most is the way Kevin is behaving toward you, his own sister." Irene sniffed as she stacked the dishwasher. "Kevin's behavior is cold and cruel and there are actually times when he behaves as though we're his *enemy* or something! It must be that Evans girl who's making him behave this way." Irene admitted to herself that she didn't like Kevin's attachment to Judy Evans one bit. But what bothered her the most was that she was losing her hold on him. He was coming into his own too soon, too fast.

"Yes, Mama," Beth answered idly. "It is Judy's influence. He acts as though he doesn't even have a family who loves him. But I know how Kevin feels deep down, Mama, and he doesn't really think I'm his enemy. Kevin loves me, Mama. He's loved me from the time we were little. He'll get over this, I just know he will. You'll see, Mama. Why, it could happen tomorrow! Kevin will open his eyes and see how much I mean to him." Beth cuddled her secret closer to her. She was going to tell Kevin about her secret tonight. She had to. It was her duty. Look how Mama was worried about him! She owed it to her family, didn't she, to make Kevin see how much he loved his little sister?

"You're right, of course, honey. I suppose it's just a stage boys go through, to rebel against their families." Irene began to hum tunelessly again as she wiped the counter. It occurred to Beth to wonder if Irene had a secret too. Mama had been all glowing lately, humming around the house and singing all those old love songs from years ago. And just look at the pounds she had taken off since the beginning of the summer and all those long visits to the hair-dresser. Not to mention a complete renovation of her wardrobe. Beth looked at her mother again, questions rising in her green eyes. Whatever secret Mama had, it couldn't be as wonderful as her own secret.

Beth left Irene humming in the kitchen and went upstairs. On her way to her room she stopped outside Kevin's door and knocked softly. "Kevin, let me in. I want to talk to you. Mama is looking for you and I said I didn't know where you were," she lied. "I know you're in there, Kev," she whispered, her mouth pressed close against the door. Silence. "If you don't open the door, I'll tell Mama you've been in there all along and then she'll punish you and not let you go to the clambake. You know how she is, Kev, about us telling her where we are at all times. She'll say you gave her four new gray hairs today. Open the door, Kevin!"

Beth stepped back in shock at the expression on Kevin's face. His eyes looked like one of Daddy's customers. Where was the color in his face? He looked worse than one of Destry's best efforts. "Go away, Beth. I don't want to talk to you and I don't want to see you." His voice was cold, embalmed, without life.

"Kevin, don't act this way with me. I'm your sister and I love you the way you love me. You're just being mean and I don't like it!"

For answer, Kevin closed the door softly. The click sounded so final, like when Daddy closed the lid on one of his boxes for the last time. Those boxes he put all those dead people in were so final. You were dead when you were in one of those boxes. Kevin wasn't dead; she wasn't dead. That meant she still had a chance. Kevin still had a chance. She would get to him at the clambake tonight and it would all come out right.

The beach was crowded with people. The pit for the clams was smoldering. The oversized grill for the franks and hamburgers was red hot and ready for the first slap of cold meat. Two big tents stood ready to be opened for the dancing on the makeshift wooden floors. Musical instruments were being tuned up and everywhere there was the sound of laughter and happiness.

Beth stood in the shadows and watched as Kevin raced after a Frisbee, his long, muscular body glowing in the orange torchlight that bathed the beach in its eerie glow. How could he be having such a good time? How could he be so happy when she was so miserable? Her eyes narrowed as she watched Kevin race after another Frisbee only to collide with Judy. They both went down in the sand, laughing and rolling over and over each other. Kevin helped Judy to her feet and put his arm around her as they walked away down the beach out of sight of the orange light and the other happy frolickers. Where were they going? What were they going to do? Hot, searing jealousy ripped through her as she stepped from her secluded spot and headed away from the narrow strip of beach and the bright, smoking torches.

She knew the kids were staring at her, but she didn't care as she raced along the sandy beach. She had to hurry and get out of the light. If Kevin and Judy were in darkness, then so would she be.

If she hadn't heard Judy's giggle, she would have passed them. She stopped, hardly daring to breathe. They were right above her on the shelf of sand. She lay down and stretched out, straining to hear words she didn't want to hear. She had to hear them. There were no words, only soft moans. She had heard those moans before. Kevin wouldn't do that with Judy. He knew Judy was nothing but a tramp. He might kiss her, but that was all he would do, wasn't it? It was too quiet. It must be a long kiss, she decided. Judy was like that. She would clutch and hang on to him and never let him go. Quietly, she slithered closer to the high shelf of sand and drew in her breath as her hands closed around something soft and silky. Her eyes widened in the darkness as she clutched the minuscule piece of nylon. Boomer said that when a guy got a girl for the first time, he tossed her panties over his left shoulder. A tradition, he said. Boomer should know. Boomer knew everything when it came to girls. Only instead of her panties, Judy lost the bottom of her bikini swimsuit.

Shaking with rage, she slid backward. Quietly, she got to her feet, the bikini bottom still clutched in her hands. Her knees were like rubber as she walked back up the beach to the gala festival. She got a plate of clams and a Coke and sat down next to a girl she barely knew and began to eat. The food was like sawdust in her mouth and she washed it down with Coke. It was important that no one should see something was wrong. She waited, her eyes riveted to the dark stretch of sand beyond the torchlight. She set her empty Coke can down next to her and felt her hand go to the big patch pocket of her sun dress. When someone lost something and someone else found it then that someone was responsible for returning it. That's what Mama always said.

Beth walked down the beach, out of the light and into the dark, back toward the secluded spot where she had left Kevin with Judy. As she approached the place, she could hear voices, now hushed whispers, actually.

"Where is it, Kevin? I can't find it anywhere! God! I can't walk around in this short dress without anything covering my behind! C'mon, Kevin! Help me look, we've got to find it!" Judy's whisper held a note of panic.

Beth patted the large pocket of her sun dress and smiled in the darkness. *Now, I wonder what they could be looking for?* It just wouldn't be Christian to bother Judy with the fact that she had her old bikini bottom right here in her pocket, would it? Not when Judy was so busy looking for something.

"I am looking, Judy," Kevin said. "I know they've got to be here somewhere!"

"Hi!" Beth said brightly as she stepped within range. "What are you two doing way down here? The party's going full blast now, music and everything. Can't you hear it?"

"Beth. What the hell are you doing here?" Kevin asked bitterly. "Jesus H. Christ! Can't a guy have any privacy?"

"Kevin Thomas! If you keep swearing like that, I'll have to tell Mama. Maybe she can have Reverend Conway have a talk with you. I just was taking a walk. I didn't know you were here," she lied. "Looks like you lost something, Judy. Can I help? What was it?"

"... er ... my rings!" Judy said hastily, her nervousness making her voice shaky.

"Rings! You'll never find them with all this sand and in the dark!" Beth said smugly, her hand covering her pocket. "You sure you lost your rings?"

"Yes ... it ... it was my rings." Judy answered, smoothing the short skirt of her sun dress down over her thighs.

"Where'd you lose them?" Beth asked stubbornly, relishing Judy's discomfort. She almost pulled the bikini bottom out of her pocket, wanting to see Judy's face as she dangled them in front of her. But something held her back. After all, wasn't it only proper that Judy should tell her the truth? When somebody lost money or something, didn't they have to tell how much it was or identify it somehow?

"Will you get out of here, Beth?" Kevin growled. "Can't you see we're busy?"

"I want to talk to you, Kevin," Beth said sweetly. "It's important."

"Not now, for Crissakes!"

"Yes, now, Kevin. I have to talk to you. Alone!" She pierced Judy with a hateful stare.

"You ... you stay here and talk to Beth," Judy said, squirming, wanting only to get out from under Beth's knowing glare. "I have to go to the little girls' room anyway. I'll see you back at the clambake." Judy moved away from the duo, back toward the lights. After she'd gone a couple of yards, she turned and ran, holding her short, flaring skirt tight against her legs.

Kevin looked after Judy, a concerned look on his face. Beth watched Kevin, her jealousy growing by the second.

"What d'you want to talk to me about, Beth? I think I've heard everything you have to say." Kevin's tone was cold and aloof, just as it had been since the night of Jackie's party. But what she had to tell him would change all that. She could make him happier than that trampy Judy Evans could. Once she told him, he'd remember that night, and then he'd know that he didn't need Judy. He'd have her, Beth, and that was all he needed.

"C'mon, Beth. I'm waiting to hear what you have to say. I want to get back to the party."

"You don't want to get back to the party; you want to get back to Judy! But what I'm going to tell you will change all that, Kevin. After you hear me out, you'll never want to see Judy again."

"Cut it out, will ya, Beth? I don't want to listen to any more gossip about Judy that you've dreamed up in that sick little head of yours. Judy's a good kid and I like her, a lot. Nothing you could say could change that. When I get to college and get into a fraternity, I'm going to give her my pin. So just cut the crap and leave me and Judy alone."

Stunned, Beth persisted, "How can you give her your pin?"

Kevin interrupted, not allowing her to complete her thought. "Not too many people know this, but Judy's going with me to Tulane. She was accepted a few weeks ago. That's how I'm going to give her my pin. She's going to be right there with me." For an instant Kevin gloated to see the shock on Beth's face. Now, maybe she'd leave him alone. Maybe she'd realize he had his own life to live. Maybe she'd stop trying to eat him alive.

Beth almost staggered beneath the weight of what she'd just heard. Judy Evans going to Tulane with Kevin! Judy Evans getting her claws into Kevin. Making Kevin like her, making Kevin kiss her, touch her, make love to her. It couldn't be! She wouldn't allow it! Kevin was hers; he belonged to her! It had been that way ever since she could remember. Kevin and Beth. Beth and Kevin. Tears welled in her eyes; her voice was a choked, strangling sound. "How could you do this to me? How could you leave me behind and take up with that whore? After what we've been to one another. After what you did to me."

"Take it easy, Beth. We haven't been anything to one another. We're brother and sister. What more could there be? And I didn't *do* anything to you. You've got your own life to live, Beth, and I've got mine."

"You're hateful, Kevin Thomas! But I'll forgive you; I always forgive you. I . . . I love you so much, Kevin. So much. I even proved it to you."

"I don't want to listen to you anymore, Beth. I'm going after Judy." Kevin pushed Beth aside and stepped past her.

"You better listen to me, Kevin Thomas. What I have to say will make a difference in all your high and mighty plans. You love me, Kevin, I know you love me. . . ." Her words were cut off by the sight of his back, tall and straight, walking away from her.

Suddenly, he turned, his eyes burning into her. "I'd like to love you, Bethy. I'd like you to be the little sister I always cared about. But you've changed. You won't let me live my own life. You hang around my neck like the albatross. Right now, this minute, I wonder that I ever cared anything about you at all."

"You do love me, Kevin, I can prove it. I know!" Beth was so overwrought with emotion that her teeth chattered. "Remember the other night? The night when you came home late? I heard you talking to Dad downstairs. You said something about drinking. Then I heard you come upstairs and get into the shower."

Kevin stood stock still. He knew she was going to tell him something he didn't want to hear and yet he was powerless to stop her, to stop himself from listening. He'd had bad vibes about that night. And now, the answer was there on her face, waiting to be read.

"I . . . I didn't feel well. I . . . I was sick. I went into your room, Kevin, and . . . I got into bed with you. It was only to keep warm. But you liked it, Kevin, I know you did. I could tell by the way you touched me. . . ."

Kevin's face went white. His fists doubled and clenched. He knew if he hit her, he would kill her. If she was telling the truth, it was what he had been afraid of, what he had refused to remember. Lightning flashes of memory charged through his mind and the gorge rose to his throat. The defenses to maintain his sanity rose to the fore. She was lying! She *had* to be lying!

"Why are you looking at me that way, Kevin? It wasn't so terrible. It was nice. I liked it. Please don't look that way, Kevin. I didn't mean to make it sound as though it was all your idea, as though you'd done something terrible to me. I *love* you, Kevin, and you love me! I know you do. It was almost like when we were kids and we used to go into Mother's room and look at Daddy's magazines." Her hand reached out to touch him, wanting him to draw her near, to comfort her, to tell her that he loved her and that everything was going to be all right again. Only better. That they'd have each other, and no one, not Judy, not anyone, would ever come between them again. She waited for Kevin to tell her that he wouldn't see Judy anymore, that he'd wait for her to go to college and be with him.

Kevin's face crumpled before her eyes. Revulsion twisted his handsome features into a mask of agony. "Get away from me,

Beth!" he menaced hoarsely. "Get away from me and don't ever come near me again!"

He backed away from her. One step, two. Then he broke into a run, his breath coming in gasps that she could hear across the widening distance he put between them. "Kevin, wait! Kevin, don't go! Don't leave me like this! Kevin! Don't leave me alooooone!"

She watched, long after he disappeared into the darkness, heading back toward the lights, toward the party, toward Judy. Judy. Nasty, dirty, whoring Judy.

CHAPTER SIXTEEN

———◆———

 *K*evin stood outside the tent where the five-piece band played their rendition of Neil Sedaka's "Bad Blood" and tried to regain some sense of normalcy. He felt a light touch on his shoulder and turned to see Reverend Conway.

"You probably won't believe this, but I used to stand where you're standing, right here, and listen to the band, wishing I had the nerve to ask someone to dance. I was young once, you know. I just saw Judy. She's your date, isn't she?"

Kevin flushed and nodded.

"I just saw Beth a while ago too. Who'd she come with?"

"I guess she came alone. Where'd you say you saw Judy?"

Damion pointed in the direction of the restrooms on the far end of the sandy strip. "Girls haven't changed much since my day. Always having to comb their hair and join in a little gossip in the john."

"Then I guess I'd better wait for her here," Kevin murmured.

"Want a little company? Say, I can get us a couple of Cokes. Rank has its privileges, you know. No waiting in line for me. Wait here."

Within moments, Damion was back carrying two cans, a Coke

and a beer. Kevin sank down onto the sand, legs crossed. He accepted the Coke from Damion and, after popping the tab, leaned back on his elbows.

"Might as well relax," Damion said with a chuckle. "That's a pretty long line outside the john." He looked off in the direction of the portable toilets and saw Judy standing in line, shifting her weight from one foot to the other. "Judy's a pretty girl. She has her mother's good looks."

Kevin only nodded, seeming to be lost in his own thoughts. He took another swallow of Coke and leaned back again, staring off into the distance. Something was troubling the boy, Damion would bet his boots on it, but the annual clambake was hardly the place to question him about it.

A group of kids passed by on their way into the tent and, when they saw the Reverend, carefully picked up their feet so they wouldn't kick sand. One of the girls hanging on Boomer's arm called out to Kevin, "If you're looking for Judy, she's over there in line for the john."

Kevin merely nodded, lost in his own thoughts as he pushed the empty Coke can deep into the sand. He wished he could bury himself the same way he did the bright aluminum. Deep, beneath the soft, loose sand. So deep that it would cover his ears and eyes and hide him from himself. And from Beth.

Beth stood just beyond the edge of light, looking across to the tents, seeing Kevin sitting there with Reverend Conway. Her relief that Kevin was not with Judy came to a swift end and was replaced with a pang of fear that Kevin could be confiding in the Reverend about what had happened between them. She quickly rejected the idea. Kevin would never tell. Never.

Beth's eyes surveyed the crowd, looking for Judy. She was somewhere, but where? Her attention fell on the long, snaking line of giggling girls waiting to use the john. She saw Judy, standing sullenly amid the others, her hands still protecting her skirt against a wayward wind that might reveal her bare behind. Beth was pleased by the discomfort she had caused her.

Crouching low, working her way through the scrub pines that lined the slight ridge just behind where the portable toilets had been set up, Beth maneuvered till she was just a few feet away from Judy. If she stood far enough back into the scrub, the light wouldn't touch her. She would make Judy come to her. Judy was dumb. Everybody knew that except Kevin.

The door to the portable john was set facing the ridge, away from the beach, to afford the greatest possible privacy. Just one more girl to come out of the john and then it would be Judy's turn.

The area near where Beth waited lighted momentarily as the door swung open. The girl inside stepped around the front of the john, signaling that it was ready for the next occupant. Judy's turn.

Beth waited, holding her breath. Judy rounded behind the building. "Oooh, Judy, is that you? Can you come over here a minute? I think I have something that's yours."

"Beth? Is that you?" Judy's spine stiffened at the friendliness in Beth's tone. And what was she doing hiding just beyond the light behind the toilet? The meaning of Beth's words suddenly struck Judy. Could she possibly . . . ? No. It wasn't possible! Beth couldn't have the bottom of her bikini, could she? That would mean she knew about her and Kevin and just how she had lost the bottom to her bathing suit.

"Judy? Come over here," Beth called again in a hushed whisper. "I have something I know you're looking for."

One backward glance toward the toilet. Should she go tell the next girl in line to go ahead of her? Deciding against it, Judy walked into the scrub, out of the light, toward Beth.

"I think these are yours." Beth held the bikini bottom aloft. "At least I think they are because they have a tape in them with your name on it. Don't you think you're old enough not to have your mama sew your name into your clothes?"

"Give me those!" Judy rasped, reaching for the bikini. Beth snatched them away with a lightning movement of her arm. "Beth Thomas, give me those!" she hissed, glancing behind her to see that no one could hear.

"Not until you tell me why your mama sewed your name into them," Beth teased wickedly, hiding the bikini behind her, out of Judy's grasp.

"So when I go to the swim club I know which is mine in the locker room. Now, give me those!"

"No! Not right now at least. First, you have to promise me something."

"Stop being a baby. Now, hand them over."

"No. First you have to promise."

Exasperated, Judy grumbled. "All right. What do you want me to promise?"

"That you stay away from Kevin."

"Stop being stupid. I can't promise that. Now, will you give me those before I . . ."

"Before you what? I've made you angry, haven't I? I didn't mean to. I'm just trying to do what's right. You know that, don't you? I only want to save Kevin from you. Now, will you promise to stay away from Kevin, or should I go and tell my mother how I found your bikini bottom?" she taunted, enjoying the misery on Judy's face and the power she held over her.

"Cut it out, Beth. Now, give me those!" She reached again and grabbed Beth's shoulders, struggling with her for the bikini.

"You don't seem to understand," Beth said levelly. "I want you to stay away from Kevin. I'll *make* you stay away from him. I'll do anything I have to do to make you stay away from him. You're bad for him, Judy. You make him forget about his family and everybody. You make him forget he even has a sister who loves him a lot."

"Grow up, huh? Give me that bikini!" Judy said forcefully, muscling Beth aside, groping for the silky bottom.

"Nothing will stop you, will it, Judy? You don't care if my mother knows you're been screwing around with Kevin. You don't care if anybody knows it, do you? All you care about is getting your pants back on so you can go back down the beach and be with Kevin. You're bad, Judy, and somebody should stop you before you hurt Kevin. Before you take him away from the people who really love him!"

Judy stared in amazement at Beth, whose voice was becoming strident with hysteria. *This kid is off the wall,* Judy thought. *Right off the wall!* She sensed that Beth was becoming desperate to hear her say she would stay away from Kevin. There was a strange look in Beth's eyes, a glittering, menacing look that was visible even in the darkness as though a sly and clever creature were peering out at her from behind Beth's eyes. And the way she was talking through clenched teeth, spitting really, sounded dangerous. Deciding she'd never get her bikini back by arguing, she began to humor Beth.

"All right, Bethy, anything you say, only give me back the bikini. I can't very well up and take off for home without them, can I?"

"Then you promise? I don't want to tell my mama about you and Kevin. I don't want to get him into trouble, but I will if it means saving him from you."

"I said you win, Beth. I won't go near Kevin again. Now, give me that bikini." Judy was shaking with barely controlled panic. She'd never seen anyone act like Beth before and didn't know how to handle it. Kevin would have to know that his sister was getting drugs from Boomer. That had to be it. Normal people just didn't behave like this!

Beth brought the silky bottom around in front of her, tentatively handing them out to Judy. Judy made a quick grab to snatch the bikini away, but not before Beth caught the smug look that flashed over her features. Too late. Judy had the swimsuit.

"You . . . you tricked me! You aren't ever going to leave Kevin alone, are you? You bitch!" Judy was bending down to step into the bikini before Beth could tear them away from her.

Taking advantage of Judy's precarious balance as she stood on one foot, Beth knocked her to the ground and struggled to retrieve the bikini. But Judy was bigger and outweighed her. Beth had to stop her. She couldn't let her win. Judy would have the bikini and Kevin too.

Her hand touched a rock in the sparse grass beneath the trees. Forcefully, she brought it down on the side of Judy's head with a crack. Instantly, Judy fell limp, the bikini still clutched in her hands.

Beth scrambled to her feet and stood looking down at the still form. Swiftly, as though still fighting for their possession, she snatched the bikini out of Judy's unprotesting fingers and stuffed them once again in the pocket of her sun dress.

A sound behind her brought her to full alert. "When are you coming out of there? Didn't fall in, did you?" the voice called. Beth realized it must be the next girl in line for the john. "Hey! There's nobody in here! Whoever it was must have gone out around the other side. I've been waiting all this time for an empty toilet!" Beth stood motionless in the cover of the shadows and watched the girl step into the cubicle and close the door behind her.

She knew she couldn't stay here. She couldn't be found. What if the girl saw her when she stepped out of the portable john, when she was facing in the direction of the trees? Beth bent over and grasped Judy beneath the arms and tugged, pulling until they were both hidden deeper in the shadows. A tiny, whining sound escaped from Judy's throat as Beth moved her. It reminded Beth of the sick kitten she and Kevin had found when they were little. She couldn't stay here, and she couldn't leave Judy here either. Someone might see them and Judy would tell what she had done.

Back through the scrub pines Beth pulled Judy. It would be easier out on the sand down toward the river. Through the shadows, across the darkened sand, away from the party, away from Kevin, Beth dragged Judy. Little by little. Carefully, stopping every few seconds to listen for sounds of activity. Pulling, pulling, until she thought her arms would break. It was easier on the sand. Down the rise, toward the river, she almost lost hold of her burden. Against the sky, the dark tree limbs lining the shallow rise became apprehending wraiths reaching out for her, to hold her, to tell what she had done. Moonlight lit oblique patterns on the sand, lighting the way for what she had to do. For Kevin.

She was tired, so tired. *How much farther? Don't look,* she told herself. *Just do it! Do it for Kevin. For Kevin.* Judy was struggling back to consciousness, but she was too stunned, too weak to do more than moan a barely audible protest. *Quickly, quickly,* Beth told herself. *Hurry! Don't give up. For Kevin. For Kevin.* She dragged Judy's semiconscious form almost to the place where she had found her with Kevin. The party was a safe distance away, around the bend, farther up the river. So far, no one had seen her, not even the sea birds which sometimes traveled this far into the Delta to escape a storm.

Beth stopped. Something was wrong. Something didn't fit. The dress. Judy's dress. She wouldn't go in swimming with her dress on. Or her shoes. Hurriedly, carefully, so as not to tear the material, she removed the sun dress. After pulling the strapped sandals off Judy's sandy feet, Beth looked down at her too-still form. She marveled at her own strength in managing to pull the heavier girl across the sands. Judy's legs and hips were full-fleshed. Unlike her own too-thin, narrow hips and thighs. And Judy had so much hair down there. She would too, someday, she promised herself.

Quickly, before she could think a second time, she ran back toward the overhanging shelf of sand and rock and deposited the dress and shoes and ran back to Judy.

Panting with exertion, Beth brought her burden to the water's edge. Just a bit more. A little bit more. Her own feet were in the water, feeling the soft clay bottom oozing between her toes. Soon. Soon. For Kevin.

Judy struggled to consciousness. Felt her legs being dragged across the small stones at the water's edge and into the soft clay. The water was cold, icy cold. Something held her around the chest and under the arms. It was strong and tight and she found it hard to breathe. Her legs were getting wet. Now her hips. She moaned. Awareness shot into her brain like a flare. It was Beth's arms around her chest, holding her, dragging her, pulling her into the water. She felt herself become buoyant. Her legs sought the bottom, struggling for footing.

She had no breath to scream. Her head hurt; her eyes wouldn't focus. She realized her arms were free, but they felt useless and leaden. With mighty effort, her hands groped, fingers clawing, reaching behind her, reaching for Beth.

Judy's hand broke the water's surface for an instant, and she caught a glimpse of Beth's face. Beth's lips were compressed into a grim line; the cords in her neck bulged with the exertion of pushing Judy back under the surface of the inky black water. But her eyes, her eyes! Slitted, cold, dead, yet behind them was that sly creature again. Sly and evil and deadly.

The night was still, with only distant sounds of music playing somewhere. Stupidly, amid her struggles, incongruously, she recognized the tune as "Help Me Make It Through the Night." Water lapped around her; she realized her struggles were useless. The force holding her was strong, becoming stronger. Her head was plunged beneath the water. With a last desperate strength from her trapped body, Judy fought. Her head surfaced. She couldn't touch bottom. She had been dragged into the current where she knew the shelf of mud and river bottom dropped off to a depth of over fifteen feet. Still, the force held her. Beth. Beth was the force.

Wet loops of hair covered her eyes, twisting around her neck. Gulping for air, she took in water. It seemed as though she were inhaling the whole river. Writhing, struggling, fighting with the last of her diminished strength, she managed to twist around to face her killer. Under, under, water pouring into her mouth and nose, filling her ear cavities, blurring her wide-eyed stare. She felt the fabric of Beth's sun dress in her hands and clutched at it frantically. Then the black waters of the river crashed through the last of her defenses. The slim cord of her life was strained, stretched taut into a black vortex of oblivion.

The last sound she heard was Beth's voice hissing, "I hope you go to hell, Judy Evans. I hope you go straight to hell!"

Kevin had wandered away from Reverend Conway and went to look for Judy. Several girls told him that Judy had been on line for the john, but she wasn't there now. He knew she hadn't come down to where the band was playing; he had just come from there.

He wondered if she had gone off in search of her bikini bottom and headed off in that direction along the beach.

A thousand thoughts tormented him as he pushed his feet through the sand, and he didn't see the discarded dress and shoes until he nearly tripped over them. Recognizing the articles immediately, he frowned and scanned the surface of the water.

All reason left him as he ran to the river, stumbling and rolling down the incline from the ridge, his eyes never leaving the two shadowy struggling figures in the water. He splashed toward them, silent prayers forming on his lips. His legs felt heavy, leaden, refusing to work in coordination with each other. He felt the clay bottom slope downward, the water rise to the height of his hips. The sky was black, the water blacker. The now solitary figure reflected the thin, wavering moonlight. Beth!

He swam with long, powerful strokes to reach his objective. Reaching it, he dove beneath the water and groped blindly, his fingers brushing against cold flesh and tangling in long hair. Fighting the need for air, he seized the form and heaved it to the surface.

Beth pounded on his back. "No! Let her die! Kill her, Kevin! Kill her!"

Kevin pulled Judy's inert form back toward shore, his feet searching for bottom. *God, don't let her die; please, don't let her die.*

"Kevin! Didn't you hear me?" Beth wailed. "Let her die, let her die!" She swam toward him, pulling at his arms, trying to push Judy's head under the surface.

"Don't touch her," Kevin growled. "Don't ever touch her again."

Beth backed away, a madness in her eyes. "I did it for you, Kevin, because I love you," she sobbed. "I love you. . . ."

"Your kind of love is sick, Beth. Get away from me. Get away from Judy and me."

For an instant he thought she would strike him, fight him for possession of Judy. His muscles tensed, ready for her onslaught. Instead, she backed away from him, then turned and pushed for shore. As he was struggling with Judy's weight, pulling and dragging her onto the beach, he saw Beth scrambling over the ridge.

He worked feverishly over Judy, tears and river water blurring his vision. Judy's head rolled as she spit and gagged. She was alive.

Kevin's stomach was churning so wildly he could barely carry Judy. He had to get her home, safe, away from Beth, away from everyone. He had hastily dressed her in the discarded sun dress and shoes that Beth stripped off her. He couldn't think about Beth, he didn't want to think about Beth. He had to take care of Judy and get her home safe and sound. Thank God no one had seen what happened, and thank God he had come looking for Judy. A cold chill washed over him. Another minute and he would have been too late. Another five minutes and Judy would have been dead and his sister would have been a murderer.

"Kev," Judy whimpered, "take me home, please. I want my mother," she said, burrowing her head against his chest.

"It's okay, it's okay," Kevin soothed. "Beth is gone and I'm taking you home. It's all right now, you're safe. Beth is gone."

"I can walk, Kev. Put me down. I want to walk, really I do."

Gently, Kevin set Judy on her feet and protectively put his arm around her to steady her. "What's your mother going to say and do?" Kevin worried aloud.

"Let's sit down a minute," Judy said shakily. "We have to talk about this. My mother will . . . she'll . . . what she'll do . . . she'll go off the deep end. She's just getting it together for herself, and I don't think she could handle this. I'll just say I don't feel well. I can carry it off. It's you who has the problem, Kev. What are you going to do? Are you going to tell?" she asked fearfully.

Kevin's arm tightened around Judy's shoulders. "Oh, God, I

don't know what to do," Kevin groaned. "How can I let Mom know that Beth . . ."

"Kev," Judy shivered against him, "Beth isn't . . . she's . . . crazy!"

"Are you okay now? Do you think you can make it?"

"Sure," Judy said, forcing a weak grin.

"Are you sure you don't want your mother to know?"

"I'm sure. I'm okay now, but there's no way I'll ever get within a hundred feet of your sister, ever again. There's no point in upsetting Mom. You do whatever you think you have to do. If you decide we should tell, then I'll do it. It's up to you, Kevin, after all, Beth is your sister."

Kevin wanted to throw up. Here Judy was, walking alongside him after his sister almost killed her, telling him to handle it, placing her trust in him. If her mother, who was a grown, sensible, reasonable adult, couldn't handle it, why did Judy think he was going to fare any better? Judy smiled up at him, and he knew that he could handle it. He fought down the bile rising in his throat and tightened his hold on her shoulders. He could handle it.

A dim orange light glowed from the Evanses' front porch and an even dimmer light glowed from within. "Mom's in bed, but not asleep. That's the night light she left on for me. If we're quiet, we can just walk through the door."

Kevin gathered Judy in his arms in the shadows of the gnarled oak tree. They said nothing, did nothing, but reveled in the comfort each gave the other. It was Judy who broke away and gazed up at Kevin. "Everything is going to be all right, Kevin. I can feel it and so can you. It's going to be all right," she reassured.

"Judy, you mean so much to me, I can't leave you. I don't want to stay here in Hayden, I want to go away to college and never come back. I can't wait, Judy. . . ."

"Shh . . ." She silenced him by touching her fingertips to his lips. "We're going away together. You're going to Tulane and I'll be right there with you. We'll be together, Kevin, and we'll put this behind us."

"It's late; you better go in," Kevin said softly. Judy squeezed his hand and smiled. Kevin watched her run up the steps, stop at the top and wave at him. His heart started its wild thumping. Jesus God Almighty, if he had been one minute later, he wouldn't be standing here watching Judy go through the front door. In the quietness he could hear the soft snick of the bolt. His shoulders slumped as he turned and headed for home.

Kevin scuffed his feet as he moped along, dragging one foot after the other. He had always loved the sound of the crickets late at night, but tonight he paid them no heed, his mind on only one thing. If he had only one wish in the world, he would wish he was at Tulane, never to return, never to set his eyes on Beth again. He stopped short under the yellow glow of the street lamp and stared at the car swerving into the driveway behind the sporting goods store. Cader was going into the store. Vaguely, he wondered why, since he himself had set the burglar alarm. He shrugged; maybe Cader forgot something. Before he realized what he was doing, he was running after the car and shouting, "Hey, Cader, can I talk to you a minute?"

Cader Harris climbed from the car and frowned. *Now, what in the living hell . . . ?* "Kind of late for you to be prowling the streets, isn't it?" he said sternly.

"If there's one thing I don't need right now, it's my boss sounding like my father." Cader felt the blood leave his face. "Can I talk to you about something? I wouldn't ask, but it really is important."

"Must be the night air and all these damn crickets, makes me go off the deep end sometimes," Cader said gruffly. "Come on in. I have a couple of beers in the cooler. That's why I stopped by, as a matter of fact; there isn't any in my apartment. Don't just stand there; you said it was important."

A bottle of Heineken in his hand, Kevin gulped and stared at the man sitting across from him. Cader Harris was a guy who had been around. If anyone knew what to do, it would be Cader. But first, he had to get the words out. Jesus, this was almost as hard as going to Aunt Cledie's that first time.

Harris's eyes narrowed. Whatever was about to pop from the boy's mouth wasn't going to be good, he could feel it in his gut. "Help me," he mouthed silently to a God he had never called on before.

"Remember the night we sat here talking?" Kevin asked. Cader nodded and waited. "Well, I had more to drink than I should have, and I was a little drunk. I took a shower but it didn't help much. I guess I passed out and I was dreaming that Viola was in bed with

me and we were . . . you know. I thought I was dreaming, but I
wasn't. I wasn't dreaming at all. It was Beth in bed with me. We . . .
I think . . . she said . . . I don't know what I did." Kevin took a swallow of beer as he watched Cader's frozen face. He didn't look
shocked. "Tonight, Beth tried to drown Judy Evans. I got there just
in time. A few more minutes and I would have been too late. I can't
handle this, Cader. I don't know what to do. Judy doesn't want to
tell her mother and she's trusting me to take care of . . . of . . . Beth."

A wild, alien surge of parental protectiveness shot through
Cader Harris. He wanted to grab Kevin and hold him, to stroke his
hair the way a mother would do and then thump him on the back
the way a father would do. He raised his eyes upward. There was
no bolt of lightning, no roll of thunder to help him. He was on his
own. He had to tell his son what to do. He swallowed hard, forcing
himself to remain in his nonchalant position in the swivel chair.

"Kevin, the dream, the actuality, isn't important. Whatever it
was, it's over and you can't do anything about it. The problem now
is something else. My best advice and my only advice to you is to
go home, wake your . . . your father and talk to him. He's got to be
a good man if he has a son like you. He'll know what you should
do. I think you've known all along that is what you should do. You
saw me coming here at just the right moment, and you needed to
talk at that moment. You need your old man, kid, not me." He
made his voice purposely gruff as he spoke. He didn't want Kevin
ever to regret coming to him. "This is between you and me; it
won't ever go any further."

"I know that, Cader; that's why I wanted to talk to you. You're
an okay guy. I'd like to keep in touch with you after I get to
Tulane, if you don't mind. My dad is an okay guy too. I love my
dad, Cader, and I'm not ashamed to tell you that. That part about
the dream, that was one thing, but I didn't want to hurt Dad by
telling him about Beth. I was all mixed up there for a while.
Thanks," Kevin said, sticking out his hand. Cader pretended not
to see it as he got up from the swivel chair. If he touched the boy
now, it would be all over. He wanted to put his arms around
Kevin, to put in a claim for his son. He loved the boy, enough not
to succumb to his own needs, but to think of Kevin. The boy was
too close to the brink; the last thing he needed was something to
confuse him even further.

"I didn't do anything, Kevin. Look, do you want a ride home? It's late."

"No, I think I'll walk. You won't forget, will you . . . about keeping in touch?"

Now, what in the goddamn hell was that lump in his throat? Cader nodded as he held the door open for Kevin and then carefully locked it. "I'd like that. I really would . . . son."

"See you tomorrow," Kevin said, loping off down the street. He could handle it if Cader said he could.

Arthur and Irene Thomas sat in the dark, paneled study and listened to Kevin's tortured words. Only once did their eyes meet and then both carefully looked away. Arthur laid a paternal hand on Kevin's shoulder. "Your mother and I will take care of this. We're both proud of you that you didn't take the easy way out and say nothing. I know what it must have cost you to come to us like this. Trust us, Kevin, to do the right thing. Tonight there are no answers. Tomorrow is something else. Try to get some sleep."

Kevin looked at his parents, loving his father and respecting his mother. He did as he was told and left the room. His hands and arms seemed to have a mind of their own as he found himself wedging the desk chair beneath the doorknob. He knew he wasn't going to sleep, but he felt better with the door secured. He'd never feel safe in this house again.

CHAPTER SEVENTEEN

Irene Thomas laid the hairbrush down on the dresser and walked to the window. Foster Doyle Hayden was climbing from the sleek car, his face a murderous mask of fury. It was time. By now, Foster Doyle would have gotten wind of her traitorous plea to the Board of Education the day before.

"Irene!" the furious voice bellowed.

"Just a moment, Father," Irene called down the stairs. She took her time, glancing in the mirror and then straightening her dress. Deftly, she rubbed her index finger over her lips and then reached for a tissue. Her movements were slow, unhurried as she descended the stairs. She was numb. As numb as she had been the night before in Arthur's study when Kevin had spelled out the sordid truth about Beth and she had to face Arthur's stony silence.

"I want to speak with you, Irene. Now!"

"Why don't we go into the study, Father? Beth is having her breakfast in the kitchen. You go along and I'll bring some coffee," Irene said firmly, heading for the kitchen.

"Mama," Beth whined, "this milk is sour." Irene ignored her daughter and started fixing a tray. "Mama, did you hear me?" Irene continued her fluid movements, completely ignoring her daughter. Later, after her father left, she would acknowledge the child, unless she could think of another way to get through the day pretending she wasn't there.

"I'm sorry, Mama. Look at me and tell me you aren't angry with me. Mamaaaa," she shrilled. Irene picked up the laden tray and moved the door with her shoulder. Beth watched her, her eyes narrowed and her bottom lip trembling.

"Here, Father. Black, no sugar, right?" Irene said, pouring the fragrant brew into a delicate china cup. She poured herself a cup and held it lightly in her hand, her eyes fixed on her father. "What did you want to talk to me about?" she asked quietly. "If you raise your voice, I'll leave the room," she said warningly.

Foster Doyle took a deep breath, aware of the rattle of the cup against the saucer. "How dare you defy me the way you did at the Board of Education meeting? How dare you go against me? What possessed you to endorse Delta Oil? Good God, Irene, have you lost your senses?"

"No, Father, I haven't lost my senses. I think I just came to my senses, as a matter of fact. I really don't want to discuss it. It's done; I've taken my stand and that's the beginning and the end of it."

"Cader Harris put you up to it, don't deny it," Foster Doyle thundered. "You never used your brain before he came here, admit it. All of a sudden Harris shows up on the scene, and he had you eating right out of his hand. You're his puppet, Irene. He told you what to do and you did it."

"And what if I did?" she asked defiantly. "I love him and he loves me. He's got a secure future with Delta Oil and will be able to take care of me. It's not like before when we were younger. Now, he has something to offer me and I intend to take him and his offer."

Foster Doyle's face turned ashen and then purple. His clawlike hand reached out to grasp the back of a chair. His breathing was labored and he looked like he was going to drop to the floor. Irene watched her father without emotion. He was old; he had lived his life. "And you think because Cader Harris has money that it's going to be all right?" the old man gasped. "Well, he had money once before and he didn't take you with him. He sold out. To me. I bought him off. That's why he went away. Is it your intention to leave or stay here? Are you going to flaunt your affair in front of me? What do you have to say to that?"

"Not much." She couldn't, she wouldn't, give him the satisfaction of knowing what the spoken words were doing to her. "Tell me," she said, setting the fragile cup down on a cherry wood table. "How much did I go for?" she asked softly.

"Too much," the old man gasped as his knees began to buckle. Only with supreme effort did he manage to stay on his feet. "He didn't care that you were pregnant with his child. The only thing that interested him was money and a chance to leave this town. Don't you understand, Irene? He didn't care about you then and he doesn't care about you now. He knows Kevin is his son. If he does say he wants you, it's because of Kevin." This time Foster Doyle's knees did give out and his flimsy hold on the back of the wing chair gave way.

Irene picked up the phone and dialed a number, then spoke softly. "Father, if you can hear me, the ambulance is on the way." There was a detached, vague look on Irene's face as she picked up her coffee cup and sipped the cool liquid. Her eyes met Beth's as the child backed off one step and then two, finally swiveling and running out the front door. "I think you've had a stroke, Father," Irene said, peering down at the inert man. "Don't worry about anything. I'm more than capable of running your affairs. I'll see that you receive the best care available."

The shrill whine of the siren heralding the arrival of the ambulance made one of Foster Doyle's legs twitch.

Irene stood aside as the ambulance attendants entered the room, pushing the stretcher. Quietly, she stood near the fireplace and watched as the men checked her father's vital signs. Their faces revealed nothing as they lifted his body onto the stretcher and then covered him. "Do you want to ride to the hospital with us, Ma'am?" one of the men asked.

"No, thank you." The attendants looked at one another and picked up the stretcher.

From her new position at the window Irene watched the scene at the rear of the ambulance. She frowned when the rear doors were closed and locked. It sounded so terminal.

Beth's eyes were hate-filled as she ran through the room and out the door. She hated them all. She ran, looking neither to the left nor to the right, her thin legs pumping rhythmically. She'd show them all. When she reached the mortuary, she slowed to regain her breath. Her knuckles were white on the heavy doorknob as she thrust open the door. Daddy would be in the office. She made her way through the meadow of thick carpet and marched into Arthur Thomas's private office. He was alone. She stared at him as she kicked the door shut. "I know Kevin told you what happened at the clambake. She deserved it, Daddy," Beth said with vitriolic vehemence. "She's a slut; even Mama said so."

"And because of that you decided you had the right to kill her, an innocent person," Arthur said coldly.

"I knew you would be on Kevin's side. You don't care about me; all you care about is Kevin. Kevin isn't even your son. He's Cader Harris's son. I heard Grandpa tell Mama this morning. I heard them talking. I think Mama is going off with Mr. Harris. I bet they take Kevin with them. And you think they're all so wonderful. What do you think now? How do you like it that Cader Harris is Kevin's father?"

"Do you think I care?" Arthur said, sitting down behind the desk. "I love Kevin and he's my son. I'm *your* father and look how you turned out."

"I always knew you and Mama loved Kevin best. He's not even my real brother. But I only wanted to protect Kevin from Judy Evans. I was helping!"

Arthur Thomas's voice was deadly when he spoke. "Go home, Beth."

"You're hateful, Daddy. You're just hateful. I don't care if you die like Grandpa. The ambulance came for him. You didn't know that, did you?" she said, running from the mortuary.

"And another pillar of the community bites the dust," Arthur said through clenched teeth.

Somehow, he had known all along that Kevin wasn't his son. He had never wanted to face the truth behind Irene's eager submission and hasty, panicked phone call. He smiled. It made no difference. He loved Kevin as much as he loved life. Kevin was his son by the right of love.

By the time Beth reached the sporting goods store her eyes were wild like those of a trapped animal. She raced up the loading dock steps and into the stock room. Frantically, she searched the area for some sign of Cader Harris. A hiss of sound escaped her parted lips as she saw him near a display of football helmets. "You're Kevin's father," she shrilled. "I heard my grandfather and mother talking this morning. My grandpa told my mother that you took money from him and went away because you didn't want Kevin. That was a disgusting thing to do. And it was disgusting of my grandfather to give you money; you're nothing but white trash. I heard my mother ask how much you took, but Grandpa wouldn't tell her. You want Kevin, don't you? Everyone wants Kevin. I told Daddy you were Kevin's father."

Cader Harris, stunned for the moment, could only stare at the wild-eyed girl in front of him. "You what?" he shouted, grabbing her by the arm.

"You heard me. I told Daddy you were Kevin's father, and do you know what he said? He said he didn't care. He said he loved Kevin. Everybody loves Kevin. Even Grandpa loves Kevin best, and now he's in the hospital. The ambulance took him a little while ago. And it's all because of you. Everything went wrong when you came back here. You don't belong here with the rest of us. You're nothing but trash," Beth said spitefully.

"You know something, kid? You're absolutely right. I don't belong here. I never did. But there's one thing you're wrong about. It's not me who's trash, it's you. They should lock you up and then throw away the key."

Long after Beth was gone, Cader Harris sat thinking. How

could he have ever thought he loved Irene? She was just like Beth. In her own clutching way she would destroy Kevin just as Beth had tried to do. He shouldn't have talked to the girl that way; there was no excuse for it. He was an adult and she was a sick child. Jesus! And Arthur. Should he go to see him, say something? What the hell was there to say? Kevin was with the only father he knew. He wasn't that much of a bastard. A bastard, yes, but he would never do anything to hurt Kevin or Arthur. They had something special and he was fortunate to have been permitted to know them both even for a short while. He hadn't lost a thing. If anything, he was a better person for this experience. He wasn't so tough after all. He hadn't lost a thing. He hadn't lost Irene because he never really had her. He hadn't lost Kevin; he had found Kevin. So he would leave, neither losing nor winning.

Arthur Thomas drove slowly down Jatha Hayden Boulevard. A deep crease of concern formed between his heavy brows. Christ! What a day! He still hadn't recovered from what Kevin had told him the night before about Beth trying to kill Judy Evans. But he didn't doubt his son's word for a minute. His son. Cader Harris's son. No, his son. All the years of love and companionship had to count for something. His feeling hadn't changed for the boy just because he had learned the truth. Nothing could stop him from loving Kevin.

Arthur's direction took him past Harris's sporting goods store. He frowned again when he noticed Irene's black Continental parked in the lot. His heart sank and his stomach churned. She was probably in there with Cader, breaking the wonderful news that he, not Arthur, was Kevin's father.

Making an illegal turn on the boulevard, he pulled into the lot beside Irene's car. As he parked, he pictured the scene he would have with Irene. She had been behaving strangely lately and now he knew why: Cader Harris.

Arthur glanced at the left rear tire of Irene's car. It looked like it could use air. He kicked at it to test it and suddenly wished he were kicking Irene. He realized in that split second that he had never liked her. Never had and never would. All that lovely Southern charm and grace had never done him one bit of good. It never had and never would.

Everything was going wrong. The whole town was off its axis.

Ever since the beginning of the summer, after the high-school graduation. Ever since Cader Harris had come to town.

The town had already changed, and now that Delta Oil was a shoo-in to get that beach front, it would never be the same again. He was beginning to hate the town of Hayden and he was beginning to hate Irene. He leaned against the fender of her Continental and waited.

Irene stood facing Cader in the office of his shop. She ignored the cold light she saw in his eyes. She had come to tell him about Kevin, but she didn't know how to approach it. It wasn't something you could just blurt out.

Earlier that day, Beth had come running into the house. Her eyes were red with crying, and although Irene had determined to ignore the girl, Beth stood in front of her and screamed, "I did it! I went and told Daddy and I told Cader Harris what you and Grandpa were talking about this morning. And do you know what, Mama? They don't care! They don't care!" she shrieked on a higher note. "They don't care about anything except Kevin. They don't care about you any more than they care about me."

So, the cat was out of the bag at last. There was no going back, there was only the beautiful future to look forward to. Foster Doyle was struggling for his life in the hospital, but they said he would never be the same. That meant that she could finally take over where Foster Doyle left off. *She* would be the most important person in town. It was *her* decision that would count. And Cader too would profit from this new importance.

"Cader," she said, trying to get his attention. "I have the most wonderful news to tell you."

"Spit it out, Irene; I don't have time for games."

"It's about Delta Oil and you have me to thank for it," she hedged, pushing back the issue of their son, Kevin. She was still frightened that Cader would bolt and run. He might see Kevin as a responsibility, and she knew from experience that that was one fact of life Cader Harris couldn't handle. "The deal was closed a few minutes ago. I just came from the Town Hall."

Cader staggered under the news. Joy lit his face. He could almost feel the weight of the payoff from Delta in his pocket. "When? How?" he asked, temporarily forgetting about Kevin.

"Actually, it's still top secret. Two men from Delta Oil came into town a few days ago and clinched the deal with the town council this morning. Of course, everything is very hush hush. Delta is going to build a municipal swimming pool for the young people in place of the beach they'll be taking over. Also, they've promised to help with the school budget. No more sewing new gold braid on old band uniforms. Isn't it wonderful?"

Cader managed a smile through his confusion. Why hadn't he been told? Suddenly, he realized why he hadn't heard from Delta Oil in two days. Just about the time the reps from Delta had come to town. Just when Sunny had told him about the two strangers and finding the executive ball pen with DELTA OIL inscribed on its side. Through his confusion, his smile brightened. What did it matter if they told him or not? They had to know it was due to his efforts that the deal was pushed through. Now he could leave with a quarter of a million bucks in his pocket as well as a contract as public relations man for their commercials. Irene was still babbling. He focused his attention on her and listened.

"And by the way, Cader," she said happily, "you'll be pleased to know that your reputation as our town celebrity has preceded you. One of Delta's men asked if I knew you, and, of course, I said yes. Anyway, he had a message for you. Some kind of football tactic, but it sounded so funny at the time that I laughed."

"What was it, Irene?"

"He told me to ask you if you'd ever heard of a kiss-off."

Cader's face fell. His stomach churned. Disbelief registered on his features and his fist tightened. Through fuzzy vision he could see Irene smiling up at him, pleased with herself. What had she said? He had her to thank? He got the message, all right, and he knew what a kiss-off was. It was a big foot right up your ass.

Irene was puzzled by Cader's silence. He seemed to be thrown off balance. "Cade, there's something else, something I've got to tell you. . . ."

"If you're going to tell me that Kevin is my son, Irene, I know all about it."

"I know you do. Beth told me she came to see you. . . ."

"You don't understand, Irene. I didn't need Beth to tell me Kevin is my son. I've known all these years. Ever since I saw the announcement of his birth in the paper and I counted back on my fingers."

Irene was stunned by this announcement. Wildly, her mind raced, putting together the pieces of the puzzle. "You . . . you knew? And you never came back? For Kevin . . . for me?" she asked weakly.

"And if I had it to do all over again, Irene, I still wouldn't come back. Not for Kevin and especially not for you. I'm not Kevin's father, I only sired him. Arthur is the boy's father."

Irene snapped her gaping mouth shut. She refused to believe what she was hearing. "How much did my father pay you, Cader? What did I go for? What price did you put on your own child and me?"

"Around five thousand a year, tuition at Tulane and a Mercedes Benz. Four years, Irene, and a new car every year."

"I see. I came cheap, didn't I?" Slowly, as though she were being dragged down into the depths of hell, she turned to him, a world of pleading in her eyes. "It doesn't matter. That was then; this is now. I love you, Cader; nothing can change that. And you love me, I know you do." She extended her hand, reaching to touch him.

Cader stepped backward, avoiding her touch, but his eyes held hers. "The same way you love Kevin?" he asked, his voice harsh. At her questioning look, he continued. "Kevin came here last night. He told me about Beth. I told him to go to his father. Now, I'm asking you, Irene, what are you going to do about it?"

"Do? What do you mean 'do'?"

"Yes," Cader smiled bitterly, "I can see why that question would be beyond your understanding. Beth tried to kill someone last night and she almost succeeded. She's a very sick girl and she's destroying Kevin. She crept into his bed, took advantage of the fact that he was blind drunk . . ." Exasperated, he demanded, "I'm asking you what you're going to do about it!"

Irene bristled. "What should I do? Expose the whole nasty business? Throw myself on the town's mercy? That little tramp Judy isn't going to say anything. . . ."

"You'd sacrifice Kevin so you could maintain your standing in the community," he said flatly. "I'm not concerned with you, Irene. What about Kevin?"

"He'll live with it and some day even forget it. . . ."

"That's not good enough and you know it!" he shouted. "You

would destroy that kid; you'd throw him together with Beth until it happened again and again, until there's nothing left of him. Between you and your daughter, you'd eat him alive!" Sudden realization dawned on Harris. "Yes, you'd like that, wouldn't you? He's too strong for you now, but soon, after Beth bites away everything he believes in, everything he stands for, Kevin would be yours. He would never leave you. He'd be broken and as sick as Beth. And you would have won."

Irene shook her head in denial. "No, you're wrong. . . ."

"Kevin is the only decent part of your life, Irene. And I'm counting on Arthur to save him from you. Get out of here, Irene. I can't stand the sight of you. And I'm warning you, if Arthur doesn't make the right moves to protect Kevin from you, I'll have to take things into my own hands. And that you won't like, Irene, I promise you."

Irene lunged toward him, locking her arms around his neck. Her voice was shrill with desperation and her words came in a rush. "No, don't leave me. I'll do anything you say, only don't leave me. I love you, Cader. I don't want Beth; I don't need Kevin. . . ."

Cader wrestled her arms from their frantic clutch. "Arthur can save Kevin from your grip, Irene. But if I stayed with you, who would save me?" His words fell like stones. "Get out of here, Irene, you disgust me."

Slowly, in a moment that seemed tike an eternity, Irene shrank away from him. He turned away from her, expecting to feel her claws rake his back. Instead, he heard the back door open and close.

When Irene Hayden Thomas walked out of the dim coolness of the sporting goods store and into the heat of the parking lot, she was startled to see Arthur leaning against her car. With an enormous amount of willpower, she managed to regain a semblance of composure. As she approached, she fidgeted with the sleeves of her blouse and flushed guiltily.

"What are you doing here, Arthur?" she managed to ask, choking back the tears she knew she would shed in private.

"Waiting for you, Irene." His voice was toneless, his eyes unreadable. "How nice to see you speechless for once," he added snidely. "I suppose you're expecting me to create a scene. Well, I won't. You're not worth it, Irene. I suppose I waited here to tell you I was leaving."

"Arthur! You can't! What about the children? And your business? You just can't leave. Where will you go?"

"I'm leaving, Irene. I think I would have eventually left even if I hadn't found out about you and Cader Harris."

"Arthur, what about me?" she whined in a shaky voice.

"What about you, Irene?"

"What will the children and I do without you? We need you, Arthur."

"You only need me to look respectable, Irene. You don't need me, Arthur Thomas, the man. You never did. I'll be by the house after dinner to pick up what I need. I'd appreciate it if you weren't home when I arrive. And I won't embarrass you by remaining in town. Kevin will be leaving with me."

Irene stared after him as he climbed into his car and started the engine. Her mind couldn't grasp what was happening to her. Yesterday she had so much and today she was left with nothing. Her eyes flicked back to the loading dock and the door into the store.

As Arthur backed his car out of its parking place, Irene waved frantically, mouthing something he couldn't hear over the whir of the air conditioner. He stopped and rolled down the window, leaning out to her.

Breathlessly, she ran over to him, her eyes wide and questioning. "Arthur . . . I have to know . . . is this a kiss-off?"

Arthur expelled air from his lungs. He wouldn't ever understand her, not if he lived to be a hundred. With great patience he nodded and said, "Yes, Irene, this is a kiss-off." He gunned the motor and left her standing alone in the parking lot. It was one of the few times he had ever seen genuine comprehension in his wife's eyes.

CHAPTER EIGHTEEN

*K*eli McDermott sat on the edge of her bed, her suit-case open but empty. What should she take with her? What did one take to the hospital to have one's breast removed? There was no doubt whatsoever in her mind that she would return less than whole. But she would return, and she would be alive, even if it was just for a little while.

Toothbrush, comb and brush, slippers, robe, nightgown. Those few things didn't fill the yawning suitcase. Different clothes to come home in? Was this home? Could it ever be home again?

As she packed, she could hear the furious sounds of Gene's typewriter. He had said he was nearing the completion of his book. He wanted the world to know that Colonel Gene McDermott, USAF, Ret., had done his bit.

The click-click of the typewriter followed Keli down the hall. She heard it stop for a moment as she passed the open door of Gene's study with her suitcase in hand. She took the luggage out to the car, and, when she returned, the rhythm of the electric machine had altered slightly. Almost as though it was drawing to a close. She could always tell when Gene was winding down. Did that mean the book was finally finished? Would he come out of that room now? He had closeted himself in there ever since the after-noon Marsha had come over begging her to keep her appointment in New Orleans. The afternoon Keli had told both Gene and Marsha that she had already decided to go and do whatever was necessary to save her own life.

After Marsha had left, pursued from the house by an irate, enraged Gene, he hadn't said a word to Keli. He had just looked at her as though she were a stranger to him. Then he had gone into his study, and his typewriter had clacked almost ceaselessly until now. No words, no explanations, nothing. It was almost as though she had simply ceased to exist.

She could tell him she was leaving. She could risk his trying to stop her. Or she could simply drive into New Orleans tomorrow and sign herself into the hospital. Later. She would decide later.

As Keli stood at her open bedroom window, she thought what a beautiful night it was. The crickets sounded joyous. She smiled. The world would be such a beautiful place if everyone could be happy.

Keli needed support and comforting; something she could never find behind the locked study door where Gene worked on his book. More, she needed these things from Damion. Desperately. Something inside her told her that Damion needed her too. Damion.

Keli had no second thoughts. There was no fear or daring in her as she picked up her car keys from the dresser. Damion told her she had a choice. Choice. Damion *was* her choice.

Through the door and down the stairs, out the door and down the porch and across the lawn to her car. Damion was her choice. She needed; she wanted.

Out of her car, across the parking lot, up the parsonage steps. She blinked and stood back as the sound of the door chimes rang in her ears. Soft yellow light from the porch lantern cloaked her in its aura.

Damion Conway opened the door and smiled down at his visitor. Keli didn't move but stood gazing up at him, her face quiet and serene. "I've decided to go to New Orleans tomorrow. I'll check into the hospital and see the surgeon Marc Baldwin told me about. My bag is in the car. It is my choice. Mine alone."

So many words, Damion thought. So many words from Keli. She seemed to need to tell someone, to talk until her words were exhausted. She needed someone to listen to her. Just listen. Silently, he stood aside, motioning her to enter.

A veil dropped over Keli's eyes and her resistance became a reality. Damion sighed forlornly. The need to talk, to be understood, was there, but his finely honed instincts concerning Keli told him she hadn't been able to muster the courage she needed to confide her feelings.

Looking into his eyes with a silent plea he could not answer, Keli turned and walked away, her back straight and unyielding.

"Keli," he called softly after her, "I'm here when you need me. I want you to need me, Keli. Not to make decisions for you, but to support you in your own decisions. Don't do this to yourself, Keli. Don't do this to us."

Feeling as though he were locked in a vacuum, he watched her continue down the walk. No sound came to his ears but the slight click of her heels against the flagstones; no sight filled his senses except the vision of her slight frame, dark hair swinging around her hips as she turned away from him.

Head held high, tears blinding her vision, Keli returned to her car in the parking lot next to the church. She had made her decision, but, God help her, she was afraid. Afraid of being mutilated, afraid of dying, afraid of being alone. Afraid that she would never know what it was to reach out to someone who loved her, someone that she loved.

She imagined she heard Damion close the door as she walked down the path. A lonely sound, a sound that shut her out. She had shut herself out. Away from Damion.

She stood there in the half-light for what seemed an eternity. Thoughts whirled around in her head, questions beat at her, and always she knew her answers would be found with Damion.

Shoulders squared, chin lifted high, eyes bright with triumph, Keli walked determinedly back to the parsonage. As she took the last few steps she felt as though her feet weren't touching the ground. Thrusting the door open, she called for him.

The first floor was deserted, and, as she mounted the stairs, she heard the running shower. She followed the sound, noticing the cigarette burning away in the large ashtray on Damion's nightstand and the trail of discarded clothing leading to the bathroom.

Not allowing herself a second thought, she pulled off her clothes, kicked her shoes beside Damion's near the bed, and stalked into the steamy tiled bathroom. Seeming to have a will of its own, her hand flung back the shower curtain and she stepped in.

Surprise marked Damion's face. A warm, welcoming expression lighted his dark eyes as he smiled and gathered her to him under the warm, needle spray.

As Keli felt the imprint of his eyes on her water-beaded body, she experienced a thrill tingling the insides of her thighs. She pressed closer to him as she raised her open lips to his, and he kissed her as though he were sipping the sweetest wine.

His hands possessed her tenderly, bringing her closer, always closer.

Damion gazed down at her with such love and tenderness that Keli began to tremble. With an answering look from her, he lifted her into his arms and carried her out of the shower stall and into the bedroom. He settled her down on the bed and lay beside her, encircling her in his arms and breathing in the delicious scent of her.

Keli pulled away from him, rising up from his arms and turning to face him. "Not yet, Damion," she protested, "I want to tell you something first." Her soft doe eyes locked with his and her intensity moved him. "Tonight, I am a whole woman. By tomorrow, I may not be. I want you to make love to me, Damion. To me, Keli, the whole person. Tonight. Now. I want to know what it is to lie beside the man I love while I'm still whole. I've never been with a man, Damion. I'm a virgin. I want to know, to remember, while I still can."

Damion looked deeply into her eyes and found peace there. His love shone upon her as he said gently, "Keli, you will always be a whole woman. A whole person. Surgery won't change you, or what's inside here," he touched a finger to her breast over her heart.

"Do you want me?"

"God only knows how I want you. I love you, Keli. You're the most beautiful creature I've ever seen. I've loved you from the moment I first saw you. It's something that's been growing inside me ever since time began to have any meaning for me. You have to know that it's you I love, Keli, not your physical perfection. I love the woman you are, not the woman's body. When I make love to you, it will be as a man who loves a woman. You must understand that, Keli, and know it with your heart. Because it won't be just for tonight, but forever. And when you leave for New Orleans tomorrow, you won't be alone. I'll be with you."

Keli looked down into his beloved face, tears welling in her eyes. Tears of happiness. It would have to be forever. He wouldn't be used. Not even because he loved her. "I understand, Damion. And the woman you make love to will love you as a woman loves a man," she told him, her eyes shining brightly as she fell into his arms and whispered, "Show me how you love me, Damion. Show me."

Gene McDermott typed the last word of his manuscript just as Keli closed the car door. It was finished. Carefully, his movements sure and precise, he stacked the pages of his book and placed them inside his desk drawer. He covered the typewriter, but not until after he had pulled the plug and wrapped the cord around the carriage knobs.

When the engine of Keli's car sprang to life, he walked over to the table and withdrew his service revolver. There was no point to looking to see if the bullet was in the chamber. Only fools kept empty guns as a threat.

He clicked back the hammer and stood in front of the full-length mirror on the closet door. The moment he heard the car pull away from the curb, he placed the gun to his temple and pulled the trigger.

CHAPTER NINETEEN

*D*amion opened the door for Keli and then climbed behind the wheel of his car. "Are you certain, Keli, that you don't want to stop at your house before we leave?" he asked quietly.

"There's no reason for me to stop. My bag is in the trunk. It is my choice, my decision. I will not return. I told you last night when we talked. I'm so glad you're going with me, Damion."

Damion's voice was gentle, loving, when he spoke. "I'll always be with you, honey."

Keli smiled. No matter what happened, no matter what the outcome of her appointment in New Orleans, all was right with her world.

"I called the Bishop early this morning, and he's sending a new minister on the afternoon plane." Keli touched his arm, her hand gentle, her eyes understanding. "It's just as well that we're leaving. Hayden will never be the same again. It will grow and prosper with Delta Oil calling the shots."

"What happened, Damion?" Keli asked hesitantly.

"I wish I knew. I've tried to think it through and analyze it, and the only thing I can come up with is Cader Harris. As soon as he arrived, he brought out the worst and the best in all of us. He's a catalyst; he makes things happen. No matter where Cader Harris goes, he takes trouble with him, and if he fails in that, then he stirs it up. I suppose he'll be leaving soon too."

Damion pulled the car over to the side of the road and turned to Keli. "Look back if you want to; we're leaving Hayden. Once we get on the interstate, Hayden will be part of the past, nothing more than a memory."

"I don't need memories, Damion. I have the one I want, and he's sitting here beside me."

Arthur rummaged throng the assorted litter that had accumulated in the rear storage closet for the past eighteen years. Deciding he had chosen those things he wanted to keep, he tied the large cardboard carton with rope, looping the knot tightly.

He walked to the back of the mortuary and called through the door of the preparation room. "Destry, can you come out here a minute?"

Destry stood in the doorway, his spotless white smock fitting him as though it were tailor-made. Arthur sighed. He had rented his smocks from the same laundry, and his whites never fitted him that way. Destry looked down at the heavy, bulging carton.

"This is the last of it, Destry. You're on your own now." His tone, instead of sounding melancholy as Destry would have expected, seeing that Arthur had run the business for eighteen years, sounded relieved. As though a two-ton weight had been lifted from his squat shoulders.

Arthur extended his hand and Destry shook it warmly. "Good luck to you, Mr. Thomas."

"The same to you, Destry. I know you'll make a go of it. You know the business inside and out. I guess this is goodbye."

Destry watched him until he was out of sight. He had never seen such an unhappy man. Yet, there was something in Arthur Thomas's eyes that sparkled with hope. Destry shrugged. With a proprietorial eye, he cast his glance around the office. This was his now, all his. Who would have ever thought it? He hadn't believed Arthur when he approached him yesterday afternoon about buying out the business. As if a black man could ever have that much money. But Arthur had been serious, so serious he had dragged Destry off to the bank to make the necessary arrangements. Monthly payments and terms stating a percentage of the profits to be paid at the end of each fiscal year, after taxes. It was an opportunity not to be refused.

Destry carried himself with new authority as he sashayed through what now belonged to him. His long brown fingers possessively touched the furniture and the light fixtures. This was his, all his. He became reflective and wondered if Mr. Thomas were telling the truth when he said he was going back to medical school to become a medical examiner. Destry smiled. Arthur intended to give Quincy, that TV M.E., a run for his money.

Destry leaned back against an ornate bronze coffin in the display room and pondered his next move. He would have to hire a white mortician. Black men weren't supposed to embalm white folks. Not in the heart of Dixie, anyway. He laughed. Wait till he told Aunt Cledie he was taking over the business. Destry laughed, a great roaring, booming sound as he slapped the cold metal coffin. Aunt Cledie would piss her drawers.

Arthur parked the car the curb near the sporting goods store and motioned for Kevin to remain seated while he went inside. Kevin was puzzled, but nodded. Arthur opened the door and walked over to Cader Harris. "Mr. Harris, I'm Arthur Thomas," he said, holding out his hand. "I'm sorry we haven't had a chance to meet before this. I wanted to stop by before leaving Hayden to tell you I appreciate what you've done for Kevin. I know that he came here first the other night and that you sent him home to me."

"Mr. Thomas, the boy would have gone to you on his own. He just happened to see me first. I gave him the best advice a friend could give. I hope you understand that." Arthur's eyes smiled at the word "friend." Cader continued. "If it's all right with you, I would like to keep in touch with Kevin, but only if you agree."

"The boy needs both of us, Mr. Harris. I want you to know that I'll always do the best I can for Kevin."

"What more could I ask?" Cader grinned, sticking out his hand. That damnable lump was back in his throat and from the looks of Arthur Thomas he had the same in his own throat.

"Kevin's in the car. He wanted to come in, but I asked him to wait outside. I'd like it if you'd come out and say goodbye."

"I'm sorry we didn't meet under other circumstances," Cader said honestly.

"I am too. Good luck with the store."

Cader laughed. "You aren't the only one leaving. I'm closing up shop and leaving here . . . alone."

Arthur Thomas watched Cader as he stuck his head in the window and talked with Kevin. Arthur should hate Cader, hate him, and Irene too, but he didn't. Kevin was the only one who was important. Arthur understood that and Cader Harris understood.

Cader Harris stood back from the curb and watched the car drive off. Jesus, he felt good. And it had nothing to do with his cock. Goddamn, he felt good. Yo!

Cader Harris hefted the duffel bag over his shoulder and grimaced. He was leaving Hayden almost the same way he had left it the first time. With all his worldly possessions stuffed in an army surplus duffel bag. Only this time he didn't have the prospect of college or a burgeoning career on the gridiron. So he bombed out. It happened to the best of men. At least he had his Beechcraft in the hangar at the airport. When he ran out of cash for fuel, he supposed he could sell it.

Cader wasn't sorry to leave Hayden. Christ! He couldn't wait to shed the stink of the place. "This has got to be the hellhole of the universe," he muttered, "and that's being kind."

He couldn't let it get to him; if he did, he was finished. It was New York and the rounds of seeing the ad boys. All those long-distance phone calls he had charged to Delta Oil would certainly bear some kind of fruit. He had four nibbles for commercials. He was photogenic; he couldn't miss. Just flash the old ivories. What the hell, a buck was a buck.

"And where do you think you're going?" Sunday Waters demanded as she closed the door of the shop.

"New York and commercials. That's all that's left, baby. I blew the deal, and I can't wait to wash the stink of this town off me."

"I'm coming with you. My bags are on the way to the airfield. You're not getting away from me again. See this?" She waved an oblong strip of green paper under his nose. She danced away as he made a grab for the paper. "No strings, no ties, just this little piece of paper. If either of us wants to walk, no explanations are necessary," she teased, still waving the slip. "A yes or a no, Cade."

"It would help if I knew what you've got there."

"It's the same thing as a marriage license, Cader. You want this, you've got to marry me." She held out her hand, offering him the strip.

Cader Harris stared in amazement at the narrow slip. A check for one hundred and fifty thousand dollars, compliments of Delta Oil, made out to Sunday and Cader Harris. Cader's mind raced. "Look, Sunny . . ." he stammered, "you can believe this or not. But I was going to stop by to ask you if you wanted to see the big city. I've been looking for someone to wash my socks for a long time." He grinned sheepishly. "Besides, you're the best piece of ass I've ever had."

Sunday laughed. "You're a first-class fuck, Cader Harris. Every time you tell a lie, you grin and show all forty-two teeth. But face it, I've got you by the short hairs . . . and every time you stray, I'm gonna reel you back in."

He knew he should ask her how she managed to wrangle the check out of Delta, but it didn't seem important right now. All that mattered was that it was here in his hand and it was already beginning to burn his fingers. He looked at Sunny and could see she expected him to ask questions. She was ready to bust with the answers. "So, okay," he grinned, creasing the check and stuffing it in his pocket, "tell me how you got it."

"It's simple. For once in your life you told the truth. You told me about your deal with Delta. When it looked like they were going to leave you out in the cold, I went to see those two guys staying in the motel behind the Lemon Drop. I told them what I knew. That it wouldn't be just your word against theirs, and how, together, we could make it pretty sticky for them here in Hayden. That's our payoff. You've noticed how it's made out, of course. For some reason they assumed I was already your wife. Any other questions?"

Never one to look a gift horse in the mouth, Cader showed all forty-two teeth again and said, "Wanna get married? They'll cash the check, no trouble, in Las Vegas."

"I thought you'd never ask." Sunny laughed.

◆ ◆ ◆

The air was balmy, more like an Indian summer day than a day in late August. Irene Thomas sat in the breakfast nook and lit her ninth cigarette of the morning. She drew the smoke deeply into her lungs and then exhaled it forcefully. If she had been a gambling woman, she would have known how to lose gracefully, but since she wasn't, she felt at a loss. Arthur was gone, Kevin was lost to her, and Cader, her wild love, was gone. And all because of Beth. How was she to fill her days? What was she going to do with herself in the long winter evenings to come? Busywork bothered her and she hated it. Committee meetings were usually over by nine P.M. and then she would have to return home to an empty house. No, it would be empty only if she made a decision to send Beth away. As long as Beth was around, the house wouldn't be empty.

Irene crushed out the cigarette and glanced at the kitchen clock. It was after ten and she should be doing something, anything, but not sitting here thinking morbid thoughts. She had the day to get through. She could start by planning the dinner menu. Meat loaf could now be served without any complaints. Beth loved meat loaf, and she herself could eat it when there was nothing else available. She would make a note for Dulcie and leave it on the kitchen counter. A trip to the hospital to see her father. How depressing. She didn't want or need that feeling, and she hated all the young nurses in their tight uniforms. Foster Doyle hated it when she went to the hospital and sat in the dark brown chair, staring at him. His eyes killed her over and over as she returned his unblinking gaze. He should have died three days ago, but he was still lingering on and the doctors just shrugged and said it was a miracle that he was hanging on like he was. Those doctors could think that all they wanted. Foster Doyle Hayden would hang on until he saw her blink. Life did go on. She would go and sit in the sterile room for three hours, pat him on the hand and stare at him. She smiled slightly. What she was doing was called "the right of divine retribution." That was two decisions she had made in only the space of a few minutes. Now, she would check on Arthur's daughter and see how she was doing.

Beth sat in the window seat and watched a fat blue jay drag a worm into his nest. Her eyes went to the double-edged razor blade she had partially unwrapped. If Kevin didn't call by tonight, she would use it on her wrists. Carefully, she closed the thin paper

over the blade and laid it back on the dresser. The blue jay struggled and managed to get the bulging pink worm over the side of
the nest. If he didn't call tonight, she would give him till noon
tomorrow. Then she would use the razor blade. Perhaps that was
too soon. He had to sign in and get all settled. Tomorrow night. He
should call by tomorrow night.

The blue jay was out of sight, now content with his breakfast.
Friday or Saturday might be soon enough. She picked up the razor
blade and put it under the blotter of her desk. It would be there
when she needed it.

"Beth, I'm going to go to the hospital to see your grandfather.
Do you want to come along?" Irene called from the hallway.

"No, Mama, I'm waiting for Kevin to call."

Wild Honey

PROLOGUE

———— ❦ ————

Alabama—1818

In the deep green forest the late afternoon sunlight slanted downward, piercing the early summer foliage to illuminate the fertile mossy earth. The pungent fragrance of new grasses, still wet with the recent blessing of rain, was light and perfumed, and the tender green shoots were cool and soft underfoot. Tall trees, sycamore, pine and ash, with trunks broader than a man, reached skyward, their lowest branches forming a roof over a small, grassy clearing.

A bone-handled deer knife found its mark with an accuracy born of long practice. The red-skinned boy grinned, his black eyes filled with mischief. He folded his youthful, muscular arms across his lean chest. "Match my target, brother."

Sloan MacAllister eyed the quivering knife and whooped with laughter. "I'll do better than match it. I'll knock it right off its mark and replace it with mine. Stand back now and watch a true test of skill! When are you going to get it through your head, Osceola, that I am every bit as good as you are? The Indian blood that runs in your veins makes no difference. If only you'd admit the truth," he mocked, "you have white blood also." Not waiting for the usual angry denial whenever he teased his step-brother about his heritage, Sloan's knife sailed through the air and unseated the protruding knife, finding its own mark in the same spot.

"See!" he crowed in delight. "I told you I could topple your knife. Now what have you got to say?"

Osceola flashed a wide smile. "The wind changed; any fool can see that. When will *you* learn?" A long stream of Muskogee words rolled off the Indian lad's tongue. Sloan frowned as he tried to keep up with the rapid-fire epithets.

"Speak English, damn you. The next time you call me a horse's ass will be the last time." Osceola laughed as he sprinted away, daring his brother to chase and track him through the woods in the day's fading light.

Sloan ran in pursuit, his lean, stripling muscles carrying him swiftly and almost soundlessly through the woods circling the perimeter of his father's farm. As he had been taught by his adopted brother, he attempted to pick up some sign, some clue, to the direction Osceola had taken. His piercing gray eyes, sharp and deliberate as a wolf's, strained into the umbrella of dark shadows. The tall, rangy youth brought all his senses into play just as Osceola had taught him. The eye could see only so far; the ear could strain only so hard; but the slightest breeze could carry the scent if the hunter was aware. He moved agilely to flatten himself against a gnarled hickory, and concentrated, savoring the thick woodsy scents around him, the tangy, pungent flavor of the Southern pine, the ripeness of the moss at his feet. And something else. Osceola's body scent; the oil he used to slick down his braids, something the Indian boy had recently started doing. Sloan's nose wrinkled in delighted anticipation as he crouched low. Pacing slowly, cautiously, he stalked Osceola, all senses alert. "Got you!" he shouted with victory as he seized his brother from behind. "I win!"

Osceola shook loose, refusing to allow Sloan to see his dismay. "How? What gave me away?"

"Simple. That grease you plaster on your hair. If it weren't for that grease, I never would have found you. You would have won, brother," Sloan told him honestly.

Osceola punched Sloan's shoulder with good-natured affection, but as he turned away, Sloan caught a fleeting expression of sorrow dimming his smile. Osceola walked abruptly into the sunlight, bare arms hanging loosely at his sides. His black hair shone like the blue hues of a raven's wing. His skin, deeper, more bronze now that summer was upon them, blended into the deerhide vest he wore. Many long nights their mother had sat stitching varicolored beads and intricate patterns onto the tanned hide. As he had been so often lately, Sloan was again aware of the differences between himself and Osceola. Where last year they had been the same height, now Sloan was a head taller than his red-skinned brother. His own hair was the color of newly mown wheat, brilliant and soft, capturing the sunlight and reflecting its brightness. Osceola's was thick and coarse, straight as a fence post and blacker than night. Since the beginning of last winter Osceola had allowed his hair to grow and had abandoned trousers and shirts for breeches of deerskin. They had been together since the age of seven, and until recently Sloan had been unaware of the contrasts between himself and his brother. Of late, other children at the schoolhouse had begun to torment Osceola, calling him names. Battle after battle erupted between the brothers and the other children until the local minister visited the MacAllister farm suggesting that Billy, Osceola's given name, should not return to school but rather be tutored at home.

"I have to speak to you, brother, seriously," Osceola said, his face portraying all the melancholy Sloan had perceived in him.

The pain on his brother's face made Sloan's stomach rumble and squeezed his heart up to his throat. He had known it was coming, this talk, and he dreaded it. He could already feel a sense of loss, the absence of his brother. But it was time. In Indian tradition Osceola had counted his age at fourteen summers, a few months older than Sloan, and manhood lurked on the horizon. Soon, time would call a halt to these games they played, to the sharing and the camaraderie. But it was time. "Do you want to talk here or go back to the house?"

"One place is as good as another. It is time for me to leave here, my brother. Time for me to go to my mother's people. I must take my place among them; it is my destiny. I am not a farmer and I never will be a farmer. This world belongs to you, Sloan, never to me." His black eyes looked so sad, and Sloan felt his breath catch in his chest. "I thought to leave here in two days' time, brother." His words fell with deadly weight.

"I should have known. For weeks now your eyes have been on the eastern sky. The day you made those braids I knew you were planning this. Have you told our mother?" Some desperate hope flickered in Sloan and was immediately extinguished. Osceola's mother, a Muskogee Indian herself, would understand her son's need to take his place as a man among his own people.

Osceola's expression stiffened, forcing himself to relinquish the securities and ties of his youth. He liked it when Sloan referred to Polly as "our mother" even though Polly was actually Sloan's stepmother. "Our mother understands. She will grieve, but knows it is my destiny. She has taught you our ways. Tell me, brother, that you're happy for me and wish me well."

There was pleading in the Indian's eyes—needing Sloan's understanding, and only half expecting to receive it. His decision had been made and his fate was written in the stars. There could never be a life for him in the adult white world. There were too many prejudices, too much hatred for the red man. Perhaps if his hair wasn't quite so black or his skin quite so dusky . . . no, those were the wishes of a child, wanting to change what could not be changed. He was Osceola, son of Polly Copinger, Muskogee Indian. Somewhere, deep within him, was a burning need to belong, to make his mark in the world. Although his own blood father was a white trader and in the one room schoolhouse he was known as Billy Powell, his outward appearance pronounced him an Indian, and only among Indians would he find true acceptance. Bearing a white man's name was useless if you also bore the stamp of a red man on your face. True belonging could only be found among the Indians where he would find a welcome despite the fact he was also the son of a white man. Here, among whites, he would forever be known as a half-breed, always on the outside looking in. Even Polly knew this and understood, reluctantly blessing Osceola's decision.

"But I'm not happy," Sloan bellowed belligerently. "I'm selfish. I don't want to lose my brother. Pa can hardly leave his bed to sit by the fire and may not last through the winter. We're both needed here! Don't you think you owe him something?" he added hotly.

Osceola's eyes left his brother's face, his gaze dropping to the spongy earth beneath his feet. "I am Muskogee."

"Hell you are! You're just as much white as you are Indian!" Sloan raged through his own torment. "Christ, even our mother tells you that she has white blood herself. What about that Scotsman, James McQueen, who was your great-grandfather? And I suppose you're going to tell me that your grandmother wasn't married to a half-breed named Copinger. That was our mother's name before she married your father, William Powell, and now her name is MacAllister since she married *my* father! We are brothers through their marriage. Step-brothers!"

"I am Muskogee." The statement was flat, devoid of emotion. Only his black eyes conveyed the seriousness of his statement. "You forget, brother, my people believe a man to be a member of his *mother's* clan, and home is where the women of his clan live. The mixture of white and Indian blood is not significant. Our mother has always told me that I am Muskogee because she is Muskogee. She is Muskogee because her mother, who married the old white man many moons ago, was Muskogee. She has told me that my blood is Muskogee for more moons than there are leaves on a great tree."

The two boys fell silent for what seemed to them an eternity. There was more than friendship between them; there was a sharing of roots, the security of a family, a love of brother for brother.

At last Osceola spoke and his words were softer than the autumn breeze filtering through the treetops. "You are the one who is needed here, Sloan. You will never lose me, brother. If the day ever comes when you need me, you will only have to mention our mother's name, or my own, and my people will be your people. No, Sloan, we will never lose each other."

"Our mother. What of her?"

"I entrust her to you, my brother. She loves you as she loves me. I know you will be good to her. There is no other way for me. Tell me you understand."

Sloan saw in Osceola's eyes the look of a man. He heard the voice of a man. "I understand," he said solemnly, wondering where he drew the strength to give his much loved brother his blessing to leave. "I will be here for our mother. For the both of us."

They embraced, no embarrassment flawing the deep love they felt one for the other. And when the moon slid from its protective cloud curtain, there was a moistness glistening in the Indian's eyes while a lone, shameless tear coursed down the white boy's cheek. Arms wrapped around slim shoulders, the two youths left the woods in silence.

Occasionally a letter would arrive, obviously posted months after it had been written and routed through New Orleans. From time to time a hunting or scouting party of Muskogee would arrive at the MacAllister farm, making their campfire just outside the barnyard. They would bring Polly news of her son from his new home among the Seminoles deep in the Florida frontier. With stoic grace she would accept gifts of warm leather slippers and handwoven blankets which Osceola had sent her while she listened eagerly to news of her son.

Since the death of his father, Sloan knew that Polly often entertained thoughts of leaving the farm to join Osceola in Florida, but she was suffering from rheumatism and the journey was impossible. It was also unthinkable for her to leave the son who worked the farm to provide for her. Sloan had come softly into her heart and dwelled there as tenderly as the son she had birthed.

The year Sloan turned nineteen Polly died of what Sloan called loneliness. He buried her quietly and sold the farm for a dazzling amount of money, half of which he sent to Osceola. He was not surprised that the young Indian did not return for the burial. While Polly's physical body died, her spirit lived on. Osceola grieved, of that Sloan was certain. One day a lone Indian rider rode into the farm with a singed feather which he extended reverently to Sloan. This alone bore out to the young man the depth of Osceola's grief. No words were needed.

Carefully, Sloan placed the feather among his important papers and then wrapped them in an oilskin packet.

It was time for a new life. He had kept his promise to his brother to care for their mother. This life was over. It was time to move on.

He didn't look back, nor did he send a farewell to Osceola. He would never say good-bye to his brother. They would meet again.

Alabama—1823

The cabin rested on the side of a gently sloping hill, its roof rising unexpectedly out of the landscape like a groundhog poking its head out of its burrow. There was a fire in the hearth and Mama bent over the round iron pot, stirring their evening meal. Savannah liked this time of day best of all. Soon it would be dark and Papa would be coming in from the field, freshly washed from the water basin and strong brown soap Mama kept for him on the front porch. He'd sweep into the room, filling it with his bulk, and grab her into his arms while he kissed Mama.

Savannah was practicing her letters on the small chalkboard, carefully copying from the sample alphabet Mama had drawn for her. The kitchen was thick with the good smell of freshly baked bread and rabbit stew, and Savannah's stomach rumbled expectantly. Wiping her little hands on the blue apron Mama insisted she wear while doing her lessons, Savannah watched out the window, wishing for darkness and Papa's arrival.

Perhaps after supper Papa would play his fiddle and make Mama smile and tap her foot while she rocked near the fireplace, doing the mending. Already Mama had shown Savannah several simple stitches and the child was becoming quite proficient on her sampler.

"You shouldn't be daydreaming, child," Mama chided gently. "Soon winter will come and the daylight hours will be short. A child needs bright daylight to see to her lessons if she doesn't want to need spectacles when she's grown."

Savannah giggled as she imagined herself balancing spectacles on her pert little nose. "Papa will be coming in soon. May I set the table for supper?"

Mama laughed. "You're only trying to find some way out of finishing your lesson." She glanced toward the window, the slanting light falling on her face lighting her gray eyes and golden hair. "Does seem as though the day is in a hurry to leave us. All right, wash your hands and do the table. You're six years old now and that's time enough to learn what it takes to keep a house. Won't be too long before you have a home of your own, I expect."

Caroline James looked at her young daughter, her soft glance almost a touch. How pretty Savannah was, and so bright and intelligent. She often wondered if she and Alfred had made the right decision to leave Mobile to eke out an existence on this meager farm in the middle of nowhere. If they'd stayed in the city and Alfred had continued with his position in his father's store, Savannah would be wearing the prettiest frocks and going to school with other children her age. It was important, she knew, for a child to have companionship, something she herself hadn't been able to provide. Since giving birth to Savannah, none of her pregnancies had gone past the fourth month. "Be careful with the platters," Caroline cautioned as she watched the little girl carry the china to the table.

"Yes, Mama. I know, it was a wedding gift to you and Papa. Will I have a wedding and will I get pretty things for my house?"

"Of course you will. Only you mustn't forget that there are many things more important than pretty things. Someday you'll meet someone you'll love just as much as I love your Papa, that's the most important of all."

"Couldn't you love Papa if we had stayed in Mobile instead of coming out here to the farm? Do I remember Mobile?"

"I don't know, Savannah. That's something only you can tell. You were about three and a half when we came out to the farm. Do you remember Grandma and Grandpa James?" Something in Caroline's voice was sad and regretful.

"I remember the letters we get sometimes and their pictures we keep in the Bible right under the picture of you and Papa when you were married."

"But you don't remember them and how much they loved you? Well," Caroline sighed, "that will soon be remedied. Grandma wrote that they'll be coming to see us this Spring."

"Sometimes I think I remember them. But mostly I remember a scary man in a dark coat who was angry. The man hollered at you, Mama, and made you cry."

The child would remember that, Caroline told herself mournfully. How could she not? It had been a terrible scene. Thomas was cruel and sadistic and actually threatened Alfred's life. Poor gentle Alfred, quite ineffectual against his brother-in-law's rage. Thomas had been the primary reason for their leaving Mobile. His interference and hostility was making their lives impossible. She was sure his generosity toward Caroline and little Savannah had been contrived to make Alfred appear a failure in being a provider for his family. Not that she hadn't defended Alfred or Thomas one to the other. But his possessiveness of her was becoming a constant thorn in her marriage. When Alfred said he wanted to try his hand at farming and gave her a choice of going home to Thomas or going with him, Caroline had realized there was no contest. She loved Alfred, his gentleness, his loving nature. Her place was with her husband because that's where she wanted most to be. Thomas had never forgiven her.

Caroline glanced out the window again. The sun was almost set; Alfred should be coming up the path now, a broad grin on his face, satisfied with the day's accomplishments. The farm was going well, and this year they expected to turn a profit. Alfred was even talking about a trip into Mobile sometime near Christmas.

Savannah hummed to herself while she placed the flatware beside each plate when a sound outside the cabin made her silent. She turned quizzically to look toward the door. She hadn't heard

Papa come up the path whistling one of the tunes he liked to play on the fiddle. Something, some inner sense, made the hairs prickle on the back of her neck.

Suddenly, the door was thrown open; Savannah saw Mama jump out of her rocker, her hand clutching her throat. The sudden draft of air made the flames in the hearth leap higher and brighter; the bright gingham curtains Mama hung at the windows whipped backward as if they too wanted to escape from the horrors that had burst through the door.

The light fell on three Indians dressed in buckskin, their features contorted into frightening grimaces. Low, guttural sounds filled the small kitchen as they spoke to one another, their black, fathomless eyes scurrying like mice around the room. Caroline seemed to gain possession of herself and stood tall, facing them, her hand falling onto Savannah's head as the child buried herself in her mother's skirts.

"What do you want? Go! Leave us!" Savannah heard the authority in her mother's voice, but her eyes were squeezed shut and she dare not look up to see the fiercesome intruders' reaction.

There was another low grunt and her mother was torn away from her shrieking. Hands captured her, holding her, mindless of her kicking and scratching and cries for her mother. The child saw Caroline back across the room, nearing the hearth. The terror in her mother's eyes was communicated to the child. Caroline looked toward the window, a prayer in her eyes that Alfred would come whistling up the path.

"Food, you want food," she croaked in a quivering voice, making motions of eating by bringing an imaginary spoon to her mouth. Her hand reached for the cauldron of boiling stew, the handle of the serving ladle gripped in her fingers. Again, her eyes traveled to the window, looking for her husband.

The Indian closest to her seemed to understand this gesture. A cruel, monstrous grin split his face, accompanied by thick, indistinguishable words. In his hand he was holding a chain and cross, the last of the daylight capturing the metal and glancing off it. Caroline nearly swooned; she felt the floor coming up to meet her. Alfred's chain and cross . . . Alfred wouldn't be coming up the path for supper!

The Indian holding the chain closed the distance between himself and Caroline, cornering her between himself and the fire-place. The savage holding Savannah suddenly lunged forward, his treetrunk arm tightening around the child's middle in a rib-crushing vise, making her gasp painfully, stilling her struggles to run to her mother's side.

The third Indian, acting on Caroline's distraction, circled around the table, coming up behind her. But not quickly enough. In a last act of desperation, her hand, gripping the ladle, whipped forward, carrying with it boiling stew, which she deliberately threw at his eyes.

A horrible sound echoed and bounced off the walls as the man clutched his face, doubling over in excruciating pain. The cabin seemed to fill with sound. The Indian's screams of pain, Caroline's shrieks of terror and Savannah's throat-tearing cries for her mother.

Savannah was still screaming for Mama when she was carried outside into the twilight. Mama was lying very still near the hearth, a bright red ribbon of blood around her throat. Nearly par-alyzed with terror, Savannah was very still, allowing herself to be put atop a horse, knowing only in the very deepest recesses of her mind that one of the Indians had climbed up behind her, holding her in front of him while they rode. Wide, staring eyes filled the lit-tle girl's face as they rode through the barnyard. The chickens clucked and the pigs snorted expectantly for their evening slops.

"Papa, Papa," her lips soundlessly whispered as she recognized a shapeless form heaped near the path. He was still, so still. Why hadn't he come to help her? To help Mama? So still.

It seemed forever before the Indian holding her kneed his pony into action. By this time the man Mama had thrown the stew at had come out of the cabin, a cloth tied around his head, covering one eye. He carried Papa's shotgun from over the mantle and Mama's bedspread stuffed with household items. The third Indian had already loaded his pony with food from the larder and was wiping his mouth in satisfaction the way Papa sometimes did after eating supper.

Savannah's eyes focused on the cabin, seeing the light inside become brighter and brighter. Within moments, flames spread to the roof and out the door. Even at her tender age she knew that all that had been was no more. The night seemed to swallow her as she felt the pony move forward, away from Mama and Papa, away . . . away. . . .

CHAPTER ONE

---◆---

Galveston—1836

*J*ust off the eastern coast of Texas, placed precariously in the volatile waters of the Gulf of Mexico, the island named Galveston rested in the last light of a setting sun. The month of November was ritually a wet season, and this year was no exception. The winding streets leading from the docks to the soft rise of land on which the main town sat were knee-deep in mud. Several well-traveled thoroughfares were paved with stone, making progress easier, but not the far end of Santabel Boulevard, where Annemarie Duval's house was located.

The sky from the south was blackening with the threat of still another rainstorm as Sloan MacAllister picked his way over the high spots from the stables to Annemarie's front door. It would be a relief to sit in front of her fire and warm his icy toes and sample her private store of cognac before going up the long, winding staircase with Beaunell to the warmth of her bed and the heat of her clinging arms. It had been at least two years since he'd seen her, but he knew from the blacksmith, in whose care he'd left Redeemer, that Beaunell Gentry was still in Annemarie's employ.

Puddle jumping his way to the three-storied mansion's front steps, he paused a moment to shake the last remaining droplets from the shoulders of his topcoat and to rake a hand through his thick, light hair, smoothing it into respectability before replacing his wide-brimmed Stetson.

Almost before his hand was lifted from the door it was opened by a huge negress in a dark dress and white cap and apron.

"Mastah Sloan!" Aunt Jenny cried in surprise. "I nevah did think these old eyes would see your likes agin. C'mon in, Miss Annemarie's gonna fall down at the sight of you."

Sloan found himself captured in Aunt Jenny's plump arms and squeezed against her massive bosom. "You come at jest the right time, Mastah Sloan. Miss Annemarie is in the parlor and that handsome face of yours is jest what she needs to brighten her day!"

As Aunt Jenny helped him off with his topcoat, her pleasure in seeing him was evident in her dancing black eyes and wide, toothy smile. "Law's sake, if'n you ain't a sight fer sore eyes. Mus' be about two years since Miss Annemarie last throwed your hide outa here. An' if that's a question I sees in your eyes, yes indeedy, Miss Beaunell's still waitin' and a pinin' for you. Lawd, ain't she gonna be glad to have y'all in her bed agin! I always did say you was a right fine-lookin' man. Fer a white man, that is," she qualified.

"Aunt Jenny, you never change. Still don't think I'm good enough for you. C'mon, Aunt Jenny," he teased, giving her a salacious wink, "when are you going to take me to that back room of yours and teach me what a woman likes?"

Jenny's laughter resounded through the hallway, her double chins quivering with glee. "G'wan with you! If I ever took you up on that offer, you'd scramble outa here like a dog what's had his tail singed."

"Aunt Jenny! What's going on out here . . . Sloan!" Annemarie Duval stood frozen in the doorway for an instant, long enough for Sloan to see that the two years which had passed since he'd last seen her had left no visible trace. Her white skin, contrasted against her ebony hair, was still luminescent, and her remarkably blue eyes were wide and sparkling with a youth that was no longer hers. She was and always would be, he decided, a beautiful woman, and he regretted, not for the first time, that Annemarie insisted that their relationship remain platonic instead of finding ground on a deeper, more intimate level.

"Sloan, how wonderful to see you. I can't believe it. But," Annemarie smiled, "I should have known it was you. You're the only one Aunt Jenny crows over. Come in, come in and sit down. We have so much to talk about. Or," she said, winking devilishly, "would you rather visit Beaunell now and talk later?"

"Only if later means you instead of Beaunell. No," he said, not waiting for a response from his beautiful hostess, "I want to have a drink and talk. You can fill me in on what's been going on during my absence. You're the only one I can depend on to give me straight facts." He settled himself on a deep crimson love seat, and fumbled in his breast pocket for a cigar. "Do you mind?" he asked, indicating the cigar.

"Not if it's a good one. Wine, whiskey?"

"Whiskey will be fine. Join me, Annemarie, I don't like drinking alone."

Her long, slender hands poured the whiskey from a crystal decanter. Annemarie sat down across from Sloan and smiled warmly. "I've missed you, Sloan. I miss those long talks we used to have, the long dinners with you falling asleep on this very sofa. Your letters told me how well you were doing in Europe. Did your luck run out, is that why you've come back to the States?" A slender brow lifted in askance, her ruby lips parted to reveal white teeth.

Sloan spread his hands and smiled. Annemarie could always be counted upon to be direct to the point. "You're a good friend, Annemarie. I wanted to see you. I wanted to see Beaunell. I've been gone a long time, too long, I think." He paused a moment, then frowned, and blurted out with more honesty, "I have this gut feeling that something's wrong. I've been in Europe, Russia to be exact. Brought back the most wonderful piece of horseflesh. Name's Redeemer." Sloan's pride and pleasure in his acquired animal was evident by his broad grin.

"A horse!" Annemarie scoffed. "Why didn't you bring back a wife and give up your wild, whoring life. It's time you settled down, Sloan. One of these days you're going to wake up old and no sweet young thing is going to take a second look at you. Then what will you do?"

"Take Redeemer and ride into the sunset, I expect," Sloan shrugged. "Just a man and his horse. Someone will take pity on me. You'd never cast me out to drift alone, would you?"

"Only if you gave me the bill of sale for your horse. Redeemer, you call him? You obviously set great store by him. What's he like?"

"He's no thoroughbred, that's for sure. He's a little bit of everything, I suspect. I bought him from a Cossack who stole him from some gypsies, or at least that's what he'd have me believe. Annemarie, you've got to see him to believe it. Biggest damn horse I ever laid eyes on. If I were to guess, I'd say he's a mutt breed of

Arabian, Russian Cosar and plough horse. A great beast with great heart. Won't let anyone else ride him but me."

"Sloan, you make him sound like a Crusader's destrier."

"In a lot of ways, he is," Sloan told her, beaming with pride.

"It's settled, then. I would definitely demand ownership of this Redeemer to look after you in your old age," Annemarie laughed, a quiet, ladylike sound.

"Cold as ever. You always were a shrewd businesswoman. You must be worth a fortune by now."

Annemarie shrugged. "I have a high overhead." Languidly, she waved her hand to call his attention to the lavish furnishings.

Sloan followed her gesture. She kept her establishment in top order, he had to give her that. Like Annemarie, it was tasteful and expensive. Only the best whiskey and wine were served, and he knew for an absolute fact that she paid her girls well, and when their youth was diminished and they could no longer catch a man's eye, she either pensioned them off or found suitable husbands for them. It was a full-time occupation, according to Annemarie.

In all things, she was a lady of breeding and quality. Born in Atlanta of good family, she married a blueblooded aristocrat from New Orleans. Childless, bored and definitely out of love with her husband, she became infatuated with a Creole gambler from the low country for whom she gave up everything. She traveled with her lover for several years, learning about the seamier side of life, accepting the fact that she had become a scandal to her family, and was totally ostracized by them. When her lover had met his end at the heated end of a poor loser's pistol, she had taken everything she owned and set up business here in Galveston. With barely enough to set up shop, so to speak, she managed to open her establishment and keep it running productively. The secret, she claimed, was turning people away at the door. Demand for something not readily available always drove the price up. Her taffeta petticoats rustled softly, as she crossed the turkey-red Oriental carpet to sit beside him on the love seat. Her expression underwent a subtle change, and Sloan knew from long association that what she was going to tell him next was serious business.

"Sloan; unfortunately, it would seem, none of my letters ever reached you. In fact, several were returned to me. I know that if you had received them you would have returned home before this.

I hope your adventures proved to be profitable, because I have a feeling you're going to need every cent you can lay hands on. Tell me, Sloan, how long has it been since you've been in touch with Osceola?" Annemarie's voice was too intense. Her aquamarine eyes seemed accusing.

At the mention of his brother's name Sloan felt his stomach muscles tighten. Several years ago, in a particularly nostalgic mood, he had confided his relationship with the Indian to Annemarie. "I docked only hours ago and spent most of that time at the blacksmith's. Then I came straight here. I've heard nothing from my brother for years now."

The last he had heard from Osceola was that he had found a place for himself among the Seminoles in Florida, becoming a member of the nation in full standing because of his marriage to a Seminole widow woman. Some mention had been made at that time that Osceola also hired himself out as a scout to army regiments who were developing forts in the Florida wilderness for the purpose of mapping and charting the area. Sloan also construed from the message that Osceola had decided it was in his own best interest to conceal his affiliations with the white race. The missives were signed in a hastily scrawled B.P., signifying Osceola's given name of Billy Powell. As far as Sloan knew, only himself and Annemarie knew of the Indian's beginnings.

Seeing Sloan's distress, Annemarie's tone softened, filling with compassion. "Your brother and his people are in a great deal of difficulty. All the Seminole nation is. I've tried to help, surreptitiously of course, but it isn't easy. I did it out of my friendship for you, but," she shrugged, "I'm afraid it isn't nearly enough."

"Trouble? What kind of trouble? There's always been bad air between the Seminoles and the United States Government, but nothing the Indians couldn't handle. Since that last disaster they call the Seminole War ended nearly twenty years ago, I had assumed things were under control. Now what kind of trouble?" he barked, almost rearing up from his place beside her.

The aquamarine eyes went momentarily blank. How could he not know? "The newspapers are full of the conflict between the Seminoles and President Andrew Jackson's determination to drive them out of their homelands. For the most part, the general consensus is sympathetic with Jackson, but there's always an acid-tongued reporter who dissembles to the Indian plight. I know it's contrived and only for drama, something like the rumblings of the Northern abolitionists, but you know the saying, "where there's smoke, there's fire.' "

"What kind of smoke?" he demanded impatiently, his broad shoulders hunched, his muscles rigid, ready for action at the word that Osceola was in trouble and might need him.

"They're starving, Sloan. Literally starving. I thought you would have heard something. Somehow gotten your hands on an American newspaper."

"Well, goddamn it, I didn't know! How can they be starving? That's supposed to be rich, fertile land . . . a paradise, grazing land, fishing . . ."

Placing a quieting hand on Sloan's arm, Annemarie said quietly, "Calm down, Sloan. I see I'd better start at the beginning." Taking a deep breath, she began. "The entire drama seems to have begun several years ago, although nothing ever seemed to be reported to the general public. There's a battle on for the Florida territories. Six or seven months after you left for Europe I began reading the first accounts of the Indian situation in the newspapers. When I first learned of the situation, as I've already told you, I managed to send a little help to your brother through a courier. I knew it was something you would have wanted me to do. In fact, I sent it in your name. It was risky, and to this day, I've no idea if the gifts I've sent have ever been received by Osceola. Because of our friendship, I watch the newspapers for the smallest mention of the Seminoles."

"If it's money Osceola needs, then he has it! I was successful in Europe, Annemarie. Especially in Russia. I was offered a chance to buy into some European bank stocks in payment for a gambling debt. It was a lucky break. Right now, I'm sitting pretty and I'm in a position to help. Osceola's problems are over. I'll leave for Florida first thing in the morning."

"Your money is useless. In my opinion the only thing that can help the Indians now is a miracle."

"To hell with miracles, Annemarie, tell me what the hell happened when I was gone. I want to know everything!" he said bitterly.

Sloan grimaced as he once again settled himself beside her, feeling somewhat comforted by the touch of her hand on his arm.

"The Seminoles are on the run, Sloan. They're being forced off their reservation by government land grabbers. They can't farm, they can't hunt and how can they fish when it's forbidden? They receive government rations that are barely adequate and, at best, hardly edible. They break away, go to the swamps and try to eke out a meager existence."

"They can't do that," Sloan pounded his heavy fist into the other palm. "Where do they expect the Indians to go? Where do they want them to live?"

"There's something about them being relocated with the Creeks out in Alabama."

Sloan's face froze into granite lines. "That's impossible. You may not know this, but there's a lot of bad feelings between the Creeks and Seminoles. My brother's people would never consent to that! Who's responsible for that stupid idea?" he asked derisively.

"None other than President Andrew Jackson himself. Bad blood, you say? Then that would explain why a contingent of Creek warriors have offered their services to the United States Army. One reporter even accused the government of sanctioning piracy. You see, Sloan, it's understood that enlisted volunteers are entitled to bounty, the spoils, so to speak. Reports have been published that land, cattle and even the blacks who live among the Indians have been taken captive and forced back into slavery."

Annemarie allowed Sloan time to digest this information before continuing. "President Jackson replaced General Scott with Richard Call several months ago and installed him as governor of the Florida territory. Now, he's combined his civil post with that of commanding a field army. He started a fighting force of over a thousand men, according to reports. Something went wrong with his strategy and his forces dissolved before they could reach the battlefield."

"Battlefield!" Alarm rang in Sloan's voice.

"Are you going to rant and rave, or do you want to hear the rest? The Congress learned how foolish it is to enlist volunteers for only a three-month period, so they've raised it now to twelve months. Governor Call then increased his fighting strength with volunteers from Georgia, Alabama and Tennessee, and succeeded in recruiting Creeks also. Everybody wants anything they can get, all at the expense of the Seminoles. Even the Creeks in Alabama signed a contract to furnish men for service until the Seminoles can be conquered."

Sloan's agitation was evident but he waited for her to continue, to bring him up to date. He was mortified that he hadn't been available to help his brother's people when they most needed it. And the whole time he'd been carousing around Europe having the time of his life.

"Last summer Governor Call's troops fell ill," Annemarie told him. "The Seminoles took the opportunity to store what provisions they could muster somewhere near the Withlacoochee River. Call's driving ambition was to devastate the villages along the river and lay claim to the plunder."

"Well, did he?" Sloan thundered. "Did he succeed?"

"No, he didn't. When he got to the cove, the log villages were empty. In a rage he burned everything to the ground. But he did succeed in one respect. The Indians are now on the run with no place to go, and what little food they had is now gone. They're starving and it's going to be a hard winter for them. No crops, no harvest. But the Seminoles are still resisting and that's something. Several of the letters I sent you contained newspaper clippings. I felt they could say all this much better than I ever could. If you had received them, you would have seen Osceola's name continually mentioned. It would seem that your brother has made a name for himself as a warrior among his people. They refer to him as a chief."

Sloan's mind raced. Twenty years since he had last seen Osceola. What must he be thinking and feeling now? What kind of man had he become to have made his way to the position of chief? Did he feel that Sloan had abandoned him? Sloan hoped not. The bond between them was too strong. "I hadn't the slightest idea that Osceola had become so influential among the Seminoles to be appointed a chief."

"According to accounts," Annemarie volunteered, "this status is fairly recent. There was a small biography concerning him in a New Orleans paper. Apparently, your brother's intimate knowledge of the United States Army, earned while he hired out as a scout, has served him well. I would also gather that he has kept it his secret that he's well versed in the English language. I read something about him using an interpreter named Abraham."

Sloan smiled. "That fox. It would be just like him to pretend ignorance of English. No one is going to pull the wool over his eyes by trying to trick him into something he doesn't fully understand. He probably gets great enjoyment out of watching them try. I can imagine he's thought to be quite wise and cunning among his people."

Annemarie tapped her tooth with her fingernail. "Hmmm. Yes, it would seem to fit. There was something about Osceola attending a treaty meeting as a bystander. Apparently, the army interpreter was translating exactly what he had been told, but there was some behind-the-scenes conversation between Governor Call and General Scott that contradicted what the Indians were being told. It's said that Osceola rose up and claimed treachery. Another chief attending the council praised your brother, calling him wise and brave, and evidently welcomed him into the Seminole hierarchy of leaders."

"Will you be able to help the Seminoles, Sloan?" Annemarie asked anxiously.

"Of course," Sloan replied with more confidence than he felt.

"Then you should know that the man who replaced Call is a major general with a mixed reputation. His name is Thomas Sidney Jessup. It's said that Jessup is a card playing man and likes to play for high stakes."

Steely gray eyes took on a hard sheen as he stared at Annemarie. "Does he, now?" His voice was suddenly lazy as his mind raced. A poker-playing general who wanted to do Osceola and his people in. Not, by God, while he had any say in the matter. "I don't suppose you would happen to know where this Jessup is quartered about now, would you, Annemarie?"

"Indeed, I would. Try New Orleans. The Floridas are too uncivilized for his tastes." Suddenly, Annemarie's face portrayed her concern. "Sloan, you aren't thinking of doing anything foolish, are you? I mean, smuggling foodstuffs into Osceola is one thing, but to become actively involved is quite another. It's . . . it's treason!"

"I've been skidding along by the seat of my pants for some time now, Anne, and I don't suppose now is the time to worry about it. I've been lucky with my investments, and I've been lucky at the card table. The friends and connections I made in Europe were very helpful with both. There's no reason for me to believe that my luck is going to run out."

"You're very confident," Annemarie told him. Her voice was quiet and solemn, betraying her doubts and fears for this young, virile man who, on more than one occasion, had proved himself her friend. But then, Sloan MacAllister had been born confident. He had proved this when she was having difficulties with old enemies of the lover for whom she had left her husband and family.

When word broke that Phillipe had met his end in a crooked game leaving Annemarie a healthy stake, the scurves began crawling out of the woodwork. Shortly after opening this establishment in Galveston she discovered her problems weren't nearly over. Sully Birdson, a menacing, evil man, claimed that he held gambling markers belonging to Phillipe which totaled to a huge amount of money. Birdson would content himself with Annemarie's business. If it hadn't been for Sloan, she would have been left with nothing, walking the streets to make a living. Mistakenly, Birdson underestimated young MacAllister's sense of justice, as well as his expertise with a pistol. One foggy night, Birdson expected to dispense with the interfering MacAllister once and for all by ambushing him as he was leaving Annemarie's house. But it was Birdson who died, with a surprised expression on his ugly face.

A spark shot upward in the fireplace and caught Sloan's attention. He stared into the orange flames, eyes narrowed, elbows on knees. How quickly he had decided to aid Osceola in his struggle against the United States Government. It wasn't until Annemarie uttered the word "treason" that he realized the full implications of helping the Seminole. Treason. It wasn't a pretty word. But neither were starvation, or injustice, or landgrabbing, or slavery pretty words. For years Sloan had known that the Seminole gave sanctuary to runaway slaves, and somewhere in the midst of this political genocide grew this ugly issue. It wasn't very difficult to see that the dispersion or annihilation of the Seminole would profit the government and those men who had the most to gain by declaring themselves patriots. If labeling himself a patriot meant he must sit by and watch the extermination of a people, then he preferred treason. There were ways, he knew, to petition Washington, to speak out publicly in favor of the Seminoles, to grease palms and influence the influential. But all that took time, too much time, and there was no guarantee of success, none at all. He only had to think of the support and organization of the Northern abolitionists and their fervor to abrogate slavery to realize how ineffective this course of action would be. And in the meantime Osceola's people would die, victims of government and greed. Osceola's chances for even a small victory would be slim, but at least there would be honor in trying. And Sloan was determined to give Osceola that chance.

Annemarie watched Sloan slump back against the love seat, raising his arms and running his hands through his golden hair. There was an expression of resolution about his mouth. So, he had decided. Osceola would soon be hearing from his brother.

"You're tired, Sloan. Would you like to go upstairs? I have a spare room where you can be alone—sleep. Or are you more inclined to forget your troubles in Beaunell's company?"

A slow smile appeared and Sloan winked at her. "What do you think?"

"I should have known," she laughed, glad to see that he was restored to himself. If Sloan had rejected the offer of Beaunell's company, Annemarie would have been gravely concerned.

He stood, pulling himself to full height, which seemed to dwarf Annemarie's sitting room. "Do you think Aunt Jenny would see to having my clothes laundered? If I'm going to New Orleans I'll have to spruce up a bit."

"I can tell by your sheepish expression that you've already made arrangements to have everything sent up from the ship to be delivered directly into Aunt Jenny's capable hands. Everything will be ready for your trip to New Orleans so you can pretend to be a gentleman acceptable to General Jessup's society."

"That transparent, am I?"

"To me, anyway. I saw the wheels turning in your head when I mentioned the man and his penchant for cards. For now, I think there's someone upstairs who finds you more than acceptable. Even the score for Osceola, Sloan, and tonight is on the house."

Annemarie was speaking of Beaunell, he knew. "Don't get up, Annemarie. I know the way."

Sloan loped up the stairs in search of Beaunell. He deliberately thrust all thoughts of Osceola and the past conversation with Annemarie from his mind. Tonight was his. Tomorrow and every day after would be devoted to helping his brother. He needed this evening. It had been a long time since he'd lain in a woman's arms.

At the top of the stairs he headed toward the guest bathroom, as Annemarie called it. No man, no matter who he was, dared to set foot in one of her beds with one of her girls until he was scrubbed down either by Aunt Jenny or some other house servant. Aunt Jenny always saved her special attentions for Sloan. He groaned as he saw the wicked anticipation in Jenny's eyes. He also remembered her less than gentle touch. No soft washcloth for Jenny. She much preferred a stiff, bristly brush that he knew in his gut Annemarie used to curry her horse.

"Now you just shed all them there clothes and hop in this tub. Ize gonna scrub you till you sparkle. Miz Beaunell is goin' to get the cleanest, ugliest man in this here house."

Sloan obeyed. He always obeyed Aunt Jenny. He also sat very still. "Yo' is goin' brush them there teeth, ain't you, Mastah Sloan? Yo' is goin' shine like a beacon in the night for Miz Beaunell. Miz Beaunell got herself a fancy wrapper all the way from New York."

"It's not her fancy wrapper I'm interested in, Aunt Jenny."

"I know that and you know that, but Miz Beaunell don't know that. She's been prettying herself up ever since she found out you wuz here. You're just like all men, you want soft, silky skin and bones." Sloan felt the brush dig deeper into his back but remained still. He knew better than to speak when Jenny was off and talking up a storm. "Now, you take me; look at all this fat on me. More for old Ezekial to love, I say. We do make those mattress ropes shake. He never go away unhappy." Sloan nodded fretfully as the brush worked its way down his chest.

"You are some kind of woman, Aunt Jenny," he said fervently. "I know you make Ezekial happy. He brags about you all over Galveston."

"He does, does he? And what might he say, Mister Sloan?"

Oh, Christ, now he had gone and done it. "Well, only good things of course."

"What kind of good things?" Jenny persisted. The brush was below his navel now and swirling the suds into a tent of lather.

"About how warm and soft you are. How pretty you are. Why, he said he wouldn't trade you for all the girls in Annemarie's," he added desperately.

Jenny forgot the brush for a minute. "Tell me some more lies, Mister Sloan. I jest love it when you lie. Here, you can finish your private parts yourself."

Sloan heaved a sigh of relief that he was certain could be heard all the way downstairs. "Hell, Jenny, a man's got to tell the truth when he's talking about a woman and how good she is in bed. Ezekial says you're the best and that's good enough for me."

"You ever have a hankerin' for me?" Jenny asked curiously.

"You're too good for me. Annemarie would have my hide and you know it." Jesus, he was sweating like a pig in summer, and the water was just tepid. He had to get out of here and find Beaunell. This was no time to get caught up with Jenny and her views on men.

Hopping out of the tub, he draped a towel around himself and made tracks for the hallway, calling over his shoulder, "I need my clothes by morning, Jenny. I'm heading for New Orleans at first light."

Jenny nodded, her wide chocolate eyes on the slim hard body beneath the bath sheet. Sloan felt as though he was being chewed alive. He had a feeling he would be if he didn't get out of the bathroom. "I'll settle with you later, Jenny."

He hurried down the carpeted hall, eager to escape Aunt Jenny's clutches, and skidded to an unmanly stop as he approached Beaunell's door. What had Aunt Jenny told him—something about a wrapper all the way from New York? Probably all laces and froufrous, and it would take him an hour to get to the soft, silky skin beneath.

Taking a deep breath, he knocked softly and entered the room without ceremony. Beaunell had lusty appetites, almost as hungry as his own, and she never stood on formality where he was concerned.

She turned to face him, pretending to be startled by his entrance. He knew better. Beaunell had a talent for knowing everything just as soon as it happened. Little vixen, he thought smugly, I can almost smell the lust radiating from her body. The stage was set, he was flattered to see, for his pleasure. The lamp behind her glowed softly, outlining her slim, lithe body beneath the most outrageously red wrapper he had ever seen. Gauzelike, it just skimmed her body, accentuating her shining dark hair and ivory skin. She hadn't changed since the last time he'd seen her. Her small, perfect breasts were thrust upward. Her legs, nicely turned and slightly voluptuous, were exposed between the folds of her wrapper as she stood perched on feathered slippers with incredibly high heels. But it was her smile that entranced him, holding him captive under its spell. She was tiny in stature, but experience had taught him she was a veritable tornado once she found her way between the sheets. A long moment was spent allowing him to drink in the sight of her before she flung herself into his arms, squealing a joyous greeting.

His hands found her breasts, her hips, holding her against him, crushing her mouth with his own. The last thing he remembered saying before Beaunell revealed her full beauty to him was what a lovely dressing gown she wore.

"Sloan," she whispered throatily, allowing his name to fill the room, her being. "Why did you wait so long before you came back to me? I knew you'd come back. I always knew it."

Her perfume engulfed him, setting his pulse racing in a sensuous throbbing that was echoed in his loins. She was beautiful, this little desirable sweetmeat. He wanted to lose himself in her, drink her in. He nuzzled the soft skin at the base of her throat and delighted in hearing her gasp her pleasure. His hands covered her breasts, found her tapering waist, caressed her flaring womanly hips. Every remembered curve and crevice filled him with renewed hunger for her.

She yielded beneath his touch, welcoming him, needing him as desperately as he needed her. Her hands found the smooth muscles of his back, the lean, taut lines of his haunches, arousing him to great heights with her fingers and lips. Sloan MacAllister was an enigma to Beaunell Gentry. She was jealous of the friendship he shared with her employer. Why couldn't Sloan take her into his confidence the way he had taken Annemarie? But it was always to *her* bed that Sloan would finally come, hungry and needing, making love to her as no other man ever had. He knew every pressure point, every caress. She loved the way his hands took possession of her, the way his lips found her most sensitive areas, the strength of him and the weight of him between her thighs.

He was a considerate lover, and there was never a need to pretend satisfaction when she was with him. No other man, not one in hundreds, could leave her panting and breathless and always wanting more. No other man could give her more.

With the perception known only to a practicing whore, she knew this man appreciated and savored a woman. When Sloan MacAllister made love to a woman, it became art, a deliberate and intense pleasure that left her pulse pounding and blood racing.

She loved it when he crushed her in his arms, holding her prisoner, touching and kissing her, demanding to be loved in return. When she was in his arms this way, she could forget all her jealousies and grievances, and just love him. For the moment Sloan was hers and that was all that mattered.

Sloan pulled her atop of him, demanding she seek her own pleasure, helping, thrusting while she rode him in a wild rhythm in which ecstasy was its own reward. Her thighs gripped his haunches, applying and releasing pressure. Her body was sacrifice to his touch, her breasts, her hips, the place where their bodies met and became one. Sloan's eyes locked with Beaunell's, watching her, enjoying her passion, reveling in it.

Tremor after tremor seized her body. Bold, shameless eyes gazed into his. At last, body arching, head thrown back, she groaned with relief that she had captured the sensual gratification she had been chasing.

Slowly, deliberately, Sloan seized her by her firm, white buttocks and rolled her over, following her with his body, keeping himself deep between her soft, gripping thighs. He buried himself in her, taking his pleasure of her, moving in slow, unhurried thrusts. Imperceptibly, his movements quickened, making her gasp, pulling his name from her lips in a deep, contented groan.

Beaunell drew in her breath and writhed sensuously beneath him, meeting each thrust with one of her own. Her body glistened with a veil of perspiration and she reached up to grasp handfuls of his golden lion's mane. She cried out in a voice that was more animal than human, "Love me, Sloan, love me!"

He reached beneath her, lifting her tight, white bottom, savagely bringing her to him.

Their lust for each other blazed and their bodies sought to quench its devouring flames.

They slept, Sloan with his head nestled between Beaunell's soft, full breasts. Twice during the night he woke to stifle the pleas of desire whispered in his ear. At first light he was about to slip from the warm bed when Beaunell pulled him backward. He groaned inwardly. She was insatiable, among other things.

Long, silken strands of hair fell over Beaunell's cheeks as she leaned toward Sloan. Her heavily fringed sapphire eyes were tear-filled, purposely so. "Sloan, take me with you to New Orleans. It's time I thought about leaving this place. I can arrange it with Annemarie."

Sloan was startled. And here he had thought all she wanted was another go-round on the sheets. If there was one thing he didn't need now, it was Beaunell trailing him all over New Orleans. He realized he had to be careful, not make his denial seem an outright rejection. Gently, he cupped her delicate oval face in both hands. Hell, what was one more lie. "There's nothing I would like better than to take you with me, little chicken, but I can't. I have Indian business to take care of. Now, you wouldn't want one of those savages to get their hands on your lily white body, would you?" At her blank look he posed another question, "Or would you?"

"I'm not a fool, Sloan. New Orleans is civilized. I hardly think I would be attacked by savages in your apartments. You're wealthy now. Aunt Jenny told me all about your time in Europe and how you're into the banking business. You have your own ship now. You can afford to take care of me and buy me the finery I like. Why can't you be as good to me as I've been to you?"

Sloan felt an itch start between his shoulder blades. Why did women always have an ulterior motive? Why couldn't women just accept what they had and let it go at that? Why did they always want to get married and settle down? Beaunell was right about one thing, she was no fool. And he would have to be very careful when he answered. "Look, Beau," he said tenderly, "I'm not the marry-ing kind. If I was," he added hastily, "you can be sure you would be my first choice. Would you be prepared to hang up all this fin-ery, give up this glamorous life, give up meeting all the rich, fancy men who come in here and give you presents and perfume? No girl in her right mind would want to part with all of this." He hoped he sounded convincing. She was thinking. He didn't know if that was good or bad.

"That doesn't make any sense, Sloan. You're wealthy now; why would I have to give up the finery? You could buy me presents. I know I'm not a very good cook, but I could learn or you could hire servants."

Sloan heard a whining threat in her voice. Goddamn women, they were never satisfied. You bought them a horse, and the next thing, they wanted a carriage. You took them to bed, enjoyed each other's passions, and they demanded marriage. He conveniently ignored the fact that he had taken to Beaunell's bed many times over a five-year period of time. A fact of which she quickly reminded him.

"Honey, I would like to stay and argue with you, but I can't. I really do have pressing business in New Orleans. I can't even promise when I'll be back." Without another word he was off the bed and dressing.

"Damn you, Sloan, is there someone else? Are you ever going to marry me?"

"No, there is no other woman in my life. You know how I feel about marriage." Hell, he could do worse than Beaunell. But he had to be realistic. If he ever did marry her, she would probably kill him by the end of the first year. A smirk of pleasure played around his mouth as he flexed his muscles. He wondered what they would put on his grave marker. Died in his bed? Died smiling?

He didn't like the sudden, calculating look in Beau's eyes. She was up to something, planning something that was going to blow an ill wind in his direction. "Tell you what, Beau. Here's two hundred dollars. You buy yourself whatever pleases you, and when I get back, we'll do this town up right. I've been thinking of setting you up in an apartment," he added rashly as he slipped into his jacket. The calculating look was rapidly turning murderous. He swallowed hard as he measured the steps to the door. Thank God Aunt Jenny had hung his clean clothes on the hook outside the door sometime in the wee hours of the morning. The rest of his baggage should be waiting near the front door. Breakfast suddenly seemed like a poor idea.

"Damn you to hell, you bastard! Set me up in an apartment!" Beaunell shrieked in outrage. "But you won't marry me, is that it? I'm not good enough to marry, is that it? Well, let me tell you a few things. You were nothing but a clod farmer with dirt between your toes when you first came here. You didn't know the first thing about making love to a woman. I taught you everything you know.

You had the fastest, clumsiest hands of any man who ever crossed Annemarie's doorstep. You're a bastard. You led me to believe that when you got back we would get married. Why did you lie to me?" she continued to shriek.

Sloan shrugged as he inched closer to the door. "It seemed like the thing to say at the time," he defended honestly.

"Get out of here," Beaunell screeched. "Now!"

A look of disgust washed over Sloan's face as he exited the room in a near frenzy. A tear or two would have made it all believable. Not that he could blame her. He *was* a rotter. A bastard. He deftly added another hundred to the amount on the dresser. By noontime Beau would hardly remember his name as she tripped from store to store in search of the finery she loved. Love, bah! Marriage? Never!

CHAPTER TWO

Sloan MacAllister took in the remembered sights and sounds of his favorite city. New Orleans. Colorful, bewitching, wicked New Orleans. Street vendors hawked their wares on busy corners, their voices lifting in a lilting patois that was somewhere between French and English. It belonged only to this magical city set between the blue-green waters of the Gulf of Mexico and the murky, gray fog over Lake Ponchartrain. Even the air was different here—perfumed with the flowers of a thousand gardens and smoky cook fires wisping up the chimneys.

It felt good to be back here. He felt alive and eager, as he contrived a means to make contact with Brevet Major General Thomas Sidney Jessup. If he was lucky, and he usually was, he would be sitting across a poker table from the general this very evening. He intended to become quite good friends with the general by making sure Jessup would go home with a considerable chunk of his bankroll. Experience told him that beating a man hands down at poker never encouraged his friendship.

He cut a fine figure as he strolled along Saint Mark's Place. Aunt Jenny had worked wonders pressing his European tailored suits and had laundered his shirts to an elegant whiteness. The diamond stickpin in his silver-gray cravat and sapphire pinky ring were exactly correct. They spoke money, not too loudly, but loud enough to hint at a healthy bankroll, all of which would find a new home in Jessup's hip pocket. But first things first.

At the top of the list was registering at a respectable hotel and having his baggage brought up from the docks. Secondly, accommodations must be found for Redeemer, and last, but not least, he would inquire, discreetly, of course, the whereabouts of Jessup and see to it that he was included in the general's next game of chance.

This last, he expected, would be quite simple. Any man with a known appetite for poker was always eager to prove himself against a professional gambler. For the time being, that was exactly how MacAllister intended to present himself.

General Thomas Sidney Jessup, in full uniform, sat in the library of his rented house on Magnolia Street, looking approvingly across his massive desk into the gilt mirror on the far side of the book-lined room. He deliberately lifted the corners of his mouth into what passed for a smile. He liked to think of this as his pose for his Presidential portrait. Other military men had made it to the country's capital, why not himself?

Jessup was as American as apple pie or, in the analogy he preferred, the Winchester rifle. An American, that's what he was. Staunch, upstanding, fighting for the right of good over evil. He had insisted that his rented house be in the American side of the city rather than in the glamorous French Quarter, where some of the wealthiest and most influential people in New Orleans resided. An all-American. And now, at last, he had the opportunity to be of some real value to his country. To say nothing of the advances it could mean in his own career and his future political ambitions.

Before he'd taken over command of the Florida forces from that procrastinating fool, Richard Call, who had botched things with the Seminoles so badly, Jessup had been transferred from one Indian War to another. A flare-up among the Creeks in Alabama the previous spring had produced a near panic in Washington, fear rising that the Seminoles and the Creeks would forego the hostilities between them to reinforce one another. Accordingly, commanders in the Creek country were ordered to seal off the routes from Alabama to Florida.

It had been early May when Jessup had been sent to take command against the recalcitrant Creeks, but he had hardly had his tent pitched when Winfield Scott arrived from Florida to supersede him and steal his thunder as senior officer. Even now, Jessup's face drew down in a scowl at the reminiscence. He had finally been given the opportunity to prove himself only to find a fool like Scott standing in his way!

Scott, with his usual fetish for details, was using Georgia as a staging area where he was trying to assemble enough men and material to crush the Creeks. He offhandedly ordered Jessup to pass on into Alabama to assume command of the Alabama troops and to be prepared to later join in a converging movement against the Indians.

Join, indeed! Jessup glowered at his own reflection in the mirror. It should have been *his* command, *his* glory! Victory would have assured him favor with the President and his cabinet, and it was no mean feat to bask beneath the favorable eye of Andrew Jackson.

Bitterly, Jessup recalled how he had followed Scott's orders, to the point of making contact with the Alabaman militia.

Once taking command, he made sure those Alabama hillbillies knew they were under orders from a first-rate military man. With an iron hand he had moved his troops into the field and began operations without notifying Scott.

Scott sent a letter by Indian runner through hostile territory and it reached its destination the next day. ". . . I desire that you stop all offensive movements on the part of the Alabamans until the Georgians are ready to act!"

Jessup later claimed that he had not kept Scott informed because of the press of responsibilities; he had not averaged three hours' sleep out of twenty-four in two weeks. But in his written response to Scott he excused himself by claiming he had acted because the situation demanded it. "I have none of that courage," he wrote in his best hand, "that would allow me to remain inactive when women and children are daily falling beneath the blows of the savage."

This, Scott knew, was an excuse. He was well aware of Jessup's hatred for the Indians, having heard somewhere that Jessup's only sister was murdered in a massacre and his six-year-old niece had never been found. A personal tragedy, but the battlefield was no place for a man with prejudices that clouded his duty. With this knowledge and with private suspicions that Jessup was trying to take full credit for subduing the Creeks, Scott fired off another letter. "Who gave you the authority to roam at pleasure through the Creek nation?"

When Jessup read the latest letter the blood pounded between his ears. The audacity of the man! Commander or not, Jessup was determined to take this opportunity to prove his military strategy and strike a heavy blow against the Indians. He hated the red man with zealous fervor. All red men.

Jessup had fifteen hundred Indian warriors with him, Creeks fighting Creeks as usual, who would defect if he hesitated and waited as Scott had ordered; he also had to keep moving to retain the Alabama militiamen. He decided to advance in spite of Scott's order, and by doing so, he secured a good many prisoners.

A second order came from Scott. Not daring to disobey again, Jessup halted his force and hurried off to Fort Mitchell to confront Scott. Unable to locate his commander, he wrote another message smoothly stating his belief that if Scott would make his move the war could be won before the next night. Realizing Scott's suspicions, Jessup added that he was not ambitious of the honors of Indian warfare and merely felt he could prevent the escape of the enemy, suggesting that if Scott were to attack from a frontal position the honor would belong to him.

"Again that addlepated malingerer failed," Jessup swore beneath his breath, conscious of the aide-de-camp stationed outside the library door. Reflexively, his fist smashed down on the desk. "We could have had them! We could have annihilated them all!"

In red-faced fury he shuffled through the papers lining his desktop. With a thin-lipped grin, he recalled the stir his letter to the editor of the *Washington Globe* had created. Francis Blair was a political crony of President Jackson's, and Jessup knew the Commander in Chief would be apprised of its contents. He had accused Scott of delaying the battle that would have terminated the war and saved the government hoards of cold, hard cash. He painted himself in the most favorable light, claiming that the success of his progress was terminated by orders from Scott—progress that would have tranquilized the entire American frontier.

"Eight days," Jessup chortled, "only eight days and Scott was ordered to transfer command of the Creek country to me!" It had been a stroke of genius to write to Washington. And Scott, ignorant of the letter, had believed Jessup had acted in good faith. At least until he was recalled to Washington, where he learned of Jessup's letter to Blair. His gorge rose and he called the letter a treacherous instrument that had stabbed him in the dark.

Jessup laughed aloud. From that moment the war between Scott and Jessup was on, but Jessup emerged clearly as the victor.

"And that pompous fool calls me shifty," Jessup sneered once again into the mirror, admiring his steady, intelligent eyes and prominent square jaw emphasized by prematurely white hair. "Whatever name he puts to me, I'm the man Washington judged most able to run the Florida War!"

The aide-de-camp standing just outside the library door shifted uneasily from one foot to the other. The general was alone in the library, he knew, and it always sent chills up his spine to hear the officer laugh so uproariously to himself.

Sloan ordered whiskey neat and gulped it down. He ordered another and carried it to a small table in the lounge of the hotel. Damn, it had been three days since he'd arrived in New Orleans. Three days of letting everyone know he had a more than adequate bankroll and would be willing to part with it in a poker game. If he didn't receive an invitation from Jessup soon he would have to take other measures. According to the hotel desk clerk, General Jessup hosted a high-stakes poker game every Friday evening. This was Friday. A new man in town with money was always invited, or so said the desk clerk. Sloan was just about to grab the man by the scruff of the neck and demand his twenty dollars back when a messenger came up to him and handed him a sealed envelope. Sloan tipped him and noted the smirk on the desk clerk's face.

Sloan read the terse invitation. If he cared to attend, he was invited to Brevet Major General Jessup's home for a game of cards. Refreshments, cigars and chips would be provided. Game to begin promptly at eight o'clock. There was no mention of how many others would play or what the stakes would be.

Sloan smiled. There were few situations in poker that could surprise him. There were few tricks he couldn't sniff out. He had learned at the hand of a proficient teacher, Annemarie. The lady had taught him all she had learned during her years with Phillipe, one of the most successful Mississippi gamblers. Sloan had sharpened his abilities on some of the best cardsharps in Europe. After being fleeced on numerous occasions, he quickly realized an honest game of poker was a rarity. Knowing that a smart man always played by existing rules, Sloan had taken to do a bit of fleecing himself.

Bathed, shaved and dressed in a carefully chosen somber suit and subdued burgundy brocade waistcoat, Sloan made his way down the magnolia-lined street. Promptly at eight, he dropped the knocker against a heavy brass plate. The door was opened by a slim negro youth dressed in white livery. He reached for Sloan's hat and then ushered him into the library.

A balding, white-haired man in uniform walked toward him and extended his hand. Sloan disliked him on sight. Shifty was the description that popped into Sloan's mind, after noting the beady snake eyes, deep wrinkles and a severe slash for a mouth.

"General Thomas Jessup," the man introduced himself in a rasping authoritative voice. "And you are Sloan MacAllister, I presume."

Leading him to a round table arranged in front of a fireplace, Jessup made the introductions. "Our leading banker, Mr. Calvin Willer, on his left, Mr. Nathaniel Devereau, cotton broker and owner of one of the largest plantations in Louisiana. Here, on my right, is Major Henry Cooper." Obviously, Jessup was, among other things, a social climber, given to surrounding himself with wealthy, influential people. "Gentlemen, Mr. Sloan MacAllister. You've recently returned from Europe, if my sources are correct."

"Correct," he admitted, watching a slow, serpentine smile widen the general's thin mouth.

"And I trust you've brought some of that European money home with you? We always like fresh money, MacAllister. Can't guarantee you're going to leave with it. We play for money and blood."

Sloan grinned, acknowledging the general's statement. "It's the only way to play." His eyes went to Major Cooper, who was dangling a gold watch fob in his right hand. Sloan wondered where a man like Cooper would get the money to sit in a high-stakes poker game. His insignia said he was a cavalry man. Why would Jessup allow a common horse soldier to sit in on one of his games unless, of course, it was rigged to the general's advantage.

It was Jessup who assigned the positions at the table, and it was Jessup who motioned for Cooper to sit directly across from him. Sloan immediately picked up the odd arrangement of furniture in the room. Either Jessup was a very vain man or the many mirrors had other functions. Small tables with assorted bric-a-brac cluttered the room. He wondered vaguely if there was a Mrs. Brevet General. Not likely, the room was a horror. Tall brass vases that were shiny as mirrors sat on both ends of the marble fireplace. They held nothing. They were also out of place.

Sloan sat down and bought his chips; all his senses alert to pick up the slightest irregularity.

"Jacks or better," Jessup said as he waited for the others to buy their chips. The going stake seemed to be a thousand dollars. Sloan anted up and took possession of the small stack of chips. The military must be paying well these days, or else he was getting a bonus for Indian scalps, Sloan thought sourly.

Within minutes, a fog of thick, gray smoke circled toward the ceiling. Sloan played clumsily, deliberately losing to Jessup. He enjoyed the greed in the beady eyes as the general used both hands to pull his chips toward him. In true greenhorn style he lost three games, won a small hand and lost three more. There was no small talk as the men slid cards to the middle of the table. He noticed that when Jessup was ready to bluff he clamped his cigar between his front teeth. Cooper sucked on the spit he allowed to accumulate in his mouth and then spit it out into the spittoon at his feet. They were a team, there was no doubt about it. Not that he cared.

He was here to ingratiate himself, to be seen in the general's company, to be accepted and hopefully somehow, to pick up some vital information. It would be good for Jessup's ego to blather around that he had milked a professional gambler. He, in turn, would say that the military man was just too good for him and come back to lose another thousand.

Jessup was a cheat. An obvious cheat. Sloan would stake his life that the Friday night card game would become a Monday and Wednesday night game as long as his money held out. They were amateurs, the lot of them, hardly worth the trouble and effort. His attention wandered as the men made their bids. Between the two brass vases on the mantle stood a portrait of a beautiful blonde woman. Too young to be Jessup's wife. He wondered who she was.

He had lost another hand, to Jessup's delight.

"What do you say to some refreshments and a stroll outside. The room is smoky. Cooper, open the windows and serve the whiskey. Bad night, MacAllister," he said slyly, turning his attention to Sloan.

"It happens that way sometimes," Sloan said nonchalantly. "I've been in Europe too long. You gentlemen are perhaps a little too good for me."

"Come now, MacAllister, are you telling us that we have those European gamblers beat to hell and back? Why, we're nothing but country bumpkins when it comes to cards. Hell, man, this is just a friendly little game. We do like our cards. Matter of fact, we play on Mondays sometimes when military business is slow. Would you care to join us and maybe win back some of your losses this coming week?" His voice was oily, unctuous, and grated on Sloan's nerves.

"If it's an invitation, I'd be more than glad to join you." He pretended not to see the amused looks on the other men's faces. "Tell me, General, who is the lovely woman who adorns your mantle? Your wife?"

"My sister," Jessup replied curtly. "Are we all ready for some air?" As an afterthought, he turned to Sloan. "Caroline was murdered in Alabama by marauding Indians."

As the men strolled the grounds in the brisk chill of late evening, Sloan tried to draw Major Henry Cooper out concerning the Seminoles. "What's the military's next move? Do the poor bastards have a chance against your forces?"

Major Cooper laughed, "Hardly, at least not with General Jessup in command. There's no organization among the Seminoles. They're spread all over Florida, which, I admit, makes it difficult for us, but it also puts them at a disadvantage. They work as independent groups instead of a single force. And each separate group seems to have its own chief. Actually, the army is only dealing with the chiefs who are in the vicinity of our established forts. Although, to their credit, they do seem to appoint intelligent leaders to speak for their people. In the St. Augustine area on the eastern coast, there's Phillip. *King* Phillip, if you would," Cooper said laughing. "Now, he's a wily old fox. We know he's at the center of the uprisings we're having in that area. Coacoochee is his son, a warrior; we'd love to get our hands on that troublemaker."

Sloan allowed the major to talk, inserting his own opinions of the Seminoles, listening intently for Osceola's name to enter the conversation.

"On the west coast," Cooper informed him, "where we've been most successful in establishing forts, there's an old man called Arpeika. Some say he's a medicine man, whatever the hell that is. He's got to be the oldest man alive. And a pain in the ass he is. We're hoping to have more luck with another thlacko, that means chief in Seminole, by the way," Cooper told Sloan, wanting him to believe he was conversant in the language.

Sloan drew deeply on his cheroot, casually exhaling the fragrant smoke, his heart beating expectantly for the sound of his brother's name. "Who is this Indian? Have I seen his name in the papers?"

"More than likely. Some of the correspondents seem to think he cuts a romantic figure. His name is Osceola. Young, quite presentable, by Indian standards, of course. About your age, I'd say. In my opinion, this Osceola is going to be the man of the hour. He seems to command a good deal of respect among his people because the old man Arpeika has more or less taken him under his wing and sanctioned him. Wish we knew more about this Osceola; perhaps it would be useful in convincing him to move out of the territory and take his scruffy lot with him." Cooper spit into the bushes. "I'll tell you one thing; if anyone can move those savages out of Florida, it'll be General Jessup. Never saw a man who hates Indians more than the general. Mark my words, MacAllister, if the general has anything to say about it, the Seminoles are an extinct people."

At midnight the game ended with Sloan the clear loser to the tune of fifteen hundred dollars. Twelve hundred found its way to Jessup's pocket with the remaining three hundred sitting neatly in Major Cooper's pocket. Not bad for an evening's work. Arrangements were made for the following Monday. The game to be played again at Jessup's house.

"Good meeting you," Jessup held out his hand. Sloan fought the urge to belt the man right between his eyes. Instead, he smiled and made inane remarks about recouping his money come Monday.

"Cooper, find that blasted dog and walk him outside till he does what he's supposed to do." To Sloan, he added, "Damn fool dog is so fat he can barely walk. If you don't walk him on a lead, he sits down and goes to sleep. I should have him shot and put out of his misery like those goddamn Seminoles."

Sloan attended six more fleecings, six more poker games at the general's home. He was forced to admit to himself that he would never learn anything from Jessup concerning future strategy against the Seminoles. The man was quite professional and staunch when it came to military information.

This would be Sloan's last chance to gather any crumb of information. Jessup should be at home this evening since it was Tuesday and between poker sessions. Sloan grinned in the darkness. He imagined that every time Jessup clapped eyes on him he was trying to decide just how much more of a seemingly endless bankroll he could gouge out of MacAllister in future games.

Nestling the bottle of aged plum brandy under his arm, Sloan pounded the door knocker.

General Jessup himself answered the door and was more than a little surprised to see Sloan standing in the stream of light shedding through the doorway. "MacAllister, what brings you here?" His keen, shifting gaze fell to the brandy bottle.

"I came to say good-bye and to offer this excellent brandy in thanks for your hospitality."

Dismay was written on the general's face. "You're leaving? Come in, come in. We'll have a drink together." Turning quickly to hide his disappointment, the general led the way into the library. He had taken this golden goose for a hefty sum, and there was more for the taking, he was certain of it. He almost snorted in disgust at the title Sloan had bestowed on himself—professional gambler. If the good-looking man was a "professional," then he himself was Andrew Jackson.

MacAllister watched with amusement as Jessup poured a stingy amount of the plum brandy into a large snifter. His own was filled a full inch higher.

After the first glass of brandy, Jessup declared it a too sweet drink and brought out a bottle of his favorite rotgut whiskey, known in the cavalry as horse liniment. Sloan sipped cautiously and watched Jessup down glass after glass. Once he saw the glassy, marble eyes start to twitch, he started to ask what he hoped were leading questions concerning the Indians.

"It's obvious there is little sympathy for the Seminoles in the Floridas," Sloan said quietly, conversationally. "I've been following the newspaper accounts, and only once in a great while is anything mentioned about the Indian side of the argument."

"They're goddamned savages is what they are," Jessup growled, slurring his words. "They should be slaughtered the day they pop out of their dog mother's womb!"

A sudden surge of rage made Sloan's fingers clench the glass in a white-knuckled grip. The pig! As if he knew anything about Indian women or the loving, gentle-natured mothers they were. He struggled to contain his temper and pretended to be sympathetic with the general's feelings.

"They *should* be slaughtered, the way they slaughtered my sister. Murdered her, you know. Her and her husband. I told Caroline not to follow that stupid bastard into Indian country. But would she listen to me? No. And she paid for it with her life. She had a daughter. A little girl who looked just like Caroline. The child, Savannah, was never found. Damn dirty Indians killed my baby sister. If it's the last thing I ever do, I'll annihilate those red-skinned savages." He drank greedily and poured his tumbler half full. His small, round eyes were closing sleepily.

This wasn't enough, MacAllister told himself. If Jessup fell asleep, all hope would be lost of learning anything of his military plans in Florida. Having witnessed the general's excitement when he spoke of his sister Caroline and her young daughter, he persisted in keeping the subject open. "Are you speaking, sir, as a soldier or a man whose sister and child were . . ."

"Say it! Say they were slaughtered. Massacred. And my niece never found. Those savages are responsible for that and they'll pay. As long as there's breath in my body, they'll pay. The Bible teaches: An eye for an eye! They'll pay. I'll see to it!"

"How?" Sloan asked bluntly.

"By the most expedient method, of course," the general told him. "Divide and conquer. The Seminoles are in for a rough winter. We've seen to that. They'll starve for certain unless they throw themselves on my mercy." Sloan noted wryly that Jessup considered it *his* mercy that would or would not save the Seminoles. The audacity of the man!

"Also," Jessup continued, "I've asked Washington to deploy more troops into the area. They'll be outnumbered three to one before we're done. Naturally, it's President Jackson's hope the Seminole will surrender and join the Creek nation. I hope for this myself. Get them all in one place, I say, and it'll be my pleasure to massacre them!" He took a deep swallow from his glass.

"General, you speak of divide and conquer. How do you plan to achieve this?" Sloan's tone was casual, yet it held enough of a challenge to force Jessup's answer.

The general leaned forward, elbows on knees, the snifter balanced in his hands. "How long do you think the Indians will follow their chiefs if they're starving and sick? When they watch their children dying before their eyes, they'll come to their senses. Another thing, I've more or less given my sanction for any whites in the territory to claim any property, livestock and slaves they feel were stolen from them by the Seminoles. And to claim it by any method that seems appropriate at the time."

Sloan understood. Open season on the Seminole had been declared. White farmers in the area might find it tempting to acquire a new cow or slaves under full protection of the law. All they had to do to receive this protection was to kill a few Seminoles in the process. Bitter gall rose into Sloan's throat and he had to choke it down. If he had had any doubts about sacrificing his patriotism to help Osceola, they were gone. Jessup's policies were those of the United States and they disgusted him, totally repelled him. After a long moment, he spoke. "Major Cooper told me of a Seminole called Osceola. From what the major said, I'd count this Osceola to be a man of extraordinary strength and wisdom."

"Bah! Cooper believes that rot those newspaper correspondents sell papers with. . . . Osceola is no different from any other redskin. He's weak and stupid, and from what I hear, he's as used to a full belly as any other man. As a matter of fact, I might use this Osceola to convince the Seminoles under him to move out of the Florida territory. If one group leaves, you understand, the rest will follow like sheep."

Sloan put his glass to his lips to hide the smirk he knew was forming there. Jessup had quite a surprise coming to him if he thought Osceola would give up so readily. "When do you leave for

Florida, General? I may find myself back in New Orleans before too long to try to win back some of my losings. You will give me an opportunity, won't you?"

"I'll be leaving for Florida shortly. When I've strengthened my forces. Yes," he brightened, "I'd be glad to give you a chance to recoup your losses. I'll be here another few weeks, at any rate. There are supplies being sent down from Washington, and I must be here to receive them. Then I'll be off to a place in central Florida called Silver Springs. We intend to try another treaty with the Seminoles. I expect I'll be meeting this upstart, this Osceola, face to face."

This was all Sloan needed to know. Osceola would be somewhere in the Silver Springs area. Annemarie had said the newspapers reported he was somewhere on the Withlacoochee River. With the general's information he could pinpoint the area where he could find his brother. Testing his luck again, Sloan pressed for more information. "What do you think this treaty will accomplish?"

For an instant it appeared the general was about to answer his question. Then, drawing himself into military attention, "A good soldier never reveals his strategy. Never!"

Sloan's mouth gaped as he watched Jessup's position falter. Jessup attempted to straighten himself, failed miserably and slid from his chair onto the floor. MacAllister grinned. He'd once seen a girl in Annemarie's, named Rowena, do exactly the same thing. It had taken them nearly three days to drive the liquor out of her. Damn rotgut whiskey. It would be days before he got the taste out of his mouth.

Standing over the general's prone figure, MacAllister was tempted to at least lift the man back onto his chair. On second thought, he decided, a night on the cold, hard floor would do the man some good. Get him used to the rigors he'd be facing in Florida. The general considered the frontiers of Florida to be too uncivilized and preferred the comforts of his home in New Orleans whenever possible. His lame excuse was that messages from Washington were more quickly relayed to New Orleans than to the wilds of the southernmost territory.

Sloan was almost to the door when he turned. He'd be damned if he would leave a good fourteen-year-old brandy for that swine. Corking the bottle tightly, he carried it in the crook of his arm and left the house.

✦   ✦   ✦

The following morning after breakfast Sloan read the latest newspaper, his teeth clenched tightly. His meal lay forgotten, congealing in bacon grease. One large fist pounded the table, setting the cream pitcher dancing. Jessup's words of last night were coming true. Seminoles were reported to be stealing chickens, cattle and anything else they could get in their hands. The farmers were organizing with army troops to recover their goods, or if that was impossible, retribution. Retribution, Sloan scoffed. Retribution in the form of slaves, most likely. A good slave was worth six cows many times over. Open season on the Seminole had been declared. All in the name of justice when, in reality, it was greed. Greed. A greedy government that wanted to give white settlers an incentive to remain in the Florida territory.

And who wouldn't be tempted to steal—when they were starving, and watching their children die of hunger? Any man would—white, red, black *or* yellow. His anger threatened to choke him. By God, he wasn't going to waste another minute. He tossed a few bills on the table and stormed out of the hotel dining room.

Two hours later he was watching the last sack of corn being weighed and hauled into the hold of his ship, the *Polly Copinger*. He'd named the ship in honor of the only mother he'd ever known. She was a sturdy vessel, sporting twin masts and a high, proud bow. Her origin was Portugal, and she was well caulked and ready to sail the blue waters of the Gulf. You're going home, *Polly*, he said silently. To Florida. Sail swiftly and steadily. Your people need you.

The pack mules were readied at the smithy to be taken aboard ship. Several goats were also standing in wait, used for the tranquilizing effect they had on horses and mules at sea.

By the time he signed out of the hotel and paid his bill, the stores for Osceola would be stowed. They could sail on the next tide.

"Three hours to high water, Laddie."

The voice belonged to Captain Enwright Culpepper, a salty old man who could spit whiskey and reef a sail at the same time. A Scotsman, he was spare with his words, but Sloan had come to depend upon his friendship and expertise at the helm.

"We're ready and waiting, Captain. I hope none of the crew decided New Orleans was more alluring than shipping out. This isn't the time to go about trying to round up a crew." Sloan scowled.

"Not to worry, Laddie. These men have drunk all they can hold and fornicated till their family jewels have about shrunk to the size of grapes. Aye, they're a ready bunch. Have you decided where we're putting in when we get to the Floridas?"

Sloan laughed at Culpepper's colorful descriptions. "A place on the west coast. Cedar Key. There's a good harbor there on the leeward side of the islands, according to those charts in your cabin. The *Polly* needs a draft of one-and-a-half fathoms, isn't that right?"

"Aye, Laddie. And where to from there? That's wilderness if I'm not mistaken." Culpepper shifted his weight from his game leg to the other. He was almost sixty, salty as the sea and twice as deep. After nine months of close living with the man, MacAllister still knew little about him except that he could be counted upon to follow orders and captain the *Polly* with a loving hand.

"From there I go ashore with the pack mules and what supplies they'll carry. The remainder will be stored in the hold until I send for it." Captain Culpepper didn't press for more information. If his employer wanted to disclose his plans, he could wait for that time. For now, last-minute preparations must be made for the *Polly's* voyage.

When the last streaks of daylight threw their golden hues across the sky, the Polly left her berth in New Orleans and headed into the dusk over the Gulf's warm, blue waters. Dressed in buckskins and soft deerhide boots covering his legs to his knees, Sloan felt fourteen years old again. He was ready to face anything that would be required of him. Ready to face the consequences of love and brotherly devotion.

CHAPTER THREE

Sloan's knees clamped tightly against his mount's flanks. He was certain he was being followed. The fine golden hairs at the back of his neck stood at attention, his pulses throbbed, his senses alerted to danger. Before embarking on this trip into

Seminole country, he had calculated the odds against arriving at Osceola's camp undiscovered by Jessup's forces. Relying on his knowledge of deep forests and spurred by the needs of his brother's people, he chanced it.

Beneath him, Redeemer sensed his master's tension. He raised his massive black head, ears pricked forward, waiting for the instant when Sloan would spur him and give him rein to run. But no signal came. Instead, Sloan kept a tight seat, handling the reins gently yet with anticipation.

The mid-afternoon sun streamed through the trees, falling in dappled shadows, never really penetrating the darkness beneath the hovering branches of scrub pine and ash. The flesh of Redeemer's splendid curving neck quivered. He had heard it also.

Sloan smiled. Soon now, very soon, he would make contact with the Indian who so expertly imitated the call of the owl. His skin prickled as he heard the rustling of undergrowth. Redeemer's pace had slowed, but Sloan knew he could have kept his animal at a steady canter and still would have found it difficult to elude these hidden pursuers. Seminoles were renowned for their stamina on a long run. They would have kept pace with him, and only when Redeemer tired would they have closed in for the attack. He reined in the animal, holding him back, allowing himself to become a sitting target for the advance of the red men.

A footfall, a rustle, a war whoop and Sloan was surrounded by braves whose austere features were streaked with yellow and red war paint. Redeemer reared, blowing and snorting in defense, pawing the air, as his powerful hind legs tore the turf.

Sloan's knees gripped Redeemer's flanks, forcing the beast to remain still, keeping his seat on the saddle. His broad shoulders and straight back made an easy target for a Seminole lance, and he bridled the animal to turn about to face them.

From high atop Redeemer's back Sloan cautiously turned his head to survey his pursuers. His broad-brimmed hat cast a shadow over his face, and with a jaunty thumb he pushed it back on his head, revealing his steady gaze and firm jaw. He understood the Indian's uncanny ability to read a man's face and to know his mind. He wished he felt the composure that he fought to portray. Redeemer snorted, a soft, blowing sound. Not even daring to make a move to quiet his mount, he remained still and apprehensive.

The circle of warriors closed around him, reaching up with strong hands and powerful arms. He offered no resistance, allowing them to tumble him to the ground, waiting until they stood back to look down at him. Their expressions were inscrutable, showing only the dignity that was the stamp of Indian visage. Sloan noticed the feathers in their headdresses were fresh, signifying a recent and successful hunting expedition. But the leather pouches used to hold dried grain, hung at their necks, were limp and empty, confirming for Sloan the reports of their poverty. Dried corn was the Indian staple, used to fortify them during long days away from home. Yet, there was something about these braves in their bright leggings and feathered turbans that hinted at a controlled elation. He couldn't believe that capturing him was reason enough for their mood. More likely, they had participated in a very recent raid upon the cavalry and were successful.

The Indians remained still, lances pointed at Sloan's breast, as they examined their quarry. The initial gesture would have to come from Sloan. Watching them intently, and careful to make no quick motion that would seal his death, he rose to a half sitting position, balancing himself on his elbows. He tried smiling toward the warrior who stood closest to him. He looked into the impenetrable darkness of the man's eyes, judging him, being judged. He opened his mouth to speak, struggling to recall the language of his brother. "I travel through the land of my brother, Osceola. I seek shade from his trees and drink from his springs. I sleep beneath his moon. Your leader is my brother."

The tall brave standing closest to him made a motion with his lance, its red-dyed feathers dancing in the sun. The warrior scowled and his eyes, if possible, darkened. Distrust and hatred were apparent in the man's look, and Sloan realized that hearing a white man speak in their tongue was not a novel experience. Too often they had been betrayed by government representatives in their own language.

Feeling the distinct disadvantage of his position there on the mossy earth, Sloan made a move to get to his feet. Without ceremony he was pushed backward and held down by two braves. This time Sloan noticed how thin the men were, the flesh of their bodies stretched over sinewy muscles and high cheekbones. Pity was an emotion that MacAllister was unfamiliar with, but there was pity in him for these brave people of his brother.

Forcing his mouth to work, he wet his lips and spoke, "The mules carry food for the Seminole. It is my gift to my brother." He kept his gaze steady, looking directly at the young man before him.

"He speaks our tongue; he asks for our chief," one brave exclaimed, a young man who wore but one feather in his turban.

The tall warrior growled, an unintelligible sound. Then he broke into angry speech, glaring at each of his men, his authority unquestionable. "Many white men speak our tongue. All white men lie." With incredible swiftness, he grabbed Sloan's buckskin shirtfront and hauled him to his feet.

"I am not other white men. I do not lie. Osceola is my brother." His words were slow, heavy with meaning. He faced the tall warrior, his head high, his eyes steady.

The circle of braves mumbled amongst themselves, keeping their voices low, muttering their puzzlement over this man who claimed to be their War Chief's brother. Sloan heard them address the tall warrior, "Mico, we must bring this white face to our thlacko. If he has such a brother, he will tell us."

Mico's face darkened with rage. "Do you take this dog's word over mine? Do you think I would not know if our thlacko had such a brother?" He sneered, showing his hatred of all the white race.

Sloan remained still, waiting to be addressed and questioned, but the opportunity never arose. Mico turned his back and signaled for his men to follow, bringing the white interloper with them.

MacAllister was dragged to his feet. His belt and holster were taken from him as was his hat. In the manner of all hostages his boots were pulled from his feet and he was divested of his shirt. Naked except for his buckskin breeches, his hands were bound behind his back and a loop of leather thong strung around his neck. Like a dog on a leash, he was pulled and shoved into his place among the ranks of warriors.

Sloan's eyes fell on Redeemer, who stood, pawing the ground. Chancing a low whistle, he commanded the giant black beast to follow. Knowing that to a Seminole a horse was a prize above and beyond a king's ransom, Sloan assured himself that Redeemer wouldn't be left behind. The pack mules might find their way into a Seminole cookfire, but not Redeemer.

The tallest warrior, Mico, gestured toward the animal, ordering it to be taken. The man's eyes perused the quivering horseflesh lovingly, no doubt thinking that as leader of this raid Redeemer would become his booty. When the young brave approached the beast, Redeemer reared up, pawing the damp forest air. His eyes blazed, his nostrils flared, blowing and snorting. In spite of his situation, Sloan smiled. Redeemer would fight and threaten, refusing to allow anyone save Sloan himself to handle him.

Three other braves stopped in front of Redeemer, their arms flailing, carefully avoiding the sharp hooves that could knock them senseless. They made soft hawing noises, seeking to calm this horse who reared and whinnied and whose eyes spoke rebellion rather than terror. Sloan whistled softly, and Redeemer quieted immediately, the muscles in his chest heaving with excitement. Bobbing his great head, the black animal fell into step behind his master. Sloan saw the amazement on his captors' faces, and he listened to their low mutters of appreciation for so glorious a beast.

Pack mules in tow, the small party traveled eastward through dense forest and over marshy ground. Considering the pace the Indians were forcing on him, Sloan figured the camp must be nearby, reason enough for these warriors to be so menacing. Inadvertently, he had come very close to their camp. It was little wonder that Mico and his band were so hostile. Allowing a stranger to travel so closely said little for their vigilance as scouts and sentries.

Thick branches of long-needled Southern pines scratched Sloan's bare chest. Insects fed on his perspiring skin. The harsh forest floor with its nettles and sharp twigs stung his bare feet. Yet he kept pace with Mico, following the moccasined Indian step for step, stride for stride. It had been too long since he had run along-side Osceola, but he remembered the rigors of those runs. He controlled his breaths, exhaling and inhaling in long measures. He concentrated only on the feel of ground covered by his long strides, blocking out all pain and exhaustion. The terrain was flat with little rise or fall to break his pacing. He wouldn't falter; he couldn't. To do so would bring disgrace upon himself and, more importantly, his brother. The leather thong around his neck was tugged harshly, nearly knocking him off balance. Mico had changed direction. Several hundred yards later the village became visible through the trees.

The low-lying thatch and bark structures were built on low

stilts, and emitted aromas from cook fires through the smoke hole in their roofs. Children played their games, and women went about their business of preparing food and other household duties. The camp was quiet and serene, and yet the activity around the cook fires created an air of celebration. Sloan suspected that he had been correct in assuming there had been a successful raid upon the blue-shirted soldiers. Sacks of grain, bearing government stamps, were stacked beneath a roofed structure without walls. Army blankets were heaped in a pile as were assorted foodstuffs and cookware. From the way the spoils were assembled, Sloan knew it had been a fairly recent undertaking and that the village had not yet had the opportunity to divide the plunder.

Mico entered the camp—the returning warrior victorious. It was the children who noticed first. They ran and clustered around the captive, pointing and calling to one another, catching the notice of the women. Other men gathered around Mico and his braves, their eyes raking over MacAllister, measuring his strength and seeking his weaknesses.

Sloan stood tall, squaring his broad shoulders. Behind him, he heard Redeemer whinny as a brave threw a blanket over the animal's head and another brave quickly hobbled his front legs with a double loop of rawhide. Sloan was pushed roughly toward the center of the camp—the area around which the huts and long houses had been built.

Mico stood proudly, arms crossed over his chest, as he retold the capture of the white dog who had dared to enter Seminole territory. Sloan noticed how Mico avoided telling how close to camp the interloper had been found and how the tall warrior avoided his eyes as he told his tale. The young brave who had dared to question Mico out in the forest was also quiet. Sloan knew that to speak aloud and protest his capture by repeating that Osceola was his brother would make Mico his enemy for life. Better to keep his counsel until Osceola could come to his rescue.

Quickly, Sloan perused the encampment, seeking his brother. He sighted a longhouse, larger than the others, off to his right. Outside the entrance was the shield and lance of the War Chief, but to his dismay, the standard of yellow and red feathers, usually set into the roof announcing the thlacko was in residence, was absent. A low rumble of apprehension stirred in the pit of his stomach.

The rest of the camp gathered around. Black faces, runaway slaves who had found sanctuary with the Seminoles, were present. There were young people who, from their coloration and features, shared a heredity of both Indian and black, descendants of runaway slaves generations ago. Children, half naked, curiosity widening their dark eyes, darted between the legs of the adults. The women, long black hair pulled back from their handsome faces and brightly colored skirts swishing, pressed forward, amusement lifting the corners of their mouths and dancing in their eyes. The rumblings in MacAllister's gut increased. He could almost see the women wet their lips in anticipation. He knew it was considered unmanly for a hostage to be tormented by the men. That task was left to the women. And as fierce and ferocious as the men were in battle, so were the women when faced with the opportunity to vent their rages upon an enemy of their people.

Mico spoke, his voice barely concealing his contempt. "The women are greedy for their enjoyment. It is not every day a white dog is brought to them for their amusement."

Sloan's stomach lurched, his eyes flew to the hut bearing the banner of the thlacko. "Osceola is not in camp on this day," Mico smiled, his thin lips lifting over his teeth like a badger's. "And when the women are through with you, there will be little left to recognize." His eyes dared Sloan to contradict him, to plead with him. Instead, Mico found himself staring into Sloan's defiant flinty glare.

An ominous buzz trebled through the camp. The men and children had withdrawn to a respectful distance. The women came closer, huddling around their prey. Several held long sticks and willow branches, and some had scoured the ground for small rocks and stones. Suddenly, a commotion erupted in the ranks. A feminine voice, shrill with authority, demanded to be brought forward. At another time the voice might have been light and melodious, but now it was shrieking, aggressive, clamoring for attention and demanding obedience. "The dog is mine!" it repeated.

From out of the flurry of activity stepped a tall woman. Her long streaming hair was flaxen and shone against her honey-colored skin. Her eyes, deep and green as the forest itself, blazed with arrogance, as full, sensuous lips parted in a derisive smile over perfect white teeth. It was the face of an angel beneath the mask of a savage. Slender, lithe and graceful, she circled MacAllister, testing the length of the serpentine whip she trailed on the dry ground. Curls of dust eddied around her feet, and the slanted rays of the setting sun glanced off her smooth skin. Bright bands of color danced as her skirt swirled about her slim legs. Her open-necked blouse strained across her proud breasts. She was a vision; she was a nightmare.

Her intensity was almost tangible as she moved in his direction. A hush seemed to fall over the spectators, and Sloan stared dazedly at the brilliant-haired wraith who was stalking him.

He watched with fascination as she wound the trailing leather over her hand. Wordlessly, almost expressionless except for the fires burning in her eyes, she jabbed the whip's handle into his gut, pushing him backward nearly off balance. Quickly, he stepped back, grappling for balance. With his hands tied behind his back it was a difficult maneuver, but one he was determined to accomplish. The last thing MacAllister wanted was to be curling in the dust, looking up at this she-demon.

Again she jabbed; and again he moved backward, more easily this time since he had expected the thrust. Back and back she maneuvered him until he was standing in the center of the clearing.

She began to move about him, swaying slightly, crooning an obscure chant, her voice low and throaty, the syllables unintelligible. His eyes followed her—first to the right, then to the left. Her movements were hypnotizing, having the effect of a snake charmer's flute. Somewhere in his head was a great roaring, a portent of danger. Suddenly, she sprang toward him, spraying spittle at his face—a display of utter contempt.

With a crack, the whip snapped the air, its tasseled tip beating the dust mere inches from his bare feet. Sloan forced himself to remain still, fighting the reflex to leap away from the expected blow. The girl stood before him, their gazes locked. The whip flicked again, this time around his ankles, sending a rush of pain up his legs. It flicked again, at mid calf and again at his knees. The pain was intense, even through his buckskin breeches. The she-devil raised her arm to strike again, and he flinched before the blow fell. The braided snake found its mark at mid thigh, nearly rocking him off his feet.

As the women giggled and the men jeered, pure unadulterated

terror coursed through Sloan as he visualized where the whip would strike next. Instead the creature lashed out again and again, striping his shoulders and chest. He could feel the heat of pain as the welts rose on his flesh. Still he stood, freezing his face into a display of indifference. The brother of the thlacko must not disgrace himself by crying like a child at punishment from a woman.

A querulous voice overrode the others, its strident quality clamoring to be heard. "Chala! Chala!" it addressed the light-haired demoness. "You overstep your bounds!" the voice complained. It belonged to an older woman who broke through the circle of spectators. Her clothing was somber, dipped in berry juice until its normally bright colors were dulled to a mottled brown. Her hair, streaked with gray, was tied at the back of her head and clubbed short. The absence of beads or ornamentation on her body marked her as a widow, as did the smudges of ashes rubbed into her face and the backs of her hands. In a flash, Sloan remembered Polly, Osceola's mother, grinding still-warm ashes into her own pretty face after witnessing Jeb MacAllister's death. For the rest of her life she had dressed in the drab, unornamented garb of a warrior's widow, sacrificing her love of bangles and beads.

"The white-eyes is mine!" Chala protested. "Stupid woman, open your eyes and look! His skin is white, as is mine. And his hair is golden as the sun, as is mine. What better reason?"

"The reason of a widow," the woman stated loudly. "Did I not lose my protector beneath white-eyes' thunder stick? I will step out of my half death into the world of the living for this one reason. I will take my revenge on this enemy of my husband and my people!" As she cried the words, she beat her formidable breast with both fists, her sleeves falling away from her arms and revealing hard-muscled forearms and the calloused working hands of the Indian woman. Quick as a fox, the woman reached for the whip.

With lightning reflexes the girl known as Chala backed away. "Do not force me to assert rights," she hissed. "I have claimed this dog for myself. I would not like to fight you for him." Her tone was venomous; her eyes spewed fire.

Sloan sensed the unease of the crowd. An Indian girl would never speak to an older woman with anything but respect, but the woman's position as a widow left her without standing in the tribe. Without a husband or a son to support and protect her, she was a virtual nonentity.

"Fight me you will," the woman threatened. "By your own words you declare yourself not a member of this tribe."

The woman's words seemed to ignite a spark of wild fury in Chala. Her eyes darkened, her grip on the whip tightened. "Step no further, Yahi, the half-dead have no rights," she warned.

Unheeding, the woman lurched for her, screaming a cry of vented rage. Immediately, the focus of the crowd swung to the grappling women. Men cried out and children squealed. But it was the women who stood by silently—watching, waiting.

Chala's skirt became a whirl of color as the two women rolled and wrestled on the ground. Teeth bared, hair flying, she pit her weight and strength against the older woman who was of brute proportions. Grunts and cries erupted from the opponents, each tossing and turning to gain the topmost position. Sloan heard the renting of cloth and saw the shoulder of Chala's blouse part from her body. In the wake of the fabric was the clawing and scratchings left by Yahi's nails. Like the cobra and the mongoose, they tumbled, clawing and tearing, each fighting for supremacy. Chala's skin glistened with sweat as she strained to overturn Yahi, who had pinned her back to the ground with the sheer force of her weight. Panting, groaning with determination, Chala scrambled atop the widow, holding her down by pushing her forearm across the woman's throat. Breasts heaving, breathing rapid, she claimed victory for herself. "Know when you have been beaten, Yahi. Or would you have me snatch you baldheaded?" she threatened, plunging her free hand into the woman's hair and yanking it viciously.

Hesitantly, and with a great lack of grace, Yahi relaxed and ceased her struggles. A long moment later, Chala lifted herself from atop the woman's prone body and stood tall and proud. "Is there any among you who would deny me my right?" she challenged. Hearing no argument, she bent to retrieve her whip. When she lifted her arm to strike, she put the full force of her weight behind the blows. With a shriek that could have come only from a wild cat, she snapped the whip over Sloan's shoulders, lashing him again and again until his legs dissolved beneath him and he rolled in the dust, plagued by the fury of the lash and the cries of the woman.

The howls and jeers of the crowd became a roar in MacAllister's ears. The twilight sky darkened to a blackness, and the stars that shone through the breaks in the trees were sparks in his head. He turned his body in on itself, exposing only his back to the bite of the whip. Suddenly, he realized that the lash had failed to fall, and through pain-dulled senses, the camp had fallen silent.

The orange flames of the ever-burning campfire in the center of the clearing were shooting toward the sky. In the silence, the song of the crickets could be heard blending with the hoots of the owl. A tingle of expectation buzzed through the gathering as they stood in respectful silence. Only a child, with the innocence of the young, dared to breathe his name. "Thlacko!"

MacAllister lifted his head and saw through the dim a prominent figure standing near the edge of the clearing. His erect bearing and feathered turban lent him a certain majesty. Slender, with the corded body of the natural athlete, he stood with easy grace as his flashing eyes read the scene before him. His gaze fell on Chala, who stood with head high and eyes level.

"And so, Chala, I have heard that you caught yourself a wild dog. Is this why you have helped yourself to the lash which once hung on the wall of my chikkee?"

"Dogs must be trained, my chief. I did not disgrace your lash." She glanced at the prone figure of MacAllister and back at Osceola. "From the look of him I would say I have brought honor to your weapon."

Osceola glanced down at Sloan and back at Chala. "And to bring this honor to my lash was it necessary for you to be unkind to our sister, Yahi, who honors her husband by walking among the half-dead?"

Chala's serpentine green eyes lowered in shame.

"My scouts ran out to greet me and share the news of my camp," Osceola explained.

Chala raised her head brazenly, shaking back her wealth of shimmering hair. "It was my right!" she said defiantly. "See him. His skin is white; his hair is yellow. As he is like me, so it was my right!"

"And so is your heart Seminole. Was this your right to defy the wishes of Yahi, who is your elder? To invade her world of the half-dead and come to physical blows?"

Instantly contrite, Chala hung her head, grateful for the curtain of hair that covered her shame. "I yield to you, my chief," she murmured. "But I would have you know that I would have fought your bravest warrior for the joy of beating a white dog!"

"A dog who claims to be our thlacko's brother," chirped the youngest brave, who had brought Sloan in from the forest.

Osceola's chiseled features hardened as his eyes found the prone figure sprawled on the ground near Chala's feet. He frowned and quickly handed his lance to a scout beside him. He covered the distance between himself and Chala's victim in three long strides, and his people stepped backward, allowing their thlacko to move forward unhindered.

Chala saw the haunted expression on Osceola's face, and unable to understand the shadows of ghosts in his eyes, felt the stirrings of dread grow in her belly. Standing her ground, hoping against hope, she turned on the young brave. "You are mad! The sun never rose on the day when our thlacko would call a white man his brother!"

Osceola stood for a long moment over Sloan, staring with disbelief into his dust-streaked face. Dropping to his knees, he reached his hand to touch the thick, sun-gilded hair, his fingers tracing the strong, square jaw. Gently, he cupped Sloan's face and turned it toward him. The face of the boy was still stamped on the man's features.

A terrible searing pain tightened Osceola's chest. A knowledge of all that was lost between them for so many years swelled in his heart, climbing up his throat and he released it in a soundless cry. This man, closer to him than any other could be, had come when the need was the greatest.

Slowly, Sloan opened his eyes to stare into his brother's face. Though no blood was shared between them, their hearts still beat in a shared rhythm. Though no words were spoken, each knew the soul of the other. Sloan longed to take Osceola into his embrace, to feel again, after these long years, the unity between them. Too weak, too helpless, to do more than initiate the gesture, he fell backward into the dust, only his steady gaze holding on to the boy who was now a man and a chief of his people.

Osceola bent closer, lifting Sloan's shoulders to take him into his arms. Quietly, in a whisper that was choked with grief and rife with hope, he uttered the words that healed the soul and bridged the past, "My mother's son, my brother."

Through his pain, Sloan gripped Osceola's shoulder, his voice hardly more than a gasp. "My brother." Joy sparked between them, two men who were in more ways true brothers than if they had sprung from the same womb. The years which had separated them now brought them together.

Osceola looked up at Chala, Sloan still held in his arms. "Indeed the sun has risen on such a day," he spoke in low, vibrant tones. Every ear in the village was intent on the words of their thlacko. "My brother will reside with me in my chikkee. He will sleep at my side. And you, Chala, will be quick to undo the damage you have done to this man whose heart is never far from my own."

A gasp went out from the crowd. In simple, loving terms Osceola, War Chief of the Seminoles, had placed this white man beneath his own protection and equal to himself.

Tears glazed the cheeks of the women and the men stood at respectful attention. Even the children were silent, stilled by the awesome emotions they had just witnessed.

Osceola rose to his feet, muttering instructions for Sloan to be brought into his chikkee. Several braves moved forward, quick to do their chief's bidding, honored by the opportunity to care for the man he called brother.

Before following Sloan into his chikkee, Osceola turned once again to the astonished Chala. "I trust my brother has shown himself to be a man of courage." Immediately, voices called out, elaborating on the courage of the man who had stood the test of Chala's whip without a whimper.

"I have you to thank for allowing my brother to display his bravery, Chala."

Although the chief's words were said with humor, her face reddened. The thlacko was showing her forgiveness, and his piercing black eyes were compelling her to open her heart. She knew what she must do.

Slowly, she walked to where the widow Yahi was watching. In a voice loud enough for all to hear, she humbled herself. "I ask you to come with me to help the brother of our thlacko."

Yahi's eyes lowered, but when she lifted them again, it was to look directly at this golden-haired girl who had lived so long among her people. She gazed at Chala with gratitude. To nurse the brother of the thlacko was a great honor. It would be a great service to the chief, and would reinstate her in the tribe as a member of Osceola's household.

Yahi's glance searched the clutch of women who had gathered around to bear witness to Chala's humiliation. Her eyes fell on Ina and Che-cho-ter, Osceola's wives. Seeing each of them nod their heads in affirmation, she once again faced Chala. With great dignity Yahi pulled herself to full height and began to bark orders to bring her ointments and medicines.

The chikkee of Osceola was filled with the pungent aroma of ointments and salves. The cook fire, which was the focal point of every Seminole household, burned slowly as Yahi stirred and chanted over a miniature cauldron of herbs and roots which were to become a dressing for MacAllister's wounds.

Chala wiped the dust from Sloan's face and body with a sweet-scented lotion made from flower petals and animal fats. Her face was pinched into a scowl, and he felt her abhorrence of him as she touched his flesh. The hatred he saw in her eyes made him want to recoil from her even more than when she had held the whip.

The chikkee was larger than usual for a Seminole dwelling, denoting Osceola's privilege and station. Sloan estimated it was nearly twenty feet square and thoroughly chinked with mud to keep out the wind and rain. The roof was thatched with the necessary smoke hole directly over the fire. The chief sat on his rug near the back of the chikkee while the two women hovered nearby, serving him food and drink. It was not surprising to Sloan that his brother did not sit close to him exchanging news of the years that had passed between them. That would come later. For now, Osceola was allowing Sloan the privacy to have his wounds tended. The chief sat on his animal skins near the back of the chikkee, thoughtfully watching as the women ministered to his brother's wounds.

As Yahi knelt down beside her patient, Chala followed her instructions to tend the pot of simmering herbs. "That is Ina and Che-cho-ter, wives of our thlacko," Yahi explained when she noticed Sloan's curious glance. Her tone was solicitous and respectful as was due the brother of her chief. Also, there was an air of gratitude about her, no doubt because this white-eyes was instrumental in having her services called upon and installing her in the most notable household in the village.

The younger squaw handed Osceola a cup and their hands touched. Sloan saw them look into each other's eyes and witnessed the love and tenderness they shared.

"That is Che-cho-ter, our thlacko's second wife," Yahi commented as she swabbed MacAllister's shoulders.

"In your tongue she is known as Morning Dew," Chala interjected, not wishing to be outdone by Yahi. "Often I hear our chief call her by that name," she confessed, intending for Yahi and Sloan, both, to know that she was on intimate terms with Osceola's household.

"Che-cho-ter's father was a runaway slave," Yahi continued, disregarding Chala's inference of intimacy. "Her mother was a Seminole of Micanopy's people."

Sloan glanced toward Che-cho-ter again, noting her exceptional beauty and her dusky skin. It was evident that Osceola was devoted to her. Unfamiliar with polygamy, Sloan directed his attention toward Ina, who was much older than Osceola.

Again sharing his thought, Yahi explained, "Ina was the daughter of a famous warrior. She and our thlacko have shared the same chikkee for many summers. Our chief was very young and without a home or people. It is the way of the Seminole to be received by the woman's people. Ina was a widow, like myself, when Osceola took her under his protection. He fished for her and hunted for her and built her a chikkee."

There was a sadness about Yahi when she spoke of the chikkee. No doubt she was thinking of her own which had to be burned to the ground along with all her other possessions at the death of her husband.

"Gifts were exchanged with Ina's brother-in-law, and she became Osceola's woman. Her people became his people. Now Ina is like a mother to our thlacko and Che-cho-ter and like a grandmother to their three daughters. There is no jealousy, only respect and much love. Ina is blessed by the spirits of the forest," Yahi sighed.

"And what of your people?" Sloan asked curiously of Chala, who was holding the small cauldron of steaming brew nearby, ready for Yahi's use. Yahi's medicines were working their magic and the pain was seeping from his body. But there was no doubt that Chala had nearly whipped him within an inch of his life.

The girl lifted her head, her delicate chin jutted arrogantly. "The

Seminoles are my people," she retorted. Her agitated movements splattered the scalding liquid over onto MacAllister's bare belly. When he gasped, she taunted him. "Your skin is not as thick as you would have us believe, white-eyes."

Something in this girl's haughty, aristocratic bearing haunted Sloan. He had seen her face before. Somewhere. Or had it only been a dream? The sudden recognition faded, and he could think no more about it. Yahi had pressed a cup to his lips and sleep was quick in coming, diffusing the edges of his misery into welcome oblivion.

For the next two days Sloan slept, being awakened only for meals and Yahi's brew, then succumbing again to the healing power of sleep. On the third day he awakened feeling considerably better, and insisted upon doing for himself rather than to succumb to the women's attentions. His personal belongings were brought to him, and after a good wash he proceeded to shave, catching Yahi's attention by stropping the razor against the thick leather strap. With unabashed curiosity, she watched Sloan scrape the whiskers from his face and chin. For the most part Indian men had no need to shave. An occasional grooming with the blade of a knife was all that was ever necessary.

After attending to his grooming, Sloan felt he looked himself again although the lash-induced welts on his skin were still tight and burned. He watched the women silently leave the chikkee to allow Osceola and his brother privacy.

Seated on a rug not far from the central fire, the two men looked warmly into one another's eyes, finding there the friendship and camaraderie so familiar to their relationship. Sloan allowed his brother to speak first.

"It has been many summers since last my eyes looked upon you. We were boys and now we are men, and yet I can see the joy in my heart echoed in your eyes." Osceola spoke in the Seminole tongue, encouraging Sloan to do the same.

"It has been too long and the years have taken us on separate trails." Sloan's understanding of the Seminole language did not aid his use of it after all these years. The syllables and flowery phrases came awkwardly to his lips. "Have you forgotten the use of English?" he asked Osceola.

Osceola laughed. "No more than I have forgotten my brother,

Sloan," he stated in perfect English. "There are very few people who know of my knowledge of English. I find it's an asset to use Abraham, our interpreter, when dealing with the military officials. Some things are better understood when heard the second time. It's most enlightening to hear what's said about oneself when the others think you cannot understand."

Sloan laughed. "You wily old fox. Well, it's not going to be easy for me to remember my Seminole vocabulary, but I'll try if you insist."

"Only when there are others present. I know whom I can trust; leave it to me to decide when we will speak in your tongue."

"Agreed. You aren't ashamed of the MacAllister name, are you, brother?"

"Ashamed, never. But giving an enemy a clue to your past gives him an advantage in deciding your future. Some of my heritage has been known and too accurately."

A quiet moment passed and Sloan spoke. "I had no idea of the troubles you were having until I returned from Europe several months ago. My first inclination was to come directly to you, but then I decided to hang around to see what information I could pick up from government sources. Things look bad for the Seminole, brother. Washington insists on emigrating your people into Arkansas territory and assimilating you among the Creeks."

"Creeks!" Osceola spit the word. "I will resist with the last breath in my body. 'The Creek nation will open their arms to the Seminole' we have been told. Bah! Surely, they will open their arms and accept us, *as slaves*. Also, I fear for our black brothers who have run away from cruel masters. They live beside us and many have their own villages. For this we Seminoles are condemned. We regard the blacks as our brethren and allies. In the past, before times were so hard, many of us purchased black slaves from the white men. The blacks would work and repay the price of their freedom. The Creeks have often raided Seminole settlements seeking slaves. Bah!" he spit again. "The only sentiment we Seminole feel for the Creek is contempt!"

"There are stories of Seminoles raiding white settlements here in Florida," Sloan stated.

Osceola's indignation was almost palatable. "There is no denying it. The Treaty of 1823 denied the Seminole our cultivated fields and good hunting grounds. We were placed in a wilderness unsuitable for farming or hunting. Because of this we have been left with the wretched choice of starving within our prescribed limits, or roaming among the whites to search for subsistence. Between the Seminole and the greedy land-grabbing white settlers there is an unceasing contest for survival. It is not right. None of it is right. Tell me what you have heard, brother, spare me nothing."

Sloan hesitated, not knowing where to begin. Finally, after taking a deep breath, he said, "Washington pretends to have lofty motives. They recognize that the Seminole can't continue to live this way. To relieve this situation, they propose moving the Seminole nation west, as you said, among the Creeks. Also, there has been a change of command. General Thomas Sidney Jessup has been assigned to the Florida territory. I've met the man; he's dangerous. He bears a contempt for the red man and seeks to further his career in the military, especially if it is at Seminole expense."

Osceola's chin sunk into his chest, his shoulders hunched with weariness. His voice, when he spoke, was barely audible, his words meant only for Sloan's ears. "Do you remember when we were boys, that day we chased each other through the forest, and I told you that I must go to meet my destiny?"

"I will never forget the day you left the farm. There was a great emptiness."

"Yes, here within me also," the Indian brought his fist to his heart. "Perhaps if I had known what destiny I was chasing, I would have stayed with you. Life has put on my shoulders great responsibility. I am thlacko, leader, chief. I am thirty-three summers and already I bear the sorrows of an old man."

Sloan listened silently, knowing that Osceola had an enormous need to bare his soul and share at least a small part of his burden with his brother.

"I had no desire to be a leader among my people. I was content to live among them, to hunt their land and fish their streams. But war has come and with it confusion. I was considered a man of honor. I had the respect of the other men and a place near the council fire. It was all a man could want. When we, as a people, saw we were in danger of losing our home, many became bewildered. Which way to turn? What to do? Should we risk all and protest or should we meekly accede to the wants of the whites? Fear for our children beclouded some men's minds. The uncertainty of the future caused chaos. But not for me, brother. Not for me. In my mind there was never a question of my beliefs. I have lived among the whites. I know too well their prejudices and fears and hatreds. I have seen firsthand how they treat their slaves. I know what it would mean to leave here to join the Creeks in Arkansas. No, in my mind, there was never a doubt. The Seminole must stand and fight for what is rightly theirs. A man known to us as Arpeika saw this determination in my heart. He is an old medicine man and also a great warrior. Fearing there would be none to come after him who would uphold his beliefs, he raised me up in the eyes of the people. I became a chief by Arpeika's design, not my own."

"This, then, is the destiny you chose when we were boys," Sloan told him.

"My destiny and my damnation. As always, in times of war, confused minds listen to the strong voice. It is not always the voice which speaks the wisest or the greatest truth. But it is a voice, and the timid and bewildered will follow it."

"My brother's voice is only one among many," Sloan comforted.

"Yes, one voice among many. Although not as many as you would think. There are those among us who believe the Seminole should join the Creeks. They are dazzled by the promises of the army to give us cattle and grain and money. But if we join the Creeks, we become their slaves and all that we own will become theirs." Osceola laughed, a hard, bitter sound. "We are a small nation, brother. For the most part, we are broken into three main groups. King Phillip and his followers are north of here along the eastern coast just outside of St. Augustine. Phillip is a fierce fighter and as cunning as a fox. His voice rises with Arpeika's and my own. I am here with Arpeika. This village is the smaller of the two. We had to separate from Arpeika's settlement because it is easier to feed smaller groups of people than one large camp."

Moving aside a reed mat near his foot, Osceola exposed the dirt floor of the chikkee. Scratching with his finger, he drew a rough map. "We are here, along the banks of the Withlacoochee River that runs from central Florida to the Gulf. Arpeika is here," he pointed to a spot centrally located. "Here, in the east is King Phillip. South and west is the village of Coa Hadjo. These are the main camps;

there are many other small groups between these points I have shown you. For the most part, the blacks have formed villages of their own. Most of them lie along the banks of the Withlacoochee with only a few farther south closer to Coa Hadjo. We are scattered, we all scratch the forest for our living, but we are all Seminoles."

Sloan watched as Osceola raised his head, his black eyes burned with fervor and outrage at the injustices committed against his people. "Our numbers are few," he said with strength and confidence, "but the white soldiers will feel the power of every man, woman and child before we see the end of this. We will speak more about this tomorrow. For now, I can see you need your rest."

It was true; Sloan was exhausted, yet he was exhilarated being here with his brother. A thought occurred to him. "I brought pack mules with me, carrying foodstuffs and necessities for your people. Also, I want to see Redeemer."

"We thank you for the supplies. They will bring a momentary respite from hunger. Right now, that is our most pertinent problem. As for that magnificent animal who carried you into Florida, Mico has seen to him. My bravest warrior will look after him through the night. Redeemer, did you call him? It's fitting, then. The old wise ones in our village have said that the beast's spirit represents the aggressive determination of our people. Your Redeemer is fast on his way to becoming a legend among the Seminole. Come, we will walk out together to see this prize of yours."

Sloan smiled. Redeemer was worthy of Indian legend, he was certain. "That horse has traveled across the ocean with me from Russia. Supposedly, he was bred for a Russian Tsar. We've seen a lot of the world together. I'm only glad he didn't have to witness what one little honey-colored girl could do to his master. He might get the idea he could take advantage of me himself." Sloan followed Osceola outside the chikkee.

Reverting to the Indian tongue and wordlessly encouraging Sloan to do likewise, Osceola remarked on Sloan's wounds. "As the victim of an unfair flogging, you are entitled to restitution," he told his brother.

Chala, who was sitting cross-legged near the thlacko's chikkee, directed her attention to the two men. She heard Osceola's statement and glared with undisguised hatred at the white man who had been the cause of her humiliation before the entire village. This stranger would be well within his rights under Seminole law to return the public beating threefold. Silently, she waited for his reply.

"I'm no woman beater, brother. There are other ways to bring the girl to heel."

Chala jumped to her feet. The movement caught Sloan's attention. She spat at him venomously. "I am not a coward, or a creeping she-dog, wary of a man's foot. Beat me if you will and see for yourself that the bite of the lash is little more than the bite of the flea!"

Osceola looked at Chala, the authority in his glance silencing her. Sloan, on the other hand, was amused by her display of belligerence. "Don't tempt me, little one," his smile was a raw mockery that grated her self-esteem and riled her contempt.

Forgetting this man's relationship to her chief, Chala retaliated, "You are not a man to be tempted by any woman. You forget, it is you who bears the stripes from *my* lash." Her words were a satisfied hiss.

Still, the mockery did not leave Sloan's smile. Her words were insignificant, tossed off like the complaints of a child. She stood before him, daring him to defend himself, to make some move to deny her accusations. Her bright hair was tossed back from her face, her eyes blazed with scorn and defiance.

Never taking his eyes from her, Sloan spoke to Osceola. "I will demand my restitution." He spoke slowly, quietly, waiting for the reaction on her face. "Give Chala to me."

Her indrawn breath was a harsh rasp. In the name of all of the Spirits in the forest, she had never expected this. Her fingers curled into talons, she flew at the tall, golden-haired man like a screech owl in the night. The sounds that escaped her lips were savage, echoing in his ears. Her movements were swift and deadly. She buffetted against him, reaching for his face, intent on scratching out his eyes.

Sloan was swift, his reflexes quick and certain. He held her off, grabbing her by the shoulders and wrestling her away from him. Chala's feet kicked out, high and wild, aiming for the vulnerable flesh between his legs. Kicking and thrashing, she continued her attack, heedless of the harsh orders of her chief to cease and desist. She flew at Sloan again, hating him, wishing him dead, knowing only that she wanted to kill him, kill herself before she would ever belong to a white man.

One of her wild kicks caught Sloan high on the thigh, wickedly close to her target. Anger boiled in him as he shook himself free of her. Her strength amazed him; her unleashed fury astounded him. She flung herself again, locking her arms around his shoulders, reaching for his hair to yank it unceremoniously from his scalp.

With all her untamed rage, she wrestled him to the ground, rolling with him in the dust, impervious to the hands of her thlacko, who was unsuccessful in his attempts to pull her off. Sloan's hands discovered her wealth of long hair and he mercilessly pulled, drawing her head back in a neck-breaking hold. Still, her legs thrashed wildly, aiming for dead center and seeking to render him helpless.

The advantage of his weight and height enabled Sloan to overturn her, pressing her back into the dust and holding her fast with his superior strength. She writhed beneath him, still flailing, breasts heaving against his chest. He accomplished drawing her arms up over her head, stretching her out beneath him, quelling her frantic actions. Suddenly, she was still, looking up at him from beneath lowered lids. Her incongruously dark lashes cast elongated shadows on her cheeks. Her skin was flushed pink beneath the honey tones, and her lips parted in a soundless cry.

Sloan filled himself with the sight of her. Beneath her savagery was an undeniable beauty that stirred his senses and quickened his pulse, and he knew he wanted her. As he had never wanted another woman.

Seeming to read his thoughts, Chala mocked him with her eyes and beckoned him with a slow, sensual smile that made a roaring in his ears and was repeated in his loins. "I claim my restitution," Sloan said loudly to Osceola, never taking his eyes from Chala. "I want this woman for my own."

"I would sooner give my brother a water moccasin than burden him with a woman such as this," Osceola smiled, understanding the attraction Chala held for Sloan. "However, if it is your wish, the girl is yours."

Hearing the dreaded words of her thlacko, Chala knew defeat. Her heart raced like a rabbit and her stomach fluttered in dread. The deed was done. The years with the Seminoles had taught her obedience even if they had not stifled her defiance and independence. It was decreed; she belonged to this golden-haired giant whom she could never hope to overpower. Even as she realized her defeat, something alien and unknown stirred within her, and quickened her breath and flushed her cheeks. Something that left her feeling cold and alone when Sloan lifted his body from hers and pulled her to her feet. She heard him mutter something concerning his horse to the thlacko and both men moved away from her. She felt discarded and repudiated. As Sloan walked off with Osceola, her eyes burned into his back. Whatever else this man would do to her, Chala was determined that he would never ignore her.

CHAPTER FOUR

ᨆ

*C*elebration was in the air. The thlacko's brother had come to share his chikkee and the War Chief smiled. Children's voices were raised to a higher, more gleeful note; women bustled about tending their fires, preparing the food that had been divided from the supplies the thlacko's white brother had brought to them.

The aroma of fresh Koonti bread, made from the flour of the briar root, filled the air, reminding Sloan of his boyhood when Polly would sing her tri-note songs and prepare supper for her men.

Everywhere he looked, happy smiles lit the people's faces; the thlacko was smiling, so should they. Happy faces, save one, the girl called Chala. If ever MacAllister saw a murderous expression, it was hers. Even Beaunell in her worst humor couldn't approach Chala's rage. Sloan made a mental note not to turn his back on this hellcat. This one was a tiger, and even Osceola with his stern warnings and even-tempered words would have little effect on Chala's vengeance. Sloan remembered too well the joy she took in wielding the whip, and the strength in her brown arms and slender legs. There was no doubt in his mind that given half a chance she would cheerfully kill him and worry about the wrath of Osceola later.

"Your eyes follow our Chala," Osceola noted standing beside

him. His handsome face smiled knowingly. "I have seen other men's eyes watch that one."

Sloan shrugged. "She's a hellion. It's beyond my imagination how you and your people put up with her. And where in the hell did you get her? She's no Indian, not with that hair and skin."

Osceola gazed fondly at Chala. "She came to us by chance of fate. Chala was found wandering in the forests, protected by the Spirits who guard the children. At the time she was merely six or seven summers. A scout found her and brought her here to us, to live among our people and make them her own. This she has done. The hearts of the Seminoles are soft for the little ones. Would it were so with the whites. Perhaps there would be an end to war."

"All whites don't crave war. All whites are not alike just as all Indians are not alike," Sloan told him gravely.

"What you say is true, brother. Tell me, do your eyes follow Wild Honey and smile upon her?" Osceola translated Chala's name into English.

"Wild Honey." Sloan rolled the name around his tongue a few times. "I like my life as it is. Up till now it's been fairly uncluttered, and I have no desire to set up a chikkee with your Chala. However, I was serious about your giving her to me."

Creases of puzzlement formed over the warrior chief's brow. "If you have no desire to make a chikkee with Chala, then why do you burden yourself with such an obvious . . ." he sighed wearily. "I must be honest with you. I am giving you no prize, my brother. Once you take her from my chikkee she cannot be returned. Ina and Che-cho-ter have been waiting for the day when some fool tries to tame Chala. My women rule my chikkee. They would refuse to take her back. I, myself, would consider my duty as her chief finished. No amount of pleading will change my mind," Osceola added hastily, watching for Sloan's reaction.

"That bad, is she? I thought as much. Well, I'll soon change all of that."

An expression of amused pity crossed the Indian's face. "Perhaps we should sign something in the way of the white man. No return," he said adamantly.

"Agreed. But I'll soon mend her ways and have her rubbing against my knee like our mother's old cat."

Osceola laughed uproariously. His brother was soon going to

discover that Chala, like Polly's old cat, had claws. There was no need to tell him of the young girl's screeching and caterwauling that made everyone in the camp run for cover. No need to tell him of the frenzied hours the women of his own chikkee suffered at her hands. Or of Chala's lack of expertise at the cook fire or the stingy way she had with soap and water when laundering clothes. He would soon see for himself. And then it would be too late—for Sloan. Osceola decided he wanted it written, treatied, the way the government men did it.

Sloan joined in the laughter, knowing it was at his own expense. "You will see, brother. That little hellcat will soon be obeying my every command. She'll know who is the master."

"And will you make her a slave? I think not, my mother's son. I think not. Look, your slave approaches with your dinner. She has cooked it for you herself," he said gleefully, anticipating Sloan tasting the thick mess in the bowl.

Che-cho-ter respectfully came to where they were sitting and handed her husband his meal. Sloan's eyes followed Chala as she walked in Che-cho-ter's wake, her head thrown back proudly, flaxen hair tumbling over her shoulders and swaying in a gentle rhythm which echoed the swinging of her hips. When he accepted his dinner from her, he was quick to notice the difference between his meal and Osceola's. Not only in appearance but definitely in aroma. He was also quick to notice his brother's amused expression.

Cautiously, Sloan sampled his dinner. He managed to swallow by sheer willpower alone. Rising from his position beside Osceola, he gripped the bowl in his hand and walked toward Chala. All conversation in the village seemed to stop. Everyone was watching, waiting, and it was not to their disappointment when Sloan said harshly, "Come with me!" Chala cowered backward, not liking the authoritative expression on the man's face. Her lips drew back, showing perfect white teeth.

"NO!"

"You're going to behave yourself and do as I say. I won't tolerate your vindictiveness or this slop you call food. Now, get over here and follow me!" His voice thundered through the clearing, seeming to bounce off the overhead clouds and fill the twilight.

"No!" Chala cried desperately. "The thlacko was making a joke when he gave me to you; I don't have to go anywhere with you!"

Her eyes blazed fire and she advanced toward him, brazenly staring up into his face, allowing him to see her hatred.

Sloan's outstretched arm froze in midair. His mouth opened in astonishment. In his rage he had spoken English rather than Seminole. And *she had understood him!* Gathering his wits, he menaced, "So, the little hellcat is conversant in English, is she? From this moment on you will speak English to me. Each time you revert to Seminole, I'll have you whipped before the entire village. When I tell you something, I tell you once! If you don't obey, I'll turn you over my knee and spank you. And don't pretend not to understand me!" Not waiting for a screeching reply, he reached for her arm and dragged her across the encampment to where Redeemer stood waiting for his evening portion of oats. Sloan held out the bowl Chala had served him to the animal who sniffed, whinnied and reared back.

"This meal isn't fit for my horse! You're a disgrace to Osceola and a disgrace to me. It's clear now I made a poor bargain with my brother. He wanted to be rid of you so badly, he'd do anything, to have you taken off his hands. You will cook for me again, Chala. And this time it'd better be edible."

"You lie!" Chala hissed in slightly accented English. "My chief made no poor bargain with you. You lie through your teeth, like all white men. Osceola is my father, and he treats me as his own child. You lie!" she spat.

The bowl he held clattered to the ground, spilling its unappetizing contents near his feet. His hands seized her shoulders, capturing her in an unrelenting vise. "I never lie!" he told her, his face so close to hers she could feel his breath on her cheek. "If you were so wonderful, why was my brother so eager to be rid of you?"

"Because . . . because you brought him food for our people, and he was obligated to repay you." Her voice held a tremor she desperately hoped was unnoticed.

"I would have been satisfied with a simple thank you. After all, he is my brother. He gave you to me because you humiliated me and your chief with your barbaric behavior. You behave like a savage, and you are unworthy of the Seminoles. It's time someone taught you to behave like a lady. If that's possible!" Each of his sentences was punctuated by a ruthless shaking of her shoulders till Chala thought her neck would snap.

"*Halpatter*," she sneered derisively, slipping back into the Seminole tongue.

"What did you say?" He shook her savagely. "What did I tell you about speaking English!"

"Alligator! Alligator! That's what you are. A smiling lizard, teeth ready to snap and grind and devour! There is no English word to tell you how much I hate you!" She faced him, eyes blazing, her breath coming in great heaves, daring him to strike her as would be his right by Seminole rule. No woman ever spoke to a man thus; even the lowest man was above a woman's scorn.

"Snake, toad, weasel!" she shrieked. "You will not speak to me in such a manner. Regardless of what Osceola says, you will not take me from this village, from my people. I belong here. And you will not make me into a lady. And," she threatened defiantly, "I will not cook your food. Starve!"

Sloan's actions were quick and sure. His hands slid from her shoulders, pinning her arms behind her back, anticipating the blow she would have cracked to his face. "We can do this the easy way or we can do it your way. Which is it to be?"

At the sight of her stony resolve, he grimaced. "That does it, woman. I'm going to tether you. And I want silence too, Chala. One more word out of you and I'll gag you!"

Chala's eyes widened. She could feel the amused glances of the village upon her! Tethered! Gagged! She'd be damned, the target of everyone's jokes, easy prey for the women's scorn. Shame vanished, replaced by a blind fury. Before Sloan knew what was happening, Chala's foot swung out and up. Sloan doubled over as she brought her clenched fists down hard on the back of his neck. Without a moment lost she thrust both hands out and pushed, standing over him when he toppled like a sapling before the wind. A hoarse cry of pain escaped him. Chala crouched low, her arms held straight in front of her to ward off any retaliation. Seeing him helpless, she stood, shouting to him in the Seminole language, daring him to stand up and fight her.

Damn. Damn. Did he live under some black Indian curse, leaving him fair game for this honey-haired savage. Warily, he struggled to his knees, aware of the deep burning in his groin. Willing himself to his feet, Sloan and Chala circled and stalked one another. The people of the village stood silently watching. From their expressions, Sloan couldn't know if they were waiting for him to beat Chala to an inch of her life or for him to go running into the woods yelping like a whipped dog.

Without warning, Sloan dropped lower to the ground, reaching a long arm toward Chala's ankle. A lightning bolt seemed to rip through his wrist as she punched down hard. To his credit, he hung on to the girl's slim ankle, dragging her to the ground. It took more strength than he anticipated to hold her prone beneath him. In some obscure way, he was enjoying her struggles, feeling her writhe beneath him, powerless.

Imprisoning her hands in one of his, he found the loop of rawhide around her neck on which various beads and trinkets were strung. Slipping it over her head, he swung his body around, straddling her, feeling her fists beating against his back and haunches. Oblivious to the pelting, he hurriedly and deftly secured the rawhide around her ankles, successfully tethering her like a runaway colt. Seizing her arms once again, he dragged her to her feet.

Shrill, venomous shrieks ripped through the cool night air. Furiously, he ripped the sleeve from her wide-necked blouse, rending the fabric, leaving her shoulder and the side of her breast exposed for all to see. Wadding the material into a ball, he then stuffed it into her open, complaining mouth. Silence relieved his ears. Suddenly, loud clapping and laughing resounded. The thlacko's brother had won; Chala had received her justice.

And just what had he won? Sloan thought frustratedly. One look into Osceola's laughing, smirking face told him. Not much except perhaps a chikkee full of trouble. With Osceola's "no return" policy it appeared as though he was stuck with a girl who could almost kill with her eyes. Deciding to make the best of a bad situation, he wrapped his arm around her slim waist and hefted her onto his hip. Carrying her, squirming in protest, he set her down near the fire where she had prepared the mess she had served him for dinner. "Now cook," he said, pushing her to her duties. She stumbled, the tether around her legs affording her only inches of walking room. "You even *think* about removing that rag from your mouth, and I'll pull out each and every one of your teeth!"

In the dim glow from the numerous fires outside the chikkees, Chala's green eyes spewed flames. Tomorrow was another day when the thlacko's mighty brother would not gain the advantage again! She hoped.

The two brothers sat long into the night, sometimes talking, sometimes enjoying the easy camaraderie they had formed in their youth. The sky above was black, lit by a spattering of stars and a slice of yellow moon. The night had brought a coolness and freshness to the air, and the fire crackling before them provided a welcome warmth.

From time to time Sloan's eyes drifted to the pouting girl across the compound. She would not be permitted to enter the chikkee until she presented a decent, edible meal to MacAllister. She stirred the contents of the black, iron pot with a vindictiveness that neither surprised nor alarmed him. The blouse sleeve was clenched between her teeth. To remove it under pain of suffering further humiliation would be more than she could bear. He realized he was going to have to watch Chala closely and not expose his back to her.

Sloan turned back toward his brother, and noticed the yellow pallor of the chief's skin.

"Osceola, I see something that's eluded me before this minute."

"What do you see, my brother?"

"A sickness, not of the spirit but of the body. You look as though you've suffered. Tell me truthfully."

"It is no secret. This summer past the horse soldiers had an outbreak of the country fever. I and many of my people brought it into our chikkees. I have recovered, but at a great price to my physical stamina. It stays in my body, and from time to time it shouts to be released. Even now, I feel it between my shoulders, and in seven sleeps it will render me to my pallet."

"Malaria?"

Osceola shrugged. "Malaria, country fever. It is the same. When the sickness falls upon me, I am weakened. It is bad for my people to see their chief sweating and raving like a madman. Only white men rant and rave. The Indian is silent and suffering." A wry smile touched the corners of his mouth as he watched for Sloan's reaction.

Sloan said nothing in retort. He had no wish to be baited by his brother over white man versus red man. He was sick of public wars and tired of private ones that tore his guts apart.

"Tomorrow," Osceola told him, "we leave this camp. It is good you arrived when you did or you would have found me absent. It is time for me to seek out the medicine man, Arpeika. The whites call him Sam Jones. We travel to the Panasoffke Swamp near the Withlacoochee River at first sun. It is time to join with our black brothers. Loyal black brothers," he said defiantly, almost daring Sloan to disagree.

"I'm going with you. This is my fight too. I'm just sorry that it's taken me so long to get here. I ask your forgiveness."

"It is given." Again the wry smile tugged at the corners of the Indian's mouth. "You appear to have need of the medicine man yourself. Chala was heavy with her hand. You'll mend. A man needs to be beaten occasionally to remind him of the power he has over those weaker than himself. For a soft white man you managed very well." There was pride in the Indian's tone. Sloan accepted the compliment, making no comment.

"What will the blacks do for you?" he inquired, changing the subject away from himself.

Osceola was thoughtful for a moment. It was important for Sloan to understand the prominence the blacks were playing in the present hostilities between the Seminoles and the United States Government. "Did you know, brother, that when the wild buffalo still roamed the open plain and when the white settlers came from across the sea to settle the northern states, the Spanish held this place of the Floridas?"

Sloan nodded, placing the time of which Osceola spoke as more than one hundred years before.

"At that time," the Indian continued, his voice deep and unhurried, "the Spanish governor opened Florida to runaway slaves from English plantations. Not out of sympathy for a race of people, but rather to plague the English for encroaching on Spanish territories. This Spanish governor armed the blacks and treated them as free men. It drew the slaves from the Carolinas in droves, all seeking freedom here in this land. Word spread of this land where a black man could be free. Many came into the western parts of Florida, as did the Creeks, who, as you know, are cousin to the Seminole. The tide of runaway slaves rolled in higher and higher, pledging service to the Seminole because in no other tribe are they so highly revered. The blacks live in separate villages and enjoy

equal liberty with us. For sharing our land, the blacks pay us tribute with the products from their fields."

Sloan could understand why the blacks preferred to live among
the Indian rather than among more "civilized" white owners. For
the protection of the Seminole they paid a small tribute. No racial
bars were ever raised against them, and intermarriage was common. Theirs was a mutual trust between the Negro and Seminole
in both war and council.

Osceola continued, "Among the blacks here are recent fugitives
certain to be reclaimed by their masters if any white authority lays
hands on them. But I fear as well for the blacks born among the
Seminole who are the descendants of runaway slaves. The white
man is greedy for the Florida land and the slaves to work that land.
But the Seminole rightfully own this land, brother, and have sheltered the runaways and we will never give either of them up."

"You seem so certain of the black's loyalty," Sloan said
somberly, testing his brother's faith in the Negroes.

Osceola nodded. "I realize that all bands of our people cannot
be controlled by me alone. But my lieutenants have been well
trained and fight wisely. This man Jessup is said to have great
numbers of troops. We're sadly outnumbered, but with small parties of our black and Indian warriors, it is possible to move quickly
and harass small bodies of white soldiers. As you know, no alligator eats the whole calf; the *halpatter* rolls and churns to rip off
pieces he can swallow. Eventually, the calf disappears."

Sloan looked doubtful. Was Osceola aware what a "great number" of troops meant? At best, his attacks would be those of a flea
biting a dog.

Sloan listened as Osceola explained why the Negroes would
fight as warriors beside the Seminole. Not only could they accept
discipline, but the forefathers of many of them had been fierce warriors in Africa. Most of the Negroes were caught in a war they could
not escape and fought bravely. Their race had more to lose; more to
remember. Whether it was the overseer's lash at the plantation, or
the wife sold at auction, or the raped sister; or the endless future of
work in the fields until the slave was kicked aside to die. Fighting
beside the Seminole might be a form of suicide, but at least the
Negroes were taking part in their own destiny, fighting for their
rights as human beings. It was right, Sloan decided. It was good.

The campfire burned low, the sapling logs hissing and flaring as they broke apart. Sloan raised his flinty gray eyes upward. The orange sliver of moon rode high in the sky toward its own destiny. A chill shivered up his spine. Nearly twenty years ago he had heard his brother tell him he was leaving the MacAllister farm to search out *his* destiny. Now, looking at the man Osceola had become, Sloan wondered where that destiny would take the young boy who had taught him to hunt and fish Indian fashion. Clouds darkened his vision, or was it the mercy of the gods who hid the future from the sight of mortal man?

It was time for sleep. Yet, Osceola sat warming himself near the diminishing fire. When he made no move to add more logs, Sloan reached for several logs and tossed them into the smoldering embers. They caught flame, sparks spewing. "My stomach rumbles. I believe it's time for my meal." Not wishing to shout to Chala, he rose from his cross-legged position and sauntered to where she waited. He helped himself to a generous portion of what appeared to be watery gruel like Polly used to make when the boys were sick. Cautiously, he sampled the new fare. The only difference he could discern between the original dish and this was the texture. It tasted the same. He grimaced, spat to show his displeasure and then tried it again. He felt as though his innards were turning in on themselves, but he had to eat; there was no choice.

"Tomorrow, you'll do better or you'll cook in that pot along with this concoction. You can spit out that gag for now, but one word from you and back in it goes. The village is sleeping, and my brother feels a fever coming upon him. Do you understand me?"

The girl nodded, watching him warily as she took the fabric from between her teeth. Sloan felt a moment of pity for the wretched beauty as she attempted to wet her lips and mouth.

"You will sleep now. Your chief tells me that tomorrow at sunup we leave for Panasoffke Swamp. We'll pretend that today never happened and start afresh. Go to sleep." His tone was not unkind when he spoke, looking deeply into the dark green eyes that could appear as black as night in the firelight. She did not speak but turned in the direction of Osceola's chikkee.

Sloan returned to his brother near the fire. "I think I'll sleep under the stars tonight. I'll wake at first light to help ready the pack mules and supplies for the trip."

"Sloan." It was part declaration, part question, part command. Sloan waited expectantly. Osceola rarely called him by his given name and for some reason the hairs on the back of his neck bristled. "If I seem preoccupied since your arrival, it is because I am deeply worried about my people. I cannot know how much more suffering they can carry. I want you to know that save for the births of my children, the day of your arrival will remain always with me. When I needed you, you came without my having to ask. You are truly our mother's son." Osceola extended his hand for the white man's salutation of greeting. It was Osceola's tribute to Sloan and to his boyhood with Jeb MacAllister.

Sloan accepted the handshake soberly. When Osceola withdrew his hand, Sloan quickly embraced him. "And you are truly more my brother than if the same blood coursed in our veins. I see your Che-cho-ter has placed a blanket for me near the chikkee. Good night, Osceola, sleep well."

Chala stood silently in the darkness watching the exchange between her chief and the white man called Sloan. She frowned as she saw Osceola offer his hand. What a foolish custom. But a smile touched her face when she watched the man with the golden hair embrace his brother. For a moment she forgot her humiliation and anger. A warm feeling settled over her until she remembered the predicament she was in. Her eyes narrowed as she saw MacAllister pick up his blanket and spread it farther away from the chikkee. Her own folded blanket hung over her arm. She no longer belonged in Osceola's chikkee. Wherever this man went she would be forced to go. The moment he settled himself she approached his blanket. Without a word, she unfolded hers and lay down, careful to stay as far away from his side as she could. She must keep telling herself she belonged to this man. At least for the present.

Sloan lay a long time waiting for the girl to explain her presence near him. Instead, he heard light, even breathing. It was a trick. She probably had a knife hidden in her moccasin, and as soon as he was asleep, his blood would run in the dust. He lay quietly for what seemed hours, his nerves strung as tautly as bow strings. It wasn't that he was afraid to die, just that he didn't want his death to be at the hands of a young girl. There was no honor in that kind of death.

Deliberately, he pretended a few loud, raucous snores. He

moved slightly, pretending restlessness and settled again. Now. She would make her move now! He counted to two hundred. Another snore, followed by a slight gnashing of teeth. Then a sound caught his ear. She was crying!

This was not the way Beaunell cried; it was soft, heartbrokenly soft, and the sound tore at his heart. If it were Beaunell, he would perhaps give her money for a new pair of slippers and offer her his handkerchief. Beaunell would blow her nose lustily, kiss him wetly on the mouth and everything would be fine. He felt at a loss with the strange, heart-rending whimpering.

Without stopping to think, he rolled over onto his side and gathered Chala close. Gently, he brushed her wild hair from her brow and from her wet cheeks. He murmured soft, soothing words. Eventually, she settled into the crook of his arm, making a nest for herself. He liked the feel of her beside him. She fit perfectly against him. Soon, she was asleep. Sloan lay a few moments longer, savoring the feel and womanly scent of her. Stirrings of desire rushed through him. He knew he could take her here and now. He also knew she would fight him. But he had never taken a woman against her will, and he wouldn't start now. There would be other times, other places, when the moment would be the same. He was certain of it.

The last thought that entered his mind before he drifted into dreamless sleep, still holding Chala's warm body against him, was that now he had a serious responsibility. He now had a woman to protect and support. A feisty she-lion of a woman who would not give him a moment's peace. Damn Osceola's generosity.

In the darkness of his chikkee, Osceola lay down beside his young wife, Che-cho-ter. In the white man's tongue, she was Morning Dew, a fitting name for her beauty. Her dusky skin was smooth, fresh, like the petal of a hibiscus in the first light of day. Her eyes were soft, loving, filling with admiration and burning passions whenever she looked at her husband. She was graceful, tender, and she was his, completely, without reservation. And to his greatest delight, this woman who was worthy of so much more was his friend.

Even in sleep she turned to him, caressing his cheek with her hand, settling her head upon his shoulder, reminding him that once she had told him it was her favorite place to be. In his arms her world was secure and held meaning.

Nearby, behind the colorful blanket hanging from the rafters, their three daughters slept. He could hear their quiet, restful breathing. A good sound, he had discovered so long ago, when their first daughter was born. What else did a man need from life, he questioned, finding sleep elusive. A warm, loving woman in his arms, his children fed and sleeping nearby. This was life and only this.

How then, he wondered, had he become responsible for the lives of so many people when simplicity and peace were all he wanted from his life?

As he turned his head to breathe the fragrance of Che-cho-ter's hair, he thought back to the day two years ago, an eternity ago, when his service to his people became clear. He had been becoming more involved with the politics of his tribe and, on several occasions, had had the opportunity to declare his views before the ritual council fires. Osceola's thoughts spun backward, recalling to mind each detail of that day when the destiny he had chased as a boy had reached out to seize him.

Under Arpeika's tutelage, he had taken great care with his dress for the visit with the chiefs and elders of his tribe to discuss the worsening situation growing between the United States Government and the Seminoles. His knee-length dress-frock bore intricate patterns of geometric design, each symbolic of a legend from his heritage and patiently embroidered by Che-cho-ter. Slim, fitted leggings ended in soft doeskin moccasins that silenced his movements across the trail. Even now, lying here beside Che-cho-ter, he could smell the forest as it had been on that day. He had run ahead of his people to scout the area, and had positioned himself in a hickory tree where he could observe the military fort and at the same time watch the trail for the arrival of Arpeika and the other spokesmen for the Seminoles.

As the dawn slowly outlined Fort King, Osceola had watched, becoming aware of the distinctive smell of soldiers who were packed too many to a barrack. There had been an odor of woodsmoke, horses, and stale cooking, and the aroma of baking bread.

Because of his past Osceola knew much more of the ways of the white man then either the soldiers or his fellow Seminoles suspected. He knew the whites' penchant for living according to the clock, and their compulsion for routine. The soldiers rose together, dressed alike, ate when ordered, and as the day progressed, they drilled obediently or labored in the sun until permitted to rest. At last tattoo, all but the sentries slept. Such was the routine, day after day.

To an Indian, this was strange behavior, but Osceola had learned the merits of such a routine from his step-father. Jeb MacAllister had taught him that soldiers who worked as a unit and fought on command presented a greater strength to their enemy. For the Seminoles to fight the white man, learning and obedience would be imperative.

Osceola had perched in the tree to watch the day begin at Fort King. On this dark morning, the forest had been ripe with the cool, wet aroma of greenery. The air was still and heavy. The quiet and silence had settled on the warrior's ears like a welcome friend. The only presence had been his own, except for a wolf, gaunt from hunger, whose howlings had been interrupted by the approach of day.

Dawn had whitened the eastern sky; a single bird screamed shrilly and was answered by another in the distance. In the tall, scrubby pines, squirrels had chattered at the form of the silent Indian who presented a threat to their lofty nests.

The thick foliage of the hickory had offered him cover and also gave an excellent view of the proceedings behind the stockades. He had watched and listened as the fort came to life. Before the sun would make a quarter arc in the sky, he would be joined by the most important chiefs in the Seminole nation. It was the day that would decide whether or not the Seminoles would make war against the white man.

He was to meet with Alligator and Arpeika and various of the other leaders opposed to the Florida Indian emigration into Arkansas. They had only recently received word that the Paynes Landing and Fort Gibson treaties for emigration had been ratified and proclaimed by the President. When word of this action had reached the Seminoles, they were stunned. Such a thing could not be. The Indian nation had not been consulted about moving! This was an unparalleled land grab.

The affairs of the Seminoles had been brought to crisis. Many starving bands were preying upon the cattle herds and provisions of the whites just to stay alive. The Treaty of 1823 had deprived the Seminoles of their cultivated fields and of a region of country fruitful with game. They had been placed in a wilderness that was unsuitable for farming or hunting, and people were dying.

And in answer to all this misery the government had demanded that the Seminoles move west and be assimilated into the Creek nation in Arkansas. This added insult to injury. The Creek were their enemy. There was unremitting bad blood between the two nations concerning the ownership of slaves. The runaway black slaves that the Seminoles had accepted into their nation had married and had children among the Indian. The Creeks had frequently raided Seminole villages, seeking slaves, oftentimes taking Indian as well as black man. The only sentiment the Seminoles felt for the Creeks was hatred. If the white man had his way, the Seminoles would become slaves to their enemies.

The sun had risen, and as he looked at the preparations taking place behind the stockades, Osceola heard the approach of many feet from a great distance away. His people had come to face the white-eyes and defy the terms of the treaty.

Within minutes he could see the feathered turbans of the warriors and the brightly banded skirts of the women who had come to bear witness and stand against the soldiers. When the head line was almost beneath the tree where he sat, Osceola lightly jumped to the ground, saluting Alligator and the old man Arpeika.

"I see the women have followed," he stated simply.

"Che-cho-ter follows with your daughters," Arpeika answered the question it would have been unseemly to ask.

His eyes searching, he finally saw her, leading their three little daughters along the trail. When she saw her husband, Che-cho-ter had smiled. "You have found me, my husband." Her voice was low, a pleasant thrum in his ears. He had not shared his chikkee with her for ten nights and he was hungry for her. The emotion was reflected in her eyes as she stood proudly before him. "We have dressed in our best so as not to bring shame upon you. Even little Lilka," she said, holding the baby out for him to approve.

Osceola had reached out and touched his youngest daughter, stroking the silken skin of her cheek. So like his Morning Dew was this youngest one. Even her quick smile and gentle features were her mother's. Turning his attention to eight-year-old Hola and five-year-old Mic-canna, he embraced them lovingly.

The more precocious of the two, Mic-canna had asked, "Do we have to be very quiet as our mother told us?"

"Yes, little one. You must be very quiet and show the soldiers how well behaved Seminole children can be." He smiled, looking up into Che-cho-ter's face. Only she could read there the great weight he bore on his shoulders. Only she knew his agony at the thought of their people's blood being shed. Brave talk was for young boys; only men knew the meaning of death and separation.

"You must leave us, my husband. You must take your place among the leaders of our nation. We will be strong for you." Che-cho-ter had masked the emotion in her voice, and looked intently at her husband, hiding her fear and dread.

It was Thursday. Agent Wiley Thompson had convened the meeting at the agency within the stockade of Fort King. The Seminole chiefs had gathered within the building while lesser warriors crowded the porch or squeezed into the main room. The women sat beneath the trees surrounding the building, lending emotional support to their men. This was an important day for all Seminole women. Today would be the day the Seminole chiefs would decide whether to leave their homes for an unknown land and fall into slavery at the hands of the Creeks, or to make their stand against white authority. If war was declared, many of the women sitting beneath the shade trees in Fort King would become widows.

Agent Thompson, who represented the government, had addressed the gathering with a long speech, interpreted by Abraham, the Negro. The tone of his message suggested that he considered the removal of the Indians all but accomplished.

Slim and tall, Abraham had delivered the speech to his friends, repeating Thompson's words in the language of the Seminole. "Your noble cousins to the west have invited the Seminoles to settle among them."

Groans and angry mutterings had filled the agency. Such behavior was a breach of Seminole etiquette and so rare that even Abraham had been astonished. The main cause for concern was the deep fear that the Creeks or white slave-catchers would claim the Negroes who lived among them.

The conference fire in Fort King had burned brightly for many days as each thlacko, or chief, had had his say. Abraham, the Negro interpreter, was present at each meeting as a trusted friend. He would represent them at the conferences with the white man.

Osceola had kept silent through most of these conferences, careful to keep his rage from erupting. At last, it was his turn to speak. Controlling his voice, he had addressed his leaders.

"Brothers, talk is good and helps to heal the wounds of betrayal. But now we must prepare for the worst. The Seminole is of this land. Our spirits walk the forests and fish the streams. Away from this land the Seminole does not exist. Our people must agree not to follow the dictates of the whites who want this land for their own. Our people must realize their blood may soak this earth. But we need to be united as a people, just as the white soldiers come together under their leaders."

"Some of our chiefs are willing to walk to the west," Alligator said, the deep lines in his face drawing his face down in a scowl. "Holata Emathla and his brother, Charley Emathla, believe it is good for the Seminole. Coa Hadjo first said he would not move, but now his mind is changing."

Osceola had stood, his slim, straight form outlined by the fire. "No! There is no good in it. To move is to become enslaved by the Creeks. Have we not seen the misery of slavery in the black faces who run from their masters to work beside the Seminole? We must turn their minds. We must also persuade Micanopy to stand firm. Micanopy, above all. He is a great chief and has many warriors under him. Arpeika can influence him." He turned toward the old medicine man who was known by the whites as Sam Jones.

"So can anyone influence Micanopy," Arpeika had observed wryly. The old man sat cross-legged, arms folded against his breast. "We know of my kinsman's weakness. Yet I believe Micanopy would die before being driven from his home. He will stand when others strengthen him."

"As we know, brother," Alligator had agreed. "But words are not enough. The white warriors will try to move us by force." There had been a note of regret and resolution in his tone.

"If we must fight, we will fight!" Osceola had shouted. "And we should be ready to fight. We must save all lead and buy kegs of powder. Every warrior must be ready!" Voice shaking with emotion and fervor, he had glanced around the campfire, searching the faces of the gathered chiefs. He saw sorrow and in some cases—defeat.

So it was that Osceola had raised his voice, speaking the hearts of his people, setting them on a course that would mean victory at a terrible price or total defeat. But his words were strong, his voice unquavering, and in time of confusion and indecision his keenness and self-assurance made his voice the one to be heard and his heart the one to follow.

Arpeika, Osceola's mentor, had chosen his protégé well. In the soul of this young Seminole burned the love of his people and the vigor of a mighty warrior. He would see to it that Osceola would gain more and more influence over the tribe and all the Seminole nation would know him as chief.

Che-cho-ter moved in her sleep, bringing Osceola back into the present. Sleep would elude him this night, he knew. Wrapping his arm about his wife, he silently thanked the Great One that his brother had come to his aid. If this heaviness in his heart was prophetic, it would seem that Osceola, thlacko to the Seminole, was in the habit of leaving his women in his white brother's care.

Sloan woke as dawn crept close to the campsite, completely aware of where he was and his surroundings. The soft grays and purples of early light comforted him somehow. It hit him instantly that the warm presence of the girl was missing. Tentatively, he rolled onto his side to see where she was. To his left, talking agitatedly to Chala, was the handsome buck Mico, who had led the scouting party which had brought him to the village. Comprehension dawned suddenly. Sloan imagined that he could feel deep hatred fan out from the brave's body. Chala's back was to him, so it was impossible to see her response, but he couldn't miss the heavy-handed expressions the brave was using during his agitated conversation with Chala. Sloan decided not to interfere. This was something that must be settled by Chala herself. If she had been promised to Mico, then Osceola would never have given him the girl, regardless of whether Sloan was his brother or not.

Chala's blanket lay folded neatly beside him. When he rose, he knew the girl would walk over, fold his blanket and place it on top of her own. For the second time it occurred to him that asking for the girl in a pique of anger had been a mistake.

A stray dog slinked past Sloan's legs, making him step sideways. He wondered vaguely how the scrawny animal had managed to survive the stew pot. It was a slat-ribbed dog with mangy fur and the saddest eyes Sloan had ever seen. He watched as the animal rubbed against Chala's bare brown leg. Absently, as if from long practice, the girl bent to scratch behind the dog's ears. Suddenly, she stiffened and then looked furtively over her shoulder at Sloan. He busied himself with tying the laces of his deerskin boots. When he looked up, Chala and the dog were gone. So, he grinned to himself, the little savage has a heart after all. The tears and the mangy dog were her release, her defense against things she couldn't control.

The fires burned low, the cook pots had simmered through the night. Each man was served his morning portion. Unable to eat Chala's contribution, Sloan made himself obvious near Osceola's chikkee. Without hesitation, Morning Dew ladled a large, generous portion of the fragrant stew into an earthenware bowl. She smiled in approval as Sloan wolfed down the food and held out his bowl for a refill. Within mouthfuls it was gone. Osceola's first wife, Ina, held out a slab of Koonti bread which Sloan ripped apart and savored to the last mouthful.

Osceola had not yet made his appearance. He inquired of Ina, who shrugged elaborately, a sad look on her face. It clearly said it was not her place to comment on Osceola's absence.

Preparations for the move were underway. Yahi, the widow woman, was to stay behind to tend the chikkee. She accepted the order with pride, feeling needed once again in her old life. Within the hour all was in readiness. The last two things to be removed from the chikkee was Osceola's yellow and red standard, and the glowing, smoldering embers from the fire that were to be placed in a clay container which was affixed to a stick. At sundown, when they camped, the embers would need nothing more than pine straw to catch and flame, making the evening fire.

Small children capered to and fro, enjoying the thrill of early morning. It was amazing what warmth and a full stomach could do for a child's happiness. At that moment in time Sloan swore to himself that no matter what, he would do his best to make sure these children and all the people under Osceola's protection survived.

The cook pots seemed to the most important items of all, and Sloan watched the reverent way Osceola's women handled their precious possessions. Still, Osceola had not made an appearance. Chala was nowhere to be seen. The mongrel dog had long since disappeared.

Everything stood in readiness, waiting for Osceola to exit his chikkee and remove the yellow and red standard. Once it was removed, it meant the chief was not in residence. It was the last thing to be removed and the first thing to be hung upon making a new camp whether it was temporary or permanent.

Crisp, cold air made Sloan draw in his breath. He hadn't realized how chilly the morning was until he saw a cloudy vapor of his own breath. With the fires almost extinguished, he felt the chill creep into his boots and beneath the buckskin he wore. He knew from long practice that within the hour he'd be perspiring, and no doubt he'd remove the buckskin tunic. But Florida mornings were still cool in the winter, something to which he was slowly adjusting.

At last all was in readiness. Osceola's wives stood near the children, awaiting the signal from their husband to begin the long walk to their destination in the Panasoffke Swamp. Their party was a small one: Osceola, his two wives, three daughters, Sloan, Chala and three warriors. Eleven, not counting the six pack mules and, of course, Redeemer. Sloan stood waiting for Osceola, Redeemer's bridle in hand.

"Give my brother any trouble, you cantankerous beast, and I'll see to it you find yourself in the same cook fires those mules are heading for, hear me?" Redeemer raised his head, the whites of his eyes showing, snorting vapors of clouds in the early morning.

When the chief exited his chikkee, he removed his standard with little ceremony. Quietly, he stood as the smoking pot of embers was affixed to a long stick. There was religious significance in bringing a fire from home to light the fires along the trail. It ensured safety, security and an uneventful night's rest.

"My brother will ride this unworthy beast I have brought all the way from Russia," Sloan told him, eyeing the horse speculatively. Ordinarily, Redeemer never allowed anyone but himself to mount him.

As Osceola put his foot into the stirrup, Redeemer looked back at him over his massive black shoulder. Sloan pulled hard upon the reins, giving fair warning. Redeemer must have sensed the association between his master and this strange, dark man with feathers in his turban. Or perhaps he sensed the man was ill and he was needed to carry him. Osceola mounted with little difficulty; it had been years since he had ridden a horse because they were so scarce among the Seminole. Redeemer showed himself to be a gentleman. The others in the camp nodded their approval that their chief was able to ride the black stallion with such little effort. He was truly a great man in close company with the spirits of the forest. They had all witnessed the battle the animal had waged with anyone who had tried to approach him, save the white-eyes.

Osceola at the head, the small party followed single file behind Redeemer. Yahi's face was stoic, giving no hint of her feelings as her new family left the little village. Sloan was the last to fall into line. Suddenly, Chala was beside him. She refused to meet his eyes, aware of her tears during the night. It was one more humiliation she had to bear.

The daylong trek was wearying. By sundown, it was apparent to Sloan that Osceola was more than a little ill. The medicine man, Arpeika, could help him if they had left in time. By noon of the following day they would set up their new camp and decide what they would do in order to survive Jessup and his men. It wounded Sloan to see the effect the trek was costing Osceola.

Ina and Morning Dew saw to their husband's comfort. His daughters stared at their father with dark, somber eyes. The littlest let her lower lip tremble when she clutched at her father's leg. Always before he would bend down, pick her up and whisper words that made her laugh in delight. This time he merely placed a tired, weary hand on her shiny black head. The child swayed back and forth, enjoying her father's gentle touch. With shaking hand, Osceola affixed his standard, and then with a deep sigh allowed Che-cho-ter to lead him to a pallet, where he lay down heavily and seemed to drop instantly into a sleep.

The Indians began their preparation for building new fires and the evening meal. There was nothing for Sloan to do. The women wouldn't tolerate him standing around their fires; the children were content to play among themselves. The Indian braves stood in awe of him now that they were convinced he was their chief's brother.

Settling himself in a comfortable position against a sturdy

Southern pine, Sloan watched Chala as she began to prepare his food. In a generous, forgiving gesture he had removed her tether for the long trek. He hoped it wasn't a mistake. She worked with an economy of motion and appeared to know what she was doing. If that was the case, Sloan wondered how the food could taste so awful. As he continued to stare at her, he became aware of the fact that she had combed her hair and pulled it behind her ears. Her profile shone in the light of the cook fire. She was a beautiful young woman. Something teased at his mind, niggled away at him as he watched her make the Koonti bread. Certainly, there was no likeness to Annemarie or Beaunell, but she reminded him of someone he knew. Perhaps someone he had seen, some brief acquaintance in Europe. Whatever, it would come to him sooner or later. He had a good memory for faces and rarely forgot names and places. He would remember. What he did remember now was the desire that rose in him while Chala slept in his arms and how he had to force himself to resist temptation. He closed his eyes and slept, knowing the girl would wake him when the food was ready. He was tired, he admitted to himself. The journey and ever-increasing worries had left him drained.

Osceola lay in exhaustion on his pallet while the women prepared the last meal of the day. His mind was rolling with the situations he faced. The calendar year was soon coming to an end, and the portents for the future were ominous. The information Sloan had given him about this new commander, General Jessup, had been enlightening, but it was Osceola himself who was more clearly apprised of the general's actions. Immediately after taking command, Jessup had ordered the building of several small forts in the heart of Indian territory. The new white commander of the Florida army must have left New Orleans shortly after Sloan because word had reached Osceola that his arrival was anticipated within days. And Jessup didn't come alone. There was word that he had recruited a unit of no less than four hundred Tennessee volunteers, experienced Indian fighters, to accompany him. It had come to his ears that these little forts were to be manned by navy marines and sailors, and were calculated to surround the Withlachoochee area and provide readily available supplies.

Turning over, eyes closing in sleep, Osceola smiled. Jessup's bringing the supplies directly into the area was encouraging. The winter would not be a hungry one after all. The Seminole would not have to travel far to find meat for their fires.

It was expected that the Withlachoochee area would be the target of concentrated attacks. In conference with the chiefs, Osceola had suggested that the bands spread out and gradually move southward. These chiefs, Arpeika, Alligator and Micanopy would shift toward the headquarters of the Oklawaha River. Alligator would operate in the vicinity of Lake Apopka. The oldest and most wily of all the Seminole leaders, King Phillip, was to maintain his position south of St. Augustine, where his periodic attacks on the city terrified its occupants.

For now, Thlacko Osceola was content with his decision to move to the Negro village in the Panasoffke Swamp. The sickness was coming fast upon him, and he believed he and his family would be more comfortable with the Indian-blacks who virtually worshipped him. And Arpeika was expected to be in the area, possibly staying in the Panasoffke village, and Osceola desperately needed his medicine.

Sleep came at last, giving the harried Indian peace, even if it was momentary.

CHAPTER FIVE

In the black night, trees overhanging like a canopy to hide them from the stars, Chala walked beside Sloan, leaving the cook fire of Ina and Che-cho-ter behind. The moon was high in the sky as it peeped down at them through the branches. The rustling of brush and the silent whoosh of an owl's wing fell on their ears.

They had left the camp while Che-cho-ter tried to get the children to sleep. This was an exciting adventure for them, traveling with their father, sleeping out. Sleep would be long coming to them this night. Sloan was aware of Chala beside him, the scent of her hair, so remembered from the night before, came pleasantly to his nostrils.

Chala, herself, was silent, absorbed in her own thoughts. When she wasn't railing against him, she could be a quiet, peaceful woman. The Seminole ways had been well learned and practiced. He wondered if he had succeeded in taming her somewhat, if she was beginning to accept the fact that she now belonged to him. Or was it the presence of the warrior, Mico, that gentled her? Back at the camp the young brave's eyes had never left Chala as she moved about the fire, and he wasn't mistaken about the fury he'd witnessed in the Indian's eyes when Chala had brought Sloan his dinner.

Sloan's own eyes had followed Chala, knowing there was something astoundingly familiar about her, yet unable to place where he had seen her before arriving at Osceola's village. This evening, she had taken the time after their long walk through the forest to brush her wild, honey-colored hair back from her face, pulling it into a single, thick braid that trailed down her back. Wayward strands escaped and curled around her face, creating a nimbus of gold that softened her features and accentuated her wide, luminous eyes. Eyes as green as the waters of the Withlacoochee fringed with startlingly black lashes. Eyes he knew he had looked into once before. Her long, arching neck was set gently above sloping shoulders. Her body slim and lithe and delicate in proportion, offset by high, proud breasts and tiny waist. But it was the face, well defined, open and beautiful, that strained his memory. Now, in the shadows of the moon, he could look at her, even touch her, but recognition eluded him.

"Why do MacAllister's eyes constantly search me?" she demanded, breaking the silence they had shared. She turned to face him, her eyes seeming to ignite with sudden anger. Her full lips were drawn into a pout, yet were appealingly curved, as if able to erupt into a beatific smile at the slightest provocation.

"You remind me of someone, and yet I can't quite place who. And it must have been fairly recent. Galveston, New Orleans, perhaps I saw a face in a crowd, in a passing carriage . . ." It suddenly dawned on him. Jessup. The portrait over the mantle. The same honey blonde hair, the curving mouth, the insolent green eyes.

Jessup's sister, who had been killed by the Indians in Alabama. Memory flooded back. What had Jessup said? A child? A daughter? Savannah. Savannah James. The sister's name was Caroline. . . .

Abruptly, he caught her arm, swinging her around so the moonlight could fall on her face. Fingertips held her chin, turning her face into a portrait-like pose.

"What do you see, MacAllister?" Chala demanded.

"Tell me, Chala, what do you know of your beginnings?"

Her eyes dropped, refusing to look at him, as though she were ashamed to admit that her heritage was white instead of Indian.

"You must tell me. I must know! It may be of the most vital importance to Osceola."

This last statement seemed to prompt her to answer. "I only know what the old ones have told me. Nothing more."

"You're lying. You do remember something, and for some reason you don't want to admit it." His voice was urgent, sharp and insistent. "Whatever it is, no matter how small or how painful, you must tell me. You may be the only living soul who can help the Seminole. You claim them for your people; don't you think you owe them something?"

Still, Chala's face was set, her eyes downcast, lips pressed firmly into a thin, grim line.

"Let me tell you what I know about you," Sloan said gently, leading her over to a low hummock that bulged from the soft, fresh earth. She was watching him intently, her eyes expressionless, listening to his voice.

"You were a little child when your parents were killed by Indians, most likely the Creeks in Alabama. I'd venture a guess that you were taken by them back to their camp. Being warriors on the move, they probably brought you into Florida with the intention of selling you as a slave to the Seminoles. How close am I to the truth, Chala?"

Her eyes fell away from him; he imagined he could hear her heart beating a tattoo in her breast. "To the Seminole, beginnings are the least important. It is only the person you become that matters. I was six summers old when Osceola and his old wife Ina took me to their chikkee."

"Do you remember your mother's name?" he asked her, his voice quiet, in a tone he would use to gentle a skittish colt.

"No." A long pause sent his hopes crashing. Then, "I only called her Mama." There was such a deep sadness in her, setting her lower lip to quivering.

"And what did your father call her?"

The question seemed to astound her; she had never thought of it before this. The syllables came hesitantly; they were nearly a sob. "C . . . Caro . . . line. Caroline."

"And she called you Savannah. Isn't that so? Savannah." He repeated the name Jessup had uttered with such drunken harshness.

She seemed to roll the name over her tongue as dagger-sharp shafts of memory pierced her. A lone, silent tear trickled down her cheek, but she didn't seem to be aware of it.

"Savannah James," she told him at last. "They killed my mother. I saw them. Papa wasn't in the house, but they killed him too. They . . . they took me. Carried me with them. I was afraid of them and I screamed and cried, but they didn't listen; they didn't care. They had paint on their cheeks and feathers in their hair. The horses they rode were big, and wild, and I had to be carried across their laps. . . ." It seemed impossible for her to continue. She had told him enough. This was the girl General Jessup thought dead. The man wouldn't need any more proof that Savannah was indeed his niece. The comparison between Savannah and the portrait would convince him.

Chala's shattered cry broke the stillness, her low, tormented moans filling the forest with the sadness, terror and grief she hadn't been able to express as a child.

When he took her into his arms and held her, she continued to sway and issue low, tormented sounds. But there were no tears. They had been expressed through a lifetime of abandonment.

Her grief had exhausted her. She lay there weak and pale, unable to move. Sympathy and tenderness welled up in Sloan and with great care he lifted her in his arms, carrying her as easily as Redeemer carried him. She cradled there, resting her head against his shoulder, accepting this show of concern with relief.

The way back to the camp was a short distance, the overhead moon gave enough illumination to see the path clearly. Following the light from the camp fire, Sloan broke into the clearing, carrying Chala, and ran straight into Mico, dark and smoldering with hostility. The man's burning eyes followed Sloan to where Savannah had laid their pallets. Dropping to one knee, Sloan gently placed her on the blankets, pulling the covers high under her chin to protect her from the chill night air. When at last he stood, it was to find Mico standing directly behind him, his face a mask of controlled rage.

"If the white-eyes was not called brother by my chief, I would have the pleasure of fighting you for her!" He spoke in guttural tones, not caring if Sloan knew his disgust. "I, Mico, Mikasuki Seminole, have looked upon the squaw with the honey hair."

Sloan knew that for a Seminole brave to "look at" a woman was the first step in claiming her for his own. But any regret for the upheaval he had brought into Chala's life and for the disappointment he had brought to one of Osceola's finest warriors, was immediately erased by Mico's brash threat. "You will never take her from this land," he told Sloan, so forcefully that spittle formed on his lips. His black eyes boiled menacingly.

Drawing himself up to his full height, Sloan peered down into the warrior's eyes. "Chala will do what she must for her people. Just as you must fight at my brother's side. You will not approach me again, Mico, or threaten me. Not because I am your chief's brother, but because I am not a man to be threatened." Authority rang in his voice.

Unconsciously, Mico's hand went to the knife he wore in his belt. "This will be settled at another time, white-eyes, when my chief no longer has use for you. Chala will belong to me, and the wild dogs will dig beneath the forest floor to consume your flesh."

For a long moment Sloan stared unswervingly into the warrior's eyes. Then he turned his back on the man and slid down into the pallet beside Chala. He half expected to feel Mico's knife plunged between his ribs.

After a moment he heard the Indian's footsteps take him away. Mico, passing the fire, in unrelenting frustration, kicked the shallow pile of embers in Sloan's direction, showering glowing sparks onto the blanket he shared with Chala. The pungent stink of singed wool filled Sloan's nostrils, but he pretended not to notice what the man had done. It would be difficult for Osceola to place himself impartially between his brother from so long ago and his most valuable warrior.

He touched Chala's shoulder and she turned toward him, sliding into his embrace and placing her head on his shoulder. She was sleeping, he knew, yet she had instinctively sought his comfort. A tenderness welled within him that was the most overpowering emotion he had ever felt.

Raucous calls erupted in the forest as brightly plumed birds greeted the dawn. A fox was skulking through the trees, pausing to sniff the smoking vapors from the campsite's banked fires. The forest was awakening to a new day, and Chala nestled into the warmth of Sloan's body, instinctively pushing her slim back and sloping haunches against him. His arms had wrapped around her during the night; his face was buried in her hair and she could feel his breath warm and soft against the nape of her neck.

Suddenly her green eyes flew open, instantly aware of her position. Scenes from the evening before assaulted her, bringing new pain. It had been years since she had allowed herself to remember her parents and the circumstances that led her into Osceola's guardianship. And MacAllister had forced her to remember, had stripped her naked of all her defenses, leaving her weak and frightened as though she were a child of six again.

Her life had become hellish since this man had come to her village. She had been chastised and humiliated before the entire village, forced to fetch and carry for a man she detested and constantly reminded by his mere presence that she was not a Seminole, but a white woman. He forced her to speak a language she had thought she had long forgotten, and to add to her misery, she must now share a pallet with him, allow him to intrude upon her, even in sleep.

Chala lay perfectly still, suddenly noticing a change in the rhythm of MacAllister's breathing. His arms, which moments ago had been heavy and lifeless, were now tightening around her, imperceptibly drawing her closer into his body's embrace.

Sloan had woken, driven by a shrill cry of birds praising the new day. Chala's weight lay warm and soft against him, the fresh woodsy scent of her hair was in his nostrils and the tender feel of her body was yielding in his arms. His first thought was of the misery he had caused her the night before when he dug into her past. She had been exhausted and near collapse when he'd carried her back to the campsite and placed her on their pallet. Throughout the night he had felt her tremblings and heard the tormented sounds she made in her sleep, both of which had made him curse himself for his cruelty and insensitivity. He wanted to hold her and protect her, even from himself. Like a kitten she had crawled against him, seeking his warmth, placing herself in his total care.

Fully awake now, Sloan's embrace deepened, his lips tenderly nuzzling the graceful sweet curve of her neck.

Wrenching herself from his arms, Chala jumped from the warmth of the pallet. Her cheeks were flaming, her eyes blazing with unbridled hostility. Her golden hair fell across her face in wild abandon. Still on her knees she turned to face him, her anger ripping through her, making her voice a lethal hiss. "MacAllister takes too much upon himself!" Her face was only inches from his, her tone low so as not to awaken the others, but strong and so intense he was taken aback. "I must cook for you. I must speak your language. I must fetch and carry for you like a slave without importance. I must even warm your pallet. These I will do because my chief says I must. Osceola does not say I must like it! And he does not say I must comfort MacAllister's nights and offer my body!"

Sloan was astounded. *She* had turned to him these nights, pressing her body against him. *She* had nestled her head on his shoulder, throwing her arm across his belly! *She* was offering a temptation any other man would have already taken to his own advantage! And to think he had pitied her, actually accused himself of cruelty!

Chala read the accusations in MacAllister's flinty gray eyes, and the color in her cheeks deepened. She knew what he was thinking and it was all true. Frustration bubbled in her breast and boiled to the surface, seeming to choke off her air. Her fingers curled into claws, itching to dig his eyes from his head.

Seeing her intent, Sloan seized her wrist in a bone-crushing grip, and pulled her forward, sending her sprawling onto his chest. The fingers of his left hand tangled in her hair, snapping her head around to face him. "You little savage!" He gave her hair a terrible yank, making her wince with pain. "I've heard about the Spirit who walks the forest looking for defenseless children to eat them up in one bite!" He spoke of the Seminole version of the bogeyman. "What I didn't know was that the Okeepapa had honeyed hair and green eyes!"

Despite his grip on her, Chala was moved to action by this insult. Twisting, she dug her elbow into his groin, enjoying the pain flashing across his face and the sudden intake of his breath. "Be careful, MacAllister. This is one Okeepapa who has a taste for white flesh and grown men."

Bringing up his knees to protect himself, he released her. Instantly, Chala was on her feet looking down at him. "I will bring MacAllister his Koonti bread. He will need his strength to fight the Okeepapa again this night." Her tone was sarcastic and her lip curled into a malicious smile.

Sloan glared up at her, deciding if he should drag her to the ground and beat her or wait and take her by surprise. His decision was made for him by the appearance of Osceola's daughters, who were looking for their morning meal.

It was early the next day when Osceola's party entered the Negro village in the Panasoffke Swamp. Nearly four hundred blacks lived here in abject poverty since the army had made farming and raising cattle impossible. Sloan walked beside Redeemer, who carried Osceola into the compound. Just outside the perimeters of the camp Sloan noticed how his brother, greatly weakened by the rising tide of his malarial attack, had willed himself to straighten in the saddle. Back straight, head proud and high, he determined to face his black compatriots a strong man, strengthening their confidence in him.

The compound's leader, a heavily muscled black named Artemus Woods, greeted them. At a glance Sloan knew the runaway slave instantly saw Osceola's feverish condition. Raising one heavily muscled arm, he hailed the Seminole chief. "Our friend, Osceola, has come to share with us." His dark, fathomless eyes settled questioningly on Sloan.

"This is my brother, MacAllister," said Osceola. His voice was strong and unwavering at a great price to himself. "Behind us follow pack mules with supplies we have brought as gifts."

Women and children stood around the perimeters of the encampment. Men armed with rifles stood watching warily, their eyes never leaving MacAllister. Bare chested, the sun glinting off their ebony bodies, they appeared a formidable troop. Osceola had told him they were fearless fighters, worthy allies to fight beside the Seminole.

The largest thatched hut was assigned to Osceola and Che-cho-ter, and Ina immediately took the children inside to rest after their long morning's walk. Watching his brother slide heavily down from Redeemer's saddle, Sloan was aware of what this display of strength was costing him. Beads of sweat streaked down Osceola's face, and even in the warmth of the day, the blanket wrapped around his shoulders was pulled high to his chin. Soon now, he knew, the racking chills would begin, rendering the Indian a help-less victim to the fever.

Seeing to Redeemer's needs himself, Sloan led the animal to a watering trough, leaving him to drink while he went to the pack mules to rescue Redeemer's sack of oats before it found its way into the Negroes' storehouse. Chala had joined the women in the hut assigned to her chief, leaving Mico and the two other warriors to stand guard outside the hanging blanket which served as a door.

Sloan rejoined Osceola as he was speaking to a council of blacks. They were seated in the shade of an ash tree, and their faces were grave and contemplative. The Seminole chief's voice was strong and rang with timbre. It was important that the blacks not desert the opposition against the United States Army now, espe-cially not now when there was so little to be gained.

"The Seminole policy toward the Negro is as clear as the water in the Silver Spring," he told them, watching their faces for signs of argument. *"No Negro should ever be surrendered to the whites!"* His voice thundered: his eyes blazed with conviction. "The dilemma is a clear one. If the Seminoles abandon their resistance and move to the west as the government decrees, our Negro allies here in the Floridas will either perish or will be captured once more for slav-ery beneath the lash of the white man. If the Negro walks with us to the far side of the Great River, it will be with the same results. All of us then would fall prey to the slave catcher's rifle. Do not depend upon those dog cousins of the Seminoles, the Creeks, to raise a hand in defense of the black man."

Osceola's eyes read the black faces uplifted toward him. He pointed to Sloan, introducing him to the others as his white brother, a champion of their causes. "How do you see it, MacAllister? Speak and let your voice count among us!"

Sloan did not hesitate to bring forward his views. He affirmed the possibilities Osceola had already mentioned to the Negroes, who, he was certain, were already doomfully aware of them. "Your only hope," he told them, "is to fight the army. Stand beside your Seminole brother when he takes the warpath. Stand beside Osceola! He fights not only for the Seminole and his rights, but also for you!"

"This white-eyes with the hair of the lion's mane speaks the truth!" A voice rose above the others. It belonged to the medicine man, Arpeika, Osceola's mentor. He was a cantankerous, lean old man with dirty white hair and the skin of an ancient turtle. From everything Osceola had told Sloan, the man seemed to be as brusque and ill-tempered as ever. Standing beside the wizened medicine man were two Mikasuki, an exclusive rank of warriors.

Exercising his authority, Arpeika drew Osceola away from the gathering. With a backward glance, Osceola signaled for Sloan to follow. When they were out of hearing distance, the old man said, "I have a plan."

If Arpeika's wrinkled eyes took in Osceola's sick and weakened appearance, he gave no sign. Brushing aside the customary greeting, the medicine man said, "I am going to lead warriors. I expect many Mikasukis will follow me."

"That is as you wish," Osceola said in a weak voice.

"As you wish, as you wish," Arpeika mimicked furiously. "I can still fight better than most of the young fools."

"Then it is good. Does that mean you haven't changed your mind about moving west among the Creeks?"

"Never!" the old medicine man cackled shrilly. "If I am to die, then I will die on my own soil."

"Well spoken. I also will die on my own soil," Osceola said gravely.

"No," the old man and prophet exclaimed. He stared at Osceola through glassy, red-veined eyes. "I don't think you will die on this soil. And I don't think you die beyond the Great River Mississippi. But you die."

"A story!" Osceola said bitterly. "You spin white man's fairy tales. If you don't do something for me, I will die at your feet, and how will you explain that to my people."

"Yes. I will do something now for you. I have waited all the morning hours." Following Osceola into his assigned hut, Arpeika then sent Ina, Morning Dew and the children from him. He then pointed to Chala. "You, too, leave us." He ignored Sloan as if he didn't exist.

Alone with Osceola, the old man administered some boiled herbs and began a ritual chanting that was the most important part of every medicine man's business.

Arpeika was not only a warrior-priest but he also practiced curative medicine. Herbs, such as snakeroot and sassafras, were used along with many others. Medicine men were more interested in the words of the chants believing that ritual drove out the disease: the herbs were only of minor significance.

When the old Indian left, Osceola slept and dreamed he raced after a deer, running at full speed, until he reached a lake where snags probed from the water like black, broken fingers. The deer swam between them, spreading ripples on the dark water, and Osceola plunged in to follow. On the far shore, he pursued the deer to a strange place where a cave gaped in the side of a hill. When the deer entered the cave, Osceola shuddered at the idea of following. But he entered the cave where, suddenly, in the blackness, there was a loud popping sound.

Osceola wakened to find Sloan and his two wives bending over him. Three warriors stood behind them. The popping sound continued, rifle shots, still at a distance, but approaching fast. His two wives were scooping up blankets and cookwear, the children clinging to their skirts.

"Soldiers!" Sloan barked. "Can you move?"

"I will walk," Osceola said hoarsely. To the three Mikasuki he ordered, "One of you ahead, the other behind me, the third behind my family. Sloan at my side if I falter."

They did as ordered. Debilitated or not, he was their thlacko. To Sloan, he whispered, "Tell me."

"It was quick. Too quick. It's my guess the attack was ordered by Jessup, probably one of his probing battalions. We can do nothing here."

"We must move on," Osceola affirmed Sloan's decision. "I know a hiding place on the Withlacoochee. Ready everything, brother, time is everything. I want as few casualties as possible.

More Seminoles will come to help if I can reach the cove and send word."

Later, Sloan would learn that Jessup's battalion made a successful sweep of the village. More than fifty blacks would be taken prisoner with the rest escaping into the forest. If Osceola had been captured at that time, future victories in the Seminole cause would have been impossible.

Rushing across the clearing that was surrounded by low thatch huts, Sloan kept a firm grip on Osceola's arm, half carrying him, half dragging him, in the opposite direction of the gun shots to the shelter of the forest. The main fighting was still a good distance away, having been discovered by sentries guarding the village. Glancing back over his shoulder, he saw Ina pulling Osceola's daughter Mic-canna along, the little girl's toes dragging in the dust, fear widening her eyes. Che-cho-ter carried Hola, and Chala balanced the baby Lilka. The children were silent, their faces pale and sallow against the dark cloud of ebony hair. Che-cho-ter's face reflected her fear for her husband as she searched ahead to where Sloan assisted him.

They had almost reached the forest behind the huts when Sloan heard a woman's scream. Pushing Osceola into the arms of the lead Mikasuki, he ran back in time to see Chala thrust the baby she was carrying into its mother's arms.

With lightning velocity and seemingly without second thought, she pulled the knife from its sheath on her belt and rushed back toward the huts. Hair flying, teeth bared, she ran, knife raised in menace. Looking ahead of her, Sloan saw a black woman had been knocked to the ground, a bare-legged Indian straddling her. The scream hadn't been Chala's; it had been the Negress's.

Before thought could become action, Chala came up behind the attacking Indian and stabbed her knife through the back of his neck. He seemed to crumple forward into a lifeless heap, an expression of total surprise contorting his face.

Standing beside Sloan was Mico, a look of satisfied approval on his face. "It was a Creek," the young warrior said, spitting on the ground as if to be rid of a bad taste. "Chala is a brave one," he said, "a true Seminole!" This last was said as a reminder to Sloan that whatever he may think, Mico thought of Chala as a woman of her people, and although Osceola may have given her to MacAllister,

Mico had not abandoned the possibility of claiming her for his own.

Ignoring Mico's veiled meaning, Sloan questioned. "A Creek? What's he doing here?"

"The army is using them as scouts. They fight beside the white soldiers. Like the fox, they mean to be the first at the chicken house. All blacks and Seminoles they capture the soldiers allow them to keep."

After seeing that the Negress who was being attacked was able to fend for herself, Chala ran back to join the women, sheathing her knife as she ran. Sloan had already returned to Osceola's side after giving orders that the Mikasukis should help the women with the children. As they entered the depths of the swamp, the vision of Chala plunging her knife into the Creek's neck haunted him. Like Mico, he admired her. Her commitment to the Seminoles was total. She was a hellcat, a tigress defending her cubs. A slow smile worked over his mouth as he thought of how at night, thoroughly feline, she could become a kitten, warm and soft in a man's arms.

Had it not been for Redeemer carrying Osceola, Sloan doubted they would have been able to escape and make the long, hurried trek through the swamp, following paths that were ventured only by the Indians. Several times the Seminole chief motioned for one of the children to be placed across his lap, relieving their fatigue and silencing their tears.

Sloan led the way, recalling all the things his brother had taught him in the woods surrounding their farm back in Alabama. Time was of the essence. Osceola was desperately weakened. The medicinal herbs Arpeika had administered seemed to have quelled the fever for the time being at least, but there was the man's dreadfully weakened condition to consider. By the evening, Sloan knew, the racking chills and fever would again have him in their grip.

The night birds were chirping their last song of the day. Mico and the two other warriors quickly set about making a low fire. Their faces were set in grim lines. Tonight the fire would be fresh; there had been no time to collect embers from the fire they had brought from their village. There would be no protecting Spirits watching over them.

The children complained of hunger, and Che-cho-ter looked at them balefully. Tonight her little ones would go to sleep hungry.

There had been no time to gather supplies. The pack mules and foodstuffs they had brought with them to the Negro village were now in the hands of the army.

Chala laid out a sleeping pallet, using one of the hastily rescued blankets to cover a hummock of soft pine boughs that would separate their bodies from the cold, hard ground. The cove Osceola had led them to was sheltered by a ring of thick forest which broke out onto the banks of the Withlacoochee River. Here the waters narrowed and a man could throw a stone from one side to the other. It was a natural place for game to come out of the forest to drink. Tomorrow, when it was light, they would fish for their morning meal and set traps. Mico would hunt the squirrel and the coon and they would feast. The women would find wild potatoes and celery for the cook pot. Tomorrow the children would not be hungry.

Thought of preparations for survival thrummed through Chala's head. She could not allow herself to think of how her knife point had sunk into the Creek's neck and the sound he had made as he choked on his blood. The vision kept reappearing despite her determination to put it from her mind. It left her shaking, her trembling fingers unable to complete the simplest task. Even now, as she prepared MacAllister's pallet, there was a shuddering inside her, making the blankets quiver and the pine boughs rustle.

She had killed a man. That he was her enemy did not comfort her. That he would have killed her without compunction did not soothe her. Often, as a child, she had regretted being a female, sentenced by her sex to the care of children and a household. She would have liked to join the young braves who were learning to hunt and fish and fight. Now, contrary to those longings, she was grateful she could leave the killing to the men. Looking at Checho-ter and Ina as they rocked and sang the children to sleep, she realized that the Great Spirits had designed that women be the caretakers, the healers. Now she understood why strong warriors would return to the village weary and sick, looking to their women with haunted, questioning eyes for warmth and comfort. Being a wife and mother was as necessary as being a warrior. It was more difficult. The blood that stained a woman's hands belonged not to an enemy but to a loved one. She tended their wounds, choking back tears, praising and chanting the bravery of her husband, who would be revived to challenge the enemy another day.

Chala's eyes drifted to MacAllister. He was sitting near Osceola's pallet speaking to his brother in low, gruff tones. She had listened while he spoke to the black men, telling them their only hope was to continue fighting with the Seminole against Jessup's army. A pride had filled her that this strong, intelligent man was her master.

Doffing her moccasins, she slid onto the pallet, her thoughts a maelstrom of confusion. Only this morning she had wanted to dig his eyes from his head. Yet this afternoon she had stood and listened to him with admiration. And she had killed a man. A terrible quaking overtook her and she tried to still her traitorous body with little success.

Minutes later MacAllister crawled onto the pallet beside her. At that moment she wanted nothing more than to turn to him and lie in his arms and have his nearness chase away the devils that were pursuing her. In his areas she had found peace, but after this morning she must even deny herself that small respite. Pride was a cold companion here in the night and offered no shelter from the misery of her thoughts.

"Are you cold, little one?" he murmured, mistaking her shuddering emotions for a night chill. Her silence piqued his curiosity and he lightly touched her chin, turning her face toward him. Her misery was marked in her eyes and he seemed to understand. "Poor little kitten," he said softly, opening his arms for her, drawing her close against him. "You've discovered the secret of all men. Killing freezes the soul. Even the blood of an enemy stains the spirit. There is no greater sin and those who must kill know the doom of their own damnation."

MacAllister's sympathy and compassion choked Chala with tears. For a long time she lay in his arms, accepting his comfort, allowing the cleansing tears to flow. At last he whispered, "Sleep now, kitten. Tomorrow is another day and I will be here if you need me."

Exhausted, Chala nestled in his embrace. He had chased away the night devils and promised her a brighter day. It was good to sleep in this man's arms, she told herself. It was good to share his warmth.

For the first time since putting eyes on him, Chala wondered what it would be like to share a chikkee with him and feel his body enter hers for the pleasure of the flesh and a meeting of the souls.

MacAllister must have a beautiful soul. She had never known a man that way but she had heard other women speak of it. Again, she shivered, feeling him hold her closer still. She smiled and pressed her face into his shoulder, wrapping her arm around his midsection, enjoying the closeness, hearing his breaths fall and rise evenly, knowing he slept.

An unknown tenderness welled in Chala's heart for this man who seemed to read her thoughts. Little did she know he was formulating a plan that would have her wishing she had never placed eyes on him.

It was midmorning when Morning Dew finally acknowledged Sloan and allowed him to approach her husband. He left Chala behind, whose tender thoughts of the night before had been replaced by a smoldering rage.

When Osceola struggled to a sitting position to greet him, Sloan failed to mask the alarm in his eyes at his brother's weakened condition. He held up his hand to show that no formality was required on his brother's part. "Stay comfortable, I came only to talk and then will leave quickly. I have much to say and want to hear what you think of a plan I have devised." Osceola nodded and leaned back onto his pallet.

"Tell me what manner of secret you have been hiding from me." It was a feeble attempt at humor on the Indian chief's part, but Sloan appreciated the effort it cost him.

"It concerns Chala. Her face has haunted me from the moment I first saw her, but I could not place it. A few days ago it finally dawned on me where I had seen her before. I saw a picture of her mother in General Jessup's home. You recall how I told you I played poker at his home in the hopes of picking up some valuable information to help you? Well, in his library there was a picture over the mantle of a woman who looks just like Chala. It can't be anyone but her mother." Quickly, he recounted the story Jessup had told him. He saw the Indian tiring before his eyes. "It's my plan to take Chala to New Orleans and let Jessup find her by accident. I'll make sure that she has some brief training from a friend of mine to make her into a lady. I've spoken briefly to Chala of this and, of course, she is fighting me. I need you to tell her there is no other way that I can think of to get you the information you need.

She'll be in the perfect position to find out any military maneuvers. I'll concoct a cover story that will hold water; have no fear. I don't know what else to do for you, Osceola. I think it's our only hope at the moment."

"Send the girl to me. At this moment in time I must rely on your judgment. What you say sounds feasible to me. Please, brother, wipe the concern from your eyes. This disease you call malaria has laid me low before. I'll recover as I have in the past, but it takes time. Today, I feel stronger. Each day after will be better. Ah, I see the doubt in your eyes. Have I ever lied to you, son of our mother? Speak with Ina and Morning Dew. They will tell you I am on the mend."

"Your word is good enough for me. What kind of brother would I be if I wasn't concerned about your health? Chala and I will sail the *Polly Copinger*. Mico tells me this river leads to the keys where she is anchored. Send a few of your men with me as far as the ship so that they can bring you the rest of the stores from my hold. Somehow, I'll get word to you of our progress. Hopefully, when we lock eyes again, you will be hale and hearty."

There was such pain and sorrow in Osceola's eyes, Sloan felt a lump rise in his throat. "It is decided then. As soon as you speak with the girl, we will leave." There was no need for further words. Osceola knew sure as the sun would set this day that Sloan would be back with the promised aid of one kind or another.

Sloan motioned for Chala to approach her chief. She shot him a baleful look but did as she was told, quite different from the way she had railed and protested when he had first presented the plan to her.

Chala scuffed at the dust as she approached her thlacko's pallet. How could she have fooled herself into thinking that MacAllister understood her? Read her heart. Bah! He understood nothing. He thought she had softened toward him and, for a time, she had. Becoming aware of a man and wondering what it would be like to share his chikkee was one thing, being told she must leave her people was quite another. However much she had protested to MacAllister, Osceola was her thlacko and she must be obedient to him.

Twenty minutes later when Chala left Osceola she was more subdued than Sloan had ever seen her. She spoke quietly, careful to avoid his eyes. Her terse, "Chala will travel with you," was all he needed to hear. And now was as good a time as any to broach the next hurdle.

"From this moment on you are Savannah James. Chala is a Seminole. Savannah is a white lady." He stressed the word "lady" and wondered how in hell Annemarie would make silk purse from this sow's ear.

Dappled sunlight penetrated the thick overhead branches as Sloan and Chala, astride Redeemer, picked their quiet and cautious way through the woods toward the west coast of the Floridas. Mico and the two other warriors, whose names Sloan had never learned, followed at an easy pace behind them. Once reaching the coast where the forest thinned to give way to sandy beaches, the traveling would be easier northward to Cedar Key, where the *Polly Copinger* and Captain Culpepper waited. He hoped. It was quite possible that marauding Creeks or a chance regiment of cavalry had happened upon the *Polly* sending Culpepper out to sea in order to save his ship. There would be no explaining to the United States Army what the *Polly* was doing berthed in the center of Indian territory stocked to the hatches with supplies. About the only worry Culpepper wouldn't have was the possibility of his crew jumping ship. With nothing but miles and miles of dense forest ahead of them, the crew would wisely stay with the *Polly.*

Chala's multibanded skirt of bright colors rode high on her tanned legs, exposing their lightly muscled roundness. Ordinarily the sight of a well-turned limb would have pleased Sloan, but he only frowned when he noticed. Due to her dress and exposure to the sun, Chala's body was probably patches of white and brown. No lady ever exposed herself to the sun, and the latest fashions revealed wide expanses of shoulder and breast as well as upper arms, fashions that Chala would soon be wearing. Worried creases formed between Sloan's brows. Something was going to have to be done! And her hands! No lady of quality ever had hands as work worn as Chala's. As Savannah James she would need soft, manicured fingers, buffed to a pampered gleam.

He couldn't bleach her skin, but he *could* even her out so she was one color! He hoped. But where? Their voyage across the Gulf would take only two days, three at the most, if the *Polly* met head winds. There wouldn't be enough time to solve the problem, even if he hung her nude from the halyards. And the beaches were no good, too much danger of being discovered. The coastlines were always under surveillance. . . . The outer islands of Cedar Key. It would be perfect! MacAllister smiled to himself. How many men, he wondered, had dreamed of spending time on a deserted island with a woman only *half* as beautiful as Chala?

Redeemer carried both Sloan and Savannah effortlessly. It had been more than three hours since they'd reached the coast, and Sloan took the animal down near the water's edge, where the hard-packed sand made for easier footing. Savannah laughed as Redeemer sometimes ventured too close to the surf and skidded crazily sideways to avoid soaking both himself and his master. Her laugh was light and musical, and Sloan realized that it was the first time he'd ever heard it. Even the two braves, jogging behind them, seemed to find something humorous in Redeemer's antics. Only Mico, his face like a dark cloud before a storm, soundlessly kept pace.

In the distance, less than a mile away, Sloan spotted the foremasts of the *Polly*. He raised his arm and pointed, calling it to the attention of the Indians. His knees dug into Redeemer's flanks, and he flew ahead of the following Indians along the curving coast to where the *Polly* waited. He was relieved that she hadn't found the need to put out for sea to save herself from Indians or the calvary.

The sea was deep azure blue rippling along the edge of a narrow strip of sand. Here the trees were different, palms with tall, graceful trunks and full heads of long, spikey green leaves, swaying gently in the wind.

"Ahoy, Laddie!" Enwright Culpepper called from the bridge of the *Polly*. Sloan noticed that several of the crew were standing ready and armed with rifles. The *Polly* rode her berth nicely, moored remarkably close to the beach. A larger ship would have had to lay out at least three times that distance.

While they watched, Captain Culpepper was lowered in the *Polly*'s dinghy to come ashore. Chala's eyes were wide with fright as she studied the *Polly*. She'd never seen so large a ship before and the thought of boarding and sailing it across the blue waters of the Gulf was almost more than she could comprehend. More familiar with the Seminole dugout canoes and rafts, for Chala the *Polly* was an awesome sight.

Mico and his two companions seemed to share Savannah's feelings. They stood on the beach, water lapping at their moccasins, arms raised to cut the glare of the sun, staring out at the *Polly*. Quickly, to put them at their ease, Sloan explained how the stores were to be unloaded and stashed at a place of their choice until everything could be transported back to the Seminoles.

Culpepper eyed Mico and the braves with wary glances. He'd never been this close to an Indian before, and for all intents and purposes, he didn't like it now. If he was surprised when MacAllister told him he wanted a week's supply of food for two, blankets and various other necessities, he didn't let it show.

Sand, sun, sky and sea . . . as far as the eye could stretch. Sloan had taken the *Polly*'s second dinghy and loaded her with supplies, taking Chala across the inlet to the out island, last in the chain of Cedar Key.

If she knew what he had in mind for her, she didn't say. She had followed his directives to the letter. If she was frightened about crossing such an expanse of water in a little boat, she was silent. They had hauled onto the flat beach ringed by low growing trees that withstood the constant buffetting winds. Sloan had dropped anchor, burying it deep in the sand.

The first order of the day had been to set about creating a makeshift shelter to spend the nights, safe from rain and winds. At this, Chala was most adept, showing Sloan which branches and palm fronds she wanted to fall beneath the blows of his hand axe. Two hours later a flat-roofed shelter had been created, and although it stood no more than four feet off the ground and demanded that one double over almost in half to enter, it would provide shelter from the elements.

Their evening meal had consisted of prepared food brought along from the *Polly*. Simple fare, it had been sufficient to satisfy their hunger. Exhausted after their long, hard day, they silently crept into the lean-to, falling asleep almost instantly. Sometime during the night, Chala realized that she was again sleeping with her head tucked away on Sloan's shoulder, and listening to the comforting sound of his deep, even breaths as he slept, gave her a sense of welcome security.

When Chala awakened it was to the aroma of fresh brewed coffee and the sizzle of eggs in the heavy black pan. Fresh corn cakes baked on smooth, flat stones near the edge of the cook fire. Rubbing the sleep from her eyes, Chala watched in amazement. Even on the trail, Seminole men ate only food brought from the village and occasionally a rabbit or fish caught in the wilds. Never did they bake bread or make eggs, especially if there was a woman about who would do the cooking for them. She smiled at this unusual treat and momentary respite from her chores. If all white men were as good to women as MacAllister, perhaps the future wasn't so bleak after all.

"C'mon out, sleepyhead. Your breakfast is waiting!" He smiled at her, seeing her surprise that he had manned the cook fire this morning.

The coffee, something Chala never remembered drinking in her life, was bitter until MacAllister added several spoonsful of a white, grainy substance he called sugar to sweeten it. One sip told her she liked the black brew that was so fragrant in the chill of early morning.

As she wiped the last of the egg yolk from her dull tin plate with the last bit of corn cake and popped it into her mouth, she sighed in contentment. Her forest green eyes found his. "What does MacAllister need on this island?" she questioned, turning her face up toward the sun, liking the feel of it on her skin.

Sloan wasn't quite certain how to approach the real reason he'd brought her out here to this desolate place. Now she gave him the perfect opportunity. "I'm glad to see you like the sun, Savannah."

She looked at him questioningly.

Sloan began to stammer and then decided the best way to approach it was directly. But how did he begin? "It's the color of your skin, Savannah . . ."

Immediately, like all women, she bristled, indignantly insulted to be told there was something about her which displeased him. "And what is wrong with the color of my skin? I'm as white as you are! Whiter even! See?" she pulled down the neck of her blouse to display her creamy white shoulder.

"I see. And that's the problem." He tried to keep his voice clinical like a schoolteacher's or a doctor's, but he had seen the swell of her breast and the sweet cleft between its firm roundness and her arm. "In New Orleans, wherever, a lady, a lady of breeding and quality, that is, never exposes herself to the sun. We won't be able to take your tan away, but we can even you out a little, so when you wear fancy ball gowns, your shoulders won't be white and your neck and arms brown. It just won't do, do you understand?"

Chala stood, knocking her plate to the ground with a resolute clatter. "MacAllister is right; it *won't* do. If the white man thinks he can sit me out in the sun to cook my hide, he's wrong. Wrong, wrong, wrong!" She stamped her foot on the ground, punctuating her defiance.

"That's exactly what you're going to do," he told her, his voice holding a thinly veiled menace. Damn, how could one woman be so sweet one minute and so damned ornery the next?

"MacAllister is wrong!" She spit forcefully at his feet. "So much for roasting me like a chicken!" Crossing her arms over her breasts she glared at him, smoky green eyes staring levelly into his.

"No, MacAllister is right!" he told her, judging the distance between them, fully expecting her to run into the patch of woods directly behind them. "Another thing, Savannah, ladies don't spit! No matter what, ladies *never* spit!" In one swift moment he reached out his arm, intending to capture her and bring her to heel. Anticipating his action, Chala jumped backward, nearly tripping. She was just out of his reach and she intended to stay that way. Sloan saw the determination in her eyes, saw the way she brought her lower lip between her teeth and knew, if he didn't get his hands on her right now, he'd have to chase her around the island. He extended his arms, holding them wide apart, shoulders hunched, every muscle ready. He began to circle her, his flinty eyes never leaving hers, making her feel like a trapped rabbit.

Chala was more than his match. She backed up, feeling her way with the heel of her foot. Finding the path clear behind her, she turned and broke off into a run. The trees were just ahead of her. Hair flying, arms pumping, she ran as fast as she could. The loose sand beneath her feet impeded her progress, and she imagined she could almost feel his hot breath on the back of her neck. She had to get away from this crazy white man whom Osceola called brother. If her chief had known what a lunatic he was, he never would have given her to MacAllister. Everyone knew it was death to lie out in the sun! Anybody with half a mind. She had nearly reached the safety of the woods when she felt him grab hold of her skirt, pulling her backward, ripping the fabric from her waist. Backward, Chala sprawled, fingers curled, ready to fight him off. But before she could prepare herself, he was upon her, seizing her wrists in both hands and dragging her out to the beach.

"No, no!" she screamed, pulling against him, trying to use her weight to an advantage. But he was strong, stronger than she would have imagined. A fleeting memory of her wielding the whip against him, hurting him, bringing him to the ground with pain, flew through her thoughts. It would be good to whip him again, and this time she wouldn't stop. She would like to whip him to a bleeding pulp. "No! No!"

"Yes! If I have to strip you naked myself, you're going to go out there and sit in the sun! We're going to even you out if it's the last thing we ever do!"

"MacAllister is crazy! Crazy!"

"Crazier than you know for asking Osceola for you in the first place. If I'd known what I was taking on, I never would have opened my stupid mouth!"

Chala struggled against him, attempting to win her freedom. Her feet kicked out, her body writhed, anything to escape his grip. She wanted to shriek, to cry, to scream, but there was no one to hear her. How could this man, who had held her so gently in the chill of the night, who had comforted her tears, do this to her?

He held her fast against him, feeling her great, heaving breaths shudder throughout her entire body. "Are you going to come willingly, or do I have to drag you out and tie you down? Remember, I'm quite capable of tying you up."

She raised her head, allowing her golden curtain of hair to reveal her face. Her eyes were dark, almost black, with hatred. Her nostrils flared and her lips were drawn into a thin, mean line. Suddenly, she spit, spraying his face with spittle.

Too late he moved to stop her. His fingers gripped her under the chin in a steely, painful hold. "I told you, ladies *never* spit. Only men and spoiled brats!" For the first time since he had tethered her for all the village to jeer, she was frightened of him, truly frightened. He seized her arm, dragging her with him, oblivious to her struggles. Chala gulped. She had gone too far. Enraged him beyond reason. And now he was going to kill her!

Her shrieks were heard only by the birds overhead and by the man dragging her across the sand, back to the cook fire, where sat a twenty-pound barrel of flour. Sitting on the barrel, he pulled her over his lap in one terrifying show of strength. On her way down she caught a glimpse of his face. Stern, square features set in granite line; lips drawn back over his white strong teeth, hair glinting gold, falling rakishly over his sun-darkened forehead. Sinewy cords stood out in his neck like twisted hanks of rope. He was mad, crazy, and he was going to kill her!

Her rump was face up, leaving her helpless. Her fists pounded blows anywhere she could reach: his thighs, his legs, his haunches. At the first slap her eyes widened in surprise. He was hitting her! Spanking her like a child, repeatedly landing his blows to her backside, hurting her.

Her indignant screams resounded in his ears, piercing and shrill. He was ashamed of what he was doing, what she had driven him to, but before she could learn to be a lady, she had to relinquish the ways of a savage. Like a naughty child, this was one lesson she'd learn well.

Disgusted with himself and her, he landed one last healthy smack to her backside and abruptly stood up, toppling her to the ground. Stepping over her, he walked down to the water's edge, not caring if she ran away into the woods, wishing she would. Later, he would send Mico to look for her. Let her belong to Mico; let her stay with him; let her poison him with her cooking!

The Gulf waters lapped against the beach in a soothing, steady rhythm. Sloan stared into the distance, wondering how he had ever come to this: beating a woman! Regardless of how angry she made him, he was ashamed of his actions. Not that he'd ever admit it to her, the little savage. He almost chuckled aloud. Look who was calling whom a savage!

The sound of his name came to him over his right shoulder. There were tears in her voice and he dreaded facing her. After a long moment, after he heard her call him a second time, he steeled himself to look at her. What he saw made his eyes widen in astonishment. She stood there on the sandy beach, hair flying in the gentle breeze, face tear-streaked, full mouth quivering in fright, eyes swollen from crying . . . naked.

"If MacAllister says I am to sit in the sun, then I will sit." Slowly, without any shame or coyness, she spread a blanket over the sand, and placing herself on top of it, stretched full out to catch the golden rays.

Her body was beautiful. The nights she had fallen asleep in his arms and he had felt her warm body pressed close against his had only been a hint of her womanly charms. Breasts, high and full and creamy white, tapered to a slender waist and round, full hips. Her legs were straight, lightly muscled and gracefully turned. Her body was totally feminine and yet athletic with none of the bony angles he had seen on women heavier than she.

Stretched out to full length, she propped herself up on both elbows, studying him, "Is this how MacAllister wants me to roast?"

In spite of himself, he laughed. "Exactly. Not too long now, it's got to be done over a period of days."

"Days?"

"Of course, the sun didn't make your arms and face brown in one day, did it? At least you've had time to pale from last summer and that's in our favor." He fought to keep his eyes away from her body. He mustn't allow himself to be aroused by this little hellcat, he warned himself. He was too involved as it was.

"Stay here, I'll be right back."

Leaving her at the water's edge, he went back to the campsite under the trees. He had to get control of himself! He had to keep reminding himself that he liked to travel light, and Chala, Savannah James, was certainly anything but light. But he couldn't seem to get the vision of her out of his mind. He took the shovel into the woods beyond the rim of trees and began to dig, placing shovelfuls of loamy, black earth into a bucket, and still he thought of her. Right now he was thinking of how he was going to make mud from this dirt and wondering how he was going to smooth it over her brown face, arms, throat and legs without falling completely to pieces. He could imagine how soft and silky her skin would feel and of the gentle curves and hidden delights he would discover as he applied the mud.

Backbreaking work, pulling aside the weeds and underbrush, digging between the tree roots, and still he thought of her. And he still had to go back there!

Passing through camp again, he stopped to pick up one of his extra shirts. One way or another Savannah James was going to drive him completely crazy.

She was positioned on the blanket in the sun just as he had left her. "Here," he threw her the shirt, "drape this over your . . . er . . . cover yourself with this."

"Why? MacAllister said I must sit in the sun. I am sitting."

"Yes, that's right . . . you don't want to burn, do you?"

"That is what I am telling MacAllister! To sit in the sun is to die! Creeks torture their enemies by staking them down in the sun. Soon the mouth is thirsty, the skin burns. . . . Why is MacAllister trying to kill me?" Her temper flared, words fired at him in rapid succession, green eyes blazing.

"MacAllister . . . I mean, I'm not trying to kill you, Savannah, just, er . . . just even you out a little. Here, put this over your breasts and stomach. The skin is so white and tender, I don't want you blistering on me."

She took his shirt, touching the unfamiliar fabric, liking its texture. "What kind of cloth is this, MacAllister? Who weaves this?" Her fingers stroked the shirt in admiration.

"Worms," came the short reply. He was mixing the loamy earth he had dug with seawater.

"Worms?" she laughed, light and melodious and totally different from her shrieking tirades. "Who can make looms so little for worms?" She laughed again, indicating a small space between her fingers.

"No, no," a chuckle escaped him, there was so much Savannah didn't know. So much he could teach her. "Worms spin the thread, like the caterpillar spins his cocoon. Then it is gathered and spun into cloth called silk. If you like it, all of your new clothes when we get to Galveston will be made of silk."

A troubled expression muffled her laugh. "Galveston? Where is this?"

"Out there," he pointed westward with his hand. "It's an island off the coast of Texas."

"Texas, I know," she told him. "An island? Like this?"

"No, no, much bigger." He had mixed the dirt into a thick, sticky mud. As he applied it to her lower arms and neck, he explained that he didn't want these areas to become more tanned than they already were. During this intimacy, he kept up a steady stream of chatter, answering her questions about the ship, *Polly Copinger*, telling her it was the name of Osceola's mother, which seemed to please her greatly. He told her about Annemarie Duval and her house in Galveston, about New Orleans and the lovely dresses she would wear. And the entire time he was sweating profusely, each agonized little droplet reminding him that this woman had him babbling like a schoolboy when all he wanted to do was tell her how beautiful she was. How smooth and soft her skin was, and how he wanted to touch her, really touch her, the way a man touches a woman when he's making love to her. The sun burned into his back, on the top of his head.

"MacAllister is burning . . . do you have a fever?" she asked quietly, and when he lifted his gaze to meet hers, he saw the invitation in her eyes.

She couldn't . . . he told himself. He was imagining it. It was what he *wanted* to see there. . . . "You stay here and in a little while, turn over. But be sure to keep that shirt over that sweet little behind of yours, or you won't be able to sit down for a week!"

"Already I can't sit for a week," she told him, pouting, turning over briefly to show him the red marks his spanking had left there.

"Just sit!" he hollered, running away as though a bee had stung him.

"MacAllister! Where do you go?"

"Fishing! For our dinner!"

He followed his own footsteps back to the camp, irritated by the pounding of his heart that had nothing to do with the short sprint.

Keeping a careful count of the time, he went back down to the water's edge, staying just within shouting distance. Out of the corner of his eye, he saw her turn over, obeying his directions and dropping the shirt over her derriere. Sloan shook his head to clear it. The Seminole believed the body was a beautiful gift of the Spirits and false modesty was definitely frowned upon. Savannah was an example of her upbringing, and she was completely enchanting.

Three fish later, he decided she had had enough sun. Loping over to her blanket, he told her to wash the mud off in the sea while he brought the fish back to the campsite. He missed the sudden dismay in her eyes.

Ten minutes later, she still hadn't returned. Looking down to the beach, he saw her, feet just touching the edge of the lapping surf. She was almost comical with her bare arms and lower legs caked with mud, the exposed portions, except for her torso, pink from the sun. She turned and saw him looking and waved, beckoning him.

"MacAllister, MacAllister!"

"Hell fire!" he swore, not wanting to go near her until she was fully dressed. She called again, waving furiously.

It wasn't until he was almost abreast of her that he saw the fear in her eyes. "What's wrong?" he asked sharply, disliking more and more the effect she was having on him. Mud and all.

"MacAllister wants me to go in the sea? No, no! You want to kill me?"

"You know I don't want to kill you, stop saying that! What's wrong with the sea? Too cold for you? You've been swimming in the Withlacoochee River, haven't you?" His tone was impatient, bordering on hostility.

"The Withlacoochee is a river, so deep," she placed her hand at hip level, drawing his eye to her slender haunches and the triangle of golden fleece only slightly darker than her hair.

"And the sea is only 'so deep,' " he mocked, "if you only go in so far."

"No. MacAllister goes with me or I do not go! I will share his pallet just as I am." Stubbornly, and with a gesture he was becoming more than familiar with, she crossed her arms over her chest.

"All right, I'll go with you. Damn, woman. You're going to drive me crazy yet! I wasn't counting on a cold bath today." He was already barefoot, so he stripped his shirt off, leaving his buckskins.

Savannah cocked an eyebrow. "Everything," she toned authoritatively, wagging a finger at his buckskin breeches. "If it is good enough for me, it is *more* than good enough for MacAllister!"

"Fool woman," he muttered to himself as his britches dropped to the sandy shore. He felt insulted for some reason at her clinical inspection of his naked body. What had she expected, he wondered sourly. He raced to the water and made a headline dive. He came up snorting and sputtering. Christ, it was cold! "All right, get in here and wash off," he muttered.

Tentatively, Savannah waded out till the water was at mid calf. She hung back, obviously reluctant to go any further. Sloan swam closer, and before she knew what was happening, she was under the water. She came up whooping and hollering as if she had been shot. "For God's sake; will you shut that mouth of yours. Every Creek from here to Arkansas will hear you. Now, wash!" he ordered.

Savannah's shrieks continued to pierce his ears as she splashed and floundered in the water. "Are you telling me you can't swim?" he asked in horror as he grabbed her hair and pulled her up for the third time.

"That is what I'm telling you, MacAllister. I cannot swim. I do not like water. If my feet do not touch bottom, I do not go in. It is simple. I will hold on to your shoulders and you wash me."

"Oh, no, none of that." He pulled her slightly in front of him. "Now your feet touch the ground. Wash!"

"Why? Do you think I am ugly? My sisters in Osceola's camp think I am ugly with my green eyes and yellow hair. I look like you, MacAllister."

Sloan groaned. "All right, come here." He clenched his teeth as he briskly washed the caked mud from her body. Christ, a minute ago he was worrying about freezing to death, and now he was hot as one of Che-cho-ter's cook fires. She didn't feel cold either. Why should she, he thought, she had sixty pounds of mud caked on her. But why were her eyes burning the way they were. Like hell it was from the mud. The same thing that was running through his veins was running through hers. Jesus, even Beaunell's eyes had never been this hot.

"C'mon, we have to get out of this water before we freeze to death," he said, dragging her from the water's edge.

Savannah sighed. White men had many problems. She followed him docilely and waited for him to toss a blanket over her shoulders. She wasn't cold. She wiggled a bit on the sand and threw her arms behind her to flex her muscles. Sloan's groan made her frown. Now what was wrong with him?

The night fell, and a spectacular galaxy of stars appeared overhead, so close they thought they could almost reach out to touch them. Dinner had been good, more than good, delicious. Savannah had surprised Sloan with her culinary efforts. After cleaning and scaling his fish, she had impaled them on sticks and roasted them over the fire, cooking them slowly until the flesh was white and delicate, flaking easily. Sloan had brewed the coffee she liked so well while she cooked a skillet of fresh greens she had searched for in the woods. Recognizing sheep's sorrel as one of the vegetables, he made a face but found it delicious.

All through dinner she quizzed him about life amidst "civilization," she called it, with a sour expression on her face that made him laugh.

"You'll soon spoil, little one. And then Lord knows what I'll do with you!" The words he had thoughtlessly uttered brought a scowl to his face. What *would* he do with her? She was his now; Osceola had said that under no circumstances would he accept her back. "Mico!" he uttered aloud. He would give her to Mico, and they could build a chikkee together and have children and grow old together. . . . The thought made him angry, so angry he spilled hot coffee on his hand. "Clumsy . . ."

"What did MacAllister say?" she asked, looking up from her fire.

"I said I was clumsy . . . I spilled coffee on my hand . . ."

Immediately, she was beside him, turning his hand over to see what damage he had done and proclaiming it insignificant. "What did you say about Mico?" she asked, questions forming in her eyes that were now lit by the fire and seemed to glow with a life of their own.

"Nothing. Nothing!" he denied too loudly even for his own ears. "Get back to your cooking. That corn bread smells like it's burning."

Obediently, she turned back to her work, looking up from time to time, trying to puzzle him out.

Later, after a nearly silent meal, Sloan said, "Savannah, you'd better get some sleep. It's been a long day. Tomorrow, you sit in the sun again."

Standing just at the edge of the pallet she expected they would both share, she casually dropped her clothes into a heap near her feet. The indigo-blue blouse and brightly banded skirt was a riot of color against the dull green carpet of wild grass. Slowly, she slipped into the silk shirt he had given her earlier that day. "MacAllister does not mind," she said softly, her eyes meeting his in a statement he dare not interpret. She was his charge; she was in his care. By Seminole law she belonged to him, but that didn't mean he could take advantage of her and then toss her back to Mico as used goods.

"Get to bed, Savannah. I'm going for a walk on the beach." Even as he said it, he realized it was going to be a long night. Every blanket they had was layered on the pallet to keep them warm through the night. The little lean-to they had built was little protection from the too-cool night. And he also realized that, more than anything else, he wanted to crawl between the covers with her, feeling the warmth of her nestled softly in his arms. But he couldn't. Not tonight or any other night, it would seem. Not ever. He just couldn't trust himself! Not after the effect she had had on him while they were swimming, when he had experienced the wet smoothness of her skin and felt her soft, gentle curves slide against his nakedness. She had almost driven him crazy, and he was crazy now for not just taking her, gruff and hard, long and sweet, all through the night, every night until he had had his fill of her. Some niggling thought plagued him, and he feared that once tasting the delights she had to offer he would *never* have enough of her!

"Where does MacAllister go?" she demanded cruelly, freezing him in her icy-cold accusations.

"I told you. Down to the beach." His voice was more intense than he would have liked. Gruff and angry.

"Among my people," she told him snidely, "we cast aside those warriors who will not look upon a woman and share a chikkee with her. MacAllister is man enough to beat a woman but not to lie between her legs!" Her tone was derisive, insulting. "Poor, poor MacAllister. He does not have the juices of a real man!" She stood before him, incongruous in his silk shirt that covered only half her thighs. Her hair was tossed back, her sneer was in full evidence.

Rage and indignation coursed through him. In two steps he was beside her, looking down into her insolent face lit by the fire's flames. "You stupid woman! Can't you see that I'm protecting you?" He savagely seized her shoulders, shaking her with his terrible rage, rocking her head back and forth on the slim column of her neck.

Gaining control of himself, he went to push her away, only to find that she was holding on to his arms, pressing closer to him. Her eyes looked into his and what he read there sent his pulses throbbing, echoing through him. With a sound that resembled a groan and a plea, he brought her to him, crushing his mouth against hers, tasting her, feeling her lips yield to his. When he broke away he saw the flush in her cheeks, the way her lips parted, lifting once again for his kiss.

"What are you doing to me?" he demanded harshly.

"What has MacAllister done to me?" she asked, breathless, husky. "What is this when you put your mouth to mine?"

"A kiss, damn you. A show of affection, of liking you!"

"MacAllister likes me? Seminole do not kiss. Kiss again, damn you," she mimicked him, "I think I like white men's ways. What else do white men do to show aff . . . affection?"

Throaty, deep, her voice resounded in his head. She knew what she was doing to him and he was powerless against her.

"Kiss again, damn you," she repeated, lifting her face to his.

Helpless, hating himself, Sloan brought her closer, aware of the sea's scent in her hair. Her skin smelled of sunshine and delicious womanly scent that was hers alone. Her arms wrapped around his neck, tighter, pulling him with her down to the pallet. She was seducing him! Seducing *him!*

Something inside him rebelled, some part of his manhood and his pride. *He* wanted to the aggressor; *he* wanted to be the one to show her how it could be between a man and a woman. Mico, be damned!

She lay in his arms, fragile as the first flower of spring. He buried his face in her hair, luxuriating in its lushness, surrounding himself in her warmth.

As Sloan gazed at her form in the starlight, all of his pent-up yearnings, feelings he hadn't realized existed until this day, rose to the surface, and he slid down beside her. The feel of her satiny skin, the voluptuous curves beneath the silk shirt she wore, exhilarated him.

Once again his lips clung to hers, and Savannah's head spun as she felt her body come to life beneath his touch. He was gentle, his hands unhurried as he intimately explored her body. His mouth moved against hers and her senses reeled as she strained against him, trying to be closer to him, trying to make them one.

With infinite tenderness, Sloan loved her, realizing that in spite of her wantonness, she was inexperienced. He put a guarded check on the growing feverishness in his loins, waiting for her, patiently arousing her until her passions were as demanding and greedy as his own.

His hands burned her flesh as they traveled the length of her, stopping to caress a pouting breast, a yielding, welcoming thigh. The silken shirt she had put on with such delight was now an irritant and she wished to be rid of it. Hasty hands found the buttons, opening them, exposing her skin to his touch.

His lips left the sweet moistness of her mouth to find the tender place where her throat pulsed and curved into her shoulder. Down, down, his mouth traveled, turning her in his arms, finding and teasing places that brought consummate pleasure and sent waves of desire through her veins. The ivory luster of her breasts beckoned him, their pink rosy crests standing erect and tempting. Her slim waist was a perfect fit for his hands, her firm, velvet haunches accommodating the pressure of his thigh. He placed a long, sensual kiss on the golden triangle her nudity offered, and Savannah gave herself in panting surrender.

As the stars twinkled overhead, his lips touched her body, satisfying his thirst for her, and yet creating in him a hunger deep and raw. The intricate details of her body intoxicated him with their perfection. The supple curve of her thigh, the flatness of her belly, the dimples in her haunches, the lightly muscled length of her legs. But it was always to the warm shadows between her breasts that he returned, imagining that they beckoned him in a silent, provocative appeal.

Savannah's body cried out for him. She offered herself completely to his seeking hands and lips. And Sloan, sensing her passion, furthered his advances, hungry for her boundless beauty and placing his lips on those secret places that held such fascination for him. He indulged in her lusty passion that met and equalled his own.

Beneath his touch her skin glistened with a sheen of desire. She slid her hands down the flat of his belly, eager to know him and satisfy her yearning need. She strove to learn every detail of his flesh, touching his rippling muscular smoothness, feeling the strength beneath. She kissed the hollow near the base of his throat, tasting the saltiness left by the sea. And when she cried his name, it tore from her throat, painful and husky, demanding he put an end to her torment and satisfy the cravings he had instilled in her.

The galaxy of stars overhead became one world, fused together by the white hot heat they created. Together they spun out beyond the moon reveling in the beauty each brought to the other, seeing in each other a small part of themselves. Two golden-haired spirits, one pale as starlight and the other spun honey, came together in their passion, creating an aura of sunlight in the dark, endless night.

CHAPTER SIX

On the first day of the New Year, the *Polly Copinger* set sail for Galveston. If he lived to be a hundred and ninety, he would never forget the expression of fear on Savannah's face when she climbed aboard. Sloan knew she feared this journey. On the out island of the key she had grilled him, often, about sailing out of sight of land, how it felt, things that could go wrong . . . among the Seminoles, she had never sailed anything larger than a canoe or raft and the grassy tree-lined banks were always in sight.

The sun had achieved the required effect on Savannah's skin. She was still a trifle pink, instead of the deep, golden brown needed to even out her skin tone, but there were still at least three days to Galveston and the weather promised to be fair. Inwardly, he groaned. He'd probably have a fight on his hands when he tried to explain that she must not strip down to the buff in front of the crew.

The memories of the past five days flooded back at him like a raging storm tide. Five days in paradise with a sun goddess. Loving her on the coarse yellow sand, where he could see the passion rising in her sultry green eyes; loving her in the night; feeling the heat emanating from her body as if it had captured the golden warmth from the sun and burned with a light of its own.

Enwright Culpepper found himself more than a little curious about his new passenger. Snapping blue eyes peered at the girl from beneath bushy white brows. He'd seen scared rabbits with more nerve than this scrap of a girl in her indigo blouse and wide, multicolored skirt. Her beads and trinkets were obviously Indian in origin, and despite her honey-colored hair and golden skin, he knew she must belong to a tribe of savages. It would be interesting to see if a whole tribe of Indian braves came charging through the woods to rescue this pretty young thing. It never occurred to him that Sloan had done anything less than kidnap her and manage to get away by the skin of his teeth. Or, he had paid for her with the shipload of stores he had brought from New Orleans. Lord amighty, he was getting the best of the bargain, but then Sloan MacAllister always came out on top.

"Does she cook?" Culpepper asked thoughtfully. Anything prepared by a hand other than the one in the galley would be an improvement. Culpepper's one weakness, aside from the liniment he rubbed on his game leg, was food. A man had to be strong, true, but there were certain comforts he owed himself.

"Christ, yes," MacAllister snapped. He shouldn't be taking his annoyance out on his captain, but he was disappointed that he hadn't won Savannah's complete trust, despite the intimacies they'd shared. Didn't she know he wasn't going to allow anything to happen to her? Why, in the name of all that was holy, did she have to look as though she'd just been whipped?

Rubbing his palms together in gleeful expectation of a decent meal, Culpepper pressed, "If it isn't too much to ask, do you think you could get the little lady to rustle up something for the crew? I'm fearing we'll have a mutiny on our hands if they don't get something more to eat than dried beans and fat back. That's all that dog in the galley seems to know. Dried beans and fat back. Enough to make a good man turn mean! Not as if there's no fresh supplies, but the man doesn't seem to know what to do with a chicken or a potato. Pretty little thing like her ought to be able to cook like an angel."

Sloan grinned. "Something like that."

Savannah sat on the hatch of the rope locker, her eyes riveted on the shore. It was true. She was leaving with this strange man Osceola called brother. In spite of the growing feelings between herself and MacAllister, she was frightened, feeling torn away from all she knew and held dear. Even Osceola's promise that she could return when MacAllister's mission was complete, did not cheer her. To what and where would she return? Would there even be Seminole people left to walk and hunt in the Floridas or would they all fall before the soldiers' bullets? She wanted to help her Indian brothers and sisters, but to live among white people, to look like them, talk like them, forget the ways of the Seminole . . . and to pretend to love a strange man she was going to call "uncle," the very man the Indians feared and hated—General Jessup . . . she couldn't do it! It was too much to ask! There was so much she didn't know . . . she would make a grave mistake, she knew it, disappointing Osceola, who had been her protector, father, brother. She must remind herself it was for Osceola and her people that she was making this terrible sacrifice.

Her life had changed irrevocably, the day MacAllister appeared in the village. She had been humiliated by him, had suffered the jeers and insults from her people for insulting the chief's brother. Yet he was a white man and weren't white men the enemy? Why was one better than the others? She hadn't understood. And then to have him see her cry. A stupid, silly mistake. More than the color of her skin and the lightness of her hair, this, most of all, set her apart from her Indian sisters. That, to this day, after all the years of living in the chikkee with Osceola and his family, she could still shed tears. No tear ever stained the dark, soulful eyes of a Seminole woman.

Now she belonged to MacAllister, and she would never make a chikkee with Mico who had wanted to defy their chief and protest. She had convinced the young, handsome brave that it would be useless. The thlacko's word was law.

A slow crimson flush settled in her honey-colored cheeks as she recalled the days and the nights on the island where he toasted her in the sun. Her skin tingled with the memory of late night hours and afternoons when the sun would kiss their hot, passionate bodies. She had always wondered what it would be like to make a chikkee with a man, and now she knew. Many times she had heard some of the Indian women laugh and whisper behind cupped hands, but they would not answer when she questioned them, telling her she would know soon enough when she and Mico made their own chikkee.

MacAllister's touch had been soft, gentle, making her come alive beneath his fingers and his lips. In her heart, she knew Mico would never have been such a lover. Mico was a warrior, and there was no place in his life for gentleness and softness. Nor would Mico have whispered the tender words that could send her pulses racing and create the warm, hungry stirring deep inside her. Now she belonged to MacAllister; she was his woman. A shudder of excitement and apprehension rippled down her spine. She belonged to a white man, but no matter what she had agreed to do, no matter how many nights she lay with him, she would never be a white woman in her mind or her heart. She was a Seminole. To her death she would remain a Seminole.

Through narrowed eyes, she watched MacAllister approach.

"Savannah, the captain would like you to go below and prepare the food. We're all hungry. Come with me and I'll take you to the galley."

"Don't call me that name! Don't ever call me that name again!" she hissed through clenched teeth, suddenly frightened that she was losing something; that things would never be the same for her again. So many years she had strived to be one of her people, an Indian, despite the fact she was white. He wasn't going to take it all away from her now. Not now!

Sloan was staggered by this sudden change in her. For five days on the island, he had called her Savannah, and she had never complained. Angry, he growled through clenched teeth. "It's your name and you'd better get used to hearing it. As soon as we make port in Galveston, it's the only name you're going to hear. I'm not asking you; I'm telling you." For an instant he pitied her. How lonely and frightened she must be with the changes in her life. "Now come with me and prepare some food."

"I'm not hungry. MacAllister said nothing about cooking on this ship. Do it yourself!" she spat.

"I didn't ask if *you* were hungry. I said I was and so are the crew." Sloan took a deep breath. "I'm responsible for this ship and the men on it. I pay their wages and they expect to be fed. I don't want to hear another word out of you. If you persist in defying me, I'll turn you over my knee and whack the bejesus out of your backside. I can do it, remember?"

"You wouldn't!" Savannah said, steadily and evenly. "MacAllister is supposed to be civilized and I'm supposed to be the savage!"

Sloan was taken back momentarily. "Oh, wouldn't I? Don't try

me, Savannah. Come to the galley with me. I meant it about pad-
dling you, and I won't tell you something twice!" He reached out a
long arm and the moment he grasped her wrist, she tightened it,
pulling forward. Sloan had expected some resistance, but not this
display of strength. She was tough as rawhide and twice as rigid.
He lost his balance on the pitching deck and literally sailed past
her. Squeals of delighted laugher sounded in his ears.

Enwright Culpepper's deep-bellied guffaw made Sloan's
breathing difficult. Bitch! Little she-lion!

"Madame," Enwright Culpepper addressed Savannah, bowing
from the waist. "It is a pure pleasure to have your beauty aboard
this clumsy ship. Excuse my employer for his rudeness; he's not
experienced when ladies are involved. Insensitive, if you know
what I mean. Surly and crude, not to mention crass and unrefined.
A lady such as yourself deserves much more. Allow me to escort
you to the galley, where we do our cooking. While I'm certain
you're not used to cooking for the scurvy likes of us, as a special
favor to me, I wonder if you mightn't prepare a little something
just to take the edge off our appetites? You don't necessarily have
to make enough for Mr. MacAllister. After the way he's insulted
you, you needn't be generous."

Sloan watched in stunned amazement as Savannah smiled
serenely and allowed her hand to be kissed. He swallowed, not
believing his eyes when she fluttered her long lashes and then lowered them coquettishly. Beaunell wasn't as adept at flirting, nor
Annemarie. As the twosome walked away leaving him dumbfounded, he heard Culpepper say in his soft, Scottish burr, "Dear
lady, you're quite the most lovely creature I've seen in a long time.
But I'm afraid I haven't learned your name. What is it?"

"Savannah James," she told him. She heard, rather than saw,
MacAllister's fist hit the *Polly*'s rail.

It was early twilight three days later when Captain Enwright
Culpepper ordered the anchor dropped in the Galveston Harbor.
He liked Galveston and a certain widow lady who had a mind of
her own. A man needed a woman and Maeve Carpenter was one
hell of a woman. Hell, when she got done with him, even his game
leg had a new spring to its step. Now, if MacAllister would take
Miss Savannah James and move on into town, Culpepper could

see to his own needs. The captain was always the last to leave the ship. Tonight, he wished he could change the rules a little. He felt an urgency he hadn't felt in months.

MacAllister didn't disappoint him. The minute the dark curtain of night dropped completely, he was standing waiting for the ship's plank to be lowered. He was as antsy as Culpepper and a little apprehensive about the reception he would receive from Annemarie. Beaunell he refused to think about altogether. Together they waited on the wharf for Redeemer to be led down by one of the hands. They would ride directly to Annemarie's, and he would stable the horse after he made the final arrangements. He was leaving nothing to chance. With Redeemer tied to the hitching post out front he could make a speedy exit if Annemarie took it in her head to show the pair of them the door, refusing to have anything to do with his plan.

Aunt Jenny herself opened the door. Her squeal of delight was quickly stifled when she set dark, liquid eyes on Savannah. For the first time in her life she was at a loss for words. A new working girl? Sloan's woman? God have mercy on us, she prayed silently. Should she let them in the front door or order them around the back? MacAllister was a favorite customer and he tipped heavily. On top of that he was Miss Annemarie's very special friend. Better to invite them in and ask questions later. The door opened wider. Sloan pushed a stiff-backed Savannah into the bright glare of the foyer. He was amused as she looked around the colorful room. There was awe in the bottle-green eyes. Jesus, if the foyer awed her, wait till she saw Annemarie's ruffles and bows in her private quarters.

He admitted to himself that he would rather take a trip into a lion's den than go through with the upcoming interview with Annemarie and Savannah's unpredictable behavior. He danced nervously behind Aunt Jenny, shoving and pushing Savannah every step of the way.

Annemarie laid down her newspaper, a smile of pleasure on her features as she rose to greet the tall, fair-haired man who had been a good friend all these years. Her smile froze as Savannah skidded to a stop just inches from her. Annemarie's milk-white hands flew to her throat to stifle a gasp. Her eyes questioned Sloan.

"I was in the neighborhood," he said flippantly. "Annemarie, I need some help and you're the only one I could think of to help me." Quickly, he introduced Savannah and explained what he wanted, ending with, "A month, sooner if you can do it. What do you think, Annemarie?"

"A month!" Annemarie's voice was almost shrill, but she caught it just in time and lowered her tone. No lady ever raised her voice except perhaps in the bedroom. "Try a year, maybe two," she said crisply. "Just how savage is she?"

"You'll know soon enough. Look, I don't want a miracle. Polish her up, smooth over the rough edges, teach her how to eat and how to talk. She speaks English, almost perfectly, but it has to be smoothed out so it sounds natural."

"Just like that? I thought you said you didn't expect a miracle."

"You can do it, Annemarie. All you're going to need is a lot of patience and a strong whip. You have to let her know you're the boss," he said mockingly, knowing Savannah was listening with rapt attention to every word.

"And while I'm doing all this, where are you going to be?" Annemarie asked sourly.

"I'm going to register at the hotel. I'll be around to check on her progress. I don't want to interfere by stopping in all the time, and besides, I'm not quite certain how she feels about me."

"If you want to know, just ask me," Annemarie said grimly as she stared into green, hate-filled eyes.

"Then it's settled, you'll do it?"

"I'll try, Sloan. You'll owe me for this one."

"I wouldn't have it any other way. You take care of her and I'll go upstairs and have a bath myself." Turning to Savannah, his voice was deliberately cold and hard, "You're to do as Annemarie says. Remember your promise to Osceola, so don't think about running away because there's nowhere for you to go. Do you understand? There's no way to get back to Florida unless I take you." In the face of her blank expression, he pressed further. "One word of warning. It's frowned upon for a white woman to live with Indians. If you so much as make a move without Annemarie's approval, you could be thrown into prison. You'll never see the Seminoles again." He knew he was exaggerating the situation but could not think of anything else that would force Savannah's obedience.

He bent down with the intention of kissing her lightly on the cheek. She lunged with both hands, trying to bring her nails down his face and neck. A high-pitched shriek split the serenity of Annemarie's sitting room. One moccasined foot lashed out, hitting him squarely in the midsection. Every nerve in Savannah's body was stretched taut and screaming. How could he? How could he treat her this way, especially after what they'd shared on the island? He was making a fool of her in front of this woman! Tears of rage filled her eyes and she willed them not to spill onto her cheeks. She half suspected this was retribution for the way she had behaved aboard the *Polly Copinger*, but it wasn't fair. It just wasn't fair! He wouldn't get away with this, not if she could help it.

"She has a bit of a temper," Sloan said, gasping for breath. "I know I can depend on you to control it. I think you should call Aunt Jenny or some of the servants to help you. Sometimes you have to tie her up. Bath time is probably one of those times," he smirked mockingly in the face of Savannah's fury. "Do it now, Annemarie, before I leave." He whispered softly, "If she really gets bad, threaten to pull her teeth, every one of them. Sometimes that works."

Annemarie looked doubtful, almost fearful. "Sloan, I don't know if this is such a good idea. What I mean is, I can't keep this child tied up all the time."

"Why not?" Sloan barked, carefully keeping his eye on Savannah. "The first chance she gets she'll tie you and slit your throat, and, Annemarie, if there's one thing I've always admired about you, it's your lily white throat."

Casually, he dropped a sheaf of bills on the endtable. "Be sure you get her some proper clothing. She doesn't even wear bloomers," he said in an amused tone. "A parasol too, but make sure she understands it isn't to be used as a weapon." Seeing the doubtful eyes, Sloan went on. "Annemarie, look upon this as the ultimate challenge. I'm depending on you. You have to do this for me. I'll be forever in your debt."

"All right," Annemarie said firmly. She tinkled a small bell and three husky-looking Negresses came into the room. Within minutes Savannah had her hands tied behind her back and her ankles neatly bound. Sloan saw the shriek that was about to erupt and stuffed his handkerchief into her mouth. "I'll check on you later," he said breathlessly as he sprinted from the room.

Once the door to Annemarie's quarters closed, Sloan heaved a mighty sigh of relief. He took the circular staircase two steps at a time, stopping by the foyer to pick up his roll of fresh clothing. He was anxious for a warm, soothing bath and a clean shave. Aunt Jenny met him, bath sheet in hand and a fresh bar of soap. "I been waitin' for you, Mastah Sloan. Now you shuck those evil-smelling clothes and hop right in this tub."

"Jenny, go downstairs and help Annemarie. She needs you. I can see to my bath myself."

Jenny grinned toothily. "No, siree, my place is here with you to scrub you down. Now you'll get in that water and hush. Miz Beaunell don' want a no account, smelly man 'tween her pretty sheets."

"Annemarie needs you, Aunt Jenny. If you don't go, I'm going to drag you back down the hall and show you what us no account white men do to women who don't mind their manners." He advanced a step and then two, leering seductively at Jenny. Frightened that he might mean what he said, the old woman turned and fled the room muttering that all she ever got was promises and more promises.

Sloan grinned as he stepped out of the deerskin boots and buckskin britches. His shirt fell in a heap. He stepped into the round tub and immediately relaxed in the steamy wetness. A man could fall asleep in this comfort, he told himself. As he sank lower and lower into the soapy water, he realized how tense he was. Was he waiting for a crash, a scream? The sound of a bullet meaning Annemarie couldn't cope and had shot Savannah? The thought brought perspiration to his brow.

He had hated tying her up, hated the betrayed look he read in her eyes, but she had given him no other choice. Osceola came first. If she wouldn't voluntarily help, then it would be involuntarily. Circumstances being what they were, he had to make the decisions for both of them. The first time he had tied her it was different. She had been nothing to him, just a girl with exceptionally bad manners. Now it was different. He knew her, had been intimate with her, had loved her body and touched her soul. He also knew if he hadn't tied her, Savannah would have run from Annemarie, and that gracious lady would not have allowed her to return for any reason, any bribe. Still, his conscience pricked him because of his cruelty. Annemarie, with her soft manner and soothing voice, might be able to make it right for the frightened Savannah. And it was more fright than hostility, Sloan was certain of it.

As the tenseness began to drain from his body, Sloan allowed his mind to wander to the nights on the island and how Savannah had felt in his arms. She had trusted him, for a short while at least. Even on the ship her behavior had been above reproach, thanks to Captain Culpepper. She had been frightened then also, on the strange ship, crossing vast waters, traveling to a strange place. She was out of her element. Little wonder she had fought back. He would have done the same thing if the Creeks had managed to get hold of him. Old Jeb MacAllister had always warned him never to push a dog against a wall, because when the dog's done looking at you, he wasn't going to just stand there, he was going to get himself away from that wall somehow. Now, this evening, he had pushed Savannah against a stone wall. One way or another she was going to get away. It might take her a while, but somehow she would manage to get back to the Seminole.

He was feeling worse by the minute for his shoddy treatment of the frightened girl when the door opened a crack and then widened. Beaunell, in a rich creation of feathers and lace and incredibly high-heeled slippers, pranced into the room. "I knew you were here," she breathed sultrily.

Sloan groaned silently. The last thing he needed was Beaunell. It had been his intention to spend the night aboard his ship and set up temporary headquarters at the hotel the following morning. Beaunell had not been in his plans at all!

"Here, let me wash your back," she said, reaching for the brush Aunt Jenny had laid on the side of the tub. "I've thought of nothing else but you since you left my bed on your last visit."

"I already used the brush," Sloan lied. "Listen, Beaunell, I can't . . ." The sounds of a crash and a high-pitched shriek exploded through the open door. "What the hell was that?" He was about to stand up and then thought better of the idea.

Beaunell was frowning. If there was one thing Annemarie insisted upon, it was quiet. Peace and quiet. Every sound was muffled, even the clink and clatter of silver had a muted sound. Again, the high-pitched wail ricocheted up the stairs. Sloan's mind raced. He didn't want Beaunell to go downstairs to see what was going on. If Beaunell and Savannah locked eyes and tongues, it would be a more violent confrontation than the war between Jessup and the Seminoles. When at last they did meet, which was inevitable, he didn't mean to be within shouting distance. He smirked, knowing he was the prize for the winner. "Pay no attention, Beau. I think Annemarie hired a new cook who breaks crystal. Tell me," he said, speaking louder than usual, "where is that beautiful dressing gown you wore the last time I was here? What pretties did you buy yourself with the money I left you?"

Beaunell answered automatically, her ears trained on the doorway. Something was going on. Something Sloan didn't want her to know about. "I didn't hear anything about a new cook. What happened to Dulcie? She's been with Annemarie forever."

Sloan shrugged. "I don't keep track of women's business. I'd like to keep talking to you, honey, but I have to get back to the ship."

Beaunell's eyes widened and her jaw dropped. "Back to the ship? You mean you aren't coming to my room, to my bed?" she asked stupidly, hardly believing her ears.

"Business, Beau, strictly business. I'll be back when I have time."

"You'll be back when you have time!" she parroted his words.

"Do you mind leaving and closing the door? It's not that I'm modest, but there are some things a man likes to do in private. I'll look in on you soon. Nice of you to stop by." He was babbling like an idiot. Time to get out of here before she went downstairs. He had to beat her to Annemarie. How in the hell had he managed to disregard Beaunell's jealousy?

"If that's how you feel about it, then I'll leave," Beaunell pouted haughtily, her delicate nostrils flaring angrily.

Now he'd gone and done it! He didn't know which was worse—Savannah's screeching or this one's pique. Whatever, he wasn't going to stay around long enough to find out.

Sloan grimaced. He thought his teeth shook loose with the slamming of the bathroom door.

Within minutes he was dried and dressed in fresh clothes and racing down the stairs to Annemarie's apartments. He rapped quietly. Annemarie herself let him in. "Shhh," she said, laying a finger to her lips. "We got her to sleep. I gave her a mild sleeping draught, but the poor thing was exhausted, half scared out of her wits. We bathed her and washed her hair and gave her something pretty to wear. Come see for yourself." Sloan's eyes widened. Sleeping in Annemarie's high tester bed was a tiny figure dressed in a dimity nightdress with a delicate ruffle around the neck. Golden hair fanned the pillow. His eyes traveled downward to her bound wrists and ankles. The sight tore at his heart.

"She's beautiful, Sloan. Quite the most beautiful creature I've ever seen. I just hope this works and I can help you."

"Keep Beaunell out of here and don't let her find out about Savannah if you can help it. She came into the bathroom and heard the noise and the screams. She's a mite put out with me now and could cause a lot of trouble if she had a mind to. I'm going back to the ship and will check in tomorrow. Try to keep it a secret at least for a few days. Beau's jealous rages are something neither of us needs at the moment."

Annemarie's eyes rolled back in her head as she envisioned the forthcoming days. "I'll do my best," she whispered fearfully. Lord, all she had ever wanted, all she had ever asked for, was peace and quiet. Sloan was doing his best to see she didn't get it.

The *Polly Copinger* pitched to and fro in the gentle swell of the harbor water, lulling Sloan into a fitful sleep. He dreamed and then woke throughout the night. Toward dawn he fell into an agonized sleep, dreaming he was chasing Osceola through the woods back on the old farm. At the end of the dim tunnel created by the dense hickory trees stood Chala, Wild Honey. There was a winsome, dutiful smile on her lovely face as she watched Osceola take a slight lead in the boyhood chase. But it was to Sloan that she held out her arms, and when both boys crossed the invisible boundary at the same split second, she laughed, a rich, wonderful sound of happiness that seemed to blend and melt with the golden sunshine of late afternoon.

Sloan thrashed about on the narrow bunk as his dreams continued to torment him. The dream was the past, the present and the future. Chala was spitting and snarling, refusing to board the *Polly Copinger*. Thomas Jessup was racing along the shoreline atop a surefooted steed, shouting obscenities, his Winchester rifle aimed at Sloan's midsection. Annemarie, her parasol in front of her, was standing next to Osceola, who was braving the situation out with a stony look and his own rifle at his side. It wasn't till Jessup got within close eye range that Savannah pointed for Sloan to see what she was shrieking about. Seated behind Jessup and clinging to him for dear life was Beaunell in her scarlet wrapper, bare legs swinging wildly against the horse's flanks. "Help me, MacAllister," Savannah begged, clinging to him. "Help me and I'll do anything you want! Anything . . . anything . . . anything!"

Sloan woke, his body drenched in perspiration. The dream had been so real he could almost feel Beaunell next to him, breathing fire. He had heard, no doubt from Annemarie, that there was no hell like that of a woman scorned. And in his dream Beaunell was definitely scorned. Christ Almighty, how could he have forgotten Beaunell? Something was going to have to be done. Maybe Annemarie could send her away. A bogus trip, anything to get her out of Galveston. His gut churned. He knew it was too late. He also knew by the time he got to Annemarie's house Beaunell would be fully apprised of the situation through no fault of Annemarie's. Beaunell was an industrious young woman. One way or another she would have found Savannah by now and was probably plotting some dastardly act of jealous revenge, not only for the poor, unsuspecting Savannah, but for himself as well.

The sun was directly overhead when Enwright Culpepper tottered up the gangplank. Sloan suppressed a grin. Wherever he had been, the old salt had had a time for himself. "My head feels like a bloody powder keg," the captain complained. "I'll be no good to ye this day, Laddie. Perhaps if some of the hair of the dog that bit me were available, I might be able to see your handsome features," he said slyly.

"That I can arrange," Sloan grinned as he fetched a bottle from the cabin. As he handed over the bottle, he watched the captain closely. The damage he was suffering wasn't from the drink. "She must be one hell of a woman," he chortled.

Bleary red eyes blinked. "That she is, Laddie. The good Lord don't make them like Maeve anymore. She's the only woman I've thought of taking for a bride. She loves me," he ended stupidly. "Can ye be believing that, Laddie?"

"I've led a precarious life, Enwright, as you well know. I don't think anyone or anything can surprise me. However, you've come this far without taking a bride, so why don't you give it some more serious thought. I want to talk to you about something that might put a crimp in your plans, so listen to me," Sloan said, taking a second breath. If there was one thing Enwright Culpepper enjoyed it was danger and adventure, and not necessarily in that order.

"Speak up, Laddie, there's nothing wrong with my hearing. It's my nether regions that are feeling pain."

"This is serious business. My brother, Osceola, needs help. I want you to take the *Polly Copinger* back to Cedar Key with as many supplies as we can load aboard. You'll have to wait till one of his men spots the ship, though. You cannot allow anyone other than Osceola's men to take possession. It's dangerous; you may be fired upon by the Creeks or Jessup's men. Do you think you can handle it?"

"Aye, Laddie, I kin handle it, but there's one small problem. One Indian looks like another. How will I know your brother's men from those ornery bastards, the Creeks."

"Christ, Culpepper, where the hell have you been? The Seminole wears yellow and red war paint, the same colors as Osceola's standard. I'm going into town now to order supplies. You're to take mules just the way you did the last time. I'll be back late this afternoon, and I want you to set sail with the tide. Will you do it?" Sloan hoped his voice wasn't as anxious as he felt. Of late, he had been putting all of his eggs in one basket, something he usually avoided doing.

Culpepper shrugged. "Dying never bothered me, Laddie, it's the way of dying that gets to my innards. If I had my druthers, I'd just as soon go by an Indian's hand than a woman's, if ye know what I mean."

Sloan suddenly developed a sensitive spot between his shoulder blades. He knew exactly what Culpepper was talking about. Without another word Sloan was down the gangplank and swinging himself onto Redeemer's saddle. Culpepper watched the young man with a mixture of envy and tiredness. Two more swigs from the brandy bottle made his spirits rise considerably. He set about to tidy his ship much the way an old woman with no one left to care for would do. It was spit and polish from stem to stern, but that didn't stop him from spitting on his handkerchief and rubbing at some of the brass here and there. He was home. He belonged, along with his sixty-four years, aboard ship. Just the thought of making the change to a landlubber set his nerve ends to twanging. A brief moment of insanity. Thank heaven he had the good sense to head back for the ship before Maeve worked more of her seductive magic on him. Thank heaven for young MacAllister and his Indians. A man, by God, needed a purpose in life. Lollygagging around with the voluptuous likes of Maeve couldn't be taken seriously. Not today, anyway. A week from today, a month from today, might tell a different story. There was a decided spring to his step as he made his way to the helm.

Annemarie walked softly down the carpeted hall to the room she had assigned to Savannah. It wasn't even nine o'clock in the morning and already she was up and dressed. Muttering beneath her breath, she swore she should have told Sloan to take his "little problem" elsewhere. As a rule, Annemarie kept late hours because of the business, and her clients expected to see her cheerful and entertaining. If she kept these hours, all they would see was a woman with dark circles under her eyes who found it difficult not to yawn with exhaustion.

Aunt Jenny was already with Savannah when Annemarie entered the femininely decorated bedroom. The morning light, with which Annemarie was so unfamiliar, was streaming in the lace-curtained window illuminating the cherry wood furniture and rose-colored hangings. Savannah was seated in front of the dressing table, quietly allowing Aunt Jenny to brush her hair. The girl did not acknowledge her hostess's presence but merely stared toward the window with a trapped look in her eyes.

"Sure is a pretty child," Aunt Jenny said enthusiastically. Not for the first time Annemarie wondered where the old woman got her energy. She kept hours almost as late as her employer and always seemed to be up and about at the crack of dawn.

"Aunt Jenny, I don't know how you do it," Annemarie said.

Mistaking her meaning, Aunt Jenny smiled a toothy grin. "I jus' take dis brush and pull it through like this. This gal's got some head o' hair. Jes look how long and silky it is and watch the way it wants to curl around my fingers."

Scrutinizing Aunt Jenny's demonstration, Annemarie said, "Yes. Lovely. Now put it up for her. Our job is to make her into a lady, and we might as well start with making her look like one. Something simple, Aunt Jenny, something she can learn to do for herself." Turning to the clothes press, Annemarie withdrew a morning wrapper of pale blue trimmed with ecru lace and satin bows. Sighing, she remembered the girl hadn't even come equipped with her own underwear. She sized her up and thought that some of Beaunell's things might fit her until some could be made for her.

"Aunt Jenny, do you think you can get hold of some of Beaunell's lingerie without going into her room to explain why you want it?"

"Yes, ma'am. There's a whole stack of Miz Beau's laundry downstairs. I wuz gonna bring it to her after she woke up."

"Beau's a flighty thing. She won't miss a few garments. Go and get them for me, please. I'll finish dressing Miss Savannah's hair."

As Aunt Jenny left the room, Annemarie picked up the brush, finding that the old Negress hadn't overstated the luxuriousness of Savannah's hair. "Lovely," Annemarie complimented. Still there was no reaction from the girl, whose sullen eyes were focused on the window. It was a rare woman who could sit in front of a mirror and look at anything besides herself. Trying another tack to get Savannah's attention, she said offhandedly, "I'll bet Sloan loves to run his fingers through your hair. Has he told you how beautiful it is?"

Immediately, Savannah glanced into the mirror, looking back at Annemarie. Her green eyes had come to life at the mention of Sloan's name and a fragile pink blush brightened her cheeks. "He tells me I have captured the sunlight." After a moment, "Where is MacAllister? Why does he not come? How long will he leave me here?"

There was something pitiful about the child that wrung Annemarie's heart. That blasted rogue, MacAllister, had no right to leave her with this frightened child whose very act of bravado was pathetic.

"Sloan had business in town. I've no doubt he'll come to see you soon. He was very worried about you, Savannah. He wants you to be happy, but he also needs your help. You will help him, won't you. You will help Osceola?"

Savannah turned to look up at Annemarie. "I promised I would help. Am I fighting? Are my hands tied? Am I gagged?" Quick tears glistened on her dark, thick fringe of lashes.

Putting down the brush, Annemarie sat beside Savannah on the dressing bench. Instinctively, her arms went around the child, holding her and giving comfort and reassurance. "Poor kitten," Annemarie crooned, "thrown out in this big, cruel world. I want to be your friend, Savannah. I want to help you learn to behave like a white woman. You have a very important task ahead of you, and Sloan wants you to be prepared. For your sake. For your safety. Did you know he came into your room last night after you fell asleep? He wanted to be certain you were all right. He wouldn't have brought you here to me if he didn't think I would take care of you."

Savannah stiffened, refusing to yield to the gentle pressure of Annemarie's embrace. "You know my MacAllister too much. Too . . ."

"Too 'well,' is the word you're looking for, child. Yes, I've known him for several years now, and he's always proved himself to be my friend. Friends help one another. That's why I'm helping him now. But rest your heart, child. MacAllister does not sleep in my bed, if that's what's peeving you, and he never has. A man and a woman can be friends."

Savannah instantly relaxed. Even though she had lived in a society where polygamy was the rule rather than the exception, she couldn't bear the thought of sharing MacAllister with another woman. Any other woman, even a Seminole woman! Annemarie's tone was soft, reassuring, and Savannah believed she really wanted to be her friend.

"Now, little one, if you'll try to learn quickly, you'll be back with Sloan in no time. And think of how proud you'll make him. Watch me while I dress your hair, so you can do it for yourself. Something simple and elegant," Annemarie told her, already standing behind Savannah with the brush in her hand. Perhaps if she could keep up a steady chatter, Savannah would be too preoccupied to think about her fears. Even as she spoke, Annemarie thought about Beaunell Gentry and how she was going to accept Sloan's interest in this girl. Sighing, Annemarie stroked the bristles through the long golden hair. That was something Sloan himself was going to have to worry about. For now, she had the education of Savannah James to accomplish.

In the space of one short hour Savannah had made long strides in her education to be a lady. To Annemarie's delight, Savannah remembered many things her mother had taught her and what she was not taught she had seen Caroline do herself. This, added to the fact that Savannah was totally female and enjoyed being pampered, made the lessons go surprisingly well.

Savannah learned the easy method of bringing her thick, honeyed hair to the top of her head and winding it into a smooth coronet. She liked the scented water Aunt Jenny had brought in a basin and she washed with the perfumed soap from Annemarie's own supply sent from Paris. Savannah already appreciated the feel of silk against her skin, and with no difficulty, Aunt Jenny and Annemarie taught her how to carefully roll expensive silk stockings up her long, pretty legs and fasten them with frilly garters. Shoes were going to be a problem, Annemarie realized, but they would jump that hurdle later. Perhaps Dolores, another of Annemarie's girls, would have a pair to fit her. The first resistance displayed by Savannah was when Aunt Jenny produced a lightly boned corset that would squeeze Savannah's figure into the fashionable style of the day, which demanded an incredibly tiny waist, rounded hips and a high, voluptuous bosom.

Dressed in chemisette and ruffled pantalettes, Savannah stood while Aunt Jenny placed the white satin corset with its long laces under her breasts and tied it at the back. It was only as she began to tighten the laces that were crisscrossed through a long series of eyelets that Savannah complained. "No!" she gasped. "What are you doing, Aunt Jenny? You're killing me!"

"Not too tight, Jenny," Annemarie snapped the order, realizing that Savannah's ribs were unused to being constricted in corsets and would offer resistance. "We don't want to crack her ribs, Jenny. She's not used to being strapped into one of these things like the rest of us. Thank heavens she has a naturally small waist, and we can camouflage it by making her skirts wider and adding a little more width in the shoulders. Besides, no one is going to look at her waistline once they see that spectacular face of hers."

"Yes, Ma'am," Aunt Jenny intoned, mentally disagreeing with her employer and biting her lower lip as she strained at the laces. "We gots to make it as tight as she can stand it, otherwise she ain't gonna walk and sit like the rest o' you white ladies." Jenny had a point, Annemarie conceded, and sympathized with Savannah, whose complexion was turning a decided shade of blue from lack of air.

"Loosen it, Jenny. She'll need time to get used to it."

"Why do I need this . . . this . . . thing? MacAllister likes to touch *me*, not a lot of clothes!" Savannah gasped with relief as Jenny loosened the corset.

"The idea is not for him to touch you, Savannah, but to make him *want* to touch you," Annemarie instructed. She could see that her logic was completely lost on her protégé. Savannah's hands were braced on the bedpost, and Annemarie noticed the rough skin and unkempt nails. Sighing, she told Jenny that a manicure was in order and said it should be accomplished while she gave the girl a few lessons in behavior. Manners were most important at the dinner table and she decided that's where she would start. "Jenny, ring for Odile in the kitchen and have her bring my breakfast in here."

"You nevah eats breakfast before two in the aftahnoon. . . ."

"Just do as I say, Jenny. If I'm going to keep these hours, I'll also need to keep up my strength."

Seated across a narrow table from Aunt Jenny, who clicked her tongue in dismay as she performed a manicure, Savannah devoted her attention to Annemarie, who had assembled a small table and a chair nearby and was demonstrating proper table manners. Enjoying this demonstration immensely, Savannah listened carefully to what her tutor was saying.

"The way a woman comports herself at the dining table must be as pleasant and agreeable to her companions as the meal itself. A lady sits with her back perpendicular to the seat and never rests back against it. Instead, her back must be slightly at a distance from the back of the chair. Her feet are placed so"—Annemarie lifted her skirts and petticoats for Savannah's benefit—"flat on the floor and touching lightly at the ankles. One hand in the lap, so, the other gracefully on the table."

Savannah nodded, knowing this was something she could easily accomplish. Being a lady seemed to be filled with silly rules and all she needed to do was remember them. MacAllister would sing her praises!

"Now, pay attention, Savannah, I'm going to show you how to unfold your napkin." At Savannah's quizzical glance, she sighed.

"This!" she said, holding a square of linen. "It is used to delicately wipe the mouth when eating." Savannah glanced at the back of her own hand, which, until now, had served the purpose just as well and was easier to wash.

"The unfolding of the napkin," Annemarie told her, "should be in a manner which reflects breeding and taste. A woman who picks up the napkin between her thumb and forefinger and then shakes it open shows she lacks principle and a certain looseness of character."

Aunt Jenny shook her head and laughed. "Miz Annemarie is saying you don't wanna act like no whore and go wavin' your napkin around."

"What's a whore . . . ?"

"Ahem!" Annemarie cleared her throat to caution Aunt Jenny. "A woman of breeding and taste," she raised her tone to override Savannah's question, "discreetly removes the folded napkin to her lap, where she unfolds it and leaves it doubled lengthwise across her lap."

"But my mouth is up here," Savannah pointed, "not between my knees."

"Just watch and listen and learn." Annoyance riddled Annemarie's voice. "Most of these things are only common sense, and the rest make no sense at all. Nevertheless, it will be expected of you if you're to become a lady."

Chastised, Savannah gave her full attention.

"Now, when eating. A lady cuts all pieces of food into tiny morsels, which she decorously raises to her mouth. She never bites, chews or crunches her food but nibbles noiselessly and daintily." Cutting into her already cold egg, Annemarie put the morsel into her mouth and demonstrated.

"I sure am glad I ain't never had to be no lady," Aunt Jenny said, giving special attention to buffing Savannah's nails with a grainy pink paste. "Gals like me always goes on picnics."

"Picnics! Good thought, Jenny," Annemarie exclaimed, thoroughly entrenched in her lessons. "Now, Savannah, it's possible that you may be invited to a picnic. That's where food is packed and taken outside to be eaten. Usually, you'll be required to sit on a blanket . . ."

"This I know how to do!" Savannah said confidently.

Annemarie looked doubtful. "Well, I'd better show you anyway." Snatching a cover from the bed. Annemarie spread it on the carpet. "When you sit on a blanket for a picnic, it's very important that you behave modestly. Do you know what modesty is?" Savannah gazed at her blankly. "No. It's not calling attention to yourself, especially not to your body. Here, I'll show you. First, you accept the support of your escort, that's the gentleman you'll be with. Aunt Jenny, come here. Let's do this right."

"No siree, Miz Annemarie, you is on your own! When I goes to a picnic, it's to enjoy myself. Ain't none of them fancy modesties gonna spoil my good time."

Exasperated, Annemarie continued. "Let's pretend there's a gentleman here with me, and he's going to help me get down to the blanket. See?"

Chewing on the inside of her lip. Savannah remarked, "Only old women need help. Are you old, Annemarie? I am not old! I can get down to the blanket myself."

"That's because you ain't tried it while you're wearin' that corset," Aunt Jenny interjected. "Just wait till I pull them laces another inch or two. You're gonna need all the help you can get!"

"Quiet. Both of you. Now watch. First, you accept the support of your escort by lightly laying your hand upon his arm and slowly bend your knees. See? It should be light and graceful, like a leaf falling from a tree. Now, once you're down here, you must turn your legs to the side and, above all, keep them under your skirts. Sit with your back straight and keep your hands in your lap. Never, never, never should you lean or slouch. And never, ever raise your arms above your head!" Annemarie lifted her arms to show what a lady must never, ever do. Her heel caught in the hem of her skirt and, losing her balance, she toppled backward.

Savannah and Aunt Jenny broke into a shrieking laughter as Annemarie shot them lethal looks.

"An' nevah, nevah, child, sprawl with your legs open and your back flat on the ground. *That's* the difference between a lady and a whore!"

Comprehension dawned on Savannah's face as she broke into peals of laughter.

Savannah lay across her high four-poster bed, the light from the oil lamp falling across the covers. Though it was only a few hours past dark, Annemarie had sent her to her room, telling her that it had been a very long day and she needed her rest. Savannah was exhilarated rather than exhausted. So many things a lady had to know. So much yet to learn. And all of it, Annemarie had promised, she *would* learn.

Trying to turn the page of an illustrated fashion book Annemarie had given her to look at, Savannah was again irritated by the gloves Aunt Jenny had insisted she wear to bed. First, a greasy cream had been rubbed into the chafed skin on her hands and the gloves were then pulled on. She must leave them until morning and as her reward she was promised prettier hands. Every night, Aunt Jenny had cautioned, she must perform this ritual. Perhaps for now, Savannah frowned, but not when she again was with MacAllister. He would not like the gloves. He would want to have her touch him with her hands, and in the dark he would not care if they were pretty or not.

Several minutes ago there was the sound of a piano coming from downstairs. She knew it was a piano because a vague memory of her mother's playing had come back to her. There were also the sounds of voices, men's and women's, and she harbored a bare hope that MacAllister had come to see her.

She would have liked to go to the top of the stairs and peek down, but Aunt Jenny had locked her door saying it was to keep other people out. What other people? She wondered when would she meet the other girls who she knew also lived here at Annemarie's house. Was her hostess also teaching them to become ladies? Everything was so secret. Why had she been kept in this room all day? Didn't ladies ever go out in the sunshine?

Still straining to hear the familiar timbre of MacAllister's voice, she closed her eyes and found sleep.

Annemarie sat quietly on the edge of the sapphire-blue settee, pretending to listen to the conversation of Mr. Lionel Bradshaw, an elderly gentleman of Galveston who liked to frequent Annemarie's establishment mostly for the companionship.

As she nodded her head from time to time, Annemarie kept her eyes fastened on Beaunell Gentry, who was draped across the lap of one of her clients. Catching Aunt Jenny's eye, Annemarie gave a signal that Beaunell wasn't to be given any more wine. Her voice was too loud and her words thick. Ever since the other night, when Sloan had deposited Savannah and had refused Beau's companionship, she had been imbibing too freely of alcohol. While Annemarie could understand Beau's disappointment, she couldn't forgive her actions. Her business had never been managed as a common bawdy house, and she would not allow it now. Beaunell Gentry would have to be sent somewhere, at least until Sloan could come to take Savannah away. "Oh, Sloan," Annemarie sighed to herself, "you've cost me my sleep, my peace of mind, and now you're going to cost me my percentage of Beaunell's earnings."

Deciding that Beaunell must leave Galveston for a while, Annemarie's mind searched for the method. What was Mr. Bradshaw saying? "Did you hear me, Anne? I said I would be leaving tomorrow for Mobile. I'm restocking my store, and I can't trust the job to that idiot who works for me. Last time he brought back a dozen banjos. Banjos! I can't even give them away! I will certainly miss my evenings here for the next three weeks. Er . . . perhaps you can suggest somewhere I can spend my off hours in Mobile? It's been some time since I was in that city and you know how discriminating my tastes are."

Annemarie's eyes swung from Beaunell to Mr. Bradshaw and back again. It was an answer from heaven. Beau was too dangerous to have around for the next few weeks; there would be no telling what she would do if she ever learned of Sloan's little scheme. One thing Annemarie did know about Beau was that she was vindictive and dangerous when crossed.

"Mr. Bradshaw," Annemarie said sweetly, smiling and openly flirting. "I, myself, have need of several things from Mobile, and I was thinking of sending one of my girls to get them. It would mean so much to me if you would volunteer to be protector and guardian to her while she was away. She would be no trouble, I assure you, and she would be a ready companion for the wonderful restaurants and theatres I'm certain you would want to attend. A refined gentleman, such as yourself, would find little to satisfy himself in the establishments I've heard of in Mobile. It's a wicked city, Mr. Bradshaw. Wicked!"

The old man's eyes showed immediate interest. Loneliness was the plight of the aged, and he wasn't looking forward to being alone and friendless in a strange city. "Whom were you sending to Mobile?" he asked, struggling to keep the excitement from his voice.

"Why, Beaunell. She's the only one I would trust to do my business." She watched as Bradshaw's eyes turned to Beau. She saw him lick his lips and smiled. Was it possible that Mr. Bradshaw would find himself with renewed passions in Beau's company? Playing her hunch, she leaned forward, lightly placing her hand on his arm. "Of course, dear Mr. Bradshaw, Beaunell would be expected to be remunerated for the pleasure of her company. You understand, don't you? A girl must prepare for her future."

"Of course, of course," Bradshaw agreed, already thinking of the pleasure Beaunell had to offer. Perhaps he wasn't as old as he thought.

Now, all Annemarie had to do was inform Beau. That would be no problem, she assured herself. Mr. Bradshaw was one of the richest men in Galveston, and Beau was expert at parting a man from his money.

It was mid-afternoon when Sloan let himself in through Annemarie's kitchen door. Silence pervaded. A small worm of agitation crawled around in his belly as he tried to imagine the reason for such silence. Why was the kitchen empty? Where was everyone? Usually, at this time of day dinner preparations were in progress and tantalizing aromas wafted about. Tentatively, he inched his way across the kitchen on tiptoe. It occurred to him that he might appear ridiculous to anyone who might be watching. Worry lines creased his brow as he entered Annemarie's formal dining room. But a loud sigh of relief escaped him as he saw Savannah bring a delicate bone china cup to her lips. She seemed to be doing fine. Fine, that is, until he looked into her eyes. She met his gaze. Daintily, she set the cup down on the saucer and folded her hands primly in her lap. She said nothing.

He stood there returning her gaze. He would rather have taken a beating than see the recriminations in her eyes. Guiltily, he counted the days since he had left her at Annemarie's. Nine days. Nine. From the expression on Annemarie's face, the thought that he had deserted Savannah seemed to be the general consensus. Shifting his weight from one foot to the other, while fidgeting with his hat like a schoolboy, he began to explain that business had kept him away. He realized how ridiculous that would sound to Annemarie and decided he would have to brave this one through. That he was afraid to face Savannah and had had to force himself to check on her progress today was something he didn't want to admit aloud.

"There you are," Annemarie kept her tone light and friendly, not wanting Savannah to know she thought Sloan's neglect deplorable. "Savannah has been worried that you might have forsaken her. I tried to assure her that wasn't the case. You are her reward. I thought a buggy ride around town might help. She's doing marvelously, Sloan. She learns very quickly. You can be proud of her."

Sloan had trouble with his breathing. He had known Savannah was beautiful, but this breathtaking creature dressed in bright yellow, the color of new daffodils, was more than he had ever imagined. She was a vision. Honey gold hair piled smoothly atop her head revealed the elegant curves of her throat and shoulders. Her breasts rose high and firm, their supple roundness making his hands ache to caress them. Her skin had evened to the color of ripe peaches, and he knew it would be smooth and yielding beneath his touch. He had missed her, had longed for her beside him at night, and seeing her here like this sent a stab of remembered passions through his loins. His heart started to pound in his chest as other thoughts raced through his mind. It was all he could do to nod and still remain on his feet.

"Good afternoon, MacAllister," Savannah said in an exaggerated singsong voice. He knew she was deliberately baiting him, poking fun at her lessons. Annemarie knew it too, but said nothing, preferring to have Sloan handle his charge's mocking behavior.

"Is that the best you can do?" he said tersely.

"Because I am your woman does not mean I must do everything you say. I am being obedient, am I not?" she questioned Annemarie, who nodded her head. "You can see that I am not bound nor am I gagged." The singsong voice grated on Sloan's nerves. "I am doing what you asked because I belong to you. If the way I do it does not please you then send me back to my people." Sloan could see the pulse working at the base of her throat. Aha, so that was what she was up to. She would go through with every-

thing and stop just short of success. Then when she returned to
Osceola she could truthfully say she had been obedient and done
what she was told.

Sloan schooled his face to sternness. "Savannah, half measures
do not count. You must give one hundred percent for this trick to
work for Osceola's benefit. Even if I were to send you back for
whatever reason, do you think Osceola would be proud of you?
No. If you fail, you'll shame him among his people. He's counting
on you, depending on you. This is no game. You're not a child any
longer playing with grown-ups. You're a woman now, and
Annemarie wants only to help you. I am not proud of you this day.
I expected more." He turned as if to leave but not before he added
one last thing. "You have made me lose face among my friends."

This was something Savannah understood completely. The
emerald eyes filled with tears as she looked around at Aunt Jenny,
Annemarie and the three handsome Negresses from the kitchen.
As if on cue, all the women lowered their heads. Sloan could see a
satisfied smile play around Annemarie's generous mouth.

"Good afternoon, MacAllister. It is a lovely day, is it not? Please
join us in some tea," Savannah said in perfect English. A gentle,
winsome smile lit her features as she waited to see Sloan's reaction.

Sloan laughed. "You see, I knew you could do it! I told
Annemarie you're smart." Then more formally, "I would love to
join you for tea, Miss James, but I thought we might take a ride
around town so you can see what it looks like in daylight."

"Aunt Jenny, fetch Miss Savannah the yellow ruffled parasol,"
Annemarie said with amusement in her voice. "Sloan, you'll stay
for dinner." It wasn't a question but a statement. "You'll get firsthand knowledge of what Savannah has learned in the short time
we've had so far."

"Depends on what time you plan to serve dinner. I have a meeting with a man who is selling me flour and cured beef. I'm storing
it at the docks until Captain Culpepper can take the *Polly Copinger*
back to Cedar Key with another full load for Osceola. I want to see
that he gets under way with no problems." This was said to
Annemarie, but his eyes were on Savannah making sure she
understood he was keeping his bargain to his brother and she
could do no less. He could see that she understood by the way her
eyes thanked him.

"It's no problem, Sloan. We'll plan on a late dinner. We don't have to worry about interruptions. If you had come around sooner, I would have told you that a certain friend of ours," her eyes lifted to indicate the room Beaunell usually occupied, "is traveling in Mobile. Did you take a room at the hotel."

"I've heard you speak of a hotel. What is it?" Savannah asked out of the blue.

"A place where you sleep and you pay for the privilege. It's a temporary room while visiting or a resting place between stops if a person is tired," Annemarie volunteered.

Savannah's green eyes turned murky. "But I'm your woman. Why don't you take me to the hotel? I belong to you," she told Sloan. "When we were on the island, you said we were one. One in this house, one in a hotel. I don't understand. Am I your woman or not?"

"Savannah," Annemarie interrupted, "go upstairs with Aunt Jenny and she'll give you a parasol to match your dress." In the habit of obeying her hostess, Savannah left the room behind the Negress, stopping only to throw Sloan a questioning glance.

Annemarie struggled to hide a wicked grin. "Let me see you wiggle out of that one, oh mighty MacAllister. This young lady is not going to be fooled for one minute. And I think you're going to have a rough time of it if that certain friend of ours discovers what's going on around here. It must be wonderful to be so in demand by two beautiful women. I hope you have the good sense not to make a mistake you'll regret later."

"So do I, Annemarie. So do I," he told her fervently. "You say our friend is out of town?"

"Only until Mr. Bradshaw's heart or money give out. I'm betting on his money. My quarters are off limits to the girls, as you know. But Savannah has met Dolores and Lina and a few of the others. They think she's perfectly charming. Women will talk, Sloan. You know that. I don't anticipate any problem for the time being, but if that certain someone should return sooner than expected, we could be faced with one. Which," Annemarie said quietly, "will be turned over for you to handle."

Sloan enjoyed seeing the sights of Galveston, seeing them through Savannah's wide eyes as if it were the first time. From time to time she asked a shy question or two and then settled back.

He watched in amusement when she would turn in the carriage to look after a strolling woman. He knew she was cataloging her entire wardrobe. Savannah was a woman. And, she appeared to be liking her new role. There were moments when she let her guard down, and her shining eyes would light at something that pleased her. Then, seconds later, a curtain would drop over the green eyes, making her remember who she was and what she was doing. If she did make the decision in the end to go back to the Seminoles, she would be hard pressed to forget the white man's luxuries. The thought that she might really and truly want to return bothered him, tore at his insides and made him jittery. It would be difficult to explain to her why he couldn't join her and make a chikkee, as she called it. What did he feel for this beautiful young woman sitting beside him. Desire? Certainly. But he couldn't be falling in love with her. MacAllister frowned. Annemarie would have picked up on it immediately. He wasn't the marrying kind. He had things to do and places to go, and this time was merely an interlude devoted to helping the Seminoles. Savannah just happened to be caught in the middle. He couldn't help it if one went with the other. He'd be like Enwright Culpepper, a man unto himself. The thought made him grimace.

Savannah watched Sloan out of the corner of her eye. She had preened under his compliments and admiring glances. Being a lady had its rewards, she admitted. She had progressed much further than he had expected. Her English was nearly faultless, and she had learned her manners well. It was only when she was upset that she groped between the two languages, making her English seem stilted.

Was this plan of MacAllister's going to work? If she did what was expected of her, it would. It wasn't at all difficult to sleep in a soft bed with sweet-smelling linens. The food was delicious and sitting at a table, eating with a fork, was second nature to her. Unconsciously, she allowed her fingers to play over the soft fabric of her dress. It was luxurious. She admitted she still didn't like being confined in a corset, and MacAllister wasn't going to like it either. It took a long time to dress in underwear, and it took almost as long to take it off. She wondered if he would let her sleep in his hotel. She liked sleeping with him. He was hard and warm. Comforting. Most of all she liked their lovemaking. She turned in the seat to face Sloan. "When will you make love with me again?" she asked bluntly.

Sloan was taken off guard. He had been busy watching some workmen lay a new foundation for still another church. "Soon," was all he could manage to say.

"When? How many nights?" she demanded.

Sloan shrugged.

"What does that mean?" she imitated his gesture.

"It means when I'm ready. Ladies don't ask questions like that."

"Why?" Savannah asked nonplussed. "I liked it."

"I know you did," Sloan blustered as he remembered the way she had responded to his touch and how she had given herself to him.

"Did I not give you pleasure with my body? I am your woman. Tell me when?"

Goddamn it. "Of course you gave me pleasure, but I can't give you a calendar date. It doesn't work like that. I have to feel . . . I have to be in the . . . what I mean is, it isn't time," he faltered lamely.

Savannah shook her head sagely. She had heard of such things with the older men in the tribe. "How many summers are you?" she asked anxiously.

Sloan didn't like the turn the conversation had taken. "Not summers, years. Thirty-two years." He hated the way the girl's eyes widened. He wasn't that old. Blast! How had he let this conversation develop to this point?

"The twilight of your life is running on swift moccasins to catch up with you, MacAllister."

By God, there was a touch of smugness to her voice. "Now, listen, Savannah, there's nothing wrong with me! While you live in Annemarie's house, we cannot . . . you can't . . . it isn't done. Now, that's all there is to it. I don't want to hear another word."

"You will not take me to the hotel when it is dark? You will not wrap your body about mine and make me love you? Not this night. Not in four or five nights. Maybe one month. Too much time!" she said emphatically.

"Maybe I can work out something. Right now, it's time to get you back to Annemarie's, and I have to keep an appointment. We'll talk about this some other time. Hold on," he said, slapping the rump of the horse lightly with his buggy whip. The obedient animal did a complete about-turn and headed back toward the stable.

Savannah smiled at the tiny beading of perspiration that dotted MacAllister's forehead. She liked the slight twitch that played around his eye, but, most of all, she liked the sight of his muscular thigh in his tight britches. She was his woman. MacAllister better remember that or the twilight she was speaking of would creep up at an alarming rate of speed to end in the final sleep. She was his woman!

A week passed and then two and then three. When the last, lingering days of winter came to Galveston, Savannah developed an acute case of cabin fever. She became sharp-tongued and belligerent, refusing to obey Annemarie, saying she had had enough of fancy white ladies' ways. She wanted to race through a wild meadow filled with flowers.

Annemarie sympathized. She knew what was really troubling Savannah was Sloan's neglect. He had come by two weeks ago to explain he had business in Florida. He would accompany Captain Culpepper with the latest hold of supplies for Osceola and then sail around the tip of the southernmost territory up to Atlanta. Blankets, cookware and mules were more readily available there. She remembered how Savannah's lower lip had trembled with Sloan's news, and she had entreated him to take her with him. She was feeling alone and was homesick for her people. If only she could see them, talk to them. . . . No! Sloan had roared at the mention of her idea. She hadn't accomplished her lessons yet, and there was no time to bring her back to Galveston before sailing on to Atlanta.

Savannah lay atop her bed listening to the music coming from below. She had met Rufus, the black man who came to play in the evenings, one afternoon when he had come to tune the piano. He was a small man with a gold tooth in the front of his mouth. And when he played, he bounced on his stool in rhythm with his music. She could imagine him now, smiling broadly to show off his tooth, his dark fingers dancing across the keys.

The door to her room hadn't been locked since a few days after arriving at Annemarie's, and often she had crept to the top of the stairs and hid behind a large chest of drawers that Annemarie called an armoire to watch the people below. At first, she hadn't understood what she had witnessed until she confronted Odile, the black kitchen maid.

"Why, honey, them gentlemen come here for a little entertainment. Miz Annemarie has the most entertainin' girls in the Texas territory. Men like to see them in their underwear, watch them smile and be invited to their rooms."

"Why?" Savannah had persisted. Perhaps if she behaved like one of Annemarie's girls, MacAllister would think she was entertaining and would come to see her more often. Perhaps there were things about being a white woman Annemarie wasn't teaching her.

Odile had laughed as she took away Savannah's breakfast dishes. "Why? Because they like to sleep with the girls. 'Specially Miz Beaunell. Why, she's the most popular girl here! Yes siree! Miz Beaunell flashes them eyes and takes 'em upstairs for her good lovin' and them gentlemen can't stay away! Yes siree!"

"Who is Miss Beaunell?" Savannah demanded.

Odile turned with a blank look. "That's right! You nevah met our star boarder. She's travelin' in Mobile right now with Mistah Bradshaw and havin' a time for herself! Yes siree! She's havin' a fine time for herself."

After that conversation Savannah was more curious than ever to see how the girls conducted themselves downstairs while Rufus played the piano. She had seen Dolores flash her huge dark eyes and smile enchantingly at a man who seemed to have difficulty keeping his eyes off her bosom, which was carelessly concealed by a thin, gauzy dressing gown. Lina's bright red hair hung seductively over one pale and creamy shoulder as she sat on a man's lap, tickling his ear with her tongue. He seemed to be enjoying it from the way he kept laughing and kissing her and fondly rubbing her little bottom. Suzann flashed her blue eyes at a man in a soldier's uniform, and he carried her up the stairs at a dead run, heading for her room. Blossom was the girl who interested Savannah the most. She had even practiced some of Blossom's expressions in the mirror when she was alone and found she could imitate the girl surprisingly well. First, she would tuck her chin down to her chest and look up with a hot, sultry expression in her eyes. Lips parted in a wet, sensuous pout, she would run her tongue over them from time to time. Blossom liked to dress in black stockings with red garters and very little else. The silky petticoats and chemise she wore left very little of her anatomy to the imagination.

She had already learned that the girls made several trips to their rooms each night and often with a different man each time. There was only one man she wanted to take up to her room, and that was MacAllister. She was constantly reminded by her surroundings how much she missed the delicious feel of his arms around her and the touch of his mouth upon hers. All around her people were making love, and it was having a strange effect on her. There was an emptiness in the center of her that only MacAllister could fill. There was a hunger for him, a yearning that went deeper and sharper than any she had ever known.

Once, when she had been spying on the group below, she had been discovered. Lina was bringing a man up the stairs when he saw her hiding behind the armoire.

"And what have we here?" he had asked, coming toward her, reaching out a hand to touch her.

Savannah had shivered at the way he had looked at her, undressing her with his eyes. It was the way he had been looking at Lina downstairs, and it sent a tiny thrill through Savannah. This was the way she wanted MacAllister to look at her.

"Leave her alone," Lina had said, pulling him by the arm. "She's not one of us. She's Annemarie's special guest."

"What's your name?" the man asked, ignoring Lina. "I'll ask for you the next time I come in."

"Leave her be, I told you!" Lina warned. "Annemarie won't like it."

"Oh, I get it! She's a virgin and Annemarie's saving her for a good price! Well, I'll never have more in my pocket than I do right now. Where's your boss?"

Lina was angry as she looked from the man to Savannah. "Get out of here," she told Savannah, her eyes snapping. "You know you're not supposed to be here. Now, git!"

Running back to her room and slamming the door shut behind her, Savannah gasped for breath. She hadn't liked the man, and she was worried that Lina would stay angry with her and tell Annemarie.

Lina hadn't said anything to Annemarie, but Savannah hadn't dared to hide at the top of the stairs again. The man had frightened her and she couldn't risk Annemarie's anger. She would have to content herself with listening to Rufus's music and dreaming of MacAllister.

Several nights later Savannah paced her room. Boredom was a curse, and she whispered every Seminole oath she knew, and each one was directed at the absent MacAllister. Ladies' fashion books held no interest for her. She was sick of practicing how to write her name on the slate Annemarie had given her. Her days were spent in abject misery as she practiced her table manners and her English. Lately, a seamstress, commissioned by Annemarie, was fitting her with a new wardrobe. She had to stand for hours on end being stuck with pins and hung with fabrics. She wanted to rail and scream. She wanted to kick and cry and tear the room apart. Where was MacAllister and why had he forgotten her?

She prepared for bed, thinking that at least sleep would bring relief from the empty, endless hours. She pulled the pins from her hair and brushed it to a gleaming softness the way she had been taught. Odile had filled the copper tub with hot water, and she had bathed, hoping the ritual would relax her. After donning a white silk wrapper, she sat on the edge of her bed and buffed her nails the way Aunt Jenny had instructed. Always her thoughts turned to MacAllister. When she heard a familiar voice, she thought her mind was playing tricks on her. Only by looking outside her window and seeing Redeemer tied to the hitching post did she realize it wasn't a dream. He was here! He was here!

Her first thought was to leap from the bed to her dressing table to do up her hair. Mentally sorting through her dresses, she wondered which one she should wear for him. She wanted to make a good impression. She didn't want him to forget her again!

Halfway between the bed and the dressing table she stopped, frozen by a sudden thought. The hairstyle and dresses and her manners hadn't stopped MacAllister from forgetting her before; why should now be any different? This time she would be certain he would never forget her. Never!

Sloan was ushered into Annemarie's as usual by Aunt Jenny, who manned the door in the evenings. If nothing else, Aunt Jenny's bulk and handy iron skillet deterred the clientele from becoming too rambunctious. Stepping into the parlor, his eyes scanned the room for Annemarie. The girls were in their usual state of disarray and the men were panting after them. Aunt Jenny told him her boss was in her private quarters but would see him. Picking his way through half-naked women and men with sala-cious expressions in their eyes, Rufus's music bounced off his ears. God, he'd be glad to get Savannah out of this environment. Even if Annemarie's was a distinguished establishment, it was still a bawdy house. Before he knocked on the door to the private quar-ters, he laughed at himself. Since when had his sensibilities become so delicate? It wasn't too long ago since he was one of the customers with a hot look blazing in his eyes. Of one thing he could be grateful. Beaunell didn't seem to be in evidence. Unless of course she was upstairs in her room with someone. Beads of per-spiration broke out on his upper lip. Talk about walking into a lion's den. Only these felines had soft breasts and willing hips. But they had claws, he reminded himself. And hungry mouths!

"Come in," Annemarie's voice answered his knock. She was lying on her sofa, a cloth pressed over her brow.

"Headache, Anne?" he asked consolingly.

"Have I ever. And it's all of your making. When, Sloan? When are you going to take her out of here? And how dare you go off and leave me to answer for you. She doesn't believe for one minute that you're coming back. Now, at least, she can see I wasn't lying to her."

"Aren't you going to offer me a cognac?" he asked, avoiding her questions.

"Over there," Annemarie pointed. "You know where it is. As a matter of fact, pour one for me. I need it."

Handing her the glass, he settled himself opposite her. "I'll take her out of here as soon as Culpepper gets back from Florida."

"What?" she cried, sitting up and throwing the wet cloth at him. "How can your ship be off to Florida? When did you get back to Galveston?"

"Only hours ago. Listen to me, Anne. I would have stopped in Florida on the way back, only I wanted to see how Savannah was doing. The crew jumped ship in Atlanta, and it wasn't easy finding another we could trust. We couldn't take that chance on them leav-ing us here, so Culpepper dropped me off and set sail again. I could have stayed away another week."

"You are too kind, Sloan, too kind. When do you expect him back? You've got to get that girl out of here. Beaunell will be getting back soon, and I don't want her tearing this place to pieces. Besides, although it's never been said between us, the less she knows about what you're doing, the better. She can be vicious when she wants to, and whether you want to face it or not, you are committing treason by helping Osceola."

"Damn it! Don't you think I know that?" He smacked one fist into the palm of the other. "Even with the help I've been giving, things aren't much better for the Seminoles. Jessup's raiding parties have been taking their toll. Do you think Savannah is ready to meet her uncle? She'd better be. We can't wait any longer."

"She's as ready as she'll ever be, Sloan. If she still wants to cooperate, that is. You know, that girl needs you, and you've made her feel abandoned. You don't know what I've been through with her. She's hardly better than the savage you dragged through my door the first time you brought her here. She doesn't obey; she won't listen. She's spending more and more time with the girls and learning things that you couldn't imagine."

"Spending time . . ." Sloan was speechless. "Why didn't you keep her locked in her room? I depended on you. . . . I thought you'd take care of her. . . ."

"Calm down, Sloan. Nothing's happened yet. I can't keep the girl chained in her room. She's got a raging case of cabin fever. I've even allowed her to go into town with Aunt Jenny or Odile. Unfortunately, several of my clients happened to see her and made inquiries. I hedged, but only tonight someone asked me who my new girl was. It's time to take her away from here, Sloan, or I may find myself with a new employee. You know, sweet, it's quite difficult to live in this environment and resist all these earthly temptations. I must admit, even I get sorely tempted."

Sloan's eyes widened. Annemarie had never spoken to him this way before, never revealed her womanly drives and passions.

"Oh, spare me, don't look so surprised. No, I haven't taken to sharing my bed for a profit, but I do have a certain friend who comes to see me whenever he's in town. It's been some time since he's been here, and I can understand what Savannah is going through. She still thinks you're the only man she wants to share her bed with; don't let her find out differently, Sloan. Now, get out of here and leave me alone with my headache and my cognac."

Sloan's thoughts spiraled. Annemarie had had enough of

Savannah James. What in hell had the girl been up to, and why was Annemarie trying to warn him that he'd regret it if he didn't take Savannah away soon? Did she know something he didn't?

Backtracking through the parlor, he anticipated picking his way through much the same scene as he had witnessed before seeing Annemarie. Only this time, something was different. Lina and Dolores were standing in the doorway with their hands on their hips, their lips curled into snarls. Rufus was playing the piano and hitting a few off notes because his attention was riveted to the far side of the room. Suzann was sitting on a sofa, a sulky expression pouting her mouth. Something was going on. Their clients were packed in a circle around the love seat, and it wasn't until he heard a soft, familiar laugh that he skidded to a halt. It wasn't! It couldn't be!

Elbowing his way between manly shoulders, he saw her, laughing and smiling at someone's inane joke. The sight of her nearly took his breath away. This wanton couldn't be Savannah!

She was perched on the love seat, one black-stockinged leg propped up on the arm of the chair. She wore nothing, save a white silk wrapper and lip rouge. Her hair fell in a heavy cascade around her shoulders, curling around one barely concealed breast. She held a drink in her hand and a slim black cheroot between her fingers. When she looked up and saw him, she offered him the most sexually inviting smile he had ever seen. Her green eyes looked up at him through the thick, dark fringe of her lashes and her mouth was parted and glistening from being constantly moistened by her tongue. Speechless, he stared down at her, muscling his way through the circle of her admirers until he stood before her.

Instead of lowering her eyes in shame and at least trying to appease him that way, she pouted her rouged lips and traced a line from her throat to a place between her breasts, the motion of her fingers opening the gap in her dressing gown still wider. The flash of black silk against her honeyed thighs distracted him and he reached down to cover them with the hem of her gown.

"What do you think you're doing?" he roared, a lion ready for the kill.

"What is it I'm doing?" she taunted, batting her lashes at him.

"I know what it's called! I've seen whores before!"

"A whore lays on her back with her legs open; Aunt Jenny told me," she volunteered. Her voice was not as confident as she wanted it to be. The rage in his eyes was deadly, making goose bumps break out on her arms and legs. Why was he looking at her this way? What had she done? The other men seemed to approve; why not Sloan? What was the matter with these crazy white people? Wasn't this the way a woman could keep a man from forgetting her?

Shock froze MacAllister's features into a mask of fury. She couldn't have just said what he'd thought she'd said! Where had she learned what a whore did? Something in Sloan cracked. His hands doubled into fists and he wanted to beat her, wipe that sultry, knowing look off her face. He should beat her, he told himself. Then he should have himself beaten. This was all his fault. He never should have neglected her the way he had.

"Get upstairs," he commanded through clenched teeth.

Seeing this order as a way to rid himself of her, Savannah rebelled. "No. I think I like it down here," she said, trailing her fingers along the flesh of her thigh, watching for his reaction. "I don't want to go upstairs. I want to drink and dance and listen to Rufus play the piano!"

Sloan's eyes widened until she could see the whites. Just like Redeemer's eyes before he threw a strange rider. Fury was unleashed. Before she had a chance to blink, he had her in his arms and slung over his shoulder. Raucous calls issued from the men who protested this interloper escaping with their latest entertainment. Hardly aware of her weight, Sloan ran up the stairs two at a time before he was forced to fight over her. If he had to fight, he'd end up killing someone.

Down the hall to her room, he carried her. She could hear his labored breathing, like the panting of a huge animal just before it devours its prey. He wasn't panting from exertion, she knew, it was anger, white and hot. Never had she seen such anger! Her fists beat at his back, her legs kicked, aiming for his tender parts; she screamed and hollered and swore in Seminole. Nothing would stop him. Instead, he slapped her elevated bottom and told her to shut up.

Reaching her room, Sloan kicked open her door and threw her on the bed. Never taking his eyes from her, he went back to the door and turned the key. The lamplight struck his face, and she saw the raw emotion contorting his features.

"If it's a whore you want to be, maybe you'd better get some firsthand knowledge of that timely profession." His eyes never left her, and they hardened to silver as his hands worked at his belt.

Savannah was thunderstruck. Why was he so angry? Why couldn't he like her the way the men downstairs seemed to like her? She only wanted him to desire her, to love her, not to forget her again. The other girls were never treated this way. Why did he hate her so much?

MacAllister crossed the room, the golden hairs on his body seemed to glow in the yellow light. His flat belly and lean hips tapered down to strong, muscular legs. His upper body was powerful and sinewy, deceivingly slim and lithe beneath his clothes. Savannah already knew the power in his arms. She had felt his strength and had been the object of his anger. And this time MacAllister was more angry than she knew a man could be. He stalked the bed with slow, deliberate steps. His broad chest heaved with each breath he took, his hands were doubled into fists.

Cringing, Savannah scuttled back across the covers. Her eyes flashed to the door and back again. There was no escape.

The slash of his mouth was set in a hard line. His flint-gray eyes never left hers. His hands were rough and cruel as he pulled her toward him; the bed sank beneath his weight. The white silk wrapper was torn open, exposing her vulnerable flesh to the onslaught of his hands and mouth. There was no tenderness, only rage. There was no pleasure, only anguish as he forced her legs open and held her arms above her head to save himself from her frantic, clawing fingers.

Savannah's heart stopped with fear. A silent cry for mercy swelled in her throat. *This* was not MacAllister. Not *her* MacAllister!

Suddenly, he fell on top of her, and she braced herself for his brutal entry. Instead, he wrapped his arms around her and buried his face in her neck. For long, long moments he held her, stilling her fears, murmuring indistinguishable words that only the heart could hear.

At last she spoke, softly, soothingly, following her womanly instincts, caressing the muscular expanse of his back, yielding her body to his. "I wanted only to belong to you, MacAllister. I thought if I was like the other girls you would like me better. I thought you wouldn't forget me again. The other men come back again and again. They never seem to forget Blossom and the others."

He heard the truth in her voice, the plea in her words. She was so innocent, so loving, and he had almost brutalized her because of his own guilt at having left her for so long. She had felt abandoned and he was responsible. "Savannah, you are my woman. I could never forget you. Never. You should hate me for what I almost did to you. I was an animal. I never want to touch you unless it's with tenderness."

She lifted his head from her shoulder and looked into his pain-filled eyes. There was a curious glistening there, and his voice was thick with emotion as though his heart was breaking. Cradling his head against her breast, she crooned to him, knowing how to heal the wounds as every woman since the beginning of time has known. "Touch me, MacAllister," she whispered. "Show me your tenderness. I am your woman."

His lips closed over hers in a gentle caress, softly, sweetly, as though he were drinking at a cool spring. Her arms closed around his neck, answering his embrace, her mouth tasting the bittersweet saltiness of their shared tears.

When Annemarie learned of Savannah's parody from Blossom the next morning, she hastily climbed the stairs to her pupil's room, expecting to find her bruised and beaten. Sloan had already left, she knew from Aunt Jenny, and she was steeling herself to comfort the poor child he had left behind.

Instead, upon entering the rose-colored room, she found Savannah dressed and sitting before her mirror, a dreamy, contented expression on her lovely face. She was humming one of the tunes Rufus liked to play on the piano.

"What happened?" she asked, breathless from her run up the stairs.

Savannah turned, questions in her eyes. "Happened? When?"

"Last night, you little fool. Haven't I told you to stay in your room in the evening? Do you realize Sloan might have killed you? And me too, for that matter!" Annemarie's anger blazed. Her friendship with Sloan was too valuable to her to have this child destroy it.

"MacAllister is still your friend, Annemarie. He's not angry with you or with me." The dreamy, romantic expression returned, and she began to hum that silly tune again.

"Well, what happened? You look like the cat that ate the canary!

Wasn't he angry when he found you downstairs behaving like one
of the other girls?"

"Angry? Oh, yes, but I forgave him. It was wonderful!"

"You're not making any sense at all!" Annemarie scolded.
"Why did you go downstairs?"

"Because I didn't want to be forgotten again. Blossom says men
have a short memory and you have to give them something to
think about."

"You certainly gave him something to think about from the
account I heard," Annemarie said, her voice softening somewhat.
"I hope you made him understand it was all your own idea and
that I had nothing to do with it."

"Oh, yes. Sometimes my ideas are good, aren't they? *This* time
MacAllister won't forget me. He told me I'm leaving with him day
after tomorrow."

"That's a relief," Annemarie said, moving across the room to
the window. Lord, she still hadn't become used to keeping these
early hours since Savannah had been left in her charge. She never
realized how strongly the sun shone through these lace curtains.
Perhaps she should have new ones made that would filter out the
morning light. It's a wonder that Dolores, whose room also faced
the front of the house, hadn't complained seeing as how the girl
never left her room before three in the afternoon.

"Day after tomorrow? We'll have to contact the dressmaker and
rush her on the last of the gowns she's making for you. Where's
Sloan now? Aunt Jenny said she heard him leave at the crack of
dawn."

"No, it wasn't that early," Savannah told her offhandedly, her
cheeks flushing slightly as she remembered their passionate lovemaking before he had left. "He told me he has business and not to
worry, that he'd be back day after tomorrow."

Annemarie was barely listening. She was watching a carriage
drive up to the top of the hill and park outside the door. A groan
erupted in her throat as she dropped the curtain and peered
through the lace. Beaunell Gentry was stepping lightly from the
hired vehicle and was instructing the driver to carry her trunks to
the house.

"Savannah, listen to me," Annemarie said hurriedly. "I want
you to stay in your room. I don't want you to come out for any rea-

son, do you understand? Not for any reason!" She heard the panic in her own voice. Calming, she said slowly and distinctly, "I don't want Sloan to be angry with you or with me. Later, when I send for you, you'll come downstairs and stay with me in my private quarters. Aunt Jenny will move your things. Now, remember, stay in your room and don't come out! I want you to lock your door after I leave and be quiet as a mouse. Don't open it or answer to anyone except Aunt Jenny or myself."

Savannah nodded her agreement, her green eyes wide with puzzlement over Annemarie's erratic behavior.

Downstairs, Beaunell was telling the driver where to put her baggage when she saw her employer at the top of the stairs. "Annemarie, what are you doing up so early? I never remember seeing you before noon. I had the most wonderful time in Mobile. I can't thank you enough for arranging everything with Lionel."

"Lionel, is it? When you left I recall you dreading the idea of spending a few weeks with a man old enough to be your grandfather," Annemarie said sarcastically.

Beaunell gave an elegant shrug. "It's Lionel now. How could I continue to call him Mr. Bradshaw after all the beautiful things he bought me? I swear, I haven't brought back a single rag I took with me. Everything is new. Everything! And very expensive. Where's Aunt Jenny? I need her to unpack for me. Do you want to come to my room and see what I bought?"

Annemarie rubbed her temples. She was fast developing another headache. Why couldn't Beaunell have stayed away for another two days? "Not now, Beau. I've got this headache coming on. I really must lay down."

"Annemarie, has anyone come looking for me while I was gone?" Beau asked brushing imaginary lint from the shoulders of her new burgundy cape, hoping the new sparkling ring she wore would be noticed. "I mean, has Sloan come here to see me?"

"No, he hasn't," Annemarie told her honestly, watching Beau's expression change from smugness to consternation.

"Has he left Galveston?" Consternation turned to disappointment.

"Yes, I think he has. Now you must excuse me, Beau. I really must get something for this headache." She couldn't get back to her rooms quickly enough. She knew she was being a coward. She should just tell Beau how things stood between Sloan and Savannah and let the devil take them. Beau really wasn't such a bad sort, and she'd been in Annemarie's employ for quite some time. Although Beau was given to put on airs and was a trifle trying at times, she still owed something to the girl. But she didn't want to be around when all hell broke loose.

Beau still had designs on Sloan and intended to marry him one day. It was hard enough to lose at love, and when a woman was approaching thirty, like Beau, it could be devastating. And Beau wasn't one to take things lying down. If she ever sniffed out what Sloan was up to, she'd see to it that he was hanged for treason. If she couldn't have him, she'd be damned certain no one else ever would either. Annemarie laughed. Had she just told herself that Beau wasn't such a bad sort? Lord, this headache was really clouding her thinking!

Shortly after the noon hour Savannah was installed in Annemarie's quarters. Aunt Jenny had assured her that Dolores, Lina and Blossom had agreed not to mention Savannah's presence to Beau as a special favor to Annemarie. Suzann was another matter entirely. She would love to break the news to her arch rival that Sloan had found himself a young, golden-haired girl who was everything Beau wasn't. At Annemarie's fearful look, Aunt Jenny soothed. "Don't you worry, Miz Annemarie. I told her if'n she breathed one single word about *anything* to Beaunell I was gonna scorch every stitch of her clothes with my flat iron. She don' want that pretty behind of hers stickin' out through her drawers. Don't you worry, that Suzann will keep her mouth shut good!"

Annemarie laughed in spite of herself at the picture Aunt Jenny made as she shook her stubby finger, her many chins quivering and her mammoth hips jouncing. "Sometimes, Aunt Jenny, I think *you're* the boss around here. Not me!"

Savannah spent the remainder of the day with Odile in the kitchen, an area of the house where Beaunell never set foot. If she wondered why she was being secluded from everyone else, she never mentioned it. She contented herself with learning from Odile the workings of the magical wood stove and memorizing the recipe for bread pudding. She took her dinner with Annemarie and, shortly afterward, a delivery was made to the kitchen door for her. Sloan had sent her a package from Bradshaw's store containing a gold-tipped quill pen and lovely inlaid inkpot. Enclosed was a note saying simply, "Never forget. S."

Annemarie had to read the note for her. "I must learn to read," Savannah said, admiring the iridescent feather on the quill. "I have practiced signing my name and I know my letters. Now I must learn to read."

Seeing an opportunity to occupy her pupil until Sloan could come and take her away, Annemarie seized on the chance. "There's no time like the present to begin. You already know your letters and the way they sound. Now, all you have to do is learn to put them together. I think I have a book here . . ." Annemarie paused, looking at Savannah, who was holding Sloan's note, her eyes closed. That the girl was in love there was no doubt. Something akin to pity struck a chord within her. Sloan hadn't expressed any thoughts for Savannah's future. It seemed he simply felt that once the girl's mission was completed she would be eager to return to her people in Florida. Men are fools, Annemarie thought sadly, and Sloan MacAllister, you're one of the biggest fools I know.

The next morning before lunch another package was delivered from Bradshaw's. This time a bottle of scent directly from Paris. Savannah was elated and begged Annemarie to read his note. "Tomorrow," it said. "Never forget. S." For the rest of the day Savannah struggled with her reading lessons, determined to learn in the quickest time possible.

That evening when Annemarie had completed dressing for the evening ahead of her, she was surprised to find Aunt Jenny leading Sloan into her apartment. Savannah was in the bedroom, practicing her letters from a chart Annemarie had made for her.

"Sloan, I hadn't expected you until tomorrow. You don't know how glad I am to see you. Beaunell is back and she's getting frisky. If I had a dollar for every time she's knocked on my door, I could retire and live a life of leisure. She knows something is going on. What amazes me is she hasn't found out. And Savannah is starting to ask questions about why she hasn't met Beaunell and why she's being confined to my apartment. Where have you been?"

"I have a problem, Anne. Culpepper returned from another trip to Florida. Right now, with the provisions I've sent, food isn't a problem for the Seminoles. But they desperately need ammunition and guns. According to Culpepper, Jessup is making inroads and there was a skirmish that lasted for six days. A band of Creeks were determined to take my ship. Culpepper and the crew had quite a fight on their hands, and the only way they were able to save the cargo was to pull out for sea and anchor at another spot. Finally, the Creeks lost interest and the *Polly* was able to go back to Cedar Key. Not only do I have to get artillery, but I also have to find another anchorage to rendezvous with Osceola's men. I hate to ask you this, Annemarie, but do you know someone who deals with munitions? Wasn't there a man I met here sometime ago? Was he from Cuba?"

Annemarie flushed. The sight stunned Sloan and he realized Annemarie herself was intimate with the man. He had simply thought he was a client of one of the girls. "I'm sorry, Annemarie, I didn't mean to embarrass you . . ."

"You seem to be doing that quite a lot lately. Forget it, Sloan, the day had to come when you had to realize I wasn't the epitome of virtue. It's just that I don't care to share my personal life. I'll write a letter. You take it to him and he'll help you. For a price, of course. A bonus wouldn't be out of order if you follow my thought. He'd be sticking his neck out."

"Where is he?"

"New Orleans. He keeps an office there. For the right price you might be able to convince him to arrange delivery of the cargo. It's risky, Sloan. If the government finds out what you're doing that handsome neck of yours might swing. Sending food and provisions are one thing, artillery is quite another."

"You let me worry about my neck. Write the letter; we'll set sail on the morning tide. We'll have to go back to Florida first to arrange a delivery point. No sense going on to see your man without knowing where he should deliver the goods. Savannah will enjoy seeing her people again, even if it's only for a few days. Do you think she's ready to go through with her part in this?"

"As ready as she'll ever be. If you can get her to keep her shoes on," Annemarie sighed. "Every chance she gets, off come the shoes."

"I'll see what I can do," Sloan promised. "Where is she?"

"In the bedroom with Aunt Jenny."

"Write the letter for me. I'll get Savannah. Are her things packed. Does she have everything she'll need?"

"For the most part. A shopping trip or two in New Orleans will take care of the rest. I've included a list in her baggage. . . ."

Savannah suddenly appeared in the doorway.

"MacAllister! It's you!" Savannah's face lit like a thousand lanterns.

Sloan opened his arms to her and she ran to him. "Savannah, are you ready to leave in the morning? Annemarie is pleased with your progress and says you're ready to be presented to society. How would you like to put on that blouse and skirt you're so fond of and come with me to Florida for a few days before we sail to New Orleans?"

Stepping backward, Savannah smoothed her hands over the pink striped silk gown she wore and frowned. Her frown deepened as she remembered the coarse fabric of her indigo blouse and the short, colorfully banded skirt. How could she have become accustomed to satins and silks in so short a time? After an instant's dismay, she realized that she was going to be with MacAllister again. Such happiness filled her that she would have worn sackcloth and ashes and not minded one bit.

In her joy, Savannah rushed toward Sloan, tripping over her shoes and falling headlong into his arms. Savannah was enthusiastically planting kisses on his mouth and cheeks when the parlor door opened. When Sloan glanced up and looked over Savannah's shoulder, he was staring directly into Beaunell's stormy, dark eyes.

"I knew it! I knew something was going on! Who is this person?" she demanded arrogantly. "I've known all along that something fishy was going on. It was a conspiracy, wasn't it?" Not bothering to wait for a reply, she rushed on, her anger hissing and sputtering like water droplets on hot coals. "Take advantage of me, will you? Use me when the mood strikes you! Take me when you need me? I'll be damned if I'll let you use and abuse me. Do you hear me, Sloan? Who is this woman?"

Sloan stepped back, unsure of his next move. "You're acting like a child, Beaunell. Behave yourself. I've been busy."

"I can see that," Beaunell said icily. "Liar! Cheat! You found someone younger, firmer, is that it? Well, I don't want to hear about it. All I want from you is payment for the hours I spent waiting for you. Hours that could have been put to more productive use. Who is she? Damn you, answer me!"

"My name is Savannah. I am MacAllister's woman," Savannah said sweetly.

"That's what you think. I've been his woman. I guess he didn't tell you about me, did he? Well, he didn't tell me about you either. You aren't getting any bargain, let me tell you."

"*I* belong to MacAllister," Savannah said more firmly.

"That's a line he hands all the women," Beaunell snarled. "Don't believe a word of what he tells you. Liar!" she shrieked in Sloan's direction.

"I *am* his woman," Savannah repeated. "You lie!" Suddenly a thought occurred to her. "Where do you sleep?"

Beaunell stopped to think before she answered. "Upstairs. Why?"

"MacAllister sleeps in the *hotel*. It is simple. You lie."

"What?" Beaunell exploded. "All men sleep in hotels. He comes here when he feels like taking a bath and climbing in my bed. He snores; what do you think of that? *And* he has three moles, here, here and here," Beaunell said, pointing to her derriere.

Aunt Jenny rolled her eyes back in her head. This was one place she didn't want to be. Wasn't Miss Annemarie going to stop this? Was she going to let the handsome Sloan stew in his own juice?

Savannah looked from Sloan to Beaunell. She was trying to make up her mind about something, some plan of action. Whatever it was going to be, Sloan knew he wasn't going to like it!"

"He promised to *marry* me," Beaunell said imperiously.

"Now just a damn minute, Beaunell. I did no such thing. You were the only one who talked of marriage. I never agreed, never consented, to anything."

Beaunell was so angry, saliva sprayed from her mouth as she tried for a fitting comeback. "I knew you were a liar, but I didn't think you would make a fool out of me in public."

"I'm not doing any such thing. You're doing it yourself."

"*I* will take care of this witch," Savannah said, advancing on Beaunell.

Before Sloan could stop her, Savannah had her hands in Beaunell's hair and was pulling her forward. She slapped, kicked and pushed the screaming Beaunell without mercy. "You will apologize to MacAllister and to me for what you said," Savannah said, gasping for breath.

"I should have known. You work as a team, is that it?" Beaunell said, bringing her elbow up and hitting Savannah square in the neck. A string of bitter Seminole curses erupted from Savannah's throat as she grabbed both of Beaunell's ears and banged her head against the wall.

Sloan tried to pull the battling women apart, only to find himself the object of several well-aimed kicks. "Annemarie! Annemarie, stop them!"

"Why?"

"Someone is going to get killed! You have to stop Beaunell. Send her upstairs, fire her. I don't care what you do, just do it!"

"Very well, but after all the fuss and bother you've caused me, why should I quibble over a little sitting-room brawl? Beaunell, you will stop this unladylike behavior this instant." Annemarie clapped her hands imperiously.

If Beaunell heard, she gave no sign. She was busy pelting away at Savannah, who was herself busy trying to rip the feathered wrapper from Beaunell's creamy white shoulders. In that instant, Annemarie pulled her free and literally threw her in Sloan's direction. "Go to your room, Beaunell, until I'm ready to talk to you about your disgraceful behavior. You know I deplore fighting of any kind. And as for you, Savannah, what has gotten into you? Ladies do not fight, scream or carry on like this. For shame!" To Sloan she added, "This is the very last time I pull your chestnuts out of the fire. You got yourself into this mess, and you're going to have to get yourself out. It's good that you're taking Savannah with you. Perhaps I can salvage my relationship with Beaunell. If I lose her because of this, the price is going to be heavy, Sloan. I'm a businesswoman, you know."

Sloan didn't like Savannah's silence. For some reason he knew that up till now he hadn't truly known the meaning of trouble. He could have taken her shrilling screams, her fighting tirades, but her silence unnerved him, made him jittery. It had to be because of Beaunell. He had thought he was going to die on the spot when she had asked the enterprising Beaunell where she slept. That was it, he was sure of it. A good Indian always covered his trail one way or the other. He knew in his gut he better do the same thing and do it before Savannah had a chance to think too long and too hard.

CHAPTER SEVEN

*L*ights rimmed the outline of Galveston harbor. Savannah sat beside Sloan in the borrowed carriage, her baggage stowed in the back. In his pocket was Annemarie's letter of introduction to the arms manufacturer from Cuba, Senor Rico Mendoza. She had cautioned Sloan to see to it that Savannah purchased a more extensive wardrobe in New Orleans. Even the prospect of frilly gowns and silken lingerie did not seem to lighten the dark shadows in the girl's eyes.

Captain Enwright Culpepper had come to Sloan with a problem. "It's the tiller bracings, sir. We must have damaged them when we were looking for a deepwater anchorage on that last trip to the Florida territory. I suspected it, but it didn't seem to be giving us trouble or I would have seen to it in Galveston. Seems to me we'll have to change course for New Orleans."

Sloan had been disappointed, for Savannah was eagerly looking forward to seeing Osceola and his family again. "We can't take a chance on being marooned, Culpepper. Change course for New Orleans. There's a gentleman there I must see."

Sloan was more than a little surprised when Savannah boarded the *Polly Copinger* and went straight to her cabin. There were no comments about sharing Sloan's cabin, no comments about making love. The fine hairs on the back of his neck stood at attention. Perhaps a little manly talk with Enwright Culpepper would be in order. He needed crystal-clear thinking from here on out.

All night he lay in his narrow bunk, remembering, imagining he could taste the times he had shared with Savannah. Twice he swung his legs over the side of the bed only to groan and lie back down. As far as Savannah was concerned, Beaunell was bitter medicine, and while she had been forced to swallow it at the time, that didn't mean she had to like it. Perhaps there was a way to explain, a way to salve Savannah's womanly pride. He hadn't scorned her, hadn't cast her aside in favor of Beaunell. Beaunell was the past, and he had no intention of making her a part of the present or his nebulous future, whatever it might be.

Sleep was out of the question. A walk around deck might settle his nerves. A couple of swallows of some good brandy should take the edge off his twanging nerves. This was the perfect place; it could be the perfect mood for making love to a willing Savannah. He grunted as he climbed the steps to the deck.

Warm, sultry breezes washed about him as millions of stars glittered, chasing one another across the boundless sky. Bright moonlight bathed the *Polly Copinger* in a silvery glow, the shiny brass and highly polished deck sparkling as they never did in bright, golden sunshine. A night for romance. A night for lovers to lie entwined in each other's arms. Was Savannah sleeping or was she lying in her narrow bunk as tormented as he was? Savannah was being stubborn. A woman's trait that he had run up against on more than one occasion. A trait he detested, because it made him feel weak and ineffectual.

His gut churned and he wiped at perspiration on his brow that had nothing to do with the warm breezes wafting about him. Goddamn it, he wanted Savannah, wanted to feel her in his arms, wanted to know that she wanted him as much as he wanted her. The hell with it, a glib tongue had always been one of his major attributes. If he was careful, he might still be able to convince Savannah of . . . what?

If he kept prowling about like this, he would never know, never be able to force himself to go back to his narrow, hard bunk alone.

Once his mind was made up, his long legs raced down the deck to the stairway and down the companionway. Cautiously, he opened the door and quietly stepped inside. Soft moonlight circled the room from the porthole. Deep, even breathing greeted his own labored, uneven breaths. He forced himself to a calmness he didn't feel. She couldn't be! But she was, sound asleep, her breathing deep and regular. How could she sleep at a time like this? Didn't she feel what he was feeling? Didn't she want him as much as he wanted her?

He stood for a long time, undecided. Should he wake her or not? Should he bend down and kiss her gently on the mouth, hoping to wake her? A frown worked its way across his forehead. Indians were supposed to sleep with one eye open and one ear ready for the slightest sound. And he had thought she was as Indian as Osceola. Disgust coursed through him. Annemarie, in the space of a month, had wiped away one of the most valuable skills an Indian has.

In the soft moonlight he noticed that Savannah still slept in his shirt. The thought pleased him when he remembered how Savannah had fought tooth and nail to keep the shirt in place of one of Annemarie's soft plisse gowns trimmed with ruffles and bows.

Savannah heard Sloan's footfalls the moment he hit the last step on the ladder. She waited, her tears long since dried. She forced her body into the relaxed pose of sleep, making her breaths low and deep. She stirred slightly, trying to afford herself a better view through her heavily fringed lashes of the man who stood inside her cabin. She should hate him, but her body ached for him to hold her in his arms. The way he must have held the woman adorned in feathers and ribbons. No, she didn't hate MacAllister, but she did hate the beautiful woman she had attacked with such vengeance. Was she his woman or wasn't she? Osceola had two women. MacAllister might need two women also. Her heart pounded at the thought of sharing a chikkee with MacAllister's other woman. If he wouldn't take her to his hotel, she didn't want him. Didn't need him. Chikkees were from her other life. She knew now that she belonged more to the white man's world than the Seminole. Whatever she was supposed to share with MacAllister she would share alone, not with the woman in feathers and ribbons who wore cherry-red paint on her cheeks and mouth. To Savannah the bright glossy paint on Beaunell's cheeks and mouth meant the woman was prepared to go to war to have MacAllister for herself. Annemarie lied to her when she told her that ladies do not fight. Even MacAllister lied. The thought was like an arrow in her heart.

Savannah felt rather than saw Sloan approach the bunk, felt the slight movement of his body when he bent down on his knees. She stirred, the sooty, dark lashes opening slightly. The moment his lean, strong hands reached for her, she had both his wrists in a viselike grip. "Do not ever sneak up on an Indian, MacAllister, for you could be dead in seconds. I could kill you now without a weapon. Why have you invaded my cabin? What is it you want from me in the middle of the night?"

"To talk with you," Sloan said honestly. He realized the words he spoke so defensively were true. He did want to talk to her, to make things right between them. And he wanted the pressure on his wrists released. She had him in the worst of all positions. He was on his knees, and her grip on his arms was that of a warrior's. All she had to do was bring her knee up to his chin and snap his neck. He swallowed hard as he waited for her to make her decision. A white woman's decision.

"So you can tell me more lies? I have no wish to hear lies from your mouth, or from Annemarie's."

"I didn't lie to you. As far as I know, Annemarie didn't lie to you. You haven't been among us long enough to understand certain things, certain ways people resort to when they feel that . . . what I mean is, sometimes when a person feels cheated for no reason he retaliates in ways that are hard to understand."

"I understand better than you know, MacAllister. I believed you. I trusted you. All because you are Osceola's brother, and he said to trust him was to trust you. I believed those words, MacAllister. I was your woman. You left me in that house where your other woman sleeps. That is not trust. You refused to let me sleep in your hotel. I have no wish to hear your weasel words. You sound like the white man who makes treaties with Osceola's people. They make promises, and as soon as the words are on paper, they say it is not so. *All* white men lie!" The last was said so emphatically, Sloan clenched his teeth.

"I am not like *all* white men. All I'm saying is you don't understand. I do not lie and I do not cheat. My brother would listen to me, why can't you do the same?"

Forgetting the hold she had on Sloan's wrists for a second, Savannah raised her hand and pounded her chest. "Because you have wounded me here," she cried dramatically.

That was all Sloan needed. He rose off his knees and threw Savannah back against the bunk, his lean, hard body on top of hers, intent only on saving himself from her scathing nails once she recovered herself. Her disappointment in him made him angry, implausibly so, he realized, but angry. He had done nothing to cause her this pain which she seemed to think he had deliberately inflicted. Manly pride, ego, stupidity, would not allow the comforting words to come to his lips.

"Let me go, MacAllister!" She seethed, heaving his weight,

attempting to slide out from beneath him. "Go back to Galveston and your painted lady! Go back and take what you want from her! You won't find me so stupidly willing to share your bed again!" Glistening tears welled in her eyes. There was just enough light spilling through the porthole to see them sparkling on her lashes.

Sloan looked at her incredulously. This couldn't be the same woman who had seduced him for the first time on the Cedar Key island. He must have dreamed that the day he'd taken her for a buggy ride she had openly compromised herself, practically begging him to take her back to the hotel with him? Not possible, he thought irrationally, not this hellcat with curved claws and hair-raising screams!

A sly smile formed on his lips, and his eyes took on the gleam of a fox with a rabbit within its clutches. Savannah's blood ran cold at the sight of him advancing on her, reaching out for her. Like the rabbit, she stood frozen, unable to move, to breathe. She saw his outstretched hand come close, so close. She wanted to run, to escape, but still his hand came, touching her. His fingers were warm against her cheek, his palm burning where it came to rest near her lips. His touch was gentle, soothing, quenching some of the hurt and disappointment that was stabbing her heart.

"I touch you only with tenderness," he told her, his tone soft and intimate.

In the light spilling through the porthole he saw her and had never known her to be more beautiful. Her hair gleamed with silver that belonged to the stars alone; her skin smooth and glowing, softer and sleeker than the silk shirt she wore. At his touch on her cheek she leaned her face into his hand, eyes closing, lips parting. Wordlessly, he smoothed her golden curls, feeling the satiny strands between his fingers, thinking that her hair was like the moon itself, shining and sleek.

When she turned to him, it was to offer her lips to him, clinging softly with arms wrapped tightly around his middle, pressing herself against him. Her appetite for their lovemaking was as intense as his own, and the knowledge of this heightened his desire for her. She was the most exciting woman he had ever known: soft and lovely one moment, scrapping and feisty the next, but always, always beautiful.

Savannah's emotions found an answering response in Sloan as

his mouth took hers hungrily, desperate to satisfy his need for her. Their hands reached for one another, softly touching, rediscovering each sweet caress.

Sloan brought her back to her bunk, stopping only to remove the shirt that guarded her most tender, sensitive spots from his greedy lips. He kissed her neck, tasting the sweetly perfumed skin of her ear lobe, the gently curving softness of the arch of her throat, that hollow between her breasts which constantly beckoned to him. The intricacies of her, the delightful differences invisible to the naked eye that made her different from all other women. His lips lingered, taking and giving pleasure.

Savannah's hands found the smoothness of his back beneath his shirt, luxuriating in his warmth and solid physique. He shrugged out of the confines of his shirt, freeing himself for her touch. Her mouth tenderly nipped at the place where muscular shoulder yielded to his neck, and she was aware of the quiver of delight that rippled through him.

MacAllister moved away from her, and when they touched again, he was naked. His hands slid down her body to worship her, adoring her, lifting her into a realm of passion and desire known only to lovers.

His arms encircled her, drawing her tightly against him, reveling in the length of her body pressed against his.

Her hands were woven in his hair, pulling it back from his forehead as she kissed him, opening her lips, bidding him enter. Straining against him, her body rose and fell rhythmically, desperately seeking to fill this sudden need that throbbed within her.

Seizing his shoulders, she pressed him backward against the bed. His breathing came in short, rapid rasps, and when she leaned over him, pressing the fullness of her breasts against the fine furring of hairs on his chest, she heard him emit a low, deep groan.

Beneath her fingers his skin glistened with a sheen of perspiration and the long, hard length of him heightened her lusty appetite and hungers. Learning her lessons well, lessons taught by him, she tasted every detail of his body, luxuriating in the rippling, muscular hardness of him.

Her legs tangled with his as she held herself above him, melting herself to him, rubbing against him, bringing him to the height of his desires. The contact between their bodies was as smooth as the silken fabrics she so admired. She crushed his face into the firm plentitude of her breasts, giving . . . wanting to give . . . only to give. In giving she was receiving and being filled with a sense of power that she could evoke these emotions in this strong, masculine man. Bringing him pleasure, pleasuring herself.

He was alive beneath her touch, and she felt his expectancy throb between them. His eyes were upon her, delving the darkness, perceiving her with more than his eyes. She was a goddess, golden and fair, bringing the warmth of the sun to his cold, hungry needs.

She mounted him and the flatness of her belly was hard against his, drawing the aches and the hunger from his loins. Her breasts were offered to his hands and her mouth was as greedy as his own, and he knew there was more between them than finding a momentary respite from the urgency of passion.

The moonlight smiled on the *Polly Copinger* as she braced the rolling tide toward the city of New Orleans. Belowdecks, Sloan lay beside Savannah, body curled around hers, hands lovingly stroking her arm, brushing her hair back from her face. The ship rolled gently, rocking them in their bunk.

Her skin was warm and smooth, smelling faintly of himself. Placing his lips close to her ear, he held her gently, whispering low and soft, "Savannah, you are MacAllister's woman!"

Murmuring in her sleep, she fit herself closer into the curve of his body, never hearing the words that would have made her heart fly the path of the bumble bee whose nectar she was named for.

The *Polly Copinger* sailed into New Orleans' harbor, sails crisply catching the breezes. Her hull was high on the water, seeming to skip ahead of the rollers bringing her into land. Sloan and Savannah stood on the deck near the bow, the warm wind ruffling their hair and caressing their cheeks. Behind them, Captain Culpepper shouted orders to the crew to reef sail and lower the main jib. Anticipation and excitement danced through Savannah's veins. This was her first pleasure trip.

Sloan watched Savannah's face as she peered off into the distance, watching the busy harbor and the activity beyond. Her green eyes flashed with a sense of adventure; her skin glowed from the freshets of wind blowing across their faces. He was enjoying her excitement. She had already told him how many gowns she wanted to buy and petticoats and those naughty silk stockings Annemarie had told her every lady wears. When he mentioned suitable negligees and shoes, she frowned. She much preferred sleeping in his own silk shirt, she told him unabashed, and as for shoes, she could hardly bear to keep them on her feet!

He had roared with laughter, pleased that she liked his shirt so well and promptly rewarded her with another, his best, with his monogram embroidered over the left pocket.

Her only request before Sloan left the *Polly* to accomplish business ashore was a tub of hot water for her bath. Her lids lowered in sultry invitation, and it was with great reluctance that Sloan had to remind himself that business came before pleasure.

Hailing a hansom cab, he entertained himself all the way to Rue du Belle Fleur with images of Savannah lowering her naked sun-kissed body into the tub and luxuriating in its fragrant water. He couldn't wait to get back to her, all soft and sweet and so willing.

It was still early in the day when Sloan opened the door to Rico Mendoza's offices. The lightly scented letter of introduction from Annemarie rested next to his heart. He didn't anticipate any trouble, a denial of his wants for the Indian. Money was the only thing he needed, and in his right breast pocket was enough money to outfit the entire United States Government with guns. The thought that he was being un-American didn't enter his mind. Osceola's face, along with those of hungry women and children, was all he needed to remind him he was doing the right thing. If the United States Government couldn't honor its commitments to the Seminole, then he was justified in what he was doing. He would never lose sleep over this transaction.

A scholarly-looking individual accepted the letter Sloan held out. "One moment, Señor, I will return. Please, make yourself comfortable. There is a recent newspaper on the table, if you care to read it."

Sloan settled himself comfortably and had just turned the page when Señor Rico Mendoza himself came out to greet him. "Señor MacAllister," he said, holding out his hand, "it is a pleasure to make your acquaintance. Come into my offices, where we can talk privately."

Sloan followed the tall, lean man and knew why Annemarie felt as she did. He was a soft-spoken, handsome man with silvery hair that was almost white. He guessed his age to be around fifty. Clear, unwrinkled skin the color of tanned leather complemented the frosty hair. He poured brandy from a decanter, which was as elegant as himself, into fine crystal glasses. A heavy gold ring with a diamond the size of a pig's eye winked at Sloan as strong, sundarkened hands closed over the fragile stem of the brandy snifter. The two men leaned back comfortably in deep leather chairs.

They discussed the weather in New Orleans as opposed to that of Galveston. Annemarie's name did not come up in the course of the conversation. It was Mendoza who changed the conversation to the matter at hand.

Mendoza's voice was low, cultured and pleasant to Sloan's ear. He liked the man immediately. "As you are aware, we are talking about a very large transaction. For me it is no problem. I am a businessman and have no loyalties to either the American or the Seminole. I want to be certain you understand the matter. Miss Duval has explained your position in her letter to me."

"Can you help me?" Sloan asked carefully, not sure where Mendoza was leading the conversation. The packet of bills in his breast pocket felt very comfortable.

"But of course. Was there any doubt in your mind when you came here?"

Sloan shook his head. Money always spoke more eloquently than any words man could devise. "I'm not a soldier. I know that you shoot a rifle and it can kill. I can shoot and am quite accurate. That's the extent of my knowledge, Señor Mendoza."

"Then let me give you a brief lesson. The American infantryman relies on the shoulder arm. Generally speaking it is a flintlock muzzle-loading musket of a standard .69 caliber. What that means is it is fired by a flint and steel mechanism, is loaded downward through the muzzle, and has no rifling and bore. Believe me when I tell you, it is not the latest in weapons. The army does have some rifles but the ratio is one to twenty-two muskets."

Sloan frowned. He didn't want a lesson in American weaponry. All he wanted was guns for Osceola. Still, he had to be polite and hear the man out. After all, according to Annemarie, he was an expert.

"Thanks to the expert craftsmanship of my people that is not and has not been the case with the Seminole. They use a small-bore Spanish weapon manufactured in Cuba. Unfortunately for the Seminole they use the weapons carelessly. After the first shot they seem to flounder. All the guns in the world won't help them if they don't use the weapons wisely. In short, Señor MacAllister, your Seminole needs to be trained in the use of the rifle. Many tales have filtered back to me. It's said that they take pains with the first shot, but after that, more often than not, shoot carelessly. The cavalry seems to be of the opinion that a Seminole shot is not dangerous beyond twenty feet. As much as this may cause you dismay, I must tell you that the Seminole shoot, not necessarily aim, whoop and then shoot again. They must be taught and reeducated."

"I didn't know this, Señor Mendoza," Sloan said briskly.

"I thought as much. I can sell you rifles from a small stockpile but no more than three hundred at this point in time. By early summer I can give you another two thousand. My plan would be to ship you the Hall rifle. It can strike hard at four hundred yards compared to the one hundred yards of the musket. Because of the breech-loading, it can be fired four times as fast. I have to caution you on one factor. It's said that because of the mulelike kick oftentimes the stock breaks. We can fix that. We can work out the kinks for the right price. It's a superior weapon to what the Seminole is now using. It's your decision, Señor MacAllister."

"I'll take them providing you work out the kinks, as you say. What is the price?"

"Twenty-five thousand dollars now. Twenty-five thousand *American* dollars. Twenty-five thousand upon delivery. If I run into problems, the delivery price will rise. Acceptable?"

"Acceptable," Sloan said, drawing the packet of money from his inside pocket. He counted out twenty-five crisp one-thousand-dollar bills and laid them in a neat pile in front of Mendoza. "Let us discuss the point of delivery. If possible, I would prefer it to be six or seven miles south of Cedar Key on the west coast. I'll have my captain, Enwright Culpepper, send you word of the exact location. He tells me it's a deepwater harbor."

"It's as good a place as any. General Jessup's troops have the shoreline well guarded. Gun running is not something I'm fond of doing. Let me think on the matter. If I need to get in touch with

you, I'll get word to Miss Duval. Is that agreeable?" Sloan nodded.
"The matter of the three hundred rifles for now is no problem. I
can have them taken to wherever your ship is berthed. Or did you
come by horseback?"

"Ship."

"In a few hours they will arrive at the harbor in barrels that
resemble water barrels. My men know how to handle such things.
It would be wise if your men do not split the containers. Once they
leave my hands I deny all complicity. *Comprende?*"

Again Sloan nodded. He stood. The meeting was over. Mendoza
made no move to pick up the money lying in front of him as though
not wanting to dirty his hands. They shook hands; Mendoza's was
firm and hard and confident. A slight smile played around the
smooth mouth of the Spaniard. "We will meet again one day, I'm
sure of it."

Sloan's eyes blazed into the coal-black eyes of the man standing
next to him. "I doubt it. Unless of course something goes wrong.
Like the kinks not being worked out of your Hall rifle. I trust we
understand one another."

"We understand each other perfectly, Señor MacAllister,"
Mendoza said coolly.

Redeemer galloped down the cobbled streets, intent on getting
Sloan back to the *Polly Copinger* in record time. The warm, near
spring breezes buffeted him as he gave the galloping horse his
head. He couldn't wait to share his news with Savannah. She
would be elated at the munitions deal he had made for Osceola. He
felt so good, so pleased with himself for Osceola's sake, he decided
to take Savannah on a shopping spree in downtown New Orleans
and let her pick out anything that pleased her. A few bangles and
beads, a new hat, a new parasol would do the young girl a world
of good. He felt as though he were twenty years of age and about
to court a young girl. It was a good feeling.

Culpepper shouted from the ship's railing. Savannah stood
next to him dressed in a persimmon-colored dress. Her back was to
the brilliant sunshine throwing her in shadow. It looked as though
she was smiling as broadly as Culpepper. Was it just because they
were happy to see him? The thought pleased him. He had been
alone too long without anyone to care about what he did or where
he went. Every man needed someone to care about him.

Quickly, he shared with them the results of the meeting with Mendoza. To Culpepper, he added, "Be on watch for the supply wagon. I'm taking Savannah shopping, and if we have time, we might stop for tea at a sidewalk cafe I know. Can we fetch anything for you, Captain Culpepper?"

"Not a thing, Laddie. You two go off and shop for Miss Savannah. I'll be keeping a sharp eye peeled for the wagon. Go along with you."

"It's a beautiful day, Savannah. Would you mind walking? The shopping district isn't far and we can hire a buggy for the ride back."

"I would like that, MacAllister. What will we buy?" she asked, her sea-green eyes sparkling with delight. It would be her first shopping trip. Annemarie had been afraid to take her to the shops in Galveston and had ordered dressmakers to the house. It would be exciting with Sloan voicing his opinion. She would purchase only things that he liked. Things that made his gray eyes soft and happy. She felt confident about using money. Annemarie had been most careful to make sure she understood how much each piece was worth and how to tell them apart. She even liked the feel of the money in her hand. While she had barely enough to buy a few ribbons, she still felt rich. If she was truly MacAllister's woman, he would give her more.

Savannah walked beside Sloan, feeling happier than she had felt in her entire life. There were times these past weeks when she had almost forgotten about Osceola and his people, and the life she had left behind. This was all so new and exciting.

When they reached the main shopping area, Sloan stopped and groped in his pockets. He handed her a sheaf of bills and assorted coins. He didn't bother to count it, but just handed it to her. "Buy what you want. Get whatever pleases you. See that cafe?" he said, pointing down the street, "I'll wait for you there. Gentlemen do not shop with ladies."

"How will I know if I'm buying the right thing and that you will like it?" Savannah asked apprehensively.

"You must buy what pleases you. If you like it, then I'll like it. Take your time. I'll have a drink or two and smoke a cigar."

Savannah looked doubtful but accepted Sloan's orders. In the first shop she bought a reticule with a twisted braided drawstring and a peach-colored shawl with long silken fringe. When she held it to her cheek, she smiled. How good it would feel on bare shoulders. In the second shop she bought six pairs of gloves. Simply, she told herself, because she didn't like to wash them. One could never have too many gloves, Annemarie had cautioned. Shell combs, then a mirror with a shell back, were added to her spoils. A frothy, lacy petticoat that made her blush was next. MacAllister would like it, she was sure of it. The camisole with even more lace kept the flush on her cheek till she left the store. Her last stop along the avenue was the milliner's.

Sloan settled himself comfortably, knowing he was going to have a long wait. He lit a fragrant cigar, propped his feet on another chair and defied the proprietor with his eyes to tell him to remove them. It was mid-afternoon with little business and the rotund man saw Sloan as a profitable hour or so. After all, he had ordered a whole bottle and he looked like a man who would tip well. He felt in a generous mood, knowing the tip would be good. He handed a wrinkled week-old newspaper to Sloan with a toothy grin. Sloan accepted it, but soon tired of reading old news. His attention wandered as he watched shoppers walk up and down the streets. A figure that looked familiar suddenly caught his eye. It was Brevet Major General Thomas Sidney Jessup. Dressed in full uniform in mid-afternoon. He seemed to be out for a stroll. There was nothing hurried about his saunter as he stopped to peer first into one window and then another.

Suddenly, he bolted upright in the cane chair. Savannah was in one of the shops Jessup was peering into. He knew that Jessup had spotted Savannah when he saw the general's back stiffen and the way his hand went nervously to his brow. He was even more convinced when he watched the general bend closer to the window and press against it. Of all the rotten damn luck. What to do? Wait for Savannah to come to the cafe or approach Jessup and try to sidetrack him? Blast it, she wasn't ready yet! Not for the likes of Jessup. She still didn't have the confidence needed to carry off the scheme.

Sloan's gut churned when he saw the general square his shoulders and enter the shop. It was too late now to do anything. He poured another drink with hands that were less than steady and waited.

Savannah was trying on a tantalizing creation with tiny scarlet ribbons. She turned this way and that admiring herself in the milliner's mirrors. She was aware of the tinkling bell over the door and assumed it was another customer.

A warning bell went off in Savannah's head when she noticed the man's intense stare. Her green eyes darkened as she took in his military uniform. This could be her first test. She deliberately averted her gaze from the man and looked into the mirror again. "I'll take this one and the one with the blue ribbons," she said quietly.

"Will there be anything else."

"No, thank you. Perhaps another time." Her breaths were quickening as she sensed the man approaching her. She widened her eyes at his obvious bad manners in addressing a woman without formal introduction. Annemarie had told her never to speak to a stranger!

"You must forgive me, but you remind me so much of . . . of someone I used to know. Please, don't be frightened." Savannah backed off a step and then two, her hands going to her throat at the man's audacity. She said nothing, looking beyond him, calculating escape. He reached into his pocket and withdrew a card. He extended it to Savannah, who reached for it, knowing it wouldn't help her since she couldn't read. She recognized the letters that Annemarie had begun to teach her, but she couldn't remember them now. Reading and writing were her next lessons.

Savannah let her eyes drop to the card. "Should this mean something to me?" she questioned coolly.

"I was hoping it might," the general said in a trembling voice. There couldn't be another woman in the world who was an exact duplicate of his sister Caroline. It had to be Savannah, her daughter and his niece. "Might I ask you your name and what you're doing in New Orleans?"

Savannah wanted desperately to make Sloan proud of her. She had to remain calm and cool and be very careful of how she answered this man. A pity she didn't have a fan to hide behind. Annemarie said a woman always flirted behind a fan. Well, she didn't have one, so she would have to make do. "Yes, you might ask my name," she said coyly. "Savannah James. I'm traveling with friends. Why do you ask?"

Jessup's face paled, then reddened and then paled again. "I

knew it!" he exclaimed. "I knew it! My dear, you are going to find this hard to believe, but I'm your uncle, your mother's brother. I've searched for you for years and years and finally gave up. And now this," he cried in agitation. "It's almost more than I can bear. Child, I'm your uncle, doesn't that mean anything to you?"

Savannah backed away another step. "I'm afraid not, sir. You see, my parents died when I was quite young. I barely remember them, and I have no memory of an uncle. I'm sorry. Perhaps you have me confused with someone else. If you'll excuse me, I must be leaving."

"No. No, you can't leave. You must let me explain how you became separated from your family, from me! It was because of those savages, the Indians. Please, I beg of you, meet me tomorrow afternoon at the cafe down the street and let me convince you. Bring your friends with you if that will make you feel better. I can prove that I'm your uncle. I have credentials. I have all of your parents' papers. I even have a picture of you when you were five years old."

Savannah allowed doubt to creep into her face and voice. MacAllister was going to be so excited at her news. "I'll speak to my friends about the matter. It's possible that I may join you, but I cannot make a promise. I barely know you. I can't promise you anything."

Savannah was astounded at how steady her hands were when she paid for her hats. The moment the door closed behind General Jessup her knees buckled. She grasped the edge of the ornate desk where the salesgirl was busily writing a receipt for her. "I think," Savannah said in a clear, high voice, "I will leave these parcels and pick them up later. Will that be all right?"

"Of course. It's almost closing time and I don't anticipate many more customers. I'll wait for you; it's no problem. I live behind my shop." Savannah thanked her and left. She stood outside a moment, staring up and down both sides of the street to see if the general was in sight. The moment she was certain the coast was clear she picked up her persimmon skirts and raced to the cafe. Her cheeks were flushed, and her eyes sparkled with her news when she sat down on the cane chair opposite Sloan.

"You will not guess who just approached me! You cannot guess what he said to me!" Her eyes widened till they were like round pools of green water. Tomorrow I am to meet him and bring my friends to this very cafe. MacAllister, can you hear me? Why aren't you saying something? Look, he gave me his card. I pretended to read it, and he didn't know I was fooling him. I cannot read, MacAllister." The thought seemed to bother her more than it should. A month ago learning letters would have seemed the most foolish thing in the world. Now it seemed like the most important.

Sloan took the card. "Brevet Major General Thomas S. Jessup."

"That's because you can read. I wanted you to guess." She was clearly disappointed. Sloan hated to spoil her fun but he had to. "I saw him while he was staring at you through the window. There was nothing I could do at the time but wait. Did you tell him your name?"

"But of course!" His face drained of all color. "I did not make any promises. I thought that best in case you might want to think this matter over. Did I do well, MacAllister?"

"Very well." Sloan smiled. He ordered her a cup of tea and forced his mind to think. This changed everything. He barely noticed Savannah as she poured a healthy jolt of the whiskey into her steaming tea. Now he had a problem. He continued to smile as Savannah sipped at her "tea."

An hour later Sloan stood up. "All right, now this is what we're going to do. We have to register you in the most respectable hotel here in New Orleans. Tomorrow you'll meet Jessup as planned. I want you to go to the meeting alone. Culpepper and myself will be here just in case anything goes wrong. You'll tell him that you have some business to attend to and you want to think about his offer to move into his house with him. That's the first thing he's going to suggest to you. You must not appear eager. I want you to demur, to stall him as long as possible."

"MacAllister, I cannot read or write. What if . . ."

"You'll just have to cover yourself the way you did with the general's business card. I'm sure he's going to arrive at the meeting with a picture of your mother to prove what he's told you this afternoon. He won't want to take no for an answer. You will be charming but firm in your refusal to go with him until you're ready."

"MacAllister, what of your plans to sail to Florida to deliver the guns to Osceola and train his warriors?"

"I can't leave you now. I won't leave you. I must stay in case anything goes wrong. We've come too far to have things go wrong now. At this moment Osceola is holding his own. He has foodstuffs to see him through till summer. Culpepper told me that he showed Mico the navigation charts and explained to him as best he could where to meet him the next time he lays the *Polly* at anchor."

"What of the new guns? Who'll train my chief's men?" Savannah was agitated. He knew she was frightened of the prospective move to her uncle's house. Frightened that she would do something wrong and that harm would come to Osceola through her mistakes. The Seminoles were again first and foremost in her mind and this he understood and admired. She loved her people and wanted to help them, just as he did. But he knew that one day, when all this was over, settled either to the Seminoles' advantage or the government's, he would resume his life in the world he knew. The world of the whites. And Savannah? Which world would she choose for herself? He had promised her she could return to the Seminoles. He hated the thought and refused to dwell on it.

"Culpepper can give them a brief instruction, for now," he told her, answering her question. "For now, this is more important. I didn't mean for Jessup to discover you this quickly, but what's done is done. We'll arrange to meet here at this cafe from time to time so that you can keep me informed of what's happening. There's nothing for you to worry about now. Clear Osceola from your mind and concentrate on your uncle. Tomorrow you'll move into your hotel room. We'll spend this last night aboard the *Polly Copinger*."

Savannah's eyes shimmered. It was right that her last night with him be spent aboard the ship where she had found such happiness.

It was early evening when Sloan guided Savannah up the narrow gangplank. Culpepper met them at the rail. "Ye be late for dinner, Laddie. Cook made a mess he calls rabbit stew. Fresh-killed rabbit that he bought off a hunter early noontime. 'Tis nothing like the ambrosia ye made fer me, Miss Savannah," he added hastily. After the first and only day of Savannah's cooking, Captain Culpepper had never asked her to enter the galley again. Next to women, Maeve Carpenter in particular, the most important thing in Culpepper's life was good wholesome food and a bottle of whiskey.

✦   ✦   ✦

Shortly before noon the following day Sloan and Savannah registered at New Orleans' finest hotel, the New Grand America. Sloan took a room down the hall from Savannah just to reassure her. The last thing Sloan had done before depositing Savannah's luggage in the spacious hotel lobby was to open a sizable bank account in her name at the Merchants' Bank of New Orleans, where she had oohed and aahed at the amount of money Sloan was entrusting to her.

Savannah sat on the bed in the hotel room and looked about. So this was what a hotel looked like. She wasn't impressed. There was too much floor space carpeted in a green and blue design that made her grimace. The Bouncy coverlet on the bed felt soft and downy but appeared dirty to her eye. She bent down to smell it. Her nose wrinkled. A few hours in the bright sun with a strong wind would work wonders. The room smelled stale as if a thousand different bodies had shared it, and, now that she understood the meaning of the word hotel, she knew this to be true.

Savannah unpacked her belongings and hung them in the cedar closet. She liked the sweet, pungent smell of cedar that wafted about her from the depths of the closet. One long finger reached out to trace the knot hole in the rough wood. It was different, and she liked it. But did she like this hotel or not? With the door closed she had to remain inside and she liked more space. She needed more space. But it did have its advantages. She was finally in a hotel with MacAllister. She was truly his woman now that he had taken her to this hotel. The thought warmed her all over.

How weary she felt with this new life. How tangled her emotions were becoming. Sometimes it was difficult to bring Osceola's face and those of her people into sharp focus. It was easier to picture Sloan, Annemarie and Captain Culpepper. Tiredly, she fell back against the down pillows. MacAllister had told her that her uncle would bring a picture of her mother for her to see. How was she going to feel? Would long-forgotten memories rise to the surface to torment her? Would she be able to accept long conversations about her parents and hear of shared memories between her uncle and mother?

She had been only six summers. No, six *years* old when she lost them both. The years with the Seminole had been good to her. She had been free to remember or not remember if she chose.

Sometimes late at night, when the camp was asleep, she would remember her bed and the doll that had been a Christmas present. Christmas. How strange that she should remember that holiday and the word Christmas. An evergreen with a candle. A festive dinner with . . . linen napkins and then a present. The china doll with green eyes and golden curls. As if a long-locked door opened, memories came flooding back helter-skelter. There was a spotted pony. A tall man with laughing blue eyes picking her up and swinging her onto the animal's back. And she remembered fear, when the tall man was out of her range of vision. His arms had been strong and protective. And the beautiful woman who looked just as she did, with her hands crossed under her throat in fear that her little girl would topple from the frisky pony's back. So long ago.

Tears for all that was lost burned her eyes. The thwack and thump of the loom while her mother sat weaving cloth. It had been red. A cape, a red cape with a blue lining. Rain pelting the windows. Apple muffins baking in the oven. Did she wear the red cape or was it her mother's cape? She wished she knew. She knew the material would have been coarse, unlike the fine materials she now had. If only she had the cape to touch. Just once. Just to be able to hold it to her cheek and remember still more.

She was tired. Tired of memories that hurt her. Tired of memories she could do nothing about. She didn't want to cry. Only small children cried. Had she cried when she was a child? Of course. When one of the arms fell off the china doll, she cried. And she had whooped and hollered with pain when she fell from the pony. Memories, from the forgotten recesses of her mind, came flooding back, haunting her, filling her with stabbing pain. Through the long night, she remembered, smiling, laughing, crying, finally sleeping. Never knowing that Sloan had crept into her room in the dark of night to brush away the tears that lingered on her cheeks.

An hour ahead of schedule Sloan and Enwright Culpepper stationed themselves at a far table in the outdoor cafe. Sloan held a newspaper in front of him. Culpepper devoted himself to the bottle in front of him, his eyes raking the nearby streets. At the first sign of a military uniform he would kick Sloan under the table. Savannah had been told to take a corner table at the entrance and to be there fifteen minutes ahead of schedule so Jessup would have to join her, not the other way around.

"What's going on, Culpepper?" Sloan asked two hours later.

"Not much. The general seems to be doing all the talking. Miss Savannah just handed back a miniature. I suppose it was the likeness of her mother ye told me about. She seems to be in control. She's sitting like a real lady, and she hasn't spit or snarled once in her uncle's direction. Miss Savannah's acting like a real lady."

"Why shouldn't she act like a real lady? She is one." He didn't realize how curt and terse his voice was when he answered the old sea salt. Culpepper smirked to himself.

"She's shaking her head 'no' over something. She's doing it again. Now she looks stern. Now she's reaching out her hand and touching the general on the arm. She's still shaking her head. Put down yer paper, Laddie, and look at the angel smile on the lass's face. That's a powerful beautiful woman ye been squiring around, Laddie. Tell me," he said, a slight slur to his words, "what will ye be doing when the general matches her up with some handsome cavalry officer. Women swoon over a uniform. Ye might be finding yourself adrift on the sea without a paddle. Ye can't count on a woman to remain faithful with all that handsome flesh culling about her. This man Jessup looks a might dandyish to me."

Sloan frowned behind the newspaper. Damn it, why hadn't he thought of the uniforms? What Culpepper said was true. For some strange reason women found themselves drawn to tailored, brass-buttoned uniforms and spit-polished boots. A lump settled in his stomach. How would Savannah react to a bevy of handsome young men paying her court? He thought of all the young officers who hung about General Jessup, and his fists clenched till the knuckles showed white.

Culpepper found himself amused once more. It would do the lad good to squirm a little. There were other fish in the sea, as Maeve had pointed out to him on more than one occasion.

Sloan rustled his newspaper in agitation. "I hope he's buying Savannah's story that she was taken in by a merchant and his family and that they took her with them to Baton Rouge. I rehearsed it with her often enough."

"Aye, Laddie. As I well know. The whole story is plausible. Savannah was taken in by John Palmer and his wife, Sophie, a dry goods merchant who only recently settled in Baton Rouge. Don't worry, Maeve Carpenter was a personal friend of theirs so Miss Savannah is on safe ground if Jessup gets curious and decides to check on her story. The Palmers both went on to their reward a year or so ago, and Maeve would back up anything I told her. But rest your mind, Laddie. From the way Jessup is looking at Miss Savannah he's only too ready to believe she's lived on the moon if that's what she tells him."

"I pray you're right, Captain. I'd hate to have put Savannah through all this for nothing." Sloan was grim and tight-lipped. "I've learned not to count on anything, and where Jessup's concerned, that goes double. The only thing I can be certain of is that Savannah will follow my instructions and not appear too eager to move in with Jessup. I told her she had to make him convince her over a period of time. At least a week." A sudden black thought crossed his mind. "Culpepper, do you think he'll want to take her in? That's what we're counting on. That when Jessup discovers Savannah is all alone in the world he'll want to take her under his protection."

"Easy, Laddie. Easy. Things will be just the way you want them. Even that black-hearted Jessup couldn't resist Miss Savannah. No doubt about it. He'll want to take her in, all right. I've seen his kind before. All arrogance and pride, thinking himself noble. After all, Laddie, it would be the correct thing to do, and if he has aspirations to the Presidency, it wouldn't hurt to have someone as pretty as Miss Savannah to act as his official hostess."

"Looks like the meeting is breaking up, Laddie. The general is standing up, and Miss Savannah is batting her eyes at him and shaking her head again. The man is frowning but accepting it in good grace. He wants to touch her so bad he can almost taste it, Laddie. The look in his eyes is one I used to see in me old mum's eyes when I was but a tad. He's looking for family ties, and he's not about to let the lass get away from him. He's writing something on a card, and now he's handing it to her. Most likely his address. He's walking down the street now. All right, ye can lay down the paper now. Miss Savannah is leaving. Ye best help me polish off this bottle and be on yer way. I'll be taking the *Polly Copinger* out with the tide. By my best calculations I'll be returning in a week's time. Any messages for that surly Mico?"

"What?"

"Any messages for that Indian, Mico?" Culpepper repeated sourly. He hated to see a man so caught up in a woman's charms that he had to be spoken to twice. But he forgave Sloan because he was nothing more than a whippersnapper with too much money and in love with a woman who was turning him into a jealous man. Culpepper wondered if Sloan knew he was in love. Not likely. Men were always the last to know.

Savannah's spirits were in the doldrums. Nothing, it seemed, could move her or bring a smile to her face. For dinner Sloan took her to one of the finest New Orleans restaurants, ordering steamed crayfish, thinking the familiar food that she had eaten while living among the Seminoles would lift her spirits. She ate them only because he had practically ordered her to do so. A light white fish baked in a wine sauce, oysters, fresh vegetables, even the flaming crepe suzettes were viewed without an appetite. Knowing her to be a ravenous eater, Sloan's brows drew down into a scowl.

"It's delicious, MacAllister," she said softly, forcing a smile to her lips.

He knew she neither saw nor tasted anything. Her thoughts were preoccupied with General Jessup and the fact that she would see him the next day with the news that she would be glad to accept his offer to move into his household in order to get to know and love her mother's brother. It was a lie, a sham, and he had come to know that Savannah disliked it intensely.

"You're thinking about Jessup," he told her, bringing the subject to the fore. "What's worrying you, Savannah?" he asked gently. "Whatever it is, tell me." A sudden thought occurred to him. "Are you troubled because you've finally met someone from your own family? Someone who is really connected to you and who knew and loved your mother? He did, you know, really love your mother. In spite of everything else the man is, his feelings for his family are noble."

Savannah's lips drew into a sneer, and he thought that if she hadn't been so well schooled by Annemarie, she would have spit.

"MacAllister wants to know if I can love that man like I should love my uncle. The answer is no. No, no, no! How could I? Not the way he hates the Indians. The very people who gave me my life! And for what he's doing to the Seminole . . . MacAllister, I have no doubt here," she said, thumping her small fist against her heart, "that even if I told the general it was Osceola who saved me and made me a member of his tribe, it would not make any bit of difference. The man is half crazed when he speaks of those with red skin. I know what you said about him is true. He wants to win the war against the Seminole because he hates them, and because he can gain glory for himself. Do you know he even told me that if I were to come and live with him, some day we would go to the capital, Washington, where he would seek a political career. MacAllister, the man believes with luck he can become President like Andrew Jackson! I hate Jackson and I hate General Jessup!"

"Uncle Thomas, Savannah, you must remember. Uncle Thomas!"

At his correction, Savannah narrowed her eyes to mere slits, "And I can hate you too, MacAllister!" Tears sprang to her eyes, and drizzled down her cheeks.

Sloan painfully understood what the girl was suffering. There were confused loyalties churning inside of her. Whom to love? To whom to be faithful? Much as she claimed she hated Jessup, and she believed herself to be telling the truth, there was still a familial tie. Blood relations. Living among the Seminole she had learned how important family and blood ties were. How could she help but feel something toward the general? The trouble was she hated herself for it.

Walking back to the hotel from the restaurant, Savannah was still too quiet for Sloan's liking. Instead of enjoying the sights; the city streets lit with deeply glowing lanterns, the ornate carriages carrying handsome couples dressed in their finery to and from various parties and socials, she silently walked beside him, her hand on his arm quivering from time to time with the trembling she felt within. He led her back to the Grand America as though she were in a trance. He hated to leave her at the door and told her he would return shortly.

Savannah entered her room and lit the oil lamp on the bedside table. Try as she might, she couldn't seem to pull herself out of this depression. Soon, within days, she told herself, she would be moving into the enemy's camp. She was to spy for Osceola, gather information no matter how insignificant and pass it on to MacAllister.

Carelessly tossing her shawl and bonnet onto the chair, her gown and undergarments quickly followed. Usually so careful of the clothing Annemarie had given her, she left them in a pile, not caring if she ever wore them again, hoping she wouldn't. What she wanted was her indigo-blue blouse and colorful banded skirt. She wanted her moccasins and beads. She wanted to be back in Florida before MacAllister had come to help Osceola. It was safe then, even though the Seminole nation was at war, it had been safe. She knew who she was then and what life could promise her. Now, everything was upside down and inside out. She was Savannah James; she was Chala, Wild Honey. She had thought she might become Mico's woman and had ended being MacAllister's. Nothing was true any more, nothing was safe. Drawing Sloan's silk shirt over her nakedness, she pulled the covers back from the pillows and crawled in. It wasn't so long ago when she had slept on a layer of blankets in Osceola's chikkee. Now the blankets were comforters made of down and the sheets, something she had never known before, were smooth and white and ironed. Where had her life gone? What had she come to? As she laid her head against the plump, feather pillow, she faced the question she had been avoiding for longer than she wanted to remember. After being here in the world that was hers by birthright, could she ever go back to the Seminoles? Would she want to?

Leaving Savannah inside her door and slipping the key into his pocket, Sloan went downstairs to the lobby to check if Culpepper had left any messages for him. Finding nothing that would inhibit his quick return to Savannah, he strode into the dining room, requesting a bottle of fine wine and two glasses. She was going to sleep tonight and erase those dark circles from under her eyes if he had to get her drunk to do it!

"I would be happy to have someone bring the wine to your room, sir," the waiter told him obligingly.

"No, that's quite all right," Sloan told him, slipping a bill into the man's hand, "this is something I'd rather do myself." Realization dawned on him that when it came to Savannah, he'd rather do everything himself. He didn't want anyone else to do for her, only him. A sad smile turned the corners of his mouth down as he thought of her pain and hoped he could lessen it just a little, to help her get through the night.

Opening her door, he was glad to see she was prepared for bed. Good, the wine would help. Putting the tray on a table in front of the windows, he inserted the corkscrew and uncapped the bottle. He filled her glass generously, and sat on the edge of the bed, encouraging her to drink.

At first she wrinkled her nose but then drank deeply, savoring the light, fruity wine and holding her glass out for more. "Sweetheart, you're not supposed to chug it down like a stevedore. Wine is to be sipped slowly; it is to be enjoyed."

"I am enjoying it, MacAllister," she told him solemnly, her face drawn into a pretty scowl. "More please."

By the third glass her eyes were growing heavy. Suddenly, her lower lip began to quiver and tears filled her eyes. Taking her glass from her, Sloan thought his heart would break in sympathy. She was a lost little girl who wasn't certain where she belonged or what lay ahead. He sat on the bed beside her, propping himself against the pillows and took her in his arms. She nestled against him, wrapping her arms around his midsection, holding, clinging, trying to chase away her fears.

"Tell me, Savannah," he whispered, his voice soft, gentle.

"I'm so afraid, I don't know where I belong," she answered.

He wanted to tell her that she belonged with him—always. But the words wouldn't come to his lips. She already had so much to contend with, so much to know and deal with, he couldn't add to her burden and confuse her still further. Now was not the time to ask her not to go back to the Seminole, to Osceola, but to stay with him forever and always be his woman—his wife.

Cradling her as though she were a little child, he offered her solace and protection from those night fears that steal sleep and seem to grow into monsters in the dark. Long, long into the night he held her, loving her.

Savannah whimpered, her face pressed in the hollow between his neck and shoulder. She felt the caring in his touch, in the way his lips rested against her hair. She knew he understood and no words were needed. He held her and asked for nothing in return, giving all he had to give. She was his woman, only his; she found comfort in the thought, not daring to ask herself the question: Was he her man?

CHAPTER EIGHT

———————⋎———————

*B*y the end of the week Sloan's nerves were stretched wire-tight. Savannah alternated between fits of crying and outright sullenness. The day her personal belongings were brought down to the hotel lobby, Sloan found himself almost as sullen, almost as taciturn. Six trunks, twelve hatboxes, four portmanteaus, eight shoe cases, along with assorted cartons and boxes, littered the lobby of the new Grand America Hotel. The desk clerk with his beak nose and narrow eyes surveyed the assortment with a jaundiced look. His face changed quickly when Brevet Major General Jessup himself entered the lobby to see to the supervision of his niece's baggage. One had to keep on the right side of the military. You just never knew when the Indians would take it into their heads to invade New Orleans.

Savannah descended the wide staircase to the lobby in time to see the last shoe case being carried out to the carriage by one of Jessup's men. If only she could turn back the clock and calendar. She knew she had to go through with the charade. She was even accepting it, but that didn't mean she had to like it. She didn't like her uncle, Thomas Jessup, with his possessive eyes and his white hands. She had wondered on more than one occasion why she had no memory of her uncle, especially when he told her he had dandled her on his knee when he visited the farm where she lived with her parents. He spoke kindly, lovingly, possessively, of his sister, Caroline, but he rarely mentioned her father. Perhaps MacAllister was right, and Jessup resented Alfred James for taking his sister from him. It made sense to her. No matter what, she did not like him and dreaded the move into his house. What would she do with her time? How would she fill her hours? Reading and doing needlepoint her uncle had said, like all ladies amuse themselves. Behind her smile Savannah felt disgust. She would have to pretend to stare at printed words that held no meaning for her. Needlework was something ladies learned from childhood, a skill she could never accomplish, she knew, remembering Annemarie's handi-work. Perhaps she could take long walks. Jessup had said he owned a very old dog who needed exercise. She wondered what had happened to the mangy dog from the village. Had he starved to death or had someone remembered to slip him scraps from time to time? It was difficult now to visualize the slat-ribbed dog with the soulful eyes.

Thomas Jessup held out his arm for his lovely niece, a truly delighted smile widening his mouth. It was true! At last he had found her, and she was so much like Caroline it was almost like having his sister with him again. She was lovely today in her green voile gown with lace edgings and her pert little hat that perched so coquettishly over her brow. Caroline's hair and skin had been a tri-fle lighter, more golden than honey, but her features were perfectly echoed in her daughter's face. Savannah James. His own precious Caroline's child. A quick frown appeared between his thick, white brows. Perhaps, at a later date of course, Savannah might agree to have her last name changed to Jessup. It would please him most heartily. Alfred James had been a milk-livered sop in his opinion, and what Caroline had ever seen in him had always been a won-der. Why should Savannah want to carry the name of a man she barely remembered? Jessup, he told himself, would someday be an honored name in Washington, and she would do her uncle honor and show her gratitude by adopting it for her own.

Savannah tried to show some enthusiasm for her uncle's home, but the brace of four soldiers standing outside the door and the aide-de-camp sitting at a desk just inside the foyer frightened her. Jessup, seeing the bleak look in her eyes, questioned, "What's wrong, dear? Are you disappointed in my home?"

"I hadn't expected to be under guard, Uncle . . ."

Jessup laughed, the first time she had ever heard him do so. "No, you mustn't think you're under guard. A man of my position requires assistance," he told her pompously. "Actually, the guard outside my door dignifies my rank, and the aide-de-camp merely sits there to carry out my orders and receive messages and such. In essence, they are there to protect us from outside invasion. There's a great many people who would like to approach me on matters of their own concern. Feel better now, Savannah?"

"Yes, Uncle," she told him; her eyes narrowed, thinking how

difficult it would be to escape the general's notice when there were no less than six pairs of eyes ready to report her actions to him.

The interior of Jessup's house had a pleasing austerity, but the lack of a woman's touch was noticeable, so different from Anne-marie's, where frills and ornaments abounded. The only concession to decoration was the carefully displayed military memorabilia consisting of medals and mounted maps and framed documents.

"Come over here, Savannah. I want to show you something." The general opened a door and led her inside a room obviously of masculine decor with its leather chairs and various tables. She immediately noticed a round table covered with a soft, green cloth around which six chairs were drawn. This must be the place where MacAllister played cards with the general, Savannah thought, feeling somehow a little closer to MacAllister and a bit less alone.

Jessup led her over to a fireplace and pointed above the mantle. "Look," he told her, "I've kept it all these years. It goes with me wherever I go," he said, emotion softening his voice.

Looking down at Savannah was the portrait of her mother, Caroline. For a moment, it could have been a portrait of Savannah herself. She drank in every detail, instinctively knowing the artist's rendering was accurate. Caroline's smooth, white hands were folded in the lap of a peach-colored gown. Her neck was long and graceful and her shoulders sweetly sloping and white. But it was her mother's eyes that struck Savannah. Turquoise and fringed with dark lashes and gentle, so gentle. Savannah remembered those eyes, looking down at her before she went to sleep; those hands, touching, smoothing her own curls. Those shoulders where she had nestled her head and listened to Caroline's soft croonings. Mother.

Tears sprang to Savannah's eyes, trickling down her cheeks. Jessup noticed immediately. "There, there, child," he clucked, reaching for his linen handkerchief to dry her tears. "She was lovely and she loved you dearly. She wouldn't like to see you cry. She was my baby sister and I thought the world of her. I still do. If only she hadn't run away with that no-account Alfred James, her life would have been so different. . . ."

"She loved my father," Savannah said harshly, refusing to hear anything the general had to say about the man who had been the world for both her mother and herself.

Jessup immediately knew he had blundered. "Of course, child," he told her, not wanting to alienate her, wanting more than anything else that she should come to love him as her uncle and her mother's brother. Later, when they knew each other better, they could share memories about Caroline.

A tall, kindly-looking woman with slate-gray hair stepped into the room. Her eyes flickered over Savannah in cursory inspection and apparently found the girl to her liking. "Savannah, this is Mrs. Bouvier, my housekeeper. So, you see, you won't be the only female in the household. Mrs. Bouvier, this is my niece, Savannah James, whom I've told you about. You will please see she has everything she needs to make her comfortable."

"Of course, sir. Miss James, would you like to see your room now?" The woman smiled, the gesture lifting the corners of her eyes, showing her amiable personality.

"Yes, I would," Savannah answered softly, glancing once again at the portrait on the wall. "Will you be joining me for dinner, Uncle?" Was that cultured, feminine voice really hers? She marveled at her own ability to carry off this charade. For a charade it was. She couldn't seem to find any feelings for the man regardless of his obvious affection. Perhaps her mother had also run away from her brother's possessiveness, wanting instead the love Alfred James offered, although he had little else he could claim. Now that she thought of it, there was a certain sadness in Caroline's gaze, a certain trapped look.

Jessup's eyes softened. She had forgiven his blunder in demeaning her father. "I will, my dear. I can think of nothing that would please me more than being your dinner companion."

Smiling sweetly, Savannah turned and followed the housekeeper into the hall.

Taking her up the curving staircase, Mrs. Bouvier carried on a running conversation. "I've already had your luggage brought to your room. If you like, I can help you unpack and put things away."

"Not right now, Mrs. Bouvier, thank you. I think I'd like to rest awhile."

"That's what you will do, cherie. The general is so delighted you've agreed to come and live with him. I've only known him a short time since he's come to New Orleans, but you have made his step lighter and his eyes brighten with a smile. We are all happy you've come to New Orleans. Your resemblance to your mother is quite remarkable. Both of you beautiful women."

When Savannah entered her room she would have thought she was entering a garden. Bouquets of flowers filled the room with their fragrance. Special pains had been taken with the room in anticipation of her arrival. In spite of herself, Savannah showed her delight, touching the soft flower petals and inhaling their perfume.

"Your uncle arranged everything, Miss James. You can see how happy he is to have you with him. Would you like me to help you undress? If you like, I'll see to hiring a personal maid for you. Or would you prefer to do that for yourself?"

"Actually, Mrs. Bouvier, I'd . . . I'd rather do it myself. You see . . ." she stammered with the erupting lie, "I've sent for some-one from home. It will be several weeks before she can arrive and I'd rather wait."

"Of course, Miss," Mrs. Bouvier eyed the young girl. It was strange that a lady of Miss James's obvious quality would consider doing for even a day without a personal maid, much less for weeks. But it would be nice to have a lady in the house. The all-male household and the limited occasions where Mrs. Bouvier could dis-play her talents were sometimes annoying. Now there would be balls and dinner parties and teas and socials . . . the thought sud-denly struck her that she had no idea in what condition the table linens were. It was something she must see to immediately.

"If you will excuse me, Miss. I have duties to attend to."

"Of course, Mrs. Bouvier. Would you please close the door behind you?"

Alone at last, Savannah sat in the little boudoir chair near the window looking down at the overgrown gardens. She sat there for a very long time, thinking of nothing and thinking of everything. Mostly, she found her thoughts returning again and again to MacAllister and the night he had come into her room and held her until the first light of day, soothing her, comforting her, giving her the strength to do what she must.

And with the first light of day, when things were clearer to her, he had turned her over in his arms and traced a delicate path of kisses from her ear to his most favorite of places between her breasts. And when, with the impatience of desire, he had ripped his shirt from her to expose her body for his lovemaking, he had swept her away with him to a place far beyond the stars where time has no meaning and being MacAllister's woman filled her world.

✦ ✦ ✦

Two days later Savannah's uncle informed her that a dinner party was being planned in her honor. Savannah found her throat muscles tightening at the thought. Upon learning that the dinner party was for twenty-four, she almost succumbed to a fainting spell. Annemarie's wise words of, "If you find yourself suddenly in the midst of something you can't handle, plead a headache or smile and flirt. Never open your mouth unless you're sure of what's going to come out!" were suddenly recalled to her. She wondered if the advice included being able to swallow. She was terrified. Officers and their wives, adjutants and their wives and a few close friends would make up the dinner party.

"Savannah, what do you think would be suitable for dinner? It makes little difference to me. That's one of your duties from now on. You'll be overseeing the kitchen. I do like Creole shrimp and am partial to gumbo, but don't let me influence you. You arrange whatever pleases you. Every eye will be upon you, my dear, and no one will notice what is being put in their mouths. I don't want to be overbearing, so you just make your plans accordingly. I realize that this is all new to you. I must even seem like a stranger to you after all these years, but I hope the feeling deserts you quite soon. I want us to have a full, wonderful life now that we've found one another. We're the last of my side of the family."

"What of my father's family, Uncle, do you have any knowledge of them?"

Jessup's face closed. "Not in recent years. I believe there was a brother in the Dakotas, but my memory isn't what it used to be."

Savannah stared at her uncle, recognizing his defensive tone. She knew he was lying. Evidently, he wanted her all to himself and wasn't about to share her with her father's people. The thought saddened her. Her father's people. Not her people, the Seminole. Not Osceola and his people, but *her* people, her father's people. She smiled. Her uncle seeing her warm smile laughed. "You see, I knew you would like it here in our house."

Savannah pretended not to hear the word "our." It would never be her house no matter how long she lived in it. She didn't like the stiff, ugly furniture with the polished tables that smelled like wax. Everything was spartan and unattractive. The house needed a woman's touch, one that a housekeeper could never give it. But not her touch. She would never dare tamper with this austere dwelling. Hopefully she wouldn't be here long enough to develop more than an acute dislike for the unattractive house.

The fat dog followed her around on his short, stubby legs, wheezing and breathing hard. She detested thinking Jessup had ordered the ugly animal to guard her. She knew the thought was silly but she couldn't shake it. Even when she slept, the animal was outside her door, sniffling and trying to catch its breath. Why her uncle didn't put it out of its misery eluded her.

A week passed and then another. With each day she missed MacAllister more and more. Several times a week she made a pretense of going shopping and she would meet him in the Vieux Carré and escape with him to his hotel room. The added secrecy and danger gave a new flavor to their loving, especially since Jessup had insisted that his niece not go shopping alone and had appointed his aide-de-camp as her escort. After purchasing a few trifles in the shops Savannah would insist the aide go and find some refreshment for himself while she kept an appointment with the dressmaker, fitter, milliner. She giggled when she thought of the way the aide-de-camp would look with disdain at the few boxes she carried, more than likely thinking her a very vain woman. If he only knew, she giggled, that while he was waiting for me, I was wrapped snugly in MacAllister's arms, feeling him touch me, kiss me . . . she must stop this line of thought. She could feel the heat burning in her cheeks!

It was the day of her first dinner party, and her uncle seemed keyed up, anxious about something. That afternoon Savannah had told Sloan she had an idea that it had nothing to do with the dinner party but rather it was some sort of military business. When she had tried to draw Jessup out, he had turned taciturn and told her she wouldn't be interested in hearing about savages. How wrong he was! Savannah decided not to press the issue but hoped that something would come of his remark over dinner conversation with other army officers.

Savannah's elaborate toilette preparations took close to three hours. Time and again she cursed herself for not allowing Mrs. Bouvier to hire a personal maid for her. At the time she didn't want to complicate her personal life with still another pair of eyes watching her. But now, nervous about the coming evening, she was all thumbs. First she was dissatisfied with her hair and then her dress, changing her choices not fewer than seven times. Her petticoats didn't seem to lie right, and her silk stockings itched; the camisole was too confining. Out came the hairpins and combs, and another hairdo was arranged. In the end she simply brushed it back and tied it with a lavender velvet ribbon that matched her gown. She added another around her throat with a cameo Jessup had given her, saying it had once belonged to her mother. She had no idea how he came to have it in his possession, but had accepted it gratefully. She didn't like the man, uncle or no. She had come to believe her dislike had nothing to do with his antipathy toward the Indians.

Savannah stood beside her Uncle Thomas to greet the guests as they arrived. Introductions were made and cordials were served in the little-used front parlor. Mrs. Bouvier had hired a staff of servants for this evening to help serve the guests. Through it all, Savannah smiled and made pleasantries. She knew that Annemarie and MacAllister would have been proud of her.

The women examined one another's gowns, complimented each other and generally lied with straight faces. Of the ten women present, Savannah felt the best dressed and the prettiest, certainly the youngest. She smiled till she thought her face would crack with the effort. Not one of the women so far had mentioned the Indians. Savannah herself was about to bring up the subject when Mrs. Bouvier announced dinner.

Thomas Jessup walked proudly over to his niece and held out his arm. Daintily, she placed her hand on his wrist and walked with him to the elaborately prepared table. For a second she panicked as she tried to recall the place setting at Annemarie's table. Her sigh of relief when it came into focus amused the general. "I grant you this is a rather big dinner party for your first introduction. But as you can see, these are my favorite people, and I wanted you to meet them all at one sitting. It's time that you and the ladies became acquainted. You can't spend all of your time reading and sewing. A casual luncheon, a walk in town or along the waterfront is an excellent means of ridding oneself of boredom."

Dinner conversation was casual. There was talk of the weather, how nice spring was going to be this year. Several of the women couldn't seem to make up their minds if they should plant flowers or not since they didn't know if their husbands would be relocated by early summer. A vegetable garden was a necessity, one stout lady said loudly and literally defied Jessup to comment. A needle-thin woman with a beak of a nose asked if anyone at the table was going to see the outrageously wicked play at the newly renovated theatre on Rue de la Paix. All the women blushed and shook their heads. "I plan to go," Savannah said brightly. "Just as soon as I can get a ticket."

"My dear, is that wise?" her uncle demanded in a tart voice.

"But of course. It was all the rage when I was in Baton Rouge. I wanted to see it then, but my plans were changed suddenly. Perhaps you would join me, Uncle." Jessup smirked and allowed as how he would.

A woman named Clarisse said her old mare had passed on and now what was she going to do. Savannah again came to her aid by telling her to buy another one. One must be able to get about, she said in her best and haughtiest voice. Again, her uncle agreed with her. At that point she felt she had contributed enough to the conversation and left the talk up to the other women. All of them suddenly became tongue-tied. Jessup started small talk on a variety of subjects. This was getting her nowhere, Savannah thought sourly. It was time to do something.

"Tell me, Uncle Thomas, how do you fare with the Indians? Now," she said, wagging a playful finger in the air, "don't tell me that the Seminole problem is not fit dinner conversation. I just know that all of us are fascinated with what you men are doing to secure our safe futures." She smiled such a charming smile that Jessup melted and smiled in return.

"You're right, my dear, we are making all the states safe and secure from the savages. I have no objection to telling you now that in two days' time we'll be signing a treaty with the Seminoles." He waited for gasps from the women. He wasn't disappointed. Encouraged, he continued. "We've been negotiating for over a month now at Camp Dade. We've decided to stop fighting. Osceola and his people have promised to go to Tampa Bay by April tenth and board ships for the west. They'll travel to the Texas coast and from there we'll march them north into Arkansas, where they'll assimilate themselves among those other savages, the Creeks." Smiling and bowing slightly, Jessup addressed his female companions. "The original plans were to take them through Louisiana, but I've convinced Washington that this fair city, with its lovely occupants, was not to be threatened or exposed in any way to their disagreeable presence. Texas is wild, a fitting place for the likes of them.

"Our government plans to support them for a year. We had to make concessions, I can tell you that. The Seminoles have insisted that they be secure in their lives and property from the Creeks especially, and the negroes whom they consider to be their property shall accompany them west. We're calling it the Capitulation of the Seminole Nation."

Savannah was stunned at her uncle's words. What should she say? How should she act? This was no flirting, laughing matter. She had to manage to get in touch with MacAllister. Did this change things? Was it a trick, a lie, on her uncle's part? She schooled her face to impassiveness as Jessup continued. "It's important that the Seminoles feel secure. If they become alarmed and hold out, the war will be renewed. That's one of the main reasons the treaty specifically mentions the word 'allies,' the free blacks who were assured their life and property. It also guarantees that those blacks who are the property of the Indians would go west with their masters. There's a Seminole black named Abraham who wanted that assurance, and so did the army. If the runaway blacks are assured their safety from white slaveholders, they will not be a barrier to Seminole migration. What we don't know and can't anticipate at this point is how the Florida settlers and the white slaveholders are going to react. It could become a sticky mess if we aren't careful."

Savannah's heart dropped to her stomach. At what price had Osceola agreed to this treaty? She knew instinctively that it was her thlacko who had insisted that provisions be made for the blacks in this agreement. He, above all men, treasured life and freedom. But to give up his homeland! To leave the Floridas for a precarious life within the Creek nation! To save lives, to share peace, she told herself, wanting to cry in sympathy for Osceola's pain.

MacAllister. She needed MacAllister to grieve with her, to share their sorrow for Osceola.

Savannah could sense that her uncle didn't like this treaty. He would just as soon kill every Seminole in Florida. MacAllister had told her of his meeting with Jessup before he came to Osceola's camp and how Jessup hated Osceola and his people. No, it had to be some trick, some sleight of hand to force Osceola and his people to move and keep moving. How could he have agreed? Abraham, she could understand, but not Osceola. Did he understand? Did he fully understand? Did he sit in the treaty negotiations? Could it be possible that he believed these white eyes? There she was thinking like an Indian again. Damnation. She had to think like these people seated at the table. And it was time she said something; they were all looking at her. Since she was the one who invited her uncle's confidences, it was up to her to reply. "How wonderful," she cooed. "Ladies, isn't it wonderful what my uncle and all your husbands are doing? How proud we are that the United States Government brought the Indians to their knees." There was a chorus of agreement. Jessup positively basked in her praise.

"I am humble in your praise, my dear," he smiled thinly. "I have always maintained the belief that this great country was civilized by white men and therefore should belong to our race." The smile turned to smugness as he made his speech and more than one person at his dinner table thought he was already campaigning for the White House.

"The papers say there is a good deal of hostility between the Seminoles and the Creeks, General. Do you think this settlement will incur further outbreaks of Indian hostilities on our western frontiers?" This was asked by the wife of an officer. From the way she spoke, Savannah knew this had been thoroughly discussed between the woman and her husband.

"Hostility, yes. And that would seem to be their problem, wouldn't it? Also, it is good military strategy to have the red man located in one territory. Perhaps we'll be lucky and they'll massacre one another, saving us the trouble."

Savannah thought she would choke. She could feel the blood draining from her face, leaving her white and shaken.

"Dear one," Jessup immediately rose from his chair and was swiftly at her side, supporting her with his arm before she collapsed onto the floor. "Forgive me, please. It was unthinkable of me to allow this turn of conversation. I've injured your sensibilities."

Savannah was regaining her composure. She wanted to shrink away from her uncle's touch. Smiling bravely, she murmured that she was quite herself again and please not to mind her. Reassuring himself that she was sincere, Jessup once again took his place at the table, eyes full of concern continually returning to her, making her feel like a fish in a bowl.

After dinner the women once more separated from the men. Savannah watched her uncle herd the men out to the verandah after offering fat Havana cigars all around. She didn't fail to notice the smug, self-satisfied look on his face. She was instantly suspicious. She excused herself prettily, promising to be right back to join the chattering ladies. She moved on silent feet to stand within inches of the open doorway leading to the wide verandah. She listened unashamedly.

Brigadier General Davis slapped Jessup on the back. "That was a pretty fairy tale you spun for your niece at the dinner table. For a minute you almost had me believing we were going to honor that asinine agreement."

"What I say and what I do are two different things," Jessup said smugly. "Women only want to hear the fair, nice things. They don't want to think about the hard trading and the blood and gore that goes with any deal made with those goddamn savages. I expect to be under great pressure from southern slave owners as well as Florida landowners. If I must," he said casually, as though his decision had nothing to do with human life, "I will draw the line between those blacks who have lived with the Seminoles *before* the war and those who have run off to them or who have been picked up by them *during* the war. I will do all I can to urge the Seminoles to accept this distinction and hand over all the wartime runaway slaves."

Savannah thought she would choke on her own saliva. She did indeed have a headache now. Osceola was going to sign a false document. He had to be stopped! Her mind swiftly calculated the distance between New Orleans and Cedar Key and then the overland ride to Camp Dade. She had to reach MacAllister as soon as possible. When was this damnable evening going to end? How soon could she sneak away? Thirty minutes was all she was going to give Jessup and then she would faint dead away from excitement.

Thirty minutes turned into sixty and then ninety. By the time the last guest was through the door Savannah thought she would go out of her mind. She couldn't bear to look at her uncle, couldn't bear to have him kiss her cheek. Her hand went to her head just as a grimace slashed across her face. He would have to walk the fat dog himself. There were a lot of things he was going to have to do by himself from now on. Filthy, lying white man, she spat as she flounced into her room. The door slammed shut with such force she thought the wood would come off the hinges.

The minute her uncle's door closed, she had hers open. Silently, she crept down the stairs and let herself out quietly. Before racing down the verandah steps she slipped off the kid slippers and placed them neatly under a wicker chair. Gathering her skirts in her hand, she fled down the street on winged feet.

Once she reached the Grand America Hotel she skidded to a stop. She had no shoes. What would the desk clerk think? Who cared what the desk clerk thought. Within seconds she was up the wide, circular hotel stairway and down the hall to MacAllister's room. She let her eyes rake the numbers on the doors. The upside-down six, just the opposite of her own room number when she stayed at the hotel. She banged on the door with clenched fists. Sloan opened the door and stepped backward. "What happened?" was all he could manage. The words tumbled out as tears cascaded down Savannah's cheeks. "We can do nothing for Osceola now. It is too late. MacAllister, what are we to do? My chief is signing a false document. Your people have tricked us again. My uncle," she made the title sound obscene as her lip curled back in anger, "leaves for Camp Dade tomorrow. He goes overland. If you took the *Polly Copinger* by water, could you get there first?" Her grass-green eyes pleaded with him to say yes.

"I can try." He was already pulling on his boots as Savannah continued her tirade against the white man. Without answering her, he pulled a wrinkled shirt over his head, and then stuffed his personal belongings into a small case. "Come with me, I'll walk you back to the house."

"I refuse to go back there. I'm going with you," Savannah said adamantly.

"You have to go back. I can't take you with me now. I'll do my best and then I'll return. This is something I didn't expect, didn't foresee. You must stay, Savannah. In truth, what could you do? Be honest with me now. There is every possibility that you will be more help here. You can sit in the cafe where the military gathers and possibly pick up some more information. At luncheon with some of the ladies who are married to those closest to the general. Pick their brains. I'm counting on you, depending on you. The general will be gone and you'll be alone. You won't have to look at him. Promise me, Savannah, that you'll stay here. I don't want to have to worry about you."

If he hadn't said he was depending on her, counting on her, she would have fought to go with him. He was right, what could she do?

"Come," Sloan said, taking her by the arm. He bent to kiss her, thinking to reassure her, and noticed her missing shoes. He said nothing, knowing she had run the distance from her uncle's house to the hotel.

"This is no time for kisses, MacAllister. You must hurry. I can find my way back to the house alone. You must take Redeemer from the stable and ride to the harbor. I will do as you ask. Sail on safe waters, MacAllister, for my heart is with you."

"I'll be back as soon as possible. Remember, Savannah, I can make no promises, there isn't much time." In the darkness outside the hotel he stared deeply into her eyes for a minute. "On my return I'll arrange to meet you at the cafe, or else I'll send Culpepper. Go now."

Without another word, Savannah turned and fled down the darkened tree-lined street. Tears of betrayal coursed down her cheek. Her very own uncle, her very own flesh and blood. Oscela would never understand.

Eleven uneventful days passed before Thomas Jessup returned to his house on Mulberry Street. Savannah was sitting on a white wicker chair on the verandah, the fat old dog close by. She had been staring at him for what seemed like a long time. There was something different about the animal. She stared a moment longer. Of course, he wasn't breathing. He was dead. The thought pleased her, knowing Jessup would grieve over the dead dog. She was trying to make up her mind what she should do about the animal when Jessup rode up in a swirl of dry dust. Her decision was made. How she hated this man she was forced to call uncle. She felt a momentary pang for the dog lying on the floor. It was a dumb animal and couldn't fend for itself. The slat-ribbed dog from camp could at least move. Hunger always kept one on the move and on the alert. Jessup's dog ate better than the Indians. His food for one day could have fed three braves. No, she felt no pity for the man or his dog.

Jessup tied his horse to a small hitching post next to a giant hickory tree. He rubbed the dust from his blue sleeves with gloved hands and literally bounded up the steps. Exuberantly, he pecked Savannah on the cheek. "I can't tell you how good it is to come home to someone. My dear, I've missed your presence and your beautiful face. Up to now the only welcome I've received is from my dog and the housekeeper."

Savannah allowed her eyes to go to the dog. Jessup followed her gaze. "Oh, no," he breathed sadly. "Not old Henry. When did this happen?"

"I have no idea. I thought there was something strange about the way he was lying. He's been there since last evening." She hoped the viciousness didn't sound in her voice. On second thought, she really didn't care. Now perhaps was the time to talk to him when he was overcome with grief for the dog. "Did you sign the treaty, Uncle? Did everything go according to plan?"

"What? Oh, yes, my dear. All the chiefs were there. You know, of course, that the treaty was ready in early February but we had to wait for all the chiefs. They arrived on schedule. I didn't anticipate any problems. The Seminole trust their white brothers. A pity we can't trust them in the same way."

Bitter gall rose in Savannah's throat. It was all she could do to remain quiet. If things went the way her uncle had wanted, it meant MacAllister had been too late. Her heart soared momentarily at the thought that he would be returning soon. She didn't need details of the treaty signing, didn't want to hear Jessup gloat. It was enough to know that Osceola and the other chiefs had been tricked.

"Child, why don't you go for a walk while I take care of old Henry. I'd like to be alone with my old friend." Savannah stared at her uncle for a moment. How sad that he could feel so much for an old dog and nothing for the lives of human beings. Perhaps he personally wasn't responsible for this particular treaty signing, but he had helped. He was elated by the fact that the Indians had been duped again. She wouldn't allow herself to feel anything but hatred for Thomas Jessup.

Gathering her skirts in her hand, she descended the stairs and walked slowly down the street. Her heart would sing if she saw MacAllister or Culpepper in the cafe.

It took Sloan three days more before Culpepper docked the *Polly Copinger*. It was mid-afternoon when Savannah set her lemonade glass down on the glass-topped table and spotted MacAllister. She wanted to leap from the chair and run to him. How sad and disheartened he appeared. He had failed, it was obvious.

Both men sat at the next table and ordered a bottle of whiskey.

Savannah waited till both men were settled then she spoke. "My uncle returned three days ago and said things went well. Osceola signed the treaty along with the other chiefs." She hated the sound of reproach in her tone, but she couldn't help it.

"We couldn't dock the goddamn ship, much less take to the ground. The Creeks were thick as flies over rotten fruit. At one point Redeemer and I took to the water and got to shore, only to be turned back by soldiers. We tried everything. It was a mistake and one I should have recognized. The military planned this for a long time. Every footpath, every trail, every waterway was guarded. A stray dog would have had a hard time going through the guards undetected. I had no bona fide business there. We were forced to return. I'm sorry, Savannah, we tried but it was fruitless."

Savannah left, followed by Culpepper, who said Maeve was granting him an all-night audience. Sloan sat for a long time. He didn't ever remember feeling so alone, so cut off from everyone and everything. He was well into a second bottle of whiskey when he felt a presence next to him. "Beaunell!" was all he could manage.

Beaunell Gentry approached Sloan's table, the little cockade feather on her fashionable hat bobbing with each diminutive step she took. She wore a sapphire silk gown trimmed with military-style braid and tiny brass buttons. Her dark hair was piled into fat curls at the back of her head, and her pink glistening lips parted in a demure smile. Beaunell appeared every inch a lady; her bedroom profession completely hidden.

"Sloan, I thought it was you, but I wasn't sure. What are you doing in New Orleans?"

Sloan hedged. "What are you doing here? Has something happened at Annemarie's?"

Beaunell gurgled with laughter. "Something is always happening at Annemarie's house, as you know. We parted company. It was time for me to move on. A dashing major invited me to New Orleans and being at loose ends I decided to accompany him. He's very handsome and most generous," Beaunell said quietly, hoping to make Sloan jealous.

"I'm happy for you, Beau. I'm glad you found someone who pleases you. Do you plan to stay here or move on with the major?"

"What do you mean, you're happy for me? What did you expect me to do, sit and twiddle my thumbs waiting for you? That's not my style, Sloan. How could you cast me aside the way you did after all we had, after all we shared. You led me to believe . . ."

"Beau, stop right there. I never made any promises. I paid for everything you gave me and may I say I was also more than generous. If you chose to misinterpret, that is not my fault. I'm fond of you; I have always been fond of you. In my own way. I care for you, Beau, but I'm not in love with you. I have no intention of marrying you. We had some good years and a lot of pleasant memories. Why can't we let it go at that? If you need money . . ."

Rage suffused Beaunell's face. "I don't want your money. I don't need your money. You aren't fooling me for one minute. It's that damn savage, isn't it? The one who attacked me in Annemarie's sitting room. Don't worry, your precious Annemarie didn't spill the secrets but Jenny did. Fat old Jenny couldn't wait to tell me all there was to tell. I knew you were up to something, and whatever it is, it isn't finished, is it? I'll fix you, Sloan, one way or the other. I won't let you get away with what you've done to me," she snarled hatefully.

"Jesus, Beau, will you shut up before everyone in New Orleans hears you. When are you going to get it through your head that we couldn't make a go of it? So we were good in bed, but there are other things in life besides rolling between the covers."

"Like making whoopee with the Indians, right?" Beaunell snapped. "I'll find out what it is you're up to and then you'll regret the way you've treated me."

"Go find your major and marry him if he's so inclined. Have some kids and settle down. That's what life is all about. Forget about me, make a new life for yourself."

"I could make a new life if it were you I was marrying, Sloan. You know I've always loved you. I thought you loved me. When I spoke of marriage, you didn't say no. You let me assume, let me think . . ."

Sloan hated the whine in her voice, detested the tears that were filling her round eyes. They meant nothing. He had more money than the major; it was as simple as that. Still, he had to be gentle with her, convince her that he wasn't for her before she set eyes on Savannah and made trouble. His gut churned at the thought of what Beaunell was capable of doing.

Several days later Savannah opened the door to her room and was walking past her uncle's room when she noticed the door was wide open. Stealing a peek inside, she found him packing his personal belongings into a case. He was going away. Her heart thumped in her chest. She said nothing, but her eyes questioned these strange actions. After all, he had just returned. Something must be wrong.

"My dear Savannah. How pretty you look. I'll be leaving in the morning. I have to go to the front and wipe out those damn savages. It's an all-out attack. We're going to squelch any resistance right from the beginning."

Savannah's mind raced. "But you just signed the treaty. You said . . ."

"I know what I said, and I know what I'm saying now. Every last one of those savages is going to be wiped out. I'll see to it personally. I thought we would dine at Antoine's tonight. I want to remember you in a pleasant setting and Antoine's is the perfect place. The service is impeccable and the food is wonderful. I must leave before sunup to be at the rail depot to see my troops assemble. It's my duty. There's no reason for you to rise so early. We'll have dinner, some wine, and say our good-bye's this evening. I've arranged everything. I've added additional monies to your bank account. Mrs. Bouvier will continue to run the household. Your every comfort will be seen to. I know you're going to be lonely, but my officers' wives will visit with you. I'll try to get back as often as possible to see you. Now that I've found Caroline's daughter, I don't ever plan to lose her again. I can't tell you how happy you've made me. Having you here in my home is like having my beloved Caroline again."

Savannah was thunderstruck. Another shoeless trip to MacAllister's hotel room was all she could think of, but first she would have to go to dinner with her uncle. What would MacAllister say to all of this news?

"Will an hour be enough time for you to change for dinner?" Savannah nodded. She could change in five minutes if she had to. Five minutes to change her gown and fifty minutes to think, or was it forty minutes in an hour. She couldn't remember. Not that it made a great deal of difference. Her uncle would wait for her if she were two hours late. He might chastise her, but he would smile and tell her how much he loved Caroline's daughter.

Savannah changed into a gown elegant in its simplicity. The color matched her eyes perfectly. The velvet ribbon with the cameo was tied around her neck. She debated over changing her shoes. She hated shoes of any kind, and once the miserable things were on her feet she preferred to keep them on till she was ready to retire for the evening. It was torture to take them off, rummage for a pair to match the gown. But she did it. Quickly, she brushed her hair, letting it fall in loose waves about her shoulders. MacAllister said he liked her hair when it fell about her shoulders, telling her she looked like an angel. Perhaps she would see MacAllister in the dining room and she could flirt with him. Annemarie had been right; it was very easy to flirt. She even enjoyed the look of discomfort on MacAllister's face when she batted her lashes at him. She loved it when his eyes took on a sleepy look and he squirmed in his chair as though ants had crawled into his pants.

Thomas Jessup looked over the tables in the dining room, finally selecting one where he felt Savannah and himself would be shown off to the best advantage. It was a small, intimate table surrounded by potted plants. To the left was a gilded cage with a pair of lovebirds sitting together on a perch. Anyone entering the room would immediately notice the decor first and then the patrons at the table. Anyone sitting would find their eyes drawn to the gilded cage and Caroline's daughter.

Jessup ordered for both of them: roast lamb, parsleyed potatoes, a crisp green salad, along with fingertip carrots. Soft, mouth-watering rolls, along with thick, yellow butter ended the meal. The wine, he ordered firmly, was to be properly chilled. Coffee and fresh strawberries would be the perfect dessert. She was having trouble with the mint jelly. Annemarie had overlooked lamb with jelly. When in doubt, play with the food, stirring it about on your plate till someone came to take it away. Savannah stirred and stirred.

"Aren't you hungry, my dear?" Jessup asked, concern in his voice.

Startled, Savannah looked at her uncle. "No, I was thinking about you leaving in the morning."

"That's exactly what I thought. Now, you must not worry. I'll be back as soon as I can. Nothing is going to go wrong." His voice was gentle with what Savannah thought was concern for her. She stirred some more, the mint jelly melting around the meat on her plate. The small, white potatoes, with their flecks of parsley, were long since mashed and soaking in the jelly. Her stomach turned at the mess on her plate.

"This is quite good, but Mrs. Bouvier makes a better roast, I think. It's probably in the spices she uses. No two cooks cook alike," Jessup said in a knowledgeable voice.

"I'm sure you're right, Uncle."

A small stir was being created at the entrance to the dining room. Savannah gasped. The woman who had attacked her in Annemarie's sitting room. MacAllister's old woman! She bit down on her tongue and felt the salty taste of her own blood. What was she doing here? Would she come over to the table? For the first time in her young life Savannah knew gut fear. There was no place she could hide, no place she could go. All she could do was brazen the situation out. Beaunell, on the arm of a handsome man in uniform, sailed down the center aisle, her head held high, paying no attention to anyone. That was good. Savannah sighed as she attacked the luscious red strawberries in front of her. She wished she could pick them up in her fingers and pop them in her mouth. It was so hard to cut a strawberry with a spoon the way her uncle was doing.

Where was MacAllister's former woman sitting? Would she see her and her uncle when they rose to leave? She wished she had paid more attention to the seating arrangements in the dining room when they entered. She couldn't do anything about it. Now she had two things to tell MacAllister. They lingered over coffee and the remainder of the wine. Savannah made small talk about inconsequential things, such as her latest needlepoint pattern and the color of thread she was using opposed to what the pattern called for. She could tell her uncle was not excited with her boring habits. Nor was she.

"If you're finished, my dear, I think we can be on our way. I would like to retire early. The train leaves at seven, and I must be there a good hour ahead of time. Let me say, I enjoyed this precious time we've had this evening. It's almost the same as having Caroline next to me. Come along, my dear," he said, rising to hold out her chair.

Savannah tried to wiggle out of the chair without turning so that the woman from Annemarie's wouldn't notice her. She failed miserably. Even from where she stood, she could hear the woman's gasp. She turned deliberately and stared straight at Beaunell, defying her to make a scene.

"Who is that?" Beaunell demanded of her companion, Major Steven Foxe.

"That's Miss Savannah James. Do you know her? If so, I would like an introduction."

"I just wager you would. Not her, the man she's with. Who is he?"

Foxe stared at Beaunell. "That's Brevet Major General Thomas Jessup, my commanding officer. Do you wish to make his acquaintance? Miss James is his niece. Every officer serving under Jessup is waiting anxiously for a dinner invitation to the general's home."

Beaunell seethed and fumed. So, that was the way it was. Her agile mind clicked away trying to make sense out of what was going on. Toward the end of the meal she thought she knew. Foxe's words startled her, shaking her from her deep thoughts. "Jessup is leaving by railroad in the morning. He's heading for the front. I'm staying behind to clean up a few details. Then I'll join him in a week's time. If he needs me, I'll be leaving sooner."

"In the morning, you say?" At his nod, Beaunell bit into a bloody red piece of meat. She chewed viciously, her eyes narrowed with what the major thought was lust.

Savannah settled herself in a highbacked windsor chair in the sitting room. When was her uncle going to go to bed? Why did he persist in prowling around as he was doing? His bags were packed and resting near the front door. Perhaps he was anxious, uncertain about how he was going to slaughter Osceola's people. Perhaps he was conscious of his own safety too.

It was midnight when Savannah finally climbed the stairs to her room. She couldn't go to Sloan now. The morning would be soon enough. Just as soon as her uncle left for the rail depot.

She slept badly, tossing and turning. She woke while it was still dark, bathed in perspiration. She washed and donned a fresh gown. She quietly crept below stairs and entered the kitchen. Mrs. Bouvier was already about. Coffee was bubbling on the stove. The ingredients were on the tabletop for a hearty breakfast, something Jessup always insisted upon. The thought of food gagged her, but she knew she would have to join her uncle at the breakfast table and wish him a safe trip as he swilled down his coffee and ate his way through a half-dozen eggs and a stack of wheatcakes.

Savannah was already seated at her place at the table when Jessup entered the dining room. Surprise and pleasure lit his features. She was her mother's daughter. How kind of her to rise so early to see him off. Caroline would have done the same thing. "Good morning, my dear. May I say it is a pleasure to see you this morning. The sight of you will make my departure that much more bearable. I can't tell you how pleased I am. I just wish I could sit and converse with you, but my men are waiting for me." He dabbed at his lips and rose from the table. Savannah rose too and followed him to the front door. Standing outside at attention was his aide-de-camp. He immediately gathered up the general's bags and loaded them in a buckboard. He saluted smartly and drove off. Jessup embraced Savannah and smiled down into her eyes. "You are truly a likeness of Caroline." Without another word he was gone.

The minute the door was closed Savannah raced up the stairs to her room for a shawl. At the last minute she splashed on some cologne and brushed out her hair. She was arranging a pretty lavender shawl about her shoulders when a knock sounded on the front door. Her eyes widened as she peeped over the upstairs railing. Mrs. Bouvier answered the door and invited a young woman inside. Savannah's hand flew to her mouth—the woman from Annemarie's.

"I'd like to see General Jessup please before he leaves," Beaunell said quietly in what Savannah later called a very ladylike voice.

"The general's gone, Miss. But you should be able to catch him at the depot. His train leaves at seven."

Beaunell digested the information. "And the general's niece, Savannah, is she at home?"

"Yes, Miss, she is. Would you like me to call her? She just retired to her room when the general left. I expect she's feeling quite alone now and saddened at the general's departure."

"I'm sure you're right. We won't disturb her. I can call again when she's more up to things. I'll just go along to the depot and see General Jessup off." Beaunell turned and left, her bearing regal, as though she paid visiting calls at six in the morning every day of the week.

Savannah's knees trembled so badly she could barely stand. Her breathing was harsh and labored as she fought to bring herself under control. She had to get out of here before the woman got to the depot. She had no idea where the depot was, much less how long it would take to get there. She raced to the window in time to see the woman's carriage turn the corner. Off came the shoes and on went her moccasins. No one would notice them beneath the gown. From the looks of things outside her window not too many people were stirring at this time in the morning.

Quietly she crept down the stairs and let herself out. Once she was on the street in the cool morning air she ran like the wind. When she reached the hotel, she was breathing heavily. She paid no mind to the disgruntled desk clerk but raced up the stairs. She didn't bother to knock. Frantically she threw open the door. Obviously, he had been asleep. How could he sleep at a time like this?

"What the hell!" Sloan sputtered alarmed at seeing her at his door at such an ungodly hour. "Savannah!"

"Listen to me, MacAllister." Quickly she recounted Jessup's words of the previous day leaving nothing out, not even the death of the dog. She finished up with Beaunell and her trip to the depot.

Sloan ripped off his nightshirt and pulled on his trousers and boots. "Beaunell," he muttered, giving the woman from Annemarie's a name. "Little bitch. I should have known to expect trouble from her. No time to pack. There's nothing here I really need." He fished for money in his wallet and drew out a sheaf of notes.

The desk clerk looked at the pile of money fluttering on the counter. His eyes widened as he stared at Savannah and Sloan's backs. Such an odd couple, he mused to himself. But his mother liked to hear about all the strange customers the hotel drew in. She was going to like the fifty-dollar tip the anxious man had left even better than the story.

Sloan dragged Savannah to the stable, threw another sheaf of bills at the stable hand and then saddled Redeemer. Even the huge beast seemed to know it was time to move on.

The first thing Jessup would do, Sloan knew, after Beaunell told him what she knew about Savannah, would be to streak back to the house to confront his niece. After pondering the question of why Savannah had lied to him about where she'd been all these years and why she had suddenly decided to turn up when he was involved in the most heated war with the Seminoles, he would have his answer. Savannah, living among the Seminoles, had placed herself back into Jessup's life to spy on him for the Indians. Beyond that, he would neither know nor care. Quite possibly, he would have murder on his mind. After what Savannah had told him, MacAllister knew that Jessup's devotion toward her was only because of his sister, Caroline. Savannah was only a replacement.

Down through the Vieux Carré to the wharf. The *Polly Copinger* sat neatly in her berth. Hopefully, Culpepper wouldn't have much difficulty in rounding up the crew. At least, MacAllister told himself, Beaunell knew nothing about his ship. That was one little piece of information she couldn't impart to Jessup. They would be safe enough for the time being. But feeling as though the hounds of hell were on his heels, Sloan wanted to pull out of New Orleans. Soon.

The hour was late, the lights from the harbor fell onto Savannah's face, lighting it to his tender gaze. "We should be going below," he told her, touching her arm in soothing little caresses. "We've done all we can here. Culpepper has rounded up the crew and he plans to sail on the next tide. Less than five hours from now. We'd better get some sleep."

"MacAllister, I keep thinking that it was all for nothing. All of it. I would have been more help to Osceola if I'd stayed with my people and cared for the wounded. Nothing. All for nothing."

"That's not true," Sloan scolded. "You did everything you could, all anyone could. All of the information you gathered was valuable; it was my own blundering that made it impossible for me to deliver it to Osceola." His fist hit the rail with such force that Savannah winced.

Tender emotions rushed within her. No, she corrected herself, it was not all for nothing. If she had stayed behind with the Seminoles she would never have known who Thomas Jessup was. Never would have learned enough to find her father's family some day. There were things she learned about her mother that she never would have known. She would have spent the rest of her life wondering, missing a piece of herself.

Their cabin was softly lit by an oil lamp. Savannah changed into a silk shirt that MacAllister had left behind. She felt his eyes watching her, drinking her in. This was where she was meant to be, here with MacAllister, preparing for bed and the passion they would share. But tonight it would be different. Tonight they would solace one another and soothe their disappointment.

Sloan's arms reached out for her, drawing her close to stand between his knees. "You always wear one of my shirts; it pleases me."

Her hand ruffled his hair, liking the thickness and feeling the golden strands slip through her fingers. Even if he didn't say it, she was his woman. Only his.

Arms wrapped around her hips, he pressed his face against the flatness of her belly. He held her this way for a moment before pulling her down on the bed beside him. His lips made delightful excursions along her jaw, down over her throat to his favorite place between her breasts.

Savannah yielded to him, offering herself, anticipating the pleasure he would bring her. Pleasure that would help to heal the sorrow, pleasure that would make her forget, for a little while, at least, her fears.

Sloan had told her that they were going to Florida. Back among the Seminoles. Together. At last, she told herself, as his hands found the smoothness of her thighs and the center of her desires, she would be with MacAllister and together they would build a chikkee.

CHAPTER NINE

t was the end of March; balmy breezes blew off the Gulf of Mexico across Osceola's land. The hardwood trees were green and in bud. Spring had touched the earth and new life was born. Young fox pups nuzzled their mothers' bellies in hungry anticipation; birds were busily finding food for their nestlings, and wild flowers praised the sun with their radiant colors.

The *Polly Copinger* had made anchor at the mouth of a secondary river which emptied into the Gulf, far enough north of the Fort Dade area to remain undiscovered by the army.

Making contact with a band of blacks who had been instructed to be on the lookout for the *Polly*, Sloan and Savannah were led to a temporary camp inland, grateful that the crew could remain aboard with Culpepper. Each Negro would carry a crate of rifles on his strong back.

Savannah quickly readapted to the rigors of the forest and made the day's walk easily. It was just approaching nightfall when they entered the Seminole camp.

There was much embracing from Osceola and many words passed across the campfire. "What went wrong?" Osceola demanded.

"General Jessup is not a man of his word. I tried to reach you earlier when I sailed here and could not get near the shore line. The Creeks and Jessup's men were patrolling every strip of beach. I was forced to return to New Orleans. I have brought three hundred Hall rifles with me. A promise of two thousand more will arrive by the end of May, the latest the first week in June. You and the other chiefs signed a false document. By now, you must know this. Jessup was behind it, as you might have guessed. Bring me up to date; tell me what has been going on. How can we help?"

Osceola pondered Sloan's questions for several moments before he answered. "Only to you, my brother, would I admit my worry. My nation, my people, are losing strength. My best warriors are the blacks, and soon they will walk from me. They think for themselves. I am proud of my black brothers. There is an ugly rumor that Coa Hadjo, a chief who has many under him and makes his camps to the south of us near Lake Okeechobee, has been parleying with General Jessup. Just yesterday, word came to me that a band of blacks defied Coa Hadjo to send them back to the whites. They said Coa Hadjo had not captured them, so it was not up to him to return them. I am inclined to believe the story. We are now a divided people, and one does not know who speaks true words and who speaks false words. I myself had sharp words to say to Coa Hadjo last week in council. He wanted the runaways returned. I spoke out in anger against this change in policy. As long as I am in the nation, it will never be done. What more can I say, brother?"

"It is my intention to train your men with the new rifle, to show them the discipline they need to fight the white man. Without discipline and organization you cannot hope for victory. Our success will depend largely on your men's cooperation. I'll start with your lieutenants and they can train others. Jessup will bring all of this to a head by late summer. Your people must be ready." He quickly recounted his and Savannah's time spent in New Orleans. "We wouldn't be here now if it wasn't for Savannah. She feels, my brother, that she was of little help to you. She wanted to return tall and proud for your eyes. A kind word, perhaps, by you would not go unnoticed."

"It will be done. I am grateful to both of you. Your foodstuffs are almost gone, but we will survive. And if we are to die as the great God in the sky predicts then our spirits will live on. You, brother, are in danger as long as you stay with us. An unauthorized white man caught in these parts is dead. You will have to dress as one of us. Your ship, the *Polly Copinger*, where is it? I worry for your safety, brother."

"Don't. I've heard this all before from a friend in Galveston. I assure you, brother, I have long before this weighed the odds. I am an American. A white man. But I cannot live with the trickery and deceit I see being staged here. I don't think of my actions as treason. I am merely attempting to even the odds, if only in a small way. If most Americans understood what was being done to the Seminoles, they would not find me guilty. Enough said." The gravity in Sloan's voice subsided and in a lighter tone he added, "As for the *Polly*, she's in a deepwater inlet with a sharp-eyed sea salt who will shoot at the first sign of trouble. My crew is well paid and will do as ordered. Our mother's namesake will not sink to bottom, and she may be just the vessel to get us out of a tight spot."

"One day I must see this ship you named after our mother." A smile played around the corners of his mouth as he stared into the flames, remembering long-ago days when he grew under his mother's watchful eye.

The silence was not uncomfortable. When Osceola spoke again, it was in a gentle tone. "And the girl, has she come to mean something to you? You will make a chikkee when the time is right or has this been done?"

Sloan laughed. Right to the core. "You always did want to know the answer before the question was asked. Yes," was all he said.

Amusement glittered in the coal-black eyes. "You tamed the wildcat!"

"More like she tamed me," Sloan grinned.

"The hour grows late, brother. I'll dispatch a runner to have my lieutenants here by first light. We will talk again tomorrow. My children were promised a story before sleep, and they wait for me. What do you think, Sloan, should this story be about two brothers who grew only to love one another more?"

"If I had such lovely daughters as you do, it is the story I would tell them. Sleep well, brother. Tomorrow is the start of a new day. For all of us. We'll work together to build something no man can take from you." Both men stood at the same time. Jet black eyes stared deeply into silvery gray ones. Simultaneously, their arms reached out, and each touched the other's shoulders gently. It was right that they were united again.

Sloan was tired and he went in search of Savannah. She stood at a distance talking quietly to one of the women. When she noticed Sloan, she moved toward him. He noticed in the flickering light of the fire that she had shed her silk dress and donned a sky blue cotton skirt with yellow overblouse. A gift, she told him later, from Morning Dew, for what she had tried to do for her husband. Sloan watched her as she spread the blankets in a secluded spot near the fire, but far enough away to afford them some privacy.

Mico had night guard. When he saw Savannah spread the blankets, his teeth clamped shut. His dark eyes swallowed the two forms as Sloan took Savannah in his arms.

For two weeks Sloan drilled Osceola's men till they pleaded with their chief for mercy. Osceola turned a deaf ear to all such pleadings, calling his braves sick women. "My brother wants only to secure your life and the lives of our women and children. Any further mewlings will be punished." Dark eyes snapped and crackled as the young lieutenants loaded, aimed and fired. Again and again, they worked with the new Hall rifle till their shoulders ached with the strain.

One day Sloan announced that the men were ready and he promised an exhibition for Osceola and the rest of the camp. The braves donned their war paint and their best dress.

Osceola sat cross-legged near his chikkee. Both little girls sat next to him, their mother behind. "You must be the one to order your lieutenants to train the others as they have been trained. If they don't follow procedure and work the men mercilessly, it will be for naught. Now that they have mastered the art, they must continue the way I've trained them. It is not my place to issue orders."

"It will be done. I see the confidence; the exuberance, that you have instilled in them, shine from their eyes. They are proud men, my braves, and I can count on each of them. We will have no problem. Rest easy, brother."

"They can shoot better than any front-line army soldier, Osceola. Discipline was all that was needed. I'm only glad I could make this deal for the guns."

"You have done much for our people. It will never be forgotten."

The exhibition lasted well over two hours. The braves lined up, shot at targets for starters. Then they fired in unison at another target. Each time Sloan raised his arm or lowered it, they would crouch and shoot or run and aim and then fire. They were expert at dropping to the ground, rolling to the right, and firing, and then rolling to the left to reload. They never fired from the same position twice. At the end of the exhibition the braves lined up, their guns at attention. They waited. Sloan stood and then walked in front of the men the way an inspecting general might do. To each he had a personal word. To Mico, the last in line, he said quietly, "You are by far the best shot in this camp. I'm proud of you." Jet black eyes revealed nothing as Mico returned his level gaze.

Sloan turned to the camp. "Completely acceptable!" he shouted. There were whistles and shouts of approval from the camp.

Osceola himself stood, one of his small daughters perched on his shoulder. "You have made me proud this day. We owe my brother thanks. Thanks that can never be paid by words alone. He is truly your brother from this day on." A wicked grin stretched across his generous mouth. "Dismissed!" he shouted loudly. Aside, he whispered to Sloan, "Did I do that right?"

Sloan matched his grin. "Better than any general could have done."

Osceola sat near the council fire, listening, holding his tongue, until it was time for him to speak. His rage burned inside him, making the flickering flames from the fire cool by comparison. When would it be his turn to speak? To turn the heads of his brothers to face in one direction? Sloan, sitting behind his brother, could sense the Indian's outrage and admired his control in keeping his tongue until his time came. Sam Jones, Arpeika, sat across the fire from Osceola, his hooded, ancient eyes never leaving the tormented chief's face.

Osceola brooded, furious with what he was hearing. Micanopy, Holacoochee, Alligator, Jumper . . . all voiced their intention to assemble at the detention center at Tampa Bay with their people to ready themselves for the trip westward aboard the ships the Government was to supply. And in so doing, they were surrendering the Negroes taken during the war, delivering them to the commanding officers of the posts on the St. Johns.

Already Sloan and Osceola had witnessed the hardships imposed on their black brothers. None of them willingly accompanied the Seminole chiefs to the stations on the St. Johns River. Being warriors, they resisted. When at last they were overcome by their Indian brothers, they were brought in bound and tethered. Never, Osceola told himself, did he ever expect to live to see the day when the Seminole would betray the Negro. Yet, it had come. Perhaps he had lived too long.

The time had come, he told himself, when he must assert himself again and seize control. Over at Fort Mellon, Coa Hadjo, King Phillip and Coacoochee had already turned in their Negroes.

Prior to the council, during which each thlacko would have his turn to speak, Arpeika and Osceola had discussed the expected outcome. Both were puzzled and aggrieved as to what should be their next move. The idea of turning in runaway slaves was inconceivable, even worse than any agreement about going west. Now they were being isolated from the rest of the Seminole Nation.

"We have one choice," Osceola had told the old medicine man. "Phillip and Coacoochee have gone to Fort Mellon. I think they will agree with us to resist the whites. They can't come out to join us without causing a great deal of trouble, but *we can go in* to join them!"

When Micanopy finished speaking, encouraging his equals to put an end to this war, it was at last Osceola's turn to speak. So involved was he with his own thoughts that Sloan had to prod a finger into his brother's back to remind him. Standing before the council fire, Osceola lifted his voice, bringing strength into its timbre, placing the facts before the War Council.

Savannah, sitting among the women, listened with rapt attention, hated tears springing to her eyes at the emotion her chief brought to his words.

"We are brothers together here in the Floridas beneath the watchful eyes of the Great Spirits. We are brothers to the blacks who have been our friends and have served us well. It is to profane the eyes of the Spirits to turn the blacks over to the white soldiers who will give our brothers back to the slavers." Here Osceola reminded the chiefs of how many Seminoles had taken black women in marriage and of the children whose blood was Seminole and Negro mixed. "Phillip and Coa Hadjo have committed themselves to turning in the blacks. It is because *we* were not strong enough to unite and give strength to their decisions. But if we group at Fort Mellon and go in to join them, I know they will fight beside us." For nearly two hours Osceola spoke, recounting past victories and past defeats, returning always to the belief that by displaying unity King Phillip and Coa Hadjo would reverse their decision to surrender.

Hope was reborn amidst the council. Osceola had said the words they wanted to hear. Instead of living with defeat, the Seminole might claim victory for his own.

Sloan was overcome with emotion and pride. Glancing past the now low-burning fire, his eyes met with Savannah's and he saw her smile. Arpeika nodded his dirty gray head and he thumped his breast with a gnarled, old hand. The Seminole would be men again. They would release the prisoners from the detention center. He had heard rumors that the nation of Seminoles would be loaded and crammed into the twenty-six ships waiting in Tampa Bay and drowned at sea before reaching Texas en route to the Arkansas Territory.

Why, why, Arpeika asked himself, wouldn't the white-eyes allow the Indian and their allies to go south where the land was swamp and the game was plentiful? There, living on land that no one else would ever want, they could live in peace. The land called the Everglades would provide subsistence for his people. Shaking his head with sorrow, Arpeika thought that he was getting much too old to lead Mikasukis, warriors, into battle. His weary gray head filled more and more with thoughts of peaceful hunting and fishing instead of the fiercesome war cry of his braves.

Following Osceola's orders, Sloan had stayed behind to lead the Indians when the thlacko sent for them. Together with Arpeika, Osceola arrived at Fort Mellon and reported to Lieutenant William Harney, telling him they were prepared to emigrate.

Osceola was thin and weary, another recent bout of malaria had laid him low and his spirits were sagging, but he was determined to follow the plan. He would release his people from the white soldiers or he would die trying. Standing tall, displaying strength and conviction, he reported to Lieutenant Harney that more than twenty-five hundred Seminoles were expected to arrive at Fort Mellon shortly.

News traveled quickly to General Jessup, and he prepared to journey to Fort Mellon, at last to witness the infamous Osceola's defeat. Jessup had been irritated by the outbreak of measles in the detention camp farther south at Tampa Bay. The Indians were frightened, rumors of smallpox were reported, further delaying the emigration.

Osceola was prepared for the visit from his esteemed enemy, General Jessup. The day was warm, too warm for late May, and his leggings of scarlet and decorated turban felt hot and clinging.

Demonstrating his annoyance over the slow progress of the

Seminoles into the detention camp, Jessup unceremoniously strode up to the waiting chief; his complexion was flushed with anger. "Osceola," he began perfunctorily, his antipathy for the Indian bringing his mouth down into a scowl, "your people are delaying in assembling at Tampa Bay!"

Although Osceola understood and spoke perfect English, his dark, haunted eyes swung to the Indian interpreter Jessup had brought with him.

Answering the interpreter, he said, "My people are fearful of the white man's disease, smallpox. Is it necessary to kill them even before they leave on the boats the army provides? Is not their sorrow heavy enough because they must leave this land they have called home long before the white man came with his rifles and hatred?"

Jessup sputtered when he listened to the interpreter's message. "You tell this savage I'll brook no more delays!" he roared. "Tell him that I intend to send exploring parties to every part of the country throughout the summer, and that I shall take all Negroes who belong to the white people. Tell him to be careful not to allow Indians to mix with the runaways because they'll be taken also." Pausing for a moment, Jessup's small, shifty eyes glittered with frustration. "And tell this savage that I am sending to Cuba for bloodhounds to trail his people, and I intend to hang every one of them who does not come in of his own volition!"

Osceola listened to the interpreter with his full and solemn attention. He had understood the general implicitly. He also understood, to his amusement, that General Jessup was almost at the end of his rope. He wanted this war done with, and he expected to step out of it with full honors. If only the Seminoles wouldn't keep delaying the outcome. Osceola suppressed a smile. He could almost smell the general's desperation oozing out of his pores.

Osceola and Arpeika had left for Fort Mellon, and by this time would have made contact with Coa Hadjo and King Phillip, who had defected from the Seminole viewpoint to accede to the demands of the government. Sloan knew Osceola would not be able to convince his fellow chiefs of the wisdom to resist the army's demands without many long nights before the council fire. Once having committed themselves publicly to turn over the blacks under them and to migrate to Arkansas, it would appear to be a loss of face to withdraw from the treaty.

Most of Sloan's time was spent with Osceola's lieutenants training the warriors in the use of the rifle. Mendoza's shipment had arrived from Cuba, and the weapons were being dispensed. Now would be the most difficult assignment: waiting for the signal from Osceola to take action to free those Indians and blacks who had followed their chiefs into the army's hands.

MacAllister was anxious to make the move, to set into action the training he had provided, to share in the success the Seminoles so desperately needed. He knew that until now Jessup had been raiding the Indians mostly for a show of strength to force them into agreeing to the Dade Treaty. The man had his public image to protect. Knowing the general as he did, Sloan felt Jessup wouldn't satisfy himself with moving the Indians and returning the blacks to the slave market. He was out for much bigger game—the annihilation of the Seminoles, and if it couldn't be accomplished here in Florida, then it would be done in Arkansas, where he could also destroy the Creek nation. It was Sloan's opinion that Jessup would wait until he had migrated the Florida Indians; it would be a matter of two birds with one stone. Both the Seminole and the Creek would fall under the concentrated blows of his Army.

In the hours before dawn, long after the council fire had burned low, Arpeika and Osceola sat beneath a willow tree on the shore of Lake Munroe and watched the fish snap at hovering insects. The Indians had been given the freedom of the area because it was realized that it was impossible to confine the Seminoles behind the stockade fences. The chiefs would not wander far, the Army reasoned, not with their people being held hostage at the fort. The two men sat in silence, each intent on his own thoughts. It had been many days since turning themselves in to the fort to make contact with King Phillip and Coa Hadjo, but tonight had been their reward. At last, the two chiefs had capitulated and agreed to join forces with Osceola and resist the migration.

A bugle sounded from the fort to signal reveille, and Osceola felt a stirring of excitement as he always did before a battle. All that needed to be done was to decide when Sloan should organize the attack.

"So, the great thlacko closes his eyes in sleep," Arpeika taunted, spitting into the still, black waters of the lake.

"Not sleep," Osceola defended, "I dream."

"Yes, with one eye open, like the alligator stalking the bird. Tell me your dream," the cantankerous old man grunted.

"I dream that this time tomorrow night I take my warriors to Tampa Bay." Osceola voiced his intention to send Sloan the signal for the next night. "When all are asleep, we free Micanopy and our people. A word to Coacoochee and his people scatter also. I dream that Micanopy, a traitor to his people, will no longer be a chief. I dream there will be a new chief, elected to lead all the Seminoles under one heart, one brain."

"Phillip?" Arpeika growled, spitting again to show his disapproval.

"No, not Phillip. This great chief must be a great warrior with great wisdom. He must be a Mikasuki. His name is Arpeika."

"Hieah," the old warrior-medicine man grunted. "If the Spirits allow me to live so long. And what of yourself? You are younger, stronger. You should be chief of all the Seminole."

"Not I, old man. I have another dream. It is as you once told me. I do not die here on Seminole land. I do not die in Arkansas beyond the Great River. But I die."

Arpeika was silent, listening to the chirping of crickets in the tall grasses. What Osceola said was true. He had read it in the signs and in the sand. Only his own stubbornness prevented him from laying a comforting arm on the younger man's shoulder.

Sloan watched the women of the camp through narrowed eyes as they gathered together their few belongings. It was a hard life at best. They were always moving, always on the run just to stay alive. How hungry they looked. But how proud as they herded their children near them. They would move as often as necessary, go hungry as often as necessary. They were used to this gypsy life that Sloan hated.

He dreaded the forthcoming scene with Savannah more than he would admit. What was he going to say to her to make the parting easier? Of late, the words failed to sail past his lips. He found himself thinking more and speaking less. Events were moving too fast for him to comprehend what was happening. The day Culpepper was dragged into camp by three blacks, screaming that he was Osceola's uncle, would be a day he would never forget. By the time Sloan had the sea salt's bonds cut, he knew that Maeve was closing in for the big wedding, and Culpepper had gotten away by the skin of his teeth. He was demanding to fight alongside Sloan for something he had believed in thanks to Sloan and all of his brothers. "If it's me time, Laddie, I want to go to me Maker doing something I believe in. And I do believe in your cause. So, hand me a rifle and I'll be next to ye fer whatever good I'll be."

Sloan was delighted with the old man. He proved himself invaluable as they set about storing what provisions he had brought along with the two thousand rifles. "The price was high, Laddie. Yer man charged $35,000. I paid up as ye said without a word."

"There is no price on life, Enwright," Sloan said using the captain's Christian name to show he was serious. "For my brother's life and the lives of his people, it is a cheap price. The dozen horses will save our lives. Don't tell me where you got them, I don't want to know."

"Ye wouldn't be believing me anyway. They were a wedding present from Maeve. I just took them and skedaddled," he said sourly. "Appaloosas," he said proudly.

"Christ!" was all Sloan could say. "Enwright, you have style. There aren't many men who would do what you did. I'm proud of you," he said, slapping the old man on the back. Culpepper grinned sheepishly as he set about carrying rifles into the forest.

Inside of an hour the camp was dismantled. The women were ready for their long journey. Something tugged at Sloan. How alone Savannah looked, how frightened. He hated good-bye's of any kind, but this was unlike anything he had ever felt before. He walked over to her slowly. Gently, he drew her close to him. "Go now. Make as much progress in daylight as you can. Take good care of the children. My brother and I are depending on you."

Tears gathered in Savannah's eyes. "Why can't I go with you? I know these forests better than you. I do not want to go with the women and play nursemaid to children. I want to be at your side."

"We've talked this over before, Savannah. Captain Culpepper said there is an outbreak of measles. We both know that the Indian cannot resist that disease. You must go deep into the forest. I gave you the map. Follow it the way I showed you and I'll join you as soon as possible."

Savannah wiped at her eyes with the back of her hand, but took her place behind Ina and Yahi. Sloan knew he had never seen anything sadder, more heartbreaking, in his life. A lump settled in his throat, making it hard to swallow. Culpepper patted him on the shoulder in a friendly manner. Together they joined the others and headed in the opposite direction. There was nothing more he could do.

All two hundred of the men assigned to Sloan by Osceola filed into the dense forest. Sloan and Culpepper were the last to leave the camp. Sloan cast a long, angry look around before he turned to Culpepper. Just then, a Seminole runner appeared. Sloan waited as he spat out his information. "It is said General Jessup is considering unleashing bloodhounds from Cuba if the holdouts continue. Those Indians in the detention camp would be hanged if the delay continues." Sloan considered the statement.

"Let it be known that the Indians are on the way. When stomachs are empty, moccasins move slowly." The runner departed, not liking the message he would let filter back to one General Jessup.

The trek to join Osceola was a long and arduous one. Only Culpepper lagged at times. Feeling sorry for the sea captain, Sloan ordered him atop one of the Appaloosas. Culpepper protested bitterly at this undignified betrayal on Sloan's part, saying he felt like a woman.

"I'm concerned with your lame leg. I want you in fighting condition when we join Osceola." Culpepper grimaced, relieved secretly that he could ride and see over the heads of the Indians and the blacks.

The moon rode high in the heavens, majestic in its shimmering brightness, when Sloan reached the rendezvous point. His men settled themselves comfortably to await their chief. Tampa Bay was but a stone's throw from where they were quartered.

Osceola was the first to arrive. Within minutes the men behind him joined Sloan's men. Whispered words passed in the stillness of the forest surrounding them.

"Mico, Yahoola, Culpepper, come with me." Seeing that his brother was about to object, Sloan spoke to him in English. "No, I will go. If something should happen to me, you will be safe. Your people need you. I am expendable. We go only to survey the guards and the garrison. Have no fear, brother, I have become attached to my skin. I have no wish to die in Tampa Bay. I plan to live to a ripe old age with many grandchildren at my feet. How do you think they would like it if the story I tell them does not include some foolhardy bravery." Without another word he fell in behind Mico, Yahoola and Culpepper at his heels.

An hour later they returned to the temporary camp. It was to Osceola that Sloan addressed himself. "A mounted company and more than a hundred Creeks surround the camp. The number is closer to one hundred fifty. We can outnumber them and overtake them without too much trouble." Osceola nodded to show that he would agree to anything Sloan said. In the bright moonlight Sloan broke off a stout branch and proceeded to draw a rough map, in the loamy earth, of the detention camp. Osceola's lieutenants were given their positions. There were nods; no words spoken among the assembled men.

Sloan raised his arm and the men broke apart, their moccasins making no sound as they surrounded the camp.

It was a silent, bloody battle. The Creeks, angry at their white employers because of abuse to their families by the whites in Alabama, had no desire to fight to the death and the expertise of Osceola's warriors quickly overpowered them. They fled into the bay, wading out into the water. When Osceola raised his arm high overhead fifty minutes later to show the battle was over, Sloan dropped to the ground. He had taken a bullet alongside his neck that stunned him. Next to him, he saw Mico with a vicious chest wound. His head reeled and then he knew no more.

Osceola strode into the detention camp and searched the long, barrackslike room for Micanopy. He was disgusted with the looks of the fat chief. Evidently, he had been fed well with white man's rations. Anger that he had slept through the attack further disgusted him. Osceola yanked on his plump leg. Micanopy sat up, snorting and bellowing, and was pulled into the dim lights at the far end of the room. "As you can see, we have you surrounded. You will come with us."

"I cannot go with you. I promised, gave my word to go west," Micanopy protested fearfully.

Hatred fanned Arpeika's features. "Either you come or you die."

"Then kill me now," Micanopy blustered.

"Put the old fool on a horse," Arpeika snarled, turning to the warriors behind him. "He'll change his mind tomorrow."

Osceola let his eyes go to Alligator and Jumper. His gaze locked with Jumper's. "Where's your horse?"

"I sold it," Jumper bleated.

"Then you walk. We'll talk later."

"I only obeyed Micanopy," he said fearfully.

"Later. I said we would talk later," Osceola said sharply, dismissing the whining Jumper from his thoughts. He must find his brother. Spotting Culpepper, he raced toward him. "My brother? Have you seen him?" Culpepper was astounded at the dread he saw in the Indian's eyes. Dread and concern that something had happened to Sloan.

Culpepper forced a jovial note into his tone. "He took a bullet alongside the neck, but he'll live. I meself treated the lad and he's resting easy over there out of sight. Your men are making litters for the wounded. We only have three dead and seventeen wounded. Mico is among them and even with expert doctoring, he will not live. There is hope for the others." The relief in Osceola's jet eyes made Culpepper feel good. He wished he had a brother, someone to share feelings with, someone to care if he lived or died. Sloan was the closest thing to a son he had ever had. His hand had shook when he tended the wound and then it had gentled more than any woman's hand. He loved this strange breed of man who fought an Indian battle alongside an Indian he called brother.

Sloan sat with his back to a gnarled, deformed sea-grape tree. His grin was lopsided as he stared up at Osceola. "On many occasions you have made me proud to call you brother," Osceola said softly. "Today you have made me proud once more. I am only sorry that you were wounded." He dropped to his knees, his face within inches of Sloan's. "There are no words in your language or mine to convey my deep feeling for you and what you have been doing for my people. Sloan," his voice rose slightly, "did I tell you that my people have bestowed a title upon you. It is truly an honor, one to tell those grandchildren some day. They call you the Swamp Fox. Truly you are."

Sloan heard the words, but the only thing he locked in on was Osceola's use of his Christian name. It warmed him greatly and his pain seemed to ease. He smiled weakly. "Now when I tell that story when I'm old and gray, I can add a little blood, embellish my wounds and add my title. I shall hold them spellbound."

Osceola laughed, a deep, rich sound. "I trust you will make the story brilliant with your golden tongue. I must bid you farewell now."

Sloan hated to see his brother leave, but he knew there was no other way. His people needed him. "Brother," he said softly, "I plan to take our mother's namesake to Galveston as soon as Culpepper thinks we can travel. I'll bring back what supplies I can. I'll do my best to fill the *Polly*'s hold. Horses, foodstuffs, mules and some trinkets for the children."

Osceola's voice was suddenly shy. "I would like to make a very large request of my brother. Would it be possible for you to buy presents that would be seemly to give my family. I know nothing of such things, but I did see Morning Dew's eyes brighten over Chala's dress and the adornment she had around her neck. Something beautiful."

Whatever it was that burned his eyes moments ago had come back, making it almost impossible to see. "I think I can arrange that for you. Culpepper has exquisite taste when it comes to women." He held out his hand and Osceola's shot out to grip it. His clasp was firm and hard. "I think our mother would be proud of both of us this day," Sloan said softly.

"You only think," Osceola smiled. "I know she would. Good luck, Sloan." Before Sloan could reply, Osceola was off and running into the forest to join his men.

The women and children followed their chief's orders, breaking into camps of small numbers to await their men in the forest. Many more women with their children in tow were beginning to drift in after being released from the detention camp at Tampa Bay. This, Savannah told herself, was proof that Osceola's and MacAllister's raid on the camp had been successful. The newly arrived women talked of guns being fired and some wounded. Many soldiers, they told the eager ears, were killed, falling down dead in their tracks. They elaborated on the strength and bravery of their own warriors, but their eyes were pained and anxious. Would it be their own men who were being killed? And what of the men, lying wounded in this dampness that seemed to make injuries fester and suppurate? Even the strongest medicine sometimes failed.

Savannah realized Osceola's wisdom in ordering that the women were not to gather in a single large encampment. It would have been too easy for the soldiers to capture them. This way, while some may be captured, many more would find the opportunity to escape.

Che-cho-ter and Ina, along with the children, were camped to the north, awaiting word of their husband and father, Osceola. Only Yahi, the widow woman she had battled for the privilege of whipping MacAllister, elected to come with Savannah here to the camp closest to Tampa Bay. It seemed a lifetime ago that Savannah had first set eyes on MacAllister, and she dreaded that it might be still another lifetime until she saw him again.

Stoic and silent, except for a small group chanting prayers in unison, their light voices lifting softly to the treetops, the women went about preparing medicines and putting children to bed. Secunna, a white-haired old woman, who many believed talked with the Spirits, padded around the camp on her moccasined feet, shaking a string of bones and chanting in her aged voice to keep the bad spirits away from the camp.

Because this camp was closest to the fighting, the wounded and dead would be brought here. Silently, Savannah prayed a mixture of prayers learned from the Seminole and taught by her mother. Feverishly, her eyes pierced the darkness beyond the torches for signs of the first runner.

Since having returned to Florida with MacAllister nearly two moons . . . eight weeks ago, she corrected, they had not been apart for a single day or night. Now she was bereft without him. This was long past the time of night when they would be asleep in their chikkee, the thick, thatch walls separating them, isolating them from everyone and every thing. There, together, they would renew the wonder they had found in one another, touching, kissing. . . . She was his woman. MacAllister's woman. And when passion was reborn with an urgency of its own, they would satisfy it, feed it, nurture it like the Spirits fed the fish in the streams and the birds in the woods, with a loving touch. The words he would whisper in her ear were soft, appealing, and could excite her beyond the plains of the earth to a place behind the moon where nothing else existed, only the two of them. He would tell her how beautiful he thought her, how soft to his touch, how exciting . . . "Please, please"—she stared upward to the heavens where MacAllister's God looked down—"please bring him back to me!"

She saw her fears reflected in the eyes of every woman who had a loved one, husband or son, out there beyond the darkness at Tampa Bay. Tonight could be the turning point of the war. Tonight the Seminole must put the white soldier down and make his voice heard above the tallest trees in the forest. Tonight. Tonight.

Every moment they had shared together became most precious to her. The days when she had watched him drill Osceola's lieutenants, the nights when he would fall exhausted onto their pallet, but never too exhausted to take her in his arms and crush her against his chest and hold her until she fell asleep. The afternoons at the river where they would bathe, washing one another with gentle, exploring fingers and never seemed to tire of one another. Afternoons when the sun would beat down upon them, warming their skin, stirring their blood. Closing her eyes, she could see him, water glistening on his magnificent body, the sun lighting his hair to a shade between silver and gold. And his eyes, always his eyes, flinty gray, deepening to ash when he looked at her, wanting her, smoldering embers burning in their depths.

"Please . . . please . . ." she prayed.

The night was hushed, crackling with expectancy. Most of the children seemed to be asleep; only the women sat waiting, eyes peering in the darkness, ears anxiously awaiting their men's return.

Beyond the rim of light from the camp were sounds, running feet, panting breaths. Savannah steeled herself. This was not the sound of soldiers' approach. This was too quiet, too expert. She braced herself, hand reaching out, feeling the rough bark of the southern pine under her palm. "Please . . . please . . ." seemed to sound with every heartbeat.

Chakika, a young brave of seventeen summers, led the forward movement. His face dripped with perspiration from his long run, but his eyes were glowing with victory. The women converged on the youth, demanding answers to their questions. Only Savannah held back, awaiting news of the Swamp Fox.

Speaking rapidly, Chakika recounted the events of the night, reporting many wounded. Unable to give them news of their men, the women asked about their chief. "Thlacko Osceola is well. I saw this with my own eyes. He is going ahead to the camp where Che-cho-ter and Ina await him. Arpeika is also safe and well. He joins our chief to plan the next move." Chakika was full of news, reporting the escape from the detention camp. Suddenly, he was silent, feeling Savannah's eyes boring into his back. The youth turned, meeting her eyes levelly, "I have no news of Swamp Fox. The last I saw him he was with Mico and Yahoola. The old uncle, Culpepper, was with him also. I know no more of him."

Breath strangled in Savannah's throat. Please . . . please . . .

As she had expected, the wounded were brought into this camp, it being closer than the others. Her eyes searched for the bright head of MacAllister as she went about her duties of fetching water and binding injuries. Every woman whose man had not yet returned watched the edge of the darkness, eyes straining, searching faces and asking the returning warriors of news of their men. Secunna visited each wounded, laying her gnarled, old hands upon their heads, chanting medicine words and peering with clinical interest at their various wounds, clicking her tongue and issuing orders for their treatment.

The night air was filled with the joyous sounds of reunions and the piercing shrill cries of grief. Savannah stood helplessly by as a woman she was working with heard news of her husband's death. Raising her fists to the sky, the woman called her husband's name, the sound stabbing icy fingers into the heart of every woman whose husband had not yet returned.

Savannah attended her duties, still listening, still searching. Many more wounded were being brought in now. Faces she knew and recognized. Faces from her own village. Yet, she could not bring herself to ask about MacAllister, as if postponing the dreaded inevitable.

"Chala, Chala!" an anguished cry called her name. The sound was guttural, like a drowning man beneath the water. She turned, bracing herself. Mico!

Someone had already laid him upon a pallet and bound his chest with strips of cloth. The blood was seeping through the bandages, trickling down his side onto the blankets. The light from the fire illuminated his strong, hawklike features, and he was pale, dark shadows forming beneath his eyes.

She went to him, going down on her knees at his side, her tentative fingers reaching out to touch him. Death was upon him, taking his life in deep, greedy swallows. His breathing was labored, the excruciating pain he was experiencing evident in his ebony eyes.

Savannah took his hand, pressing it against her breast. This man whom she had known from childhood was dying. This man, whose woman she had once thought she would become, was leaving this world of sorrow to ride beyond the earth on the wings of the Spirits. Deep loss and grief filled her for an old friend.

"Chala," he breathed, contented now that she was beside him, a costly smile turning up the corners of his mouth as he lifted a trembling hand to touch her honeyed curls.

"Mico," she whispered, "you must not talk, you must save your strength."

"Women, always telling a dying man to save his strength. Always wanting the last word, never allowing a man to speak his heart."

Savannah was quiet, waiting for him to catch his breath. The hand she held in her own momentarily tightened as a wave of pain engulfed him. She must not cry, she told herself. For once she must be the stoic Seminole woman Mico expected her to be.

"I have wanted to build a chikkee with you, Chala, to claim you for my own . . ." his eyes closed with the effort of speaking through his vale of pain. "I was not quick enough . . . I waited . . . too long. When MacAllister took you . . . I wanted to kill him, feel my knife plunge between his ribs . . ."

Mico's head fell back in exhaustion, but his eyes flickered open again, determined to speak his heart. "My thoughts have always been with you, Chala. Even though you sailed the great sea with the white man, I knew you would return." A sob erupted in Savannah's throat. This man was telling her he loved her, something pride would never allow him to say until now.

"I hated MacAllister. I was wrong. He was a brave man, true to his brother. And when I saw him fall beneath the soldier's bullet, I knew how wrong I had been to be jealous of the love you found in his chikkee." Mico winced with pain, his back arching up from the pallet.

What was he saying? MacAllister fall? Dead? No, no!

"Chala," Mico breathed, the sound softer than the owl's wing beating the air. He tried to raise himself, to touch her. Savannah leaned closer, taking his head into her arms, holding him, comforting him, her heart breaking. She must think of Mico now, make his last moments peaceful. There would be time to cry later. Pressing her lips against his brow, a tear fell down onto his face.

An eternity later, someone took Mico out of her arms, leading her away. There was no feeling, no tears. Without MacAllister there was no life.

The "abduction," as General Jessup preferred to call the escape from the detention camp, brought his peace plans crashing down, and with them his quest for glory. Fiercefully bitter, the general blamed various factors: the Creek spies who were supposed to give warning; Captain Graham, who had been in charge of the detention camp; and the greedy slaveholders who had pressed too hard for the return of their property. In contrast, antislavery advocates blamed Jessup himself. Had he scrupulously adhered to the agreements in the March 6 Treaty and not gone back on his word concerning the runaway slaves, there would have been no foray at the Tampa Bay detention camp.

The impact of the "abduction" on General Jessup was inescapable. At first, he was thrown into a deep depression. "This campaign for the Indian migration," he wrote the Adjutant General, "has entirely failed." Now the only way to eliminate the Seminoles from Florida was to exterminate them. Knowing the stain such an action would leave on his record, he had to abandon this plan.

Ever since learning of Savannah's duplicity, the general had little heart for campaigning. It was as though he had lost his precious sister for a second time. That Savannah could have been raised among those savages seemed entirely implausible until, after leaving Miss Gentry at the depot and rushing home, he had found Savannah gone. Throughout the day he had waited for her, dispatching his officers to comb the city for her. She had escaped, disappeared without a trace, and he had no word of her since.

Jessup had been personally wounded by the Indians. First, his sister and then his niece. Growing more and more cynical by the day, he was willing to employ treachery to carry out his orders to quell the Seminole, despite the sour press he was receiving in the tabloids.

He had no confidence whatsoever in the promises made by the Seminoles, and he felt little compunction about violating his promises to them. The war was entering a new phase where all was fair, and winning was its own reward.

His new strategy in this campaign was one that he had the most confidence in: divide and conquer. His first effort was to split the milder Alachua bands away from the Seminole nation. He would promise the Alachua that if they fought against the others, he would secure permission for them to remain in Florida. The policy worked poorly. If a few Alachuas came over to the white cause, it only stiffened the resistance of the Seminoles. Micanopy was degraded and Arpeika became chief of all the Seminoles, fulfilling Osceola's dream. The scrawny, old warmonger and his warriors fought with renewed vigor, successfully eluding capture.

The divide-and-conquer plan could still work, Jessup told his officers. Now they would try to separate the blacks from the reds. What had given Jessup this idea was the news that some of the runaway slaves were slipping away from the Seminole and going back to the plantations. It would do Jessup service for rumors of privation and mistreatment to reach the ears of the antislavists who had become the general's most severe critics. No one seemed to consider that after twenty months of hardship in combat only fifty of the black fugitives from the St. Johns region decided to trade freedom for food. Among them was John Phillip, a slave of Chief Phillip.

Another reason for the black defeatism which the general refused to consider was the great loss in their leadership, suffered when several of their outstanding men were taken into custody.

Jessup seized his chance. He put out offers of freedom and safety to blacks if they would leave the Seminole. More and more blacks took his offer and came in, most of them reported to be starving. The general knew he had no legal power to grant them the freedom he had promised, and those who could be proved to be the property of whites would be reclaimed as slaves.

This was exactly what the slaveholders wanted to hear; they were certain the blacks were better off in slavery than in any other condition. They propagated tales of extreme hardships and torture their blacks had suffered at the hands of the Seminoles.

General Jessup paced his sparsely appointed office. Tales of starvation were true for the scattered blacks who could not find their way back to Seminole camps. Damn! He pounded a heavy fist on his desk. Where were those savages getting their supplies? At first he had doubted the reports he had heard concerning a mystical man known among the Seminoles as the Swamp Fox, who was running supplies and foodstuffs in to the Seminole. And those blasted rifles! Where did the Indians get them? They were Cuban made, he knew, but what surprised him and his officers more was the fact that somewhere the Seminole had learned to use them! No longer did they fire off a volley and then whoop, missing their target with greater frequency than hitting it! Where had they learned? Who had taught them? Some of the blacks spoke of a golden-haired white man the Indians called Swamp Fox who was the benefactor of the Seminole. Who was he? Where did he come from? Did he actually exist?

Rubbing his hand over his chin, Jessup collapsed into his chair. With the Indians so well supplied, the army would need a new consignment of goods to see them through the forthcoming campaign. The list he was composing for these supplies lay beneath his hand. He scrutinized it, looking for something he had overlooked.

Dearborn wagons. Most important items were listed first. Valuable because they had large wheels and could travel through boggy swamps. They could even be used as boats when needed.

Horses, mules and wagons. Pack saddles, steamers for the rivers and hundreds of small hand tools. The general was even willing to try new firearms, such as Colt's revolvers and Cochran's repeater. Shotguns were needed for use by the light companies. More Mackinaw boats were useful, flat bottomed with a double set of oars, each capable of carrying twenty men.

Haversacks, wall tents, common tents, hospital tents, camp kettles, mess kits, canteens, axes, spades, hatchets, all must arrive in time. Large sheets of lumber, sheepskins for saddle blankets, halters, hobbles, wagon harnesses, whips, saddler's tools and several thousand horseshoes must be on hand for the mounted men. And of course, food.

Jessup smiled bleakly as he once again perused the letter he had received from the Secretary of War in Washington. The government would supply any and all requisitions made by Jessup if he would agree to delay the start of his operations until November. The summers were intolerable, the Secretary of War stated, and it would be impossible to gather a large supply of commissioned goods until that time.

Stuffing the list for commissioned supplies into an envelope and sealing it, he smiled wryly. That his list was complete, he was certain. Now it would be in the hands of the Secretary of War. His would be the most completely outfitted army in the history of the United States. Not even the Swamp Fox could boast bringing such supplies to the Indians!

CHAPTER TEN

Arriving in Galveston, Sloan registered for himself and Culpepper at a hotel close to Annemarie's house. Both men treated themselves to long baths, close shaves and clean clothes. Sloan departed for Annemarie's, his intention to get the latest newspaper and devour it while drinking some of her best cognac.

Annemarie greeted him with open arms, all her aggravation over past encounters forgotten. She wanted details of Savannah's life in New Orleans, news of Rico Mendoza and Sloan's own adventures. "I want to know everything," she cried excitedly, "don't leave out a single detail."

Quickly, he filled Annemarie in on recent occurrences, expressing his hopes that he had had a hand in the turning point of the war between the Seminoles and the United States.

"How awful for Savannah to be separated from you. The poor child must be beside herself. You should have brought her back with you. She could have stayed with me. I know, I know, she feels she can be of some use to the Seminoles. But I also know, Sloan, that she considers herself a part of your world now. If it came to a choice, she would choose this side of the fence." Annemarie's certainty pleased Sloan. He knew the day was going to come when Savannah would be forced to a choice.

The newspaper Annemarie offered was read from front to back.

"What's this?" Sloan chortled gleefully. "Brevet General Thomas Jessup has written Washington asking to be relieved of his command unless he was given full sanction and support by the government to deal with the Seminoles with expediency." Sloan's smile became a glower and his flinty gray eyes held shadows of disgust. "For a minute there I was hopeful. But any fool can see that Jessup is holding up the government by threatening to leave his command because he knows that assigning a new commander would only drag this business on indefinitely. If the government refuses Jessup's resignation, in essence Washington is giving its permission for Jessup to slaughter the Seminoles without regard to humanity or to policy." The news correspondent went on to say that in his own opinion Jessup had only one goal in mind: stop the war by stopping Osceola, whose influence over the Seminoles was almost spiritual. While other chiefs were important, all were shadows compared to the determined Osceola.

"The correspondent is right, you know, Annemarie. When I first went to Florida, Osceola was a chief of minor importance. True, he held a large section of Seminoles under him and he had gained some influence, but nothing like he has now. The fires of justice burn brightly in my brother; he seems to glow from within. I swear, there's something saintly about him and his people see it. He is the only one, aside from the old man, Arpeika, who has never turned his sights. The others, Phillip, Coa Hadjo, Micanopy and all the others have all vacillated. With my brother there is only one way. He demands justice for his people and he will fight until he has it."

Annemarie listened with rapt attention. "It would seem that same fire burns in you, Sloan MacAllister. I've never known a man more committed to an ideal. You've risked a lot to help the Seminole, and you're still risking your neck. Be careful, Sloan, from what you tell me of Jessup, he'll put the rope around your neck himself!"

"Truer words were never spoken, Anne. He's been thwarted

one turn after another. He still can't claim any major success in this war and, God willing, he never will. I see here in the newspaper that Jessup describes the battle at the Tampa detention camp as a 'mere abduction.' No mention that we cleared the camp out and 'freed' the emigres."

Time dragged for Sloan while gathering supplies. It was most difficult. The United States Army was paying top dollar to supply the southern army and they bought in huge quantities, creating a shortage in the marketplace. Sloan and Culpepper rode up and down the coast, stopping at each town for a sack of this, a bag of that, a few pounds of something else. Annemarie and the girls in her employ did their share by helping to accumulate as much as they could. But it was not nearly the load Sloan and Culpepper had taken out on previous trips.

Word reached Sloan in early August that some of the Indians were arriving at some of the posts, particularly Fort King. Jessup, whose resignation Washington rejected as Sloan had expected, agreed to a conference with Coa Hadjo, Tuckose Emathla and Tuskeneho. It was also said that Osceola and Arpeika would send representatives but not attend themselves.

Several days after the conference Sloan read in a newspaper that Jessup had said he would never agree to recognizing Arpeika as chief, and that the general was extending the time of emigration to October. It went on to conclude that he threatened to execute Seminole prisioners the moment fresh depredations were committed. Jessup was quoted as saying he had "a thousand Creek warriors ready to kill the Seminole."

Sloan knew Osceola must be in a turmoil trying to decide what his next move should be. Up to this point, Osceola's war had been a defensive one, and Sloan knew he wanted to keep it that way. If attacked, he would fight. Sloan also knew his brother would never stay in the boundaries Jessup devised. Nor would Arpeika, Phillip and Coacoochee, who was Phillip's son.

It was the first week in September that the *Polly Copinger* set sail once more with supplies, horses and mules. In Sloan's cabin, in gaily beribboned boxes, were the gifts that Annemarie had bought for Osceola's family.

For Morning Dew there was a delicate lace shawl the color of the sky on a summer day. A string of matching beads lay next to the gossamer wrap. For Ina, a flowered skirt trimmed with bright fringe. For Yahi, who now resided in Osceola's chikkee, a pair of scarlet slippers lined with lamb's wool. For the children, a doll in Indian dress, harmonicas, several colored bracelets and pretty yellow shell combs. In a closed canister some candy sticks of assorted colors and flavors. For the baby, a Golliwog, a soft rag doll popular with English children, and a box of brightly colored wooden building blocks.

The *Polly Copinger* dropped anchor in a deepwater inlet off the Halifax River. Sloan and Culpepper waited for two days before the Seminoles arrived. Sloan was anxious, barely able to contain himself with his forced inactivity. "Something is wrong, I can feel it here," he said, pounding at his stomach.

A little past noon on the second day an Indian named Hola Alto crept aboard the *Polly Copinger*. Sloan's heart lurched at what he read in the Indian's eyes. "Tell me," he croaked.

"Four days ago King Phillip was captured by an underling of Jessup, General Hernandez. As far as we can tell, he was camped at a ruined plantation thirty miles south of St. Augustine. They surrounded Phillip's camp sometime near midnight and attacked at first light. No guard was posted. No horse neighed; no dog barked. There were no injuries. Tomoka John, a Negro, was captured also. They say he offered to guide the troops to a Yuchis' camp six miles away and again they circled the camp during the night and attacked at first light. They captured Yuchi Billy and his brother, Jack." There was disgust on Hola Alto's face. The soldiers could never have reached the camp, for it is a pine barren placed like an island in the middle of the swamp. Only one familiar with the trails could get there. "Tomoka John betrayed the Seminole."

Sloan wasn't surprised. To Culpepper he said, "I feared something like this would happen. It makes for a serious breach in Seminole leadership."

Sloan knew there was more to come from the Indian standing in front of him. "Give me the rest of it."

"General Jessup ordered Chief Phillip to send out a runner to call in his sons, Coacoochee and Bluesnake. When they came in with the white flag, the general detained them, ignoring one of the most respected rules of war. My people are angry," he said, stony-faced.

"They have a right to be angry. What happened to Bluesnake and Coacoochee?"

"The general liberated Coacoochee and sent him out to bring in more of his followers, knowing that Phillip, his father, was being held as hostage."

Sloan stared at Culpepper a moment, dreading the next question he had to ask. "What of Osceola? Where are his people?" He couldn't ask about Savannah.

The Indian's eyes were defiant when he replied. "Osceola and Coa Hadjo sent word to General Jessup that they would parley. It is to take place near Fort Peyton near Moultrie Creek. They have erected a log work and they have a garrison with a detachment from the Second Dragoons."

"When is Osceola due to parley?" he demanded in a harsh voice.

Hola Alto shrugged. "Nothing is for certain. A few days' time, a week, a moon. Swamp Fox knows that my chief will not parley, he will be captured in the same manner as King Phillip and Tomoka John. Your brother flies the white flag over his camp."

"What?" Sloan exploded. "What of the yellow and red standard?"

"Your brother flies a white flag," Hola Alto said stubbornly.

"How many days' ride to the camp?"

"On horseback, on that monster you ride, perhaps a day and one half. I will have to lead you. I have no horse. Our time will be slow."

"On our ride to Osceoloa's camp will we pass any of his smaller camps?"

"One, maybe, two, but only women and children. They cannot help you."

"Culpepper, bring Redeemer topside along with horses for yourself and Hola Alto. Once we get to land you will signal for your people to meet me, here," Sloan said pointing a finger at a spot on his map. "A three-hour ride at top speed. We can make our presence felt, if nothing else. I can't sit here and do nothing. We'll rendezvous along Moultrie Creek and attack in darkness."

"The Swamp Fox has the eye of the eagle in darkness?" There was amusement in the Indian's tone.

"Hell, no. We're just going to fight them by their own dastardly ways. While they sleep. That's the way they attack the Indian. We'll turn their own strategy around and do the same. They won't be expecting us. Jessup is probably sitting in some soft easy chair swilling brandy and smoking cigars while some other bastard does his dirty work."

Sloan followed behind Hola Alto with the wind at his back. The Indian rode the horse like demons were on his heels. Sloan looked behind him once to see Culpepper hanging on to his mount for dear life, his watery eyes squeezed closed.

The three men rode for six hours before reaching the arranged meeting place which Hola Alto had ordered. Darkness was complete when the first Seminole reached the temporary camp. The others followed swiftly until they numbered sixty-seven. Sloan was pleased. He recognized some of the men from his training program. All of them looked at him with respect.

"I don't like this," Yahoola said sharply. "Why is your brother, our chief, flying a white flag over his camp?" His voice was bold and full of anger.

Sloan stared at the man in front of him. He was an expert marksman, better than himself, as a matter of fact. "Osceola has not spoken with me. Perhaps he thinks it is time to make peace. I have no answers for you."

"Peace. It is impossible with the white men! They lie, cheat, steal and kill our women and children. You talk to me of peace. Save your breath, for it will not work. My people who stand here before you, ready to fight, think as I do. Do you believe your white generals will parley with Osceola? If you do, you're wrong. It is one more white-eyes trick to capture all of our chiefs. Mark my word, Swamp Fox, for I speak true. A runner is on his way to Osceola to advise him of this foray we plan. Also to advise him of the general's troops that are headed in his direction. The *wrong* direction. If the intention was to parley as Osceola thinks, then why are Ashby and Hernandez heading for his camp?"

"Goddamn it, I didn't say you were wrong. I'm not even saying that Osceola is wrong. I don't know what's going on. I've just arrived yesterday. My brother never does anything without a reason. We must all trust to his good judgment. It is just possible that he and his men are planning an ambush on their own. Did you consider that?"

"Of course it has been considered." Yahoola spat into the ground to show what he thought of Osceola's methods.

"Then why are you here? Why are these men here? If there's no hope, why are we planning a raid on the white camp?"

"Because it is my time to die, and before my spirit leaves my body, I want to take my enemies with me. The others feel the same way. When the troops descend on Osceola's camp, there will be that many less white-eyes for our chief to look upon."

Sloan grimaced understanding perfectly Yahoola's logic. "We are not women; let us not think like women. Whatever we accomplish will be better than doing nothing. Are we all agreed?" There were loud mutterings and much shuffling of feet as the men stared at him.

"Agreed," Yahoola said firmly.

"Good. Now show me the way we travel. How many hours before midnight will we be close enough to make our plans work?"

Yahoola squatted down on his haunches and proceeded to draw a rough map for Sloan in the dirt. "We do not have many horses among us. My brothers can outrun that monster you ride, so have no fear. We do not travel as one. We scatter and meet when the moon is high, here," he said, pointing to a spot he drew in the dry ground. One by one the men filed past the crude map, and Yahoola spoke to each. They scattered silently till there was just Culpepper and MacAllister left.

"Do you get the feeling, Laddie, that those brothers of yours aren't too keen on being seen with the likes of us? Do ye think we be tainted or something?"

Sloan laughed. "Never! An Indian travels best alone. Even on horseback we'll be hard pressed to keep up with them. You're forgetting that we can't arrive in numbers and horses make noise. A good scout can pick up a horse's hoofbeats as much as a mile away."

There was a vicious ache between Sloan's shoulder blades when he rode into dense undergrowth to meet Yahoola and his men. Culpepper looked done in. Twelve hours on horseback was something the old man wasn't used to. Nor was he, Sloan admitted to himself.

"How far?" he demanded of Yahoola.

"An hour by foot."

An hour by foot. Leave the horses or take them? Sloan pondered. Perhaps it would be best to go up the creek, wade through the water and attack from the rear. If there were Indian scouts in the white camp, he would have to use every trick, every wile he knew, to attack under cover of surprise.

"We'll ford the creek. Tether the horses on a marshy bank for a quick exit once we depart. Any objections?" It was clear from the surprised looks on the Indians' faces they never would have thought of the creek. The Swamp Fox was a good man to join in battle. Sloan demonstrated how the men were to carry the guns once they were immersed into waist-high water. The ammunition belts hung from their necks. They knew what would happen if they got wet.

The moon was slipping behind thick cloud cover, and the water was cold, making Sloan's teeth chatter.

Culpepper prayed that the moon would stay hidden as he floundered in the dark, murky water. He liked the water as long as he was in a ship on top of it. This evil-smelling swampy water was enough to make a man want to toss up his innards. Once he slipped and would have gone under but for the help of a giant Indian with no teeth. He grinned as he hauled Culpepper up by the scruff of the neck and set him upright. "Mighty obliged," the sea captain managed. The Indian grunted and forged ahead.

"Problems, Culpepper?" Sloan asked.

"None I can't handle," the captain lied.

The quarter moon played hide and seek for the next thirty minutes, finally settling behind a dark black cloud. It was good. They would be on their way back before daylight.

Up ahead, Yahoola lifted his arm to show they had arrived within what the Indian called spitting distance of the soldiers' camp. Word came back to Sloan: dogs, first with a knife; sentries with a garotte, and from that point on anything goes.

Sloan leaped to the creek bank, shaking the water from his body and shivering in the cool night air. Culpepper was right behind him waiting for an order. So far, so good. No sound of barking dogs which, in itself, was unusual, unless of course they were Indian dogs to begin with who recognized the invaders from previous camps. The horses were quiet, something else that surprised Sloan. Either the white men felt safe or somehow they were expecting an ambush. He preferred to go with the former thought rather than the latter. It was an eerie kind of quiet and Sloan didn't like it. Culpepper's teeth were chattering so loud, Sloan was sure the entire camp would wake from the harsh clickety-clack. He pulled the red bandanna he had tied around his head to keep the hair from his eyes and handed it to the captain. "Bite down on this," he whispered. "You're making enough noise to wake the dead."

Culpepper bit down and immediately felt better. There were times when he regretted the decisions he had made. But if he had to do it all over again, he wouldn't change a thing. A man had to do what he had to do.

Sloan and Culpepper crept closer to the camp. He could almost feel the warmth from a low-burning fire. A sentry was walking slowly around the fire in a sleepy manner, his rifle held sloppily at his side. As his eyes became accustomed to the darkness, he picked out a sleeping dog at the outer edge of the fire. He watched as both sentry and dog went to their eternal rewards. Another guard at the outer perimeter fell, and then another. A third was bringing his rifle to his shoulder when a knife slashed across his throat. Sloan imagined he could hear the rush of blood flowing from the man's throat. Culpepper gagged behind him. For fifteen minutes the silent slaughter continued. Suddenly, lanterns were flaring up and gunshots sounded. Wild, frenzied war whoops echoed as Yahoola and his men attacked savagely. Sloan had just fired off three shots in quick order. Three men fell, one screaming obscenities about Sloan's origins. Another volley went off, this time from Culpepper's rifle. A man with a captain's insignia dropped at Sloan's back. "I didn't think ye noticed him, Lad," Culpepper grinned. Sloan grinned, enjoying the old man's success with the rifle. Under normal conditions, he couldn't hit the broad side of a barn. "You saved my life, Enwright. I owe you another one."

"I'll let ye know when it's time to collect," Culpepper said, firing off another shot and getting his man in the middle of his chest. He blanched slightly, but recovered quickly and reloaded.

Sloan swiveled like a dancer, firing and reloading, hitting his target each time he fired. At a signal from Yahoola he danced his way to the outer confines of the camp. "We are victorious. To stay longer will endanger our men. We leave now while they are still stunned. They must report to their superiors that it was our battle. We lost none and none were wounded. They have no liking for night fighting, unless it is to capture women and children and knifing my brothers while they sleep. We fight as they do. We are victorious!" A bloodcurdling war whoop sounded. Sloan shivered.

"Culpepper, where the hell are you? We're making tracks. Culpepper, get your ass over here before someone shoots you. Now!" Sloan ordered.

"I'm coming, Laddie, but slow it is. I picked up a shot in me foot. Some damn fool corporal thought I didn't need a foot. Well, the bastard was wrong. I shot his guts right out of his body."

A look of relief washed over Sloan's face. He was trying to decide what to do with Culpepper when the tall, toothless Indian who had fished him out of the creek approached. His dark eyes took in Culpepper's bleeding foot. Without a word he bent over and slung the captain over his shoulder. He loped ahead, following Yahoola and the others.

"This is a disgrace," Culpepper shouted to Sloan. "Make him put me down. It's indecent, I tell you!"

"Shut up, Culpepper. You'll slow us up if you walk. You want to see Maeve again to tell her how brave you were. Women love wounded war heroes." He fired off two more shots, getting one man smack in the kneecap and the other at the base of the throat. He felt nothing as the men fell, one to his death, the other moaning that he would never walk again. He had chosen his side, and he wasn't about to back out now no matter how white the man's skin was.

Sunlight dappled through the trees, falling softly upon Che-cho-ter's face. This was the way he always wanted to remember her, Osceola told himself. Fresh from the waters of the river where she bathed, preening beneath his eye. She had given him children, this woman with the dusky skin and thick sweep of black hair. Soon, he told himself, before the moon makes another arc in the night sky, he would leave her.

"My husband's eyes grow dark with sorrow," Morning Dew said softly, touching his cheek.

Osceola turned his head, burying his face in the palm of her hand. "My eyes are filled with looking at you, Che-cho-ter, breath of my soul. I have never looked at another woman such as I have looked upon you." It was important to say these things to her, to tell her what she had always known. But it brought comfort to have them said aloud. He drew her into his arms for an instant, loving the feel of her body against his. How long would he be able to hold her this way? Forever, he scolded himself. As long as there is memory, as long as I draw breath.

Che-cho-ter rested against him, her heart heavy and thoughts troubled. There was little need for words between them; then why was he saying these things to her? Did he think they had just looked upon one another and were about to build their first chik-kee? These words were for the very young who had not learned the faith and trust that comes with loving.

Taking her hands in his, he led her to the bank of the river, where they sat down, gazing at their own reflections. "I can see us as we once were, not so many summers ago. You were heavy with our first daughter. I put my hand against your belly, so, and felt the life within you." He smiled, remembering. "Such a man as you should have sons, you told me. What will we do if it is a girl child? I told you that a child from the womb of Che-cho-ter was a child given in love, a blessed child who would find the Spirits of the forest smiling. And so it was." He nodded his head, smiling with the bittersweet reverie.

"And so it was, my husband," Che-cho-ter told him. "And so it will be again. There is time for more children, for the seed of my husband to spawn in my body and grow into life."

"No, wife of my soul, there is no more time." His voice quaked, his spirit breaking under the heavy burden of sorrow and regret.

Che-cho-ter tried to break him out of his misery. "You only speak this way because your efforts go unrewarded. Soon, my husband, the other chiefs will find their courage and stand behind you."

"Yes, soon they will. But only at great sacrifice made both by my wife and myself. I know this is so and Arpeika has seen it in his dreams."

A shadow passed over Che-cho-ter's face. She too had dreams, but the mornings had always come and she found her husband at her side. When her soul talked with the Spirits at night, they lied to her. They must have lied! Unless . . . unless . . . her eyes searched Osceola's face, finding there the truth. It was to be. She must hold each precious moment and keep it close to her always. When she was an old woman, she would tell her daughters' sons of their grandfather who fought the white soldiers to keep their home in Florida. Her tales would be peopled with heroes.

The forest was suddenly still, only the shrill cry of a bird fell on her ears. There was already an emptiness in her heart, and the spark within her soul that united all living things with the Great Spirit was somehow dimmer. Yes, my husband, she wept silently. You will reunite the Seminole but it will cost us your life.

"When?" was all she asked, and he loved her for knowing him so well.

"Soon. When the time is right. I will allow myself to fall into the white general's hands. I will allow him to trick me like the fox tricks the rabbit. And there will be an outcry among my people and they will see that Jessup is never to be trusted. That his words fall without meaning like clouds brushing the treetops. Shed your tears now, Che-cho-ter, for when the time comes you must be brave. You must speak my heart to our people and let them never forget the Seminole belong in the Floridas."

Che-cho-ter was struck by his impassioned statement. His tone was bitter, his dark eyes sharp and suspicious. She wrapped her arms around him, burying his face into her breast, willing the hate to drain from his heart, leaving him pure again, receptive to her love.

Her fingers traced the planes of his face, committing it to memory. She wished, more than anything, never to forget the way he looked and the warmth of his arms when he held her. Death was a sorrowful parting for the one left behind with only memories to comfort the long nights. Lovingly, she took his beloved face in her hands and pressed her cheek against his. "My husband, my chief," she told him softly, "as long as there is breath in your wife's body, you will never be forgotten."

Osceola stood beside Coa Hadjo beneath the shade of the trees. The weather continued to be unseasonably warm for late October and the Seminoles took it as a good sign. The wild winds would come again, whipping from the east, churning the oceans into a froth, whistling through the forests and bringing torrential rains. Just the sort of weather to immobilize the white soldiers, giving the Seminole time to regroup.

For a fleeting moment, Osceola thought about Che-cho-ter and the children. Believing he had said his last farewells to them, he was now prepared for anything General Jessup might throw his way. Stiff-backed, rigid, he appeared the essence of the strong

Seminole warrior. Word had been sent to the army command post that both he and Coa Hadjo were ready to parley.

Osceola narrowed his eyes, engrossed in thought. By now General Jessup had made his decision, and if it was the one Osceola expected, the general was well on the road to disgracing himself. Counting upon Jessup's quest for glory and knowing his hatred of the Indian, Osceola planned to use the general's weaknesses to reunite the Seminole nation. When word was spread of the general's deed, the Seminoles would rise again, fighting for their land, knowing they could have no faith in this white leader's promises. Glancing upward, Osceola focused on the white flag of truce flying over the camp. "Now, Jessup," he swore under his breath, using a white man's profanity, "now you come, you bastard!"

Spies had already informed Osceola that orders were sent out to General Hernandez to reconnoiter to Fort Peyton and commandeer a detachment of Dragoons. Fort Peyton was only a mile from Osceola's camp, and the chief expected them to arrive at any moment.

Listening intently, he could hear the sounds of mounted men approaching the camp, and Osceola expected their numbers to be great. A runner came flying into camp, reporting to his chief, Coa Hadjo.

Breathlessly, he reported, "Dragoons, like mosquitos, over the swamp. So many horses, you can smell them from where you stand!" The runner's eyes were wide with alarm. He was only a young boy, inexperienced on the battleground. But today there would be no battle.

Osceola offered the boy an inscrutable smile. So, Jessup had taken the bait! The general could not resist capturing the two most important chiefs in the Seminole nation. Only Sam Jones, Arpeika, was more important to the Indians for leadership.

"We are ready," Coa Hadjo intoned solemnly.

"But we fly the white flag!" the young runner exclaimed. "Under the rules of war the flag is a sign of truce! No injury should be done!"

"So it would mean to a man of justice," Osceola told him. "Stand straight and look upon your enemy when he comes. Know that these lands in the Floridas belong to the Seminole and never forget what you are about to witness."

Osceola swallowed hard, his mouth feeling dry and parched. He had recently fought off another bout of the fever and he still did not feel his usual strength. "When they come, Coa Hadjo, you must speak for the Seminole. Let there be no slip of my tongue. Let all the words belong to the white soldiers. A man cannot be condemned for what he does not say."

Coa Hadjo looked at his old friend sadly. He knew what Osceola expected of Jessup and it lay heavy on his heart.

In a thunder of hooves, the Dragoons rode into camp, a gold-braided leader at their head who introduced himself as General Hernandez. So, thought Osceola, Jessup could not bring himself to do his own dirty work.

Dismounting, General Hernandez approached the two chiefs, two aides-de-camp flanking him on either side. Raising his hand in greeting, Hernandez made the first overture. "I have come as a friend," he began, his dour glance instinctively measuring the men before him. "As a friend, I have a question to ask. What prompted you to seek this parley?"

Osceola remained silent, listening. Coa Hadjo spoke. "We have come for the good of our people."

Not considering this an answer to his question, Hernandez asked, "At whose request did you come?"

"A message was brought from Coacoochee from his father, King Phillip."

"And what do you expect from me?" Hernandez persisted. "Have you come to give yourself up to me?"

"No," Coa Hadjo said quietly. "We want to make peace."

Quirking a heavy black brow, Hernandez said, "And are you also ready to surrender all the property you have captured?"

Pretending innocence, Coa Hadjo shrugged his shoulders. "We have no property that is not ours. We have only a few Negroes . . ."

Not allowing him to complete his statement, Hernandez glowered. "Why haven't you brought your Negroes in before as you promised at Fort King? Why did not Micanopy, Jumper and Cloud come instead of sending a messenger?"

Calmly, coolly, Coa Hadjo stated, "They all have the measles." His glance was accusatory. Until the arrival of the white man, measles and smallpox were unheard of among the Indians. Their effects had been devastating on the Seminole population.

Seeing Coa Hadjo's anger, Hernandez cooled, saying smoothly, "I am an old friend of Phillip's and I wish you all well, but we have been deceived so often that it is necessary for you to come with me. You will all see the good treatment you receive. You will be glad that you fell into my hands."

"We will see about it," Coa Hadjo said sternly, knowing that Osceola's heart was lifted in victory. This was exactly what his friend had expected and wanted. Now Jessup would lose face. It would be reported that Coa Hadjo and Osceola and their small band of people that did not number seventy were taken prisoner by two hundred and fifty Dragoons under orders of treachery given by General Thomas Jessup himself. The Indians had agreed to parley and the white general had seized the opportunity to capture them! Under the flag of truce!

Hernandez issued a prearranged signal and the Dragoons moved in, their lances pointed at their prisoners. Although the Seminoles carried guns, there was no resistance.

Before being herded out of camp, Osceola took the white flag from its place in camp. He carried it bravely for all to see. Never had there been a single instance of a failure on the part of the Seminoles to respect the flag of truce. In all civilized parts of the world it was held to be inviolable, and yet Jessup had made a mockery of it. As he mounted the horse given to him by MacAllister, Osceola told himself, soon the Seminoles will reunite when they see what sin his been committed.

Word began to spread throughout the country that Osceola, the famous Seminole leader, had been seized while attending a conference under a flag of truce. The public reaction was one of outrage: Jessup had performed a dishonorable deed, staining the honor of his country. Papers throughout the nation editorialized about the disgraceful means by which Osceola was captured. The English were shocked by the dishonorable performance of an American general. One English writer said there was "never a more disgraceful piece of villainy perpetrated in a civilized land." The writer was Andrew Welch and he pointed out with consternation that the Americans had recognized the Seminoles as a nation by making treaties with them. They were not rebels. To seize a Seminole leader under a flag of truce was as much an act of infamy as it would be for an English general to seize an American general under similar circumstances.

Fort Marion, where Osceola and Coa Hadjo were brought, was an old building formerly known as Castillo de San Marco. It had been started by the Spanish in 1672 and was the oldest fort in the United States. It had been used once before as a prison, and in 1821 a dungeon was found beneath the high turret with human bones and other indications of cruel imprisonment.

The prisoners held by the army were allowed visitors. Indeed, so much had been made of the dishonorable way the Indians had been brought into the camp that the army was setting aside many of its regulations to accommodate them.

Sloan gained admittance to the Fort early in the afternoon. All that was required of him was that he sign his name to a registry and that he be welcomed by the Indians.

He found Osceola sitting on a bed of straw, his cell door wide open to the fresh air and sunshine of the courtyard that was guarded by blue-coated sentries. It was obvious that for all intents and purposes, the prisoners were allowed to go about their business undisturbed.

Sloan stood in the entry to his brother's cell. Osceola's suffering resembled that of a captive eagle. He knew he had been betrayed, and he resented it fiercely, but his resentment was tinged with elation. Word had come to him that the chiefs who still enjoyed their freedom in the Florida swamps were pledging to fight for their rights and property.

"My brother," Sloan said softly, great sorrow creeping into his voice. "It sickens me to see you this way. Captive in your own land."

"Lift your heart, MacAllister, my brother. I have nothing to be ashamed of. My soul is free to fly with the Spirits of the air and the forest. It is for those who entrapped me to feel shame." Osceola looked at Sloan with a calm and steady gaze. He knew he was looking into the eyes of a brave and honorable man. A man who had made sacrifices for his people.

"You planned this, didn't you, old fox? To bring shame upon your enemy and make his words false to all Seminoles?" MacAllister spoke in the Seminole tongue, abiding by his brother's wishes, bringing him a taste of home.

"I am fulfilling Arpeika's prophecy. He told me I was not to die in my home, nor was I to die beyond the Mississippi. But I was to die. For this, brother, I am prepared. But my people are not. Jessup has already begun his campaign, and his storehouses are full to the rafters. But the Seminoles are ready to fight; and their storehouses will never be empty because of the generosity of the Swamp Fox." Osceola smiled sadly, his eyes showing gratitude.

"My brother's people are also mine. Can I do anything for you? Send word to someone?"

"Yes," Osceola's answer was quick. "Go to the camp where Che-cho-ter and Ina and my children are staying. Bring them here to me. It is allowed."

"Why haven't they been brought to you before this?" Sloan demanded, knowing Osceola's need to have his family surrounding him at this time.

"There was no one to trust. I could not chance that the army would take them and hold them hostage, keeping me from them. But now," he shrugged elegantly, "there is so much hostility against Jessup he would not dare to commit another act of treachery against me. Until now, I did not have you to depend upon. Bring them to me, brother. Quickly. Each day I awaken to see the sun I know not whether I am blessed or cursed. To live behind the walls of a prison breaks the spirit of a man."

For a long time they sat together, silently. No words were needed, none were said. Their camaraderie was complete.

It was mid-November with the bitter hurricanes long gone. Savannah sat before the fire with Osceola's daughters at her feet. The cruel weather and the hardships the women and children had endured had frozen Chala's heart, making it difficult to face even one more day. The children played quietly with pieces of twigs and stones, smiling up at Savannah from time to time. Mic-canna spoke softly. "You must not look so sad, Chala. My father does not like to look upon tormented eyes."

"I am not sad for your father, little one, but for something else."

"What is that?"

"Your father's brother, he is lost to me. My heart no longer sings, for he is not here to listen. My eyes can no longer weep. I have only my memories now."

"My mother is sad also. My sisters are sad. We are a sad people, is it not so, Chala?"

"It is so," Savannah replied with a catch in her voice.

"Will we be forced to leave this land?" the little girl questioned.

Would they? She didn't know. The days seemed endless and without hope. How was she to answer this child? "Perhaps, one day," she said vaguely, praying the child would be satisfied with her answer.

Idly, she poked at the ground near her with a spindly twig. How frail it was. It would crack if she exerted too much pressure. Angrily, she tossed the stick into the fire and watched it burst into flame. That was what had happened to her. She had taken life from Sloan MacAllister; she had broken into flames when he was near. But he was gone and she was nothing, a cold shell.

Sloan went in search of his brother's family. Because of the gravity of their situation, Osceola's people were scattered throughout the forests, and only by vigilant inquiry was he able to find out where Che-cho-ter and her daughters were camped. Despite the fact that he knew Savannah would stay with Che-cho-ter, Sloan's eyes would comb each encampment, searching for her bright golden head and gypsy green eyes. Only yesterday had he learned where he might find them.

Redeemer responded to the pressure of his knees, following a stream bed, watching the slow trickle of crystal water run swifter and become broader in its rush to join the sea. It had been more than a week since he had left to find Che-cho-ter—at first traveling southward and then to the west, thinking they would still be camped somewhere near Lake Okeechobee. Coming almost full circle, Sloan realized they had kept moving northeast, their migration taking them within a two days' walk of St. Augustine, where Osceola was being held captive.

It had occurred to Sloan time and again that Savannah must feel abandoned by him. Annemarie had been right; he should have taken her with him to Galveston. He hadn't known a minute's peace since he had last been with her. Even now, with the bright sun filtering through the trees, there was a coldness in the center of him, an emptiness that only Savannah could fill. He had never thought a woman could come to mean so much to him. Had never dreamed

FERN MICHAELS

that his heart could be held so softly in a woman's hands. She had surrounded him with love and he needed her beside him. Always.

His thoughts of Savannah were so intense that he thought he was dreaming when Redeemer brought him through the trees and he recognized a slim feminine form kneeling at the stream, her golden mane of hair reflecting the sun's brightness. He watched silently as Savannah glided the tortoiseshell comb she had brought from Galveston through her silky long hair. Her arms were raised above her head, back arched in delicate symmetry, accentuating the rise of her breasts, the sleekness of her haunches. She must have just finished bathing; a precious bar of perfumed soap and a towel were resting nearby. Her thin blouse clung to her damply, the wide neckline revealing a creamy, graceful shoulder.

Sloan drank in the sight of her, nourished by her presence, feeling once again the peace she brought to him. He wished he had arrived earlier to watch her bathe, remembering those halcyon days on the island, feeling the quiver of excitement only Savannah could stir within him. Her lovely face was raised to the sun, the delicate patrician nose, the sweet curve of her chin, the purity of her brow were illuminated, and she became a goddess of femininity. It was only when she turned her head that he saw the dark shadows in her eyes.

Redeemer issued a friendly snort, recognizing the slim girl who had ridden with his master atop his back. Savannah was startled by the sound, her eyes immediately turning toward him, peering into the shadows. Within the space of a heartbeat, Sloan was out of the saddle and crossing the distance between them with long, quick strides. Savannah swayed, the earth rocking beneath her. She would have fallen if Sloan hadn't captured her in his arms, holding her against him, filling her world and dragging her back from the world of the dead into a place where his love was warmer and brighter than the sun.

His hands were in her hair, his lips covered her face, tasting her, devouring her. How much he had missed her. There was a sudden relief flooding through him, as though all these long weeks he had held his breath and could now at last draw fresh, sweet air. He inhaled her freshness, recognized the scent of the soap mingled with the smoky fragrance of the woods. Having her in his arms, it was impossible to release her, to explain, to tell her where he had been and why he hadn't come to find her before this. These things would keep until later, until he had had his fill of her, if that would ever be possible.

Savannah clung to him, reveling in the feel of his arms around her, the pressure of his mouth upon hers. She could not spoil this moment with questions. Perhaps he was a ghost after all, conjured up by her dreadful longing for him, sent to her by the Spirits to help heal her lonely heart. And if he was a ghost, then she must not break the spell; she must close her eyes and welcome his embrace. And if a cry escaped her lips and she moaned his name, she would be forgiven. The sound of her name filled her ears, his touch filled her senses. There was only MacAllister and all else was a void, an emptiness where only the pain of separation penetrated the nightmare. The delicious weight of him pushed her backward to the ground, falling upon her, pressing his length upon her. She understood his sudden hunger and responded with an appetite of her own, tangling her legs with his, impatient with the scraps of cloth that separated her from him. She wanted to be naked with MacAllister, just the way they had been on the island, with the sun searing their bodies, with the salt sea breezes cooling their passions.

As though listening to her thoughts, Sloan sat up, freeing himself from her arms, his fingers working at the laces of his buckskin tunic and his belt. Savannah stood and slipped her colorful skirt from around her waist, her blouse quickly followed. Golden skin and golden hair, sultry green eyes and moist parted lips . . . . She was a goddess, made for loving, designed by the muses to spark a man's desire and fill his heart with passion's song.

They clung to each other, seeking that which the other could give, wanting to end the torment their need for each other had created. With each touch something of themselves was restored. Each caress, each kiss carried with it the power to heal, to broach the time they had been separated and melt the ice that had sprung in Savannah's heart. He loved her, had come back for her, and now he was whispering soft words against the hollow of her throat, telling her of his love.

The words were sweeter than wild honey, and she gathered them into her soul. She offered herself to him, pressing his palm over her breast, lifting her mouth to kiss his ear, opening her eyes to see him, at last believing he really was here with her.

The sunlight kissed his hair, glinted off the smooth, muscular expanse of his shoulders. His eyes locked with hers, seeming to draw her into him, and she learned there all she would ever need to know; she was MacAllister's woman and he loved her.

It was twilight before Sloan and Savannah left their haven near the stream to go back to camp. They walked with their arms around each other; Redeemer following in their steps.

The women were gathered around their cook fires preparing the evening meal while the children hovered nearby. Che-cho-ter stepped out of her chikkee, carrying her youngest daughter, and when she noticed her husband's brother she froze.

Savannah dropped her arm from around Sloan's waist, feeling a sudden guilt that she should have her love back with her while Che-cho-ter's husband was held prisoner by the white soldiers.

After a moment, Che-cho-ter seemed to regain herself, her soft, dark eyes searching Savannah's, silently telling her that she was happy MacAllister had found his way back to her. With her natural grace and dignity, Che-cho-ter walked toward Sloan, head high, bearing proud. It was only as she came closer that Sloan could see the single heartbreaking tear that glistened on her cheek. "Tell me of my husband," she entreated.

"He wants you with him, and I've come to take you. He needs his family. We'll leave at dawn. It is a long trip for the little ones, but their father wants them."

"He is well." It wasn't really a question, but a positive statement.

He couldn't lie to her. "No, he is not well. I don't know how much time he has left. There is nothing more I can do. It was your chief's choice to put himself into Jessup's hands and both of us must accept this."

"I do accept it, but it does not stop my heart from breaking, Sloan MacAllister. He is my husband. He is my children's father. What will become of our people?" Her voice broke on her last words.

"There is no need for worry. I will see to you and the children and the rest of your people. As long as there is breath in my body, you will never want. That is the only promise I can make you."

"It is enough, more than enough. Does Osceola know of this promise you make to me?"

"There is no need for such words between Osceola and myself. He knows, without asking, that I would protect you. It has been understood since we were small boys. If I could breathe life into my brother, I would do it at the cost of my own. If I could bleed for him, I would. If I can make his last burdens easier, I will do it. We are brothers."

"No man has ever had a brother such as you," Che-cho-ter said quietly as she placed a grateful hand on Sloan's arm.

Damp, clammy fog swirled about Sloan's feet as he crept from Savannah's chikkee. It was almost light but the women were already at the fire. Their breakfast finished, they waited for him. Surely, they wouldn't . . . they weren't all planning . . . he shook his head. He should have known. He was going to have to take the whole damn camp. His heart broke a little when he saw Che-cho-ter in the clammy air with nothing but the flimsy blue shawl and blue beads around her even thinner blouse. Yahi had on the red sheep-lined slippers, and Ina was dressed in the brilliant skirt. The children clutched their dolls to their chests, their dark eyes solemn and wide. Even the baby held on to the Golliwog. Gifts from their father.

Everyone was dressed in her best for the trip. The single file parade from the camp reminded Sloan of a rainbow. He smiled to himself. He wouldn't have this any other way either. If Osceola got five minutes of joy out of seeing his people, it was worth it. Savannah was the last to join the long column of people. She wore her black ribbon with the cameo around her neck. It was her only concession to her heritage.

Sloan pushed hard to lead the camp through the forest, in a northeasterly direction. He was determined to arrive at St. Augustine by noon of the following day. Grim-faced and silent, Osceola's people followed—the women, the children, the aged. There were no young braves or fiercesome warriors to protect them and scout the way. All those who were capable of fighting were with Arpeika in central Florida.

Savannah walked beside Che-cho-ter, helping her with the children, offering a silent companionship. A great sadness was heavy on her heart as she recalled the kindness Che-cho-ter had always shown her. Savannah had been almost twelve summers when

Osceola had brought his second wife to live in his chikkee with Ina and herself. From the moment the dusky-skinned maiden smiled at them with her soft, dark eyes, they were a family. Osceola was always proud of his women. There were no squabbling or jealousies between them as there sometimes were in other chikkees where two wives resided. Ina, whose marriage to Osceola had been of a mutual convenience, had stepped into the role of a mother to them all, and Che-cho-ter, always respectful, had come to love Ina in a very special way.

And now this special sister was taking her children to a prison to be near their father. Che-cho-ter's eyes were always on the horizon, measuring each step that would take her closer to the man she loved.

As the sun dipped behind the trees, Sloan gave the order to camp for the night. Provisions, prepared the night before, were brought out. Tonight, all would sleep under the stars. Tomorrow, they would arrive in St. Augustine. Savannah slept on a pallet beside Sloan. Through the night they reached for one another, touching, holding, comforting. There was no joy to be shared, only anxiety. A baby cried during the night, its mother soothing it with hushed, crooning words. Savannah nestled her head on Sloan's shoulder and listened to the sound of his heartbeat. Tomorrow. Tomorrow.

As they neared St. Augustine, the salty sea air blowing off the Atlantic was fresh and pungent to their nostrils. But there was another scent also, harsh and fetid, rotten. Sloan and Savannah recognized it instantly. It was the smell of civilization. People, crowded into the confines of a city, garbage and human offal.

The column of Seminole Indians led by a flaxen-haired white man riding a huge black horse brought immediate attention. People lined the cobblestoned streets in unabashed curiosity. Small boys, taught the sins of prejudice and hatred, hurled stones and trash until they were chastised. There was a dignity to these Indians that brooked no insult.

The Castillo, or Fort Marion as the soldiers now called it, rose above the city, the yellow cochina, from which it was constructed, shining dully in the sun. Sloan led his brother's people up the long hill to the gates. He had dismounted and Savannah walked beside him at the head of the column. Uniformed soldiers opened the draw gate, allowing the Seminoles to gather in the central court, hemmed in by the tall battlements.

"You will come with us, MacAllister?" Savannah asked hopefully.

"I brought you this far; I won't desert you now. Come, we must first ask permission to see Osceola. It is a formality and the request will be granted."

Osceola entered the compound where his family and the rest of his camp stood. He walked slowly to his wife and drew her into his arms. He kissed the children and smiled down at them. His eyes saw "his gifts" and he lifted grateful eyes to his brother.

Sloan stood to the side, not wishing to intrude in his brother's private moments. He felt Osceola's eyes upon him. Nothing more than a slight nod of his head was evident to Sloan. Words weren't necessary.

"General, general, what am I supposed to be doing with all these people, sir?" a young sergeant shouted to be heard over the chattering Indians.

"Feed them. We're not barbarians," a harsh voice replied. He could be generous now that he had Osceola, Jessup thought arrogantly. It would look good in the history books in later years. Brevet General Thomas Jessup fed and bedded the Indians from Osceola's camp when they visited their chief at Fort Marion. He preened, liking the pictures his mind was weaving.

"General, sir? Are these people moving in or are they visiting?"

"They're moving in, thanks to my generosity. See to their comfort."

"What about the white man and woman?"

Jessup frowned. "What white man and woman?"

"The white man and the white woman who brought Osceola's people here."

The young sergeant noticed something strange happen to Jessup's eyes. He looked as though he had just been handed his death sentence. "Where are they?"

"Right outside your window."

Jessup felt a pain in his chest as he walked to the window. He knew what he was going to see and he wasn't wrong. But the man standing next to his niece looked familiar. By God, it was the gambler named MacAllister from New Orleans. Sloan MacAllister.

Sloan MacAllister and Savannah. He should have known. How hard it had been that day to pretend disinterest to save his face when Beaunell Gentry called on him at the rail depot. It was easier to delude himself. Easier to not think about it. Easier to think only of his sister, Caroline. Caroline would never betray him. Once she had, but he had forgiven her. She had only been a young girl, mistaking his protectiveness for possessiveness.

Jessup straightened his military jacket, touched the braid reverently and then smoothed down his hair. He would behave like the general he was and take his cues from the couple standing outside, waiting for him.

His mind raced as he took in MacAllister's attire. A sudden insight told him this was the Swamp Fox, that the myth was indeed a reality. Savannah stared at him insolently. How dare she wear Caroline's cameo! Saying nothing, he reached out and tore the cameo from Savannah's neck. Sloan immediately stiffened, forcing his hands to remain at his sides. He wanted to pound his fists into the general's face, wanted to hear his cries for mercy, but better judgment prevented him. He couldn't chance a fight that would cause a retaliation against Osceola and his family.

"You have no right to wear my sister's cameo," Jessup was hissing. "I gave it to her. You've disgraced my sister's memory, taken up with the savages who murdered her! You're a traitor to her and to your race, and I will never forgive you!"

"I don't want your forgiveness," Savannah said calmly, as the general's face bloomed red with rage. "I know why my mother left it behind when she went with my father to the farm. She wanted to be away from you, from your disapproval and interference. You're an evil man, Uncle, and my mother knew it."

Something in the general seemed to crumble. Savannah was repeating the very accusation Caroline made before she left his life forever. "I loved your mother. Caroline was my life! There was nothing I wouldn't have done for her," Jessup protested, his voice suddenly husky and brimming with emotion.

"You would have done anything except to see her happy. And she was happy. A child knows these things. The very fact that it was my father who could make her so happy and not you is what you've hated the most. You were a fool, Jessup."

The general seemed to have difficulty catching his breath.

Savannah stood there accusingly, the same look in her eye as in Caroline's before she left him. "I loved her," his voice was a whisper now, "I only wanted . . ."

"You only wanted to own her, to possess her. You needed her gratitude, her obligation to love you in return, the same things you wanted from me when I lived with you in New Orleans. It wasn't the Indians who killed my mother. It was you! You drove her out to that isolated farm . . . you drove her away from yourself. It is this you can't live with, so you choose to blame the Indians. It was Creeks who murdered my family. The Seminoles took me in and made me one of them. Ironic, isn't it? The Seminoles saved me and you want to throw them into the hands of their sworn enemies, the very ones who murdered my parents." Savannah's lip curled into a sneer. "I could hate you, Jessup, but I only pity you."

Desperately, Jessup's hand reached out to touch Savannah's arm. "I am your mother's brother, your uncle. In time, things can change between us. Savannah, I'm asking you not to throw away all we could have . . ."

"Don't touch me!" Savannah bridled. "Look down there in the compound. That is my family. They're the ones who looked after me, loved me, helped me, and never asked for anything in return. You can't order someone to love you, General. That's something you have to earn. All you've earned is my pity."

Jessup stared as Savannah and Sloan turned and left him. He wanted to strike out, to hurt her. It would be so easy to have MacAllister arrested and held under suspicion of treason. If he was the Swamp Fox, and Jessup instinctively knew he was, MacAllister could face a firing squad. He was about to call the sergeant-at-arms but he thought better of the idea. If it were common knowledge that his own niece paid her allegiance to the Seminoles, and that the man known as Swamp Fox had been entertained in the general's own library, he would never find a political career in Washington. He would do nothing. Prove nothing. They could leave here and he wouldn't stop them. But he had the last laugh, Jessup consoled himself. He had Osceola!

Savannah rode behind Sloan on Redeemer's back. She was leaving a part of her life behind. Osceola was being held prisoner within the fort, but at least he had his wives and children with him.

Her uncle, a link with the past and her heritage, was also there, in his own way more a prisoner than Osceola.

Burying her face into Sloan's broad back, Savannah wept. Her arms gripped him around the middle, holding fast. Here was her future, she told herself. This man with the flinty gray eyes and the heart of a lion. It seemed a lifetime ago that she had given herself into his keeping and found him a gentle master. A soft smile broke through her tears.

Coa Hadjo approached Osceola in the courtyard of Fort Marion shortly before the end of the year. They had been imprisoned for nearly seven weeks, and during that time Osceola had found himself gripped in a severe relapse of fevers. But the sun felt good today, warming the bones and erasing some of the pain. Word had been received of fighting taking place far to the south of St. Augustine, miles away from Fort Marion. The Seminoles were winning small victories. Every Indian in the prison wished they too could raise their weapons against the enemy.

"I have heard rumor," Coa Hadjo said abruptly. "General Jessup does not consider this a fitting prison for such a dangerous enemy. He fears our people will come to rescue us. We are to be moved to South Carolina to a place called Fort Moultrie. Prepare your family, Thlacko. We will leave by ship before the week is out."

Osceola said nothing, his face impassive, and retreated back into his cell.

Osceola stood on the deck of the gunboat taking him away from Florida to Charleston, South Carolina, and to the prison in Fort Moultrie. That his family was allowed to travel with him was a great consolation. His shawl was tightly pulled around his shoulders, and the fever sweat was cold on his face as he watched the shores of Florida disappear in the distance. The breeze blew off the land, and he could detect, faintly, the smell of earth and grass and trees. Morning light blazed off the gray turrets and battlements of Fort Marion while gulls wheeled above the ship. Behind him was the blue streak of the Gulf Stream.

Some had whispered that the fight was over now, that the dreams of freedom had been blown on the wind, but Osceola, chief of the Seminoles, knew otherwise. Freedom always had a price, but it was there, just over the horizon, just behind the moon.

A dark shadow crossed his eyes, blinding him. It was a portent of his death. Only in Florida had life found meaning and purpose. In leaving Florida he left behind his spirit that was linked to the very forests and earth he was walked. Leaving the spirit was to leave life—it was to die.

The *S.S. Poinsett* arrived at Fort Moultrie on January 1, 1838, and the prisoners, including Micanopy, Phillip, Coa Hadjo and Cloud, along with one hundred sixteen warriors and eighty-two women and children, were brought inside the enclosure. The quarters assigned Osceola were spacious enough to include his whole family and the women immediately set about housekeeping.

In the days that followed, Osceola spent a great deal of time reviewing the events of the war. Had he been wrong to fight? Had he committed a sin against nature to lead men into battle where they would suffer injury and death? Had the white man been right in wanting them to leave their forests and streams behind for a new life in Arkansas?

No. The white man had lied and cheated and allowed them to starve. Then he had stolen the bitter dignity of starvation from the Seminole and had tried to force them at gunpoint from the land of their birth. Resistance had been the only choice.

Che-cho-ter joined him one early morning as he stared out into the southern sky. "My husband is troubled," she stated softly. His arm came around her, holding her close. "You watch the southern sky with such longing, it wounds me here," she said, thumping her breast with her fist.

"Once my brother, MacAllister, said much the same thing when we were boys. You keep your eyes on the eastern sky, he told me. And I said that was where I would find my destiny. And so I have."

A chill swept through Che-cho-ter. Not a chill of cold or ice but of death. She knew the time was fast approaching when she would be allowed to go back to Florida with their children. Only Osceola and the warriors were prisoners. The women could be released at any time.

The thought of filling her days without him brought a heaviness to her heart. He had been fighting the fever since arriving here in South Carolina, and was losing the battle. His will to live had evaporated, smothered by the mists that hung over the swamps and his hunting ground. There was nothing to be done, Che-cho-ter told herself, gasping back the cries that were swelling in her breast, but to wait with her husband for the end.

On January 28th, a nightlong vigil was held inside Fort Moultrie. The soldiers of the fort had fallen under Osceola's spell, and fires burned long into the night in respect for the Seminole. A physician was called, Dr. Strobel, who was a professor of anatomy in the college of South Carolina. When the doctor, a man in his late fifties, stocky and well fed, entered Osceola's cell, he found the chief with his head in Che-cho-ter's lap while she bathed his throat with herb-soaked clothes.

"Bring me a candle," the doctor ordered, immediately seeing that the Indian's situation was grave. Peering down Osceola's throat, he saw swollen tonsils and a mucous membrane formed over his pharynx. Shaking his head, his many chins quivering, the man intoned, "He'll suffocate if we don't scarify those tonsils."

Immediately, Pa-hay-okee, the medicine man, jumped to his feet, shaking his magic bones that were strung on rawhide. His shadow on the stone walls created by the flickering fire trembled and shifted. "No," the conjurer said, meeting the doctor's level gaze.

"He'll suffocate, man!" the physician warned, looking quickly at the interpreter to deliver his message. Still, the answer was no. No!

Several other treatments were recommended. Each time Dr. Strobel received the same answer. No.

Osceola delivered himself into Che-cho-ter's hands knowing his life was over, wanting it to be. The dark shadow that had chased him these past moons was closer now. He thought of his family, of his children, and still the darkness that seemed to be just beyond the circle of light loomed threateningly. His throat pained him gravely; the fever was raging in his body. The end was near.

Unable to speak, he looked deeply into Che-cho-ter's eyes. With motions of his hands, he signified that he wished for the chiefs and officers of the post. Pointing to where his war dress was lying, he glanced once again at Che-cho-ter. He wanted to wear them when the end came. He wanted to leave this world dressed for battle, not wrapped in a blanket like a woman at birthing time. With the last bit of his strength, he sat up in bed, helping to dress himself in his shirt, his bright red leggings and his moccasins.

Ina, the old woman whom Osceola had married to save her from the privations of widowhood, wrapped his war belt around his narrow waist and attached his bullet pouch and powder horn. His hunting knife was reverently placed beside him on the cold stone floor.

In a final gesture of defiance, Osceola signaled for a looking glass and his red and yellow paints. He streaked the vivid colors across his face and throat, a ceremony denoting the irrevocable oath of war. Shaking hands held his knife for the last time, placing it in its sheath under his belt. Carefully, with the ease of long practice, he arranged his turban on his head, aided by Che-cho-ter, who placed three feathered plumes which were an insignia of his status among the Seminoles.

Fully prepared, he turned to his wives, sharing with them a last moment of understanding. He made a signal for them to lower him down onto his pallet. Slow, unsteady hands grasped his knife and held it to his chest. Despite the obvious pain, he smiled, giving up his last breath without a struggle or a sound.

The *Polly Copinger* had been anchored in the port of Charleston since the day Osceola had been led to Fort Moultrie. Although Sloan and Savannah were not permitted to see him, they were determined to remain close by. Sometimes, Sloan secretly thought of their vigil as a death watch; reports were frequent of Osceola's failing health.

On this day, Sloan felt a prickling at the nape of his neck and his feet itched to touch dry land, but most of all, he had a desperate need for word of his brother.

Savannah joined her husband on deck, the cold Atlantic air ruffling the stray curls near her cheeks. She was wearing a thick woolen shawl around her shoulders, and the somber brown of her gown seemed to reflect her emotions. Gypsy green eyes searched the horizon as her hands found warmth within Sloan's. "Soon," she whispered, "his suffering will come to an end."

Taking her into his embrace, Sloan was aware of her thickening waistline and of the new life that grew within her. On the night she had told him she was with child, she had cried, great gulping sobs racking her body. Alarmed, he had held her against him, pleading with her to tell him why she was so unhappy. "I have everything a woman can want," she told him. "A man I love, a marriage, and now a child. Everything, and the Seminole have nothing. Not even a future."

Port Charleston was a barren harbor, all the leaves from the trees long gone since the onset of winter. Sloan felt depressed as he waved to Savannah from the dock. It was bitter cold and his teeth chattered. He didn't know if it was from apprehension or from the weather. The sooner he got a newspaper, the sooner he would know.

Inside the lobby of the closest hotel he asked for the latest paper. The banner headline shook him to his very toes. "Seminole Chief dies at Fort Moultrie." He laid a bill on the counter, but not before the startled desk clerk noticed the tears in the metallic eyes. They slipped down Sloan's cheeks and he made no move to wipe at them. The freezing cold air crystallized them and still they flowed. He walked blindly down the long, deserted street back toward the *Polly Copinger* and to Savannah. Always to Savannah. How was he to tell her?

His step lagged and he had to force himself to grasp the rope handrail to help him gain momentum. Once aboard, he sought her out. She asked no questions, correctly interpreting his news from the slump of his shoulders and his glistening eyes.

In the end it was Savannah who comforted Sloan. "Your brother's spirit lives on. It will never die as long as there is a Seminole to walk the earth. Already the chiefs are reuniting under one cause of action. Surely you read that in your newspaper."

"How do you know this?" Sloan asked, bewildered by Savannah's calm acceptance of Osceola's death.

"Because he knew this is what would happen. You forget, my husband, I lived among the Seminole for many years. Osceola was all things to me. One learns to read the signs. He wanted peace."

Savannah stood on the deck of the *Polly* for a very long time. She had realized Sloan's need to be alone and respected it. He had gone below to be alone with his grief and his memories. The gray sky had deepened to ash and the evening was calm and still; hardly a breeze rocked the *Polly* on her moorings. Gentle white flakes were falling onto Savannah's nose and shoulders. Snow. Soon it would blanket the earth with its purity, making everything seem bright and clean. She thought it symbolic that today of all days it should snow. Such a thing was a rarity in this region, and she herself had witnessed it only once before. Perhaps God and the Spirits had sent the snow to cover the dismal failures of the past and to bring hope to the future.

Gathering her skirts around her, Savannah crept below. It was time. He had been alone long enough. Soon now, his need for her would rise and she must be there for him.

Slipping into the cabin, she found him asleep on their bed. The gentle glow from the lamp revealed his grief-ravaged face, the bitter line of his mouth. Silently, she unfastened her gown, stepping out of it, feeling a sudden chill against the flesh her petticoats and chemisette did not cover. Sliding into the bed alongside him, she pressed her body against his, offering warmth and consolation.

He stirred and reached out a muscular arm to bring her closer, bringing her head onto his chest and kissing the soft golden curls that lay so sweetly on the gentle curve of her neck. She heard him sigh, felt the sudden rise of his chest against her cheek. Instinctively, he tightened his embrace, whispering her name softly. "Savannah," he whispered huskily, "come closer. Let me love you." His mouth closed hungrily over hers, blazing a path to her throat. And always he whispered her name, beckoning to her, calling for her love.

Long afterward, he lay beside her, resting his head between her breasts, his hand lovingly caressing the gentle swell of her belly where their child slept. No words were wanted, none were needed. As long as they could be together like this and their love could reach out to one another, they could look to the future and live with the past.

EPILOGUE

*O*sceola was never conquered, although he died in prison, a victim of treachery and deceit. The Seminoles never surrendered as a nation, and the United States Government was unsuccessful in its goal of removing the Indians from Florida. Despite white greed, despite dishonor, the Seminoles were the victors. Osceola's death did not end the Second Seminole War, instead his spirit inspired his people to continue their fight. In the end Osceola won his war. His people were never vanquished.